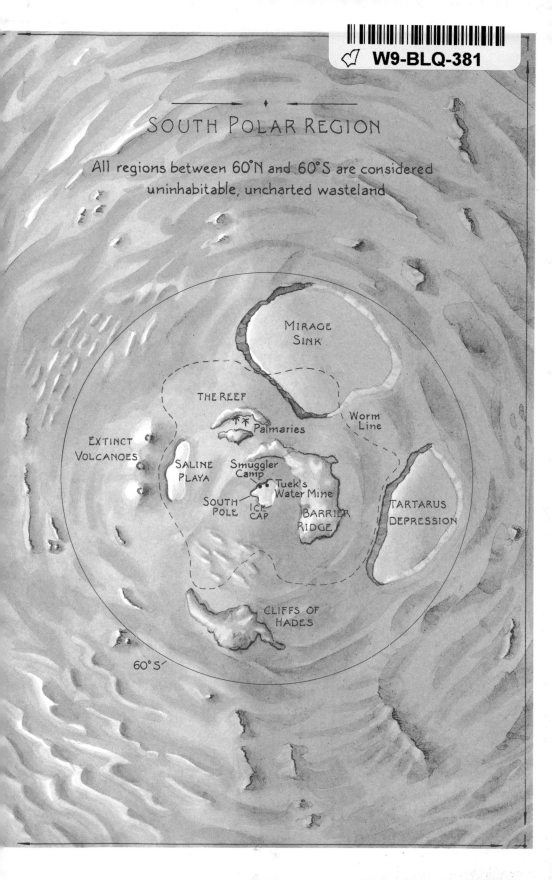

DUNE

HOUSE ATREIDES

DUNE
HOUSE ATREIDES

Brian Herbert
and
Kevin J. Anderson

BANTAM BOOKS
NEW YORK TORONTO LONDON
SYDNEY AUCKLAND

DUNE: HOUSE ATREIDES

A Bantam Spectra Book / October 1999

SPECTRA and the portrayal of a boxed "s" are trademarks of
Bantam Books, a division of Random House, Inc.

BOOK DESIGN BY CASEY HAMPTON.
MAP DESIGNS BY DAVID CAIN.

Library of Congress Cataloging-in-Publication Data
Herbert, Brian.
Dune : House Atreides / Brian Herbert and Kevin J. Anderson.
p.   cm. — (A Bantam spectra book)
Based on the Dune universe created by Frank Herbert.
ISBN 0-553-11061-6
I. Anderson, Kevin J., 1962– .   II. Herbert, Frank.   III. Title.
PS3558.E617D86   1999
813'.54—dc21   99-17726
CIP

Published simultaneously in the United States and Canada

Bantam Books are published by Bantam Books, a division of Random House, Inc. Its
trademark, consisting of the words "Bantam Books" and the portrayal of a rooster, is
Registered in U.S. Patent and Trademark Office and in other countries. Marca Reg-
istrada. Bantam Books, 1540 Broadway, New York, New York 10036.

PRINTED IN THE UNITED STATES OF AMERICA
RRH   10 9 8 7 6 5 4 3 2 1

This book is for our mentor, Frank Herbert,
who was every bit as fascinating and complex as
the marvelous Dune universe he created.

ACKNOWLEDGMENTS

Ed Kramer, for being the bridge that brought us together in the first place.

Rebecca Moesta Anderson, for her unflagging imagination, brainstorming, and plain hard work to make this novel the best it could be.

Jan Herbert, for allowing the creation of this project to continue during a wedding-anniversary trip to Europe, and for so much more.

Pat LoBrutto, our editor at Bantam Books, for helping us achieve the best possible focus and clarity in this book.

Robert Gottlieb and Matt Bialer of the William Morris Agency, Mary Alice Kier and Anna Cottle of Cine/Lit Representation, for their faith and dedication, seeing the potential of the entire project.

Irwyn Applebaum and Nita Taublib at Bantam Books, for their support and enthusiasm in such an enormous undertaking.

Penny and Ron Merritt, whose enthusiastic support made this project possible.

Beverly Herbert, for brainstorming and editorial contributions on the Dune books written by Frank Herbert.

Marie Landis-Edwards, for her encouragement.

The Herbert Limited Partnership, including David Merritt, Byron Merritt, Julie Herbert, Robert Merritt, Kimberly Herbert, Margaux Herbert, and Theresa Shackelford.

At WordFire, Inc., special thanks to Catherine Sidor, who put in many hours of hard work in preparing and revising the manuscript, and Sarah Jones, for her help in converting many old books and documents into a usable form.

And to the millions of devoted *DUNE* fans, who have kept the original novel popular for three and a half decades.

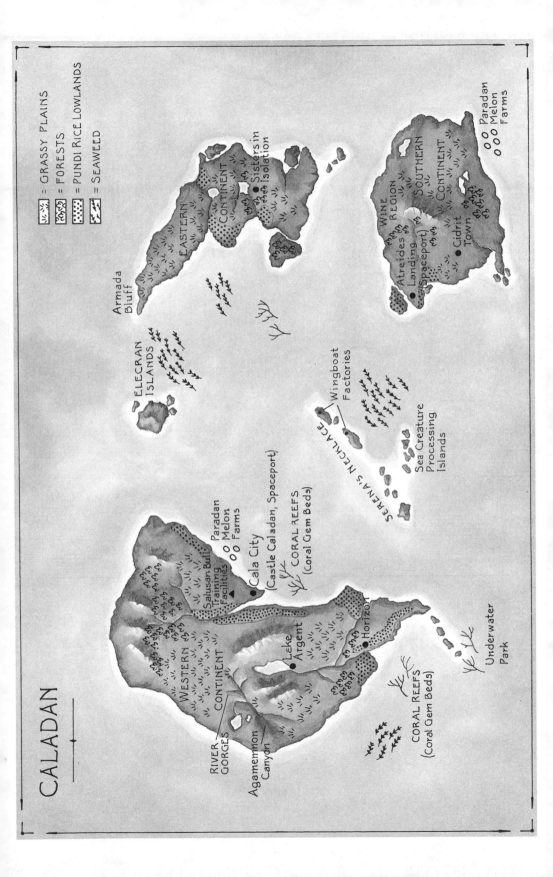

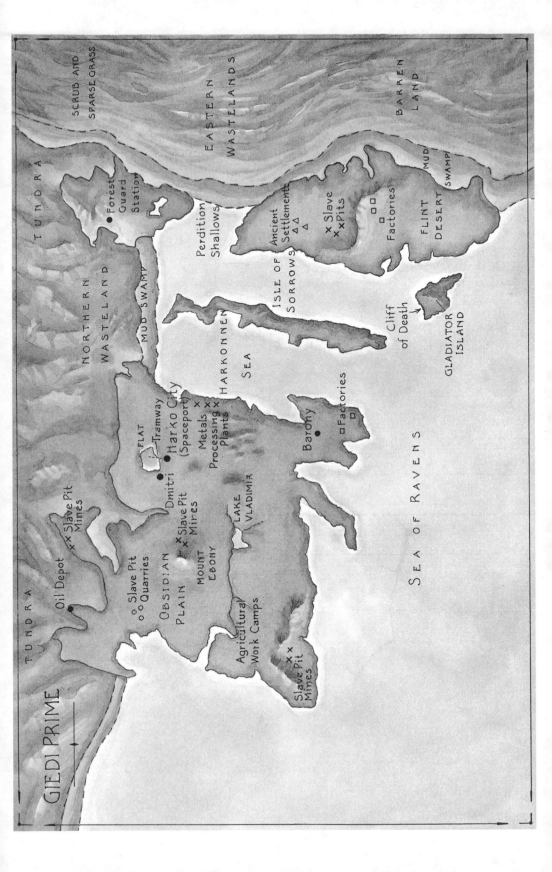

GIEDI PRIME

TUNDRA

SCRUB AND SPARSE GRASS

EASTERN WASTELANDS

BARREN LAND

TUNDRA

• Forest Guard Station

NORTHERN WASTELAND

MUD SWAMP

Perdition Shallows

ISLE OF SORROWS

Ancient Settlements △△△

× Slave ×× Pits

□□ Factories

MUD SWAMP

FLINT DESERT

TUNDRA

• Oil Depot

×× Slave Pit Mines

○○ Slave Pit Quarries

FLAT

Tramway

• Dmitri

Harko City (Spaceport)

Metals ×

Processing × Plants

OBSIDIAN PLAIN

×× Slave Pit Mines

MOUNT EBONY

LAKE VLADIMIR

HARKONNEN SEA

Cliff of Death

GLADIATOR ISLAND

Barony •

□ Factories □

Agricultural Work Camps

×× Slave Pit Mines

SEA OF RAVENS

Transmission to the galactic merchandizing conglomerate "Combine Honnete Ober Advancer Mercantiles" (CHOAM) from the Spacing Guild:

Our specific charge in this unofficial mission has been to search the uninhabited worlds to find another source of the precious spice melange, upon which so much of the Imperium depends. We have documented the journeys of many of our Navigators and Steersmen, searching hundreds of planets. To date, however, we have had no success. The only source of melange in the Known Universe remains the desert world of Arrakis. The Guild, CHOAM, and all other dependents must continue in thrall of the Harkonnen monopoly.

However, the value of exploring outlying territories for new planetary systems and new resources bears its own fruit. The detailed surveys and orbital maps on the attached sheets of ridulian crystal will no doubt be of commercial import for CHOAM.

Having completed our contract to the specifications upon which we previously agreed, we hereby request that CHOAM deposit the required payment in our official Guild Bank headquarters on Junction.

To His Royal Highness, the Padishah Emperor Elrood IX, Ruler of the Known Universe:

From His Faithful Subject the Siridar Baron Vladimir Harkonnen, Planetary Governor of Arrakis, titular head of House Harkonnen and Overlord of Giedi Prime, Lankiveil, and allied planets.

Sire, let me once again affirm my commitment to serving you faithfully on the desert planet Arrakis. For seven years after my father's death, I am ashamed to say that my incompetent half brother Abulurd has allowed spice production to falter. Equipment losses have been high, while exports fell to abysmal levels. Given the dependence of the Imperium on the spice melange, this bottleneck could have had dire consequences. Be assured that my family has taken action to rectify the unfortunate situation: Abulurd has been removed from his duties and relegated to the planet of Lankiveil. His noble title has been removed, though he may reclaim a district governorship one day.

Now that I am the direct overseer of Arrakis, allow me to give you my personal guarantee that I will use whatever means necessary—money, dedication, and an iron hand—to ensure that melange production meets or exceeds previous record levels.

As you so wisely have commanded, the spice must flow!

Melange is the financial crux of CHOAM activities. Without this spice, Bene Gesserit Reverend Mothers could not perform feats of observation and human control, Guild Navigators could not see safe pathways across space, and billions of Imperial citizens would die of addictive withdrawal. Any simpleton knows that such dependence upon a single commodity leads to abuse. We are all at risk.

—CHOAM Economic Analysis
of Materiel Flow Patterns

L ean and muscular, Baron Vladimir Harkonnen hunched forward next to the ornithopter pilot. He peered with spider-black eyes through the pitted windowplaz, smelling the ever-present grit and sand.

As the armored 'thopter flew high overhead, the white sun of Arrakis dazzled against unrelenting sands. The sweeping vista of dunes sizzling in the day's heat made his retinas burn. The landscape and sky were bleached of color. Nothing soothed the human eye.

Hellish place.

The Baron wished he could be back in the industrialized warmth and civilized complexity of Giedi Prime, the central world of House Harkonnen. Even stuck here, he had better things to do back at the local family headquarters in the city of Carthag, other diversions to suit his demanding tastes.

But the spice harvesting must take precedence. *Always.* Especially a huge strike such as the one his spotters had reported.

In the cramped cockpit, the Baron lounged with well-postured confidence, ignoring the buffet and sway of air currents. The 'thopter's mechanical wings beat rhythmically like a wasp's. The dark leather of his chestpiece fit tightly over well-toned pectorals. In his mid-forties, he had rakish good looks; his reddish gold hair had been cut and styled to exacting specifications, enhancing his distinctive widow's peak. The Baron's skin was smooth, his cheekbones high and well sculpted. Sinewy muscles stood out along his neck and jaw, ready to contort his face into a scowl or a hard smile, depending on circumstances.

"How much farther?" He looked sideways at the pilot, who had been showing signs of nervousness.

"The site is in the deep desert, m'Lord Baron. All indications are that this is one of the richest concentrations of spice ever excavated."

The flying craft shuddered on thermals as they passed over an outcropping of black lava rock. The pilot swallowed hard, focusing on the ornithopter's controls.

The Baron relaxed into his seat and quelled his impatience. He was glad the new hoard was far from prying eyes, away from Imperial or CHOAM corporate officials who might keep troublesome records. Doddering old Emperor Elrood IX didn't need to know every damned thing about Harkonnen spice production on Arrakis. Through carefully edited reports and doctored accounting journals, not to mention bribes, the Baron told the off-planet overseers only what he wanted them to know.

He swiped a strong hand across the sheen of sweat on his upper lip, then adjusted the 'thopter's environment controls to make the cockpit cooler, the air more moist.

The pilot, uncomfortable at having such an important and volatile passenger in his care, nudged the engines to increase speed. He checked the console's map projection again, studied outlines of the desert terrain that spread as far as they could see.

Having examined the cartographic projections himself, the Baron had been displeased by their lack of detail. How could anyone expect to find his way across this desert scab of a world? How could a planet so vital to the economic stability of the Imperium remain basically uncharted? Yet another failing of his weak younger demibrother, Abulurd.

But Abulurd was gone, and the Baron was in charge. *Now that Arrakis is mine, I'll put everything in order.* Upon returning to Carthag, he would set people to work drawing up new surveys and maps, if the damned Fremen didn't kill the explorers again or ruin the cartography points.

For forty years, this desert world had been the quasi-fief of House Harkonnen, a political appointment granted by the Emperor, with the blessing of the commercial powerhouse CHOAM—the Combine Honnete Ober Advancer Mercantiles. Though grim and unpleasant, Arrakis was one of the most important jewels in the Imperial crown because of the precious substance it provided.

However, upon the death of the Baron's father, Dmitri Harkonnen, the old Emperor had, through some mental deficiency, granted the seat of power to the softhearted Abulurd, who had managed to decimate spice production in a mere seven years. Profits plunged, and he lost control to smugglers and sabotage. In disgrace, the fool had been yanked from his position and sent off without official title to Lankiveil, where even he could do little damage to the self-sustaining whale-fur activities there.

Immediately upon being granted the governorship, Baron Vladimir Harkonnen had set out to turn Arrakis around. He would make his own mark, erase the legacy of mistakes and bad judgment.

In all the Imperium, Arrakis—a hellhole that some might consider a punishment rather than a reward—was the only known source of the spice melange, a substance worth far more than any precious metal. Here on this parched world, it was worth even more than its weight in water.

Without spice, efficient space travel would be impossible . . . and without space travel, the Imperium itself would fall. Spice prolonged life, protected health, and added a vigor to existence. The Baron, a moderate user himself, greatly appreciated the way it made him feel. Of course, the spice melange was also ferociously addictive, which kept the price high. . . .

The armored 'thopter flew over a seared mountain range that looked like a broken jawbone filled with rotted teeth. Up ahead the Baron could see a dust cloud extending like an anvil into the sky.

"Those are the harvesting operations, m'Lord Baron."

Hawklike attack 'thopters grew from black dots in the monochrome sky and swooped toward them. The communicator pinged, and the pilot sent back an identification signal. The paid defenders—mercenaries with orders to keep out unwelcome observers—circled away and took up protective positions in the sky.

So long as House Harkonnen maintained the illusion of progress and profits, the Spacing Guild didn't need to know about every particular spice find. Nor did the Emperor, nor CHOAM. The Baron would keep the melange for himself and add it to his huge stockpiles.

After Abulurd's years of bumbling, if the Baron accomplished even *half* of what he was capable of, CHOAM and the Imperium would see a vast improvement. If he kept them happy, they wouldn't notice his substantial skim, would never suspect his secret spice stashes. A dangerous stratagem if discovered . . . but the Baron had ways of dealing with prying eyes.

As they approached the plume of dust, he took out a pair of binoculars and focused the oil lenses. The magnification permitted him to see the spice factory at work. With its giant treads and enormous cargo capacity, the mechanical monstrosity was incredibly expensive—and worth every solari expended to maintain it. Its excavators kicked up cinnamon-red dust, gray sand, and flint chips as they dug down, scooping up the surface of the desert, sifting for aromatic spice.

Mobile ground units ranged across the open sand in the vicinity of the factory, dipping probes beneath the surface, scraping samples, mapping the extent of the buried spice vein. Overhead, heavier machinery borne by jumbo ornithopters circled, waiting. Peripherally, spotter craft cruised up and down the sands with alert watchers searching for the telltale ripples of wormsign. One of the great sandworms of Arrakis could swallow their entire operation whole.

"M'Lord Baron," the pilot said and handed the communicator wand over to him, "the captain of the work crew wishes to speak with you."

"This is your Baron." He touched his ear to listen to the pickup. "Give me an update. How much have you found?"

Below on the sands, the crew captain answered, his voice gruff, his manner annoyingly unimpressed with the importance of the man to whom he was speaking. "Ten years working spice crews, and this deposit's beyond anything I've ever seen. Trouble is, it's buried deep. Normally, you know, we find the spice exposed by the elements. This time it's densely concentrated, but . . ."

The Baron waited for only a moment. "Yes, what is it?"

"Something strange going on here, sir. Chemically, I mean. We've got carbon dioxide leaking from below, some sort of a bubble beneath us. The harvester's digging through outer layers of sand to get at the spice, but there's also water vapor."

"Water vapor!" Such a thing was unheard-of on Arrakis, where the moisture content of the air was nearly unmeasurable, even on the best of days.

"Could have stumbled on an ancient aquifer, sir. Maybe buried under a cap of rock."

The Baron had never imagined finding running water beneath the surface of Arrakis. Quickly he considered the possibilities of exploiting a free-flowing water resource by selling it to the populace. That was sure to upset the existing water merchants, who had grown too swollen with self-importance anyway.

His basso voice rumbled. "Do you think it's contaminating the spice somehow?"

"Not able to say, sir," said the crew captain. "Spice is strange stuff, but I've never seen a pocket like this before. It doesn't seem . . . right somehow."

The Baron looked over at the 'thopter pilot. "Contact the spotters. See if they've picked up any wormsign yet."

"No wormsign, m'Lord," the pilot said, scanning the reply. The Baron noticed sparkles of sweat on the man's forehead.

"How long has the harvester been down there?"

"Nearly two standard hours, sir."

Now the Baron scowled. One of the worms should definitely have come before now.

Inadvertently, the pilot had left the comsystem open, and the crew captain gruffly acknowledged over the speaker. "Never had this much time either, sir. The worms always come. Always. But something's going on down here. Gases are increasing. You can smell it in the air."

Taking a deep breath of the recycled cabin air, the Baron detected the musky cinnamon smell of raw melange scooped from the desert. The ornithopter flew in a holding pattern now, several hundred meters from the main harvester.

"We're also detecting vibrations underground, some kind of a resonance. I don't like it, sir."

"You're not paid to like it," the Baron replied. "Is it a deep worm?"

"I don't think so, sir."

He scanned the estimates being transmitted from the spice harvester. The numbers boggled his mind. "We're getting as much from this one excavation as a month's production on my other sites." He drummed his fingers on his right thigh in a rhythmic pattern.

"Nevertheless, sir, I suggest that we prepare to pack up and abandon the site. We could lose—"

"Absolutely not, Captain," the Baron said. "There's no wormsign, and you've already got nearly a full factory load. We can bring down a carryall and give you an empty harvester if you need it. I'm not leaving behind a fortune in spice just because you're getting nervous . . . just because you have an uneasy *feeling*. Ridiculous!"

When the work leader tried to push his point, the Baron interrupted, "Captain, if you're a nervous coward, you're in the wrong profession and in the employ of the wrong House. Carry on." He switched off the communicator and made a mental note to remove that man from his position as soon as possible.

Carryalls hovered above, ready to retrieve the spice harvester and its crew as soon as a worm appeared. But why was it taking so long for one to come? Worms always protected the spice.

Spice. He tasted the word in his thoughts and on his lips.

Veiled in superstition, the substance was an unknown quantity, a modern unicorn's-horn. And Arrakis was inhospitable enough that no one had yet deciphered the origin of melange. In the vast canvas of the Imperium, no explorer or prospector had found melange on any other planet, nor had anyone succeeded in synthesizing a substitute, despite centuries of attempts. Since House Harkonnen held the planetary governorship of Arrakis, and therefore controlled all spice production, the Baron had no wish to see a substitute developed, or any other source found.

Expert desert crews located the spice, and the Imperium used it— but beyond that, the details didn't concern him. There was always risk to spice workers, always the danger that a worm would attack too soon, that a carryall would malfunction, that a spice factory would not be lifted away in time. Unexpected sandstorms could come up with startling speed. The casualty rate and the equipment losses to House Harkonnen were appalling . . . but melange paid off nearly any cost in blood or money.

As the ornithopter circled in a steady, thrumming rhythm, the

Baron studied the industrial spectacle below. Baking sun glinted off the spice factory's dusty hull. Spotters continued to prowl the air, while groundcars cruised beneath them, taking samples.

Still no sign of a worm, and every moment allowed the crew to retrieve more spice. The workers would receive bonuses—except for that captain—and House Harkonnen would become richer. The records could be doctored later.

The Baron turned to the pilot. "Call our nearest base. Summon another carryall and another spice factory. This vein seems inexhaustible." His voice trailed off. "If a worm hasn't shown up by now, there just might be time. . . ."

The ground crew captain called back, broadcasting on a general frequency since the Baron had shut down his own receiver. "Sir, our probes indicate that the temperature is rising deep below—a dramatic spike! Something's going on down there, a chemical reaction. And one of our ground-roving teams just broke into a swarming nest of sandtrout."

The Baron growled, furious with the man for communicating on an unencrypted channel. What if CHOAM spies were listening? Besides, no one cared about sandtrout. The jellylike creatures deep beneath the sand were as irrelevant to him as flies swarming around a long-abandoned corpse.

He made a mental note to do more to this weakling captain than just remove him from the work crews and deny him a bonus. *That gutless bastard was probably handpicked by Abulurd.*

The Baron saw tiny figures of scouts tracking through the sands, running about like ants maddened with acid vapor. They rushed back to the main spice factory. One man leaped off his dirt-encrusted rover and scrambled toward the open door of the massive machine.

"What are those men doing? Are they abandoning their posts? Bring us down closer so I can see."

The pilot tilted the ornithopter and descended like an ominous beetle toward the sand. Below, the men leaned over, coughing and retching as they tried to drag filters over their faces. Two stumbled on the shifting sand. Others were rapidly battening down the spice factory.

"Bring the carryall! Bring the carryall!" someone cried.

The spotters all reported in. "I see no wormsign."

"Still nothing."

"All clear from here," said a third.

"Why are they evacuating?" the Baron demanded, as if the pilot would know.

"Something's happening," the crew captain yelled. "Where's that carryall? We need it now!"

The ground bucked. Four workers stumbled and pitched facefirst onto the sand before they could reach the ramp to the spice factory.

"Look, m'Lord!" The pilot pointed downward, his voice filled with awe. As the Baron stopped focusing on the cowardly men, he saw the sand trembling all around the excavation site, vibrating like a struck drumhead.

The spice harvester canted, slipped to one side. A crack opened in the sands, and the whole site began to swell from beneath the ground, rising in the air like a gas bubble in a boiling Salusan mudpot.

"Get us out of here!" the Baron shouted. The pilot stared for a fraction of a second, and the Baron swept his left hand with the speed of a cracked whip, striking the man hard on the cheek. "Move!"

The pilot grabbed the 'thopter controls and wrenched them into a steep ascent. The articulated wings flapped furiously.

On the terrain below, the swollen underground bubble reached its apex—then burst, hurling the spice harvester, the mobile crews, and everything else up off the surface. A gigantic explosion of sand sprayed upward, carrying broken rock and volatile orange spice. The mammoth factory was crushed and blasted to pieces, scattered like lost rags in a Coriolis storm.

"What the devil happened?" The Baron's dark eyes went wide in disbelief at the sheer magnitude of the disaster. All that precious spice gone, swallowed in an instant. All the equipment destroyed. The loss in lives hardly occurred to him, except for the wasted costs of crew training.

"Hang on, m'Lord," the pilot cried. His knuckles turned white on the controls.

A hammer-blast of wind struck them. The armored ornithopter turned end over end in the air, wings flailing. The engines whined and groaned, trying to maintain stability. Pellets of high-velocity sand struck the plaz windowports. Dust-clogged, the 'thopter's motors made sick, coughing sounds. The craft lost altitude, dropping toward the seething maw of the desert.

The pilot shouted unintelligible words. The Baron clutched his crash restraints, saw the ground coming toward them like an inverted bootheel to squash an insect.

As head of House Harkonnen, he had always thought he would die by a treacherous assassin's hand . . . but to fall prey to an unpredictable natural disaster instead—the Baron found it almost humorous.

As they plunged, he saw the sand open like a festering sore. The dust and raw melange were being sucked down, turned over by convection currents and chemical reactions. The rich spice vein of only moments before had turned into a leprous mouth ready to swallow them.

But the pilot, who had seemed weak and distractible during their flight, became rigid with concentration and determination. His fingers flew over sky rudder and engine throttle controls, working to ride the currents, switching flow from one motor to another to discharge dust strangulation in the air intakes.

Finally the ornithopter leveled off, steadied itself again, and cruised low over the dune plain. The pilot emitted an audible sigh of relief.

Where the great opening had been ripped into the layered sand, the Baron now saw glittering translucent shapes like maggots on a carcass: sandtrout, rushing toward the explosion. Soon giant worms would come, too. The monsters couldn't possibly resist this.

Try as he might, the Baron couldn't understand spice. Not at all.

The 'thopter gained altitude, taking them toward the spotters and the carryalls that had been caught unawares. They hadn't been able to retrieve the spice factory and its precious cargo before the explosion, and he could blame no one for it—no one but himself. The Baron had given them explicit orders to remain out of reach.

"You just saved my life, pilot. What is your name?"

"Kryubi, sir."

"All right, then, Kryubi—have you ever seen such a thing? What happened down there? What caused that explosion?"

The pilot took a deep breath. "I've heard the Fremen talking about something they call a . . . *spice blow*." He seemed like a statue now, as if the terror had transformed him into something much stronger. "It happens in the deep desert, where few people can see."

"Who cares what the Fremen say?" He curled his lip at the thought of the dirty, nomadic indigents of the great desert. "We've all heard of spice blows, but nobody's ever actually seen one. Crazy superstitions."

"Yes, but superstition usually has some kind of basis. They see many things out in the desert." Now the Baron admired the man for his willingness to speak out, though Kryubi must know of his temper and vindictiveness. Perhaps it would be wise to promote him. . . .

"They say a spice blow is a chemical explosion," Kryubi continued, "probably the result of a pre-spice mass beneath the sands."

The Baron considered this; he couldn't deny the evidence of his own eyes. One day maybe someone would understand the true nature of melange and be able to prevent disasters like this. So far, because the spice was seemingly inexhaustible to those willing to make the effort, no one had bothered with a detailed analysis. Why waste time on tests, when fortunes waited to be made? The Baron had a monopoly on Arrakis—but it was also a monopoly based on ignorance.

He gritted his teeth and knew that once they returned to Carthag he would be forced to blow off some steam, to release his pent-up tensions on "amusements," perhaps a bit more vigorously than he had earlier intended. He would have to find a special candidate this time—not one of his regular lovers, but someone he would never have use for again. That would free him of restraint.

Looking down, he thought, *No longer any need to hide this site from the Emperor.* They would record it, log it as a find, and document the destruction of the crew and equipment. No need to manipulate the records now. Old Elrood would not be pleased, and House Harkonnen would have to absorb this financial setback.

As the pilot circled around, the surviving spice crew assessed their damages on the ground, and over the comlink reported losses of men, equipment, and spice load. The Baron felt rage boiling within him.

Damn Arrakis! he thought. *Damn the spice, and damn our dependence on it!*

We are generalists. You can't draw neat lines around planetwide problems. Planetology is a cut-and-fit science.

—PARDOT KYNES, Treatise on the Environmental
Recovery of Post-Holocaust Salusa Secundus

On the Imperial planet Kaitain, immense buildings kissed the sky. Magnificent sculptures and opulent tiered fountains lined the crystal-paved boulevards like a dream. A person could stare for hours.

Pardot Kynes managed to catch only a glimpse of the urban spectacle as the royal guards marched him at a rapid clip into the Palace. They had no patience for a simple Planetologist's curiosity, nor any apparent interest in the city's wonders. Their job was to escort him to the tremendous vaulted throne room, without delay. The Emperor of the Known Universe could not be kept waiting for mere sight-seeing.

The members of Kynes's escort wore gray-and-black uniforms, impeccably clean and adorned with braids and medals, every button and bauble polished, every ribbon straightened and pressed. Fifteen of the Emperor's handpicked staff, the Sardaukar, surrounded him like an army.

Still, the splendor of the capital world overwhelmed Kynes. Turning to the guard closest to him, he said, "I'm usually out in the dirt, or tromping through swamps on a planet where nobody else wants to be." He had never seen, or even imagined, anything like this in all of the rugged and out-of-the-way landscapes he had studied.

The guard made no response to this tall, lean off-worlder. Sardaukar were trained to be fighting machines, not conversationalists.

"Here I've been scrubbed clean down to the third layer of my skin and dressed like a noble." Kynes tugged at the thick corded fabric of his dark blue jacket, smelled the soap and scent of his own skin. He had a high forehead, with sparse, sandy hair combed straight back.

The escort hurried up a seemingly endless waterfall of polished stone steps, ornately highlighted with gold filigree and creamy, sparkling soostones.

Kynes turned to the guard on his left. "This is my first trip to Kaitain. I'd wager you don't even notice the sights anymore, if you work here all the time?" His words hung on a wistful smile, but again fell on deaf ears.

Kynes was an expert and well-respected ecologist, geologist, and meteorologist, with added specialties in botany and microbiology. Driven, he enjoyed absorbing the mysteries of entire worlds. But the people themselves often remained a complete mystery to him—like these guards.

"Kaitain is a lot more . . . comfortable than Salusa Secundus—I grew up there, you know," he continued. "I've been to Bela Tegeuse, too, and that's almost as bad, dim and bleak with two dwarf suns."

Finally Kynes faced forward, consenting to mutter to himself. "The Padishah Emperor called me from halfway across the galaxy. I wish I knew why." None of these men ventured to offer any explanations.

The entourage passed under a pitted archway of crimson lava rock that bore the ponderous oppression of extreme age. Kynes looked up, and with his geological expertise recognized the massive rare stone: an ancient archway from the devastated world of Salusa Secundus.

It puzzled him that anyone would keep such a relic from the austere planet where Kynes had spent so many years, an isolated prison world with a ruined ecosystem. But then he recalled, feeling like a fool for having forgotten it, that Salusa had once been the Imperial capital, millennia ago . . . before the disaster changed everything. No doubt House Corrino had brought this archway here intact as a reminder of their past, or as some sort of trophy to show how the Imperial family had overcome planet-destroying adversity.

As the Sardaukar escort stepped through the lava arch and into the echoing splendor of the Palace itself, fanfare rang out from brassy instruments Kynes could not name. He'd never been much of a student in music or the arts, not even as a child. Why bother, when there was so much natural science to absorb?

Just before passing beneath the jewel-sparkling roof of the immense royal structure, Kynes craned his neck upward to gaze once more at the clear sky of perfect blue.

On the trip here, inside a cordoned-off section of the Guild Heighliner, Kynes had taken the time to learn about the capital world, though he had never before applied his planet-understanding skills to such a civilized place. Kaitain was exquisitely planned and produced, with tree-lined boulevards, splendid architecture, well-watered gardens, flower barricades . . . and so much more.

Official Imperial reports claimed it was always warm, the climate forever temperate. Storms were unknown. No clouds marred the skies. At first, he thought the entries might have been mere tourist propaganda, but when the ornate Guild escort craft descended, he had noted the flotilla of weather satellites, climate-bending technology that—through brute force—kept Kaitain a peaceful and serene place.

Climate engineers could certainly strong-arm the weather to what someone had foolishly decided was optimal—though they did it at their own peril, creating an environment that led, ultimately, to malaise of the mind, body, and spirit. The Imperial family would never understand that. They continued to relax under their sunny skies and stroll through their well-watered arboretums, oblivious to an environmental catastrophe just waiting to unfold before their covered eyes. It would be a challenge to stay on this planet and study the effects—but somehow Kynes doubted that was why Emperor Elrood IX had summoned him here. . . .

The escort troops led him deeper into the echoing Palace, passing statuary and classic paintings. The sprawling audience chamber could well have been an arena for ancient gladiatorial events. Its floor stretched onward like a polished, multicolored plain of stone squares—each one from a different planet in the Imperium. Alcoves and wings were being added as the Empire grew.

Court functionaries in dazzling raiment and brilliant plumage strutted about, showing off fabrics that had been spun with threads of precious metal. Carrying documents, they conducted inexplicable business, hurrying to meetings, whispering to each other as if only they understood what their true functions were.

Kynes was an alien in this political world; he would rather have the wilderness any day. Though the splendor fascinated him, he longed for solitude, unexplored landscapes, and the mysteries of strange flora and fauna. This bustling place would give him a headache before long.

The Sardaukar guards ushered him across a long promenade beneath prismatic lights, taking sharp, rhythmic footsteps that sounded like weapons fire; Kynes's stumbles provided the only dissonance.

Ahead on a raised dais of blue-green crystal sat the translucent Golden Lion Throne, carved from a single piece of Hagal quartz. And on the dazzling chair perched the old man himself—Elrood Corrino IX, Imperial ruler of the Known Universe.

Kynes stared at him. The Emperor was a distressingly gaunt man, skeletal with age, with a ponderously large head on a thin neck. Surrounded by such incredible luxury and dramatic richness, the aged ruler appeared somehow insignificant. But with a twitch of his large-knuckled finger, the Emperor could condemn entire planets to annihilation, killing billions of people. Elrood had sat upon the Golden Lion Throne for nearly a century and a half. How many planets were in the Imperium? How many people did this man rule? Kynes wondered how anyone could tally such a staggering amount of information.

As he was led to the base of the dais, Kynes smiled uncertainly at Elrood, then swallowed hard, averted his gaze, and bowed low. No one had bothered to instruct him in the proper protocol here, and he'd had little use for manners and social niceties. The faint cinnamon odor of melange touched his nostrils from a mug of spice beer the Emperor kept on a small table beside his throne.

A page stepped forward, nodded to the leader of the Sardaukar guard escort, and turned, booming out in Galach, the common language, "The Planetologist Pardot Kynes!"

Kynes squared his shoulders and tried to stand straight, wondering why they had made such a loud and portentous introduction when the Emperor obviously knew who he was—else why summon him here?

Kynes wondered if he should say hello, but decided instead to wait and let the Court determine the flow of events.

"Kynes," the old Emperor said in a reedy, scratchy voice that suffered from too many years of issuing firm commands, "you come to me highly recommended. Our advisors have studied many candidates, and they've chosen *you* above all others. What do you say to that?" The Emperor leaned forward, raising his eyebrows so that his skin furrowed all the way to the top of his cranium.

Kynes mumbled something about being honored and pleased, then cleared his throat and asked the real question. "But, sir, what exactly have I been chosen *for*?"

Elrood cackled at that and sat back. "How refreshing to see someone more concerned with satisfying his own curiosity than with saying the right thing, or pandering to these stupid clingers and buffoons." As he smiled, Elrood's face turned rubbery, the wrinkles stretching back. His skin had a grayish, parchment tone. "The report says you grew up on Salusa Secundus, and you wrote definitive, complex reports on the ecology of the planet."

"Yes, Sire, uh, Your Majesty. My parents were bureaucratic functionaries, sent to work in your Imperial prison there. I was just a child and went along with them."

In truth, Kynes had heard rumors that his mother or father had displeased Elrood somehow, and that they had been transferred in disgrace to the punishment planet. But young Pardot Kynes had found the wastelands fascinating. After the tutors were finished with him, he'd spent his days exploring the blasted wilderness—taking notes, studying the insects and weeds and hardy animals that had managed to survive the ancient atomic holocaust.

"Yes, yes, I understand that," Elrood said. "After a while your parents were transferred to another world."

Kynes nodded. "Yes, Sire. They went to Harmonthep."

The Emperor waved a hand to dismiss the reference. "But later you returned to Salusa, of your own free will?"

"Well, uh, there was still much more for me to learn on Salusa," he answered, stifling an embarrassed shrug.

Kynes had spent years by himself in the outback, piecing together the mysteries of the climate and ecosystems. He had suffered many hardships, endured much discomfort. He had even been pursued once by Laza tigers and survived. Afterward, Kynes had published an extensive treatise about his years there, opening remarkable windows of understanding to the once-lovely, now-abandoned Imperial capital planet.

"The wild desolation of the place whetted my interest in ecology. It's so much more interesting to study a . . . damaged world. I find it difficult to learn anything in a place that's too civilized."

Elrood laughed at the visitor's comment and looked around so that all the other members of the Court chuckled as well. "Like Kaitain, you mean?"

"Well, I'm sure there must be interesting places here, too, Sire," Kynes said, hoping he hadn't made an inexcusable faux pas.

"Well spoken!" Elrood boomed. "My advisors have chosen you wisely, Pardot Kynes."

Not knowing what else to do or say, the Planetologist bowed awkwardly.

After his years on Salusa Secundus, he had gone on to the swampy tangles of dimly lit Bela Tegeuse, and then to other places that interested him. He could live off the land just about anywhere; his needs were few. To him, most important of all was the harvesting of scientific knowledge, looking under rocks and seeing what secrets the natural processes had left for him to find.

But his curiosity was piqued now. What had brought him to such impressive attention? "If I may ask again, Your Majesty . . . what exactly do you have in mind for me?" Then he added quickly, "Of course, I am happy to serve in whatever capacity my Emperor wishes."

"You, Kynes, have been recognized as a true world-reader, a man capable of analyzing complex ecosystems in order to harness them to the needs of the Imperium. We have chosen you to go to the desert planet of Arrakis and work your magic there."

"Arrakis!" Kynes could not restrain his astonishment—and yes, *pleasure*—at the prospect. "I believe the nomadic Fremen inhabitants call it Dune."

"Whatever its name," Elrood said a little sharply, "it is one of the most unpleasant yet important worlds in the Imperium. You know, of course, Arrakis is the sole source of the spice melange."

Kynes nodded. "I've always wondered why no searchers have ever found spice on any other world. And why doesn't anyone understand how the spice is created or deposited?"

"*You* are going to understand it for us," the Emperor said. "And it's about time, too."

Kynes suddenly realized he might have overstepped his bounds, and he balked a little. Here he was in the grandest throne room on a million worlds, having an actual *conversation* with Emperor Elrood IX. The other members of the Court stared at him, some with displeasure, some with horror, some with wicked glee as if they anticipated a severe punishment momentarily.

But soon Kynes found himself thinking of the sweeping landscape of scoured sands, majestic dunes, and monstrous sandworms—visions he'd only seen in filmbooks. Forgetting his minor lapse in tact, he caught his breath and waited for the details of his assignment.

"It is vitally important to the future of the Imperium that we understand the secret of melange. To date, no one has spent the time or effort to unravel its mysteries. People think of Arrakis as an unending source of riches, and they don't care about the mechanics or the details. Shallow thinking." He paused. "This is the challenge you will face, Pardot Kynes. We install you as our official Imperial Planetologist to Arrakis."

As Elrood made this pronouncement, he looked down at the weathered, middle-aged man and assessed him privately. He saw immediately that Kynes was not a complex man: His emotions and alliances lay wide-open on his face. Court advisors had indicated that Pardot Kynes was a man utterly without political ambitions or obligations. His only true interest lay in his work and in understanding the natural order of the universe. He had a childlike fascination for alien places and harsh environments. He would do the job with boundless enthusiasm, and would provide honest answers.

Elrood had spent too much of his political life surrounded by simpering sycophants, brainless yes-men who said what they thought he wanted to hear. But this rugged man filled with social awkwardness was not like that.

Now it was even more important that they understand the facts behind the spice, in order to improve the efficiency of operations, vital operations. After seven years of inept governorship by Abulurd Harkonnen, and the recent accidents and mistakes made by the overambitious Baron Vladimir Harkonnen, the Emperor was concerned about a bottleneck in spice production and distribution. The spice *must* flow.

The Spacing Guild needed vast amounts of melange to fill the enclosed chambers of their mutated Navigators. He himself, and all the upper classes in the Empire, needed daily (and increasing) doses of melange to maintain their vitality and to extend their lives. The Bene Gesserit Sisterhood needed it in their training to create more Reverend Mothers. Mentats needed it for mental focus.

But though he disagreed with many of Baron Harkonnen's recent harsh management activities, Elrood could not simply take Arrakis for himself. After decades of political manipulations, House Harkonnen had been placed in charge after the ouster of House Richese.

For a thousand years now, the governorship of Arrakis had been an Imperial boon, granted to a chosen family that would wring the riches out of the sands for a term not to exceed a century. Each time the fief changed hands, a firestorm of pleas and requests for favors bombarded the Palace. Landsraad support came with many strings attached, and some of those strings felt like nooses to Elrood.

Though he was Emperor, his position of power rested in a careful and uneasy balance of alliances with numerous forces, including the Great and Minor Houses of the Landsraad, the Spacing Guild, and the all-encompassing commercial combines such as CHOAM. Other forces were even more difficult to deal with, forces that preferred to remain behind the scenes.

I need to disrupt the balance, Elrood thought. *This business of Arrakis has gone on too long.*

The Emperor leaned forward, seeing that Kynes was fairly bursting with joy and enthusiasm. He actually *wanted* to go to the desert world—all the better! "Find out everything you can about Arrakis and send me regular reports, Planetologist. House Harkonnen will be instructed to give you all the support and cooperation you need." *Though they certainly won't like an Imperial Observer snooping around.*

Newly installed in the planetary governorship, Baron Harkonnen was wrapped around the Emperor's fingertip, for now. "We will provide the items necessary for your journey. Compile your lists and give them to my Chamberlain. Once you reach Arrakis, the Harkonnens will be instructed to give you whatever else you require."

"My needs are few," Kynes said. "All I require are my eyes and my mind."

"Yes, but see if you can make the Baron offer a few more amenities than that." Elrood smiled again, then dismissed the Planetologist. The Emperor noticed a pronounced spring in Kynes's step as he was led out of the Imperial audience chamber.

Suffering is the great teacher of men," the chorus of old actors said as they stood on the stage, their voices in perfect unison. Though the performers were simple villagers from the town below Castle Caladan, they had rehearsed well for the annual performance of the official House Play. Their costumes were colorful, if not entirely authentic. The props—the facade of Agamemnon's palace, the flagstoned courtyard—showed a realism based only on enthusiasm and a few filmbook snapshots of ancient Greece.

The long play by Aeschylus had already gone on for some time, and the gathered audience in the theatre was warm and the air was close. Glowglobes lit the stage and rows of seating, but the torches and braziers around the performers added aromatic smoke to the building.

Though the background noises were loud enough, the Old Duke's snores threatened to carry all the way forward to the performers.

"Father, wake up!" Leto Atreides whispered, nudging Duke Paulus in the ribs. "The play isn't even half-over."

In the chair of his private box, Paulus stirred and straightened, brushing imaginary crumbs from his broad

chest. Shadows played across the creased, narrow face and the voluminous salt-and-pepper beard. He wore a black Atreides uniform with a
red hawk crest on the left breast. "It's all just talking and standing anyway, lad." He blinked toward the stage, where the old men still hadn't
moved much. "And we've seen it every year."

"That is not the point, Paulus, dear. People are watching." It was
Leto's mother, sitting on the other side of the Duke. The dark-skinned
Lady Helena, dressed in her fine gown, took seriously the ponderous
words of the Greek chorus. "Pay attention to the context. It's *your* family
history, after all. Not mine." Leto looked from one parent to the other,
knowing that the family history of his mother's House Richese carried
just as much grandeur and loss as that of Atreides. Richese had sunk from
a highly profitable "golden age" to its current economic weakness.

House Atreides claimed to trace its roots more than twelve thousand years, back to the ancient sons of Atreus on Old Terra. Now the
family embraced its long history, despite the numerous tragic and dishonorable incidents it contained. The Dukes had made an annual tradition of performing the classic tragedy of *Agamemnon*, the most famous
son of Atreus and one of the generals who had conquered Troy.

With black-black hair and a narrow face, Leto Atreides strongly resembled his mother, though he had his father's aquiline nose and
hawkish profile. The young man watched, dressed in uncomfortable
finery, vaguely aware of the off-world background of the story. The author of the ancient play had counted on his audience understanding
the esoteric references. General Agamemnon had been a great military commander in one of human history's legendary wars, long before
the creation of thinking machines that had enslaved mankind, long
before the Butlerian Jihad had freed humanity.

For the first time in his fourteen years, Leto felt the weight of legends
on his shoulders; he sensed a connection with the faces and personalities
of his star-crossed family's past. One day he would succeed his father, and
would become a part of Atreides history as well. Events were chipping
away at his childhood, transforming him into a man. He saw it clearly.

"The unenvied fortune is best," the old men chimed together to say
their lines. "Preferable to sacking cities, better than following the
commands of others."

Before sailing to Troy, Agamemnon had sacrificed his own daughter to guarantee favorable winds from the gods. His distraught wife,

Clytemnestra, had spent the ten years of her husband's absence plotting revenge. Now, after the final battle of the Trojan War, a chain of signal fires had been lit along the coast, sending back home word of the victory.

"All of the action occurs offstage," Paulus muttered, though he had never been much of a reader or literary critic. He lived life for the moment, squeezing every drop of experience and accomplishment. He preferred spending time with his son, or his soldiers. "Everybody just stands in front of the sets, waiting for Agamemnon to arrive."

Paulus abhorred inaction, always telling his son that even the wrong decision was better than no decision at all. In the play, Leto thought the Old Duke sympathized most with the great general, a man after his own heart.

The chorus of old men droned on, Clytemnestra stepped out of the palace to deliver a speech, and the chorus continued again. A herald, pretending to have disembarked from a ship, came onto the stage, kissed the ground, and recited a long soliloquy.

"Agamemnon, glorious king! How you deserve our joyous welcome, for annihilating Troy and the Trojan homeland. Our enemy's shrines lie in ruins, nevermore comforting their gods, and their soils are barren."

Warfare and mayhem—it made Leto think of his father's younger days, when he had charged out to fight battles for the Emperor, crushing a bloody rebellion on Ecaz, adventuring with his friend Dominic, who was now the Earl of House Vernius on Ix. In private times with Leto, the Old Duke often talked about those days with great fondness.

In the shadows of their box, Paulus heaved a too-loud sigh, not concealing his boredom. Lady Helena shot him a daggered glare, then returned her attention to the play, reconstructing her face to form a more placid smile in case anyone should look at her. Leto gave his father a crooked and sympathetic grin, and Paulus winked back at him. The Duke and his wife played their parts and fit their own comfortable roles.

Finally, on the stage below, the victorious Agamemnon arrived in a chariot, accompanied by his spoils-of-war mistress, the half-insane prophetess Cassandra. Meanwhile, Clytemnestra made preparations for her hated husband's appearance, feigning devotion and love.

Old Paulus started to loosen the collar of his uniform, but Helena reached over quickly to pull his hand away. Her smile didn't waver.

Seeing this ritual his parents often went through, Leto smiled to himself. His mother constantly struggled to maintain what she called "a sense of decorum," while the old man behaved with far less formality. Though his father had taught him much about statecraft and leadership, Lady Helena had taught her son protocol and religious studies.

A daughter of Richese, Lady Helena Atreides had been born into a House Major that had lost most of its power and prestige through failed economic competitions and political intrigues. After being ousted from the planetary governorship of Arrakis, Helena's family had salvaged some of its respectability through an arranged marital alliance with the Atreides; several of her sisters had been married off to other Houses.

Despite their obvious differences, the Old Duke had once told Leto he had truly loved Helena in the first years of their union. Over time, that had eroded, and he'd dabbled with many mistresses, possibly producing illegitimate children, though Leto was his sole official heir. As decades passed, an enmity built up between husband and wife, causing a deep rift. Now their marriage was strictly political.

"I married for politics in the first place, lad," he had said. "Never should have tried to make it otherwise. At our station, marriage is a tool. Don't muck everything up by trying to throw love into the mix."

Leto sometimes wondered if Helena herself had ever loved his father, or if it had only been his title and station that she loved. Of late, she seemed to have assumed the role of Paulus's royal caretaker; she constantly strove to keep him groomed and presentable. It bore as much on her own reputation as on his.

On the stage, Clytemnestra greeted her husband, strewing purple tapestries on the ground so he could walk on them rather than on the dirt. Amidst great pomp and fanfare, Agamemnon marched into his palace, while the oracle Cassandra, speechless in terror, refused to enter. She foretold her own death and the murder of the general; of course, no one listened to her.

Through carefully cultivated political channels, Leto's mother maintained contacts with other powerful Houses, while Duke Paulus developed strong bonds with the common people of Caladan. The

Atreides Dukes led their subjects by serving them and by paying themselves only what was fair from family business enterprises. This was a family of wealth, but not to excess—not at the expense of its citizens.

In the play, when the returning general went to his bath, his treacherous wife tangled him in purple robes and stabbed both him and his oracular mistress to death. "My gods! A deadly blow has befallen me!" Agamemnon wailed from offstage, out of sight.

Old Paulus smirked and bent over to his son. "I've killed many a man on the battlefield, and I have yet to hear one say *that* as he died!"

Helena hushed him.

"Gods protect me, another blow! I shall die!" cried the voice of Agamemnon.

While the audience was engrossed in the tragedy, Leto tried to sort through his thoughts of the situation, how it related to his own life. This was supposedly his family's heritage, after all.

Clytemnestra admitted the murder, claiming vengeance against her husband for his bloody sacrifice of their daughter, for his whoring in Troy, and for blatantly bringing his mistress Cassandra into her own home.

"Glorious king," wailed the chorus, "our affection is boundless, our tears unending. The spider has ensnared you in its ghostly web of death."

Leto's stomach churned. House Atreides had committed horrible deeds in the distant past. But the family had changed, perhaps driven by the ghosts of history. The Old Duke was an honorable man, well respected by the Landsraad and beloved by his people. Leto hoped he could do as well when it came his turn to rule House Atreides.

The final lines of the play were spoken, and the company of actors marched across the stage, bowing to the assembled political and business leaders, all of whom were dressed in finery befitting their stations.

"Well, I'm glad that's over," Paulus sighed as the main glowglobes went on in the performance hall. The Old Duke rose to his feet and kissed his wife's hand as they filed out of the royal box. "On your way now, my dear. I have something to say to Leto. Wait for us in the reception room."

Helena glanced once at her son and went down the corridor of the ancient stone-and-wood theatre. Her look said she knew exactly what Paulus intended to say, but she bowed to his archaic tradition of having the men speak of "important matters" while the women busied themselves elsewhere.

Merchants, important businessmen, and other well-respected locals began filling the corridor, sipping Caladanian wine and munching hors d'oeuvres. "This way, lad," the Old Duke said, taking a backstage passage. He and Leto strode past two Atreides guards, who saluted. Then they took a lift tube up four levels to a gilded dressing room. Balut crystal glowglobes floated in the air, flickering a warm orange. Formerly the living quarters of a legendary Caladanian actor, this chamber was now used exclusively by the Atreides and their closest advisors for times requiring privacy.

Leto wondered why his father had taken him here.

After closing the door behind him, Paulus slipped into a green-and-black suspensor chair and motioned for Leto to take one opposite him. The young man did so and adjusted the controls to lift the floating chair higher in the air, so that his eye level was equal to that of his father. Leto only did this in private, not even in the presence of his mother, who would consider such behavior unseemly and disrespectful. By contrast, the Old Duke found his son's brashness and high spirits to be an amusing reflection of the way he himself had been as a young man.

"You are of age now, Leto," Paulus began, removing an ornate wooden pipe from a compartment in the arm of his chair. He did not waste time with chitchat. "And you must learn more than your own backyard. So I'm sending you to Ix to study." He examined the black-haired youth who looked so similar to his mother, but with lighter, more olive-toned skin than hers. He had a narrow face with sharp angles and deep gray eyes.

Ix! Leto's pulse accelerated. *The machine planet. A strange and alien place.* Everyone in the Imperium knew of that mysterious world's incredible technology and innovations, but few outsiders had ever been there. Leto felt disoriented, as if on the deck of a boat in a storm. His father loved to pull surprises like this, to see how well Leto could react to a changed situation.

Ixians maintained a strict veil of secrecy around their industrial operations. They were rumored to skirt the fringes of legality, manufacturing devices that came close to violating Jihad prohibitions against thinking machines. *Why then is my father sending me to such a place, and how has it been arranged? Why hasn't anyone asked me?*

A robo-table emerged from the floor beside Leto and produced a cold glass of cidrit juice. The young man's tastes were known, just as it was known that the Old Duke would want nothing but the pipe. Leto took a sip of the tart drink, puckering his lips.

"You'll study there for a year," Paulus said, "according to the tradition of the allied Great Houses. Living on Ix will be quite a contrast with our bucolic planet. Learn from it." He stared at the pipe in his hand. Carved from Elaccan jacaranda wood, it was deep brown, with swirls that glinted in the light cast by the glowglobes.

"You've been there, sir?" Leto smiled as he remembered. "To see your comrade Dominic Vernius, right?"

Paulus touched the combustion pad on the side of his pipe, lighting the tobacco, which was actually a golden seaweed rich in nicotine. He took a long drag and exhaled smoke. "On many occasions. The Ixians are an insular society and don't trust outsiders. So you'll have to go through plenty of security precautions, interrogations, and scans. They know that dropping their guard for the briefest instant can be fatal. Great and Minor Houses alike covet what Ix has and would like to take it for themselves."

"Richese for one," Leto said.

"Don't say that to your mother. Richese is now only a shadow of what it was because Ix trounced them in all-out economic warfare." He leaned forward and took a puff from his pipe. "The Ixians are masters of industrial sabotage and patent appropriation. Nowadays Richesians are only good for making cheap copies, without any innovations."

Leto considered these comments, which were new to him. The Old Duke blew smoke, puffing his cheeks and making his beard bristle.

"In deference to your mother, lad, we've filtered the information you've learned. House Richese was a *most* tragic loss. Your grandfather, Count Ilban Richese, had a large family and spent more time with his offspring than watching his business interests. Not surprisingly, his children grew up pampered, and his fortunes fizzled away."

Leto nodded, attentive as always to his father's talk. But he already knew more than Paulus imagined; he'd listened privately to holo-records and filmbooks inadvertently left accessible to him by his proctors. It occurred to him now, however, that perhaps all of that was by design, part of a plan to open his mother's family history to him like a flower, one petal at a time.

In conjunction with his familial interest in Richese, Leto had always found Ix to be equally intriguing. Once an industrial competitor of Richese, House Vernius of Ix had survived as a technological powerhouse. The royal family of Ix was one of the wealthiest in the Imperium—and he was going to study there.

His father's words broke through his thoughts. "Your training partner will be Prince Rhombur, heir to the noble title of Vernius. I hope you two get along. You're about the same age."

The Prince of Ix. Leto's thoughts soured, hoping the young man wasn't spoiled, like so many other children of powerful Landsraad families. Why couldn't it at least have been a princess, one with a face and figure like the Guild banker's daughter he had met last month at the Tidal Solstice Ball?

"So . . . what is this Prince Rhombur like?" Leto asked.

Paulus laughed, a blustery offering that suggested a lifetime of revelry and bawdy stories. "Why, I don't think I know. It's been a long time since I visited Dominic at home with his wife Shando." He smiled with an inner joke. "Ah, Shando—she was an Imperial concubine once, but Dominic stole her right out from under old Elrood's nose." He gave a loud, impertinent chuckle. "Now they have a son . . . and a daughter, too. Her name is Kailea."

Smiling enigmatically, the Old Duke continued, "There is much for you to learn, my boy. A year hence, both of you will come to study on Caladan, an exchange of teaching services. You and Rhombur will be taken to pundi rice farms in the lowland marshes on the southern continent, to live in shacks and work the paddies. You'll travel beneath the sea in a Nells chamber, and you'll dive for coral gems." He smiled and clapped his son on the shoulder. "Some things can't be taught with filmbooks or in classrooms."

"Yes, sir." He smelled the iodine-sweetness of the seaweed tobacco. He frowned, hoping the smoke covered his expression. This drastic and unexpected change in his life wasn't to his liking, but he respected his father; Leto had learned through many hard lessons that the Old Duke knew exactly what he was talking about, and that Paulus had only the greatest desire to ensure that his son would follow in his footsteps.

The Duke lounged back in his suspensor chair, bobbing in the air. "Lad, I can tell you're not entirely pleased, but this will be a vital experience for you and for Dominic's son. Here on Caladan you'll both learn our greatest secret—how we foster the intense loyalty of our subjects, why we trust our people implicitly in a way the Ixians do not trust theirs."

Paulus became most serious now, without the slightest glint of humor in his eyes. "My son, this is more essential than anything you will learn on an industrial world: People are more important than machines."

It was an adage Leto had heard often; the phrase was part of him, almost as important to him as breathing. "That's why our soldiers fight so well."

Paulus leaned forward into the curling smoke from his last puff. "One day you will be Duke, lad, patriarch of House Atreides and a respected representative in the Landsraad. Your voice there will be equal to that of any other ruler among the Great Houses. That's a great responsibility."

"I'll handle it."

"I'm sure you will, Leto . . . but let yourself relax a bit. The people can tell when you're not happy—and when their Duke is not happy, the population is not happy. Let pressure pass over and through you; that way you can't be harmed by it." He extended a scolding finger. "Have more fun."

Fun. Leto thought again of the Guild banker's daughter, envisioning the fullness of her breasts and hips, the moist pout of her mouth, the way she had looked at him so enticingly.

Maybe he wasn't as serious as his father thought he was. . . .

He took another drink of cidrit juice; the tart coolness dissipated in his throat. "Sir, with your proven loyalty, with the known faithfulness of the Atreides to its allies, why do the Ixians still put us through their interrogation procedures? Do you think an Atreides, even with all that has been instilled in him, could ever become a traitor? Could we ever become like . . . like the Harkonnens?"

The Old Duke scowled. "Once, we were not so different from them, but those are not stories you're ready to hear yet. Remember the play we just watched." He held up a finger. "Things change in the Imperium. Alliances form and dissolve on whims."

"Not *our* alliances."

Paulus met the boy's gray-eyed stare, then looked away, into a corner where the smoke from his pipe swirled in thick curtains.

Leto sighed. There was so much he wanted to know, and quickly. But it was being fed to him in little morsels, like petit fours at one of his mother's fancy parties.

Outside, they heard people moving about, clearing the theatre for the next performance of *Agamemnon*. The actors would be resting, changing costumes, preparing for another audience.

Sitting in this private room with his father, Leto felt more like a man than ever before. Maybe next time he would light a pipe of his own. Maybe he would drink something stronger than cidrit juice. Paulus looked at him with a proud glow in his eyes.

Leto smiled back and tried to imagine what it would be like to be Duke Atreides—then felt a sudden rush of guilt as he realized his father would have to die first in order for him to slip the ducal signet ring onto his finger. He didn't want that, and was thankful that it would be a long time yet. Too far in the future to think about.

Spacing Guild: one leg of the political tripod maintaining the Great Convention. The Guild was the second mental-physical training school (see Bene Gesserit) after the Butlerian Jihad. The Guild monopoly on space travel and transport and upon international banking is taken as the beginning point of the Imperial Calendar.

—Terminology of the Imperium

From his perch on the Golden Lion Throne, Emperor Elrood IX scowled down at the broad-shouldered and too-confident man who stood at the base of the royal dais, with one of his boots, still dirty probably, on the lowest step. As polished-bald as a marble banister knob, Earl Dominic Vernius still carried himself like a popular and decorated war hero, though those days were long over. Elrood doubted anyone still remembered the man's reckless glory days.

The Imperial Chamberlain, Aken Hesban, moved swiftly to the visitor's side, and in a brusque tone ordered Dominic to remove the offending foot. Hesban's face was sallow, his mouth framed with long and drooping mustaches. The last rays of Kaitain's afternoon sunlight cast streaks high on a wall, shining golden rivers through the narrow prismatic windows.

Earl Vernius of Ix removed his foot as he was instructed, but continued to stare cordially at Elrood. The Ixian crest, a purple-and-copper helix, adorned the collar of Dominic's tunic. Though House Corrino was vastly more powerful than the ruling family of Ix, Dominic had the maddening habit of treating the Emperor as an equal, as if their past history—good and bad—allowed him to dispense with formalities. Chamberlain Hesban did not at all approve.

Decades ago Dominic had led legions of Imperial troops during the rough civil wars, and he had not truly respected his Emperor since. Elrood had gotten himself into political trouble late in his impulsive marriage to his fourth wife Habla, and several Landsraad leaders had been forced to use their House military might to enforce stability again. House Vernius of Ix had been among these allies, as had the Atreides.

Now Dominic smiled beneath an extravagant mustache, and looked on Elrood with a jaded eye. The old vulture had not earned his throne through great deeds or compassion. Dominic's great-uncle Gaylord had once said, "If you are born to power, you must prove you deserve it through good works—or give it up. To do any less is to act without conscience."

Standing impatiently on the checkerboard floor of polished stone squares—purportedly samples from all the worlds in the Imperium—Dominic waited for Elrood to speak. *A million worlds? There couldn't possibly be that many stones here, though I don't want to be the one to count them.*

The Chamberlain stared down at him as if his diet consisted entirely of soured milk. But Earl Vernius could play the game himself and refused to fidget, refused to inquire into the nature of his summons. He just stood still, smiling at the old man. Dominic's expression and bright eyes implied knowledge of many more embarrassing personal secrets about the old man than Shando had actually confessed to him—but the suspicion galled Elrood, like an Elaccan bitterthorn in his side.

Something moved on the right, and in the shadows of an arched doorway Dominic saw a black-robed woman, one of those Bene Gesserit witches. He couldn't make out her face, partially concealed as it was by an overhanging cowl. Notorious hoarders of secrets, the Bene Gesserit were always close to the centers of power, constantly watching . . . constantly manipulating.

"I won't ask you if it's true, Vernius," the Emperor finally said. "My sources are unerring, and I know you have committed this terrible act. Ixian technology! Pah!" He made as if to spit from his withered lips. Dominic did not roll his eyes upward; Elrood always overestimated the effectiveness of his melodramatic gestures.

Dominic continued to smile, showing plenty of teeth. "I am unaware of committing any 'terrible act,' Sire. Ask your Truthsayer, if you don't believe me." He flicked a glance at the dark-robed Bene Gesserit woman.

"Mere semantics—don't play dumb, Dominic."

Still, he simply waited, forcing the Emperor to state his charge explicitly.

Elrood huffed, and the Chamberlain huffed with him. "Damn it, your new Heighliner design will allow the Guild, with their damnable monopoly on space transport, to carry *sixteen percent more* in each load!"

Dominic bowed, still smiling mildly. "Actually, m'Lord, we have been able to boost the increase to eighteen percent. That's a substantial improvement over the previous design, involving not only a new hull but a shield technology that weighs less and takes up less room. Therefore, boosted efficiency. This is the very heart of Ixian innovation, which has made House Vernius great over the centuries."

"Your alteration reduces the number of flights the Guild must make to haul the same amount of cargo."

"Why, naturally, Sire." Dominic looked at the old man as if he were incredibly dense. "If you increase the capacity of each Heighliner, you decrease the number of flights required to haul the same amount of material. Simple mathematics."

"Your redesign causes great hardship for the Imperial House, Earl Vernius," said Aken Hesban, clutching his chain of office as if it were a handkerchief. His long mustaches looked like the tusks of a walrus.

"Well, I suppose I can understand the shortsighted reason for your concern, *Sire*," Dominic said, not deigning to look at the stuffed-shirt Chamberlain. Imperial tax was based on the number of flights rather than on the amount of cargo, and the Heighliner redesign therefore resulted in a substantial reduction in income for House Corrino.

Dominic spread his broad scarred hands, looking eminently reasonable. "But how can you request that we blatantly hold back progress? Ix has in no way countermanded the strictures of the Great Revolt. We have the full support of the Spacing Guild and the Landsraad."

"You did this knowing it would incur my wrath?" Elrood leaned forward on the massive throne, looking even more the vulture.

"Come now, Sire!" Dominic laughed, belittling the Emperor's concerns. "Personal feelings can have no place in the march of progress."

Elrood raised himself off the chair, standing in his billowy robes of state that hung like awnings over his skeletal body. "I can't renegotiate with the Guild for a tax based on metric tonnage, Vernius. You know that!"

"And I can't change the simple laws of economics and commerce." He shook his gleaming head, then shrugged. "It's just business, Elrood."

The Court functionaries stopped with a gasp, listening to the candor and familiarity Dominic Vernius used with the Emperor. "Watch yourself," the Chamberlain warned.

But Dominic ignored him and continued. "This design modification affects many people, most of them positively. We are only concerned about progress, and about doing the best possible job for our client, the Spacing Guild. The cost of one new Heighliner is more than most planetary systems make in a Standard Year."

Elrood stared him down. "Perhaps it is time for my administrators and licensors to inspect your manufacturing facilities." His voice carried a threatening tone. "I have reports that Ixian scientists may be developing secret, illegal thinking machines in violation of the Jihad. Yes, I have also heard complaints of repression against your suboid working class. Haven't we, Aken?"

The Chamberlain nodded dourly. "Yes, Highness."

"There have been no such rumors." Dominic chuckled, though a bit uncertainly. "No evidence whatsoever."

"Alas, they were anonymous reports and therefore no records have been kept." The Emperor tapped his long-nailed fingertips together as a real smile crossed his face. "Yes, I believe the best thing would be an unannounced inspection of Ix—before you can send a warning and arrange for anything to be hidden."

"The inner workings of Ix are off-limits to you, according to a long-established Imperium–Landsraad pact." Dominic was riled now, but he tried to maintain his composure.

"I made no such agreement." Elrood looked down at his fingernails. "And I've been Emperor for a long, long time."

"Your ancestor did, and you're bound by it."

"I have the power to make and break agreements. You don't seem to realize that I am the Padishah *Emperor*, and I can do as I please."

"The Landsraad will have something to say about that, *Roody*." Instantly Dominic regretted using the nickname and wished he could take it back. But it was too late.

33

Flushing with rage, the Emperor leaped to his feet and pointed an accusing, shaking finger at Dominic. "How dare you!" The Sardaukar guards snapped to attention, shifting their weapons.

"If you insist on an Imperial inspection," Dominic said with a contemptuous, dismissive gesture, "I will resist it and file a formal complaint in Landsraad court. You have no case, and you know it." He bowed and backed away. "I'm extremely busy, Sire. If you will excuse me, I must take my leave."

Elrood glared at him, stabbed by the pet name Dominic had used. *Roody.* Both men knew that particular personal nickname had been used only by a former concubine of Elrood's, the beautiful Shando . . . who was now Lady Vernius.

After the Ecazi Rebellion, Emperor Elrood had decorated brave young Dominic and granted him an expansion of his fief to include other worlds in the Alkaurops system. At Elrood's invitation, the young Earl Vernius had spent much time at court, a war hero to be seen as a decoration at Imperial banquets and state functions. Hearty Dominic had been very popular, a welcome guest, a proud and humorous companion in the dining hall.

But it was there that Dominic had met Shando, one of the Emperor's many concubines. At the time, Elrood had been married to no one; his fourth and last wife Habla had died five years earlier, and he already had two male heirs (though his eldest, Fafnir, would be poisoned later that year). The Emperor continued to keep a retinue of beautiful women, though primarily to maintain appearances, since he rarely took Shando or any of his other concubines to bed.

Dangerously, Dominic and Shando had fallen in love, but had kept their relationship secret for many months. It was clear that Elrood had lost interest in her after five years, and when she asked to be freed from service and to leave the Imperial Court, Elrood—though perplexed—had complied. He thought fondly of her, and saw no reason to deny her a simple request.

The other concubines had thought Shando foolish to give up such riches and pampering, but she'd had enough of the lavish life and instead wanted a real marriage and children. Elrood, of course, would never take her as his wife.

As soon as she was freed from Imperial service, Dominic Vernius married her, and they had completed their vows with minimal pomp and ceremony, but airtight legality.

Upon hearing that someone else wanted her, Elrood's male pride suddenly made him change his mind—but it was too late. He had resented Dominic ever since, feeling like a cuckold, paranoid about what bedroom secrets Shando might be sharing with her husband.

Roody.

The Bene Gesserit witch who hovered near the throne faded deeper into the shadows behind a speckled column of Canidar granite. Dominic couldn't tell if the cowled woman was pleased or annoyed with the events.

Forcing himself not to waver, not to hurry, Dominic strode confidently past a pair of Sardaukar guards and entered the outer hallway. At a signal from Elrood, they could execute him instantly.

Dominic increased his pace.

The Corrinos were known for rash behavior. On more than one occasion they'd had to make up for their hasty and ill-advised reactions, using their vast family wealth for payoffs. Killing the head of House Vernius during an Imperial audience might just be one of those rash acts—if it weren't for the involvement of the Spacing Guild. The Guild had favored Ix with increased attention and benefits—and had adopted the new Heighliner design—and not even the Emperor and his brutal Sardaukar could oppose the Guild.

This was an ironic circumstance, considering the military might of House Corrino, for the Guild had no fighting forces, no armaments of its own. But without the Guild and their Navigators to see a safe path across folded space, there would be no space travel, no interplanetary banking—and no empire for Elrood to rule. On a moment's notice, the Guild could withhold its favors, stranding armies and putting an end to military campaigns. Of what use would the Sardaukar be if they were planet-bound on Kaitain?

Finally reaching the main exit gate of the Imperial Palace, passing under the Salusan lava arch, Dominic waited while three guards ran him through a security scan.

Unfortunately, Guild protection only went so far.

Dominic had very little respect for the old Emperor. He had tried to hide his contempt for the pathetic ruler of a million worlds, but he'd made a dire mistake by allowing himself to think of him as a mere man, a former lover of his wife's. Elrood, snubbed, could annihilate an entire planet in a fit of pique. The Emperor was the vindictive sort. All Corrinos were.

I HAVE MY contacts, Elrood thought as he watched his adversary depart. *I can bribe some of the workers who are building components for those improved Heighliners—though that may be difficult, since suboids are said to be mindless. Failing that, Dominic, I can find other people you've pushed aside and taken for granted. Your mistake will be in overlooking them.*

In his mind's eye Elrood envisioned the lovely Shando, and recalled their most intimate moments together, decades ago. Purple merh-silk sheets, the sprawling bed, incense burners, and mirrored glowglobes. As Emperor, he could have any woman he wanted—and he had chosen Shando.

For two years she had been his favorite concubine, even when his wife Habla had been alive. Small-boned and petite, she had a fragile porcelain-doll appearance, which she had cultivated during her years on Kaitain; but Elrood also knew she had a commonsense strength and resiliency deep inside her. They had enjoyed doing multilingual word puzzles together. Shando had whispered "Roody" in his ear when he had invited her to the Imperial bedchamber; and she had cried it loudly during climactic moments of passion.

In memory he heard her voice. *Roody . . . Roody . . . Roody . . .*

Being a commoner, however, Shando simply wasn't suitable for him to marry. It had not even been an option. The heads of royal Houses rarely wed their concubines, and an Emperor *never* did. Dashing young Dominic, with his wiles and flattery, had gotten Shando to talk herself free, to trick Elrood, and then had spirited her away to Ix, where he had married her in secret. The astonishment in the Landsraad came later, and despite the scandal the two had remained married these many years.

And the Landsraad, despite Elrood's petition to them, had refused to do anything about it. After all, Dominic had married the girl and the Emperor never had any intention of doing so. Everything according to law. Despite his petty jealousies, Elrood couldn't claim Shando had been adulterous, not by any legal standard.

But Dominic Vernius knew her intimate nickname for him. What else had Shando told her husband? It ate at him like a Poritrin fester.

On the screen of a wrist-strap security monitor, he watched Dominic at the main gate, as pale security beams washed over him—from a scanner that was another sophisticated Ixian machine.

He could send a signal, and the probes would obliterate the other man's mind, leave him a vegetable. *An unexpected power surge . . . a most terrible accident . . .* How ironic if Elrood were to use an Ixian scanner to kill the Earl of Ix.

Oh, how he wanted to do it! But not now. The time wasn't right, and there could be embarrassing questions, maybe even an investigation. Such vengeance required subtlety and planning. In that way, the surprise and ultimate victory would be so much more satisfying.

Elrood switched off the monitor, and the screen darkened.

Standing beside the blocky throne, Chamberlain Aken Hesban didn't ask why his Emperor was smiling.

The highest function of ecology is the understanding of consequences.
—PARDOT KYNES, Ecology of Bela Tegeuse,
Initial Report to the Imperium

Over a razor-edged horizon the shimmering atmosphere was filled with pastel colors of sunrise. In a brief instant the clean stillness of Arrakis allowed warm light to flood over the wrinkled landscape . . . a sudden deluge of brightness and rising heat. The white sun lurched above the horizon, without much precursor glow in the arid air.

Now that he had finally arrived on the desert world, Pardot Kynes drew a deep breath, then remembered to put the face mask over his nose and mouth to prevent extreme moisture loss. His sparse, sandy hair blew in a light breeze. He had only been on Arrakis four days, and already he sensed that this barren place held more mysteries than a lifetime could ever unravel.

He would have preferred to have been left to his own devices. He wanted to wander alone across the Great Bled with his instruments and logbooks, studying the character of lava rock and the stratified layers of dunes.

However, when Glossu Rabban, nephew of the Baron and heir apparent to House Harkonnen, announced his intention to go into the deep desert to hunt one of the legendary sandworms, such an opportunity was too great for Kynes to ignore.

As a mere Planetologist in the entourage, a scientist instead of a warrior, he felt like the odd man out. Harkonnen desert troops brought along weaponry and explosives from the armored central keep. They took a troop transport led by a man named Thekar, who claimed to have once lived in a desert village, though he was now a water merchant in Carthag. He had more of a Fremen look to him than he admitted, though none of the Harkonnens seemed to notice.

Rabban had no specific plan for tracking one of the huge sinuous beasts. He didn't want to go to a spice-harvesting site, where his crew might disrupt the work. He wanted to hunt down and kill such a beast by himself. He just brought along all the weaponry he could imagine and relied upon his instinctive talent for destruction. . . .

Days earlier, Kynes had arrived on Arrakis by diplomatic shuttle, landing in the dirty though relatively new city. Eager to get started, he had presented his Imperial assignment papers to the Baron himself. The lean, red-haired man had scrutinized Kynes's orders carefully, then verified the Imperial seal. He pursed his thick lips before he grudgingly promised his cooperation. "So long as you know enough to stay out of the way of real work."

Kynes had bowed. "I like nothing better than to be alone and out of the way, m'Lord Baron."

He'd spent his first two days in the city purchasing desert gear, talking to people from the outlying villages, learning what he could about the legends of the desert, the warnings, the customs, the mysteries to explore. Understanding the importance of such things, Kynes spent a substantial sum to obtain the best stillsuit he could find for desert survival, as well as a paracompass, water distilleries, and reliable note-keeping devices.

It was said that many tribes of the enigmatic Fremen lived in the trackless wastes. Kynes wanted to talk with them, to understand how they squeezed survival from such a harsh environment. But the out-of-place Fremen seemed reticent within the boundaries of Carthag, and they hurried away whenever he tried to talk with them. . . .

Kynes didn't much care for the city himself. House Harkonnen had erected the new headquarters *en masse* when, four decades earlier, Guild manipulations had given them Arrakis as a quasi-fief to govern.

Carthag had been built with the rapidity of inexhaustible human labor, without finesse or attention to detail: blocky buildings constructed of substandard materials for ostentatious purposes or functionality. No elegance whatsoever.

Carthag did not appear to *belong* here; its architecture and placement were offensive to his sensibilities. Kynes had an innate ability to see how the fabric of an ecosystem meshed, how the pieces fit together in a natural world. But this population center was wrong, like a pustule on the skin of the planet.

Another outpost to the southwest, Arrakeen, was a more primitive city that had grown slowly, naturally, nestled against a mountainous barrier called the Shield Wall. Perhaps Kynes should have gone there first. But political requirements had forced him to establish his base with the rulers of the planet.

At least that had given him the opportunity to search for one of the giant sandworms.

The large 'thopter transport carrying Rabban's hunting party lifted off, and soon Kynes received his initial glimpse of the true desert. Kynes peered out the windowplaz at the rippled wastelands below. From experiences in other desert regions, he was able to identify dune patterns . . . shapes and sinuous curves that revealed much about seasonal wind patterns, prevailing air currents, and the severity of storms. So much could be learned from studying these ripples and lines, the fingerprints of weather. He pressed his face to the plaz observation ports; none of the other passengers appeared to be interested at all.

The Harkonnen troops fidgeted, hot in their heavy blue uniforms and armor. Their weapons clattered against each other and scraped the floor plates. The men seemed uneasy without their personal body-shields, but the presence of a shield and its Holtzman field would drive any nearby worms into a killing frenzy. Today, Rabban himself wanted to do the killing.

Glossu Rabban, the twenty-one-year-old son of the planet's former lackluster governor, sat up front near the pilot, looking for targets out on the sand. With severely cropped brown hair, he was broad-shouldered, deep-voiced, and short-tempered. Icy pale blue eyes looked out from a sunburned face. He seemed to do everything possible to be the opposite of his father.

"Will we see worm tracks from the sky?" he asked.

Behind him, Thekar the desert guide leaned very close, as if wishing to remain within Rabban's personal space. "The sands shift and mask the passage of a worm. Often they travel deep. You will not see a worm moving until it approaches the surface and is ready to attack."

The tall, angular Kynes listened intently, taking mental notes. He wanted to record all of these details in his logbook, but that would have to wait until later.

"Then how are we going to find one? I heard the open desert is crawling with worms."

"Not that simple, m'Lord Rabban," Thekar responded. "The great worms have their own domains, some extending to hundreds of square kilometers. Within these boundaries they hunt and kill any intruders."

Growing impatient, Rabban turned around in his seat. His skin grew darker. "How do we know where to find a worm's domain?"

Thekar smiled, and his dark, close-set eyes took on a distant look. "All of the desert is owned by Shai-Hulud."

"By *what*? Stop evading my questions." Within another moment, Kynes was sure Rabban would cuff the desert man across the jaw.

"You have been on Arrakis for so long, and you did not know this, m'Lord Rabban? The Fremen consider the great sandworms to be gods," Thekar answered quietly. "They name him, collectively, Shai-Hulud."

"Then today we shall kill a god," Rabban announced in a loud voice, causing the other hunters in the back of the compartment to cheer. He turned sharply toward the desert guide. "I depart for Giedi Prime in two days, and must have a trophy to take back with me. This hunt *will* be successful."

Giedi Prime, Kynes thought. *Ancestral homeworld of House Harkonnen. At least I won't have to worry about him once he's gone.*

"You will have your trophy, m'Lord," Thekar promised.

"No doubt about that," Rabban said, but in a more ominous tone.

Seated alone in the rear of the troop transport, huddled in his desert gear, Kynes felt uncomfortable in such company. He had no interest in the glorious ambitions of the Baron's nephew . . . but if this excursion gave him a good look at one of the monsters, it could be worth months of intensive effort on his own.

Rabban stared out through the front of the transport; his hard, squinting eyes were surrounded by thick folds of skin. He scrutinized the desert as if it were a delicacy he intended to eat, seeing none of the beauty Kynes noted in the landscape.

"I have a plan, and this is how we'll follow it." Rabban turned to the troops and opened the comsystem to the spotter ornithopters flying in formation around the transport. They cruised out over the expanse of open sand. The dune ripples below looked like wrinkles on an old man's skin.

"That outcropping of rock down there"—he gestured, and read off the coordinates—"will be our base. About three hundred meters from the rock we'll touch down in the open sand, where we'll drop Thekar with a gadget he calls a thumper. Then we'll lift off to the safety of the rock outcroppings, where the worm can't go."

The lean desert man looked up in alarm. "Leave me out there? But m'Lord, I'm not—"

"*You* gave me the idea." He turned back to address the uniformed troops. "Thekar here says that this Fremen device, a thumper, will bring a worm. We'll plant one along with enough explosives to take care of the beast when it comes. Thekar, we will leave you behind to rig the explosives and trigger the thumper. You can run across the sands and make it to safety with us before a worm can come, right?" Rabban gave him a delicious little grin.

"I—I . . ." Thekar stammered. "It appears I have no choice."

"Even if you can't make it, the worm will probably go for the thumper first. The explosives will get the beast before you become its next target."

"I take comfort in that, m'Lord," Thekar said.

Intrigued by the Fremen device, Kynes considered obtaining one for himself. He wished he could watch this desert native up close to witness how he ran across the sands, how he eluded pursuit from the vibration-sensitive "Old Man of the Desert." But the Planetologist knew enough to remain quiet and avoid Rabban's notice, hoping that the hot-blooded young Harkonnen wouldn't volunteer *him* to assist Thekar.

Inside the personnel compartment at the back of the craft, the Bator—a commander of a small troop—and his underlings looked through the weapons stockpile, removing lasguns for themselves. They rigged explosives to the stakelike mechanism that Thekar had brought along. *A thumper.*

With curious eyes, Kynes could see that it was just a spring-wound clockwork device that would thunk out a loud, rhythmic vibration. When plunged into the sand, the thumper would send reverberations deep below the desert to where "Shai-Hulud" could hear them.

"As soon as we land, you'd better rig up these explosives fast," Rabban said to Thekar. "The engines of these ornithopters will do a good job of attracting the worm, even without the help of your Fremen toy."

"I know that all too well, m'Lord," Thekar said. His olive skin now had a grayish, oily tinge of terror.

The ornithopter struts kissed the sands, throwing up loose dust. The hatch opened, and Thekar—determined, now—grabbed his thumper and sprang out, landing with spread feet on the soft desert. He flashed a longing glance back up at the flying craft, then turned toward the dubious safety of the line of solid rock some three hundred meters away.

The Bator handed the explosives down to the hapless desert man, while Rabban gestured for them to hurry. "I hope you don't become worm food, my friend," he said with a laugh. Even before the doors could close on the ornithopter, the pilot lifted off the sands again, leaving Thekar alone.

Kynes and the other Harkonnen soldiers rushed to the starboard side of the transport, crowding the windowplaz to watch their guide's desperate actions out on the open sands. The desert man had reverted to a different, feral human being as they watched.

"Excuse me. Just how much explosive does it take to kill a worm?" Kynes asked curiously.

"Thekar should have plenty, Planetologist," the Bator answered. "We gave him enough to wipe out an entire city square."

Kynes turned his attention back to the drama below. As the craft rose higher, Thekar worked in a flurry, grabbing the explosive components, piling them in a mound and linking them together with shiga-wire cables. Kynes could see tiny ready lights winking on. Then the whip-thin man stabbed his thumper into the sand next to the deadly cache, as if he were pounding a stake into the heart of the desert.

The troop 'thopter swerved and arrowed straight toward the bulwark of rock where the great hunter Rabban would wait in comfort and safety. Thekar triggered the thumper's spring-wound mechanism and began to run.

Inside the ornithopter, some of the soldiers placed bets on the outcome.

Within moments the craft alighted on the ridge of blackened, pitted rock that looked like a reef in the soft desert. The pilot shut down his engines, and the 'thopter doors opened. Rabban shoved his troops aside to be the first to stand upon the shimmering rock. The others in the party piled out afterward; Kynes waited his turn and emerged from the rear.

The guards took up watch positions, directing the oil lenses of their binoculars at the small running figure. Rabban stood tall, holding a high-powered lasgun, though Kynes couldn't imagine what he intended to do with the weapon at this point. Through a spotting-scope, the Baron's nephew stared out into the heat-addled air, seeing the ripples and mirages. He centered on the clacking thumper and the dark landmark of piled explosives.

One of the high spotter 'thopters reported possible wormsign about two kilometers to the south.

Out on the desert, Thekar ran frantically, kicking up sand. He advanced toward the archipelago of safety, the rocky islands in the sea of sand—but he was still many minutes away.

Kynes watched the odd manner in which Thekar placed his footsteps. He seemed to jitter and hop erratically, running like a spastic insect. Kynes wondered if this was some sort of arrhythmic pattern to fool an oncoming sandworm. Was this technique something that desert travelers learned? If so, who could teach it to Kynes? He had to know everything about this place and its people, the worms and the spice and the dunes. Not only was it his Imperial directive: Pardot Kynes wanted to know for *himself*. Once he became involved in a project, he hated unanswered questions.

The group waited, and time passed slowly. The soldiers talked. The desert man continued his peculiar running, moving imperceptibly closer. Kynes could feel the stillsuit micro-sandwich layers sucking up his droplets of sweat.

He knelt and studied the umber rock at his feet. Basaltic lava, it contained eroded pockets that had been formed from leftover gaseous bubbles in the molten rock, or softer stone eaten away by the legendary Coriolis storms of Arrakis.

Kynes picked up a handful of sand and let it run through his fingers.

Not unexpectedly, he saw that the grains of sand were quartz particles, shimmering in the sun with a few flecks of darker material that might have been magnetite.

At other places he had seen rusty colorations in the sand, striations of tan, orange, and coral, hinting at various oxides. Some of the coloring could also have been from weathered deposits of the spice melange, but Kynes had never seen unprocessed spice in the wild before. *Not yet.*

Finally, the spotter 'thopters overhead confirmed an approaching worm. A large one, moving fast.

The guards rose to their feet. Looking out onto the blurry landscape, Kynes saw a ripple on the sand, like an immense finger being drawn beneath the surface, disturbing the upper layers. The size of it astounded him.

"Worm's coming in from the side!" the Bator called.

"It's going straight for Thekar!" Rabban shouted, with cruel glee. "He's between the worm and the thumper. Awww, bad luck." His wide face now showed a different kind of anticipation.

Even from this distance, Kynes could see Thekar put on a burst of speed, forgetting his staggering walk as he saw the mound of the approaching worm tunneling toward him faster and faster. Kynes could well imagine the look of horror and hopeless despair on the desert man's face.

Then with a grim resolve and a sudden desperation, Thekar came to a full stop and lay flat on the sand, motionless, staring up at the sky, perhaps praying fervently to Shai-Hulud.

With the tiny footstep vibrations stopped, the distant thumper seemed as loud as an Imperial band. *Thump, thump, thump.* The worm paused—then altered its path to head straight toward the cache of explosives.

Rabban gave a twitch of a shrug, nonchalant acceptance of an irrelevant defeat.

Kynes could hear the underground hiss of shifting sands, the approach of the behemoth. It came closer and closer, attracted like an iron filing to a deadly magnet. As it neared the thumper, the worm dived deeper underground, circled, and came up to engulf that which had attracted it, angered it—or whatever instinctive reaction these blind leviathans experienced.

When the worm rose from the sands, it revealed a mouth large enough to swallow a spacecraft, ascending higher and higher, its maw opening wider as its flexible jaws spread like the petals of a flower. In an instant it engulfed the insignificant black speck of the thumper and all the explosives. Its crystal teeth shone like tiny sharp thorns spiraling down its bottomless gullet.

From three hundred meters away, Kynes saw ridges of ancient skin, overlapping folds of armor that protected the creature in its passage beneath the ground. The worm gulped the booby-trapped bait and began to wallow into the sands again.

Rabban stood up with a demonic grin on his face and worked small transmitting controls. A hot breeze dusted his face, peppering his teeth with grains of sand. He pushed a button.

A distant thunderclap sent a tremor through the desert. The sands shifted in tiny avalanches from the fingernail dunes. The sequenced bomb ripped through the internal channels of the worm, blasting open its gut and splitting its armored segments.

As the dust cleared, Kynes saw the writhing, dying monstrosity that lay in a pool of disrupted sand, like a beached fur-whale.

"That thing's more than two hundred meters long!" Rabban cried, taking in the extent of his kill.

The guards cheered. Rabban turned and pounded Kynes on the back with nearly enough strength to dislocate his shoulder.

"Now *there's* a trophy, Planetologist. I'm going to take this back to Giedi Prime with me."

Almost unnoticed, Thekar finally arrived, sweating and panting, hauling himself up to safety on the rocks. He looked behind him with mixed emotions at the faraway dead creature sprawled on the sands.

Rabban led the charge as the worm ceased its final writhing. The eager guards sprinted across the sands, shouting, cheering. Kynes, anxious now to see the amazing specimen up close, hurried along, stumbling as Harkonnen troops plowed a battered path ahead of him.

Many minutes later, panting and hot, Kynes stood awestruck in front of the towering mass of the ancient worm. Its skin was scaled, covered with gravel, thick with abrasion-proof calluses. Yet between the segments that sagged open from the explosions, he saw pink, tender skin. The gaping mouth of the worm itself was like a mine shaft lined with crystal daggers.

"It's the most fearsome creature on this miserable planet!" Rabban crowed. "And I've killed it!"

The soldiers peered, none of them wanting to approach closer than several meters. Kynes wondered how the Baron's nephew intended to haul this trophy back with him. With the Harkonnen penchant for extravagance, however, he assumed Rabban would find a way.

The Planetologist turned to see that the exhausted Thekar had plodded up beside them. His eyes held a silvery sheen, as if some inner fire blazed bright. Perhaps by coming so close to death and seeing the Fremen desert god laid low by Harkonnen explosives, his perspective on the world had changed.

"Shai-Hulud," he whispered. Then he turned to Kynes, as if sensing a kindred spirit. "This is an ancient one. One of the oldest of the worms."

Kynes stepped forward to look at the encrusted skin, at its segments, and wondered how he might go about dissecting and analyzing the specimen. Certainly Rabban couldn't object to that? If necessary, Kynes would invoke his assignment from the Emperor to make the man understand.

But as he approached closer, intending to touch it, he saw that the skin of the old worm was shimmering, moving, shifting. The beast itself wasn't still alive—its nerve functions had ceased even to twitch . . . and yet its outer layers trembled and shifted, as if melting.

While Kynes stared in amazement, a rain of translucent cellular flaps dripped off the hulk of the old worm, like scales shed to the churned sand, where they vanished.

"What's going on?" Rabban cried, his face purpling. Before his eyes the worm seemed to be evaporating. The skin sloughed off into tiny flopping amoebalike patches that jiggled and then burrowed into the sand like molten solder. The ancient behemoth slumped into the desert.

In the end, only skeletal, cartilaginous ribs and milky teeth were left. Then even these remains sank slowly, dissolving into mounds of loose gelatin covered by sand.

The Harkonnen troops stepped back to a safer distance.

To Kynes, it seemed as if he had seen a thousand years of decay in only a few seconds. Accelerated entropy. The hungry desert seemed eager to swallow every shred of evidence, to conceal the fact that a human had defeated a sandworm.

As Kynes thought about it, more in confusion and growing amazement than in dismay at losing all chance of dissecting the specimen, he wondered just how strange the life cycle of these magnificent beasts must be.

He had so much to learn about Arrakis. . . .

Rabban stood, seething and furious. The muscles in his neck stretched taut like iron cables. "My trophy!" He whirled, clenched his fists, and struck Thekar full across the face, knocking him flat onto the sands. For a moment, Kynes thought the Baron's nephew might actually kill the desert man, but Rabban turned his rage and fury on the still-dissolving, shuddering heap of the sandworm sinking into the exploded sands.

He screamed curses at it. Then as Kynes watched, a determined look came into Rabban's cold, menacing eyes. His sunburned face flushed a deeper red. "When I return to Giedi Prime, I'll hunt something a lot more satisfying." Then, as if distracted from all thoughts of the sandworm, Rabban turned and stalked away.

One observes the survivors, and learns from them.
—Bene Gesserit Teaching

Of all the fabled million worlds in the Imperium, young Duncan Idaho had never been anywhere but Giedi Prime, an oil-soaked, industry-covered planet filled with artificial constructions, square angles, metal, and smoke. The Harkonnens liked to keep their home that way. Duncan had known nothing else in his eight years.

Even the dark and dirt-stained alleys of his lost home would have been a welcome sight now, though. After months of imprisonment with the rest of his family, Duncan wondered if he would ever again go outside the huge en-slavement city of Barony. Or if he would live to see his ninth birthday, which shouldn't be too far off now. He wiped a hand through his curly black hair, felt the sweat there.

And he kept running. The hunters were coming closer.

Duncan was beneath the prison city now, with his pur-suers behind him. He hunched down and rushed through the cramped maintenance tunnels, feeling like the spiny-backed rodent his mother had let him keep as a pet when he was five. Ducking lower, he scuttled along in tiny crawl spaces, smelly air shafts, and power-conduit tubes. The big adults with their padded armor could never follow him here. He scraped his elbow on the metal walls, worming his way into places no human should have been able to navigate.

The boy vowed not to let the Harkonnens catch him—at least not today. He hated their games, refused to be anyone's pet or prey. Negotiating his way through the darkness by smell and instinct, he felt a stale breeze on his face and noted the direction of the air circulation.

His ears recorded echoes as he moved: the sounds of other prisoner children running, also desperate. They were supposedly his teammates, but Duncan had learned through previous failures not to rely on people whose feral skills might not match his own.

He swore he would get away from the hunters this time but knew he would never be entirely free of them. In this controlled environment the stalking teams would catch him again and run him through the paces, over and over. They called it "training." Training for *what*, he didn't know.

Duncan's right side still ached from the last episode. As if he were a prized animal, his tormentors had put his injured body through a skin-knit machine and acu-cellular repair. His ribs still didn't quite feel right, but they had been getting better each day. Until now.

With the locator beacon implanted in the meat of his shoulder, Duncan could never really escape from this slaveholding metropolis. Barony was a megalithic construction of plasteel and armor-plaz, 950 stories tall and 45 kilometers long, with no ground-level openings whatsoever. He always found plenty of places to hide during the Harkonnen games, but never any freedom.

The Harkonnens had many prisoners, and they had sadistic methods of making them cooperate. If Duncan won in this training hunt, if he eluded the searchers long enough, the keepers had promised that he and his family could return to their former lives. All the children had been promised the same thing. Trainees needed a goal, a prize to fight for.

He ran by instinct through the secret passageways, trying to muffle his footfalls. Not far behind, he heard the blast and sizzle of a stun gun firing, a child's high-pitched squeal of pain, and then teeth-chattering spasms as another one of the young boys was brought to ground.

If the searchers captured you, they hurt you—sometimes seriously and sometimes worse, depending upon the current supply of "trainees." This was no child's game of hide-and-seek. At least not for the victims.

Even at his age, Duncan already knew that life and death had a price. The Harkonnens didn't care how many small candidates suffered during the course of their training. This was how the Harkonnens *played*. Duncan understood cruel amusements. He had seen others do such things before, especially the children with whom he shared confinement, as they pulled the wings off insects or set tiny rodent babies on fire. The Harkonnens and their troops were like adult children, only with greater resources, greater imaginations, greater malice.

Without making a sound, he found a narrow, rusted access ladder and scrambled up into the darkness, wasting no time on thought. Duncan had to do the unexpected, hide where they'd have trouble reaching him. The rungs, pitted and scarred with age, hurt his hands.

This section of ancient Barony still functioned; power conduits and suspensor tubes shot through the main structure like wormholes—straight, curved, hooking off at oblique angles. The place was one enormous obstacle course, where the Harkonnen troops could fire upon their prey without risking damage to more important structures.

Above him in a main corridor, he heard booted feet running, filtered voices through helmet communicators, then a shout. A nearby pinging sound signaled that the guards had homed in on his locator implant.

Hot white lasgun fire blasted the ceiling over his head, melting through metal plates. Duncan let go of the ladder and allowed himself to drop, freefall. One armed guard peeled up the hot-edged floor plate and pointed down at him. The others fired their lasguns again, severing the struts so that the ladder fell in tandem with the small boy.

He landed on the floor of a lower shaft, and the heavy ladder clattered on top of him. But Duncan didn't cry out in pain. That would only bring the pursuers closer . . . though he had no real hope of eluding them for long because of the pulsing beacon in his shoulder. How could anyone but Harkonnens win this game?

He pushed himself to his feet and ran with a new, frantic desire for freedom. To his dismay, the small tunnel ahead opened into a wider passage. Wider was bad. The bigger men could follow him there.

He heard shouts behind, more running feet, gunfire, and then a gurgling scream. The pursuers were supposed to be using stun guns, but Duncan knew that this late in the day's hunt, most everyone else would have been captured—and the stakes were higher. The hunters didn't like to lose.

Duncan had to survive. He had to be the best. If he died, he couldn't go back to see his mother again. But if he lived and defeated these bastards, then perhaps his family would get their freedom . . . or as much freedom as Harkonnen civil service workers could ever have on Giedi Prime.

Duncan had seen other trainees who had defeated the pursuers before, and those children had disappeared afterward. If he could believe the announcements, the winners and their captive families had been set free from the hellhole of Barony. Duncan had no proof of this, though, and had plenty of reasons to question what the Harkonnens told him. But he *wanted* to believe them, could not give up hope.

He didn't understand why his parents had been thrown into this prison. What had minor government office workers done to deserve such punishment? He remembered only that one day life had been normal and relatively happy . . . and the next, they were all here, enslaved. Now young Duncan was forced nearly every day to run and fight for his life, and for the future of his family. He was getting better at it.

He remembered that last normal afternoon out on a manicured lawn planted high up in one of the Harko City terraces, one of the rare balcony parks the Harkonnens allowed their subjects to have. The gardens and hedges were carefully fertilized and tended, because plants did not fare well in the residue-impregnated soil of a planet that had been too long abused.

Duncan's parents and other family members had been playing frivolous lawn games, tossing self-motivated balls at targets on the grass, while internal high-entropy devices made the balls bounce and ricochet randomly. The boy had noticed how different, how dry and structured the games of adults were compared with the reckless romping he did with his friends.

A young woman stood near him, watching the games. She had chocolate-colored hair, dusky skin, and high cheekbones, but her pinched expression and hard gaze detracted from what might have been remarkable beauty. He didn't know who she was and understood only that her name was Janess Milam, and she worked with his parents somehow.

As Duncan had watched the adult yard game, listening to the laughter, he smiled at the woman and observed, "They're practicing to be old men." It became apparent, though, that Janess had no real interest in him or his opinion, for she'd given him a sharp verbal brush-off.

Under the hazy sunlight Duncan had continued to watch the game, but with increasing curiosity about the stranger. He sensed tension in her. Janess, who didn't participate, frequently glanced over her shoulder, as if watching for something.

Moments later Harkonnen troops had come, grabbing Duncan's parents, himself, even his uncle and two cousins. He understood intuitively that *Janess* had been the cause of it all, for whatever reason. He'd never seen her again, and he and his family had been in prison for half a year now. . . .

Behind him, an overhead trapdoor opened with a hiss. Two blue-uniformed pursuers dropped through, pointed at him, and laughed in triumph. Weaving from side to side, Duncan dashed ahead. A lasgun blast ricocheted off the wall plates, leaving a lightning-bolt scorch mark down the corridor.

Duncan smelled the ozone from the singed metal. If even one of those bolts hit him, he'd be dead. He hated the way the hunters snickered, as if they were merely toying with him.

A pair of pursuers charged out of a side passage only a meter in front of him, but Duncan moved too fast. They didn't recognize him or react quickly enough. He struck one stout man in the knee and knocked him sideways before dashing between the two at a full run.

The stout man stumbled, then shouted as a laser bolt singed his armor, "Stop firing, you idiot! You'll hit one of us!"

Duncan ran as he'd never run before, knowing his child's legs couldn't outrace adults conditioned for fighting. But he refused to give up. It wasn't in his blood.

Ahead, where the corridor opened, he saw bright lights at an intersection of passageways. As he approached, he skidded to a stop only to find that the cross-passage was no tunnel at all, but a suspensor tube, a cylindrical shaft with a Holtzman field in the center. Levitating bullet-trains shot down the tube without resistance, traveling from one end of the enormous prison city to the other.

There were no doors, no open passageways. Duncan could run no farther. The men surged close behind him, extending their guns. If he surrendered, he wondered if they would still shoot him down. *Probably*, he thought, *since I've gotten their adrenaline going.*

The suspensor field shimmered in the center of the horizontal shaft in front of him. He vaguely knew what it would do. He had only one place left to go, and he wasn't sure what would happen—but he knew he'd be punished, or most likely slaughtered, if the guards captured him.

So as they pressed closer, Duncan turned around and gazed into the suspensor field. Taking a deep breath for courage, he swung his short arms behind him and leaped out into the open shimmering tube.

His curly black hair rippled in the breeze as he plummeted. He shouted, the sound halfway between a despairing wail and a cry of glorious release. If he died here, at least he would be free!

Then the Holtzman field wrapped around him and caught him with a jolt. Feeling as if his stomach had just lurched to the center of his chest, Duncan found himself adrift in an invisible net. He floated without falling, hanging in the neutral center of the field. This force held the bullet-trains suspended as they careened through mammoth Barony. It could certainly hold him.

He saw the guards rushing to the edge of the platform, shouting at him in anger. One shook a fist. Two others pointed their guns.

Duncan flailed in the field, trying to swim—anything to move away.

With a shout of alarm, a guard knocked the other's lasgun aside. Duncan had heard about the nightmarish effects of a lasgun beam crossing a Holtzman field: They produced an interacting destructive potential as deadly as forbidden atomics themselves.

So the guards fired their stun weapons instead.

Duncan writhed in the air. Though he could get no leverage, at least he made a moving target as he squirmed and spun. Stun blasts arced on either side of him, diverted into curving paths.

Despite the confining embrace of the Holtzman field, he felt the air pressure change around him, sensed the currents of movement. He rotated himself, bobbing in the air—until he saw the oncoming lights of a bullet-train.

And he was at the center of the field!

Duncan thrashed, desperate to move. He drifted toward the opposite edge of the levitation zone, away from the guards. They continued to fire, but the change in air pressure pushed their stun blasts even farther off the mark than before. He saw the uniformed men making adjustments.

Below him were other doorways, ramps, and platforms that led into the bowels of Barony. Maybe he could reach one . . . if he could just escape the confining field.

Another stun blast tore past and this time caught the edge of his back near his shoulder, numbing him, making the muscles and skin crawl with a sensation like a thousand stinging insects.

Duncan finally wrenched himself away from the field and dropped. Falling facedown, he saw the platform just in time. He reached out with his good arm and snagged a railing. The bullet-train screamed past, whistling as it displaced air . . . missing him by centimeters.

He hadn't had time to pick up much momentum in his fall; even so, the jarring stop nearly ripped his other arm out of its socket. Duncan scrambled up and ran into a tunnel, but found only a tiny alcove with metawalls. He could see no exit. The hatch was sealed and locked. He pounded on it, but couldn't go anywhere.

Then, the outer door clanged shut behind him, sealing him into a small armor-walled box. He was trapped. This time it was over.

Moments later, the guards unsealed the rear hatch. Their stares, as pointed as their weapons, held a mixture of anger and admiration. Duncan waited with resignation for them to gun him down.

Instead, the hunt captain smiled without humor and said, "Congratulations, boy. You made it."

EXHAUSTED AND BACK in his cell, Duncan sat with his mother and father. They ate their daily meal of bland cereals, starch-cakes, and protein chips—nutritionally satisfying yet almost maliciously made with either foul flavors or no taste whatsoever. So far the boy hadn't been told more by his captors, just that he'd "made it." That had to mean freedom. He could only hope.

The family's cell was filthy. Though his parents tried to keep it clean, they had no brooms, mops, or soap, and very little water, which couldn't be wasted on mere sanitation.

During the months of confinement, Duncan had undergone vigorous and violent "training," while his family sat fearfully offstage, doing nothing with their days. All of them had been given numbers, slave-cell addresses, and (with the exception of Duncan) nothing to do—no labor, no entertainment. They simply awaited any change in their sentence . . . and dreaded that such a change would someday come.

Now with excitement and pride Duncan told his mother of his adventures, how he had outwitted the pursuers, how he had been resourceful enough to defeat even the best Harkonnen trackers. None of the other children had succeeded on this day, but Duncan was certain he'd done what was necessary to buy freedom.

Any minute now they'd be released. He tried to imagine his family standing together again, free, outside, looking up into a clear, starlit night.

His father gazed proudly at the boy, but his mother found it difficult to believe that such a thing could possibly be true. She had good reason not to trust Harkonnen promises.

Before long, the cell lights flickered, and the opaque door field became transparent, then opened. A group of blue-uniformed prison guards stood beside the smiling hunt captain who had chased him. Duncan's heart leaped. *Are we going to be set free?*

He didn't like the hunt captain's smile, though.

The uniformed men stepped aside in deference to a man with broad shoulders, thick lips, and big muscles. His face was sunburned and ruddy, as if he had spent a great deal of time far from gloomy Giedi Prime.

Duncan's father sprang to his feet, then bowed clumsily. "M'Lord Rabban!"

Ignoring the parents, Rabban's eyes sought out only the round-faced young trainee. "The captain of the hunt tells me you're the best boy," he said to Duncan. As he stepped into the cell, the guards hustled in behind him. Rabban grinned.

"You should have seen him in today's exercise, m'Lord," the hunt captain said. "Never had a more resourceful pup."

Rabban nodded. "Number 11368, I've seen your records, watched holos of your hunts. How are your injuries? Not too bad? You're young, so you'll heal quickly." His eyes hardened. "Lots more fun left in you. Let's see how you do against me."

He turned about. "Come with me for the hunt, boy. Now."

"My name is Duncan Idaho," the boy responded, in a defiant tone.

"I'm not a number." His voice was thin and high-pitched, but held a gruff bravery that shocked his parents. Surprised, the guards turned to stare at him. Duncan looked to his mother for support, as if hoping for some kind of challenge or reward. Instead, she tried to hush him.

Rabban coolly snatched a lasgun from the guard standing next to him. Without the slightest pause, he fired a lethal blast into the chest of Duncan's father. The man slammed against the wall. Before his corpse could slide to the floor, Rabban shifted his weapon and incinerated the head of Duncan's mother.

Duncan screamed. Both of his parents tumbled to the floor, lifeless mounds of blistering, burned flesh.

"Now you have no name, 11368," Rabban said. "Come with me."

The guards grabbed him, not even letting Duncan rush to his fallen parents. Not even giving him time to cry.

"These men will have to prepare you before we can begin the next round of fun. I need a good hunt for a change."

The guards dragged Duncan, kicking and screaming, out of the noisome cell. He felt dead inside—except for an icy flame of hatred that blossomed in his chest and burned away all vestiges of his childhood.

*The populace must think their ruler is a greater man than they,
else why should they follow him? Above all a leader must be a
showman, giving his people the bread and circuses they require.*

— DUKE PAULUS ATREIDES

The weeks of preparation for his sojourn on Ix passed in
a blur as Leto tried to drink up a year's worth of
memories and store them, fixing all the images of his ancestral home in his mind. He would miss Caladan's moist salty
air, its fog-shrouded mornings, and the musical afternoon
rainstorms. How could a stark, colorless machine planet
compare with this?

Of the many palaces and vacation villas on the water-
rich planet, Castle Caladan, perched high on a cliff over
the sea, was the true place where Leto belonged, the main
seat of government. Someday, when he finally put on the
ducal signet ring, he would be the twenty-sixth Duke Atreides to sit in the Castle.

His mother Helena spent much time fussing over him,
seeing omens in many things, and quoting passages she considered important from the Orange Catholic Bible. She was
distressed to be losing her son for a year, but would not
countermand the Old Duke's orders—not in anyone's hearing, at least. Her expression was troubled, and Leto realized
it especially alarmed her that Paulus had chosen to send
him to Ix, of all places. "It's a festering hotbed of suspect

technology," she said to him when her husband was gone, far out of earshot.

"Are you sure you aren't just reacting because Ix is the main rival to House Richese, Mother?" he asked.

"I think not!" Her long, slender fingers paused as they laced up an elegant collar on his shirt. "House Richese relies on old, tried-and-true technology—established devices that fall safely within prescribed guidelines. No one questions Richesian adherence to the strictures of the Jihad."

She looked at him, her dark eyes hard, then cracking with tears. She stroked his shoulder. From a recent spurt of growth, he was almost her height. "Leto, Leto, I don't want you to lose your innocence there, or your soul," she told him. "There's too much at stake."

Later, in the dining hall during a quiet family meal of fish stew and biscuits, Helena had once again begged the Old Duke to send him somewhere else. Paulus merely laughed at her concerns, though, until finally her quiet but firm refusal to back down drove him to rage. "Dominic is my friend—and by God our son couldn't learn at the hands of a better man!"

Trying to concentrate on his own meal, yet disturbed over his mother's protestations, Leto had nonetheless stood by his father. "I want to go there, Mother," he said, gently resting his spoon beside his bowl, then repeated the line she always told him. "It's for the best."

During Leto's upbringing, Paulus had made many choices with which Helena disagreed: putting the young man to work with villagers, taking him out to meet citizens face-to-face, letting him make friends with commoners, encouraging him to get his hands dirty. Leto could see the wisdom in this, since he would be Duke of these people someday, but Helena still objected on various grounds, often quoting passages from the Orange Catholic Bible to justify her opinions.

His mother was not a patient woman and not warm to her only child, though she maintained a perfect front during important meetings and public events. She always fussed about her own appearance, and often said she would never have any more children. Bringing up one son and running the ducal household already took up most of her valuable time, which could otherwise have been spent studying the Orange Catholic Bible and other religious texts. It was obvious that Helena had borne a son only out of duty to House Atreides, rather than out of any desire to nurture and raise a child.

No wonder the Old Duke sought out the companionship of other women who proved less prickly.

Sometimes at night, behind the massive doors of layered Elaccan teak, Leto heard the loud, reverberating arguments of his father and mother. Lady Helena could disagree all she wanted about sending their son to Ix, but Old Duke Paulus *was* House Atreides. His word was law, in the Castle and on Caladan, no matter how much his distraught wife tried to sway his opinion.

It's for the best.

Leto knew that theirs had been an arranged marriage, a bargain struck among the Houses of the Landsraad to fulfill the requirements of the important families. It had been a desperate action on the part of crumbling Richese, and House Atreides could always hope the former grandeur of the innovative technological House might rise again. In the meantime, the Old Duke had received substantial concessions and rewards for taking in one of the many daughters of House Richese.

"A noble household has little room for the swooning and romanticism lesser peoples feel when hormones guide their actions," his mother had once said to him, explaining the politics of marriage. He knew such a fate undoubtedly lay in store for him as well. His father even agreed with her in this regard, and was more adamant about it than she.

"What's the first rule of the House?" the Old Duke would say, ad nauseam. And Leto would have to repeat it, word for word: "Never marry for love, or it will bring our House down."

At fourteen, Leto had never been in love himself, though he had certainly felt the fires of lust. His father encouraged him to dally with the village girls, to toy with anyone he found attractive—but never to promise anything. Leto doubted, given his position as heir apparent to House Atreides, that he would ever have much chance to fall in love, especially not with the woman he would eventually take as his wife. . . .

One morning, a week before Leto was scheduled to leave, his father clapped a hand on his shoulder and took him along as he went about his rounds to meet the people, making a point to greet even the servants. The Duke led a small honor guard into the seaside town below the Castle, doing his own shopping, seeing his subjects and being seen. Paulus often went on such outings with his son—and Leto always considered these to be wonderful times.

Out under the pale blue sky, the Old Duke laughed easily, beaming with infectious good nature. The people smiled when the hearty man walked among them. Leto and his father strolled together along the bazaar, past the stalls of vegetables and fresh fish to inspect beautiful tapestries woven from beaten ponji fibers and fire-threads. There Paulus Atreides often bought baubles or keepsakes for his wife, especially after they had quarreled, though the Duke didn't seem to understand Helena's interests enough to select anything appropriate for her.

At an oyster stall the Old Duke suddenly paused and gazed up at the cloud-scudded sky, struck by what he considered a brilliant idea. He looked down at his son, and a broad grin split his bushy beard. "Ah, we need to send you off with an appropriate spectacle, lad. Make your leave-taking a memorable event for all of Caladan."

Leto forced himself not to cringe. He had heard his father's crazy ideas before, and knew the Old Duke would follow through, regardless of common sense. "What do you have in mind, sir? What do I need to do?"

"Nothing, nothing. I shall announce a celebration in honor of my heir and son." He grabbed Leto's hand and raised it up in the air, as if in a triumphant wave, then his voice boomed out, subduing the crowds. "We are going to have a bullfight, an old-fashioned extravaganza for the populace. It will be a day of celebration for Caladan, with holoprojections transmitted around the globe."

"With Salusan bulls?" Leto asked, picturing in his mind the spine-backed beasts, their black heads studded with multiple horns, their eyes faceted. When he had been a younger boy, Leto had often gone into the stables to look at the monstrous animals. Stablemaster Yresk, one of his mother's old retainers from Richese, tended the bulls for Paulus's occasional spectacles.

"Naturally," the Old Duke said. "And as usual, I'll fight them myself." He swept his arm out in a flourish, as if imagining a colorful cape there. "These old bones are agile enough to dodge around a lumbering monster like that. I'll have Yresk prepare one—or would you like to pick the beast yourself, lad?"

"I thought you weren't going to do that anymore," Leto said. "It's been almost a year since you . . ."

"Wherever did you get that idea?"

"Your advisors, sir. It's too risky. Isn't that why others have been fighting the bulls in your place?"

The old man laughed. "What a foolish notion! I've been out of the ring for only one reason: The bulls went downhill for a while, some genetic imbalance that made them unworthy. That's changed, though, and new bulls are being brought in now, tougher than ever. Yresk says they're ready to fight, and so am I." He put his arm around Leto's narrow shoulders. "What better occasion for a *corrida de toros* than the leave-taking of my son? You'll attend this bullfight—your first. Your mother can't say you're too young anymore."

Leto nodded, reluctantly. His father would never be swayed, once his mind was made up. At least Paulus had the training, and would wear a personal shield.

Using personal shields, Leto himself had fought human opponents, aware of a shield's advantages and limitations. A shield could block projectile fire and fast-moving weapons of death, but any blade traveling below the threshold speed could pass through to the unprotected flesh beneath. A rampaging Salusan bull, with its sharp horns, might well move slowly enough to pierce even the most finely tuned shield.

He swallowed hard, wondering about the new, enhanced bulls. The old ones Stablemaster Yresk had shown him seemed dangerous enough—they'd killed three matadors that Leto could remember. . . .

Consumed by his fresh idea, Duke Paulus made the announcement at the bazaar, over the public address system implanted in booths and stalls. Upon hearing this, people in the marketplace cheered and their eyes glittered. They laughed, partly in anticipation of the performance itself—and also because of the declared day of rest and celebration.

Leto's mother wouldn't like this at all, he knew—Paulus in the fight and Leto in attendance—but Leto also understood that as soon as Helena began to object, the Old Duke would be more determined than ever.

THE BOWL OF the Plaza de Toros sprawled under the noonday sun. The stands spread out in an immense broad grid, so filled with people that in the farthest reaches they looked like tiny colored pixels. The Duke had never charged any fee to witness his performances; he was too proud of them, enjoyed showing off too much.

Enormous green-and-black banners flapped in the breeze, while fanfare blasted from speakers. Pillars emblazoned with Atreides hawk crests sparkled with emblems that had been newly polished and painted for the event. Thousands of floral bouquets harvested from the fields and lowlands had been placed about the bullring—an unsubtle hint that the Duke liked the people to strew the ground with blossoms each time he dispatched a bull.

Below, in the preparation chambers at ground level, Paulus girded up before the fight. Leto stood with him behind a barricade, listening to the impatient crowd. "Father, I'm uneasy about the risk you're taking. You shouldn't do this . . . especially not for me."

The Old Duke brushed aside the comment. "Leto, lad, you must understand that governing people and winning their loyalty consists of more than just signing papers, collecting taxes, and attending Landsraad meetings." He straightened his magenta cape, preened in front of a mirror.

"I depend on those people out there to produce the most that Caladan can provide. They must do so willingly, with hard work—and not just for their own profit, but for their honor and glory. If House Atreides was ever to go to war again, these people would shed their blood for me. They would lay down their lives under our banner." He fiddled with his armor. "Tighten this for me?"

Leto grabbed the string fasteners of the back leather plate, tugged them, and cinched the knots tight. He kept silent but nodded to show he understood.

"As their Duke, I need to give them something back, prove that I'm worthy. And it's not just for entertainment, but to instill in their minds that I'm a man of grand stature, of heroic proportions . . . someone blessed by God to rule them. I can't do that unless I put myself before them. Leadership is not a passive process."

Paulus checked his shield belt, then smiled through his beard. " 'No one is too old to learn,' " he quoted. "That's a line from the *Agamemnon* play—just to show you that I'm not always sleeping when I appear to be."

Thufir Hawat, the stern-faced weapons master, stood beside his Duke. As a loyal Mentat, Hawat would not speak out against his superior's decisions; instead, he gave the best advice he could, whispering to Paulus the patterns he had seen in the movements of this new batch of mutated Salusan bulls.

Leto knew his mother would be up in the stands in the ducal spectator box. She would be dressed in her finery, wearing colorful gauzy veils and robes, playing her part, waving to the people. The night before, once again, there had been much heated discussion behind the bedroom doors; finally, Duke Paulus had simply silenced her with a barked command. Afterward he had gone to sleep, resting for the following day's exertions.

The Duke put on his green-bordered cap, then took the equipment he would need to conquer the wild bull: his poniards and a long, feathered *vara* with nerve toxin on the lance tip. Thufir Hawat had suggested that the stablemaster slightly tranquilize the bull to deaden its rampaging impulses, but the Duke was a man who loved to face a challenge. No drug-dulled opponent for him!

Paulus clipped the activation pack onto his shield belt and powered up the field. It was only a half shield, used to guard his side; the Duke used a garishly brilliant cape called a *muleta* to cover his other side.

Paulus bowed first to his son, then his Mentat, and then the trainers waiting at the entrance to the arena. "Time for the show to begin." Leto watched him swirl about and, like a bird on a mating display, strut out into the open Plaza de Toros. At his appearance, cheers thundered out with a roar far louder than any Salusan bull's.

Leto stood behind the barricade, blinking into the glare of the open sun. He smiled as his father made a slow circuit of the arena, waving his cape, bowing, greeting his ecstatic people. Leto could sense the love and admiration they had for this brave man, and it warmed his heart.

Waiting there in the shadows, Leto vowed to do all he could to study his father's triumphs, so that one day he would command such respect and devotion from the people. Triumphs . . . this would be another in a long list of them for his father, Leto assured himself. But he couldn't help worrying. Too much could change in the flicker of a shield, the flash of a sharp horn, the stamp of a hoof.

Tones sounded, and an announcer's voice gave introductory details of the impending *corrida de toros*. With a flourish of a sequined glove, Duke Paulus gestured toward the broad reinforced doors on the opposite side of the arena.

Moving to another archway for a better view, Leto reminded himself that this would be no sham performance. His father would be battling for his very life.

Stableboys had been tending the ferocious beasts, and Stablemaster

Yresk had personally selected one for the day's *corrida*. After inspecting the animal, the Old Duke had been satisfied, certain the crowd would be equally pleased by its ferocity. He looked forward to the fight.

Heavy gates opened with a grinding of suspensor hinges, and the Salusan bull charged out, shaking its massive, multiple-horned head in the dazzling light. Its faceted eyes glittered with feral rage. The scales on the mutated creature's back reflected iridescent colors from its black hide.

Duke Paulus whistled and waved his cape. "Over here, stupid!" The spectators laughed.

Turning toward him, the bull lowered its head with a loud bubbling snort.

Leto noticed that his father hadn't yet switched on his protective shield. Instead, Paulus snapped and fluttered his colorful cape, trying to draw the wrath of the beast. The Salusan bull pawed and snorted on the sandy arena floor, then charged. Leto wanted to cry out, to warn his father. Had the man simply forgotten to switch on his protection? How could he possibly survive without a shield?

But the bull thundered past, and Paulus swept his cape gracefully to one side, letting the creature strike the diversionary target. Its hooked horns shredded the bottom of the fabric into ragged frays. While it was coming about, the Old Duke turned his back to the bull, exposed and overconfident. He bowed mockingly toward the crowd before he stood straight—then calmly, patiently, flicked on his personal shield.

The bull attacked again, and now the Duke used his poniard to toy with it, pricking through its thick, scaled hide before slashing a stinging yet minor wound along its flank. The creature's faceted eyes saw multiple images of its colorfully garbed tormentor.

It charged again.

Moving too fast to penetrate the shield, Leto thought. *But if the bull tires and slows, he could be even more dangerous. . . .*

As the fight continued, Leto saw how his father was playing this up for all the spectacle he could muster, tantalizing the audience to amuse them. Old Paulus could have killed the Salusan bull at any time, yet he drew out the moment, savored it.

From the reactions of the spectators, Leto knew this would be an event talked about for years. The rice farmers and fishermen led such dreary, hardworking lives. But this celebration would fix a proud image of their Duke forever in their minds. Look what Old Paulus was doing, they would say, despite his age!

Eventually the bull became exhausted, its eyes reddened with blood, its snorts heavy and tired as it spilled its life fluid onto the powdery surface of the arena. Duke Paulus himself now chose to end the fight. He had dragged the sport along for nearly an hour. Though dripping with sweat, he somehow maintained his regal appearance and did not allow his manner to show weariness, or his fine clothes to be disheveled.

Up in the stands, Lady Helena continued to wave her pennants, smiling fixedly down at the spectacle.

By now, the Salusan bull was like a maddened machine, a rampaging monster that had few vulnerable spots in its black-scaled armor. As the beast ran at him again, its gait staggering, its gleaming horns pointed like spears, Duke Paulus feinted to the left, then returned as the bull surged past.

Then Paulus swung sideways, tossed his flapping cape to the dust, and gripped the shaft of his *vara* lance in both hands. He threw all of his strength into a powerful side thrust. Flawlessly performed, magnificently executed. The blade of the lance drove home through a chink in the Salusan bull's armored hide, sliding through an intersection of bone and skull, skewering straight through to impale both of the creature's separated brains—the most difficult, most sophisticated way to kill it.

The bull ground to a halt, wheezing, groaning—and suddenly dead. Its carcass slumped like a crashing spaceship onto the ground.

Planting his foot on the horned head of the bull, Duke Paulus heaved against his lance, pulled the bloodied blade out, and dropped it onto the ash-covered ground. Next he drew his sword and, raising it high, twirled it in a triumphant gesture.

As one, the people in the stands surged to their feet, screaming, howling, and cheering. They waved their banners, snatched bouquets from flowerpots, and tossed the blossoms onto the arena floor. They sang out Paulus's name over and over.

Reveling in the adoration, the Atreides patriarch smiled and turned about, opening his coat so that the spectators could see his blood-spattered, sweat-drenched form. He was the hero now; he had no need to show off his finery.

After the throbbing cheers had died down, many minutes later, the Duke raised his sword again and struck downward, hacking repeatedly until he had severed the head of the bull. Finally, he plunged the bloody sword into the soft ground of the plaza and used both hands to grasp the horns of the bull and lift its head high.

"Leto!" he shouted over his shoulder, his voice booming into the acoustics of the Plaza de Toros. "Leto, my son, come out here!"

Leto, still in the shadows of the archway, hesitated a moment, then marched forth. He held his head high as he crossed the hoof-trampled dirt to stand at his father's side. The crowd cheered with renewed enthusiasm.

Old Duke Paulus turned and presented his son with the bloodied head of his kill. "I give you Leto Atreides!" he announced to the audience while pointing at his son. "Your future Duke!"

The crowd continued to applaud and shout hurrahs. Leto grasped one of the bull's horns; he and his father stood together holding the defeated beast's head high, the trophy oozing thick red drops onto the sand.

As Leto heard the people echo his name, he felt deep stirrings within, and wondered for the first time if this was truly what it felt like to be a leader of men.

N'kee: *Slow-acting poison that builds up in the adrenal glands; one of the most insidious toxins permitted under the accords of Guild Peace and the restrictions of the Great Convention. (See War of Assassins.)*

—The Assassins' Handbook

M mmm, the Emperor will never die, you know, Shaddam." A small man with oversize dark eyes and a weasel face, Hasimir Fenring, sat opposite the shield-ball console from his visitor, Crown Prince Shaddam. "At least not while you're young enough to enjoy the throne."

With a sharp, darting gaze Fenring watched the black shield-ball come to rest on a low-scoring point. Completing his turn at the game, the heir to the Imperium clearly wasn't happy about the result. They had been close companions for most of their lives, and Fenring knew exactly how to distract him at the right moment.

From the game room of Fenring's luxurious penthouse, Shaddam could see the lights of his father's Imperial Palace glittering on the gentle hillside a kilometer away. With Fenring's aid he had disposed of his older brother Fafnir years and years ago, and still the Golden Lion Throne seemed no closer.

Shaddam went over to the balcony and drew a long, deep breath.

He was a strong-featured man in his mid-thirties, with a firm chin and aquiline nose; his reddish hair was cut short and oiled and styled into a perfect helmet. In an odd way, he looked similar to the century-old busts of his father sculpted during the early decades of Elrood's reign.

It was early evening, and two of Kaitain's four moons hung low in the sky beyond the gigantic Imperial building. Illuminated gliders rode the calm skies of dusk, chased by flocks of songbirds. Sometimes, Shaddam just needed to get away from the sprawling Palace.

"A hundred and thirty-six years as Padishah Emperor," Fenring continued in his nasal voice. "And old Elrood's father ruled for more than a century himself. Think about it, hmm-m-m-ah? Your father took the throne when he was only nineteen, and you're almost twice that age." The narrow-faced man looked with huge eyes at his friend. "Doesn't that bother you?"

Shaddam didn't respond, stared at the skyline, knowing he should return to the game . . . but he and his friend had bigger games to play.

After his long years of close association Fenring knew that the Imperial heir could not deal with complex problems when other amusements distracted him. *Very well, then, I will end this diversion.*

"My turn," he said. Fenring lifted a rod on his side of the shimmering shield globe and dipped it through the shield to engage a spinning interior disk. This in turn caused a black ball in the center of the globe to levitate into the air. With expert timing, Fenring withdrew the rod, and the ball dropped into the center of an oval receptacle bearing the highest mark.

"Damn you, Hasimir, another perfect game for you," Shaddam said, returning from the balcony. "When I'm Emperor, though, will you be wise enough to lose to me?"

Fenring's oversize eyes were alert and feral. A genetic-eunuch, incapable of fathering children because of his congenital deformities, he was still one of the deadliest fighters in the Imperium, so single-mindedly ferocious that he was more than a match for any Sardaukar.

"*When* you're Emperor?" Fenring and the Crown Prince held so many deadly secrets between them that neither could imagine keeping knowledge from the other. "Shaddam, are you listening to what I'm telling you, hmmm?" He gave an annoyed sigh. "You're thirty-four years old, sitting on your hands and waiting for your life to begin—your birthright. Elrood could last another three decades, at least. He's a tough old Burseg, and the way he gulps spice beer, he might outlive both of us."

"So why even talk about it?" Shaddam toyed with the shield-ball controls, clearly wanting to play another round. "I've got what I need here."

"You'd rather play games until you're an old man? I thought you had better things in store for you, hm-m-m-m-ah? The destiny of your Corrino blood."

"Ah, yes. And if I don't achieve my *destiny*," Shaddam said in a bitter tone, "where does that leave you?"

"I'll do fine, thank you." Fenring's mother had been trained as a Bene Gesserit before entering Imperial service as lady-in-waiting to Elrood's fourth wife; she had raised him well, preparing him for great things.

But Hasimir Fenring was disgusted with his friend. At one time, in his late teens, Shaddam had been much more ambitious to claim the Imperial throne, even to the point of encouraging Fenring to poison the Emperor's eldest son, Fafnir, who had been forty-six and eagerly awaiting the crown himself.

Now Fafnir was dead for fifteen years, and still the old vulture showed no signs of ever dying. At the very least, Elrood should abdicate with good grace. Meanwhile, Shaddam had lost his drive, and instead occupied his time enjoying the pleasures of his station. Being Crown Prince posed few hardships in life. But Fenring wanted much more—for his friend, and for himself.

Shaddam glowered at the other man. The Crown Prince's mother, Habla, had cast him aside as an infant—her only child by Elrood—and let her lady-in-waiting, Chaola Fenring, serve as wet nurse. From boyhood, Shaddam and Hasimir had talked about what they would do when he ascended to the Golden Lion Throne. *Padishah Emperor Shaddam IV.*

But for Shaddam such conversations no longer held their childhood magic. Too many years of reality had settled in, too much waiting to no purpose. His grip on hope and his enthusiasm for the job had faded into apathy. Why *not* spend the days playing shield-ball?

"You're a bastard," Shaddam said. "Let's start another game."

Ignoring his friend's suggestion, Fenring shut down the console. "Maybe so, but the Imperium has too many critical matters that require attention, and you know as well as I do that your father is bungling the job. If a company head ran his business the way your father runs the Empire, he'd be sacked. Think of the CHOAM scandal, for example, the soostone skimming operation."

"Ah, yes. Can't argue with you on that, Hasimir." Shaddam heaved a deep sigh.

"Royal impersonators—a Duke, a Duchess . . . a whole damned family of fakes, right under your father's nose. Who was watching? Now they've disappeared to a rogue planet somewhere beyond Imperial control. That should never have occurred, hmm-m-m-m? Just imagine the lost profits for Buzzell and the adjoining systems. What was Elrood thinking?"

Shaddam looked away. He didn't like to bother with serious Imperial matters. They gave him headaches. Given his father's apparent vigor, such details seemed distant and, by and large, irrelevant to him.

But still Fenring persisted. "The way it looks now, you won't get a chance to do better. One hundred and fifty-five years, and still in remarkable health. Fondil III before him lived to be one hundred seventy-five. What's the longest a Corrino Emperor has ever lived?"

Shaddam frowned and looked longingly at the gaming apparatus. "You know I don't pay attention to things like that, even when the tutor gets angry with me."

Fenring jabbed a finger at him. "Elrood will live to two hundred, mark my words. You have a serious problem, friend . . . unless you listen to me." He raised his thin eyebrows.

"Ah, yes, more ideas from the *Assassins' Handbook*, I suppose. Be careful with that information. You can get in a lot of trouble with it."

"Timid people are destined for nothing better than timid jobs. You and I, Shaddam, have much more in our futures. Think of the possibilities, hypothetically of course. Besides, what's wrong with poison? It works nicely and affects only the targeted person, as required by the Great Convention. No collateral deaths, no loss of revenue, no destruction of inheritable property. Nice and neat."

"Poisons are for House-to-House assassinations, not for what you're talking about."

"You didn't complain when I took care of Fafnir, hm-m-m-m-ah? He'd be in his sixties now, still waiting to taste the throne. Do *you* want to wait that long?"

"Stop," Shaddam insisted, digging in his heels. "Don't even imagine such a course. This isn't right."

"And denying you your birthright *is*? How effective an Emperor would you be if you couldn't exercise power until you were old and senile—like your father? Look what's happened on Arrakis. By the time we replaced Abulurd Harkonnen, the damage to spice production was already done. Abulurd had no idea how to crack the whip, so the workers didn't respect him. Now the Baron cracks it too much, and so morale is way down, leading to rampant defections and sabotage. But you can't really blame the Harkonnens. It all traces back to your father, the Padishah Emperor, and the bad decisions he's made." He continued more quietly. "You owe it to the stability of the Imperium."

Shaddam glanced up at the ceiling, as if searching for spy-eyes or other listening devices, though he knew that Fenring kept his private penthouse impeccably shielded and regularly scanned. "What kind of poison are you considering? Hypothetically speaking, only?" Again he stared across the lights of the city at the Imperial Palace. The shimmering structure seemed like a legendary grail, an unattainable prize.

"Perhaps something slow-acting, hm-m-m-m? So Elrood will appear to be aging. No one will question what's happening, since he's so old already. Leave it to me. As our future Emperor, you shouldn't concern yourself with the details of such matters—I have always been your expediter, remember?"

Shaddam chewed his lower lip. No one in the Imperium knew more about this man than he did. But could his friend ever turn on him? Possibly . . . though Fenring knew full well his best path to power lay through Shaddam. How to keep this ambitious friend under control, how to stay a step ahead of him—that was the challenge.

Emperor Elrood IX, aware of Hasimir Fenring's deadly skills, had made use of him in a number of clandestine operations, all of which had been successful. Elrood even suspected Fenring's role in Crown Prince Fafnir's death, but accepted it as part of Imperial politics. Over the years, Fenring had murdered at least fifty men and a dozen women, some of whom had been his lovers, of either sex. He took a measure of pride in being a killer who could face the victim or strike behind his back, without compunction.

There were days Shaddam wished he and the pushy Fenring had never formed a boyhood relationship: Then he wouldn't be hemmed in with difficult choices that he didn't want to think about. Shaddam should have abandoned his crib-companion as soon as he could walk. It was risky to be around such an unrelenting assassin, and at times he felt tainted by the association.

Still, Fenring was his friend. There was an attraction between them, an undefinable *something* of which they'd spoken on occasion without fully understanding it. For the present Shaddam found it easier to accept the friendship—and for his own sake, he hoped it *was* friendship—instead of trying to sever it. That course of action could be extremely dangerous.

Close beside him, Shaddam heard a voice that broke his train of thought. "Your favorite brandy, my Prince." Looking to one side, Shaddam saw Fenring offering him a large snifter of smoky-dark kirana brandy.

He accepted the snifter but stared at the liquid suspiciously, swirling it around. Was there another color to it, something not quite mixed in? He put his nose over the lip, inhaling the aroma as if he were a connoisseur—though he was actually trying to detect any foreign chemical. The brandy smelled normal. But then Fenring would have made sure of that. He was a subtle and devious man.

"I can drag out the snooper if you like, but you never need worry about poison from me, Shaddam," Fenring said with a maddening smile. "Your father, however, is in an entirely different position."

"Ah, yes. A slow-acting poison, you say? I suspect you already have a substance in mind. How long will my father live after you begin the process? If we do this at all, I mean."

"Two years, maybe three. Long enough to make his decline appear natural."

Shaddam raised his chin, trying to look regal. His skin was perfumed, his reddish hair pomaded and slicked back. "You understand, I might only entertain such a treasonous idea for the sake of the Imperium—to avoid continued calamities at the hands of my father."

A crafty smile worked at the edges of the weasel face. "Of course."

"Two or three years," Shaddam mused. "Time for me to prepare for the great responsibilities of leadership, I suppose . . . while you attend to some of the more unpleasant tasks of empire."

"Aren't you going to drink your brandy, Shaddam?"

Shaddam met the hard gaze of the oversize eyes, and felt fear course along his spine. He was in too deep *not* to trust Fenring now. He drew another shaky breath and sipped the rich liqueur.

⟨ ⟩

THREE DAYS LATER, Fenring slipped like a ghost through the shields and poison-snoopers of the Palace and stood over the sleeping Emperor, listening to the smooth purr of his snores.

Not a care in the universe, this one.

No one else could have gotten into the most secure sleeping chamber of the ancient Emperor. But Fenring had his ways: a bribe here, a manipulated schedule there, a concubine made ill, a doorman distracted, the Chamberlain sent off on an urgent errand. He had done this many times before, practicing for the inevitable. Everyone in the Palace was used to Fenring slinking around, and they knew better than to ask too many questions. Now, according to his precise assessment— which would have made even a Mentat proud—Fenring had three minutes. Four, if he was lucky.

Enough time to change the course of history.

With the same perfect timing he had demonstrated during the shield-ball game, as well as during his rehearsals on mannequins and two unfortunate servingwomen from the kitchen storehouses, Fenring froze in place and waited, gauging the breathing of his victim like a Laza tiger about to pounce. In one hand he cradled a long microhair needle between two slender fingers, while in the other hand he held a mist-tube. Old Elrood lay on his back, in the precisely correct position, looking like a mummy, his parchment skin stretched tight over his skull.

Guided by a certain hand, the mist-tube moved closer. Fenring counted to himself, waiting. . . .

In a space between Elrood's breaths, Fenring squeezed a lever on the tube and sprayed a powerful anesthetic mist in the old man's face.

There was no discernible change in Elrood, but Fenring knew the nerve deadener had taken effect, instantaneously. Now he made his thrust. A fiber-fine, self-guiding needle snaked up the old man's nose, through sinus cavities, and into the frontal lobe of his brain. Fenring paused no more than an instant to dispense the chemical time bomb, then withdrew. A few seconds and it was done. Without any evidence

or even any pain. Undetectable and multilayered, the internal machinery had been set in motion. The tiny catalyst would grow and do
its damage, like the first rotten cell in an apple.

Each time the Emperor consumed his favorite beverage—spice
beer—his own brain would release tiny doses of catalytic poison into
his bloodstream. Thus an ordinary component of the old man's diet
would be chemically converted into chaumurky—poison administered
in a drink. His mind would gradually rot away . . . a metamorphosis
that would be most enjoyable to watch.

Fenring loved to be subtle.

Kwisatz Haderach: "Shortening of the Way." This is the label ap-
plied by the Bene Gesserit to the unknown for which they sought a
genetic solution: a male Bene Gesserit whose organic mental pow-
ers would bridge space and time.

—Terminology of the Imperium

It was another cold morning. The small blue-white sun
Laoujin peeked over terra-cotta-tiled rooftops, dissipat-
ing the rain.

Reverend Mother Anirul Sadow Tonkin held the collar
of her black robe shut against the moisture-laden wind that
whipped up from the south and dampened her short bronze-
brown hair. Her hurried footsteps carried her across the wet
cobblestones, straight toward the arched doorway of the
Bene Gesserit administration building.

She was late and ran, even though it was unseemly for a
woman of her status to be seen rushing about like a red-
faced schoolgirl. Mother Superior and her selected council
would be waiting in the chapter chamber—for a meeting
that could not begin without Anirul. Only she had the Sisterhood's complete breeding projections and the full knowledge from Other Memory in her head.

The sprawling Mother School complex on Wallach IX
was the base of Bene Gesserit operations throughout the
Imperium. The historic first sanctuary of the Sisterhood had
been erected here, dating from post–Butlerian Jihad days at
the beginnings of the great schools of the human mind.

Some of the buildings in the training enclave were thousands of years old and echoed with ghosts and memories; others had been constructed in more recent centuries, with styles carefully designed to match the originals. The bucolic appearance of the Mother School complex fostered one of the primary precepts of the Sisterhood: minimal appearance, maximum content. Anirul's own features were long and narrow, giving her a doelike face, but her large eyes had a depth of millennia in them.

The half-timbered stucco-and-wood structures, a combination of classical architectural styles, had moss-streaked sienna roof tiles and beveled lume-enhancement windows, designed to concentrate natural light and warmth from the tiny sun. The simple, narrow streets and alleys, in tandem with the quaintly archaic appearance of the instructional enclave, belied the subtle complexities and sheer weight of history taught inside. Haughty visitors would not be impressed, and the Sisterhood did not care a whit.

Throughout the Imperium the Bene Gesserit kept a low profile, but they were always to be found in vital areas, tilting the political equilibrium at crux points, watching, nudging, achieving their own aims. It was best when others underestimated them; the Sisters encountered fewer obstacles that way.

With all of its superficial deficiencies and difficulties, Wallach IX remained the perfect place to develop the psychic muscles required of Reverend Mothers. The planet's intricate hive of structures and workers was too valuable, too steeped in history and tradition to be replaced. Yes, there were warmer climates on more hospitable worlds, but any acolyte who could not endure these conditions had no place among the agonies, harsh environments, and often painful decisions a true Bene Gesserit would face.

Keeping her quick breaths under control, Reverend Mother Anirul mounted the rain-slick steps of the administration building, then paused to look back across the plaza. She stood straight, tall, but she felt the weight of history and memory bearing down on her—and for a Bene Gesserit, there was little difference between the two. The voices of past generations echoed in Other Memory, a cacophony of wisdom and experience and opinions available to all Reverend Mothers, and particularly acute in Anirul.

On this spot the first Mother Superior, Raquella Berto-Anirul—

after whom Anirul herself had taken her name—had delivered her legendary orations to the embryonic Sisterhood. Raquella had forged a new school from a group of desperate and pliable acolytes still stinging from centuries under the yoke of thinking machines.

Did you realize what you were beginning, so long ago? Anirul asked herself. *How many plots, how many plans . . . so much you pinned upon a single, secret hope.* Sometimes, the buried presence of Mother Superior Raquella actually answered her from within. But not today.

From her access to the multitude of memory-lives buried in her psyche, Anirul knew the precise stairstep on which her illustrious ancestor had stood, and could hear the exact, long-ago words. A chill coursed her spine, making her pause. Though still young in years and smooth-skinned, she contained an Oldness within her, as did all living Reverend Mothers—but in her, the voices spoke louder. It was reassuring to have the comforting crowd of memories there to provide advice in times of need. It prevented foolish mistakes.

But Anirul would be accused of distraction and foolish delay if she did not get to the meeting. Some said she was far too young to be the Kwisatz Mother, but Other Memory had revealed more to her than to any other Sister. She comprehended the precious, millennia-old genetic quest for the Kwisatz Haderach better than the other Reverend Mothers because the past lives had revealed *everything* to her, while keeping the details hidden from most Bene Gesserit.

The idea of a Kwisatz Haderach had been the Sisterhood's dream for thousands upon thousands of years, conceived in dark underground meetings even before the victory of the Jihad. The Bene Gesserit had many breeding programs aimed at selecting and enhancing various characteristics of humanity, and no one understood them all. The genetic lines of the messiah project had been the most carefully guarded secret for much of the Imperium's recorded history, so secret in fact that even the voices in Other Memory refused to divulge the details.

But to Anirul they had told the whole scheme, and she grasped the full implications. Somehow she had been chosen as this generation's Kwisatz Mother, the guardian of the Bene Gesserit's most important goal.

The notoriety and the power, however, did not excuse her for being late to the council meetings. Many still saw her as young and impetuous.

Swinging open a heavy door covered with hieroglyphics in a language only Reverend Mothers remembered, she passed through into a foyer where ten other Sisters, all dressed in hooded black aba robes like her own, stood in a cluster. A low murmur of conversation filled the air inside the nondescript building. *Treasures can be hidden within a drab and unpretentious shell,* said one popular Bene Gesserit dictum.

The other Sisters moved aside for Anirul as she glided through their midst like a swimmer parting water. Though her body was tall and large-boned, Anirul succeeded in projecting a grace in her movements . . . but it did not come easily to her. Whispering, they fell in behind her as she entered the octagonal chapter chamber, the meeting place of the ancient order's leadership. Her footsteps creaked across the worn planks of the floor, and the door groaned shut, locking behind them.

White Elacca-wood benches rimmed the timeworn room; Mother Superior Harishka sat on one, like a common acolyte. Of mixed parentage, showing bloodlines from distinctive branches of humanity, the Mother Superior was old and bent, with dark almond eyes peering out from beneath her black hood.

The Sisters moved to the sides of the chamber and seated themselves on empty white benches, as Mother Superior had. Presently the rustling of robes ceased, and no one spoke. From somewhere, the old building creaked. Outside, drizzle fell in silent curtains, muffling the struggling blue-white sunlight.

"Anirul, I await your report," Mother Superior finally said with just a glimmer of annoyance at her tardiness. Harishka commanded the entire Sisterhood, but Anirul was vested with full authority to make command decisions on the *project*. "You have promised us your genetic summary and projections."

Anirul took her position in the center of the chamber. Overhead, a vaulted ceiling spread like a flower to the tops of Gothic stained-glasplaz windows; within each window section, panes contained the family crests of great historical leaders of the order.

Fighting back nervousness, Anirul took a deep breath and suppressed the multitude of voices within her. Many of the Bene Gesserit Order would not like what she had to say. Though the voices of past lives might offer her comfort and support, she was about to give her own assessment, and had to stand by it. She also had to be completely honest; Mother Superior was adept at sensing the slightest deceit. Mother Superior noticed everything, and now her almond eyes flashed with expectation, as well as impatience.

Anirul cleared her throat and covered her mouth as she began her report in a directed-whisper that carried to the ears of everyone in the sealed room, but nowhere else. Nothing escaped into the ambient air for any concealed listening device. They all knew of her work, but she gave them the details anyway, adding to the import of her announcement.

"Thousands of years of careful breeding have brought us closer than ever before to our goal. For ninety generations, a plan begun even before the Butlerian warriors led us to freedom from the thinking machines, we of the Sisterhood have planned to create our own weapon. Our own superbeing who will bridge space and time with his mind."

Her words droned on. The other Bene Gesserit did not stir, though they appeared bored with her standard summary of the project. *Very well, I will give them something to awaken their hopes.*

"With the dance of DNA, I have determined we are, at most, only three generations removed from success." Her pulse accelerated. "Soon, we will have our Kwisatz Haderach."

"Take care when you speak of this secret of all secrets," Mother Superior warned, but her delight could not be covered by her sternness.

"I take care with every aspect of our program, Mother Superior," Anirul countered, in too haughty a tone. She caught herself, kept her narrow face expressionless, but others had already seen the slip. There would be more murmurings about her brashness, her youth and unsuitability for such an important role. "That is why I am so certain of what we must do. The gene samples have been analyzed, all possibilities projected. The path is plainer now than ever before."

So many Sisters before her had worked toward this incredible goal, and now it was her duty to administer the final breeding decisions and supervise the birth and upbringing of a new girl-child, who would in all probability be the grandmother of the Kwisatz Haderach himself.

"I have the names of the final genetic pairings," Anirul announced. "Our mating index indicates that these will produce the highest likelihood of success." She paused, savoring the absolute attention the others paid to her.

To any outsider, Anirul appeared to be no more than another Reverend Mother, indistinguishable from the rest of her Sisters and not terribly talented or gifted in any way. The Bene Gesserit were good at keeping secrets, and the Kwisatz Mother was one of the greatest of these.

"We need a particular bloodline from an ancient House. This will produce a daughter—our equivalent to the mother of the Virgin Mary—who must then take the mate we choose. These two will be the grandparents, and their offspring, also a daughter, will be trained here on Wallach IX. This Bene Gesserit woman will become the mother of our Kwisatz Haderach, a boy-child to be raised by us, under our complete control." Anirul let out her last words with a slow sigh, and considered the immensity of what she had said.

Only a few decades more, and the astounding birth would occur—potentially within Anirul's lifetime. Thinking back through the tunnels of Other Memory, grasping the canvas of time that had spread out in preparation for this event, Anirul realized how lucky she was to be alive now, in this period of time. Her predecessors stood in a spectral line inside her mind, eagerly watching and waiting.

When the unparalleled breeding program finally came to fruition, the Bene Gesserit would no longer need to remain a subtle, manipulative presence in the politics of the Imperium. Everything would belong to *them*, and the archaic galactic feudal system would fall.

Though no one spoke, Anirul detected concern in the hawkish eyes of her Sisters, bordering on a doubt that none of them dared express. "And what is this bloodline?" Mother Superior asked.

Anirul did not hesitate, drew herself taller. "We must have a daughter by . . . the Baron Vladimir Harkonnen."

She read the surprise on their faces. Harkonnens? They had been part of the overall breeding programs, of course—all Landsraad Houses were—but no one would have imagined the Bene Gesserit savior springing from the seed of such a man. What did such a lineage bode for the Kwisatz Haderach? Given a Harkonnen-bred superman, could the Bene Gesserit hope to control him?

All of these questions—and many more—passed between the Sisters, without the utterance of a sound or even a directed-whisper. Anirul saw it plainly.

"As all of you know," she said at last, "the Baron Harkonnen is a dangerously cunning and manipulative man. Though we can be certain he is generally aware of the numerous Bene Gesserit breeding programs, our plan cannot be revealed. Still, we must find a way for him to impregnate a chosen Sister without telling him why."

Mother Superior pursed her wrinkled lips. "The Baron's sexual appetites run exclusively to men and boys. He will have no interest in accepting a female lover—especially not one thrust upon him by us."

Anirul nodded soberly. "Our seductive abilities will be taxed as never before." She gave a challenging look to the powerful Reverend Mothers in attendance. "But I have no doubt that with all the resources of the Bene Gesserit, we will find a way to coerce him."

In response to the strict Butlerian taboo against machines that per-
form mental functions, a number of schools developed enhanced
human beings to subsume most of the functions formerly per-
formed by computers. Some of the key schools arising out of the
Jihad include the Bene Gesserit, with their intense mental and
physical training, the Spacing Guild, with the prescient ability to
find a safe path through foldspace, and the Mentats, whose com-
puterlike minds are capable of extraordinary acts of reasoning.

—Ikbhan's Treatise on the Mind, Volume I

As he made ready to depart from home for an entire year, Leto tried to hold on to his self-confidence. He knew this was an important step for him, and understood why his father had chosen Ix as a place to study. But he would still miss Caladan terribly.

It was not the young ducal heir's first trip to a different star system. Leto and his father had explored the multiple worlds of Gaar and the fog-bound planet of Pilargo, where Caladanian primitives were thought to have originated. Those had been mere outings, exciting sight-seeing trips.

However, the prospect of going away for so long, and all alone, made him worry more than he'd expected. He didn't dare show it, though. *I will be Duke someday.*

Dressed in Atreides finery, Leto stood with the Old Duke at the Cala Municipal Spaceport, awaiting a shuttle that would carry him to a Guild Heighliner. Two suspensor-borne suitcases hovered near his feet.

His mother had suggested he take retainers, cargo cases full of garments and diversions, and supplies of good Cal-adanian food; Duke Paulus, on the other hand, had laughed and explained how when he was Leto's age he'd survived for months on the battlefield with only the few possessions in a pack on his back. He did, however, insist that Leto take one of Caladan's traditional fishing knives in a sheath at his back.

Siding with his father, as usual, Leto chose to be minimal in his packing. Besides, Ix was a rich industrial planet, not a wilderness; he wouldn't suffer many privations during his schooling.

When anyone could see her, the Lady Helena bore the decision with stoic good grace. Now she stood beside the departure group dressed in fine robes and a shimmering cape. Though he knew his mother genuinely feared for his well-being, Lady Atreides would never show anything but the most perfect public face.

Adjusting the oil lenses of his father's field glasses, Leto peered away from the shifting pastels of the dawn horizon, up into the vestiges of night. A glinting speck moved against the stars. When he touched the zoompad, the speck grew until Leto recognized a Heighliner in low orbit surrounded by the shimmering blur of a shield defensive system.

"Do you see it?" Paulus asked, standing at his son's shoulder.

"It's there—with full shields activated. Are they worried about military action? Here?" With such severe political and economic consequences, Leto couldn't imagine anyone attacking a Guild craft. Although the Spacing Guild had no military power of its own, it could—through withdrawal of transportation services—cripple any solar system. And with elaborate surveillance mechanisms, the Guild could trace and identify rogue attackers and send messages off to the Emperor, who in turn would dispatch Imperial Sardaukar according to mutual treaty.

"Never underestimate the tactics of desperation, lad," Paulus said, but did not elaborate further. From time to time he had told his son stories of trumped-up charges against particular people, situations fabricated in the past in order to wipe out enemies of the Emperor or the Guild.

Leto thought that of all the things he was leaving behind, he would miss his father's insights most, the Old Duke's brief and perceptive lessons tossed off the cuff. "The Empire functions beyond mere laws," Paulus continued. "An equally strong foundation is the network of alliances, favors, and religious propaganda. Beliefs are more powerful than facts."

Leto stared through the thick sky at the magnificent, distant ship and frowned. It was often difficult to separate truth from fiction. . . .

He watched a speck of orange appear below the immense orbiting craft. The color became a streak of descending light that resolved into the shape of a shuttle, which soon hovered over the Cala landing field. Four white gulls whipped around, soaring in the stirred air currents from the shuttle's descent, then flew shrieking out to the sea cliffs.

Around the shuttle, a shield shimmered and flickered off. All along the spaceport fences, pennants snapped in a salty morning breeze. The shuttle, a white bullet-shaped craft, floated across the field toward the embarkation platform on which Leto and his parents stood separate from the honor guard. A crowd of onlookers and well-wishers waved and shouted from the outskirts of the landing field. The craft and platform connected, and a door slid open in the fuselage.

His mother came forward to say her goodbyes, embracing him without words; she had threatened simply to watch from one of the towers in Castle Caladan, but Paulus had convinced her otherwise. The crowd cheered and shouted their farewells; Duke Paulus and Lady Helena stood hand in hand and waved back at them.

"Remember what I told you, son," Paulus said, referring to intense counseling he had given the boy in recent days. "Learn from Ix, learn from *everything*."

"But use your heart to know what is true," his mother added.

"Always," he said. "I'll miss you both. I'll make you proud of me."

"We already are, lad." The older man stepped back to the formal guard escort. He exchanged Atreides salutes with his son—an open right hand beside the temple—and all the soldiers did the same. Then Paulus bounded forward to give Leto a hearty hug. . . .

Moments later the robo-piloted shuttle rose away from the black cliffs, churning seas, and cloud-wreathed croplands of Caladan. Inside, Leto sat in a plush chair in the observation lounge, peering out a windowport. As the craft reached the indigo darkness of space, he saw the metallic island of the Guild Heighliner with sunlight glinting off its surface.

At their approach, a yawning black hole opened in the underside. Leto took a deep breath, and the immense ship swallowed the shuttle. He envisioned what he had once seen in a filmbook about Arrakis, a sandworm inhaling a spice harvester. The metaphor unsettled him.

The shuttle slid smoothly into the docking port of a Wayku passenger ship that hung in its designated berth inside the cavernous hold of the Heighliner. Leto boarded, his suitcases floating along behind, and made up his mind to do as his father had instructed.

Learn from everything. His determined curiosity pushing his intimidation aside, Leto climbed a stairway to the main passenger lounge, where he found a seat on a bench by another window. Two soostone merchants sat nearby, their rapid conversation sprinkled with jargon. Old Paulus had wanted Leto to learn how to fend for himself. So, to enhance the experience, Leto was traveling as an ordinary passenger, with no special amenities, no pomp or entourage, no indication that he was the son of a Duke.

His mother had been horrified.

Aboard the ship, Wayku vendors wearing dark glasses and ear-clamp headsets moved from passenger to passenger, selling confections and perfumed beverages at exorbitant prices. Leto waved off a persistent vendor, though the spicy-salty broths and broiled meat sticks smelled delicious. He could hear an overflow of music from the man's headset, saw his head, shoulders, and feet moving to the beat of music piped into his skull. The Wayku did their jobs, tended to the customers, but managed to live in their own sensory cacophony; they preferred the universe within to any spectacle they might experience outside.

This mass-transit craft, operated by the Wayku under Guild contract, carried passengers from system to system. A disgraced House Major whose planets had all been destroyed in the Third Coalsack War, the Wayku were gypsies now and lived as nomads aboard Guild Heighliners. Although ancient surrender terms prevented members of their race from setting foot on any planet in the Imperium, the Guild had, for undisclosed reasons, granted them sanctuary. For generations, the Wayku had showed no interest in petitioning the Emperor for amnesty or a revocation of the severe restrictions placed upon them.

Looking through the window of the lounge, Leto saw the dimly illuminated cargo hold of the Heighliner, a vacuum chamber so large that this passenger ship was, by comparison, even smaller than a grain of pundi rice in the belly of a fish. He could see the ceiling high overhead, but not the walls kilometers away. Other ships, large and small, were arrayed in the hold: frigates, cargo haulers, shuttles, lighters, and armored monitors. Strapped-together stacks of "dump boxes"— unpiloted cargo containers designed to dump material directly from low orbit onto a planet's surface—hung next to the main exterior hatches.

Guild regulations, etched on ridulian crystals mounted to the main wall of every room, prohibited passengers from leaving the isolation of their ship. Through adjacent windows Leto snatched glimpses of passengers inside other craft—a potpourri of races bound for all parts of the Imperium.

The Wayku deckhands finished their first round of service, and the passengers waited. The trip through foldspace took no more than an hour, but preparations for departure sometimes required days.

Finally, with no announcement whatsoever, Leto detected a faint, smooth purring that seemed to come from far away. He could feel it in every muscle of his body. "We must be heading out," he said, turning to the soostone merchants, who seemed unimpressed. From the quick diverting of their eyes and the way they studiously ignored him, Leto thought they must consider him an uncultured yokel.

In an isolated chamber high atop the craft, a Guild Navigator swimming in a tank of gas saturated with melange began to encompass space with his mind. He envisioned and threaded a safe passage through the fabric of foldspace, transporting the Heighliner and its contents across a vast distance.

At dinner the previous evening in the Castle's dining hall, Leto's mother had wondered aloud if Navigators might somehow violate the machine-human interaction prohibited by the Butlerian Jihad. Knowing Leto would soon be off to Ix and at risk of moral tainting, she innocently made the suggestion as she nibbled on a mouthful of lemon-broiled fish. She often used a most reasonable tone when she uttered her provocative statements. The effect was like dropping a boulder into a pool of still water.

"Oh, nonsense, Helena!" Paulus said, wiping his beard with a napkin. "Where would we be without Navigators?"

"Just because you have become accustomed to a thing, does not make it right, Paulus. The Orange Catholic Bible says nothing about morality being defined by personal convenience."

Before his father could argue the point, Leto interrupted. "I thought that Navigators just saw the way, a safe way. Holtzman generators actually operate the spacecraft." He decided to add a quote he remembered from the Bible. " 'The highest master in the material world is the human mind, and the beasts of the field and the machines of the city must be forever subordinate.' "

"Of course, dear," his mother said, and dropped the subject.

Now, he didn't notice any change of sensation upon passing into foldspace. Before Leto knew it, the Heighliner arrived in another solar system—Harmonthep, according to the transport schedule.

Once there, Leto had to wait for five more hours as cargo ships and shuttles went in and out of the Heighliner hold, as well as transports and even a superfrigate. Then the Guild ship moved off again, folding space to a new solar system—Kirana Aleph, this time—where the cycle occurred once more.

Leto took a nap in the sleeping compartments, then emerged to buy two of the sizzling meat sticks and a potent cup of stee. Helena might wish he'd been escorted by Atreides house guards, but Paulus had insisted that there was only one way for his son to learn to take care of himself. Leto had an agenda and instructions, and he vowed to do just that.

Finally, on the third stop, a Wayku deckhand ordered Leto to descend three decks and board an automatic shuttle. She was a stern-looking woman in a gaudy uniform and did not seem to be in the mood for conversation. Her headset thrummed with an undercurrent of melody.

"Is this Ix?" Leto inquired, reaching for his suspensor-buoyed suitcases. They followed him as he moved.

"We are in the Alkaurops system," she said. Her eyes couldn't be seen because of her dark glasses. "Ix is the ninth planet. You get off here. We've already jettisoned the dump boxes."

Leto did as he was instructed, making his way toward the indicated shuttle, though he wished he had been given more warning and more information. He didn't know exactly what he was supposed to do once he arrived on the high-tech industrial world, but he assumed Earl Vernius would greet him or at least send some sort of welcoming party.

He took a deep breath and tried not to let his anxiety grow too intense.

The robo-piloted shuttle plummeted out of the Heighliner hold toward the surface of a planet traced with mountains, clouds, and ice. The automated shuttle functioned according to a limited set of instructions, and conversation wasn't in its repertoire of skills. Leto was the only passenger aboard, apparently the only traveler bound for Ix. The machine planet welcomed few visitors.

As he looked out the porthole, though, Leto had a sinking feeling that something had gone wrong. The Wayku shuttle approached a high mountain plateau with Alpine forests in sheltered valleys. He saw no buildings, none of the grand structures or manufacturing facilities he had expected. No smoke in the air, no cities, no sign of civilization at all.

This couldn't possibly be the heavily industrialized world of Ix. He looked around, tensing up, ready to defend himself. Had he been betrayed? Lured here and stranded?

The shuttle came to a stop on a stark plain strewn with flecked granite boulders and small clumps of white flowers. "This is where you get out, sir," the robo-pilot announced in a synthesized voice.

"Where are we?" Leto demanded. "I'm supposed to be going to the capital of Ix."

"This is where you get out, sir."

"Answer me!" His father would have used a booming voice to wrench a reply from this stupid machine. "This can't be the capital city of Ix. Just look around you!"

"You have ten seconds to exit the craft, sir, or you will be forcibly ejected. The Guild operates on a tight schedule. The Heighliner is already prepared to depart for the next system."

Cursing under his breath, Leto nudged his drifting luggage and stepped onto the rubble-strewn surface. Within seconds the white, bullet-shaped craft rose and dwindled to a pinpoint of orange light in the sky, before it disappeared from view entirely.

His pair of suitcases hovered beside him, and a clean-smelling wind ruffled his hair. Leto was alone. "Hello?" he shouted, but no one answered.

He shivered as he stared at rugged mountain ridges dusted with snow and glacial ice. Caladan, mostly an ocean world, had very few mountains approaching this grandeur. But he had not come to see mountains. "Hello! I'm Leto Atreides, from Caladan!" he called out. "Is anyone here?"

A sick feeling clenched his chest. He was far from home on an unknown world, with no way to find out where in the vast universe he was. *Is this even Ix?* The brisk wind was cold and sharp, but the open plain remained eerily quiet. Oppressive silence hung in the thin air.

He had spent his life hearing the lullaby of the ocean, the songs of gulls, and the bustle of villagers. Here he saw nothing, no welcoming party, no signs of habitation. The world looked untouched . . . empty.

If I've been stranded here, will anyone be able to find me?

Thickening clouds concealed the sky, though he saw a distant blue sun through a break in the cover. He shivered again and wondered what he should do, where he should go. If he was going to be a Duke, he had to learn to make decisions.

A drizzle of sleet began to fall.

The paintbrush of history has depicted Abulurd Harkonnen in a most unfavorable light. Judged by the standards of his older half brother, Baron Vladimir, and his own children Glossu Rabban and Feyd-Rautha Rabban, Abulurd was a different sort of man entirely. We must, however, assess the frequent descriptions of his weakness, incompetence, and foolhardy decisions in light of the ultimate failure of House Harkonnen. Though exiled to Lankiveil and stripped of any real power, Abulurd secured a victory unmatched by anyone else in his extended family: He learned how to be happy with his life.

—Landsraad Encyclopedia of Great Houses, post-Jihad edition

Though the Harkonnens were formidable foes in the arena of manipulations, subterfuge, and disinformation, the Bene Gesserit were undisputed *masters.*

In order to achieve the next step in their grand breeding scheme, a plan that had been in place since ten generations before the downfall of thinking machines, the Sisterhood needed to find a fulcrum that would make the Baron bend to their will.

It didn't take them long to figure out the weak point in House Harkonnen.

Presenting herself as a new domestic servant on cold and blustery Lankiveil, the young Bene Gesserit Sister Margot Rashino-Zea infiltrated the household of Abulurd Harkonnen, the Baron's younger half brother. Beautiful Margot, hand-selected by Kwisatz Mother Anirul, had been trained in the ways of spying and ferreting out information, of connecting mismatched tidbits of data to construct a broader picture.

She also knew sixty-three ways to kill a human being using nothing but her fingers. The Sisterhood worked hard to maintain their appearance as brooding intellectuals, but they also had their commandos. Sister Margot was counted among their best.

The lodge house of Abulurd Harkonnen sat on a rugged spit of land that extended into deep water bordered by narrow Tula Fjord. A fishing village surrounded the wooden mansion; farms pushed inland into the thin and rocky valleys, but most of the planet's food supply came from the frigid sea. Lankiveil's economy was based on the rich whale-fur industry.

Abulurd lived at the base of dripping mountains, whose tops were rarely seen through the looming steel-gray clouds and lingering mist. The main house and surrounding village was the closest thing to a capital center this frontier world had to offer.

Since strangers were rare, Margot took precautions not to be noticed. She stood taller than many of the stocky and muscular natives, so she disguised herself with a slight stoop. She dyed her honey-blonde hair dark and cut it thick and shaggy, a style favored by many of the villagers. With chemicals, she treated her smooth, pale skin to make it weathered and lend it a darker cast. She blended in, and everyone accepted her without a second glance. For a woman trained by the Sisterhood, maintaining the sham was easy.

Margot was only one of numerous Bene Gesserit spies dispatched to the widespread Harkonnen holdings, where they would surreptitiously scour any and all business records. The Baron had no reason to suspect such scrutiny at this time—he'd had very few dealings with the Sisterhood—but if any of their female spies were discovered, the lean and vicious man would have no compunctions against torturing them for explanations. Luckily, Margot thought, any well-trained Bene Gesserit could stop her own heart long before inflicted pain could force her to reveal secrets.

Traditionally, the Harkonnens were adept at manipulation and concealment, but Margot knew she would find the necessary incriminating evidence. Though other Sisters had argued for digging closer to the heart of Harkonnen operations, Margot had concluded that Abulurd would make the perfect patsy. The younger Harkonnen demi-brother had, after all, run the spice operations on Arrakis for seven years: He *must* have some information. If anything needed to be hidden, the Baron would likely do it here, unexpectedly, right under Abulurd's nose.

Once the Bene Gesserit uncovered a few of the Harkonnens' mistakes and held proof of the Baron's financial indiscretions, they would have the blackmail weapon so desperately needed to advance their breeding program.

Dressed as an indigenous villager in dyed wools and furs, Margot slipped into the rustic great house at the docks. The structure stood tall and was composed of massive wood, stained dark. Fireplaces in every room filled the air with resinous smoke, and glowglobes tuned to yellow-orange did their best to approximate sunlight.

Margot cleaned, she dusted, she helped with the cooking . . . she searched for financial records. Two days in a row, the Baron's amiable half brother greeted her, smiling, welcoming; he noticed nothing whatsoever amiss. A trusting sort, he seemed unconcerned for his own safety, and allowed locals and strangers to wander into the main rooms and guest quarters of his mansion, even close to his person. He had gray-blond hair, long to his shoulders, and a seamed, ruddy face that was disarmed by a perpetual half smile. It was said that he'd been a favorite of his father Dmitri, who had encouraged Abulurd to take over the Harkonnen holdings . . . but Abulurd had made so many bad choices, so many decisions based on *people* rather than business necessities. It had been his downfall.

Wearing warm and prickly Lankiveil clothing, Margot kept her gray-green eyes downcast and concealed behind lenses that made them appear brown. She could have made herself into a golden-haired beauty and had, in fact, considered seducing Abulurd and simply taking the information she needed, but she had decided against that plan. The man seemed unshakably devoted to his squat and wholesome native wife, Emmi Rabban, the mother of Glossu Rabban. He had fallen in love with her long ago on Lankiveil, married her to the dismay of his father, and carried her with him from world to world during his chaotic career. Abulurd seemed impervious to any feminine temptations but hers.

Instead, Margot used simple charm and quiet innocence to gain access to written financial records, dusty ledgers, and inventory rooms. No one questioned her.

In time, taking advantage of every surreptitious opportunity, she found what she needed. Using flash-memorization techniques learned on Wallach IX, Margot scanned through stacks of etched ridulian crystals and absorbed columns of numbers, cargo manifests, lists of equipment decommissioned or placed into service, suspicious losses, storm damage.

In nearby rooms, groups of women skinned and gutted fish, chopped herbs, peeled roots and sour fruits for steaming cauldrons of fish stew, which Abulurd and his wife served for the entire household. They insisted on eating the same meals, at the same tables, as all of their workers. Margot finished her surreptitious scanning well before the meal call sounded throughout the rooms of the great house. . . .

Later, in private while listening to a blustery storm outside, she reviewed the data in her mind and studied spice-production records from Abulurd's tenure on Arrakis and the Baron's current filings with CHOAM, along with the amounts of melange spirited away from Arrakis by various smuggler organizations.

Normally, she would have set aside the data until entire teams of Sisters had a chance to analyze it. But Margot wanted to discover the answer herself. Pretending to sleep, she dived into the problem behind her eyelids with abandon, falling into a deep trance.

The numbers had been masterfully manipulated, but after Margot stripped away the masks and thin screens, she found her answer. A Bene Gesserit could see it, but she doubted even the Emperor's financial advisors or CHOAM accountants would detect the deception.

Unless it was pointed out to them.

Her discovery suggested serious underreporting of spice production to CHOAM and the Emperor. Either the Harkonnens were selling melange illicitly—doubtful, because that could easily be tracked—or accumulating secret stockpiles of their own.

Interesting, Margot thought, raising her eyebrows. She opened her eyes, went over to a reinforced window casement, and stared out at the liquid metal seas, the choppy waves trapped within the bottleneck fjords, the murky black clouds hovering above the rugged bulwarks of rock. In the bleak distance, fur-whales set up an eerie, humming song.

The following day she booked passage on the next Guild Heighliner. Then, shucking her disguise, she rode up in a cargo hauler filled with processed whale-fur. She doubted that anyone on Lankiveil had noticed her arrival or her departure.

*Four things cannot be hidden—love, smoke, a pillar of fire, and a
man striding across the open bled.*

— Fremen Wisdom

Alone in the quiet, stark desert—exactly as it should be.
Pardot Kynes found that he worked best with nothing but his own thoughts and plenty of time to think them.
Other people provided too many distractions, and few others had the same focus or the same drive.

As Imperial Planetologist to Arrakis, he needed to absorb the huge landscape into every pore of his being. Once he got into the right mind-set he could actually *feel* the pulse of a world. Now, standing atop a rugged formation of black-and-red rock that had been uplifted from the surrounding basin, the lean, weathered man stared in both directions at the vastness. Desert, desert everywhere.

His map screen named the mountainous line Rimwall West. His altimeter proclaimed the tallest peaks to be substantially higher than six thousand meters . . . yet he saw no snow, glaciers, or ice, no signs of precipitation whatsoever. Even the most rugged and atomic-blasted mountaintops on Salusa Secundus had been covered with snow. But the air here was so desperately dry that exposed water could not survive in any form.

Kynes stared southward across the ocean of sand to the

world-girdling desert known as the Funeral Plain. No doubt geographers could have found ample distinctions to categorize the landscape into further labeled subsections—but few humans who ventured out there ever returned. This was the domain of the worms. No one really needed maps.

Bemused, Kynes remembered ancient sailing charts from the earliest days of Old Terra, their mysterious unexplored areas marked simply, "Here Be Monsters." *Yes,* he thought as he recalled Rabban's hunt of the incredible sandworm. *Here be monsters indeed.*

Exposed atop the serrated ridge of the Rimwall, he removed the stillsuit's nostril plugs and rubbed a sore spot where the filter constantly brushed against his nose. Then he pulled away the covering on his mouth so he could take a deep breath of the scorched, brittle air. According to his desert-prep instructions, he knew he should not expose himself unnecessarily to such water loss, but Kynes needed to draw in the aromas and vibrations of Arrakis, needed to sense the heartbeat of the planet.

He smelled hot dust, the subtle saltiness of minerals, the distinct tastes of sand, weathered lava, and basalt. This was a world entirely without the moist scents of either growing or rotting vegetation, without any odor that might betray the cycles of life and death. Only sand and rock and more sand.

Upon closer inspection, though, even the harshest desert teemed with life, with specialized plants, with animals and insects adapted to hostile ecological niches. He knelt to scrutinize shadowy pockets in the rock, tiny hollows where the barest breath of morning dew might collect. There, lichens gripped the rough stone surface.

A few hard pellets marked the droppings of a small rodent, perhaps a kangaroo rat. Insects might make their homes here at high altitude, along with a bit of windblown grass or hardy and solitary weeds. On the vertical cliffs, even bats took shelter and surged out at dusk to hunt night moths and gnats. Occasionally in the enamel-blue sky he spotted a dark fleck that must have been a hawk or a carrion bird. For such larger animals, survival must be particularly hard.

How, then, do the Fremen survive?

He'd seen their dusty forms walking the village streets, but the desert people kept to themselves, went about their business, then vanished. Kynes noticed that the "civilized" villagers treated them differently, but it wasn't clear whether this came from awe or disdain. *Polish comes from the cities*, went an old Fremen saying, *wisdom from the desert.*

According to a few sparse anthropological notes he had found, the Fremen were the remnants of an ancient wandering people, the Zensunni, who had been slaves dragged from world to world. After being freed, or perhaps escaping, from their captivity they had tried to find a home for centuries, but were persecuted everywhere they went. Finally, they'd gone to ground here on Arrakis—and somehow they had thrived.

Once, when he'd tried to speak to a Fremen woman as she walked past, the woman had fixed him with the gaze of her shockingly blue-within-blue eyes, the whites completely swallowed in the indigo of pure spice addiction. The sight had jolted all questions from his mind, and before Kynes could say anything else to her, the Fremen woman had hurried on her way, hugging her tattered brown jubba cloak over her stillsuit.

Kynes had heard rumors that entire Fremen population centers were hidden out in the basins and the rocky buttresses of the Shield Wall. Living off the land, when the land itself provided so little life . . . how did they do it?

Kynes still had much to learn about Arrakis, and he thought the Fremen could teach him a great deal. If he could ever find them.

IN DIRTY, ROUGH-EDGED Carthag, the Harkonnens had been reluctant to outfit the unwanted Planetologist with extravagant equipment. Scowling at the Padishah Emperor's seal on Kynes's requisition, the supply master had authorized him to take clothes, a stilltent, a survival kit, four literjons of water, some preserved rations, and a battered one-man ornithopter with an extended fuel supply. Those items were enough for a person like Kynes, who was a stranger to luxury. He didn't care about formal trappings and useless niceties. He was much more focused on the problem of understanding Arrakis.

After checking the predicted storm patterns and prevailing winds, Kynes lit off in the ornithopter toward the northeast, heading deeper into the mountainous terrain surrounding the polar regions. Because the mid-latitudes were broiling wastelands, most human habitation clustered around the highlands.

He piloted the old surplus 'thopter, listening to the loud hum of its engines and the flutter of movable wings. From the air, and all alone: *This* was the best way to see the vistas below, to get a broad perspective on the geological blemishes and patterns, the colors of rock, the canyons.

Through the sand-scratched front windows he could see dry rills and gorges, the diverging brooms of alluvial fans from ancient floods. Some of the steep canyon walls appeared to have been cut by water abrasion, like a shigawire strand sawing through strata. Once, in the distance shimmering with the ripples of a heat mirage, he thought he saw a sparkling salt-encrusted playa that could easily have been a dried sea bottom. But when he flew in that direction, he couldn't find it.

Kynes became convinced that this planet had once held water. A lot of it. The evidence was there for any Planetologist to see. But where had it all gone?

The amount of ice in the polar caps was insignificant, mined by water merchants and hauled down to the cities, where it was sold at a premium. The caps certainly did not hold enough to explain vanished oceans or dried rivers. Had the native water somehow been destroyed or removed from the planet . . . or was it just hiding?

Kynes flew on, keeping his eyes open and searching, constantly searching. Diligently compiling his journals, he took notes of every interesting thing he spotted. It would take years to gather enough information for a well-founded treatise, but in the past month he had already transmitted two regular progress reports back to the Emperor, just to show he was doing his appointed job. He'd handed these reports to an Imperial Courier and a Guild representative, one in Arrakeen, the other in Carthag. But he had no idea if Elrood or his advisors even read them.

Kynes found himself lost most of the time. His maps and charts were deplorably incomplete or absolutely *wrong*, which puzzled him. If Arrakis was the sole source of melange—which, therefore, made this planet one of the most important in the Imperium—then why was the landscape so poorly charted? If the Spacing Guild would just install a few more high-resolution satellites, much of the problem could be solved. No one seemed to know the answer.

For a Planetologist's purposes, though, being lost caused little concern. He was an explorer, after all, which required him to wander about with no plan and no destination. Even when his ornithopter began to rattle, he pressed on. The ion-propulsion engine was strong and the battered craft handled reasonably well, even in powerful gusts and updrafts of hot air. He had enough fuel to last him for weeks.

Kynes remembered all too well the years he had spent on harsh Salusa, trying to comprehend the catastrophe that had ruined it centuries before. He had seen ancient pictures, knew how beautiful the former capital world had once been. But in his heart it would always remain the hellish place it was now.

Something epochal had happened here on Arrakis, too, but no witnesses or records had survived that ancient disaster. He didn't think it could have been atomic, though that solution might be easy to postulate. The ancient wars before and during the Butlerian Jihad had been devastating, had turned entire solar systems into rubble and dust.

No . . . something different had happened here.

☙

MORE DAYS, MORE WANDERING.

On a barren, silent ridge halfway around the world, Kynes climbed to the top of another rocky peak. He had landed his 'thopter on a flat, boulder-strewn saddle, then walked up the slope, picking his way hand over hand with jangling equipment on his back.

In the unimaginative fashion of early cartographers, this curving arm of rock that formed a barrier between the Habanya Erg to the east and the great sink of the Cielago Depression to the west had been forever named False Wall West. He determined this would be a good spot to establish a data-collection outpost.

Feeling the exertion in his thighs and hearing the click-ticking of his overworked stillsuit, Kynes knew he must be perspiring heavily. Even so, his suit absorbed and recycled all of his bodily moisture, and he was in good shape. When he could stand it no longer, he drew a lukewarm sip through the catchtube near his throat, then continued to trudge upward on the rough surface. *The best place to conserve water is in your own body,* said conventional Fremen wisdom, according to the vendor who had sold him his equipment. He was accustomed to the slick stillsuit by now; it had become a second skin to him.

At the craggy pinnacle—about twelve hundred meters high, according to his altimeter—he stopped at a natural shelter formed by a broken tooth of hard stone. There, he set up his portable weather station. Its analytical devices would record wind speeds and directions, temperatures, barometric pressures, and fluctuations in relative humidity.

Around the globe, centuries-old biological testing stations had been erected in the days long before the properties of melange had been discovered. Back then, Arrakis had been no more than an unremarkable, dry planet with little in the way of desirable resources—of no interest to any but the most desperate of colonists. Many of those testing stations had fallen into disrepair, unattended, some even forgotten.

Kynes doubted the information gleaned from those stations would be very reliable. For now, he wanted his own data from his own instruments. With the whir of a tiny fan, an air-sampler gulped an atmospheric specimen and spilled out the composition readings: 23 percent oxygen, 75.4 percent nitrogen, 0.023 percent carbon dioxide, along with other trace gases.

Kynes found the numbers most peculiar. Perfectly breathable, of course, and exactly what one might expect from a normal planet with a thriving ecosystem. But in this scorched realm, those partial pressures raised enormous questions. With no seas or rainstorms, no plankton masses, no vegetative covering . . . where did all the oxygen come from? It made absolutely no sense.

The only large indigenous life-forms he knew of were the sandworms. Could there be so many of the beasts that their metabolisms actually had a measurable effect on the composition of the atmosphere? Did some odd form of plankton teem within the sands themselves? Melange deposits were known to have an organic component, but Kynes had no idea what its source could be. *Is there a connection between the voracious worms and the spice?*

Arrakis was one ecological mystery built upon another.

With his preparations complete, Kynes turned from the perfect spot for his meteorological station. Then he realized with startling abruptness that parts of the seemingly natural alcove atop this isolated peak had been *intentionally fashioned.*

He bent down, amazed, and ran his fingers over rough notches. *Steps cut into the rock!* Human hands had done this not long ago, chopping out easy access to this place. An outpost? A lookout? A Fremen observation station?

A chill shot down his spine, borne on a trickle of sweat that the stillsuit greedily drank. At the same time, he felt a thrill of excitement, because the Fremen themselves might become allies, a hardened people who had the same agenda as he did, the same need to understand and improve. . . .

As Kynes turned around in the open air, searching, he felt exposed. "Hello?" he called out, but only the desert silence answered him.

How is all of this connected? he wondered. *And what, if anything, do the Fremen know about it?*

Who can know whether Ix has gone too far? They hide their facilities, keep their workers enslaved, and claim the right of secrecy. Under such circumstances, how can they not be tempted to step beyond the restrictions of the Butlerian Jihad?

—COUNT ILBAN RICHESE,
third appeal to the Landsraad

U se your resources and use your wits," the Old Duke had always told him. Now, as he stood alone and shivering, Leto took stock of both.

He contemplated his grim and unexpected solitude on the wilderness surface of Ix—or wherever this place was. Had he been stranded here by accident or treachery? What was the worst case? The Guild should have kept a record of where he'd been unceremoniously discharged. His father and House Atreides troops could rally out and find him when he didn't show up at his intended destination—but how long would that take? How long could he survive here? If Vernius was behind this treachery, would the Earl even report him missing?

Leto tried to be optimistic, but he knew it might be a long time before help could come. He had no food, no warm clothing, not even a portable shelter. He had to take care of this problem himself.

"Hello!" he shouted again. The vast emptiness snatched his words and drained them to nothing, without even bothering to echo them back.

He considered venturing forth in search of some landmark or settlement, but decided to stay put for the time being. Next, he mentally assessed the possessions he'd brought in his suitcases, trying to think of what he might use to send a message.

Then, from beside him, in a blue-green thicket of spiny plants struggling to survive in the tundra, came a rustling sound. Startled, Leto jumped back, then looked closer. Assassins? A group intending to take him captive? The ransom of a ducal heir might bring a mountain of solaris . . . as well as the wrath of Paulus Atreides.

He drew the curve-bladed fishing knife from its sheath at his back and made ready to fight. His heart pounded as he tried to guess his peril, to prepare in some way. An Atreides had no qualms about shedding necessary blood.

The branches and pointed leaves moved, then opened to reveal a round plaz pad on the ground. With a hum of machinery, a transparent lift tube emerged from beneath the surface, looking totally incongruous on the rugged landscape.

A stocky young man stood inside the transparent tube, grinning a warm welcome. He had blond, unruly hair that looked tousled despite careful combing; he wore loose military-style trousers and a color-shifting camouflage shirt. His pale, open face had soft edges from outgrown baby fat. A small pack hung on the stranger's left shoulder, similar to the one he carried in his hand. He appeared to be about Leto's age.

The transparent lift came to a stop, and a curved door rotated open. A breath of warm air brushed Leto's hands and face. He crouched, ready to attack with his fishing knife, though he could not imagine this innocuous-looking stranger to be a killer.

"You must be Leto Atreides, right?" the young man said. He spoke in Galach, the common language of the Imperium. "So should we start out with a day hike?"

Leto's gray eyes narrowed and fixed on the purple-and-copper Ixian helix adorning the boy's collar. Trying to hide his immense relief and maintain a professional, even suspicious facade, Leto nodded and lowered the tip of the knife, which the stranger had pretended not to notice.

"I'm Rhombur Vernius. I, uh, thought you'd want to stretch a bit before we settle in down below. I heard you like being outdoors, though I prefer to be underground myself. Maybe after you spend a little time with us, you'll feel at home in our cavern cities. Ix is really quite nice."

He looked up at the clouds and high-altitude sleet. "Oh, why is it

raining? Vermilion hells, I hate being in unpredictable environments."
Rhombur shook his head in disgust. "I told weather control to give you
a warm, sunny day. My apologies, Prince Leto—but this is just too
dreary for me. How about we go down to the Grand Palais?"

Catching himself rambling, Rhombur dropped both day packs inside the lift tube and nudged Leto's floating luggage inside as well. "It's
good to meet you at last. My father's been talking about Atreides *this*
and Atreides *that* for so long. We'll be studying together for some time,
probably family trees and Landsraad politics. I'm eighty-seventh in
line to the Golden Lion Throne, but I think you rank even higher
than I do."

Golden Lion Throne. The Great Houses were ranked according to
an elaborate CHOAM-Landsraad system, and within each House was
a sub-hierarchy based upon primogeniture. Leto's ranking was indeed
substantially higher than the Ixian Prince's—through his mother he
was actually a great-grandson of Elrood IX, through one of his three
daughters by his second wife, Yvette. But the difference was meaningless; the Emperor had many great-grandchildren. Neither he nor Rhombur would ever get to be Emperor. Serving as Duke of House Atreides
would offer enough of a challenge, Leto thought.

The young men exchanged the half handshake of the Imperium,
interlocking fingertips. The Ixian Prince wore a fire-jewel ring on his
right hand, and Leto felt no rough calluses.

"I thought I was in the wrong place after I'd landed," Leto said, finally letting his uneasiness and confusion show through. "I believed I
was stranded on some uninhabited rock. Is this really . . . Ix? The machine planet?" He pointed toward the spectacular peaks, the snow and
rocks, the dark forests.

Remembering what his father had told him about the Ixian penchant for security, Leto noted Rhombur's hesitation. "Oh, uh, you'll
see. We try not to make ourselves too obvious."

The Prince gestured him into the tube, and the plaz door rotated
shut. They plunged through what seemed to be a kilometer of rock.
Rhombur continued to speak calmly even as they plummeted. "Because of the nature of our technical operations, Ix has countless secrets
and many enemies who'd like to destroy us. We try to keep our dealings and our resources hidden from prying eyes."

The two young men passed through a luminescent honeycomb of

artificial material, then into a vast expanse of air that revealed a huge grotto-world, a fairyland protected deep within the crust of the planet.

Massive crowns of graceful support girders came into view, connected to diamond lattice columns so tall that the bottoms were not visible below. The plaz-walled capsule continued to descend, floating free on an Ixian suspensor mechanism. The capsule's transparent floor gave Leto the unsettling illusion of dropping feetfirst through thin air. He held on to the side railing while his floating suitcases bobbed around him.

Overhead, he saw what looked like the cloudy Ixian sky and the blue-white sun peeking through. Projectors concealed on the surface of the planet transmitted actual weather images onto high-resolution screens that covered the rock ceilings.

This enormous underworld made the inside of even a Guild Heighliner look minuscule. Hanging down from the roof of the stone vault, Leto saw geometric inverted buildings, like inhabited crystal stalactites connected to each other by walkways and tubes. Teardrop-shaped aircraft sped noiselessly through the subterranean realm, flitting between structures and supports. Hang gliders carrying people flashed by in streaks of brilliant color.

Far down on the floor of the rough cavern he spotted a lake and rivers—all deep underground and protected from outsiders' eyes.

"Vernii," Rhombur said. "Our capital city."

As the capsule slid between the hanging stalactite buildings, Leto could make out groundcars, buses, and an aerial tube-transport system. He felt as if he were inside a magical snowflake. "Your buildings are incredibly beautiful," he said, his gray eyes drinking in all the details. "I always thought of Ix as a noisy industrial world."

"We, uh, foster that impression for outsiders. We've discovered structural materials that are not only aesthetically pleasing but extremely light and strong. Living here underground, we're both protected and hidden."

"And it lets you keep the surface of the world in pristine condition," Leto pointed out. The Prince of Ix looked as if he hadn't even considered that advantage.

"The nobles and administrators live in the upper stalactite buildings," Rhombur continued. "Workers, shift supervisors, and all the suboid crews live below in warrens. Everyone works together for the prosperity of Ix."

"More levels beneath this city? People live even deeper down there?"

"Well, not really people. They're *suboids*," Rhombur said, with a dismissive wave of one hand. "We've specifically bred them to perform drudgery without complaint. Quite a triumph of genetic engineering. I don't know what we'd do without them."

Their floating compartment skirted a tube-transport path and continued to follow the upside-down skyline. As they approached the most spectacular of the inverted ceiling palaces—a huge, angled structure hanging suspended like an archaic cathedral—Leto said, "I assume your Inquisitors await me?" He raised his chin and prepared himself for the ordeal. "I've never had a deep mental scan before."

Rhombur laughed at him. "I can, uh, arrange a mind probe if you really wish to undergo the rigors. . . ." The Ixian Prince studied Leto intently. "Leto, Leto, if we didn't trust you in the first place, you never would have been allowed on Ix. Security has, um, changed a lot here since your father's day. Don't listen to all those dark, sinister stories we spread about ourselves. They're just to scare away the curious."

The capsule finally settled onto a sprawling balcony constructed of interlocking tiles, and Leto felt a holding apparatus engage underneath them. The chamber began to move laterally toward an armor-plaz building.

Leto tried not to let his relief show. "All right. I'll defer to your judgment."

"And I'll do the same when we're on your planet. Water and fish and open skies. Caladan sounds . . . uh, *wonderful.*" His tone said the exact opposite.

Household personnel clad in black-and-white livery streamed out of the armor-plaz building. Forming a neat line on each side of the tube path, the uniformed men and women stood rigidly at attention.

"This is the Grand Palais," Rhombur said, "where our staff will see to your every wish. Since you're the only current visitor, you might be in for some pampering."

"All these people just to serve . . . me?" Leto remembered the times when he'd had to scale and fillet the fish he caught, if he wanted to eat.

"You are an important dignitary, Leto. The son of a Duke, the friend of our family, an ally in the Landsraad. Do you expect anything less?"

"In truth, I'm from a House with no substantial wealth, on a planet where the only glamour comes from fishermen, harvesters of floating paradan melons, and pundi rice farmers."

Rhombur laughed, a friendly peal. "Oh, and you're modest, too!"

Followed by the suspensor-borne luggage, the young men walked side by side up three wide, elegant stairs into the Grand Palais.

Looking around the central lobby, Leto identified Ixian crystal chandeliers, the finest in all the Imperium. Crystal goblets and vases adorned marbleplaz tables, and on each side of a blackite reception desk were full-size lapisjade statuaries of Earl Dominic Vernius and his Lady Shando Vernius. Leto recognized the royal couple from triphotos he had seen.

The uniformed household staff filtered back into the building and took up positions where they would be available for instructions from superiors. Across the lobby, double doors opened and big-shouldered, bald Dominic Vernius himself approached, looking like some *djinn* out of a bottle. He wore a silver-and-gold sleeveless tunic trimmed in white at the collar. A purple-and-copper Ixian helix adorned his breast.

"Ah, so this is our young visitor!" Dominic effused with blustery good humor. Crow's-feet became laugh lines around his bright brown eyes. His facial construction looked very much like that of his son Rhombur, except the fat he carried had set into ruddy folds and creases, and his dark bushy mustache made for a striking frame around white teeth. Earl Dominic was several centimeters taller than his son. The Earl's features were not narrow and hard like the Atreides and Corrino bloodlines, but came instead from a lineage that had been ancient at the time of the Battle of Corrin.

Behind him came his wife Shando, former concubine of the Emperor, dressed in a formal gown. Her finely chiseled features, delicately pointed nose, and creamy skin suffused her appearance with a regal beauty that would have shone through even the most drab of garments. She looked slight and delicate at first glance, but carried a toughness and resilience about her.

Beside her, their daughter Kailea seemed to be trying to outshine even her mother in a brocaded lavender dress that set off copper-dark hair. Kailea looked a little younger than Leto, but she walked with a studied grace and concentration, as if she dared not let formality or appearances slip. She had thin arched eyebrows, striking emerald eyes, and a generous, catlike mouth above a narrow chin. With the faintest of smiles, Kailea executed an extravagant and perfect curtsy.

Leto nodded and responded to each introduction, trying to keep his eyes from the Vernius daughter. Hurriedly going through the motions his mother had drilled into him, Leto snapped open the seal on one of his suitcases and removed a heavy jeweled box, one of the Atreides family treasures. Holding it, he stood erect. "For you, Lord Vernius. This contains unique items from our planet. I also have a gift for Lady Vernius."

"Excellent, excellent!" Then, as if impatient with overblown ceremony, Dominic accepted the gift and motioned for a servant to come and take it. "I'll enjoy its contents this evening, when there is more time." He rubbed his broad hands together. This man seemed to belong more in a smoky blacksmith's shop or on a battlefield than in a fancy palace. "So, did you have a good trip to Ix, Leto?"

"Uneventful, sir."

"Ah, the best kind of trip." Dominic laughed easily.

Leto smiled, not certain how best to make a good impression on this man. He cleared his throat, embarrassed to confess his concerns and worries. "Yes, sir, except I thought I was abandoned when the Guild left me on your planet and I saw only wilderness."

"Ah! I asked your father not to mention that to you—our little prank. I did the same to him on his first visit here. You must have imagined yourself good and lost." Dominic beamed with pleasure. "You look rested enough, young man. At your age, space lag isn't much of a factor. You left Caladan, what, two days ago?"

"Less than that, sir."

"Amazing how quickly Heighliners can span great distances. Positively incredible. And we're making improvements in Heighliner design, enabling each ship to carry a larger payload." His booming voice made the accomplishments seem even more grandiose. "Our second construction is to be completed later today, another triumph for us. We'll take you through all the modifications we've made, so you can learn them as part of your apprenticeship here."

Leto smiled, but already his head felt as if it might explode. He didn't know how much more new input he could absorb. By the time the year was up, he would be a different person entirely.

There are weapons you cannot hold in your hands. You can only hold them in your mind.

—Bene Gesserit Teaching

The Bene Gesserit shuttle descended to the dark side of Giedi Prime, landing in the well-guarded Harko City spaceport just before midnight, local time.

Concerned about what the damned witches wanted from him now that he had come home from the desert hellhole of Arrakis, the Baron went to a shielded upper balcony of Harkonnen Keep to watch the lights of the arriving craft.

Around him, the monolithic blackplaz-and-steel towers shone garish lights into the smoke-smeared darkness. Walkways and roads were covered by corrugated awnings and filtered enclosures to protect pedestrians from industrial waste and acid rain. Given a little more imagination and attention to detail during its construction, Harko City could have been striking. Instead, the place looked *stricken*.

"I have the data for you, my Baron," said a nasal but sharp voice behind him, as close as an assassin.

Startled, the Baron turned, flexing his well-muscled arms. He scowled. The gaunt-robed form of his personal Mentat, Piter de Vries, stood at the doorway to the balcony.

"Don't ever sneak up on me, Piter. You slither like a worm." The comparison brought to mind his nephew

Rabban's desert hunting expedition and its embarrassing results. "Harkonnens kill worms, you know."

"So I've heard," de Vries answered dryly. "But sometimes moving silently is the best way to acquire information." A wry smile formed on his lips, which were stained red from the cranberry-colored sapho juice Mentats drank in order to increase their abilities. Always seeking physical pleasures, curious to experiment with additional addictions, the Baron had tried sapho himself, but found it to be bitter, vile stuff.

"It's a Reverend Mother and her entourage," de Vries said, nodding toward the lights of the shuttle. "Fifteen Sisters and acolytes, along with four male guards. No weapons that we could detect."

De Vries had been trained as a Mentat by the Bene Tleilax, genetic wizards who produced some of the Imperium's best human computers. But the Baron hadn't wanted a mere data-processing machine with a human brain—he'd wanted a calculating and clever man, someone who could not only comprehend and compute the consequences of Harkonnen schemes, but who could also use his corrupt imagination to assist the Baron in achieving his aims. Piter de Vries was a special creation, one of the infamous Tleilaxu "twisted Mentats."

"But what do they *want?*" the Baron muttered, gazing at the landed shuttle. "Those witches seem damned confident coming here." His own blue-uniformed troops marched out like a wolf pack before any of the passengers emerged from the ship. "We could erase them in an instant with our most trivial House defenses."

"The Bene Gesserit are not without weapons, my Baron. Some say they themselves are weapons." De Vries raised a thin finger. "It's never wise to incur the wrath of the Sisterhood."

"I know that, idiot! So, what's the Reverend Mother's name and what does she want?"

"Gaius Helen Mohiam. As to what she wants . . . her Sisterhood has refused to say."

"Damn them and their secrets," the Baron grumbled, as he spun about on the plaz-enclosed balcony. He strode toward the corridor to go meet the shuttlecraft.

Piter de Vries smiled after him. "When a Bene Gesserit speaks, she often does so in riddles and innuendos, but her words also hold a great deal of truth. One simply needs to excavate it."

The Baron responded with a deep grunt, kept going. Intensely curious himself, Piter followed.

On the way, the Mentat reviewed his knowledge of these black-robed witches. The Bene Gesserit occupied themselves with numerous breeding schemes, as if farming humanity for their own obscure purposes. They also commanded one of the greatest storehouses of information in the Imperium, using their intricate libraries to look at the broad movements of peoples, to study the effects of one person's actions amidst interplanetary politics.

As a Mentat, de Vries would have loved to get his hands on that storehouse of knowledge. With such a treasure trove of data he could make computations and prime projections—perhaps enough to bring down the Sisterhood itself.

But the Bene Gesserit allowed no outsiders into their archives, not even the Emperor himself. Hence there wasn't much on which even a Mentat could base his calculations. De Vries could only guess at the arriving witch's intentions.

THE BENE GESSERIT liked to manipulate politics and societies in secret, so that few people could trace the exact patterns of influence. Nevertheless, the Reverend Mother Gaius Helen Mohiam knew how to plan and execute a spectacular entrance. With black robes swishing, flanked by two immaculately dressed male guards and followed by her troop of acolytes, she strode into the reception hall of the ancestral Harkonnen Keep.

Seated at a gleaming blackplaz desk, the Baron waited to receive her, accompanied by his twisted Mentat, who stood on one side with a few handpicked personal guards. To exhibit his utter contempt and lack of interest for these visitors, the Baron wore a sloppy, casual robe. He had prepared no refreshments for them, no fanfare, no ceremony whatsoever.

Very well, Mohiam thought, *perhaps it's best we keep this encounter a private matter anyway.*

In a strong, firm voice she identified herself, then took one step closer to him, leaving her entourage behind. She had a plain face that showed strength rather than delicacy—not ugly, but not attractive either. In profile her nose, while unremarkable from the front, was revealed to be overlong. "Baron Vladimir Harkonnen, my Sisterhood has business to discuss with you."

"I'm not interested in doing business with witches," the Baron said, resting his strong chin on his knuckles. His spider-black eyes looked the assemblage over, assessing the physiques and physical appearance of her male guards. The fingers of his free hand tapped a nervous rhythm against his thigh.

"Nevertheless, you will hear what I have to say." Her voice was iron.

Seeing the blustering rage building within the Baron, Piter de Vries stepped forward. "Need I remind you, Reverend Mother, where you are? We did not invite you to come here."

"Perhaps I should remind *you*," she snapped at the Mentat, "that we are capable of running a detailed analysis of all Harkonnen spice-production activities on Arrakis—the equipment used, the manpower expended, compared with spice production actually *reported* to CHOAM, as opposed to our own precise projections. Any anomalies should be quite . . . revealing." She raised her eyebrows. "We've already done a preliminary study, based upon firsthand reports from our"—she smiled—"sources."

"You mean *spies*," the Baron said, indignantly.

She could see that he regretted these words as soon as they were uttered, for they hinted at his culpability.

The Baron stood up, flexing his arm muscles, but before he could counter Mohiam's innuendo, de Vries interjected, "Perhaps it would be best if we made this a private meeting, just between the Reverend Mother and the Baron? There's no need to turn a simple conversation into a grand spectacle . . . and matter of record."

"I agree," Mohiam said quickly, assessing the twisted Mentat with a glint of approval. "Why don't we adjourn to your chambers, Baron?"

He pouted, his generous lips forming a dark rose. "And why should I take a Bene Gesserit witch into my private quarters?"

"Because you have no choice," she said in a low, hard voice.

In shock, the Baron mused at her audacity, but then he laughed out loud. "Why not? We can't get any less pretentious than that."

De Vries watched them both with narrowed eyes. He was reconsidering his suggestion, running data through his brain, figuring probabilities. The witch had jumped too quickly at the idea. She *wanted* to be alone with the Baron. Why? What did she have to do in private?

"Allow me to accompany you, my Baron," de Vries said, already strutting toward the door that would take them through halls and suspensor tubes to the Baron's private suite.

"This matter is best kept between the Baron and myself," Mohiam said.

Baron Harkonnen stiffened. "You don't command my people, witch," he said in a low, menacing tone.

"Your instructions then?" she asked, insolently.

A moment's hesitation, and: "I grant your *request* for a private audience."

She tipped her head in the slightest of bows, then glanced behind her at her acolytes and guards. De Vries caught a flicker of her fingers, some sort of witch hand signal.

Her birdlike eyes locked on to his, and de Vries drew himself up as she said, "There is one thing you can do, Mentat. Be so kind as to make certain my companions are welcomed and fed, since we won't have time to stay for pleasantries. We must return posthaste to Wallach IX."

"Do it," Baron Harkonnen said.

With a look of dismissal toward de Vries, as if he were the lowest servant in the Imperium, she followed the Baron out of the hall. . . .

Upon entering his chambers, the Baron was pleased to note that he had left his soiled clothes in a pile. Furniture lay in disarray, and a few red stains on the wall had not been sufficiently scrubbed. He wanted to emphasize that the witch did not deserve fine treatment or a particularly well-planned welcome.

Placing his hands on his narrow hips, he squared his shoulders and raised his firm chin. "All right, Reverend Mother, tell me what it is you want. I have no time for further word games."

Mohiam released a small smile. "Word games?" She knew that House Harkonnen understood the nuances of politics . . . perhaps not the kindhearted Abulurd, but certainly the Baron and his advisors. "Very well, Baron," she said simply. "The Sisterhood has a use for your genetic line."

She paused, relishing the look of shock on his hard face. Before he could splutter a response, she explained carefully chosen parts of the scenario. Mohiam herself didn't know the details or the reasons; she simply knew to obey. "You are no doubt aware that for many years the Bene Gesserit have incorporated important bloodlines into our Sisterhood. Our Sisters represent the full spectrum of noble humanity, containing within us the desirable traits of most of the Great and Minor Houses in the Landsraad. We even have some representatives, many generations removed, of House Harkonnen."

"And you want to improve your Harkonnen strain?" the Baron asked, warily. "Is that it?"

"You understand perfectly. We must conceive a child by *you*, Vladimir Harkonnen. A daughter."

The Baron staggered backward, then chuckled as he brushed a tear of mirth from his eyes. "You'll have to look elsewhere, then. I have no children, nor is it likely I'll ever have any. The actual procreation process, involving women as it does, disgusts me."

Knowing full well the Baron's sexual preferences, Mohiam made no response. Unlike many nobles, he had no offspring, not even illegitimate ones lurking among planetary populations.

"Nevertheless, we want a Harkonnen daughter, Baron. Not an heir, or even a pretender, so you need not worry about any . . . dynastic ambitions. We have studied the bloodlines carefully and the desired mix is quite specific. *You* must impregnate *me*."

The Baron's eyebrows rose even higher. "Why, under all the moons of the Imperium, would I want to do that?" He raked his gaze up and down her body, dissecting her, sizing her up. Mohiam was rather plain-looking, her face long, her brown hair thin and unremarkable. She was older than he, near the end of her childbearing years. "Especially with you."

"The Bene Gesserit determine these things through genetic projections, not through any mutual or physical attraction."

"Well, I refuse." The Baron turned about and crossed his arms over his chest. "Go away. Take your little slaves with you and get off Giedi Prime."

Mohiam stared at him for a few more moments, absorbing the details of his chambers. Using Bene Gesserit analytical techniques, she learned many things about the Baron and his personality from the way he maintained this odorous private warren, a space that was not groomed and decorated for the view of formal visitors. He unknowingly exhibited a wealth of information about his inner self.

"If that is your wish, Baron," she said. "My shuttle's next stop will be Kaitain, where we have a meeting already scheduled with the Emperor. My personal data library on the ship contains copies of all the records that give evidence of your spice-stockpiling activities on Arrakis, and documentation of how you have altered your production deliberately to hide your private stores from CHOAM and House Corrino. Our *preliminary* analysis contains enough information to initiate a full-scale Guild bank audit of your activities and revocation of your temporary CHOAM directorship."

The Baron stared back at her. An impasse, neither of them budging. But he saw behind her eyes the truth in her words. He did not doubt the witches had used their diabolical intuitive methods to determine exactly what he had done, how he had been making a secret fool out of Elrood IX. He also knew that Mohiam would not hesitate to follow through with her threat.

Copies of all the records . . . Even destroying this ship would do no good. The infernal Sisterhood obviously had other copies elsewhere.

The Bene Gesserit probably had blackmail material on Imperial House Corrino as well, perhaps even embarrassing data on the important but surreptitious dealings of the Spacing Guild and the powerful CHOAM Company. *Bargaining chips.* The Sisterhood was good at learning the weaknesses of potential enemies.

The Baron hated the Hobson's choice she gave him, but he could do nothing about it. This witch could destroy him with a word, and in the end still force him to give her his bloodline.

"To make things easier on you, I have the ability to control my bodily functions," Mohiam said, sounding reasonable. "I can ovulate at will, and I guarantee that this unpleasant task will not need to be repeated. From a single encounter with you, I can guarantee the birth of a girl-child. You need not worry about us again."

The Bene Gesserit always had plans afoot, wheels within wheels, and nothing with them was ever as clear as it seemed. The Baron frowned, running through the possibilities. With this daughter they wanted so badly, did the witches—in spite of their denials—intend to create an illegitimate heir and claim House Harkonnen in the following generation? That was preposterous. He was already grooming Rabban for that position, and no one would question it.

"I . . ." He fumbled for words. "I need a moment to consider this, and I must speak with my advisors."

Reverend Mother Mohiam all but rolled her eyes at the suggestion, but granted him leave, gesturing for the Baron to take his time. Tossing aside a bloodstained towel, she lounged back on the divan, comfortable to wait.

Despite his despicable personality, Vladimir Harkonnen was an attractive man, well built with pleasant features: reddish hair, heavy lips, pronounced widow's peak. However, the Bene Gesserit instilled in all their Sisters the critical belief that sexual intercourse was a mere tool for manipulating men and for obtaining offspring to add to the genetically connected web of the Sisterhood. Mohiam never intended to enjoy the act, no matter her orders. Nevertheless, she did find it pleasurable to have the Baron under her thumb, to be able to force him into submission.

The Reverend Mother sat back, closed her eyes, and concentrated on the flow and ebb of hormones in her body, the inner workings of her reproductive system . . . preparing herself.

She knew what the Baron's answer had to be.

"PITER!" THE BARON strode down the halls. "Where's my Mentat?"

De Vries slipped out of an adjoining hall, where he'd been intending to use the hidden observation holes he'd placed in the Baron's private chambers.

"I'm here, my Baron," he said, then swigged from a tiny vial. The sapho taste triggered responses in his brain, firing his neurons, stoking his mental capabilities. "What did the witch request? What is she up to?"

The Baron wheeled, finally finding an appropriate target for his rage. "She wants me to impregnate her! The sow!"

Impregnate her? de Vries thought, adding this to his Mentat database. At hyper speed he reassessed the problem.

"She wants to bear my girl-child! Can you believe it? They know about my spice stockpiles, too!"

De Vries was in Mentat mode. *Fact: The Baron would never have children any other way. He loathes women. Besides, politically, he is too careful to spread his seed indiscriminately.*

Fact: The Bene Gesserit have broad genetic records on Wallach IX, numerous breeding plans, the results of which are open to interpretation. Given a child by the Baron—a daughter instead of a son?—what could the witches hope to accomplish?

Is there some flaw—or advantage—in Harkonnen genetics they wish to exploit? Do they simply wish to do this because they consider it the most humiliating punishment they can inflict upon the Baron? If so, how has the Baron personally offended the Sisterhood?

"The thought of it disgusts me! Rutting with that broodmare," the Baron growled. "But I'm nearly mad with curiosity. What can the Sisterhood possibly want?"

"I'm unable to make a projection, Baron. Insufficient data."

The Baron looked as if he wanted to strike de Vries, but refrained. "I'm not a Bene Gesserit stud!"

"Baron," de Vries said calmly, "if they truly have information about your spice-stockpiling activities, you cannot afford to have that exposed. Even if they were bluffing, your reaction has no doubt already told them all they need to know. If they offer proof to Kaitain, the Emperor will bring his Sardaukar here to exterminate House Harkonnen and set up another Great House in our stead on Arrakis, just as they removed Richese before us. Elrood would like that, no doubt. He and CHOAM can withdraw their contracts from any of your holdings at any time. They might even give Arrakis and the spice production to, say, House Atreides . . . just to spite you."

"Atreides!" The Baron wanted to spit. "I'd *never* let my holdings fall into their hands."

De Vries knew he had struck the right chord. The feud between Harkonnen and Atreides had started many generations before, during the tragic events of the Battle of Corrin.

"You must do as the witch demands, Baron," he said. "The Bene Gesserit have won this round of the game. Priority: Protect the fortunes of your House, your spice holdings, and your illicit stockpiles." The Mentat smiled. "Then get your revenge later."

The Baron looked gray, his skin suddenly blotched. "Piter, from this instant forward I want you to begin erasing the evidence and dispersing our stockpiles. Spread them to places where no one will think to look."

"On the planets of our allies, too? I wouldn't recommend that, Baron. Too many complexities setting it up. And alliances change."

"Very well." His spider-black eyes lit up. "Put most of it on Lankiveil, right under the nose of my stupid half brother. They'll never suspect Abulurd's collusion in any of this."

"Yes, my Baron. A very good idea."

"Of course it's a good idea!" He frowned, looked around. Thinking of his half brother had reminded him of his cherished nephew. "Where is Rabban? Maybe the witch can use his sperm instead."

"I doubt it, Baron," de Vries said. "Their genetic plans are usually specific."

"Well, where is he anyway? Rabban!" The Baron spun about and paced the hall, as if looking for something to stalk. "I haven't seen him in a day."

"Off on another one of his silly hunts, up at Forest Guard Station." De Vries suppressed a smile. "You are on your own here, my Baron, and I think you'd better get to your bedchamber. You have a duty to perform."

The basic rule is this: Never support weakness; always support strength.

—The Bene Gesserit Azhar Book,
Compilation of Great Secrets

The light cruiser soared out over a night wasteland unmarked by Giedi Prime's city lights or industrial smoke. Alone in a holding pen in the belly of the aircraft, Duncan Idaho watched through a plaz port as the expanse of Barony prison dropped behind them like a geometrical bubo, festering with trapped and tortured humanity.

At least his parents were no longer prisoners. Rabban had killed them, just to make him angry and willing to fight. Over the past several days of preparations, Duncan's anger had indeed increased.

The bare metal walls of the cruiser's lower hold were etched with a verdigris of frost. Duncan was numb, his heart leaden, his nerves shocked into silence, his skin an unfeeling blanket around him. The engines throbbed through the floor plates. On the decks above, he could hear the restive hunting party shuffling about in their padded armor. The men carried guns with tracking scopes. They laughed and chatted, ready for the evening's game.

Rabban was up there, too.

In order to give young Duncan what they called "a sporting chance," the hunting party had armed him with a dull knife (saying they didn't want him to hurt himself), a handlight, and a small length of rope: everything an eight-year-old child should need to elude a squadron of professional Harkonnen hunters on their own well-scouted ground. . . .

Above, in a warm and padded seat, Rabban smiled at the thought of the terrified, angry child in the hold. If this Duncan Idaho were bigger and stronger, he would be as dangerous as any animal. The kid was tough for his size, Rabban had to admit. The way he had eluded elite Harkonnen trainers inside the bowels of Barony was admirable, especially that trick with the suspensor tube.

The cruiser flew far from the prison city, away from the oil-soaked industrial areas, to a wilderness preserve on high ground, a place with dark pines and sandstone bluff faces, caves and rocks and streams. The tailored wilderness even hosted a few examples of genetically enhanced wildlife, vicious predators as eager for a boy's tender flesh as the Harkonnen sportsmen themselves.

The cruiser alighted in a boulder-strewn meadow; the deck canted at a steep angle, then shifted to norm as stabilizers leveled the craft. Rabban sent a signal from the control band at his waist.

The hydraulic door in front of the boy hissed open, freeing him from his cage. The chill night air stung his cheeks. Duncan considered just dashing out into the open. He could run fast and take refuge in the thick pines. Once there, he would burrow beneath the dry brown needles and drift into a self-protective slumber.

But Rabban wanted the boy to run and hide, and he knew he wouldn't get very far. For the moment Duncan had to act on instinct tempered with cleverness. It wasn't the time for an unexpected, reckless action. Not yet.

Duncan would wait at the cruiser until the hunters explained the rules to him, though he could certainly guess what he was supposed to do. It was a bigger arena, a longer chase, higher stakes . . . but in essence the same game he had trained for in the prison city.

The upper hatch slid open behind him to reveal two light-haloed forms: a person he recognized as the hunt captain from Barony, and the broad-shouldered man who had killed Duncan's mother and father. *Rabban.*

Turning away from the sudden light, the boy kept his dark-adapted eyes toward the open meadow and the thick shadows of black-needled trees. It was a starlit night. Pain shot through Duncan's ribs from the earlier rough training, but he tried to put it out of his mind.

"Forest Guard Station," the hunt captain said to him. "Like a vacation in the wilderness. Enjoy it! This is a game, boy—we leave you here, give you a head start, and then we come hunting." His eyes narrowed. "Make no mistake, though. This is different from your training sessions in Barony. If you lose, you'll be killed, and your stuffed head will join Lord Rabban's other trophies on a wall."

Beside him, the Baron's nephew gave Duncan a thick-lipped smile. Rabban trembled with excitement and anticipation, and his sunburned face flushed.

"What if I get away?" Duncan said in a piping voice.

"You won't," Rabban answered.

Duncan didn't press the issue. If he forced an answer, the man would simply have lied to him anyway. If he managed to escape, he would just have to make up his own rules.

They dumped him out onto the frost-smeared meadow. He had only thin clothes, worn shoes. The cold of the night hit him like a hammer.

"Stay alive as long as you can, boy," Rabban called from the door of the cruiser, ducking back inside as the throb of the engines increased in tempo. "Give me a good hunt. My last one was very disappointing."

Duncan stood immobile as the craft lifted into the air and roared off toward a guarded lodge and outpost. From there, after a few drinks, the hunting party would march out and track down their prey.

Maybe the Harkonnens would toy with him a while, enjoying their sport . . . or maybe by the time they caught him they would be chilled to the bone, longing for a hot beverage, and they'd simply use their weapons to cut him to pieces at the first opportunity.

Duncan sprinted toward the shelter of trees.

Even when he left the meadow behind, his feet left an obvious trail of bent grass blades in the frost. He brushed against thick evergreen boughs, disturbed the chuff of dead needles as he scrambled upslope toward some rugged sandstone outcroppings.

In the handlight beam, he saw cold steam-breath bursting like heartbeats from his nostrils and mouth. He toiled up a talus slope, tending toward the steepest bluff faces. When he struck the rocks, he grasped with his hands, digging into crumbling sedimentary rock. Here, at least, he wouldn't leave many footprints, though pockets of old, crystalline snow had drifted like small dunes on the ledges.

The outcroppings protruded from the side of the ridge, sentinels above the carpet of forest. Wind and rain had eaten holes and notches out of the cliffs, some barely large enough for rodents' nests, some sufficient to hide a grown man. Driven by desperation, Duncan climbed until he could barely breathe from the exertion.

When he reached the top of an exposed sandwich of rock that was rust and tan in his light beam, he squatted on his heels and looked all around, assessing his wilderness surroundings. He wondered if the hunters were coming yet. They wouldn't be far behind him.

Animals howled in the distance. He flipped off the light to conceal himself better. The old injuries to his ribs and back burned with pain, and his upper arm throbbed where the pulsing locator beacon was implanted.

Behind him, more shadowy bluffs rose tall and steep, honeycombed with notches and ledges, adorned with scraggly trees like unsightly whiskers sprouting from a facial blemish. It was a long, long way to the nearest city, the nearest spaceport.

Forest Guard Station. His mother had told him of this isolated hunting preserve, a particular favorite of the Baron's nephew. "Rabban's so cruel because he needs to prove he's not like his father," she had once said.

The young boy had spent most of the nearly nine years of his life inside giant buildings, smelling recycled air laden with lubricants, solvents, and exhaust chemicals. He had never known how cold this planet could get, how frigid the nights . . . or how clear the stars.

Overhead, the sky was a vault of immense blackness, filled with tiny light-splashes, a rainstorm of pinpricks piercing the distances of the galaxy. Far out there, Guild Navigators used their minds to guide city-sized Heighliners between stars.

Duncan had never seen a Guild ship, had never been away from Giedi Prime—and now doubted he ever would. Living inside an industrial city, he'd never had reason to learn the patterns of stars. But even if he had known his compass points or recognized the constellations, he still had no place to *go.* . . .

Sitting atop the outcropping, looking out into the sharp coldness,

Duncan studied his world. He huddled over and drew his knees up to his chest to conserve body heat, though he still shivered.

In the distance, where the high ground dipped into a wooded valley toward the stark silhouette of the guarded lodge building, he saw a train of lights, bobbing glowglobes like a fairy procession. The hunting party itself, warm and well armed, was sniffing him out, taking their time. *Enjoying themselves.*

From his vantage point, Duncan watched and waited, cold and forlorn. He had to decide if he wanted to live at all. What would he do? Where would he go? Who would care for him?

Rabban's lasgun had left nothing of his mother's face for him to kiss, nothing of her hair for him to stroke. He would never again hear her voice as she called him her "sweet Duncan."

Now the Harkonnens intended to do the same to him, and he couldn't prevent it. He was just a boy with a dull knife, a handlight, and a rope. The hunters had Richesian beacon trackers, heated body armor, and powerful weapons. They outnumbered him ten to one. He had no chance.

It might be easier if he just sat there and waited for them to come. Eventually the trackers would find him, inexorably following his implanted signal . . . but he could deny them their sport, spoil their fun. By surrendering, by showing his utter contempt for their barbaric amusements, he could gain a small victory at least: the only one he was likely to have.

Or Duncan Idaho could fight back, try to hurt the Harkonnens even as they hunted him down. His mother and father hadn't had an opportunity to fight for their lives, but Rabban was giving *him* that chance.

Rabban considered him a mere helpless boy. The hunting party thought that gunning down a child would provide them with some amusement.

He stood up on stiff legs, brushed his clothes, and stopped his shivers. *I won't go down like that,* he decided—*just to show them, just to prove they can't laugh at me.*

He doubted the hunters would be wearing personal shields. They wouldn't think they'd need such protection, not against the likes of him.

The knife handle felt hard and rough in his pocket, useless against decent armor. But he could do something else with the blade, something painfully necessary. Yes, he would fight—for all he was worth.

Crawling up the slope, climbing from rock to fallen tree, maintaining his balance on the scree, Duncan made his way to a small hollowed-out hole in the lumpy sandstone. He avoided the patches of remaining snow, keeping to the iron-frozen dirt so as to leave no obvious tracks.

The tracer implant would bring them directly to him, no matter where he ran.

Above the cave hollow, an overhang in the near-vertical bluff wall provided his second opportunity: loose, lichen-covered sandstone chunks, heavy boulders. Perhaps he could move them. . . .

Duncan crawled inside the shelter of the cave hollow, where he found it no warmer at all. Just darker. The opening was low enough that a grown man would have to belly-crawl inside; there was no other way out. This cave wouldn't offer him much protection. He'd have to hurry.

Squatting there, he switched on the small handlight, pulled off his stained shirt, and brought out the knife. He felt the lump of the tracer implant in the meat of his upper left arm, the back of the tricep at his shoulder.

His skin was already numb from the cold, his mind dulled by the shock of his circumstances. But when he jabbed with the knife, he felt the point dig into his muscle, lighting the nerves on fire. Closing his eyes against reflexive resistance, he cut deeply, prodding and poking with the tip of the blade.

He stared at the dark wall of the cave, saw skeletal shadows cast by the wan light. His right hand moved mechanically, like a probe excavating the tiny tracer. The pain shrank to a dim corner of his awareness.

At last the beacon fell out, a bloody piece of micro-constructed metal clinking to the dirty floor of the cave. Sophisticated technology from Richese. Reeling with pain, Duncan picked up a rock to smash the tracer. Then, thinking better of it, he set the rock down again and moved the tiny device deep into the shadows where no one could see it.

Better to leave the tracer there. As bait.

Crawling outside again, Duncan scooped up a handful of grainy snow. Red droplets spattered on the pale sandstone ledge. He packed the snow against the blood streaming from his shoulder, and the sharp cold deadened the pain of his self-inflicted cut. He pressed the ice hard against the wound until pink-tinged snow melted between his fingers. He grabbed another handful, no longer caring about the obvious marks he left in the drift. The Harkonnens would come to this place anyway.

At least the snow had stanched the flow of blood.

Then Duncan scrambled up and away from the cave, careful to leave no sign of where he was going. He saw the bobbing lights down in the valley split up; members of the hunting party had chosen different routes as they climbed the bluff. A darkened ornithopter whirred overhead.

Duncan moved as quickly as he could, but took care not to splash fresh blood again. He tore strips from his shirt to dab the oozing wound, leaving his chest naked and cold, then he pulled the ragged garment back over his shoulders. Perhaps the forest predators would smell the iron blood scent and hunt him down for food rather than sport. That was a problem he didn't want to consider right then.

With loose pebbles pattering around him, he circled back until he reached the overhang above his former shelter. Duncan's instinct was to run blindly, as far as he could go. But he made himself stop. This would be better. He squatted behind the loose, heavy chunks of rock, tested them to be sure of his strength, and dropped back to wait.

Before long, the first hunter came up the slope to the cave hollow. Clad in suspensor-augmented armor, the hunter slung a lasgun in front of him. He glanced down at a handheld device, counterpart to the Richesian tracer.

Duncan held his breath, making no move, disturbing no pebbles or debris. Blood sketched a hot line down his left arm.

The hunter paused in front of the hollow, noting the disturbed snow, the bloodstains, the targeting blip on his tracer. Though Duncan couldn't see the man's face, he knew the hunter wore a grin of scornful triumph.

Thrusting the lasgun into the hollow ahead of him, the hunter ducked low, bending stiffly in his protective chest padding. On his belly, he crawled partway into the darkness. "Found you, little boy!"

Using his feet and the strength of his leg muscles, Duncan shoved a lichen-smeared boulder over the edge. Then he moved to the second one and kicked it hard, pushing it to the abrupt dropoff. Both heavy stones fell, tumbling in the air.

He heard the sounds of impact and a crack. A sickening crunch. Then the gasp and gurgle of the man below.

Duncan scrambled to the edge, saw that one of the boulders had struck to one side, bouncing off and rolling down the steep slope, gathering momentum and taking loose scree along with it.

The other boulder had landed on the small of the hunter's back, crushing his spine even through the padding, pinning him to the ground like a needle through an insect specimen.

Duncan climbed down, gasping, slipping. The hunter was still alive, though paralyzed. His legs twitched, thumping the toes of his boots against the frost-hard ground. Duncan wasn't afraid of him anymore.

Squeezing past the man's bulky, armored body into the hollow, Duncan shone his handlight down into the man's glazed, astonished eyes. This wasn't a game. He knew what the Harkonnens would do to him, had already seen what Rabban had done to his parents.

Now Duncan would play by their rules.

The dying hunter croaked something unintelligible at him. Duncan did not hesitate. His eyes dark and narrow—no longer the eyes of a child—he bent forward. The knife slipped in under the man's jawline. The hunter squirmed, raising his chin as if in acceptance rather than defiance—and the dull blade cut through skin and sinew. Jugular blood spurted out with enough force to splash and spatter before forming a dark, sticky pool on the floor of the cave.

Duncan could not spend time thinking about what he had done, could not wait for the hunter's body to cool. He rummaged through the items on the man's belt, found a small medpak and a ration bar. Then he tugged the lasgun free from the clenching grip. Using its butt, he smashed the blood-smeared Richesian tracer, grinding it into metal debris. He no longer needed it as a decoy. His pursuers could hunt him with their own wits now.

He figured they might even enjoy the challenge, once they got past their fury.

Duncan crawled out of the hollow. The lasgun, almost as tall as he was, clattered as he dragged it behind him. Below, the hunting party's trail of glowglobes came closer.

Now better armed and nourished by his improbable success, Duncan ran off into the night.

Many elements of the Imperium believe they hold the ultimate power: the Spacing Guild with their monopoly on interstellar travel, CHOAM with its economic stranglehold, the Bene Gesserit with their secrets, the Mentats with their control of mental processes, House Corrino with their throne, the Great and Minor Houses of the Landsraad with their extensive holdings. Woe to us on the day that one of those factions decides to prove the point.

—COUNT HASIMIR FENRING,
Dispatches from Arrakis

Leto had barely an hour to rest and refresh himself in his new quarters in the Grand Palais. "Uh, sorry to rush you," said Rhombur as he backed through the sliding door into the crystal-walled corridor, "but this is something you won't want to miss. It takes months and months to build a Heighliner. Signal me when you're ready to go to the observation deck."

Still unsettled but mercifully alone for a few moments, Leto rummaged through his luggage, made a cursory inspection of his room. He looked at the carefully packed belongings, much more than he could ever need, including trinkets, a packet of letters from his mother, and an inscribed Orange Catholic Bible. He had promised her he would read verses to himself every night.

He stared, thinking of how much time he would need just to make himself at home—*a whole year away from Caladan*—and instead left everything in its place. There would be time enough to do all that later. *A year on Ix.*

Tired after the long journey, his mind still boggling at the weighty strangeness of this underground metropolis, Leto stripped off his comfortable shirt and sprawled back on the bed. He had barely managed to test out the mattress and fluff up the pillow before Rhombur came pounding on his door. "Come on, Leto! Hurry up! Get dressed and we'll, uh, catch a transport."

Still fumbling to get his arm through his left sleeve, Leto met the other young man in the hall.

A bullet tube took them between the upside-down buildings to the outskirts of the underground city, and then a lift capsule dropped them to a secondary level of buildings studded with observation domes. After emerging, Rhombur bustled through the crowds gathered at the balconies and broad windows. He grabbed Leto's arm as they pushed past Vernius guards and assembled spectators. The Prince's face was flushed, and he turned quickly to the others there. "What time is it? Has it happened yet?"

"Not yet. Another ten minutes."

"The Navigator's on his way. His chamber's being escorted across the field right now."

Muttering thanks and pardons, Rhombur led his confused companion to a broad metaglass window in the sloping wall of the observation gallery.

At the far end of the room another door glided open, and the crowd parted for two dark-haired young men—identical twins, from the looks of them. Small in stature, they flanked Rhombur's sister Kailea as proud escorts. In the brief time since Leto had last seen her, Kailea had somehow managed to change into a different dress, less frilly but no less beautiful. The twins seemed drunk with her presence, and Kailea seemed to enjoy their fawning attention. She smiled at both of them and guided them toward a good spot at the observation window.

Rhombur took Leto to stand beside them, far more interested in the view than in the members of the crowd. Glancing around, Leto assumed that all the people there must be important officials of some sort. He peered down, still at a loss as to what was going on.

An immense enclosure funneled into the distance where the grotto ceiling and the horizon came together. Down below he saw a full-scale Heighliner, an asteroid-sized ship like the one that had carried him from Caladan to Ix.

"This is the largest, uh, manufacturing facility on all of Ix," Rhombur said. "It's the only surface hold in the Imperium large enough to accommodate an entire Heighliner. Everyone else uses dry docks in space. Here, in a terrestrial environment, the safety and efficiency for even large-scale construction is very cost-effective."

The shining new ship crowded the subterranean canyon. A fan of decorative dorsal arrays shone from the nearer side. On the fuselage, a gleaming purple-and-copper Ixian helix interlocked into the larger white analemma of the Spacing Guild, symbolizing infinity inside a rounded convex cartouche.

Constructed in place deep underground, the spaceship rested on a suspensor-jack mechanism, which elevated the craft so that large groundtrucks could drive underneath the hull. Suboid workers in silver-and-white uniforms scanned the fuselage with handheld devices, performing rote duties. As the teams of underclass workers checked the Guild craft, readying it for space, lines of light danced around the manufacturing center—energy barriers to repel intruders.

Cranes and suspensor supports looked like tiny parasites crawling over the Heighliner's hull, but most of the machinery was clustered against the sloping walls of the chamber, moved out of the way . . . for a *launch*? Leto didn't think it was possible. Thousands of surface-bound workers swarmed like a static pattern across the ground, removing debris and preparing for the departure of the incredible ship.

The buzz of the audience in the observation chamber grew louder, and Leto sensed something was about to happen. He spotted numerous screens and images transmitted by comeyes. Numbed by the spectacle, he asked, "But . . . how do you get it out? A ship this size? There's a rock ceiling overhead, and all the walls look solid."

One of the eager-faced twins next to him looked down with a confident smile. "Wait and see." The two identical young men had widely set eyes on squarish faces, intent expressions, furrowed brows; they were several years older than Leto. Their pale skin was an inevitable consequence of spending their lives underground.

Between them, Kailea cleared her throat and looked at her brother. "Rhombur?" she said, flashing a glance at the twins and at Leto. "You're forgetting your manners."

Rhombur suddenly remembered his obligations. "Oh, yes! This is Leto Atreides, heir to House Atreides on Caladan. And these two are C'tair and D'murr Pilru. Their father is Ix's Ambassador to Kaitain, and their mother is a Guild banker. They live in one of the wings of the Grand Palais, so you might see them around."

The young men bowed in unison and seemed to draw closer to Kailea. "We're preparing for Guild examination in the next few months," one of the twins, C'tair, said. "We hope to pilot a ship like that someday." His dark head nodded toward the immense vessel below. Kailea watched them both with a worried glint in her green eyes, as if she wasn't too sure about the idea of their becoming Navigators.

Leto was moved by the sparkle and eagerness he saw in the young man's deep brown eyes. The other brother was less social and seemed to be interested only in the activity below. "Here comes the Navigator's chamber," D'murr said.

Below, a bulky black tank floated ahead on a cleared path, borne on industrial suspensors. Traditionally, Guild Navigators masked their appearance, keeping themselves hidden in thick clouds of spice gas. It was generally believed that the process of becoming a Navigator transformed a person into something other than human, something more evolved. The Guild said nothing to confirm or deny the speculations.

"Can't see a thing inside," C'tair said.

"Yes, but that's a Navigator in there. I can sense him." D'murr leaned forward so intently it seemed as if he wanted to fly through the metaglass observation window. When the twins both ignored her, intent on the ship below, Kailea turned instead to Leto and met his gaze with sparkling emerald eyes.

Rhombur gestured down at the ship and continued his rapid commentary. "My father is excited about his new enhanced-payload Heighliner models. I don't know if you've studied your history, but Heighliners were originally of, uh, Richesian manufacture. Ix and Richese competed with one another for Guild contracts, but gradually we won by bringing all aspects of our society into the process: uh, subsidies, conscriptions, tax levies, whatever it took. We don't do things halfway on Ix."

"I've heard you're also masters of industrial sabotage and patent law," Leto said, remembering what his mother had claimed.

Rhombur shook his head. "Lies told by jealous Houses. Vermilion hells, we don't steal ideas or patents—we waged only a technological war against Richese, and won without firing a single shot. But as sure as if we'd used atomics, we struck mortal blows against them. It was either them or us. A generation ago they lost their stewardship of Arrakis at about the same time they lost their lead in technology. Bad family leadership, I guess."

"My mother is Richesian," Leto said crisply.

Rhombur flushed with deep embarrassment. "Oh, I'm sorry. I forgot." He scratched his tousled blond hair just to give his hands something to do.

"That's okay. We don't wear blinders," Leto said. "I know what you're talking about. Richese still exists, but on a vastly smaller scale. Too much bureaucracy and too little innovation. My mother's never wanted to take me there, not even to visit her family. Too many painful memories, I suppose, though I think she hoped marrying my father might help restore Richese fortunes."

Below, the tank bearing the mysterious Navigator entered an orifice at the front end of the Heighliner. The polished black chamber vanished into the vessel's immensity like a gnat inhaled into the mouth of a large fish.

Though she was younger than her brother, when Kailea spoke, her voice sounded more businesslike. "The new Heighliner program is going to be the most profitable of all time for us. Large sums will be pouring into our accounts from this contract. House Vernius will get twenty-five percent of all the solaris we save the Spacing Guild during the first decade."

Overwhelmed, Leto thought back to the small-scale activities on Caladan: the pundi rice harvest, the boats unloading cargoes from ships . . . and the dedicated cheers the population had hurled at the Old Duke after the bullfight.

Grating sirens sounded from speakers mounted throughout the huge chamber. Below, like iron filings flowing within magnetic-field lines, the suboid workers evacuated from all sides of the newly constructed Heighliner. Up and down the ceiling city, lights twinkled from other large observation windows in the stalactite towers. Leto could make out tiny forms pressed close to distant panes.

Rhombur stood near Leto as the spectators around them fell into a hush.

"What is it?" Leto asked. "What's happening now?"

"The Navigator is going to fly the ship out," the twin C'tair said.

"He'll take it away from Ix so it can begin its rounds," D'murr added.

Leto stared at the rock ceiling, the impenetrable barrier of a planetary crust, and knew this was impossible. He heard a faint, barely dis-cernible humming.

"Piloting such a vessel out isn't difficult—uh, at least, not for one of *them*." Rhombur crossed his arms over his chest. "Much easier than guiding a Heighliner back *into* a confined space like this. Only a top-level Steersman could do that."

As Leto watched, holding his breath just like all the other specta-tors, the Heighliner shimmered, became indistinct—then vanished entirely.

The air inside the huge grotto reverberated with a loud boom from the sudden volume displacement. A tremor ran through the observa-tion building, and Leto's ears popped.

The grotto now stood empty, a vast enclosed space with no trace of the Heighliner, just leftover equipment and a pattern of discolorations on the floor and walls and ceiling.

"Remember how a Navigator operates a ship," D'murr said, seeing Leto's confusion.

"He folds space," C'tair said. "That Heighliner never passed *through* the crustal rock of Ix at all. The Navigator simply went from here . . . to his destination."

A few members of the audience applauded. Rhombur seemed im-mensely pleased as he gestured to the new emptiness below that ex-tended as far as they could see. "Now we have room to start building another one!"

"Simple economics." Kailea glanced at Leto, then demurely flicked her eyes away. "We don't waste any time."

*The slave concubines permitted my father under the Bene
Gesserit–Guild agreement could not, of course, bear a Royal Successor, but the intrigues were constant and oppressive in their similarity. We became adept, my mother and sisters and I, at avoiding
subtle instruments of death.*

—From "In My Father's House"
by the Princess Irulan

Crown Prince Shaddam's tutoring chambers in the Imperial Palace would have been large enough to house
a village on some worlds. With total disinterest, the Corrino heir brooded in front of his teaching machine while
Fenring watched him.

"My father still wants me to sit in training classes like a
child." Shaddam scowled down at the lights and spinning
mechanisms of the machine. "I should be married by now.
I should have an Imperial heir of my own."

"Why?" Fenring laughed. "So the throne can skip a generation and go directly to your son when he reaches his
prime, hmmmm?"

Shaddam was thirty-four years old and seemingly a
lifetime away from becoming Emperor. Each time the
old man took a drink of spice beer, he activated more
of the secret poison—but the *n'kee* had been working
for months, and the only result seemed to be increasingly irrational behavior. As if they needed more of
that!

That very morning Elrood had scolded Shaddam for
not paying closer attention to his studies. "Watch, and

learn!"—one of his father's tedious phrases—"Do as well as Fenring, for once."

Since childhood, Hasimir Fenring had attended classes with the Crown Prince. Ostensibly, he provided companionship for Shaddam, while he himself gleaned an understanding of Court intrigues and politics. In academics, Fenring always did better than his royal friend: He devoured any bit of data that could help him increase his position.

His mother Chaola, an introspective lady-in-waiting, had settled into a quiet home and lived on her Imperial pension after the death of the Emperor's fourth wife Habla. In raising the two young boys together while she attended the Empress Habla, Chaola had given Fenring the chance to be so much more—almost as if she had planned it that way.

These days Chaola pretended not to understand what her son did at Court, though she was Bene Gesserit–trained. Fenring was wily enough to know that his mother comprehended far more than her station suggested, and that many plans and breeding schemes had gone on without his knowledge.

Now Shaddam let out a miserable groan and turned from the machine. "Why can't the old creature just die and make it easy for me?" He covered his mouth, suddenly alarmed at what he had blurted.

Fenring paced the long floor, glancing up at the hanging banners of the Landsraad. The Crown Prince was expected to know the colors and crests of every Great and Minor House, but Shaddam had difficulty simply remembering all the family names.

"Be patient, my friend. All in its own time." In one of the alcoves, Fenring struck a combustible spike of vanilla-scented incense and inhaled a long breath of the fumes. "In the meantime, learn about subjects that will be relevant to your reign. You'll need such information in the near future, hmm-m-m-ah?"

"Stop making that noise, Hasimir. It's annoying."

"Hmmmm?"

"It irritated me when we were children, and you know it still does. Stop it!"

In the adjoining room, behind supposed privacy screens, Shaddam could hear his tutor giggling, the sounds of clothes rustling, bedsheets, skin upon skin. The tutor spent his afternoons with a willowy, achingly beautiful woman who had been sexually trained to Expert

Class. Shaddam had given the girl her orders, and her ministrations kept the tutor out of the way so that he and Fenring could have private conversations—difficult enough in a palace full of prying eyes and attentive ears.

The tutor did not know, however, that the girl was intended for Elrood as a gift, a perfect addition to his harem. This little trick gave the Crown Prince a large club to wield as a threat against the bothersome teacher. If the Emperor ever found out . . .

"Learning to manipulate people is an important part of ruling," Fenring often told him upon suggesting an idea. That much, at least, Shaddam had understood. *As long as the Crown Prince listens to my advice*, Fenring thought, *he could become a good enough ruler, after all.*

Screens displayed dull statistics of shipping resources, primary exports of major planets, holographic images of every conceivable product from the finest dyed whale-fur, to Ixian soothe-sonic tapestries . . . inkvines, shigawire, fabulous Ecazi art objects, pundi rice, and donkey dung. Everything spewed from the teaching machine like an out-of-control font of wisdom, as if Shaddam was supposed to know and remember all the details. *But that's what advisors and experts are for.*

Fenring glanced down at the display. "Of all the things in the Imperium, Shaddam, what do *you* suppose is most important, hm-m-m-m?"

"Are you my tutor now too, Hasimir?"

"Always," Fenring replied. "If you turn out to be a superb Emperor, it will benefit all the populace . . . including me."

The bed in the next room made rhythmic, thought-scattering sounds.

"Peace and quiet is the most important thing." Shaddam grumbled his answer.

Fenring tapped a key on the teaching machine. Machinery clicked, chimed, hummed. An image of a desert planet appeared. *Arrakis.* Fenring slid onto the bench beside Shaddam. "The spice melange. That's the most important thing. Without it, the Imperium would crumble."

He leaned forward, and his nimble fingers flew across the controls, calling up displays of the desert planet's spice-harvesting activities. Shaddam glanced at footage of a giant sandworm as it destroyed a harvesting machine in the deep wastelands.

"Arrakis is the only known source of melange in the universe."

Fenring curled his hand into a fist and brought it down with a hard thump on the milky marbleplaz tabletop. "But *why*? With all the Imperial explorers and prospectors, and the huge reward House Corrino has offered for generations, *why* has no one found spice anywhere else? After all, with a billion worlds in the Imperium, it must be *somewhere* else."

"A billion?" Shaddam pursed his lips. "Hasimir, you know that's just hyperbole for the masses. The tally I've seen is only a million or so."

"A million, a billion, what's the difference, hmmmm? My point is, if melange is a substance found in the universe, we should find it in more than one place. You know about the Planetologist your father sent to Arrakis?"

"Of course, Pardot Kynes. We expect another report from him at any moment. It's been a few weeks since the last one." He raised his head in pride. "I've made a point to read them whenever they arrive."

From the curtained side room, they heard gasping and giggling, heavy furniture sliding aside, something overturning with a thump. Shaddam allowed himself a thin smile. The concubine was well trained, indeed.

Fenring rolled his large eyes, then turned back to the teaching machine. "Pay attention, Shaddam. Spice is vital, and yet all production is controlled by a single House on a single world. The threat of a bottleneck is enormous, even with Imperial oversight and pressure from CHOAM. For the stability of the Imperium, we need a better source of melange. We should create it synthetically if we have to. We need an alternative." He turned to the Crown Prince, his dark eyes glittering. "One that's in *our* control."

Shaddam enjoyed discussions like this much more than the tutor's programmed learning routines. "Ah, yes! An alternative to melange would shift the entire balance of power in the Imperium, wouldn't it?"

"Exactly! As it is, CHOAM, the Guild, the Bene Gesserit, the Mentats, the Landsraad, even House Corrino, all fight over the spice production and distribution from a single planet. But if there was an alternative, one solely in the hands of the Imperial House, your family would become *true* Emperors, not just puppets under the control of other political forces."

"We are not puppets," Shaddam snapped. "Not even my doddering father." He flicked a nervous glance at the ceiling, as if comeyes might be hidden there, though Fenring had already run thorough scans for observational apparatus. "Uh, long may he live."

"As you say, my Prince," Fenring said without conceding a millimeter. "But if we put the wheels in motion now, then you will reap those benefits when the throne is yours." He fiddled with the teaching machine. "Watch, and learn!" he said in a creaking falsetto imitation of Elrood's ponderous pronouncements. Shaddam chuckled at the sarcasm.

The machine displayed scenes of Ixian industrial accomplishments, all the new inventions and modifications that had been made during a profitable rule by House Vernius. "Why do you think it is the Ixians can't use their technology to find a spice alternative?" Fenring asked. "They've been instructed time and again to analyze the spice and develop another option for us, yet they play with their navigation machines and their silly timepieces. Who needs to tell the exact hour on any planet of the Imperium? How are those pursuits more important than the spice itself? House Vernius is an utter failure, as far as you are concerned."

"This tutoring machine is Ixian. The annoying new Heighliner design is Ixian. So's your high-performance groundcar and . . ."

"Off the point," Fenring said. "I don't believe House Vernius invests any of its technological resources in solving the alternative-spice problem. It is not a high priority for them."

"Then my father should give them firmer guidance." Shaddam clasped his hands behind his back and tried to look Imperial, flushed with forced indignation. "When I'm Emperor, I'll be certain people understand their priorities. Ah, yes, I will personally direct what is most important to the Imperium and to House Corrino."

Fenring circled the teaching machine like a prowling Laza tiger. He plucked a sugared date from a fruit tray unobtrusively displayed on a side table. "Old Elrood made similar pronouncements a long time ago, yet so far he hasn't followed through on any of them." He waved his long-fingered hand. "Oh, in the beginning he asked the Ixians to look into the matter. He also offered a large bounty for any explorer who found even melange precursors on uncharted planets." He popped the date into his mouth, licked his sticky fingers, and swallowed the smooth, sweet fruit. "Still nothing."

"Then my father should increase the reward," Shaddam said. "He's not trying hard enough."

Fenring studied his neatly clipped nails, then raised his overlarge eyes to meet Shaddam's. "Or could it be that old Elrood IX isn't willing to consider *all* the necessary alternatives?"

"He's incompetent, but not entirely stupid. Why would he do that?"

"Suppose someone were to suggest using . . . the Bene Tleilax, for example? As the only possible solution?" Fenring leaned against a stone pillar to observe Shaddam's reaction.

A ripple of disgust crossed the Crown Prince's face. "The filthy Tleilaxu! Why would anyone want to work with them?"

"Because they might provide the answer we seek."

"You must be joking. Who can trust anything the Tleilaxu say?" He pictured the gray-skinned race, their oily hair and dwarfish stature, their beady eyes, pug noses, and sharp teeth. They kept to themselves, isolating their core planets, intentionally digging a societal ditch in which they could wallow.

The Bene Tleilax were, however, true genetic wizards, willing to use unorthodox and socially heinous methods, dealing in live or dead flesh, in biological waste. With their mysterious yet powerful axlotl tanks they could grow clones from live cells and gholas from dead ones. The Tleilaxu had a slippery, shifty aura about them. *How can anyone take them seriously?*

"Think about it, Shaddam. Are the Tleilaxu not masters of organic chemistry and cellular mechanics, hm-m-m-m-ah?" Fenring sniffed. "Through my own web of spies I've learned that the Bene Tleilax, despite the distaste with which we view them, have developed a new technique. I have certain . . . technical skills myself, you know, and I believe this Tleilaxu technique could be applicable to the production of artificial melange . . . our own source." He fixed his bright birdlike eyes on Shaddam's. "Or are *you* unwilling to consider all alternatives, and let your father maintain control?"

Shaddam squirmed, hesitating to answer. He would much rather have been playing a game of shield-ball. He didn't like to think of the gnomelike men; religious fanatics, the Bene Tleilax were intensely secretive and did not invite guests. Heedless of how other worlds regarded them, they sent their representatives out to observe and to make deals at the highest levels for unique bioengineered products. Rumor held that no outsider had ever seen a Tleilaxu woman. *Never.* He thought they must be either wildly beautiful . . . or incredibly ugly.

Seeing the Crown Prince shudder, Fenring pointed a finger at him. "Shaddam, don't fall into the same trap as your father. As your friend and advisor, I must investigate unseen opportunities, hm-m-m-m-ah? Put aside such feelings and consider the possible victory if this works— a victory over the Landsraad, the Guild, CHOAM, and the scheming House Harkonnen. How amusing to think that all the strings the Harkonnens pulled to gain Arrakis after the downfall of Richese would be for naught."

His voice became softer, infinitely reasonable. "What difference does it make if we have to deal with the Tleilaxu? So long as House Corrino breaks the spice monopoly and establishes an independent source?"

Shaddam looked at him, turning his back on the teaching machine. "You're sure about this?"

"No, I'm *not* sure," Fenring snapped. "No one can be sure until it is done. But we must at least consider the idea, give it a chance. If we don't, somebody else will . . . eventually. Maybe even the Bene Tleilax themselves. We need to do this for our own survival."

"What will happen when my father hears about it?" Shaddam asked. "He won't like the idea."

Old Elrood never could think for himself, and Fenring's chaumurky had already begun to fossilize his brain. The Emperor had always been a pathetic pawn, shifted around by political forces. Perhaps the senile vulture had made a deal with House Harkonnen to keep them in control of the spice production. It wouldn't surprise Shaddam if the young and powerful Baron had old Elrood wrapped around his little finger. House Harkonnen was fabulously wealthy, and their means of influence were legion.

It would be good to bring them to their knees.

Fenring put his hands on his hips. "I can make all of this happen, Shaddam. I have contacts. I can bring a Bene Tleilax representative here without anybody knowing. He can state our case before the Imperial Court—and then if your father turns him down, we might be able to find out who's controlling the throne . . . the trail would be fresh. Hmmm-ah, shall I set it up?"

The Crown Prince glanced back at the teaching machine that obliviously continued to instruct a nonexistent pupil. "Yes, yes, of course," he said impatiently, now that he had come to a decision. "Let's not waste more time. And stop making that noise."

"It'll take a while for me to get all the pieces in place, but the investment will be worth it."

From the next room came a high-pitched moan; then a thin squeal of ecstasy built higher and higher until it seemed that the walls themselves must crumble.

"Our tutor must have learned how to pleasure his little pet," Shaddam said with a scowl. "Or perhaps she's just faking."

Fenring laughed and shook his head. "That wasn't her, my friend. That was *his* voice."

"I wish I knew what they were doing in there," Shaddam said.

"Don't worry. It's all being recorded for your later enjoyment. If our beloved tutor cooperates with us and causes no trouble, we'll simply watch it for amusement. If, however, he proves difficult, we'll wait until after your father's been given this concubine for his own private toy—*then* we'll show Emperor Elrood a glimpse of those images."

"And we'll have what we want anyway," Shaddam said.

"Exactly, my Prince."

The working Planetologist has access to many resources, data, and projections. However, his most important tools are human beings. Only by cultivating ecological literacy among the people themselves can he save an entire planet.

—PARDOT KYNES,

The Case for Bela Tegeuse

As he gathered notes for his next report to the Emperor, Pardot Kynes encountered increasing evidence of subtle ecological manipulations. He suspected the Fremen. Who else could be responsible out there in the wastelands of Arrakis?

It became clear to him that the desert people must be present in far greater numbers than the Harkonnen stewards imagined—and that the Fremen had a dream of their own . . . but the Planetologist in him wondered if they had developed an actual *plan* to accomplish it.

While delving into the geological and ecological enigmas of this desert world, Kynes came to believe that he had the power at his fingertips to breathe life into these sun-blistered sands. Arrakis was not merely the dead lump it appeared to be on the surface; instead, it was a *seed* capable of magnificent growth . . . provided the environment received the proper care.

The Harkonnens certainly wouldn't expend the effort. Though they had been planetary governors here for decades, the Baron and his capricious crew behaved as if they were unruly houseguests with no long-term investment in

Arrakis. As Planetologist, he could see the obvious signs. The Harkonnens were plundering the world, taking as much melange as they could as quickly as possible, with no thought to the future.

Political machinations and the tides of power could quickly and easily shift alliances. Within a few decades, no doubt, the Emperor would hand control of the spice operations to some other Great House. The Harkonnens had nothing to gain by making long-term investments here.

Many of the other inhabitants were also indigents: smugglers, water merchants, traders who could easily pull up stakes and fly to another world, a different boomtown settlement. No one cared for the planet's plight—Arrakis was merely a resource to be exploited, then discarded.

Kynes thought the Fremen might have a different mind-set, though. The reclusive desert dwellers were said to be fierce to their own ways. They had wandered from world to world in their long history, been downtrodden and enslaved before making Arrakis their home—a planet they had called *Dune* since ancient times. These people had the most at stake here. They would suffer the consequences caused by the exploiters.

If Kynes could only enlist Fremen aid—and if there were as many of these mysterious people as he suspected—changes might be made on a global scale. Once he accumulated more data on weather patterns, atmospheric content, and seasonal fluctuations, he could develop a realistic timetable, a game plan that would eventually sculpt Arrakis into a verdant place. *It can be done!*

For a week now, he had concentrated his activities around the Shield Wall, an enormous mountain range that embraced the northern polar regions. Most inhabitants settled in rocky guarded terrain where, he supposed, the worms could not go.

To see the land up close, Kynes chose to travel slowly in a one-man groundcar. He puttered around the base of the Shield Wall, taking measurements, collecting specimens. He measured the angle of strata in the rocks to determine the geological turmoil that had established such a mountainous barrier.

Given time and meticulous study, he might even find fossil layers, limestone clumps with petrified seashells or primitive ocean creatures from the planet's much wetter past. Thus far, the subtle evidence for primordial water was clear enough to the trained eye. Uncovering such a cryptozooic remnant, though, would be the keystone of his treatise, incontrovertible proof of his suspicions. . . .

Early one morning Kynes drove in his trundling groundcar, leaving tracks on loose material that had eroded from the mountain wall. In this vicinity all villages, from the largest to the most squalid settlements, were carefully marked on the charts, undoubtedly for purposes of Harkonnen taxation and exploitation. It was a relief to have accurate maps for a change.

He found himself near a place called Windsack, the site of a Harkonnen guard station and troop barracks that lived in an uneasy alliance with the desert dwellers. Kynes continued along, rocking with the uneven terrain. Humming to himself, he stared up at the cliffsides. The putter of his engines served as a lullaby, and he lost himself in thought.

Then, as he came over a rise and rounded a finger of rock, he was startled to encounter a small, desperate battle. Six muscular, well-trained soldiers stood in full Harkonnen livery, cloaked in body-shields. The bravos held ceremonial cutting weapons, which they were using to toy with three Fremen youths they had cornered.

Kynes brought the groundcar to a lurching halt. The deplorable scene reminded him of how he had once watched a well-fed Laza tiger playing with a mangy ground rat on Salusa Secundus. The satisfied tiger had no need for additional meat, but simply enjoyed playing the predator; it trapped the terrified rodent between some rocks, scratching with long, curved claws, opening painful, bloody wounds . . . injuries that were, intentionally, not fatal. The Laza tiger had batted the ground rat around for many minutes as Kynes observed through high-powered oil lenses. Finally bored, the tiger had simply bitten off the creature's head and then sauntered away, leaving the carcass for carrion feeders.

By contrast, the three Fremen youths were putting up more of a fight than the ground rat, but they had only simple knives and stillsuits, no body-shields or armor. The desert natives had no chance against the fighting skills and weaponry of Harkonnen soldiers.

But they did not surrender.

The Fremen snatched at the ground and threw sharp rocks with deadly aim, but the projectiles bounced harmlessly off the shimmering shields. The Harkonnens laughed and pressed closer.

Out of sight, Kynes climbed from his groundcar, fascinated by the tableau. He adjusted his stillsuit, loosening binders to give him more freedom of movement. He made sure the face mask was in place but not sealed. At the moment, he didn't know whether to observe from a distance, as he had done with the Laza tiger . . . or whether he should aid in some way.

The Harkonnen troops outnumbered the Fremen two to one, and if Kynes came to the defense of the youths, he would likely find himself either wounded or at least charged with interference by Harkonnen officials. A sanctioned Imperial Planetologist wasn't supposed to meddle in local events.

He rested his hand near the weapon blade at his waist. In any event, he was ready, but hopeful that he would see no more than an extended exchange of insults, escalating threats, and perhaps a scuffle that would end in hard feelings and a few bruises.

But in a moment, the character of the confrontation changed— and Kynes realized his stupidity. This was not a mere taunting game, but a deadly serious standoff. The Harkonnens were out for a kill.

The six soldiers waded in, blades flashing, shields pulsing. The Fremen youths fought back. Within seconds, one of the natives was down, gushing bright foaming blood from a severed neck artery.

Kynes was about to shout, but swallowed his words as anger turned his vision red. While he'd been driving along, he had made grandiose plans of using the Fremen as a resource, a true desert people with whom he could share ideas. He had dreamed of adapting them as a grand workforce for his sparkling scheme of ecological transformation. They were to be his willing allies, enthusiastic assistants.

Now these blockheaded Harkonnens were—for no apparent reason— trying to kill his workers, the tools with which he intended to remake the planet! He could not let that happen.

While the third member of their band lay bleeding to death on the sands, the other two Fremen, with only primitive milky blue knives and no shields, attacked in a wild frenzy that astounded Kynes. "Taqwa!" they screamed.

Two Harkonnens fell under the surprise rally, and their four remaining comrades were slow in coming to their aid. Hesitantly, the blue-uniformed soldiers moved toward the youths.

Indignant at the Harkonnens' gross injustice, Kynes reacted on impulse. He slid toward the bravos from the rear, moving quickly and silently. Switching on his personal shield, he unsheathed the short-bladed slip-tip he kept for self-defense—a shield-fighting weapon, with poison in its point.

During the harsh years on Salusa Secundus, he had learned how to fight with it, and how to kill. His parents had worked in one of the Imperium's most infamous prisons, and the day-to-day environments in Kynes's explorations had often required him to defend himself against powerful predators.

He uttered no cry of battle, for that would have compromised his element of surprise. Kynes held his weapon low. He wasn't particularly brave, merely single-minded. As if driven by a force beyond the person who held it, the tip of Kynes's blade passed slowly through the body-shield of the nearest Harkonnen, then pushed hard and thrust upward, into flesh, cartilage, and bone. The blade penetrated beneath the man's rib cage, pierced his kidneys, and severed his spinal cord.

Kynes yanked out the knife and rotated halfway to his left, sliding the knife into the side of a second Harkonnen soldier, who was just turning to face him. The shield slowed the poisoned blade for a moment, but as the Harkonnen thrashed, Kynes drove the point home, deep into the soft flesh of the abdomen, again cutting upward.

Thus, two Harkonnens lay mortally wounded and writhing before anyone had made an outcry. Now four of them were down, including those the Fremen had killed. The remaining pair of Harkonnen bullies stared in shock at this turn of events, then howled at the brash boldness of the tall stranger. They exchanged combat signals and spread apart, eyeing Kynes more than the Fremen, who stood ferocious and ready to fight with their fingernails if necessary.

Again the Fremen lunged against their attackers. Again, they screamed, "Taqwa!"

One of the two surviving Harkonnen soldiers thrust his sword at Kynes, but the Planetologist moved rapidly now, still angry and flushed with the blooding of his first two victims. He reached upward, rippling through the shield, and neatly slit the attacker's throat. An *entrisseur*. The guard dropped his sword and grasped his neck in a futile attempt to hold his lifeblood inside.

The fifth Harkonnen crumpled to the ground.

As the two Fremen fighters turned their revenge upon the lone remaining enemy, Kynes bent over the seriously wounded desert youth and spoke to him. "Stay calm. I will help you."

The young man had already sprayed copious amounts of blood into the gravelly dust, but Kynes had an emergency medpak on his belt. He slapped a wound sealant on the ragged neck cut, then used hypovials with ready plasma and high-powered stimulants to keep the victim alive. He felt the young man's pulse at the wrist. A steady heartbeat.

Kynes saw the depth of the damage now and was astonished that the youth hadn't bled more. Without medical attention, he would have died within minutes. But still, Kynes was amazed the boy had survived this long. *This Fremen's blood coagulates with extreme efficiency.* Another fact to file away in his memory—a survival adaptation to reduce moisture loss in the driest desert?

"Eeeeah!"

"No!"

Kynes looked up at the cries of pain and terror. Off to one side, the Fremen had dug the surviving Harkonnen's eyes out of their sockets, using their blade tips. Then they made slow work of flaying their victim alive, stripping away ribbons of pink skin, which they stored in sealed pouches at their hips.

Covered with blood, Kynes stood up, panting. Seeing their viciousness now that the tables had been turned, he began to wonder if he'd done the right thing. These Fremen were like wild animals and had worked themselves into a frenzy. Would they attempt to kill *him* now, despite what he had done for them? He was a complete stranger to these desperate young men.

He watched and waited, and when the youths had finished with their grisly torture, he met their eyes and cleared his throat before speaking in Imperial Galach. "My name is Pardot Kynes, the Imperial Planetologist assigned to Arrakis."

He looked down at his blood-smeared skin and decided not to extend a hand in greeting. In their culture, they might misinterpret the gesture. "I'm very pleased to introduce myself. I've always wanted to meet the Fremen."

It's easier to be terrified by an enemy you admire.
—THUFIR HAWAT, Mentat and
Security Commander to House Atreides

Hidden by the thick pines, Duncan Idaho knelt in the soft needles on the ground, feeling little warmth. The chill night air deadened the resinous evergreen scent, but at least here he was sheltered from the razor breezes. He had gone far enough from the cave that he could pause and catch his breath. For just a moment.

He knew the Harkonnen hunters wouldn't rest, though. They would be particularly incensed now that he'd killed one of their party. *Maybe,* he thought, *they might even enjoy the chase more. Especially Rabban.*

Duncan opened the medpak he'd stolen from the am-bushed tracker and brought out a small package of newskin ointment, which he slathered over the incision on his shoulder, where it hardened to an organic bond. Then he wolfed down the nutrition bar and stuffed the wrappings into his pockets.

Using the glow of his handlight, he turned to study the lasgun. He'd never fired such a weapon before, but he had watched the guards and the hunters operate their rifles. He cradled the weapon and fiddled with its mechanisms and controls. Pointing the barrel upward, he attempted to understand what he was supposed to do. He had to learn if he meant to fight.

With a sudden surge of power, a white-hot beam lanced out toward the upper boughs of the pine trees. They burst into flames, crackling and snapping. Smoldering clumps of evergreen needles fell around him like red-hot snow.

Yelping, he dropped the gun to the ground and scrambled backward. But he snatched it up again before he could forget which combination of buttons he had pushed. He had to remember and know how to use them.

The flames overhead flared like a bonfire beacon, exuding curls of sharp smoke. With nothing to lose now, Duncan fired again, aiming this time, just to make sure he could use the lasgun to defend himself. The cumbersome weapon was not built for a small boy, especially not with his throbbing shoulder and sore ribs, but he could use it. He had to.

Knowing the Harkonnens would run toward the blaze, Duncan scampered out of the trees, searching for another place to hide. Once again he made for higher ground, keeping to the ridgeline so he could continue observing the hunting party's scattered glowglobes. He knew exactly where the men were, exactly how close.

But how can they be so stupid, he wondered, *making themselves so obvious?* Overconfidence . . . was that their flaw? If so, it might help him. The Harkonnens expected him to play their game, then cower and die when he was supposed to. Duncan would just have to disappoint them.

Maybe this time we'll play my game instead.

As he dashed along, he avoided patches of snow and kept away from noisy underbrush. However, Duncan's focus on the clustered pursuers distracted him from seeing his real danger. He heard a snap of dried twigs behind and above him, the rustle of bushes, then a clicking of claws on bare rock accompanied by heavy, hoarse panting.

This was no Harkonnen hunter at all—but another forest predator that smelled his blood.

Skidding to a halt, Duncan looked up, searching for gleaming eyes in the shadows. But he didn't turn to the stark outcropping over his head until he heard a wet-sounding growl. In the starlight, he discerned the muscular, crouching form of a wild gaze hound, its back fur bristling like quills, its lips curled to expose flesh-tearing fangs. Its huge, huge eyes focused on its prey: a young boy with tender skin.

Duncan scrambled backward and fired off a shot with the lasgun. Poorly aimed, the beam came nowhere close to the stalking creature, but powdered rock spewed from the outcropping below the gaze hound. The predator yelped and snarled, backing off. Duncan fired again, this time sizzling a blackened hole through its right haunch. With a brassy roar, the creature bounded off into the darkness, howling and baying.

The gaze hound's racket, as well as flashes from the lasgun fire, would draw the Harkonnen trackers. Duncan set off into the starlight, running once more.

HANDS ON HIS hips, Rabban stared down at the body of his ambushed hunter by the cave hollow. Rage burned through him—as well as cruel satisfaction. The devious child had lured the man into a trap. Very resourceful. All of the tracker's armor hadn't saved him from a dropped boulder and then the thrust of a dull dagger into his throat. The coup de grâce.

Rabban simmered for a few moments, trying to assess the challenge. He smelled the sour scent of death even in the cold night. This was what he wanted, wasn't it—a *challenge?*

One of the other trackers crawled into the low hollow and played the beam of his handlight around the cave. It lighted the smears of blood and the smashed Richesian tracer. "Here is the reason, m'Lord. The cub cut out his own tracking device." The hunter swallowed, as if uncertain whether he should continue. "A smart one, this boy. Good prey."

Rabban glowered at the carnage for a few moments; his sunburn still stung on his cheeks. Then he grinned, slowly, and finally burst out into loud guffaws. "An eight-year-old child with only his imagination and a couple of clumsy weapons bested one of my troops!" He laughed again. Outside, the others in the party stood uncertainly, bathed in the light of their bobbing glowglobes.

"Such a boy was made for the hunt," Rabban declared; then he nudged the dead tracker's body with the toe of his boot. "And this clod did not deserve to be part of my crew. Leave his body here to rot. Let the scavengers get him."

Then two of the spotters saw flames in the trees, and Rabban pointed. "There! The cub's probably trying to warm his hands." He laughed again, and finally the rest of the hunting crew snickered along with him. "This is turning into an exciting night."

FROM HIS HIGH vantage Duncan gazed into the distance, away from the guarded lodge. A bright light blinked on and off, paused, then fifteen seconds later flashed on and off again. Some kind of signal, separate from the Harkonnen hunters, far from the lodge or the station or any nearby settlements.

Duncan turned, curious. The light flashed, then fell dark. *Who else is out here?*

Forest Guard Station was a restricted preserve for the sole use of Harkonnen family members. Anyone discovered trespassing would be killed outright, or used as prey in a future hunt. Duncan watched the tantalizing light flickering on and off. It was clearly a message. . . . *Who's sending it?*

He took a deep breath, felt small but defiant in a very large and hostile world. He had no place else to go, no other chance. So far, he had eluded the hunters . . . but that couldn't last forever. Soon the Harkonnens would bring in additional forces, ornithopters, life-tracers, perhaps even hunting animals to follow the smell of blood on his shirt, as the wild gaze hound had done.

Duncan decided to make his way to the mysterious signaler and hope for the best. He couldn't imagine finding anyone to help him, but he had not given up hope. Maybe he could find a means of escape, perhaps as a stowaway.

First, though, he would lay another trap for the hunters. He had an idea, something that would surprise them, and it seemed simple enough. If he could kill a few more of the enemy, he'd have a better chance of getting away.

After studying the rocks, the patches of snow, the trees, Duncan selected the best point for his second ambush. He switched on his handlight and directed the beam at the ground so that no sensitive eyes would spot a telltale gleam in the distance.

The pursuers weren't far behind him. Occasionally, he heard a muffled shout in the deep silence, saw the hunting party's firefly glow-globes illuminating their way through the forest, as the trackers tried to anticipate the path their quarry would take.

Right then Duncan *wanted* them to anticipate where he would go . . . but they would never guess what he meant to do. Kneeling beside a particularly light and fluffy snowdrift, he inserted the handlight into the snow and pushed it down through the cold iciness as far as he could. Then he withdrew his hand.

The glow reflected from the white snow like water diffusing into a sponge. Tiny crystals of ice refracted the light, magnifying it; the drift itself shone like a phosphorescent island in the dark clearing.

Slinging the lasgun in front of him, ready to fire, he trotted back to the sheltering trees. He lay on a cushion of pine needles flat against the ground, careful to present no visible target, then rested the barrel of the lasgun on a small rock, propping it in position.

Waiting.

The hunters came, predictably, and Duncan felt that their roles had reversed: Now he was the hunter, and they were his game. He aimed the weapon, fingers tense on the firing stud. At last the group entered the clearing. Startled to find the shining snowdrift, they milled about, trying to figure out what it was, what their prey had done.

Two of the trackers faced outward, suspicious of an attack from the forest. Others stood silhouetted in the ghostly light, perfect targets— exactly as Duncan had hoped.

At the rear of the party, he recognized one burly man with a commanding presence. *Rabban!* Duncan thought of how his parents had fallen, remembered the smell of their burning flesh—and squeezed the firing stud.

But at that moment, one of the scouts stepped in front of Rabban to give a report. The beam scored through his armor, burning and smoking. The man flung out his arms and gave a wild shriek.

Reacting with lightning speed for his burly body, Rabban hurled himself to one side as the beam melted all the way through the hunter's padded chest and sizzled into the snowdrift. Duncan cut loose another blast, shooting a second tracker who stood outlined against the glowing snow. Then the remaining guards began firing wildly into the trees, into the darkness.

Duncan next targeted the drifting glowglobes. Bursting one after another, he left his hapless pursuers alone in flame-haunted darkness. He picked off two more men, while the rest of the party scrambled for cover.

With the charge in his lasgun running low, the boy scrabbled back behind the ridge where he had set up his attack, and then he headed out at top speed toward the blinking signal light he had seen. Whatever the beacon might be, it was his best chance.

The Harkonnens would be startled and disorganized for a few moments, and overly suspicious for much longer than that. Knowing he had one last opportunity, Duncan threw caution to the wind. He ran, slipping, down the hillside, smashing against rocks, but taking no time to feel the pain of scrapes or bruises. He could not cover his tracks in time, did not attempt to hide.

Somewhere behind him, as he increased the distance, he heard muffled growls and snarls, and shouts from the hunters. A pack of the wild gaze hounds had converged on them, seeking wounded prey. Duncan hid a smile and continued toward the intermittently blinking light. He saw it now, up ahead near the edge of the forest preserve.

He finally approached, treading lightly toward a shallow clearing. He came upon a silent flitter 'thopter, a high-speed aircraft that could take several passengers. The flashing beacon signaled from the top of the craft—but Duncan saw no one.

He waited in silence for a few moments, then cautiously left the shadows of the trees and moved forward. Was the craft abandoned? Left there for him? Some kind of trap the Harkonnens had laid? But why would they do that? They were already hunting him.

Or did he have a mysterious rescuer?

Duncan Idaho had accomplished much this evening and was already exhausted, stunned at how much had changed in his life. But he was only eight years old and could never pilot this flitter, even if it was his only way to escape. Still, he might find supplies inside, more food, another weapon. . . .

He leaned against the hull, surveying the area, making no sound. The hatch stood open like an invitation, but the mysterious flitter was dark inside. Wishing he still had his handlight, he moved forward cautiously and probed the shadows ahead of him with the barrel of the lasgun.

Then hands snatched out from the shadows of the craft to yank the gun from his grip before he could even flinch. Fingers stinging, flesh torn, Duncan staggered backward, biting back an outcry.

The person inside the flitter tossed the lasgun with a clatter onto the deckplates and lunged out to grab hold of the boy's arms. Rough hands squeezed the wound in his shoulder and made him gasp in pain.

Duncan kicked and struggled, then looked up to see a wiry, bitter-faced woman with chocolate-colored hair and dusky skin. He recognized her instantly: *Janess Milam,* who had stood next to him during the yard games . . . just before Harkonnen troops had captured his parents and sent his entire family to the prison city of Barony.

This woman had betrayed him to the Harkonnens.

Janess pressed a hand over his mouth before he could cry out and clamped his head in a firm arm lock. He couldn't escape.

"Got you," she said, her voice a harsh whisper.

She had betrayed him again.

We consider the various worlds as gene pools, sources of teachings and teachers, sources of the possible.

—Bene Gesserit Analysis,
Wallach IX Archives

Baron Vladimir Harkonnen was no stranger to despicable acts. Still, being coerced into this encounter disturbed him more than any vile situation he had ever been in. It threw him completely off-balance.

And throughout it all, why did this damned Reverend Mother have to be so calm, so smug?

Embarrassed, he sent away his guards and officials, purging all possible eavesdroppers from the brooding Harkonnen citadel. *Where is Rabban when I need him? Off on a hunt!* He sulked back to his private chambers, as ready as he would ever be. His stomach churned.

Nervous sweat glistened on his forehead as he stepped through the ornate arched doorway, then flicked on the privacy curtains. Perhaps if he extinguished the glowglobes and pretended he was doing something else. . . .

When he entered, the Baron was relieved to see that the witch had not taken off her clothes, had not reclined seductively on the mussed bedcovers in anticipation of his return. Instead, she sat fully robed, a prim Bene Gesserit Sister, just waiting for him. But a maddeningly superior smile curved her lips.

The Baron wanted to slash that smile away with a sharp instrument. He took a deep breath, appalled that this witch could make him feel so helpless.

"The best I can offer you is a vial of my sperm," he said, trying to be gruff and in control. "Impregnate yourself. That should be sufficient for your purposes." He lifted his firm chin. "You Bene Gesserit will just have to accept that."

"But it's *not* acceptable, Baron," the Reverend Mother said, sitting up straighter on the divan. "You know the strictures. We're not Tleilaxu growing offspring in tanks. We Bene Gesserit must have birth through natural processes, with no artificial meddling, for reasons you're incapable of understanding."

"I'm capable of understanding plenty," the Baron growled.

"Not this you aren't."

He hadn't expected the gambit to work anyway. "You need Harkonnen blood—what about my nephew Glossu Rabban? Or better yet, his father, Abulurd. Go to Lankiveil and you could have as many children as you want through him. You won't have to work so hard."

"Unacceptable," Mohiam said. She fixed him with a cold, narrow-lidded glare. Her face looked plain, pasty, and implacable. "I am not here to negotiate, Baron. I have my orders. I must return to Wallach IX carrying your child."

"But . . . what if—"

The witch held up her hand. "I've made it perfectly clear what will happen if you refuse. Make your decision. We'll have you either way."

His private chamber had suddenly become an alien and threatening place to him. He squared his shoulders, flexed his biceps. Though a muscular man, lean of body, with fast reflexes, his only escape seemed to involve pummeling this woman into submission. But he also knew about Bene Gesserit fighting abilities, especially their arcane weirding ways . . . and felt a twinge of doubt as to whether he would be the victor in such a struggle.

She got up and glided across the room with silent steps, then sat rigidly on the edge of the Baron's stained and unmade bed. "If it's any consolation, I take no more pleasure in this act than you do."

She looked at the Baron's well-made body, his broad shoulders, his firm pectorals and flat abdomen. His face had a haughty look, clearly noble-born. In other circumstances Vladimir Harkonnen might even have been an acceptable lover, like the male trainers with whom the Bene Gesserit had matched Mohiam throughout her childbearing years.

She had already delivered eight daughters to the Bene Gesserit school, all of them raised apart from her on Wallach IX or on other training planets. Mohiam had never tried to follow their progress. That was not the Sisterhood's way. Her daughter by Baron Harkonnen would be no different.

Like many well-trained Sisters, Mohiam had the ability to manipulate her most minute bodily functions. In order to become a Reverend Mother, she had been required to alter her own biochemistry by taking an awareness-spectrum poison. In transmuting the deadly drug within herself, she had passed *inward* through the long echoing bloodlines, enabling conversation with all of her female ancestors, the clamorous inner lives of Other Memory.

She could prepare her womb, ovulate at will, even choose the sex of her child from the moment the sperm and egg united. The Bene Gesserit wanted a daughter from her, a Harkonnen daughter, and Mohiam would deliver, as instructed.

With only limited details of the numerous breeding programs, Mohiam did not understand why the Bene Gesserit needed this particular combination of genes, why she had been selected to bear the child and why no other Harkonnen could produce a viable offspring for Bene Gesserit plans. She was just doing her duty. To her the Baron was a tool, a sperm donor who had to play his part.

Mohiam lifted her dark skirt and lay back on the bed, propping her head up to look at him. "Come, Baron, let us waste no more time. After all, it's such a small thing." She let her gaze drop down to his crotch.

As he flushed with rage, she continued in a soft voice, "I have the ability to increase your pleasure, or to deaden it. Either way, the results will be the same to us." She smiled with her thin lips. "Just think of the hidden melange stockpiles you'll be able to keep without the Emperor's knowledge." Her voice grew harder. "On the other hand, just try to imagine what old Elrood will do to House Harkonnen if he finds out you've been cheating him all along."

Scowling, the Baron fumbled with his robe and lurched toward the bed. Mohiam closed her eyes and muttered a Bene Gesserit benediction, a prayer to calm herself and to focus her bodily actions and her inner metabolism.

The Baron was more nauseated than aroused. He couldn't bear to look at Mohiam's naked form. Fortunately she kept most of her clothes on, as did he. She worked with her fingers until he stiffened, and he kept his eyes closed during the entire mechanical act. Behind his eyes, he had no choice but to fantasize about earlier conquests, the pain, the power . . . anything to take his mind from the revolting and messy act of male-female intercourse.

It wasn't lovemaking by any means, just a tired ritual between two bodies in order to exchange genetic material. For both of them it was barely even sex.

But Mohiam got what she wanted.

AT HIS ONE-WAY private observation window, Piter de Vries moved silently, surreptitiously. As a Mentat he had learned how to glide like a shadow, how to see without being seen. An ancient law of physics claimed that the mere act of observation changed parameters. But any good Mentat knew how to observe broader issues while remaining invisible, unknown to the subjects of his scrutiny.

De Vries had often watched the Baron's sexual escapades through this peephole. Sometimes the acts disgusted him, occasionally they fascinated . . . and rarer still, they gave the Mentat ideas of his own.

Now, he silently kept his eyes to the tiny observation holes, drinking in details as the Baron was forced to copulate with the Bene Gesserit witch. He watched his master with great amusement, enjoying the man's utter discomfiture. He had never seen the Baron so nonplussed. Oh, how he wished he had found time to set up the recording apparatus so he could enjoy this again and again.

The moment she'd made her demands, de Vries had known the unavoidable outcome. The Baron had been a perfect pawn, utterly ensnared, with no choice in the matter.

But why?

Even with his great Mentat prowess, de Vries could not understand what the Sisterhood wanted with House Harkonnen or its offspring. Surely, the genetics weren't that spectacular.

For now, though, Piter de Vries just enjoyed the show.

Many inventions have selectively improved particular skills or abilities, emphasizing one aspect or another. But no achievement has ever scratched the complexity or adaptability of the human mind.

—Ikbhan's Treatise on the Mind, Volume II

On one side of the faux-stone practice floor in the Ixian Grand Palais, Leto stood beside Guard Captain Zhaz, panting. The fight instructor was an angular man with bristly brown hair, thick eyebrows, and a square-cut beard. Like his students, Zhaz wore no shirt, only beige fighting shorts. The smell of sweat and hot metal hung in the air despite the best efforts of an air-exchange apparatus. As on most mornings, though, the training master spent more time watching than fighting. He let the battle-machines do all the work.

After his regular studies, Leto loved the change of pace, the physical exercise, the challenge. By now he had settled into a routine on Ix, undergoing hours of high-tech physical and mental training, with added time for tours of technological facilities and instruction in business philosophy. He had warmed to Rhombur's enthusiasm, though often he had to help explain difficult concepts to the Ixian Prince. Rhombur wasn't slow-witted, just . . . distant from many practical matters.

Every third morning, the young men left their classrooms behind and worked out on the automated training floor. Leto loved the exercise and the rush of adrenaline, while both Rhombur and the fight instructor seemed to find this an antiquated requirement added to the curriculum only because of Earl Vernius's memories of warfare.

Leto and the bristly-haired captain watched stocky Prince Rhombur wield a golden pike against a sleek and responsive fighting mek. Zhaz didn't train personally against his students. He felt that if he and his security troops did their jobs, no member of House Vernius need ever stoop to barbaric hand-to-hand combat. He did, however, help program the self-learning combat drones.

In its resting position, the man-sized mek was a featureless charcoal ovoid—no arms, legs, or face. Once the fight began, however, the Ixian unit morphed a set of crude protrusions and took on varying shapes based upon feedback from its scanner, telling it how best to defeat an adversary. Steel fists, knives, flexsteel cables, and other surprises could be thrust from any point on its body. Its mechanical face could disappear entirely or change expression—from a dullness designed to lull an opponent to a ferocious red-eyed glare, or even fiendish glee. The mek interpreted and reacted, learning with each step.

"Remember, no regular patterns," Zhaz shouted to Rhombur. His beard protruded like a shovel from his chin. "Don't let it read you."

The Prince ducked as two blunted darts sped past his head. A surprise knife thrust from the mek drew a trickle of blood on the young man's shoulder. Even with the injury, Rhombur feinted and attacked, and Leto was proud of his royal peer for not crying out.

On several occasions Rhombur had asked Leto for advice, even critiques on sparring style. Answering honestly, Leto kept in mind that he himself was not a skilled professional instructor—nor did he want to reveal too much of Atreides techniques. Rhombur could learn those from Thufir Hawat, the Old Duke's swordmaster himself.

The tip of the Prince's blade found a soft spot on the mek's charcoal body, and it fell over "dead."

"Good, Rhombur!" Leto called.

Zhaz nodded. "Much better."

Leto had fought the mek twice that day, defeating it each time on higher difficulty settings than Prince Rhombur was using. When Zhaz asked how Leto had acquired such skills, the young Atreides hadn't said much, not wishing to brag. But now he had firsthand proof that the Atreides method of training was superior, despite the mek's chilling near intelligence. Leto's background involved rapiers, knives, slow-pellet stunners, and body-shields—and Thufir Hawat was a more dangerous and unpredictable instructor than any automated device could ever hope to be.

Just as Leto took up his own weapon and prepared for the next round, the lift doors opened and Kailea entered, sparkling with jewels and a comfortable metal-fiber outfit whose design seemed calculated to look gorgeous but casual. She bore a stylus and ridulian recorder pad. Her eyebrows arched in feigned surprise at finding them there. "Oh! Excuse me. I came to look at the mek design."

The Vernius daughter usually contented herself with intellectual and cultural pursuits, studying business and art. Leto couldn't keep himself from watching her. At times her eyes almost seemed to flirt with him, but more often she ignored him with such intensity he suspected she shared the same attraction he felt.

During his time in the Grand Palais, Leto had crossed her path in the dining hall, on the open observation balconies, in library facilities. He had responded to her with snatches of awkward conversation. Aside from the inviting sparkle in her beautiful green eyes, Kailea had given him no special encouragement, but he couldn't stop thinking about her.

She's only a stripling, Leto reminded himself, *playing at being a Lady.* Somehow, though, he couldn't convince his imagination of that. Kailea had complete confidence that she was destined for a greater future than living underground on Ix. Her father was a war hero, the head of one of the wealthiest Great Houses, and her mother had been beautiful enough to be an Imperial concubine, and the girl herself had an excellent head for business. Kailea Vernius obviously had a wealth of possibilities.

She focused her complete attention on the motionless gray ovoid. "I've gotten Father to consider marketing our new-phase fighting meks commercially." She studied the motionless training machine, but glanced at Leto out of the corner of her eye, noted his strong profile and regal, high-bridged nose. "Ours are better than any other combat device—adaptable, versatile, and self-learning. The closest thing to a human adversary developed since the Jihad."

He felt a chill, thinking back to all the warnings his mother had given him. Right now she would be pointing an accusing finger and nodding in satisfaction. Leto looked over at the charcoal-colored ovoid. "Are you saying that thing has a brain?"

"By all the saints and sinners, you mean in violation of the strictures after the Great Revolt?" Captain Zhaz replied in stern surprise. " 'Thou shalt not make a machine in the likeness of the human mind.' "

"We're, uh, very careful about that, Leto," Rhombur said, using a purple towel to wipe sweat from the back of his neck. "Nothing to worry about."

Leto didn't back down. "Well, if the mek scans people, if it *reads* them as you said, how does it process the information? If not through a computer brain, then how? This isn't just a reactive device. It learns and tailors its attack."

Kailea jotted notes down on her crystal pad and adjusted one of the gold combs in her copper-dark hair. "There are many gray areas, Leto, and if we tread very carefully House Vernius stands to make a tremendous profit." She ran a fingertip along her curved lips. "Still, it might be best to test the waters by offering some unmarked models on the black market first."

"Don't trouble yourself, Leto," Rhombur said, avoiding the uncomfortable subject. His tousled blond hair still dripped with sweat, and his skin showed a flush from his exertion. "House Vernius has teams of Mentats and legal advisors scrutinizing the letter of the law." He looked over at his sister for reassurance. She nodded absently.

In some of his instruction sessions in the Grand Palais, Leto had learned of interplanetary patent disputes, minor technicalities, subtle loopholes. Had the Ixians come up with a substantially different way of using mechanical units to process data, one that did not raise the spectre of thinking machines like those that had enslaved mankind for so many centuries? He didn't see how House Vernius could have created a self-learning, reactive, adaptable fighting mek without somehow going over the line into Jihad violation.

If his mother ever found out, she would haul him home from Ix, no matter what his father might say.

"Let's see just how good this product is," Leto said, taking up a weapon and turning his back on Kailea. He could feel her eyes on his bare shoulders, the muscles of his neck. Zhaz stood back casually to watch.

Leto shifted his pike from hand to hand and jogged onto the floor. Taking a classic fighting stance, he called out a degree of difficulty to the charcoal oval shape. "Seven point two-four!" Eight notches higher than the time before.

The mek refused to move.

"Too high," the training master said, thrusting his bearded chin forward. "I disabled the dangerous higher levels."

Leto scowled. The fight instructor did not want to challenge his students, or risk more than the slightest injury. Thufir Hawat would have laughed out loud.

"Are you trying to show off for the young lady, Master Atreides? Could get you killed."

Looking at Kailea, he saw her watching him, a bemused, teasing expression on her face. She quickly turned to the ridulian pad and scratched a few more ciphers. He flushed, felt the hotness. Zhaz reached over to grab a soft towel from a rack and tossed it to Leto.

"The session's over. Distractions of this sort are not good for your training, and can lead to serious injury." He turned to the Princess. "Lady Kailea, I request that you avoid the training floor whenever Leto Atreides is fighting our meks. Too many hormones in the way." The guard captain could not cover his amusement. "Your presence could be more dangerous than any enemy."

We must do a thing on Arrakis never before attempted for an entire planet. We must use man as a constructive ecological force—inserting adapted terraform life: a plant here, an animal there, a man in that place—to transform the water cycle, to build a new kind of landscape.

—Report from Imperial Planetologist PARDOT KYNES, directed to Padishah EMPEROR ELROOD IX (unsent)

When the blood-spattered Fremen youths asked Pardot Kynes to accompany them, he didn't know whether he was to be their guest or prisoner. Either way, the prospect intrigued him. Finally, he would have his chance to experience their mysterious culture firsthand.

One of the young men quickly and efficiently carried his injured companion over to Kynes's small groundcar. The other Fremen reached into the back storage compartments and tossed out Kynes's painstakingly collected geological samples to make more room. The Planetologist was too astonished to object; besides, he didn't want to alienate these people—he wanted to learn more about them.

In moments, they had stuffed the bodies of the dead Harkonnen bravos into the bins, no doubt for some Fremen purpose. *Perhaps a further ritual desecration of their enemies.* He ruled out the unlikely possibility that the youths simply wished to bury the dead. *Are they hiding the bodies for fear of reprisals?* That, too, seemed wrong somehow, not in keeping with what little he had heard about Fremen. *Or will these desert folk render them for resources, reclaiming the water in their tissues?*

Then, without asking, without giving thanks or making any comment whatsoever, the first grim Fremen youth took the vehicle, its injured passenger, and the bodies, and drove off rapidly, spewing sand and dust in all directions. Kynes watched it go, along with his desert-survival kit and maps, including many he had prepared himself.

He found himself alone with the third young man—a guard, or a friend? If these Fremen meant to strand him without his supplies, he would be dead before long. Perhaps he could get his bearings and make it back to the village of Windsack on foot, but he had paid little attention to the locations of population centers during his recent wanderings. *An inauspicious end for an Imperial Planetologist,* he thought.

Or perhaps the young men he'd rescued wanted something else from him. Because of his own newly formed dreams for the future of Arrakis, Kynes desperately wanted to know the Fremen and their unorthodox ways. Clearly, these people were a valuable secret hidden from Imperial eyes. He thought they'd be sure to greet him with enthusiasm once he told them his ideas.

The remaining Fremen youth used a small patch-kit to repair a fabric rip on the leg of his stillsuit, then said, "Come with me." He turned toward a sheer rock wall a short distance away. "Follow, or you'll die out here." He flashed an indigo-eyed glare over his shoulder. His face held a hard humor, an impish smile as he said, "Do you think the Harkonnens will take long to seek vengeance for their dead?"

Kynes hurried to him. "Wait! You haven't told me your name."

The young man looked at him strangely; he had the blue-within-blue eyes of long spice addiction, and weathered skin that gave him an appearance of age far beyond his years. "Is it worthwhile to exchange names? The Fremen already know who you are."

Kynes blinked. "Well, I did just save your life and the lives of your companions. Doesn't that count for something among your people? It does in most societies."

The young man seemed startled, then resigned. "You are right. You have forged a water bond between us. I am called Turok. Now we must go."

Water bond? Kynes suppressed his questions and trailed after his companion.

In his well-worn stillsuit, Turok scrambled over the rocks toward the vertical cliff. Kynes trudged beside fallen boulders, slipping on loose footing. Only as they approached did the Planetologist notice a discontinuity in the strata, a seam that split the old uplifted rock, forming a fissure camouflaged by dust and muted colors.

The Fremen slipped inside, penetrating the shadows with the speed of a desert lizard. Curious and anxious not to become lost, Kynes followed, moving quickly. He hoped he would get a chance to meet more of the Fremen and learn about them. He didn't waste time considering that Turok might be leading him into a trap. What would be the point? The young man could easily have killed him out in the open.

Turok stopped in the cool shade, giving Kynes a moment to catch up. He pointed toward specific places on the wall near him. "There, there—and there." Without waiting to see if his charge understood, the youth stepped in each indicated spot, near-invisible handholds and footholds. The young man slithered up the cliff, and Kynes did his best to climb after. Turok seemed to be playing a game with him, testing him somehow.

But the Planetologist surprised him. He was no water-fat bureaucrat, no mere bumbler into places where he didn't belong. As a wanderer on some of the harshest worlds the Imperium had to offer, he was in good shape.

Kynes kept pace with the youth, climbing up behind him, using the tips of his fingers to haul his body higher. Moments after the Fremen boy stopped and squatted on a narrow ledge, Kynes sat beside him, trying not to pant.

"Breathe in through your nose and out through your mouth," Turok said. "Your filters are more efficient that way." He nodded in faint admiration. "I think you might make it all the way to the sietch."

"What's a sietch?" Kynes asked. He vaguely recognized the ancient Chakobsa language, but had not studied archaeology or phonetics. He had always found it irrelevant to his scientific study.

"A secret place to retreat in safety—it's where my people live."

"You mean it's your home?"

"The desert is our home."

"I'm eager to talk with your people," Kynes said, then continued, unable to contain his enthusiasm. "I've formed some opinions of this world and have developed a plan that might interest you, that might interest all the inhabitants of Arrakis."

"Dune," the Fremen youth said. "Only the Imperials and the Harkonnens call this place Arrakis."

"All right," Kynes said. "Dune, then."

DEEP IN THE rocks ahead of them waited a grizzled old Fremen with only one eye, his useless left socket covered by a puckered prune of leathered eyelid. Naib of Red Wall Sietch, Heinar had also lost two fingers in a crysknife duel in his younger days. But he had survived, and his opponents had not.

Heinar had proven to be a stern but competent leader of his people. Over the years, his sietch had prospered, the population had not decreased, and their hidden stockpiles of water grew with every cycle of the moons.

In the infirmary cave, two old women tended foolish Stilgar, the injured youth who had been brought in by groundcar only moments ago. The old women checked the medical dressing that had been applied by the outsider, and augmented it with some of their own medicinals. The crones conferred with each other, then both nodded at the sietch leader.

"Stilgar will live, Heinar," one old woman said. "This would have been a mortal wound, had it not been tended immediately. The stranger saved him."

"The stranger saved a careless fool," the Naib said, looking down at the young man on the cot.

For weeks, troublesome reports of a curious outsider had reached Heinar's ears. Now the man, Pardot Kynes, was being led to the sietch by a different route, through rock passageways. The stranger's actions were mind-boggling—an Imperial servant who killed Harkonnens?

Ommun, the Fremen youth who had brought bleeding Stilgar back to the sietch, waited anxiously beside his injured friend in the cave shadows. Heinar turned his monocular gaze to the young man, letting the women continue to tend their patient. "Why is it that Turok brings an outsider to our sietch?"

"What were we to do, Heinar?" Ommun looked surprised. "I needed his vehicle to bring Stilgar here."

"You could have taken this man's groundcar and all his possessions and given his water to the tribe," the Naib said, his voice low.

"We can still do that," one of the women rasped, "as soon as Turok gets here with him."

"But the stranger fought and killed Harkonnens! We three would have died, had he not arrived when he did," Ommun insisted. "Is it not said that the enemy of my enemy is my friend?"

"I do not trust or even understand the loyalties of this one," Heinar said, crossing his sinewy arms over his chest. "We know who he is, of course. The stranger comes from the Imperium—a Planetologist, they say. He remains on Dune because the Harkonnens are forced to let him do his work, but this man Kynes answers only to the Emperor himself . . . if that. There are unanswered questions about him."

Wearily, Heinar sat down on a stone bench carved in the side of the wall. A colorful tapestry of spun spice fibers hung across the cave opening, offering a limited sort of privacy. Sietch inhabitants learned early that privacy was in the mind, not in the environment.

"I will speak with this Kynes and learn what he wants of us, why he has defended three stupid and careless youths against an enemy he had no cause to make. Then I will take this matter to the Council of Elders and let them decide. We must make the choice that is best for the sietch."

Ommun swallowed hard, recalling how valiantly the man Kynes had fought against the ruthless soldiers. But his fingers strayed to the pouch in his pocket, counting the water rings there—metal markers that tallied the accumulated wealth he had in the tribe.

If the elders did decide to kill the Planetologist after all, then he, Turok, and Stilgar would divide the water treasure equally among them, along with the bounty from the six slain Harkonnens.

WHEN TUROK FINALLY led him through the guarded openings, past a doorseal, and into the sietch proper, Kynes saw the place as a cave of infinite wonders. The aromas were dense, rich, and redolent with humanity: smells of life, of a confined population . . . of manufacturing, cooking, carefully concealed wastes, and even chemically exploited death. In a detached way, he confirmed his suspicion that the

Fremen youths had not stolen the Harkonnen corpses for some sort of superstitious mutilation, but for the water in their bodies. *Otherwise, it would have gone to waste. . . .*

Kynes had assumed that when he finally found a hidden Fremen settlement, it would be primitive, almost shameful in its lack of amenities. But here, in this walled-off grotto with side caves and lava tubes and tunnels extending like a warren throughout the mountain, Kynes saw that the desert people lived in an austere yet comfortable style. Quarters rivaled anything Harkonnen functionaries enjoyed in the city of Carthag. And they were much more natural.

As Kynes followed his young guide, he found his attention riveted on one fascinating sight after another. Luxurious woven carpets covered portions of the floor. Side rooms were strewn with cushions and low tables made of metal and polished stone. Articles of precious off-planet wood were few and seemingly ancient: a carved sandworm and a board game that he couldn't identify, its ornate pieces made of ivory or bone.

Ancient machinery recirculated the sietch air, letting no breath of moisture escape. He smelled the sharp cinnamon sweetness of raw spice everywhere, like incense, barely masking the sour pungency of unwashed bodies packed into close quarters.

He heard women talking, children's voices, and a baby crying, all with a hushed restraint. The Fremen spoke among themselves, eyeing this stranger with suspicion as he passed, led by Turok. Some of the older ones flashed him wicked smiles that gave the Planetologist some concern. Their skin looked tough and leathery, leached of all excess water; every pair of eyes was a deep blue-within-blue.

Finally Turok raised a hand, palm outward, signaling Kynes to halt inside a large meeting hall, a natural vault within the mountain. The grotto had ample floor space for hundreds and hundreds to stand; additional benches and balconies zigzagged up the sheer reddish walls. *How many people live in this sietch?* Kynes stared upward in the empty, echoing room to a high balcony, a speaking platform of some sort.

After a moment, a proud old man stepped forward up there to look disdainfully down at the intruder. Kynes noted that the man had only one eye, and that he carried himself with the presence of a leader.

"That is Heinar," Turok whispered in his ear, "the Naib of Red Wall Sietch."

Raising a hand in greeting, Kynes called out: "I am pleased to meet the leader of this wondrous Fremen city."

"What is it you want from us, Imperial man?" Heinar called down in a tone that was ruthless and demanding. His words rang like cold steel against the stone.

Kynes drew a deep breath. He had been waiting for an opportunity such as this for many days. Why waste time? The longer that dreams remained mere dreams, the more difficult it was to mold them into reality.

"My name is Pardot Kynes, Planetologist to the Emperor. I have a vision, sir—a dream for you and your people. One I wish to share with all the Fremen, if only you will listen to me."

"Better to listen to the wind through a creosote bush than to waste time with the words of a fool," the sietch leader responded. His words had a ponderous weight, as if this were an old and recognizable saying among his people.

Kynes stared back at the old man and quickly made up his own platitude, hoping to make an impression. "And if one refuses to listen to words of truth and hope, who then is the greater fool?"

Young Turok gasped. From side passages Fremen onlookers stared wide-eyed at Kynes, amazed by this stranger who spoke so boldly to their Naib.

Heinar's face became dark and stormy. He felt a sullenness permeate him, and he envisioned this upstart Planetologist lying slain on the cave floor. He put his hand on the hilt of a crysknife at his waist. "Do you challenge my leadership?" Making up his mind, the Naib yanked the curve-bladed knife from its sheath and glowered down at Kynes.

Kynes didn't flinch. "No, sir—I challenge your *imagination*. Are you brave enough to meet the task, or are you too frightened to listen to what I have to say?" The sietch leader stood tense, holding his strange milky blade high as he stared down at the prisoner. Kynes simply smiled up at him, his expression open. "It's difficult to talk to you way up there, sir."

Finally, Heinar chuckled, looked down at the bare blade in his hand. "A crysknife, once drawn, must never be sheathed without tasting blood." Then he quickly slashed its edge across his forearm, drawing a thin red line that coagulated within seconds.

Kynes's eyes glittered with excitement, reflecting the light cast by the clusters of glowglobes that floated in the large meeting chamber.

"Very well, Planetologist. You may talk until the breath flows out of your lungs. With your fate undecided, you will remain here in the sietch until the Council of Elders deliberates over what must be done with you."

"But you'll listen to me first." Kynes nodded with utter confidence.

Heinar turned, took a step away from the high balcony, and spoke again over his shoulder. "You are a strange man, Pardot Kynes. An Imperial servant and a guest of Harkonnens—by definition, you are our enemy. But you have killed Harkonnens as well. What a quandary you present for us."

The sietch leader made quick gestures and barked commands, ordering a small but comfortable room to be prepared for the tall and curious Planetologist, who would be their prisoner as well as their guest.

And Heinar thought as he strode away, *Any man who would speak words of hope to the Fremen after our many generations of suffering and wandering . . . is either confused, or a very brave man indeed.*

My Father had only one real friend, I think. That was Count Hasimir Fenring, the genetic-eunuch and one of the deadliest fighters in the Imperium.

—From "In My Father's House"
by the Princess Irulan

E ven from the highest, darkened chamber of the Imperial observatory, the pastel glow of the opulence-choked capital drowned out the stars over Kaitain. Built centuries earlier by the enlightened Padishah Emperor Hassik Corrino III, the observatory had been used little by his recent heirs . . . at least not for its intended purpose of studying the mysteries of the universe.

Crown Prince Shaddam paced across the cold, burnished-metal floor as Fenring fiddled with the controls of a high-powered starscope. The genetic-eunuch hummed to himself, making unpleasant, insipid sounds.

"Would you please stop those noises?" Shaddam said. "Just focus the damned lenses."

Fenring continued to hum, only fractionally quieter now. "The oils must be in precise balance, hm-m-m-m-ah? You would rather have the starscope perfect, than fast."

Shaddam huffed. "You didn't ask my preference."

"I decided for you." He stood back from the starscope's calibrated phased optics and bowed with an annoyingly formal gesture. "My Lord Prince, I present to you an image from orbit. See it with your own eyes."

Shaddam squinted into the eyepiece pickups until a shape became startlingly clear, soaring silently in the distance. The image shifted between brittle resolution and murky ripples caused by atmospheric distortion.

The mammoth Heighliner was the size of an asteroid, hanging over Kaitain and waiting to be met by a flotilla of small ships from the surface. A tiny movement caught his eye, and Shaddam spotted the yellow-white flickers of engines as frigates rose from Kaitain bearing diplomats and emissaries, followed by transports carrying artifacts and cargo from the Imperial capital world. The frigates themselves were immense, flanked by cadres of smaller ships—but the curve of the Heighliner's hull dwarfed everything.

At the same time, other ships departed from the Heighliner hold and descended toward the capital city. "Delegation parties," Shaddam said. "They've brought tributes to my father."

"Taxes, actually—not tributes," Fenring pointed out. "Same thing, in an old-fashioned sense, of course. Elrood is still their Emperor, um-m-m-ah?"

The Crown Prince scowled at him. "But for how much longer? Is your damned chaumurky going to take decades?" Shaddam fought to keep his voice low, although subsonic white-noise generators supposedly distorted their speech to foil any listening devices. "Couldn't you find a different poison? A faster one? This waiting is maddening! How much time has passed anyway? It seems like a year since I've slept well."

"You mean we should have been more overt about the murder? Not advisable." Fenring took his station back at the starscope, adjusting the automated trackers to follow the Heighliner along its orbit. "Be patient, my Lord Prince. Until I suggested this plan, you were content to wait for decades. What does a year or two matter compared with the length of your eventual reign, hm-m-m-m?"

Shaddam nudged Fenring away from the eyepieces so he wouldn't have to look at his fellow conspirator. "Now that we've finally set the wheels in motion, I'm impatient for my father to die. Don't give me time to brood about it and regret my decision. I'll suffocate until I can ascend the Golden Lion Throne. I was destined to lead, Hasimir, but some have been whispering that I'll never get the opportunity. It makes me afraid to marry and father any children."

If he expected Fenring to attempt to convince him otherwise, the other man disappointed him with his silence.

Fenring spoke again after a few moments. "*N'kee* is slow poison by design. We have worked long and hard to establish our plan, and your impatience can only cause damage and increase risk. A more sudden act would certainly create suspicion in the Landsraad, hmmm? They would seize upon any wedge, any scandal, to weaken your position."

"But I am the heir to House Corrino!" Shaddam said, lowering his voice to a throaty whisper. "How can they question my right?"

"And you come to the Imperial throne bearing all the associated baggage, all the obligations, past antagonisms, and prejudices. Don't fool yourself, my friend—the Emperor is merely one sizable force among many that make up the delicate fabric of our Imperium. If all the Houses banded together against us, even your father's mighty Sardaukar legions might not be able to hold out. No one dares risk it."

"When I'm on the throne, I intend to strengthen the emperorship, add some real teeth to the title." Shaddam stood away from the starscope.

Fenring shook his head with exaggerated sadness. "I'd be willing to wager a cargo hold full of the highest-quality whale-fur that most of your predecessors have vowed the same thing to their advisors ever since the Great Revolt." He drew a deep breath, narrowing his large dark eyes. "Even if the *n'kee* works as planned, you have at least another year to wait . . . so calm yourself. Take comfort in the increased symptoms of aging we've seen in your father. Encourage him to drink more spice beer."

Miffed, Shaddam turned back to the phased optics and studied the hull patterns along the belly of the Heighliner, the mark of Ixian construction yards, the cartouche of the Spacing Guild. The hold was crowded with fleets of frigates from various Houses, shipments assigned to CHOAM, and precious records earmarked for library archives on Wallach IX.

"By the way, someone of interest is aboard that Heighliner," Fenring said.

"Oh?"

Fenring crossed his arms over his narrow chest. "A person who *appears to be* a simple seller of pundi rice and chikarba root on his way to a Tleilaxu way station. He's bearing your message for the Tleilaxu

Masters, your proposal to meet with them and discuss covert Imperial funding of a large-scale project that will produce a substitute for the spice melange."

"My proposal? I made no such proposal!" Revulsion flickered across Shaddam's face.

"Um-m-m, you did, my Lord Prince. Ah, the possibility of using unorthodox Tleilaxu means to develop a synthetic spice? What a good idea you had! Show your father how smart you are."

"Don't place the blame on me, Hasimir. It was your idea."

"You don't want the credit?"

"Not in the least."

Fenring raised his eyebrows. "You *are* serious about breaking the Arrakis bottleneck and setting up the Imperial House with a private, unlimited source of melange? Aren't you?"

Shaddam glowered. "Of course I'm serious."

"Then we will bring a Tleilaxu Master here in secret to present his proposal to the Emperor. We'll soon see how far old Elrood is willing to go."

Blindness can take many forms other than the inability to see. Fanatics are often blinded in their thoughts. Leaders are often blinded in their hearts.

—The Orange Catholic Bible

For months, Leto had stayed in the underground city of Vernii as the honored guest of Ix. By now, he had become comfortable with the strangeness of his new surroundings, with the routine, and with self-confident Ixian security—comfortable enough to grow careless.

Prince Rhombur was a chronic late sleeper, while Leto was the opposite, an early riser like the fishermen on Caladan. The Atreides heir wandered the upper stalactite buildings alone, going to observation windows and peeking in on manufacturing-design procedures or fabrication lines. He learned how to use the transit systems and discovered that his bioscram card from Earl Vernius opened many doors for him.

Leto gleaned more from his wanderings and his voracious curiosity than he did from instructional meetings hosted by various tutors. Remembering his father's admonishment to learn from everything, he took the self-guiding lift tubes; when none were available, he grew accustomed to using walkways, cargo lifts, or even ladders to go from one level to another.

One morning, after awakening refreshed and restless,

Leto went to one of the upper atriums and stepped out onto an observation balcony. Even sealed underground, the caverns of Ix were so vast that they had their own air currents and wind patterns, though it was a far cry from the Castle towers and windy cliffsides of his home. He took a deep breath, filling his lungs to capacity, but the air here always smelled of rock dust. Maybe it was just his imagination.

Stretching his arms, Leto looked out and down toward the broad grotto that had held the Guild Heighliner. Among the scars of construction and support machinery, he could pick out the already-sprouting skeleton of another massive hull, flash-welded together by teams of suboid workers. He watched the low-level inhabitants working with insect efficiency.

A cargo platform drifted by, passing directly below the balcony as it made a gradual descent to the distant work area. Leto leaned over the railing and saw that the platform's surface was loaded with raw materials mined from the crust of the planet.

On impulse, he climbed over the balcony rim, took a deep breath, and dropped two meters to land atop a pile of girders and plating destined for the Heighliner construction site. He assumed he could find a way to get back up to the stalactite buildings using his bioscram card and his understanding of the city workings. A pilot underneath the hovering platform guided the lowering load; he didn't seem to notice or care about his unexpected passenger.

Cool breezes riffled through Leto's hair as he descended toward the warmer surface. Thinking of ocean winds, he sucked in another deep breath. Here beneath the immense vault of the ceiling, he felt a freedom that reminded him of the seashore. With the thought came a pang of homesickness for the ocean breezes of Caladan, the noises of the village market, the booming laugh of his father, even the prim concern of his mother.

He and Rhombur spent too much time confined within the buildings of Ix, and Leto often longed for fresh air and a cold wind on his face. Perhaps he would ask Rhombur to accompany him up to the surface again. There, the two of them could wander around the wilderness and look up at an infinite sky, and Leto could stretch his muscles and feel real sunlight on his face instead of the holographic illumination displayed on the cavern ceiling.

While the Ixian Prince was not Leto's equal as a fighter, neither was he the spoiled son so common among many Great Houses. He had his interests and loved collecting rocks and minerals. Rhombur had an easy, generous way about him, and an unflagging optimism, but that was not to be misinterpreted. Beneath the soft shell was a fierce determination and a desire to excel in every pursuit.

In the gigantic manufacturing grotto, supports and suspensor jacks had been readied for the new Heighliner already taking shape. Equipment and machinery stood waiting near where holo blueprints shimmered in the air. Even with full resources and huge numbers of suboid workers, such a vessel required the better part of a Standard Year to construct. The cost of a Heighliner was equivalent to the economic output of many solar systems; thus, only CHOAM and the Guild could finance such massive projects, while House Vernius—as the manufacturer—reaped incredible profits.

The docile working class on Ix far outnumbered the administrators and the nobles. On the floor of the grotto, low archways and huts built into the solid rock provided entrances to a warren of living quarters. Leto had never visited the suboids himself, but Rhombur had assured him that the lower classes were well taken care of. Leto knew these crews labored around the clock to build each new ship. The suboids certainly worked hard for House Vernius.

The cargo platform levitated downward to the rocky cavern floor, and teams of workers came forward to unload the heavy raw materials. Leto sprang down, landed on his hands and feet, then stood and brushed himself off. The strangely placid suboids had pale skin dusted with freckles. They looked at him with doe eyes and didn't ask any questions or object to his presence; they simply averted their gazes and went about their tasks.

The way Kailea and Rhombur talked about them, Leto had imagined the suboids to be less than human, muscular troglodytes without minds, who simply labored and sweated. But the people around him could easily have passed for normals; perhaps they weren't brilliant scientists or diplomats, but the working class didn't appear to be animals either.

With his gray eyes open wide, Leto walked along the grotto floor, staying out of the way as he observed the Heighliner construction. Leto admired the sheer engineering and management of such an incredible job. In the heavier, dustier air on the ground, he smelled an acrid tang of laser-welding and alloy-fusing materials.

The suboids followed a master plan, using step-by-step instructions like a hive organism. They concluded each increment of the huge task without being overwhelmed by the amount of work still in store for them. The suboids did not chatter, sing, or roughhouse . . . behavior Leto had seen among the fishermen, farmers, and factory workers of Caladan. These pale-skinned laborers remained intent only on their tasks.

He thought he imagined well-hidden resentment, a simmering anger beneath calm, pale faces, but he didn't feel afraid down here alone. Duke Paulus had always encouraged Leto to play with villager children, to go out on fishing boats, to mix with merchants and weavers in the marketplace. He had even spent a month working in the pundi rice fields. "In order to understand how to rule a people," the Old Duke had said, "you must first understand the people themselves."

His mother had frowned upon such activities, of course, insisting that the son of a Duke should not dirty his hands with the mud of rice paddies or foul his clothes with the slime of a sea catch. "What good does it do for *our son* to know how to skin and gut a fish? He will be the ruler of a Great House." But Paulus Atreides had his own way of insisting, and he made it clear that his wishes were law.

And Leto had to admit that despite sore muscles, an aching back, and sunburned skin, those times of hard work had satisfied him in a way that grand banquets or receptions hosted in Castle Caladan could not. As a result he thought he understood the common folk, how they felt, how hard they worked. Leto appreciated them for it, rather than scorning them. The Old Duke had been proud of his son for comprehending that fundamental point.

Now as he walked among the suboids, Leto tried to understand them in the same way. Powerful glowglobes hovered over the work site, driving back shadows, maintaining a starkness in the air. The grotto was large enough that the construction sounds did not echo back, but reflected and faded into the distance.

He saw one of the openings into the lower tunnels and since no one had yet questioned his business there, Leto decided this would be a good opportunity to learn more about the suboid culture. Maybe he could discover things even Rhombur didn't know about his own world.

When a crew of workers emerged from the archway, clad in service overalls, Leto slipped inside. He wandered into the tunnels and spiraled down, passing hollowed-out living compartments, identical and evenly spaced rooms that reminded him of the chambers in an insect hive. Occasionally, though, he spotted homey touches: colorful fabrics or tapestries, a few drawings, images painted on the stone walls. He smelled cooking, heard low conversations but no music and not much laughter.

He thought of his days spent studying and relaxing in the inverted skyscrapers overhead, with their polished floors, ser-chrome and faceted crystalplaz windows, the soft beds and comfortable clothes, the fine foods.

On Caladan, ordinary citizens could petition the Duke whenever they wished. Leto remembered when he and his father would walk in the marketplaces, talking to the merchants and craftsmen, allowing themselves to be seen and known as real people rather than as faceless rulers.

He didn't think Dominic Vernius even noticed the differences between himself and his comrade Paulus. The hearty, bald Earl gave all of his attention and enthusiasm to his family and the workers in his immediate vicinity, paying attention to overall industrial operations and business politics to keep the Ixian fortunes pouring in. But Dominic viewed the suboids as resources. Yes, he cared for them well enough, just as he maintained his precious machinery. But Leto wondered if Rhombur and his family treated the suboids as *people*.

He'd already gone down many levels, and felt the uncomfortable tightness of stale air. The tunnels ahead became darker and emptier. The quiet corridors led deeper into open rooms, common areas from which he heard voices, a rustling of bodies. He was about to turn back, knowing he had a full day ahead of him: studies and lectures about mechanical operations and industrial processes. Rhombur probably hadn't even eaten breakfast yet.

Curious, Leto stopped at the archway to see many suboids gathered in a common room. There were no seats or benches that he could see, and so all the people remained standing. He listened to the droning, curiously impassioned words of one suboid, a short, muscular man at the front of the room. In the man's voice, and in the fire in his eyes, Leto detected emotions that he found peculiar, in view of what he had heard about the suboids, that they were placid and undemanding.

"*We* build the Heighliners," he said, and his voice grew louder. "*We* manufacture the technological objects, yet *we* make none of the decisions. We do as we are commanded, even when we know those plans are wrong!"

The suboids began to mutter and mumble.

"Some of the new technologies go beyond what is forbidden by the Great Revolt. We are creating *thinking machines*. We don't need to understand the blueprints and designs, because we know what they will do!"

Hesitating, Leto drew back into the shadows of the archway. He had walked enough among the common people that he usually wasn't afraid of them. But something strange was going on here. He wanted to run, yet needed to listen. . . .

"Since we are suboids, we have no participation in profits from Ixian technology. We have simple lives and few ambitions—but we do have our religion. We read the Orange Catholic Bible and know in our hearts what is right." The suboid speaker raised a massive, knuckled fist. "And we know that many of the things we've been building here on Ix *are not right!*"

The audience moved restlessly again, on the verge of being riled. Rhombur had insisted that this group had no ambitions, did not have the capacity for them. Here, though, Leto saw otherwise.

The suboid speaker narrowed his eyes and spoke ominously. "What are we going to do? Should we petition our masters and demand answers? Should we do more?"

He swept his gaze over the gathered listeners—then suddenly, like two sharp fléchettes, his eyes skewered Leto eavesdropping in the archway shadows. "Who are you?"

Leto stumbled backward, raising his hands. "I'm sorry. I got lost. I didn't mean anything by it." Normally, he would know how to make himself welcome, but now his confusion raised his senses to a fever pitch.

The worker audience spun about, and their eyes slowly lit with comprehension. They realized the implications of what the speaker had said and what Leto had overheard.

"I'm really sorry," Leto said. "I meant no trespass." His heart pounded. Sweat sparkled on his brow, and he sensed extreme danger.

Several suboids began to move toward him like automatons, picking up speed.

Leto offered them his most congenial smile. "If you'd like, I can speak with Earl Vernius for you, bring some of your grievances—"

The suboids closed in, and Leto bolted and ran. He rushed back through the low corridors, turning at random, ducking down passageways as the workers hurried, ineffectually pursuing and growling in anger. They flooded out, spreading into side corridors in their search for him, and Leto could not remember the way back to the open cavern. . . .

The fact that he got lost probably saved him. The suboids continued to block his retreat, attempting to intercept him in corridors that led to the surface. But Leto didn't know where he was going and took blind turns, sometimes hiding in empty alcoves, until finally he reached a small maintenance door that spilled out into the dusty air under the glaring lights of industrial glowglobes.

Several suboids, seeing his silhouette in the doorway, shouted from deep below, but Leto raced out to an emergency lift tube. He swept his bioscram card through the reader and gained access to the upper levels.

Shaking in the aftermath of a burned-out adrenaline rush, Leto couldn't believe what he had just heard and didn't know what the suboids would have done had they caught him. He had been astonished enough to see their outrage and their reactions. Intellectually, he couldn't believe they would have killed him—not the son of Duke Atreides, an honored guest of House Vernius. He had offered to help them, after all.

But the suboids clearly held a deep potential for violence, a frightening darkness that they had managed to hide from their oblivious rulers above.

Leto wondered with dread if perhaps there might be other enclaves of dissent, other groups with similarly charismatic speakers who could manage to tap into the low-level dissatisfaction of the vast worker population.

As he rode up in the lift chamber, Leto looked down and saw the workers below, innocently acting out their roles, carrying out their daily routines. He knew he had to report what he had overheard. But would anyone believe him?

He realized with a tightness in his stomach that he was learning far more about Ix than he had ever meant to know.

Hope can be the greatest weapon of a downtrodden people, or the greatest enemy of those who are about to fail. We must remain aware of its advantages and its limitations.

—LADY HELENA ATREIDES,

her personal journals

After weeks of aimless journeying, the cargo ship dropped out of the orbiting Heighliner and sped down toward the cloud-swirled atmosphere of Caladan.

For Duncan Idaho, the end of his long ordeal seemed at hand.

From his stowaway spot in the cluttered cargo bay, Duncan shifted a heavy box. Its metal corners grated across the deckplates, but he finally got the burden out of the way so he could remove the cover flange on a small windowport. Leaning close to the protective plaz, Duncan stared down at the ocean-rich world. Finally, he began to believe.

Caladan. My new home.

Even from high orbit, Giedi Prime had looked dark and forbidding, like an infected sore. But Caladan, home of the legendary Duke Atreides—mortal enemy of the Harkonnens—seemed like a sapphire sparkling with a blaze of sunlight.

After everything that had happened to him, it still seemed impossible that the surly and treacherous woman Janess Milam had actually been true to her word. She had rescued him for her own petty reasons, her own spiteful revenge, but that did not matter to Duncan. He was *here*.

IT HAD BEEN worse than a nightmare, which he relived in the brooding days as the Heighliner journeyed from system to system in a roundabout way to Caladan:

In the darkness of Forest Guard Station, as he had approached the mysterious flitter 'thopter, the woman had snatched Duncan, gripping tightly before he could defend himself. The young boy had reacted with fear and frantic struggles, but Janess yanked his arm, breaking open the hardened newskin he'd placed over the deep cut in his shoulder.

With surprising strength the dusky-skinned woman hauled him inside the small flitter and sealed the entry hatch. Yowling like a wild animal, Duncan thrashed and clawed, trying to writhe away from her grip. He pounded on the curved hatch, desperate to get out, to run once again into the night filled with armed hunters.

But instead, the flitter's door remained locked. Panting, Janess released the boy, tossed her chocolate hair, and glared at him. "If you don't stop it right now, Idaho, I'm going to dump you in the laps of those Harkonnen hunters."

Turning away from him with disdain, she powered up the flitter's engines. Duncan could feel an ominous hum travel through the small craft, vibrating through the seat and floor. He crouched back against the wall.

"You've already betrayed me to the Harkonnens! You were the one who made those men take my parents and murder them. You're the reason I had to train so hard, and why they're hunting me now. I *know* what you did!"

"Yeah, well, things have changed." She raised a dusky hand in a meaningless gesture, turning toward the piloting controls. "I'm not helping Harkonnens anymore, not after what they did to me."

Indignant, Duncan clenched his fists at his sides. Blood from the reopened wound seeped onto his tattered shirt. "What did they do to *you?*" He couldn't imagine anything that even approached the anguish he and his family had endured.

"You wouldn't understand. You're just a youngster, another one of their pawns." Janess smiled as she raised the flitter up off the ground. "But through you, I can get back at them."

Duncan sneered. "Maybe I'm just a boy, but I spent all night beating the Harkonnens at their hunting game. I watched Rabban kill my mother and father. Who knows what else they've done to my uncles, aunts, and cousins?"

"I doubt there's anyone left alive on Giedi Prime with the name of Idaho—especially after the embarrassment you caused them tonight. Tough luck."

"If they did that, it was a waste of effort," he said, trying to hide the pain. "I didn't know my relatives anyway."

Janess increased the flitter's speed, boosting them low across the dark trees and away from the wilderness preserve. "Right now, I'm helping you get away from the hunters, so just shut up and be glad. You don't have any other options."

She ran the craft without lights, keeping her engines masked, though Duncan couldn't imagine how they could ever escape from prying Harkonnen eyes. He had killed several of the hunters—and worse, he had outwitted and humiliated Rabban.

Duncan allowed himself the slightest satisfied smile. Coming forward, he slumped exhausted into a seat beside Janess, who had strapped herself into the pilot's chair. "Why should I trust you?"

"Did I *ask* you to trust me?" She flashed a dark-eyed glance at him. "Just take advantage of the situation."

"Are you going to tell me anything?"

Janess flew in silence for a long moment, racing over the bunched treetops before she answered. "It's true. Yeah, I reported your parents to the Harkonnens. I'd heard rumors, knew your mother and father had done something to get the officials angry—and the Harkonnens don't like people who make them angry. I was looking out for myself and saw an advantage. By turning them in, I thought I might get a reward. Besides, *your parents* caused the problem themselves in the first place. *They* made the mistakes. I was just trying to cash in on it. Nothing personal. Somebody else would have done it, if I hadn't."

Duncan scowled, clenching his grimy hands. He wished he had the nerve to use his knife on this woman, but that would cause the flitter to crash. She was his only way out. For now.

Her face contorted into an angry grimace. "But what did the

Harkonnens give me in return? A reward, a promotion? No—nothing. A kick in the teeth. Not even a 'thank you very much.'" A troubled look crossed her face, disappearing as quickly as a tiny cloud scudding across the sun. "It's not easy to do something like that, you know. You think I enjoyed it? But on Giedi Prime opportunities arise rarely enough, and I'd watched too many of them pass me by.

"This should have really changed things for me. But when I approached them to ask for the slightest bit of consideration, they threw me out and ordered me not to come back again. It was all for nothing, and that makes it even worse." Her nostrils flared. "Nobody does that to Janess Milam without risking plenty."

"So you're not doing this for me at all," Duncan said. "Not because you feel guilty about what you did and all the pain you caused people. You just want to get even with the Harkonnens."

"Hey, kid, just take your breaks where you can get them."

Duncan rummaged in one of the storage compartments until he found two fruit-rice bars and a sealed bubble of juice. Without asking, he tore into the packets and began stuffing himself. The bars tasted only faintly of cinnamon, a flavor-enhancer to simulate melange.

"You're welcome," Janess said sarcastically.

He didn't reply, chewed loudly.

All night long the flitter soared over the lowlands toward the forbidding city of Barony. For a moment Duncan thought she intended to dump him back into prison, where he would have to go through everything all over again. He slipped his hand into his pocket, felt the handle of his dull knife. But Janess flew the unmarked craft beyond the prison complex and headed south, past a dozen cities and villages.

They had stopped for a day, hiding out during the afternoon, replenishing their supplies at a small way station. Janess provided him with a blue singlesuit, cleaned up his wound as best she could, and crudely administered medical treatment. She tended him with no special care, but merely expressed the hope that he would not draw attention to himself.

At dusk they set off again, heading far south to an independent spaceport. Duncan didn't know the names of the places they visited, nor did he ask. No one had ever taught him geography. Whenever he bothered to venture a question, Janess invariably snapped at him or ignored him entirely.

The spaceport complex carried a flavor of rough mercantile personnel and the Guild rather than the cumbersome Harkonnen style. It was functional and efficient, with endurance emphasized over luxury or eye appeal. Corridors and rooms were large enough for the movement of enclosed tanks holding Guild Navigators.

Janess parked the flitter-thopter where she could easily retrieve it, then set her own hot-wired security systems before leaving the craft behind. "Follow me," she said. With young Duncan in tow, she marched out into the bustle and chaos of the spaceport. "I've made some arrangements. But if you get lost here, I'm not looking for you."

"Why shouldn't I just run? I don't trust you."

"I'm going to put you on a ship that'll take you away from Giedi Prime, far from the Harkonnens." She looked down at him, goading. "Your choice, kid. I don't need any more trouble from you."

Duncan clenched his teeth and followed her without further comment.

Janess tracked down a battered cargo craft swarming with workers who loaded scuffed cases on board. Using suspensor pads, they dragged heavy pallets into the holding bay and stacked them haphazardly.

"Second mate of this ship is an old friend of mine," Janess said. "He owes me a favor."

Duncan did not ask what kind of people a woman like Janess Milam would consider friends . . . or what she had done to earn herself such a favor.

"I'm not going to pay a single solari for your passage, Idaho—your family has already cost my conscience enough, ruined my standing with the Harkonnen overlords, and got me *nothing*. But my friend Renno says you can ride in the hold, just as long as you don't eat anything other than standard rations or cost anyone time or credits."

Duncan watched the spaceport activities around him. He had no real conception of what life would be like on any other world. The cargo ship looked old and unimpressive—but if it provided him with passage away from Giedi Prime, then it was a golden bird from heaven.

Janess took him roughly by his arm and marched him toward the loading ramp. His sore shoulder throbbed. "They're hauling recyclable materials and other salvage, which they'll take to a processing station on Caladan. That's the home of House Atreides . . . archenemies of the Harkonnens. You know about the feud between those Houses?"

When Duncan shook his head, Janess laughed. "Of course not. How would a little dirt rodent like you have learned anything about the Landsraad and the Great Houses?"

She stopped one of the workers guiding a precariously loaded suspensor platform. "Where's Renno? Tell him Janess Milam is here and I want to see him right away." She glanced down at Duncan, who stood up straight and tried to look presentable. "Tell him I brought the package I promised."

Touching a communicator on his lapel, the man mumbled something into it. Then, without acknowledging Janess, he pushed his load up into the squat cargo hauler.

Duncan waited, analyzing the activity around him, while Janess frowned and fidgeted. Before long, a grubby-looking man emerged, his skin smeared with colored lubricants, grime, and oily sweat.

"Renno!" Janess waved to him. "It's about damn time!"

He gave her a tight embrace, followed by a long and wet kiss. Janess broke away as quickly as she could and pointed to Duncan. "There he is. Take him to Caladan." She smiled. "I can't think of a better revenge than to deliver this boy right where they least want him to be—and where they're least likely to find him."

"You play dangerous games, Janess," Renno said.

"I enjoy games." She balled her fist and playfully punched him in the shoulder. "Don't tell anyone."

Renno raised his eyebrows. "What's the point of coming back to this scummy port if you're not here waiting for me? Who'd keep me company in a dark and lonely bunk? Nah, it wouldn't be worth my while to turn you in. But you still owe me."

Before going, Janess knelt and fixed her eyes on young Duncan Idaho. She seemed to be trying for some semblance of compassion. "Look, kid. Here's what I want you to do. When you get to Caladan, step off that ship and insist on seeing Duke Paulus Atreides himself. *Duke Atreides.* Tell him you've come from the Harkonnens, and demand to be taken into service in his household."

Renno's eyebrows shot high on his forehead, and he muttered something unintelligible.

Janess kept her face firm and intent, thinking to play a last cruel joke on the boy she had betrayed. She realized there would be no chance whatsoever that a dirty, nameless street urchin could possibly set foot in the Grand Hall of Castle Caladan—but that wouldn't stop him from trying . . . maybe for years.

She'd already had her victory by stealing the boy from Rabban's hunting party. She had known they were taking Duncan to the Forest Guard Station and so she made a particular effort to find him, to snatch him away and turn him over to the Harkonnens' greatest enemies. Whatever else happened to the boy was now irrelevant to her, but Janess amused herself by imagining all the tribulations Duncan Idaho would undergo before finally giving up.

"Come on," Renno said gruffly, pulling Duncan's arm. "I'll find you a place in the cargo hold, where you can sleep and hide."

Duncan didn't look back at Janess. He wondered if she expected him to say goodbye or thank her for what she'd done, but he refused to do that. She hadn't helped him because she cared, or even out of remorse. No, he wouldn't demean himself, and he could never forgive Janess for her part in destroying his family. Strange woman.

He walked up the ramp, looking straight ahead, not knowing where he was going. Lost and parentless, without any idea of what he would do next, Duncan Idaho headed off. . . .

RENNO GAVE HIM no comfort and little nourishment, but at least he left the boy in peace. What Duncan Idaho needed most in the entire universe was time to recover, a few days to sort out his memories and learn to live with the ones he could not forget.

He slept alone like a rat in the cargo hold of the battered transport, surrounded by scrap metal and recyclables. None of it was soft, but he still slept well enough on the rust-smelling floor, with his back against a cold bulkhead. It was the most peaceful time he'd had in recent memory.

Finally, when the ship descended toward Caladan to deliver its load and dump him alone and friendless on a strange world, Duncan was ready for anything. He had his drive and his energy; nothing would sway him from his chosen quest.

Now he just had to find Duke Paulus Atreides.

History allows us to see the obvious—but unfortunately, not until it is too late.

—PRINCE RAPHAEL CORRINO

When he surveyed Leto's bedraggled black hair, his dust-smeared clothes, and the perspiration streaks down his cheeks, Rhombur actually chuckled. He meant no insult by his response, but seemed incapable of believing the preposterous story Leto had told. He stood back and assessed his friend. "Vermilion hells! Don't you think you're, uh . . . overreacting a bit, Leto?"

Rhombur strode over to one of the broad windows. Alcoves all along the wall of the stocky Prince's room displayed handpicked geological oddities, his delight and pride. Far beyond the amenities of his station as the Earl's son, Rhombur found joy in his collection of minerals, crystals, and gems. He could have purchased more magnificent specimens many times over, but the Prince had personally found each rock in his own explorations of cave floors and small tunnels.

But in all his explorations, Rhombur—indeed, the entire Vernius ruling family—had been blind to the unrest among the workers. Now Leto understood why the Old Duke had insisted that his son learn to read his subjects and know the mood of the populace. "At the heart of it all, lad, we rule at their sufferance," Paulus had told him, "though thankfully most of the population doesn't realize it. If you're a good enough ruler, none of your people will think to question it."

As if embarrassed by Leto's dramatic news and rumpled appearance, the tousle-haired young man peered down at the swirling masses of workers in the production yards below. Everything seemed quiet, business as usual. "Leto, Leto . . ." He pointed a pudgy finger at the apparently content lower classes who labored like dutiful drones. "Suboids can't even decide for themselves what to eat for dinner, much less band together and start a rebellion. That takes too much . . . initiative."

Leto shook his head, still panting. His sweaty hair clung to his forehead. He felt more shaky now that he was safe, sitting slumped in a comfortable self-forming chair in Rhombur's private quarters. When he'd been fleeing for his life, he had reacted on instinct alone. Now, trying to relax, he couldn't keep his pulse from racing. He took a long gulp of sour cidrit juice from a goblet on Rhombur's breakfast tray.

"I'm only reporting what I saw, Rhombur, and I don't *imagine* threats. I've seen enough real ones to know the difference." He leaned forward, his gray eyes flashing at his friend. "I tell you, something's going on. The suboids were talking about overthrowing House Vernius, tearing down what you've built, and taking Ix for themselves. They were preparing for violence."

Rhombur hesitated, as if still waiting to hear the punch line. "Well, I'll tell my father. You can give him your version of the events, and I'm, uh, sure he'll look into the matter."

Leto's shoulders sagged. What if Earl Vernius ignored the problem until it was too late?

Rhombur brushed down his purple tunic and smiled, then scratched his head in perplexity. It seemed to take great stamina for him to address the subject again; he appeared genuinely baffled. "But . . . if you've been down there, Leto, you see that we take care of the suboids. They're given food, shelter, families, jobs. Sure, maybe we take the lion's share of the profits . . . that's the way of things. That's our society. But we don't abuse our workers. What can they possibly complain about?"

"Maybe they see it differently," Leto said. "Physical oppression isn't the only kind of abuse."

Rhombur brightened, then extended his hand. "Come, my friend.

This might just make an interesting twist for our political lectures to-day. We can use it as a hypothetical case."

Leto followed, more saddened than distraught. He was afraid the Ixians would never see this trouble as anything more than an interesting political discussion.

FROM THE TALLEST spire of the Grand Palais, Earl Dominic Vernius ruled an industrial empire hidden from outside view. The big man paced back and forth on the transparent floor of his Orb Office that hung like a magnificent crystal ball from the cavern ceiling.

The office walls and floor were constructed of perfectly bonded Ixian glass with no seams or distortions; he seemed to be walking on air, floating over his domain. At times, Dominic felt like a deity on high, gazing out upon his universe. He ran a callused palm across his smooth, newly shaven head; the skin still tingled there from the invigorating lotions Shando used when she massaged his scalp.

His daughter Kailea sat in a suspensor chair and watched him. He approved of her taking an interest in Ixian business, but today he felt too troubled to spend much time debating with her. He brushed imaginary crumbs off his newly laundered sleeveless tunic, turned about, and circled his quicksilver desk again.

Kailea continued to study him, offering no advice, though his daughter understood the problem they faced.

Dominic didn't expect old "Roody" to roll over and meekly accept the loss of tax revenues caused by the new Ixian Heighliner design. No, the Emperor would find some way to twist a simple business decision into a personal affront, but Dominic had no idea how the retaliation would come, or where it would strike. Elrood had always been unpredictable.

"You just have to stay one step ahead of him," Kailea said. "You're good at that." She thought of the wily way her father had stolen the Emperor's concubine right out from under his nose . . . and how Elrood had never forgotten the fact. The slightest touch of resentment darkened her words. She would rather have grown up on marvelous Kaitain, instead of here, under the ground.

"I can't stay ahead of him if I don't know which direction he's moving," Dominic replied. The Ixian Earl seemed to be floating upside down, with the solid rock ceiling and the spires of the Grand Palais above his head, and only open air beneath his feet.

Kailea straightened the lace on her gown, adjusted the trim, and bent as she studied shipping records and compared manifests again, hoping to determine a better pattern for distributing Ixian technology. Dominic didn't expect her to do better than his experts, but he let her have her fun. Her idea to send out Ixian self-learning fighting meks to a few black market dealers had been a stroke of genius.

He paused a moment for a wistful smile that made his long mustache sink into the seams around his mouth. His daughter was stunningly beautiful, a work of art in every way, made to be an ornament in some great lord's household . . . but she was sharp-witted, too. Kailea was a strange mixture, all right: fascinated by court games and styles and everything to do with the grandeur of Kaitain, but also doggedly determined to comprehend the workings of House Vernius. Even at her age, she understood that behind-the-scenes business complexities were a woman's real key to power in the Imperium—unless she joined the Bene Gesserit.

Dominic didn't think his daughter understood Shando's decision to leave the Imperial Court and come with him to Ix. Why would the lover of the most powerful man in the universe leave all that splendor to marry a weather-beaten war hero who lived in a city underground? At times, Dominic wondered the same thing, but his love for Shando knew no bounds, and his wife often told him she had never regretted her decision.

Kailea offered a stark contrast with her mother in all but appearance. The young woman couldn't possibly be comfortable in her extravagant clothes and finery, yet she wore her best at all times, as if afraid she might miss an opportunity. Perhaps she resented the lost chances in her life, and would rather be warded off to a sponsor in the Imperial Palace. He'd noticed that she toyed with the affections of the twin sons of Ambassador Pilru, as if marriage to one of them might tie her to the embassy on Kaitain. But C'tair and D'murr Pilru were scheduled to test for positions in the Spacing Guild, and if they passed the examination they would be off-planet within a week. At any rate,

Dominic was sure he could arrange a much more profitable match for his only female child.

Perhaps even to Leto Atreides . . .

A comeye blinked yellow on the wall, interrupting his thoughts. An important message, an update of the troubling rumors that had spread like poison through a cistern.

"Yes?" he said. Without being asked, Kailea walked across the invisible floor and stood next to him to read the report as it imaged itself on the quicksilver surface of his desk. Her emerald eyes narrowed as she read the words.

The smell of his daughter's faint perfume and the glitter of combs in her dark bronze hair brought a paternal smile to his face. Such a young *lady*. Such a young businesswoman.

"Are you sure you want to concern yourself with this, child?" he asked, wishing to shelter her from the grim news. Labor relations were so much more complex than technological innovations. Kailea just looked at him in annoyance that he would even ask the question.

He read more details on what he had been told earlier in the day, though he still couldn't quite believe everything Leto Atreides claimed he'd heard and seen. A disturbance was brewing in the deep-ground manufacturing facilities, where the suboid workers had begun complaining—an unprecedented situation.

Kailea took a deep breath, marshaling her thoughts. "If the suboids have such grievances, why haven't they elected a spokesman? Why haven't they delivered any formal demands?"

"Oh, they're just grumbling, child. They claim they're being forced to assemble machines in violation of the Butlerian Jihad, and they don't want to perform 'blasphemous labor.' "

The message screen went dark after they finished reading the summary report, and Kailea stood up, hands on her hips. Her skirts rustled as she huffed. "Wherever do they get such ridiculous ideas? How can they even begin to understand the nuances and complexities of running these operations? They were bred and trained in Ixian facilities—who put those thoughts in their minds?"

Dominic shook his gleaming head, and realized his daughter had raised a very good question. "You're right. Suboids certainly couldn't come up with such extrapolations on their own."

Kailea continued to be indignant. "Don't they realize how much we give them? How much we provide, and how much it costs? I've looked at the costs and benefits. The suboids don't know how good they have it compared to workers on other planets." She shook her head, and her curved mouth bent downward in a frown. She looked through the floor at her feet, to the manufactories in the cavern far below. "Maybe they should visit Giedi Prime—or Arrakis. Then they wouldn't complain about Ix."

But Dominic wouldn't let go of her first thread of conversation. "Suboids are bred for limited intelligence, only enough to perform assigned tasks . . . and they're supposed to do it without complaining. It's part of their mental makeup." He joined his daughter in staring down at the floor of the grotto, which swarmed with Heighliner construction workers. "Could our bio-designers have overlooked something important? Do the suboids have a point? The definition of machine-minds encompasses a broad range, but there might be gray areas. . . ."

Kailea shook her head and tapped her crystal pad. "Our Mentats and legal advisors are meticulous about the precise strictures of the Jihad, and our quality-control methods are effective. We're on solid ground, and they can prove every assertion we make."

Dominic chewed his lower lip. "The suboids couldn't possibly have specifics, since there aren't any violations. At least we haven't *knowingly* stepped over the line, not in any instance."

Kailea studied her father, then looked down at the bustling work area again. "Maybe you should have Captain Zhaz and a team of inspectors turn over every stone, investigate every aspect of our design and manufacturing processes. Prove to the suboids that their complaints are groundless."

Dominic considered the idea. "Of course I don't want to be too hard on the workers. I want no crackdowns, and certainly no revolts. The suboids are to be treated well, as always." He met her gaze, and she seemed very much an adult.

"Yes," Kailea said, her voice hardening. "They work better that way."

*Like the knowledge of your own being, the sietch forms a firm base
from which you move out into the world and into the universe.*

—Fremen Teaching

Pardot Kynes was so fascinated by the Fremen culture,
religion, and daily routine that he remained completely oblivious to the life-and-death debate raging around
him in the sietch. Naib Heinar had told him he could talk
to the people and describe his ideas—and so he talked, at
every opportunity.

For an entire cycle of the moons, the Fremen whispered
their opinions in small caves and dens, or shouted them
across tables in private meetings of the sietch elders. Some
of them even empathized with what the strange outworlder
was saying.

Though his fate remained undecided, Kynes didn't slow
for a moment. Sietch guides took him around and showed
him many things they thought would interest him, but the
Planetologist also stopped to ask questions of women working in the stillsuit factories, of old men tending water supplies, and of withered grandmothers operating solar ovens
or filing rough burrs off scrap metal.

The bustling activity around the sealed caves astonished
him: Some workers trampled spice residue to extract fuel,
others curded spice for fermentation. Weavers at power

looms used their own hair, the long fur of mutated rats, wisps of desert cotton, and even skin strips from wild creatures to make their durable fabric. And of course schools taught the young Fremen desert skills, as well as ruthless combat techniques.

One morning Kynes awoke refreshed, perfectly comfortable after spending the night on a mat on the hard floor. Throughout much of his life, he had slept in the open on rough ground. His body could find rest just about anywhere. He breakfasted on dehydrated fruits and dry cakes the Fremen women had baked in thermal ovens. The beginnings of a beard covered his face, a sandy stubble.

A young woman named Frieth brought him a serving tray with meticulously prepared spice coffee in an ornate pot. During the entire ritual, she directed her deep blue eyes downward, as she had done every morning since Kynes's arrival at the sietch. He hadn't thought anything of her cool, efficient attentions until someone had whispered to him, "She is the unmarried sister of Stilgar, whose life you saved against the Harkonnen dogs."

Frieth had fine features and smooth, tanned skin. Her hair appeared long enough to flow to her waist, if ever she undid it from her water rings and let it fall. Her manner was quiet but all-knowing, in the Fremen way; she rushed to fulfill every small wish Kynes bothered to express, often without his realizing it. He might have noticed how beautiful she was, had he not been so intent on noticing everything else around him.

After he had sipped his pungent, cardamom-laced coffee down to the dregs, Kynes hauled out his electronic pad to jot down notes and ideas. At a noise, he looked up to see wiry young Turok standing in the doorway. "I'm to take you anywhere you wish, Planetologist, so long as you remain within Red Wall Sietch."

Kynes nodded and smiled, disregarding the constraints of being a captive. They did not rankle him. It was understood that he would never leave the sietch alive unless the Fremen accepted him and decided to trust him completely. If he did join the community, there could be no secrets between them; on the other hand, if the Fremen chose to execute him in the end, there would have been no point in keeping secrets from a dead man.

Previously Kynes had seen the tunnels, the food-storage chambers, the guarded water supplies, even the *Huanui* deathstills. In fascination he had watched the family groups of desert-hardened men, each with his several wives; he had seen them pray to Shai-Hulud. He'd begun to compile a mental sketch of this culture and the political and familial ties within the sietch, but it would take decades to unravel all the subtle relationships, all the nuances of obligations laid down upon their kinsmen many generations earlier.

"I'd like to go to the top of the rock," he said, remembering his duties as Imperial Planetologist. "If we could retrieve some of the equipment from my groundcar—I presume you've kept it safe?—I'd like to establish a weather station here. It's imperative that we collect climate data—temperature variations, atmospheric humidity, and wind patterns—from as many isolated spots as possible."

Turok looked at him, surprised and disbelieving. Then he shrugged. "As you wish, Planetologist." Knowing the conservative ways of the sietch elders, Turok was pessimistic about the fate of this enthusiastic but not terribly bright man. What a futile effort it would be for Kynes to continue his vigorous work. But if it kept him happy in his last days . . .

"Come," Turok said. "Put on your stillsuit."

"Oh, we'll only be out for a few minutes."

Turok scowled at him, looking stern and much older. "A breath of moisture is water wasted into the air. We are not so rich we can afford to waste water."

Shrugging, Kynes pulled on his crinkling, slick-surfaced uniform and took the time to attach all the seals, though he did so clumsily. Heaving a heavy sigh, Turok assisted him, explaining the most effective way to dress out the suit and adjust the fittings to optimize its efficiency.

"You have bought a decent stillsuit. It is of Fremen manufacture," the young man observed. "In this at least you have chosen well."

Kynes followed Turok to the storage chamber where his groundcar had been kept. The Fremen had stripped it of amenities, and his equipment lay in open boxes on the cave floor, inspected and cataloged. No doubt the sietch inhabitants had been trying to determine how they could put these things to use.

They're still planning to kill me, Kynes thought. *Haven't they heard a thing I've said?* Oddly, the thought neither depressed nor frightened him. He simply took the knowledge as a challenge. He was not about to give up—there was too much left to do. He would have to make them understand.

Among the clutter he found his weather apparatus and tucked the components under his arms, but made no comment about what had been done to his possessions. He knew Fremen had a communal mentality: Every item owned by an individual was owned by the entire community. Since he had spent so much of his life alone, relying only on himself and his abilities, he found it difficult to absorb such a mind-set.

Turok did not offer to carry any of the equipment, but led the way up steep steps that had been rough-hewn into the stone wall. Kynes panted but did not complain. Ahead of him the guide shifted aside numerous barricades, moisture baffles, and doorseals. Turok flashed glances over his shoulder to make sure the Planetologist was keeping up, then increased his speed.

Finally they emerged from a cleft atop the rubble-strewn peaks. The young Fremen leaned back in the shadow of the rocks, keeping himself cool, while Kynes stepped out into open sunlight. All around them the stone was coppery brown with a few discolorations of lichen. *A good sign*, he thought. The advance footprints of biological systems.

As he stared out at the sweeping vista of the Great Basin, he saw dunes that were the grayish white and brown of newly decomposed rock grains, as well as the buttery yellow of older, oxidized sand.

From the sandworms he'd seen, as well as the teeming sand plankton in the spice-rich sands, Kynes knew that Dune already had the basis for a complex ecosystem. He was certain it would take only a few crucial nudges in the proper direction to make this dormant place blossom.

The Fremen people could do it.

"Imperial man," said Turok, stepping forward from the shade, "what is it you see when you stare out onto the desert like that?"

Kynes answered without looking at him. "I see limitless possibilities."

IN A SEALED chamber deep in the sietch, wizened Heinar sat at the head of a stone table, glaring with his single eye. Trying to remain apart from the debate, the sietch Naib watched the council elders shout at each other.

"We know the man's loyalty," said one old man, Jerath. "He works for the Imperium. You've seen his dossier. He's on Dune as a guest of the Harkonnens." Jerath had a silver ring in his left earlobe, a treasure taken from a smuggler he'd killed in a duel.

"That means nothing," said another elder, Aliid. "As Fremen, do *we* not don other clothes, other masks, and pretend to fit in? It's a means of survival when circumstances require it. You, of all people, should know not to judge someone solely on appearances."

Garnah, a weary-looking long-haired elder, rested his pointed chin on his knuckles. "I'm most incensed at those three young idiots, what they did after the Planetologist helped them defeat the Harkonnen bravos. Any straight-thinking adult would have shrugged and sent the man's shade to join those of the six dead vermin on the ground . . . with some regret, of course, but still it should have been done." He sighed. "These are inexperienced youths, poorly trained. They should never had been left alone in the desert."

Heinar flared his nostrils. "You cannot fault their thinking, Garnah. There was the moral obligation—Pardot Kynes had saved their lives. Even brash young men such as those three realized the water burden that had been placed on them."

"But what of their obligations to Red Wall Sietch and our people?" long-haired Garnah insisted. "Does a debt owed to a mere Imperial servant outweigh their loyalty to *us*?"

"The question isn't about the boys," Aliid interrupted. "Ommun, Turok, and Stilgar did what they thought was best. We are now left to decide about this Planetologist and his fate."

"He's a madman," the first elder, Jerath, said. "Have you heard him talk? He wants trees, open water, irrigation, crops—he envisions a verdant planet instead of desert." A snort, then a toying with the ring in his ear. "He's mad, I say."

Puckering his mouth skeptically, Aliid pointed out, "After the thousands of years of wandering that finally brought us here and made our people what we are—how can you scorn one man's dream of paradise?"

Jerath frowned, but accepted the point.

"Perhaps Kynes *is* mad," Garnah said, "but just mad enough to be holy. Perhaps he's mad enough to hear the words of God in a way that we cannot."

"*That* is a question we cannot decide among us," Heinar said, finally using a Naib's voice of command to focus the discussion back on the matter at hand. "The choice we face is not about the word of God, but about the survival of our sietch. Pardot Kynes has seen our ways, lived in our hidden home. By Imperial command, he sends reports back to Kaitain whenever he finds himself in a city. Think of the risk to us."

"But what of all his talk about paradise on Dune?" Aliid asked, still trying to defend the stranger. "Open water, dunes anchored by grass, palmaries filled with tall date palms, open qanats flowing across the desert."

"Crazy talk and no more," grumbled Jerath. "The man knows too much—about us, about the Fremen, about Dune. He cannot be allowed to hold such secrets."

Doggedly, Aliid tried again. "But he killed Harkonnens. Doesn't that place upon us, and our sietch, a water debt? He saved three members of our tribe."

"Since when do we owe the Imperium anything?" Jerath asked with another tug on his earring.

"Anyone can kill Harkonnens," Garnah added with a shrug, shifting his pointed chin to his other fist. "I've done it myself."

Heinar leaned forward. "All right, Aliid—what of this talk about the flowering of Dune? Where is the water for all this? Is there any possibility the Planetologist can do what he says?"

"Haven't you heard him?" Garnah replied in a mocking tone. "He says the water is here, far more than the miserable amounts we collect for our sustenance."

Jerath raised his eyebrows and snorted. "Oh? This man has been on our world for a Standard Month or two, and already he knows where to find the precious treasure that no Fremen has discovered in generations upon generations of living in the desert? An oasis on the equator perhaps? Hah!"

"He did save three of our own," Aliid persisted.

"Three fools put themselves in the way of the Harkonnen fist. I feel no obligation to him for their rescue. *And* he has seen crysknives. You know our law: Who sees that knife must be cleansed or slain. . . . " Garnah's voice trailed off.

"It is as you say," Aliid admitted.

"Kynes is known to travel alone and explore many inhospitable areas," Heinar said with a shrug. "If he disappears, he disappears. No Harkonnen or Imperium officials will ever be the wiser."

"It will no doubt be interpreted as a simple accident. Our world is not a comfortable place," said Garnah.

Jerath simply smiled. "If the truth is told, the Harkonnens may be perfectly happy to get rid of this meddlesome man anyway. There is no risk to us if we kill him."

Silence hung in the dusty air for a moment. "What must be, must be," Heinar said, rising to his feet at the head of the table. "All of us know this. There can be no other answer, no changing of our minds. We must protect the sietch above all, no matter the cost, no matter the burden it places on our hearts."

He crossed his arms over his chest. "It is decided. Kynes must die."

Two hundred thirty-eight planets searched, many of only marginal habitability. (See star charts attached in separate file.) Resource surveys list valuable raw materials. Many of these planets deserve a second look, either for mineral exploitation or possible colonization. As in previous reports, however, no spice found.

—Independent scout survey, third expedition, delivered to EMPEROR FONDIL CORRINO III

Hasimir Fenring had bribed old Elrood's guards and retainers, setting up what he called "a surprise secret meeting with an important, though unexpected, representative." The weasel-faced man had used his silken tongue and his iron will to manipulate the Emperor's schedules to leave an opening. As a fixture around the Palace for more than three decades, Fenring, by virtue of his association with Crown Prince Shaddam, was a man of influence. With various methods of persuasion, he convinced everyone he needed to convince.

Old Elrood suspected nothing.

At the appointed hour of the Tleilaxu delegate's arrival, Fenring made certain he and Shaddam were present in the audience chamber—ostensibly as eager students of the bureaucracy, intent on becoming viable leaders of the Imperium. Elrood, who liked to think he was instructing these protégés in important matters of state, had no idea the two young men laughed at him behind his back.

Fenring leaned close to the Crown Prince and whispered in his ear, "This is going to be most entertaining, hm-m-m-m-ah?"

"Watch, and learn," Shaddam said ponderously, then raised his chin in the air and snickered.

The huge embossed doors swung open, sparkling with soostones and rain crystals, etched with ghlavan metal. Sardaukar guards, standing stiff and formal in their gray-and-black uniforms, snapped to attention for the new arrival.

"Now the show begins," Fenring said. He and Shaddam kept further chuckles to themselves.

Liveried house pages stepped forward to introduce the off-world visitor in a rippling overtone of processed, electronically translated pomp. "My Lord Emperor, Highness of a Million Worlds—the Master Hidar Fen Ajidica, representative of the Bene Tleilax, is here at your request for a private meeting."

A gnomelike man with grayish skin walked proudly into the hall flanked by pasty-faced guards and his own retainers. His slippered feet scuttled like whispered gossip across the polished stones of the floor.

A ripple of surprise and distaste passed through the attendees at court. Chamberlain Aken Hesban, his mustaches drooping, stood indignantly behind the throne and glared at the Emperor's scheduling advisors as if this were some sort of trick.

Elrood IX lurched forward in his massive throne and demanded to see his calendar.

Thus caught off guard, the old reprobate might just be surprised enough to listen, Fenring thought. With surprising astuteness, Chamberlain Hesban's eagle gaze fell on him, but Fenring returned the look with only a bland, curious expression.

Ajidica, the Tleilaxu representative, waited patiently, letting the chatter and whispers flow around him. He had a narrow face, long nose, and a pointed black beard that protruded like a trowel from his cleft chin. Maroon robes gave Ajidica an air of some importance. His skin was weathered-looking, and pale and discolored blotches marked his hands, especially on the fingers and palms, as if frequent exposure to harsh chemicals had neutralized the melanin. Despite his diminutive stature, the Tleilaxu Master came forward as if he had a perfect right to be in the Imperial audience chamber of Kaitain.

From the side of the room Shaddam studied Ajidica, and his nose wrinkled, from the lingering food odors that were so characteristic of the Tleilaxu.

"May the one true God shine his light upon you from all the stars in the Imperium, my Lord Emperor," said Hidar Fen Ajidica, placing his palms together and bowing as he quoted from the Orange Catholic Bible. He stopped in front of the massive Hagal-quartz throne.

The Tleilaxu were notorious for handling the dead and harvesting corpses for cellular resources, yet they were unquestionably brilliant geneticists. One of their first creations had been a remarkable new food source, the slig ("sweetest meat this side of heaven"), a cross between a giant slug and a Terran pig. The overall populace still thought of sligs as tank-bred mutations, however—ugly creatures who excreted slimy, foul-smelling residue, and whose multiple mouths ground incessantly on garbage. This was the context in which people thought of the Bene Tleilax, even as they savored marinated slig medallions in sauces prepared from rich Caladan wines.

Elrood drew back his bony shoulders into a firm line. He frowned down at the visitor. "What is . . . *this* doing here? Who let this man in?" The old Emperor looked around the echoing room, his eyes flashing bright. "No Tleilaxu Master has ever entered my Court for a private audience. How do I know he's not a Face Dancer mimic?" Elrood glared down at his personal secretary, then over at his Chamberlain. "And since he got on my schedule at all, how do I know *you're* not a Face Dancer yourself? This is outrageous."

The personal secretary stepped back, appalled at the suggestion. Diminutive Ajidica looked up at the Emperor, calmly letting the resentment and prejudice wash past without being affected by it. "My Lord Elrood, tests can be performed to prove that none of our shapeshifters has subsumed the identity of anyone in your Court. I assure you, I am no Face Dancer. Neither am I an assassin, nor a Mentat."

"And why are you here?" Elrood demanded.

"As one of the premier scientists of the Bene Tleilax, my presence here was requested." The gnomish man hadn't moved a centimeter, and remained at the foot of the Golden Lion Throne, unflappable in his maroon robes. "I have developed an ambitious plan that can benefit the Imperial family, as well as my own people."

"Not interested," the Padishah Emperor said. He flicked a glance at his Sardaukar, began to raise his gnarled hand to issue a command of forceful dismissal. The Court attendees watched, amused and eager.

Hasimir Fenring rapidly stepped forward, knowing he had only an instant to intercede. "Emperor Elrood, may I speak?" He didn't wait for permission, but tried to appear innocent and interested. "The sheer audacity of this Tleilaxu's arrival has me curious. I find myself wondering what he has to say." He glanced over at the emotion-masked face of Hidar Fen Ajidica; the gray-skinned Master seemed impervious to any harsh treatment foisted upon him. Nothing in his demeanor betrayed his connection with Fenring, who had suggested the synthetic spice idea to *him*—an idea that had quickly found support among Tleilaxu scientists.

Crown Prince Shaddam took the lead and looked up at his father with a guileless, anticipatory expression. "Father, you have instructed me to learn everything I can from the example of your leadership. It would be most educational for me to observe how you handle this situation with an open mind and a firm hand."

Elrood raised a ring-adorned hand that trembled with faint, uncontrollable spasms. "Very well, we will hear briefly what this Tleilaxu has to say. *Briefly*, under pain of severe punishment if we determine he has wasted our precious time. Watch, and learn." The Emperor slid a sidelong glance at Shaddam, then took a sip of the spice beer at his side. "This shouldn't take much time."

How true, Father. You don't have much time left, Shaddam thought, still smiling attentively and innocently.

"My words require privacy, my Lord Emperor," Ajidica said, "and the utmost discretion."

"I will determine that," Elrood snapped. "Speak of your plan."

The Tleilaxu Master folded his hands in the voluminous sleeves of his maroon robes. "Rumors are like a disease epidemic, Sire. Once they escape, they spread from person to person, often with deadly effect. Better to take simple initial precautions than be forced into eradication measures at a later date." Ajidica fell silent, standing rigid, and refused to speak further until the audience chamber had been emptied.

Impatiently, the Emperor gestured to dismiss all the functionaries, pages, ambassadors, jesters, and guards. Sardaukar security men stationed themselves at the doorways, where they could protect the throne, but everyone else departed, muttering and shuffling. Humming privacy screens were erected to prevent any potential eavesdroppers from listening in.

Fenring and Shaddam sat at the foot of the throne, pretending to be intent students, though they were both in their thirties. Looking frail and battling illness, the old Emperor indicated for them to remain as observers, and the Tleilaxu man did not object.

In all this time, Ajidica's hard gaze never strayed from Elrood. The Emperor looked back at the little man, feigning boredom. Finally satisfied with the privacy precautions, and ignoring the Emperor's distaste for him and his race, Hidar Fen Ajidica spoke.

"We Bene Tleilax have continued experiments in all areas of genetics, organic chemistry, and mutations. In our factories we have recently developed highly unorthodox techniques to synthesize, shall we say, *unusual* substances." His words were clipped and efficient, providing no more detail than necessary. "Our initial results indicate that a synthetic could be fashioned that, in all important chemical properties, is identical to melange."

"Spice?" Elrood now gave the Tleilaxu his full attention. Shaddam noticed a twitching tic in his father's right cheek below his eye. "Created in a laboratory? Impossible!"

"Not impossible, my Lord. Given the proper time and conditions for development, this artificially created spice could become an inexhaustible supply, mass-produced and inexpensive—and it could be earmarked exclusively for House Corrino, if you wish."

Elrood leaned forward like a mummified carrion bird. "Such a thing has never been possible before."

"Our analysis shows that the spice is an organically based substance. Through careful experimentation and development, we believe our axlotl tanks can be modified to produce melange."

"The same way you grow gholas from dead human cells?" the Emperor said, scowling with revulsion. "And clones?"

Intrigued and surprised, Shaddam glanced over at Fenring. *Axlotl tanks?*

Ajidica continued to focus on Elrood. "In . . . effect, my Lord."

"Why come to me?" Elrood asked. "I should think the diabolical Tleilaxu would create a spice substitute for themselves and leave the Imperium at their mercy."

"The Bene Tleilax are not a mighty race, Sire. If we discovered how to produce our own melange, and kept the secret for ourselves, we know it would bring down the wrath of the Imperium. You yourself would send in Sardaukar, tear the secret from our grasp, and destroy us.

The Spacing Guild and CHOAM would be happy to assist you—and the Harkonnens, too, would defend their spice monopoly at all costs." Ajidica gave a thin, humorless smile.

"It's good to see that you understand your subordinate position," Elrood said, resting his bony elbow on the arm of the heavy throne. "Not even the wealthiest Great House has ever developed a military force to oppose my Sardaukar."

"Thus, we have prudently decided to ingratiate ourselves with the most powerful presence in the galaxy—the Imperial House. In that way we can reap the greatest benefit from our new research."

Elrood placed a long finger on his papery lips, considering. These Tleilaxu were clever, and if they could manufacture the substance exclusively for House Corrino, *and cost-effectively*, the Emperor would have a powerful bargaining chip.

The economic difference could be huge. House Harkonnen could be driven into the ground, bankrupted. Arrakis would become of little value, with the product there comparatively expensive to get out of the sand.

If this gnome could do as he suggested, the Landsraad, CHOAM, the Spacing Guild, the Mentats, and the Bene Gesserit would be forced to seek favors from *the Emperor* in order to get their supplies. Most of the important scions of noble families were already addicted to melange, and Elrood himself could become their supplier. Excitement blossomed within him.

Ajidica interrupted Elrood's train of thought. "Let me emphasize that this will be no simple task, Sire. The precise chemical structure of melange is extraordinarily difficult to analyze, and we must separate out which components are necessary for the substance to be effective, and which are irrelevant. In order to achieve this goal, the Tleilaxu will require enormous resources, as well as the freedom and time to pursue our avenues of research."

Fenring shifted on the polished steps and, while looking up at the old Emperor, interjected: "My Lord, I see now that Master Ajidica was right in seeking privacy for this audience. Such an undertaking must be carried out entirely in secret if House Corrino is to have an exclusive source. Ah, certain powers in the Imperium would do anything to prevent you from creating an independent and inexpensive supply of spice, hm-m-m-m?"

Fenring could see that the old man recognized the enormous political and economic advantages Ajidica's proposal could bring him—even in light of everyone's instinctive loathing for the Tleilaxu. He sensed the balance shifting, the senile Emperor coming to exactly the conclusion Fenring wished. *Yes, the ancient creature can still be manipulated.*

Elrood himself saw many forces hanging in the balance. Since the Harkonnens were ambitious and intractable, he would have preferred to place another Great House in charge of Arrakis, but the Baron would remain in power for decades yet. For political reasons, the Emperor had been forced to grant this valuable quasi-fief to House Harkonnen after ousting Richese, and the new fief holders had dug themselves in. Too much so. Even the debacle of Abulurd's governorship (he'd been installed in his position at the request of his father Dmitri Harkonnen) had not brought the desired result. The effect had been the exact opposite, in fact, once the Baron had maneuvered himself into a position of power.

But what to do with Arrakis afterward? Elrood thought. *I would want total control of it as well. Without its monopoly on spice, the place might come cheap. At the right price, it could prove useful for something else . . . an incredibly harsh military training area, perhaps?*

"You were correct in bringing your ideas to our attention, Hidar Fen Ajidica." Elrood clasped his hands on his lap, clinking gold rings together, refusing to apologize for his earlier rudeness. "Please give us a detailed summary of your needs."

"Yes, my Lord Emperor." Ajidica bowed again, keeping his hands folded in his billowing maroon sleeves. "Most importantly, my people will need equipment and resources . . . a place in which to do our research. I will be in charge of this program myself, but the Bene Tleilax require an appropriate technological base and industrial facilities. Preferably ones that are already functional—and well defended."

Elrood pondered the question. Surely, among all the worlds in the Imperium, there must be someplace, a high-tech world with industrial capabilities. . . .

Puzzle pieces snicked into place, and he saw it: a way to obliterate his old rival House Vernius—payback for Dominic's effrontery involving the royal concubine Shando, and for the new Heighliner design that threatened to wreak havoc on Imperial profit systems. *Oh, this will be magnificent!*

Sitting on the steps to the crystal pedestal of the throne, Hasimir Fenring did not understand why the Emperor smiled with such smug satisfaction. The silence drew out for a long moment. He wondered if it might have something to do with the mind-eating effects of the slow chaumurky. The old man would soon become increasingly irrational and paranoid. And after that he would die. *Horribly, I hope.*

But before then, all the proper wheels would have been set in motion.

"Yes, Hidar Fen Ajidica. We do have the place for your efforts, I believe," Elrood said. "A perfect place."

Dominic must not know until it is too late, the Emperor thought. *And then he must know who did it to him. Right before he dies.*

The timing, as in so many matters of the Imperium, had to be precise.

The Spacing Guild has worked for centuries to surround our elite Navigators with mystique. They are revered, from the lowest Pilot to the most talented Steersman. They live in tanks of spice gas, see all paths through space and time, guide ships to the far reaches of the Imperium. But no one knows the human cost of becoming a Navigator. We must keep this a secret, for if they really knew the truth, they would pity us.

—Spacing Guild Training Manual
Handbook for Steersmen (Classified)

The austere Guild Embassy Building contrasted severely with the rest of Ixian grandeur in the stalactite city. The structure was drab, utilitarian, and gray among the sparkling and ornate cavern towers. The Spacing Guild had priorities beyond ornamentation or ostentation.

Today C'tair and D'murr Pilru would be tested, in hopes of becoming Guild Navigators. C'tair didn't know whether to be excited or terrified.

As the twin brothers marched shoulder to shoulder across a shielded crystal walkway from the Grand Palais, C'tair found the Embassy Building so aesthetically repulsive that he considered turning around and leaving. In the face of the Guild's enormous wealth, the lack of splendor seemed odd, to the point of making him ill at ease.

As if thinking the same thing but coming to a different conclusion, his brother looked at C'tair and said, "Once the wonders of space are opened up to a Guild Navigator's mind, what other decorations are necessary? How can any ornamentation rival the wonders a Navigator sees on a single journey through foldspace? The universe, brother! The whole universe."

C'tair nodded, conceding the point. "All right, we'll both have to use different criteria from now on. 'Think outside the box'—remember what old Davee Rogo used to tell us? Things are going to be so . . . changed."

If he passed these examinations, he would have to be up to the challenge, though he had no real desire to leave the beautiful cavern city of Vernii. His mother S'tina was an important Guild banker, his father a respected ambassador, and—with help from Earl Vernius himself—they had arranged to give the twins this remarkable chance. He would make Ix proud of him. Maybe someone would erect a sculpture in his honor someday, or name a side grotto after him and his brother. . . .

While their father attended to diplomatic duties with the Emperor and a thousand functionaries on Kaitain, his twin sons remained in the underground city, grooming and preparing themselves for "bigger things." Over the years of their subterranean childhood, C'tair and his brother had come to the Guild facility many times to see their mother. Always before, they had been guests in the building, but this time the twins were going for a much more rigorous ordeal.

C'tair's future would be determined in a few hours. Bankers, auditors, and commerce specialists were all humans, bureaucrats. But a *Navigator* was so much more.

No matter how much he tried to shore up his confidence, C'tair wasn't certain he would pass the mind-twisting tests anyway. Who was he to think he could become one of the elite Guild Navigators? His high-ranking parents had only given the twins an *opportunity* to be *considered*, not a guarantee. Could he make the cut? Was he really that special? He ran a hand through his dark hair, found sweat on his fingertips.

"If you perform well enough on the test, you'll both become important representatives of the Spacing Guild," his mother had said, smiling with a severe pride. "Very important." C'tair felt a lump grow in his throat, and D'murr drew himself taller.

Kailea Vernius, Princess of the household of Ix, had also wished the two of them well. C'tair suspected the Earl's daughter was leading them on, but he and his brother both enjoyed flirting with her. Occasionally, they even pretended to be jealous when Kailea referred in passing to young Leto, heir to House Atreides. She played the twins against each other, and he and D'murr engaged in a good-natured rivalry for her affections. Still, he doubted their families would ever agree to a match, so it was unlikely that there could be any future in it.

If C'tair joined the Guild, his duties would take him far from Ix and the underground metropolis he loved so well. If he became a Navigator, so many things would change. . . .

They arrived in front of the embassy reception chamber, half an hour early. D'murr paced beside his anxious brother, who was entranced and noncommunicative, as if completely focused on his thoughts and desires. Though the two young men looked identical, D'murr seemed so much stronger, so much more dedicated to the challenge, and C'tair struggled to emulate him.

Now, in the waiting area, he swallowed hard, repeating the words he and his brother had shared, like a mantra, in their quarters that morning. *I want to be a Navigator. I want to join the Guild. I want to leave Ix and sail the starlanes, my mind joined to the universe.*

At seventeen, they both felt rather young to endure such a grueling selection process, one that would lock them permanently on a life-path, no matter what they might decide later on. But the Guild wanted resilient and malleable minds inside bodies that had sufficiently matured. Navigators who trained at young ages often proved to be the best performers, some even reaching the highest rank of Steersman. Those candidates taken *too* early, however, could mutate into ghastly shapes fit only for menial tasks; the worst failures were euthanized.

"Are you ready, brother?" D'murr asked. C'tair drew strength and enthusiasm from his twin's confidence.

"Absolutely," he said. "We're going to be Navigators after today, you and I."

Fighting misgivings, C'tair reassured himself that he wanted this; it would be a great credit to his abilities, an honor for his family . . . but he could not remove the spectre of doubt that nagged at him. In his heart he didn't want to leave Ix. His father, the Ambassador, had instilled in both of his sons a deep appreciation for the underground engineering marvels, the innovations, and the technological acumen of this planet. Ix was like no other world in the Imperium.

And, of course, if he left, Kailea would be forever lost to him as well.

When they were summoned forward deeper into the labyrinth of the embassy, the twins walked through the portal, side by side, feeling very alone. They had no escorts, no one to cheer them to victory or console them if they failed. Their father wasn't even present to offer his support; the Ambassador had recently been sent to Kaitain in preparation for another Landsraad subcommittee meeting.

That morning, as the ominous hour ticked closer and closer, C'tair and D'murr had sat at the breakfast table in the ambassadorial residence, picking over a selection of colored pastries while S'tina played a message their father had holo-recorded for them. They'd had little appetite, but they listened to Cammar Pilru's words. C'tair tried to hear some special hints or knowledge, anything he could use. But the Ambassador's shimmering image merely gave them encouragement and platitudes, like echoes of a well-worn speech he had used many times in his diplomatic duties.

Then, after a final hug, their mother had stared at each of them before she hurried off to her daily duties at Guild Bank headquarters, a section of the drab building that now hung before them. S'tina had wanted to be at her sons' side during the testing, but the Guild had forbidden it. Navigator testing was an intensely private and personal matter. Each of them had to do it by himself, relying on his abilities alone. So their mother would be in her office, probably distracted, probably worried for them.

As S'tina said goodbye, she did manage to hide most of the horror and despair on her face. C'tair had noticed the flicker, but D'murr had not. He wondered what his mother had hidden from them during their preparations for the test. *Doesn't she want us to succeed?*

Navigators were the stuff of legends, shrouded in secrecy and Guild-fostered superstitions. C'tair had heard whispered rumors about bodily distortions, the damage that intense and constant immersion in spice could wreak upon a human physique. No outsider had ever seen a Navigator, so how were those people to know what kind of changes might surge through the body of someone with such phenomenal mental abilities? He and his brother had laughed at the silly speculations, convincing each other how outrageous such ideas could be.

But are they so outrageous? What does Mother fear?

"C'tair—keep focused! You look upset," D'murr said.

C'tair's tone overflowed with sarcasm. "Upset? Absolutely. I wonder why! We are about to take the biggest test of our lives, and no one knows how to study for it. I'm worried we haven't prepared enough."

D'murr looked at him with intense concern, gripping his brother's arm. "Your nervousness may be your failing, brother. A Navigator test isn't about studying. It's about natural ability and the potential to expand our minds. We'll have to pass safely through the void. Now it's your turn to remember what old Davee Rogo told us: You can only be successful if you let your mind go beyond the boundaries that other people have set for themselves. C'tair, open up your imagination and go beyond the boundary with me."

His brother's confidence seemed unshakable, and C'tair had no choice but to nod. *Davee Rogo*—until this morning, he hadn't thought about the crippled and eccentric Ixian inventor in years. When they'd been ten, the twins had met the famous innovator Rogo. Their father had introduced them, imaged holograms of them with the man for the ambassadorial scrapbook shelf, then fluttered off to meet other important people. The two boys, though, had continued talking with the inventor, and he had invited them to visit his laboratory. For two years afterward, Rogo had set himself up as an offbeat mentor to C'tair and D'murr, until his death. Now the twins had only Davee Rogo's advice to remember, and his confidence that they would succeed.

Rogo would be scolding me for my doubts' now, C'tair thought.

"Think about it, brother. How does one practice for the job of moving huge ships from one star system to another in the wink of an eye?" To demonstrate, D'murr winked. "You'll pass. We both will. Get ready to swim in spice gas."

As they strode up to the embassy's inner reception desk, C'tair stared across the underground city of Vernii, beyond the glittering chains of glowglobes that illuminated the site where another Heighliner was already under construction. Perhaps someday he would fly that very vessel. Thinking of how the visiting Navigator had whisked the immense new Heighliner out of the cavern and into open space, the young man felt an infusion of desire. He loved Ix, wanted to stay here, wanted to see Kailea one last time—but he also wanted to be a Navigator.

The brothers identified themselves and waited. They stood together at the flat marbleplaz counter in silence, each brooding with personal thoughts, as if a trance might increase their chances of succeeding. *I will keep my mind completely open, ready for anything.*

A shapely female testing proctor appeared in a loose gray suit. The Guild's infinity symbol was stitched on her lapel, but she wore no jewelry or other ornamentation. "Welcome," she said, without introducing herself. "The Guild seeks the finest talent because our work is the most important. Without us, without space travel, the fabric of the Imperium would unravel. Think on that, and you will realize how selective we must be."

She did not smile at all. Her hair was reddish brown and close-cropped; C'tair would have found her attractive at any other time, but now he could think of nothing beyond the impending examination.

Checking their identification yet again, the proctor escorted the brothers to isolated, separate testing chambers. "This is an individual test, and each of you must face it alone. There is no way you can cheat, or even help each other," she said.

Alarmed at being separated, C'tair and D'murr looked at each other, then silently wished the other luck.

THE CHAMBER DOOR closed behind D'murr with a loud and frightening slam. His ears popped from the difference in air pressure. He was alone, intensely alone—but he knew he was up to the challenge.

Confidence is half the battle.

He noted the armored walls, the sealed cracks, the lack of ventilation. Hissing gas boiled from a single nozzle in the ceiling . . . thickening clouds of rusty orange, with a sharp gingery tang that burned his nostrils. Poison? Drugs? Then D'murr realized what the Guild had in mind for him.

Melange!

Closing his eyes, he smelled the unmistakable cinnamon odor of the rare spice. Rich melange, an incredible wealth of it in the confined air, filling the chamber and permeating his every breath. Knowing the value of Arrakis spice from his mother's meticulous work in the Guild Bank, D'murr sucked in another large gulp. The sheer cost of this! No wonder the Guild didn't test just anyone—the price for a single examination would be enough to build a housing complex on another planet.

The wealth controlled by the Spacing Guild—in banking, transportation, and exploration—awed him. The Guild went everywhere, touched everyone. He wanted to be part of it. Why did they need frivolous ornamentation when they had so much melange?

He felt possibilities spinning all around him like an elaborate contour map, with ripples and intersections, a locus of points, and paths
that led into and out of the void. He opened his mind so that the spice
could transport him anywhere in the universe. It seemed like such a
natural thing to do.

As the orange fog enfolded D'murr, he could no longer see the featureless walls of the testing chamber. He felt melange pressing into his
every pore and cell. The sensation was marvelous! He envisioned himself as a revered Navigator, expanding his mind to the farthest reaches
of the Imperium, encompassing everything. . . .

D'murr soared along, without leaving the test chamber—or so he
thought.

THE TEST WAS far worse than C'tair could have imagined.

No one ever told him what he was expected to do. He never had a
chance. He choked on the spice gas, became dizzy, fought to keep control of his faculties. The melange overdose stupefied him, so that he
could not remember who he was or why he was there. He struggled to
maintain focus, but lost himself.

When he eventually returned to consciousness, his clothes clean
and his hair and skin freshly washed (perhaps so the Guild could reclaim every particle of melange?), the shapely red-haired proctor
looked down at him. She gave C'tair a winsome, sad smile, and shook
her head. "You blocked your mind to the spice gas, thereby shackling
yourself to the normal world." Her next words came like a death sentence. "The Guild cannot use you."

C'tair sat up, coughing. He sniffed, and his nostrils still tingled
from the potent cinnamon stench. "I'm sorry. Nobody explained what
I was supposed to—"

She helped him to his feet, anxious to usher him out of the Embassy Building.

His heart felt like molten lead. The proctor didn't need to answer
him as she led him out to the reception area. C'tair looked around,
searching for his brother, but the waiting room was empty.

Then he learned that his own failure wasn't the worst thing he had
to face.

"Where's D'murr? Did he succeed?" C'tair's voice filled with hope.

The proctor nodded. "Admirably." She extended her hand toward the exit, but he sidestepped her. C'tair looked back toward the inner corridor and the sealed testing chamber where his brother had gone. He needed to congratulate D'murr, even though the victory was now bittersweet. At least one of them would become a Navigator.

"You will never see your brother again," the proctor said, coldly. She moved to block the way back in. "D'murr Pilru is ours now."

Recovering after an instant of shock, C'tair broke past the proctor and ran to the sealed chamber door. He pounded against it and shouted, but received no answer. Within minutes, Guild guards surrounded him—more businesslike than gentle—and peeled him away.

Still dizzy from the unaccustomed aftereffects of melange exposure, C'tair didn't realize where they were taking him. Blinking and disoriented, he found himself standing on the crystal walkway outside the blocky gray embassy. Below him, other walkways and streets bustled with traffic and pedestrians traveling from one tower building to another.

Now he was more alone than ever.

The testing proctor stood on the embassy steps, barring C'tair from reentering. Even though his mother worked somewhere inside, deep in the banking section, C'tair knew that the doors of this facility, as well as the doors to the future he had counted on, were now locked to him.

"Rejoice for your brother," the proctor called from the steps, her voice finally showing some life. "He has entered another world. He can travel to places you'll never imagine."

"I can never see him, or talk to him again?" C'tair said, as if part of him had been ripped away.

"Doubtful," the proctor said, crossing her arms over her chest. She gave him an apologetic frown. "Unless he . . . suffers a reversal. His first time, your brother immersed himself so completely in the spice gas that he started the . . . conversion process right there and then. The Guild cannot deny such talent. He has already started to change."

"Bring him back," C'tair said, his eyes tear-filled now. He prayed for his brother. "Just for a little while." He wanted to be happy for his twin—and proud. D'murr had passed the test that meant so much to both of them.

The twins had always been so close. How could they possibly go on without one another? Perhaps his mother could use her Guild banking connections, so that they would at least be able to have their farewells. Or maybe his father would use ambassadorial privilege to get D'murr back.

But C'tair knew that would never happen. He could see that now. His mother had already known it, had been afraid of losing *both* sons.

"The process is, in the majority of cases, irreversible," the proctor said with finality.

Guild security guards marched out to stand beside her, ensuring that C'tair did not become irrational and try to force his way inside.

"Trust me," said the proctor. "You don't want your brother back."

The human body is a machine, a system of organic chemicals, fluid conduits, electrical impulses; a government is likewise a machine of interacting societies, laws, cultures, rewards and punishments, patterns of behavior. Ultimately, the universe itself is a machine, planets around suns, stars gathered into clusters, clusters and other suns forming entire galaxies. . . . Our job is to keep the machinery functioning.

—Suk Inner School, Primary Doctrine

Both frowning, Crown Prince Shaddam and Chamberlain Aken Hesban watched the approach of a diminutive, scrawny man who nonetheless walked as tall as a Mutellian giant. After years of training and conditioning, all Suk doctors seemed compelled to take themselves far too seriously.

"That Elas Yungar looks more like a circus performer than a respected medical professional," Shaddam said, looking at the arched eyebrows, black eyes, and the steel-gray ponytail. "I hope he knows what he's doing. I want only the best care for my poor ailing father."

Beside him, Hesban tugged on one of his long mustaches, but made no response. He wore a floor-length blue robe with golden piping. For years, Shaddam had disliked this pompous man who hovered too close to his father's presence, and he vowed to choose a new Chamberlain after assuming the throne. And so long as this Suk doctor could find no explanation for Elrood's gradually worsening illness, Shaddam's ascendancy would be assured.

Hasimir Fenring had emphasized that even all the resources of the exalted Suk Inner School could not stop what had been set in motion. The catalyst chemical implanted in the old man's brain would register on no poison-snooper, since it was not itself poison, but would only convert to a dangerous substance in the presence of spice beer. And as he felt worse and worse, old Elrood consumed ever-increasing quantities of the beer.

No more than a meter in height, the shrunken doctor had smooth skin but ancient eyes from the vast medical knowledge hammered into his mind. A black diamond tattoo marked the center of Yungar's creased forehead. His ponytail of steel-gray hair, secured in the back by a silver Suk ring, was longer than a woman's, reaching nearly to the floor.

Wasting no time on further pleasantries, Elas Yungar broached a familiar subject. "You have our payment?" He looked first at the Chamberlain, then at the Crown Prince, where his gaze settled. "Fresh accounts must be established before we can begin treatment. Given the Emperor's age, our care could be quite prolonged . . . and ultimately fruitless. He must pay his bills, like every other citizen. King, miner, basket-weaver—it makes no difference to us. Every human wants to be healthy, and we cannot treat everyone. Our care is available only to those willing *and* able to pay for it."

Shaddam rested a hand on the Chamberlain's sleeve. "Ah yes, we will spare no expense for my father's health, Aken. It is already arranged."

They stood just inside the high-arched doorway of the Imperial audience chamber, beneath glorious ceiling frescoes of epic events from the history of the Corrino family: the blood of the Jihad, the desperate last stand on the Bridge of Hrethgir, the destruction of thinking machines. Shaddam had always found ancient Imperial history ponderous and boring, with little relevance to his current goals. Centuries and centuries ago didn't matter—he just hoped it wouldn't take that long for a change in the Palace.

In the echoing hall, the Padishah Emperor's magnificent jeweled throne sat invitingly empty. Court functionaries and a few dark-robed Bene Gesserit scuttled about in side passages and alcoves, trying to remain unseen. A pair of heavily armed Sardaukar guards stood at the dais steps, attentive. Shaddam wondered whether they would obey him right now, knowing his father lay sick in his chambers. He decided not to test the idea. *Too soon.*

"We are all familiar with promises," the doctor said. "Still, I wish to see the payment first." Stubborn tone, an impertinent upward gaze that didn't move from Shaddam, even though the Crown Prince hadn't done much talking. Yungar chose to play strange power games, but soon he would be out of his league.

"Payment before even looking at the patient?" the Chamberlain gasped. "Where are your priorities, man?"

Finally, Dr. Yungar deigned to look over at Hesban. "You have dealt with us before, Chamberlain, and you know the costs of producing a Suk doctor, fully conditioned, fully trained."

As heir to the Golden Lion Throne, Shaddam was familiar with Suk Imperial Conditioning, which guaranteed absolute loyalty to a patient. In centuries of medical history, no one had ever managed to subvert a graduate of the Inner School.

Some members of the royal Court had a hard time reconciling the legendary Suk loyalty with their incessant greed. The doctors never wavered from the clear but unstated position that they would not minister to anyone—not even to an Emperor—on a mere *promise* of remuneration. Suk doctors extended no credit. Payment had to be tangible and immediate.

Yungar spoke in an irritating whine. "Though we are perhaps not as prominent as the Mentats or the Bene Gesserit, the Suk School is still one of the greatest in the Imperium. My equipment alone costs more than most planets." Yungar pointed to a suspensor pod at his side. "I do not receive your payment on my own behalf, of course. I am only a custodian, holding it in a fiduciary capacity. When I return, your credits go with me to the Suk School, for the benefit of mankind."

Hesban glared at him with unconcealed loathing, his face turning ruddy, his mustaches twitching. "Or at least to benefit that portion of mankind that can afford your services."

"Correct, Chamberlain."

Seeing the doctor's staunch and misplaced self-importance, Shaddam shuddered. When he sat on the throne himself, he wondered if he could initiate any changes to put these Suks in their place. . . . He caught his rambling thoughts and quelled them. *All in due time.*

He sighed. His father Elrood had let too many threads of control slip right through his fingers. Fenring was right. As much as Shaddam despised dirtying his fingers with blood, removing the ancient Emperor was a necessary action.

"If cost of treatment is your paramount concern," the Suk doctor said, quietly goading the Chamberlain, "you are welcome to hire a less expensive physician for the Emperor of the Known Universe."

"Enough bickering. Come with me, Doctor," Shaddam said, taking charge. Dr. Yungar nodded, then turned his back on the Chamberlain, as if he was of no consequence whatsoever.

"Now I know why you people have the shape of a diamond tattooed on your foreheads," Hesban growled as he followed behind them. "You always have treasure on your minds."

The Crown Prince led the way to a security-shielded antechamber and passed through a shimmering electrical curtain to the inner vault. On a golden table at the center of the room lay opafire pendants, danikins of melange, and fold-pouches partially open to reveal glittering soostones.

"This will be sufficient," the Suk said. "Unless the treatment proves to be more involved than we expect." With his floating equipment pod at his side like a dutiful pet dog, the doctor shuffled back the way they had come. "I already know the way to the Emperor's chamber." Without explanation, Yungar hurried through a doorway and up the grand staircase that led to the guarded bedroom suites where the Emperor rested.

Sardaukar guards remained behind at the force field that protected the treasure vault, while Shaddam and Hesban marched after the doctor. Fenring would already be waiting at the dying old man's side, making his annoying humming noises and making sure none of the treatment could potentially be successful.

THE WITHERED EMPEROR lay on an enormous four-poster bed beneath a canopy of the finest merh-silks embroidered in the ancient Terran method. The bedposts were carved ucca, a fast-growing hardwood native to Elacca. Soothing fountains, set into alcoves in the walls, trickled fresh water, bubbling and whispering. Scented glowglobes tuned to the low range floated in the corners of the room.

As Shaddam and Fenring stood together and watched, the Suk doctor waved a liveried attendant away and mounted the two shallow steps to the bedside. Three lovely Imperial concubines hovered behind the ailing man, as if their mere presence could revitalize him. The old man's stink clung to the air, despite the ventilation and the incense.

Emperor Elrood wore slick royal satins and an old-fashioned sleeping cap that covered his liver-spotted scalp. He lay atop the covers, since he had complained about being too warm. The man looked haggard, could barely keep his eyes open.

Shaddam was pleased to see how markedly his father's health had declined since the Tleilaxu Ambassador's visit. Still, Elrood had good days and bad days, and he had the annoying habit of recovering his vitality after a significant downslide like this one.

A tall mug of cool spice beer rested on a tray beside his clawed and ring-bedecked hand, next to a second empty mug. And mounted on the bed canopy, Shaddam noted the waving insect arms of a poison-snooper.

You must be thirsty, Father, Shaddam thought. *Drink more of the beer.*

The doctor opened his suspensor pod to reveal shiny instruments, clicking scanners, and colored vials of testing liquids. Reaching inside the kit, Yungar brought out a small white device, which he passed over Elrood.

After tugging off the satin sleeping cap to reveal the sweaty scalp, Dr. Yungar scanned Elrood's skull, lifting the old man's head to check all around. Looking small and weak and *old,* the Emperor grumbled at the discomfort.

Shaddam wondered what he himself would look like after 150 years . . . preferably at the end of a long and glorious reign. He fought back a smile and held his breath during the examination. Beside him, Fenring remained calm and aloof. Only the Chamberlain scowled.

The doctor withdrew his scanner, then studied the Imperial patient's case-history cube. Presently he announced to the groggy old man, "Even melange can't keep you young forever, Sire. At your age, health naturally begins to decline. Sometimes rapidly."

Inaudibly, Shaddam released a sigh of relief.

With great difficulty Elrood sat up, and his concubines propped tasseled pillows behind him. His cadaverous, parchment face creased in a deep frown. "But only a few months ago I felt so much better."

"Aging is not a perfect downhill graph. There are peaks and valleys, recoveries and slowdowns." The doctor had the audacity to use a know-it-all tone that implied the Emperor could not understand such complex concepts. "The human body is a chemical and bioelectric soup, and changes are often triggered by seemingly inconsequential events. You have been under stress lately?"

"I'm the Emperor!" Elrood snapped, this time responding as if the Suk were unbearably stupid. "I have many responsibilities. Of course this causes stress."

"Then start to delegate more to the Crown Prince and to your trusted aides, such as Fenring over there. You're not going to live forever, you know. Not even an Emperor can do that. Plan for the future." Smugly, the doctor snapped shut his case. Shaddam wanted to embrace him. "I will leave you with a prescription and devices to make you feel better."

"The only prescription I want is more spice in my beer." Elrood took a deep drink from his mug, slurping loudly.

"As you wish," the scrawny Suk doctor said. From the suspensor pod he removed a satchel, which he placed on a side table. "These are muscle-soothing devices, in case you need them. Instructions are contained with each unit. Have your concubines use them on your aches."

"All right, all right," Elrood said. "Now leave me. I have work to do."

Dr. Yungar backed down the steps from the bed platform with a bow. "With your permission, Sire."

Impatiently, the Emperor waved a gnarled hand in dismissal. The concubines moved about, whispering to each other, watching with wide eyes. Two of them picked up muscle-soothing devices and toyed with the controls.

Shaddam whispered to one of the attendants to have the doctor go with Chamberlain Hesban, who would arrange for the transfer of payment. Hesban obviously wanted to stay in the bedchamber and discuss certain documents, treaties, and other state matters with the sick old man, but Shaddam—feeling he could take care of such things himself—wanted the dour advisor out of the way.

When the Suk was gone, old Elrood said to his son, "Perhaps the doctor is right, Shaddam. There is a matter I wish to discuss with you and Hasimir. A policy and project I wish to continue, regardless of my personal health. Have I told you about our plans on Ix, and the eventual Tleilaxu takeover?"

Shaddam rolled his eyes. *Of course, you old fool! Fenring and I have already done most of the work. It was our idea to send Tleilaxu Face*

Dancers to Ix, because they could disguise themselves and infiltrate the working classes.

"Yes, Father. We know of the plans."

Elrood waved a hand to beckon them closer, and the old man's features darkened. Out of the corner of his eye, Shaddam saw Fenring chase the hovering concubines away, then approach to hear the Emperor's words. "This morning I received a cipher from our operatives on Ix. You know about the enmity between myself and Earl Dominic Vernius?"

"Ah, yes—we do, Father," Shaddam said. He cleared his throat. "An old affront, a stolen woman . . ."

Elrood's rheumy eyes brightened. "It seems that our brash Dominic has been playing with fire, training his men with mobile fighting meks that scan opponents and process data, probably through a computer brain. He has also been selling these 'intelligent machines' on the black market."

"Sacrilege, Sire," Fenring murmured. "That clearly goes against the strictures of the Great Convention."

"Quite so," Elrood agreed, "and this isn't the only infraction. House Vernius has been developing sophisticated cyborg enhancements as well. Mechanical body replacements. We can use that to our advantage."

Shaddam frowned, leaning closer and smelling the sour spice beer on the old man's breath. "Cyborgs? But they are *human* minds attached to robot bodies, and therefore not in violation of the Jihad."

Elrood smiled. "But we understand there have been certain . . . compromises. True or not, it's exactly the sort of excuse our impostors need to finish the job—the time to act is now. House Vernius is poised on the brink of destruction, and a small nudge will topple them."

"Hmm-m-ah, that *is* interesting," Fenring said. "Then the Tleilaxu can take over the sophisticated Ixian facilities for their research."

"This is very important, and you will watch how I handle this situation," Elrood said with a sniff. "Watch, and learn. Already I have set my plan in motion. Ixian suboid workers are, shall we say, *troubled* by these developments, and we are . . ." the Emperor paused to finish his mug of spice beer with a smack of his lips, ". . . *encouraging* their discontent through our own representatives."

Setting down the empty mug, Elrood grew suddenly lethargic. He adjusted his pillows, shifted onto his back, and fell into a fitful sleep.

Exchanging a knowing glance with Fenring, Shaddam thought of the conspiracy within the conspiracy—their own secret participation in the events on Ix, and how he and Fenring had put the Tleilaxu Master in contact with Elrood in the first place. Now the Bene Tleilax, employing their own genetically altered shape-shifters, were stirring up religious fervor and discontent among Ix's lower classes. To the fanatical Tleilaxu, any hint of a thinking machine—and the Ixians who created them—was the work of Satan.

As the two young men left the Emperor's chamber, Fenring smiled with similar thoughts. "Watch, and learn," the old fool had said.

Elrood, you condescending bastard, you have much to learn yourself—and no time left in which to learn it.

The leaders of the Butlerian Jihad did not adequately define artificial intelligence, failing to foresee all possibilities of an imaginative society. Therefore, we have substantial gray areas in which to maneuver.

—Confidential Ixian Legal Opinion

Though the explosion was distant, the concussion rocked the table where Leto and Rhombur sat studying sample resource ledgers. Small chunks of decorative plascrete trickled from the ceiling above them, where a long crack had just appeared. A jagged lightning bolt zigzagged across one of the broad plaz observation windows, fracturing it.

"Vermilion hells! What was that?" Rhombur said.

Leto had already surged to his feet, knocking the ledgers aside and looking for the source of the explosion. He saw the farside of the underground grotto, where several badly damaged buildings crumbled into rubble. The two young men exchanged blank looks.

"Get ready," Leto said, instantly on guard.

"Uh, ready for what?"

Leto didn't know.

They had gone together into one of the tutorial rooms of the Grand Palais, first studying Calculus Philosophy and the underpinnings of the Holtzman Effect, and then Ixian manufacturing and distribution systems. On the walls around them, ancient paintings hung in hermetically sealed frames, including works of the Old Terran masters Claude Monet and Paul Gauguin, with interactive plates that allowed enhancements by Ixian depth artists. Since Leto had reported his adventure down in the sub-oid tunnels, he had heard of no further discussions or investigations. Perhaps the Earl hoped the problem would just go away.

Another concussion rocked the room, this one closer, stronger. The Prince of Ix gripped the table to keep it from toppling. Leto rushed over to the cracked window. "Rhombur, look out here!"

From the crosswalk streets connecting the stalactite buildings, someone screamed. Off to the left, an out-of-control transport capsule plummeted to smash into the ground far below with a spray of crystal shards and mutilated passengers.

The door to the tutorial room crashed open. Captain Zhaz of the Palace Guard burst in, carrying one of the new pulsed assault lasguns. Four subordinates followed him, all armed in the same fashion, all wearing the silver-and-white uniforms of House Vernius. No one on Ix, especially not the Earl himself, had ever thought Leto or Rhombur would need the protection of personal bodyguards.

"Come with us, young masters!" Zhaz said, breathing hard. The man's dark eyes, framed by his squarish brown beard, darted with excitement as he noted the stone fragments falling from the ceiling, then the cracked windowplaz. Though he was ready to fight to the death, Zhaz clearly didn't understand what had taken place in the normally peaceful city of Vernii.

"What's happening, Captain?" Rhombur asked, as the retinue of guards hustled them out of the room and into the corridor, where the lights flickered. His voice quavered for a moment, then sounded stronger, like an Earl's heir should. "Tell me—is my family safe?"

Other guards and members of the Ixian court ran helter-skelter, with excited shouts ringing out, high-pitched and strident, in counter-point to yet another explosion. From far below came the hubbub of an angry mob, so distant it sounded like a deep murmur. Then Leto made out the buzzing hum of lasgun fire. Even before the captain answered Rhombur, Leto guessed the source of the disturbance.

"There's trouble with the suboids, my Lords!" Zhaz shouted. "Don't worry, though—we'll have it under control soon." He touched a button on his belt, and a previously unseen door opened in the marble-mirrored wall. The captain and the household guard had drilled and prepared for so long against large-scale external attacks, they didn't seem to know how to deal with a revolt from within. "This way to safety. I'm sure your family will be there waiting for you."

When the two young men ducked under the low half door behind the mirrors, the portal sealed shut behind them. In the yellow light of emergency glowglobes, Leto and Rhombur ran alongside an electro-magnetic track, while the captain of the guard shouted frantically into a tiny handheld comceiver. Lavender light flashed from the face of the instrument, and Leto heard the metallic sound of a responding voice: "Help is on the way!"

Seconds later an armored personnel car roared along the sheltered track and screeched to a stop. Zhaz boarded with the two young heirs and a pair of guards, leaving the rest of the security men behind to de-fend their exit. Leto tumbled into a bucket seat, while Zhaz and Rhombur clambered into the front. The railcar began to move.

"Suboids blew two of the diamond columns," Zhaz said, breath-lessly consulting the lavender screen of his comceiver. "Part of the overhead crust has collapsed." His face turned gray with disbelief, and he scratched his brown beard. "This is impossible."

Leto, who had seen the signs of the gathering storm all along, knew that the situation was probably even worse than the guard captain imagined. Ix's troubles would not be solved within an hour.

A metallic-voiced report clattered in, sounding desperate. "Suboids are boiling up from the lower levels! How did . . . how could they be-come so organized?"

Rhombur cursed, and Leto looked knowingly at his stocky friend. He had tried to warn the Ixians, but he did not point out the fact. House Vernius had not been willing to consider the seriousness of the situation.

In the railcar, a safety harness snapped into place over Leto as soon as he situated himself, and the car continued to accelerate with a smooth hum, traveling at high speed upward into caverns hidden in the rock ceiling. Captain Zhaz worked a comboard at the front of the compartment, his fingers dancing over the communication keys. A blue glow surrounded his hands. At his side, Rhombur watched the guard captain intently, as if knowing he might be expected to take charge.

"We're in an escape pod," one of the secondary guards explained to

Leto. "You two are safe, for now. The suboids won't be able to penetrate our upper defenses, once we have them activated."

"But what about my parents?" Rhombur asked. "And Kailea?"

"We've got a plan for this, an option. You and your family should all meet at a rendezvous point. By all the saints and sinners, I hope my people remember what to do. For the first time, it isn't a drill."

The car made several track changes, clicking and humming along with increased speed, and then ascended steeply into darkness. Presently the track leveled off and the vehicle was bathed in light as it sped past an immense window wall of one-way armor-plaz. They caught just a glimpse of the riots down below: flares of spontaneous fires and swirling demonstrations going on beneath the city. Another explosion, and one of the transparent upper walkway tubes shattered, tumbling in shards to the floor of the cavern far below; tiny puppetlike figures of pedestrians flailed and fell to their doom.

"Stop here, Captain!" Rhombur cried. "I need to see what's happening out there."

"Please, sir, keep it to a few seconds," the captain said. "The rebels could breach that wall."

Leto found it hard to comprehend what he was hearing. Rebels? Explosions? Emergency evacuations? Ix had seemed so sophisticated, so peaceful, so . . . protected from discord. Even dissatisfied with their lot, how could the suboids have orchestrated such a massive and coordinated assault? Where could they have gotten the resources?

Through the one-way panel, Leto saw uniformed Vernius soldiers fighting a losing battle against swarms of the pale, smooth-skinned opponents down on the grotto floor. The suboids hurled crudely made explosive or incendiary devices, while Ixians cut the mobs down with purple beams of lasgun fire.

"Comcommand says the suboids are rebelling on all levels," Zhaz said in a tone of disbelief. "They're screaming 'Jihad' as they attack."

"Vermilion hells!" Rhombur said. "What does the Jihad have to do with anything? What could it have to do with us?"

"We need to leave the window, sir," Zhaz insisted, tugging at Rhombur's sleeve. "We have to make it to the rendezvous point."

Rhombur lurched back from the window as part of a tiled street collapsed behind it, and wave upon wave of the pale suboids scrambled out of the dark tunnels beneath.

The railcar picked up speed along the track and curved left into darkness, then ascended again. Rhombur nodded to himself, his face pinched and distressed. "We've got secret command centers on the upper levels. Precautions have been taken for this sort of thing, and by now our military units will have surrounded the most vital manufacturing facilities. It shouldn't take long to subdue this." The Earl's son sounded as if he were trying to convince himself.

At the front of the car, Zhaz leaned intently over the comboard, which cast his face in pale light. "Look out—trouble ahead, sir!" He wrenched the controls. The railcar rocked, and Zhaz took a side track. The other two guards brought their weapons to bear, squinting into the rocky darkness all around them, ready to fire.

"Unit Four has been overrun," Captain Zhaz said. "Suboids broke through the sidewalls. I'm trying for Three instead!"

"Overrun?" Rhombur said, and his face flushed with either embarrassment or fear. "How in the hells could suboids do that?"

"Comcommand says Tleilaxu are involved—and some of their Face Dancers. They're all heavily armed." He gasped as he stared at the reports flowing in. "May God protect us!"

Questions fell in an avalanche around Leto. *Tleilaxu? Why would they attack Ix? Jihad! This is a machine planet . . . and the Tleilaxu are religious fanatics. Do they fear Ixian machines enough to use their tank-grown shape-shifters to infiltrate the suboid workforce? That would explain the coordination. But why would they be so interested? Why here?*

As the railcar soared along, Zhaz scrutinized the comboard, where he received battle reports. "By all the saints and sinners! Tleilaxu engineers have just blown the pipelines that feed heat from the molten core of the planet."

"But we need that energy to run the factories," Rhombur cried, still hanging on to his seat.

"They've also destroyed recycling lines where the industrial waste and exhaust chemicals are dumped into the mantle." Now the captain's voice sounded more ragged. "They're hitting at the heart of Ix— paralyzing our manufacturing capacity."

As Leto thought back on what he had learned during his months on this planet, pieces of the puzzle began fitting together in his mind. "Think about it," he said, "all of that can be fixed. They knew exactly where to hit in order to cripple Ix without causing permanent damage. . . . " Leto gave a grim nod, the reason suddenly clear to him. "The Tleilaxu want this world and its facilities intact. They plan to take over here."

"Don't be ridiculous, Leto. We'd never give Ix to the filthy Tleilaxu." Rhombur looked perplexed more than miffed.

"We may not . . . have any choice in the matter, sir," Zhaz said.

At Rhombur's barked command for weapons one of the guards opened a cabinet beneath the railcar and brought out a pair of fléchette pistols and shield belts, which he handed to both Princes.

Without questioning, Leto snapped on the belt, touched a test button to confirm that the unit was operational. The projectile weapon felt cold in his hand. He checked its clip of deadly darts, accepted two additional packs from the guard, and slid them into compartments on the shield belt.

The escape pod thundered into a long, dark tunnel. Ahead, Leto saw light, which grew larger and brighter by the second. He remembered what his father had said to him about the Tleilaxu: *"They destroy anything that resembles a thinking machine."* Ix would have been a natural target for them.

The light ahead touched them now, dazzling his eyes, and they roared into it.

Religion and law among the masses must be one and the same. An act of disobedience must be a sin and require religious penalties. This will have the dual benefit of bringing both greater obedience and greater bravery. We must depend not so much on the bravery of individuals, you see, as upon the bravery of a whole population.

— PARDOT KYNES, address to gathered
representatives of the greater sietches

Oblivious to the fate that had been decided for him, Pardot Kynes strolled through the tunnels, accompanied by his now-faithful companions Ommun and Turok. The three went to visit Stilgar, who rested and healed in his family chambers.

At first sight of his visitor, a lean Stilgar sat forward on his sickbed. Though his wound should have been fatal, the Fremen youth had almost entirely recovered in a short time. "I owe you the water of my life, Planetologist," he said, and with great seriousness spat upon the floor of the cave.

Kynes was startled for a moment, then thought he understood. He knew the importance of water to these people, especially the precious moisture contained within a person's body. For Stilgar to sacrifice even a droplet of saliva showed him a great honor. "I . . . appreciate your water, Stilgar," Kynes said with a forced smile. "But you may keep the rest of it for now. I want you to be well."

Frieth, Stilgar's quiet sister, stayed by the young man's bedside, always busy, her blue-in-blue eyes darting from side to side in search of something else to do. She looked long at Kynes, as if assessing him, but her expression was unreadable.

Then she silently glided off to bring more unguents that would speed her brother's healing.

Later, as Kynes walked along the sietch passageways, curious people gathered to follow him and listen. In the midst of their daily routines, this tall, stubble-bearded Planetologist continued to be something new and interesting. His crazy but visionary words might sound ridiculous, the most preposterous of fantasies, but even the sietch's children tagged along after the stranger.

The bemused and talkative crowd accompanied Kynes as he lectured, gesturing with his hands, gazing at the ceiling as if he could see the open sky there. Though they tried, these Fremen could not imagine the sight of clouds gathering to pour rain upon the desert. *Droplets of moisture falling from the empty sky? Absurd!*

Some of the children laughed at the very idea of rain on Dune, but Kynes kept talking, explaining the steps of his process to reap the faintest breath of water vapor from the air. He would collect every sparkle of dew in the shadows to help twist Arrakis in the way he required, to pave the way for a brilliant new ecology.

"You must think of this world in engineering terms," Kynes said, in a professorial tone. He was happy to have such an attentive audience, though he wasn't sure how much they understood. "This planet, taken in its entirety, is merely an expression of energy, a machine driven by its sun." He lowered his voice and looked down at a young, wide-eyed girl. "What it requires is reshaping to fit our needs. We have the ability to do that on . . . Dune. But do we have the self-discipline and the drive?"

He lifted his gaze to someone else. "That is up to *us*."

By now Ommun and Turok had heard most of Kynes's lectures. Although they had scoffed at first, eventually the words had sunk in. Now, the more they heard of his unbridled enthusiasm and bright honesty, the more they actually began to *believe*. Why not dream? Judging from the expressions on the faces of his listeners, they could see that other Fremen had started to consider the possibilities as well.

The sietch elders called these converts optimistic and overly gullible. Undaunted, Kynes continued to spread his ideas, as outrageous as they might seem.

WEARING A GRIM expression, Naib Heinar squinted his one eye
and extended the holy crysknife, still sheathed. The strong warrior
standing rigid in front of him held out his hands to receive the gift.

The Naib intoned ritual words. "Uliet, older Liet, you have been
chosen for this task for the good of our sietch. You have proven yourself many times in battle against the Harkonnens. You are an accomplished worm rider and one of the greatest fighters among the
Fremen."

A man of middle years and craggy features, Uliet bowed. His hands
remained outstretched. He waited and did not flinch. Though a deeply
religious man, he held his awe in check.

"Take this consecrated crysknife, Uliet." Heinar now grasped the
carved hilt and yanked the long milky white blade from its sheath.
The crysknife was a sacred relic among the Fremen, fashioned from
the crystal tooth of a sandworm. This particular blade was *fixed*, keyed
to the body of its owner so that the weapon would dissolve upon his
death.

"Your blade has been dipped in the poisonous Water of Life, and
blessed by Shai-Hulud," Heinar continued. "As is our tradition, the sacred blade must not be sheathed again until it has tasted blood."

Uliet took the weapon, suddenly overwhelmed by the importance
of the task for which he had been selected. Intensely superstitious, he
had watched the great worms in the desert and had ridden atop them
many times. But never had he allowed himself to become familiar with
the magnificent creatures. He could not forget that they were the
manifestations of the great creator of the universe.

"I shall not fail the will of Shai-Hulud." Uliet accepted the blade
and held it up high, with its poisoned tip pointed away from him.

The other elders stood behind the one-eyed Naib, firm in their decision. "Take two watermen with you," Heinar said, "to collect the water of this Planetologist and use it for the good of our sietch."

"Perhaps we should take a small amount and plant a bush in his
honor," said Aliid, but no one seconded the suggestion.

Out of the stone-walled chamber Uliet walked tall and proud, a warrior of the Fremen. He did not fear this Planetologist, though the outsider spoke fervently of his wild and preposterous plans, as if he were guided by a holy vision. A shudder went up the assassin's spine.

Uliet narrowed his deep blue eyes and forced such thoughts from his mind as he strode down the shadowed passageways. Two watermen followed him, bearing empty literjons for collecting Kynes's blood, and absorbent cloths to soak up every drop that might spill on the stone floor.

The Planetologist was not difficult to find. An entourage trailed him, their faces filled with either awe or skepticism tinged with wonder. Towering over the others, Kynes walked an aimless path, lecturing as he went, waving his arms. His flock scuttled after him at a wary distance, sometimes asking questions, but more often just listening.

"The human question is not how many can survive within the system," Kynes was saying as Uliet approached, the crysknife plain in his hand, his mission clear on his face, "but what kind of existence is possible for those who do survive."

Moving forward, unwavering, Uliet stepped through the fringes of the crowd. The Planetologist's listeners saw the assassin and his knife. They stepped away and looked at each other knowingly, some with disappointment, some with fear. They fell silent. This was the way of the Fremen people.

Kynes didn't notice at all. With one finger he made a circle in the air. "Open water is possible here, with a slight but viable change. *We can do this if you help me.* Think of it—walking in the open without a stillsuit." He pointed at two of the children closest to him. They backed away shyly. "Just imagine: so much moisture in the air that you no longer need to wear stillsuits."

"You mean we could even have water in a pond that we might dip out and drink anytime we wish?" one of the skeptical observers said, his voice sarcastic.

"Certainly. I've seen it on many worlds, and there's no reason we can't do it on Dune, too. With windtraps, you can grab the water from the air and use it to plant grasses, shrubs, anything that will lock the water in cells and root systems and keep it there. In fact, beside those open ponds one could even have orchards with sweet, juicy fruit for the picking."

Uliet stepped forward in a trance of determination. The accompanying watermen behind him held back; they would not be needed until after the killing was finished.

"What kind of fruit?" a girl asked.

"Oh, any kind you like," Kynes said. "We'd have to pay attention to soil conditions and moisture first. Grapes, perhaps, on the rocky slopes. I wonder what an Arrakeen vintage wine would taste like. . . . " He smiled. "And round orange fruits, portyguls. Ah, I like those! My parents used to have a tree on Salusa Secundus. Portyguls have a hard leathery rind, but you peel it away. Inside, the fruit is in sections, sweet and juicy, and the brightest color of orange you could ever imagine."

Uliet saw only a red haze. His assignment burned in his brain, obscuring all else from his vision. Naib Heinar's orders echoed in his skull. He walked into the empty area where the people had drawn back to listen to the Planetologist's rantings. Uliet tried not to hear the dreams, tried not to think of the visions Kynes summoned. Clearly this man was a demon, sent to warp the minds of his listeners. . . .

Uliet stared fixedly ahead, while Kynes continued to wander down the corridor, taking no notice. With broad gestures he described grasslands, canals, and forests. He painted pictures in their imaginations. The Planetologist licked his lips as if he could already taste the wine from Dune.

Uliet stepped in front of him and raised the poisoned crysknife.

In the middle of a sentence, Kynes suddenly noticed the stranger. As if annoyed at the distraction, he blinked once and simply said, "Remove yourself," as he brushed past Uliet and continued to talk.

"Ah, forests! Green and lush as far as the eye can see, covering hills and swales and broad valleys. In ancient times, sand encroached on plants and destroyed them, but it will be the reverse on the new Dune: The wind will carry seeds across the planet, and more trees and other plants will grow, like children."

The assassin stood still, astonished at being so casually dismissed. *Remove yourself.* The import of what he had been charged to do transfixed him. If he killed this man, Fremen legends would call Uliet the Destroyer of Dreams.

"First, though, we must install windtraps in the rocks," Kynes continued, breathless. "They're simple systems, easy to construct, and will grasp moisture, funneling it to where we can use it. Eventually, we'll have vast underground catchbasins for all the water, a step toward bringing water back to the surface. Yes, I said *back*. Once water ran freely on Dune. I have seen signs of it."

In dismay Uliet stared at the poisoned knife, unable to believe that this man had no fear of him whatsoever. *Remove yourself*. Kynes had faced his death and walked right past it. *Guided by God*.

Uliet stood there now, knife in hand, the unprotected shoulders of the Imperial servant taunting him. He could easily drive a killing blow into the man's spine.

But the assassin could not move.

He saw the Planetologist's confidence, as if he were protected by some holy guardian. The vision this great man brought for the future of Dune had already captivated these people. And the Fremen, with their harsh lives and generations of enemies who had forced them from planet to planet, *needed* a dream.

Perhaps someone had finally been sent to guide them, a prophet. Uliet's soul would be damned forever if he dared to kill the long-awaited messenger sent by God!

But he had accepted a mission from his sietch leader, and knew that the crysknife could never be put away without shedding blood. In this case, the dilemma could not be resolved by a minor cut either, for the blade was poisoned; the merest scratch would kill.

Those facts could not be reconciled with each other. Uliet's hands trembled on the hilt of the curved knife.

Without noticing that everyone had fallen silent around him, Kynes rambled on about windtrap placement, but his audience, knowing what must happen, watched their esteemed warrior.

Then Uliet's mouth watered. He tried not to think of it, but—as if in a dream—he seemed to taste the sweet, sticky juice of portyguls, fresh fruit that one could simply pluck from a tree and eat . . . a mouthful of lush pulp washed down with pure water from an open pond. Water for everyone.

Uliet took a step back, and another, holding the knife up in a ceremonial gesture. He took a third step away, as Kynes spoke of wheat- and rye-covered plains and gentle rain showers in the spring.

The assassin turned, dizzy, thinking of the two words the messenger had said to him, "Remove yourself."

He turned away and stared down at the knife he held in front of him. Then, Uliet swayed, stopped, then swayed forward again, deliberately—

and fell on his knife. His knees did not bend, nor did he flinch or try to avoid his fate as he let himself fall facefirst onto the floor, onto the tip of the blade. The poisoned crysknife plunged below his sternum and up into his heart. Sprawled on the stone floor, his body trembled. Within moments Uliet was dead. There was very little blood.

The sietch audience cried out at the omen they had just witnessed and backed away. Now, as the Fremen gazed at Kynes with religious awe, his words finally stuttered to a halt. He turned and saw the sacrifice this Fremen had just made for him, the bloodletting.

"What's going on here?" Kynes demanded. "Who was that man?"

The watermen rushed forward to remove Uliet's body. With a rustle of robes, a shrouding of blankets and towels and cloths, they whisked away the fallen assassin, taking him to the deathstills for processing.

The other Fremen now stared at Kynes with reverence. "Look! God has shown us what to do," one woman exclaimed. "He has guided Uliet. He has spoken to Pardot Kynes."

"*Umma* Kynes," someone said. *Prophet* Kynes.

One man stood up and glared at the others gathered around. "We would be fools not to listen to him now."

Runners departed and dashed through the sietch. Not understanding the Fremen religion, Kynes couldn't grasp it all.

From that point on, however, he didn't think he would have trouble getting anyone to listen to him.

No outsider has ever seen a Tleilaxu female and lived to tell about it. Considering the Tleilaxu penchant for genetic manipulation— see, e.g., related memos on clones and gholas—this simple observation raises a wealth of additional questions.

— Bene Gesserit Analysis

A breathless Ixian woman with full Courier credentials arrived on Kaitain, bearing an important communiqué for the Emperor. She marched into the Palace without pause, stopping to answer no questions. Even Cammar Pilru, the official Ambassador from Ix, had not yet heard the message or the dire news of the underground suboid revolt.

Since instantaneous foldspace communication did not exist between planets, certified and bonded Couriers booked passage on express Heighliners, bearing flash-memorized communications for personal delivery to the intended recipients. The net result was much faster than radio or other electronic signals that would take years to cross vast space.

Under the escort of two Guildsmen, Courier Yuta Brey arranged for an immediate appointment with the Emperor. The woman staunchly refused to reveal anything to her planet's own Ambassador, who got wind of the excitement and rushed into the audience chamber. The magnificent Golden Lion Throne sat empty; Elrood was again feeling tired and ill.

"This is for the Emperor's ears only, an urgent private request from Earl Dominic Vernius," Brey said to Ambassador Pilru, turning hard eyes toward him. The Guild and CHOAM used various harsh techniques to indoctrinate official Couriers, ensuring accuracy and loyalty. "However, please remain at hand, Ambassador. I also bear vital news regarding the possible downfall of Ix. You must be apprised of the situation."

Gasping, Ambassador Pilru beseeched the Courier for more information, but the woman remained silent. Leaving her Guild escorts and the Ixian diplomat behind in the audience chamber, Sardaukar elite guards examined her credentials and ushered her alone into an anteroom adjacent to Elrood's bedchamber.

The Emperor, looking aged and drawn, wore a robe bearing the Imperial crest on its lapel. He sat slumped in a high-backed chair, with his feet on a heated ottoman. Beside him stood a tall, fussy-looking man with drooping mustaches, Chamberlain Aken Hesban.

It surprised Brey to see the old man seated in this rather ordinary fashion instead of on the massive throne. His blue-tinted eyes were filled with sickness, and he could hardly hold his head erect on its rail-thin, wattled neck. Elrood seemed ready to pass out at any moment.

With a curt bow she announced, "I am Courier Yuta Brey from Ix, Sire, with an important request from Lord Dominic Vernius."

The Emperor scowled upon hearing his old rival's name, but said nothing, waiting and ready to pounce. He coughed, hawking something onto a lacy handkerchief. "I am listening."

"It is for the Emperor's ears only," she said, staring insolently at Hesban.

"Well?" Elrood said, with a terse smile. "I don't hear so well anymore, and this distinguished gentleman is my ears. Or should I say, 'are my ears'? Does one use the plural in a situation like this?"

The Chamberlain bent over to whisper something to him.

"I am informed that he *is* my ears," Elrood said with a decisive nod.

"As you wish," Brey said. She recited the memorized words, using even the intonations Dominic Vernius had used.

"We are under attack from the Bene Tleilax under a false guise of internal unrest. Through infiltration by Face Dancer mimics, the Tleilaxu have fomented an insurrection among our working class. By these treacherous means, the rebels have gained the advantage of surprise. Many of our defense installations have either been destroyed or are besieged. Like madmen, they scream 'Jihad! Jihad!' "

"Holy war?" Hesban said. "Over what? What has Ix done now?"

"We have no idea, Monsieur Chamberlain. The Tleilaxu are known to be religious fanatics. Our suboids are bred to follow instructions, and thus are easily manipulated." Yuta Brey hesitated, with a slight trembling of her lips. "Earl Dominic Vernius respectfully requests the immediate intervention of the Emperor's Sardaukar against this illegal act."

She recited extensive details on Ixian and Tleilaxu military positions, including the extent of the uprising, the manufacturing facilities crippled, and the citizens murdered. Prominent among the victims was the Ambassador's own wife, a Guild banker, who had died in an explosion at the Guild Embassy Building.

"They've gone too far." Indignant, Hesban appeared ready to issue the order himself for the defense of Ix. The request of House Vernius was eminently reasonable. Looking down at the Emperor, he said, "Sire, if the Tleilaxu wish to accuse Ix of violating any strictures of the Great Convention, let them do so in open Landsraad court."

Although incense burned in the air, and spicy hors d'oeuvres sat arrayed on mother-of-pearl serving trays, Brey could still smell a sour odor of sickness hanging in the stuffy air of the anteroom. Elrood fidgeted under the weight of his heavy robe. He narrowed his rheumy eyes. "We will take your request under advisement, Courier. I feel as if I need to rest a bit now. Doctor's orders, you know. We will discuss the matter tomorrow. Please take refreshment and select a chamber in our visiting dignitaries' quarters. You may also wish to meet with the Ixian Ambassador."

A look of alarm electrified the woman's gaze. "This information is already several hours old, Sire. We are in a most desperate situation. I have been instructed to tell you that Earl Vernius believes any delay will be fatal."

Hesban responded loudly, still confused as to why Elrood would not take immediate action. "One does not *tell* the Emperor anything, young lady. One makes *requests* of him, no more."

"My deepest apologies, Sire. Please forgive my agitation, but today I have seen my world struck a deadly blow. What response may I give to Earl Vernius?"

"Be patient. I will get back to him in due time, after I have considered my reply."

All color drained from Brey's face. "May I ask *when?*"

"You may not!" Elrood thundered. "Your audience is concluded." He glared back at her.

Taking charge, Chamberlain Hesban stepped forward, placing a hand on Brey's shoulder and steering her toward the door as he looked curiously over his shoulder at the Emperor.

"As you wish, Sire." Brey bowed, and the elite guards escorted her from the room.

ELROOD HAD NOT failed to notice anger and despair in the Courier's expression when she realized that her mission had failed. He had seen desperation and the beginnings of tears in her eyes. So tiresome, so predictable.

But everything had proceeded perfectly.

As soon as the Ixian Courier and the Court Chamberlain were gone, Crown Prince Shaddam and Fenring entered the anteroom and stood before Elrood. The old man knew they had been eavesdropping.

"Quite an education you two are getting, eh?" Elrood said. "Watch, and learn."

"Ah, yes. You handled the situation masterfully, Father. Events are unfolding exactly as you predicted." *With a great deal of invisible help from me and Fenring.*

The Emperor beamed, then fell into a bout of coughing. "My Sardaukar would have been more efficient than Tleilaxu, but I couldn't risk showing my hand too early. A formal Ixian complaint to the Landsraad could spell trouble. We've got to get rid of House Vernius and put the Tleilaxu in place as our puppets, with legions of Sardaukar sent in afterward to crack down and ensure the takeover."

"Hm-m-m-m-ah, perhaps it would be preferable to refer to it as 'fostering a smooth and orderly transition.' Avoid using the term 'crack down.'"

Elrood smiled with his papery lips, exposing teeth in a way that made his head look even more like a skull. "See, Hasimir, you are learning to be a politician after all—despite your rather direct methods."

Though all three of them knew the underlying reasons for the overthrow of Ix, none of them spoke of the benefits they would receive after Hidar Fen Ajidica had begun the artificial spice research there.

Chamberlain Hesban burst back into the room, uncharacteristically flustered. He bowed. "Sire, pardon me, please? As I was transferring the Courier back to her Guild escorts, she informed them that you had refused to act in accordance with Imperial regulations. She has already joined with Ambassador Pilru in requesting an immediate audience with the members of the Landsraad Council."

"Hm-m-m-m, she's going behind your back, Sire," Fenring said.

"Absurd," the old Emperor snapped, then searched for his ever-present mug of spice beer. "What does a *messenger* know of Imperial regulations?"

"Though they have not qualified for full Mentat training, Licensed Couriers have perfect memories, Sire," Fenring pointed out, bending close to the Emperor in the position Chamberlain Hesban usually assumed.

"She can't process the concepts, but she may well have every regulation and codicil readily accessible in her brain. She rattled off a number of them in my presence."

"Ah, yes. But how can she contest the Emperor's decision, when he hasn't even made up his mind yet?" Shaddam asked.

Hesban tugged on one of his drooping mustaches, increasing the frown that he directed at the Crown Prince, but he refrained from scolding Shaddam for his ignorance of Imperial law. "By mutual agreement between the Federated Council of the Landsraad and House Corrino, the Emperor is required either to render immediate assistance, or convene an emergency Security Council meeting to deal with the matter. If your father does not act within the hour, the Ixian Ambassador is within his rights to convene the Council himself."

"Security Council?" Elrood grimaced and looked first to Chamberlain Hesban, then to Fenring for assistance. "What regulation is that infernal woman citing?"

"Volume thirty, section six point three, under the Great Convention."

"What does it say?"

Hesban took a deep breath. "It concerns situations of House-to-House warfare, in which an appeal to the Emperor has been made by one of the parties engaged in hostilities. The regulation was designed to prohibit Emperors from taking sides; in such matters you must act as a neutral arbiter. Neutral, yes—but you must act." He shuffled his feet. "Sire, I'm afraid I don't understand why you would wish to delay. Surely, you don't side with . . . with the *Tleilaxu?*"

"There are many things you don't understand, Aken," the Emperor said. "Just follow my wishes." The Chamberlain appeared stung.

"Um-m-m-m." Fenring paced behind the high-backed chair, then snagged a crystallized fruit wafer off one of the snacking trays. "Technically the Courier is correct, Sire. You're not allowed to delay for a day or two. The regulation also goes on to say that, if called, the Landsraad Security Council meeting cannot be concluded without a decision." Fenring placed a finger on his lips as he considered. "The hostile parties and their representatives have a right to attend. In the Ixians' case, their representative could be the Spacing Guild as well as Ambassador Pilru—who, I might add, has a son currently threatened by the revolt on Ix, and another son recently inducted into the Guild."

"Remember, too, the Ambassador's wife has been killed in the revolt," Hesban added. "People are dying."

"Considering our plans for the Tleilaxu to use Ixian facilities, it would be better to keep the Guild out of this, too," Shaddam spoke up.

"Plans?" The Chamberlain looked alarmed to learn he had been kept out of such important discussions. He turned to Elrood. "What plans, Sire?"

"Later, Aken." The Emperor frowned. Shifting uncomfortably on his chair, he tugged the robes around his sunken chest. "Damn that woman!"

"The Guildsmen are waiting with her down in the hall," Hesban pressed. "Ambassador Pilru demands an audience with you. In only a few moments other Houses will get wind of the news, and they'll insist on action as well—especially the ones with CHOAM directorships. Turmoil on Ix will have drastic economic consequences, at least for the immediate future."

"Bring me the regulations and two Mentats to run independent analyses. Find something to get us out of this!" The Emperor appeared suddenly alert, pumped up by the crisis. "House Corrino must not interfere with the Tleilaxu takeover of Ix. Our future depends on it."

"As . . . you wish, Sire." Hesban bowed and left in a rustle of his deep blue finery, still perplexed but willing to follow orders.

Minutes later a house servant entered the anteroom carrying a projector and a blackplaz oval screen. Bustling about, the servant set up the apparatus on a table. Fenring moved it into position so the Emperor could see it better.

Hesban returned, flanked by two Mentats, their lips stained red with sapho juice. Outside the door, the Sardaukar elite guard held back several representatives who clamored for entry. Clearly recognizable above the clamor was the high-pitched, agitated voice of the Ixian Ambassador.

Fenring called up recorded data on shigawire reels as Chamberlain Hesban summarized the events and the problem for the two Imperial Mentats. Images danced above the table—black words printed in Galach. Staying close to his friend, Shaddam peered into the depths of the law as if he might spot some subtlety that had eluded everyone else.

Both Mentats stood rigid, eyes distant, as they ran their separate analyses of the law and its subsidiary codes. "To begin," one of the Mentats said, "take a look at six point three."

The words scrolled across the projector field in a blur, then stopped on a particular page. One of the sections was highlighted in red, and a second holo copy of the page appeared in midair. The duplicate floated to the Emperor's lap, so that both he and the others could read it.

"Won't work," the second Mentat said. "Cross-reference seventy-eight point three, volume twelve."

Leaning close, Elrood scanned the regulation. Then he passed a hand through the page, and it disappeared. "Rotten Guild," he said. "We'll bring them to their knees as soon as—" Fenring cleared his throat to interrupt the failing Emperor's train of thought before he could reveal too much.

The holoprojector began searching again as the Mentats fell silent. Chamberlain Hesban leaned close to study pages that slowed in front of him.

"Blast these regulations! That's what I'd like to do, use atomics on all the laws." Elrood continued to fume. "Do I rule the Imperium, or don't I? Having to pander to the Landsraad, having to avoid stepping on the Guild's toes . . . an Emperor shouldn't be required to bow to other powers."

"Quite right, Sire," Hesban acknowledged. "But we're caught in a web of treaties and alliances."

"Maybe this is something," Fenring said, presently. "Jihad Appendix nineteen point oh-oh-four." He paused. "In matters involving the Butlerian Jihad and the strictures established thereafter, the Emperor is given additional latitude to make decisions regarding punishment for those who breach the prohibition against thinking machines."

The Emperor's sunken eyes lit up. "Ah, and since there is some question here about possible Ixian violations, perhaps we can legally proceed with 'all due caution.' Especially since we have recently received disturbing reports about machine developments."

"We have?" the Chamberlain asked.

"Certainly. Remember the self-learning fighting meks on the black market? That bears closer scrutiny."

Shaddam and Fenring smiled at each other. They all knew such a stance might not hold up to prolonged scrutiny, but for now Elrood only needed to delay taking action. The Tleilaxu would seal their conquest in another day or two. Without outside support, House Vernius didn't have a chance.

Hesban added, studying the precise Galach words, "According to this Appendix, the Padishah Emperor is the 'Holy Guardian of the Jihad,' charged with protecting it and all it represents."

"Ah, yes. In that case, we could request to see this alleged evidence from the Tleilaxu Ambassador, and then give Pilru a set time to respond afterward." Shaddam paused, looked at Fenring for encouragement. "By the end of the day, the Emperor could issue a request for a temporary cessation of hostilities."

"It'll be too late, then," Chamberlain Hesban said.

"Exactly. Ix will fall, and there will be nothing they can do about it."

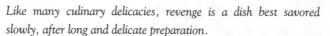

Like many culinary delicacies, revenge is a dish best savored
slowly, after long and delicate preparation.

— EMPEROR ELROOD IX,
Deathbed Insights

Half an hour later, Shaddam watched the opposing
Ambassadors enter the Emperor's anteroom for a private audience meant to "resolve the matter." At Fenring's
suggestion, he had changed into a more formal outfit with
subtle military trappings, so that while his father looked unkempt and sloppy, *he* had the appearance of a leader.

The Ixian Ambassador had a broad, flesh-fat face with
pink cheeks. His entire body looked rumpled in a serge singlesuit with wide lapels and fluffed collar. His thin gray hair
had been combed hurriedly. Since he admitted he wasn't personally familiar with the crisis conditions on Ix, he brought
along the Courier Yuta Brey, an eyewitness.

The only Tleilaxu delegate they could find, Mofra Tooy,
was a man of small stature with scruffy orange hair and
grayish skin. The man exuded a barely suppressed rage,
seething as his small dark eyes bored holes through his
Ixian counterpart. Tooy had been briefed in exactly what
to say.

Ambassador Pilru remained shocked by the entire situation, only now beginning to grasp the death of his wife
S'tina and mourn her. It all seemed unreal to him. A night-

mare. He shifted uneasily on his feet, concerned for his world, his position, and his missing son C'tair. The Ambassador's gaze flitted around the room, looking for support among the Emperor's advisors and staff. It gave him a chill to see their hard gazes turned back at him.

Two Guild agents hovered at the rear of the anteroom, looking on expressionlessly. One of them had a ruddy face with scars. The other's head was misshapen, bubbled out at the back. Shaddam had seen similar people before, people who had begun training as Guild Navigators, but had failed the rigors of the selection process.

"We will hear from Mofra Tooy first," the Emperor said in a rasping voice. "I would have him explain himself and his people's suspicions."

"And why they are taking such unprecedented and violent action!" Pilru interjected. The others ignored his outburst.

"We have discovered illegal activities on Ix," the Tleilaxu began, in a childlike voice. "The Bene Tleilax felt it imperative to stop this scourge before another insidious machine intelligence could be unleashed in the Imperium. If we had waited, the human race might have been subjected to more millennia of slavery. We had no choice but to act as we did."

"Liar!" Pilru snarled. "What makes you the enforcers of the strictures, without due process of law? You have no proof because there have been no illegal activities on Ix. We have adhered carefully to all guidelines from the Jihad."

With remarkable calm for a Tleilaxu, Tooy kept his gaze on the others in the room, as if Pilru were beneath contempt. "Our forces took necessary action before the evidence could be destroyed. Have we not learned from the Great Revolt? Once active, a machine intelligence may become vindictive *and* it can develop the ability to copy itself and spread like wildfire. Ix is the source of all machine minds. We Tleilaxu are continuing the holy war only to keep the universe free of this enemy." Though Ambassador Pilru stood two heads taller than he, Tooy screamed at him, "Jihad! Jihad!"

"Now see here, sir," Pilru said, falling back several steps. "This behavior is uncalled-for."

" 'Thou shalt not make a machine in the likeness of a human mind,' " the Tleilaxu snapped. "You and House Vernius will be damned for your sins!"

"Calm yourself." Artfully suppressing a smile, Elrood motioned for

Tooy to return to his earlier position. Reluctantly, the diminutive delegate cooperated.

Pilru and the Ixian Courier conferred in low, anxious tones, before the Ambassador said, "I ask the Emperor to require proof of such violations. The Bene Tleilax have acted as a rogue element, destroying our commercial base without first submitting their accusations to the Landsraad." Then he added quickly, "Or to the Emperor."

"Evidence is being compiled," Tooy responded. "And it will include the true motive behind the criminal acts you Ixians have committed. Your profit margins have been slipping, putting your CHOAM membership in jeopardy."

Ah, Shaddam thought, exchanging glances with Hasimir Fenring. *Those reports that we falsified so skillfully!* No one could manipulate documents as well as Fenring.

"That's patently false," Pilru said. "We're more profitable than ever, especially with our new Heighliner design. Simply ask the Guild. Your people had no right to incite such violence—"

"We had every right, the *moral* right, to protect the Imperium from another epoch of domination by machines. We see through your subterfuges to your motivation for making machine-minds. Is your profit worth more than the safety of humanity? You have sold your souls!"

Veins throbbed at Pilru's temples, and he lost his ambassadorial calm. "You lying little bastard, this is a complete fabrication!" He turned to Elrood. "Sire, I demand that you send Sardaukar to Ix to intervene and protect our people from the illegal invasion committed by forces of the Bene Tleilax. We have broken no laws."

"Violating the Butlerian Jihad is a most serious charge," the Emperor said in a thoughtful tone, though he didn't really care a whit about it. He covered his mouth as he coughed again. "Such an accusation cannot be taken lightly. Think of the consequences . . ." Elrood spoke with deliberate slowness, which Shaddam found amusing. The Crown Prince couldn't help admiring *some* things about his doomed father, but Elrood was far beyond his prime, and it was time for new blood to step in.

The Courier spoke up. "Emperor Elrood, the Tleilaxu are stalling for time while battles rage on Ix. Use your Sardaukar to enforce a cessation of hostilities, then let each side present its case and evidence in court."

The Emperor's eyebrows arched, and he gazed down his thin nose at her. "As a mere Courier, you are not qualified to present arguments to me." He flicked his glance at the Sardaukar guards. "Remove this woman."

Desperation gave her voice a ragged edge. "Pardon, Sire, but I am the one most familiar with the crisis on Ix, and my Lord Vernius instructed me to take all necessary steps. We demand that the Bene Tleilax present proof immediately, or withdraw their forces. They aren't compiling evidence. That's just a delaying tactic!"

"When can you submit the proof to me?" the Emperor inquired, sliding his gaze to Tooy.

"*Alleged* proof," Pilru objected.

"Three Imperial days, Sire."

Gasps of protest issued from the Ixians. "But, Sire, in that amount of time, they can solidify their military gains—fabricate any evidence they wish." Pilru's eyes glittered. "They have already murdered my wife, destroyed buildings . . . My son is missing. Please do not allow them to continue their rampage unchecked for *three days!*"

The Emperor considered this for a moment, while the assemblage grew quiet. "I'm sure you are exaggerating the unpleasantness to force me into making a rash decision. Considering the gravity of the charges, I'm inclined to await the evidence, or lack of it." He looked at his Chamberlain. "What say you, Aken? Does that follow the letter of Imperial Law in a situation such as this?" Hesban murmured in concurrence.

Elrood nodded at Pilru as if he were granting him an incredible personal favor. "I think, however, that the proof should be submitted in two days instead of three. Can you accomplish that, Ambassador Tooy?"

"It will be difficult, Sire, but . . . as you wish."

Aghast, Pilru flushed with anger. "My Lord, how can you side against us with these . . . these filthy *Tleilaxu?*"

"Ambassador, your prejudice is not welcome here in my Imperial anteroom. I have nothing but the utmost respect for your Earl . . . and, of course, his Lady Shando."

Shaddam looked at the Guild agents at the rear of the room. In subdued tones they conversed in a secret language. Presently they nodded to each other. A violation of the Butlerian Jihad was a most serious matter to them.

"But in two days my planet will be lost." Pilru sent a pleading look to the Guildsmen for support, but they remained silent and would not make eye contact.

"You can't do this—you'll doom our people to destruction!" Yuta Brey shouted at Elrood.

"Messenger, you *are* impertinent, just like Dominic Vernius. Tax my patience no more." Looking sternly at the Tleilaxu representative, Elrood commanded: "Ambassador Tooy, bring me your proof—*incontrovertible* proof—within two days, or withdraw your forces from Ix."

Mofra Tooy bowed. Concealed from the Guildsmen directly behind him, a slight smile worked briefly at the edges of his mouth, then faded.

"Very well then," the Ixian Ambassador said, trembling now with rage. "I hereby demand an immediate Security Council session of the Landsraad."

"And you shall have it, precisely according to law," Elrood said. "I have already acted in the manner I believe best serves the Imperium. Mofra Tooy here will address the Council in two days, and you may do the same. If you wish to return to your planet in the meantime, I will divert an express Heighliner for your use. But be warned, if these charges are indeed valid, Ambassador, House Vernius will have much to atone for."

WIPING PERSPIRATION FROM his shaven head, Dominic Vernius studied his Ambassador to Kaitain. Pilru had just delivered a shocking report to the Earl and his Lady. The man was clearly anxious to search for his missing son in the chaos of the underground city, though he had been back on the planet for less than an hour. They stood together in a subterranean operations center, deep within the ceiling of rock, since the transparent Orb Office in the Grand Palais was too vulnerable in time of war. Machinery sounds could be heard, tube transports moving Ixian troops and equipment through the catacombs of the planetary crust.

The defensive battles had not been going well. Through well-planned sabotage and carefully arranged bottlenecks, Tleilaxu now controlled most of the underworld, and the Ixians were being herded into smaller and smaller areas. The rebellious suboids vastly outnumbered the besieged Ixian defenders, and the Tleilaxu invaders took full advantage, manipulating the pale-skinned workers with ease.

"Elrood has betrayed us, my love," Dominic said, holding his wife. They had only the dirty clothes on their backs and a few household treasures they had managed to rescue. He understood everything now, though. "I knew the Emperor hated me, but I never expected such loathsome behavior, not even from him. If only I could prove it."

Looking pale and more fragile than ever, though her eyes flared with iron determination, the Lady Shando drew a deep breath. Delicate lines etched around her exquisite eyes and mouth were the only indications of her advancing age, subtle reminders to Dominic to treasure her beauty, love, and fine character more each day. Stepping to his side, she looped one arm through his. "Maybe if I went to him and threw myself on his mercy? He might be reasonable, for whatever memories he still holds of me. . . . "

"I wouldn't let you do it. He hates you now and resents me for marrying you. Roody is beyond compassion." Dominic clenched his fists and studied Ambassador Pilru's face, but found no hope there. Looking back at Shando, he said, "Knowing him, he's undoubtedly set up intrigues so complex that he couldn't withdraw now if he wanted to.

"We'll never receive war reparations, even if we are victorious. My family fortunes will be confiscated, my personal power stripped." He lowered his voice, trying to hide the despair. "And all to get even with me for taking his woman away from him a long, long time ago."

"I'll do whatever you want me to do, Dominic," she said softly. "You made me your wife instead of your concubine. I've always told you . . ." Her words trailed off.

"I know, my love." He squeezed her hand. "I'd do anything for you, too. It was worth the cost . . . even this."

"I await your orders, m'Lord," Ambassador Pilru said, deeply agitated. His son C'tair was out there somewhere, hiding, fighting, perhaps already dead.

Dominic chewed the inside of his mouth. "Clearly, House Vernius has been singled out for destruction, and there is but one alternative. All the fabricated charges mean nothing, and the paper shield of the law lies torn into shreds. The Emperor intends to destroy us, and we cannot fight House Corrino, especially against treachery such as this.

I don't doubt that the Landsraad will stall and then pounce upon the spoils of war." Glowering, he squared his broad shoulders and stood straighter. "We will take our family atomics and shields and flee beyond the reach of the Imperium."

Pilru bit back an outcry. "Going . . . *renegade*, my Lord? What about the rest of us?"

"Unfortunately, we have no choice, Cammar. It's the only way we can escape with our lives. I want you to contact the Guild and request emergency transport. Invoke any favors they owe us. The Guildsmen observed your session with the Emperor, so they know our situation. Tell them we want to take our military forces with us, too—what little we have left." Dominic hung his head. "I never imagined it would come to this . . . thrust from our Palace and our cities. . . . "

The Ambassador nodded stiffly, then departed through the shimmer of a shielded doorway.

One wall of the administrative center flashed alive with four projections on separate panels of battles raging all over the planet—color scenes transmitted by portable comeyes. Ixian losses continued to mount.

Shaking his head, Dominic said, "Now we must speak to our closest friends and retainers and inform them of the dangers they will face if they accompany us. It will be much more difficult and dangerous to flee with us than to be subjugated by the Tleilaxu. No one will be forced to go with us; it will be volunteers only. As a renegade House, all of our family members and supporters will be hunted by glory-seekers."

"Bounty hunters," Shando said, her voice heavy with mingled sorrow and anger. "You and I will have to separate, Dominic—to throw them off our trail and increase our chances."

On the wall, two image panels fizzled out, as the Tleilaxu found transmitting comeyes and disabled them.

Dominic softened his voice. "Later, after our House and planet have been restored to us, we'll remember what we did here and what was said. This is history. High drama. Let me tell you a little story, a parallel case study."

"I do enjoy your stories," she said with a gentle smile on her strong yet delicate face. Her hazel eyes danced. "Very well, what will we tell our grandchildren?"

Momentarily he focused on a fresh crack in the ceiling and water that trickled down a wall. "Salusa Secundus was once the Imperial capital world. Do you know why they moved it to Kaitain?"

"Some problem with atomics," she replied. "Devastation on Salusa."

"According to the Imperial version, it was an unfortunate accident. But House Corrino only says that because they don't want to give people ideas. The truth is that another renegade family, a Great House whose name was stripped from historical records, managed to land on Salusa with their family atomics. In a daring raid they bombed the capital and set off an ecological catastrophe. The world still hasn't recovered."

"An attack with atomics? I didn't know that."

"Afterward the survivors moved the Imperial throne to Kaitain, in a different, more secure solar system, where young Emperor Hassik III rebuilt the government." Seeing the concern on his wife's face, he drew her closer and held her tightly. "We won't fail, my love."

The last wall panels fizzled and went dead as the Tleilaxu knocked out the remaining comeyes.

Despite disastrous military losses during the unexpected revolt, many secret places still remained on Ix. Centuries ago, during the paranoid times after House Vernius took over the machine operations, engineers sworn to secrecy had laid down an unrecorded honeycomb of transmission-shielded rooms, algae-chambers, and hideouts masked from discovery by remarkable Ixian ingenuity. It would take centuries for an enemy to ferret them out; even the ruling House had forgotten half of them.

Guided by Captain Zhaz and the troop of personal bodyguards, Leto and Rhombur concealed themselves in an algae-walled chamber, which was entered via an access tube that led upward into the crust of the planet. Routine enemy scans would detect only the life signs of the algae, since massive dampening fields surrounded the rest of the isolated chamber.

"We'll only have to stay here a few days," Rhombur said, struggling to recapture his usual optimism. "Surely by then, Landsraad or Imperial forces will have come to our rescue, and House Vernius can begin rebuilding Ix. Things will all work out."

Narrowing his eyes, Leto remained silent. If his suspicions were correct, it could well take much longer than that.

"This chamber is just a rendezvous point, Master Rhombur," Captain Zhaz said. "We'll await the Earl and follow his orders."

Rhombur nodded vigorously. "Yes, my father'll know what to do. He's been in plenty of challenging military situations before." He smiled brightly. "Some of them with your own father, Leto."

Leto clapped a strong hand on the other Prince's shoulder, in a display of support for his friend. But he didn't know how many of Dominic Vernius's previous battle engagements had been desperate defensive measures like this; it was Leto's impression that Dominic's victories in the past had always been overwhelming charges against crumbling groups of rebels.

Remembering what his father had taught him—*know the details of your surroundings in any difficult circumstance*—Leto took a moment to inspect their hideaway. He searched for escape routes, vulnerable points. The algae-chamber had been hacked out of solid crustal rock, with an outer shell of thick green growth that gave the air a sour, organic taint. The bolt-hole had four apartments, an extensive kitchen complete with survival supplies, and a last-chance emergency ship that could make low-planetary orbit.

Frictionless, noiseless machinery operated nullentropy bins at the core of the chamber, keeping food and beverages fresh. Other bins contained clothing, weapons, filmbooks, and clever Ixian games for hidden refugees to while away the time. The endless waiting could be the most difficult part of this protected sanctuary, and boredom was an often-overlooked part of isolation and escape. The Ixians, though, had thought of all necessary preparations.

It was already evening, as determined by their chronos. Zhaz set up his guards in the outer corridors and at the camouflaged door-hatch. Rhombur rattled off an endless stream of questions, most of which the captain could not answer: What was going on outside? Did they dare hope to be freed by Ixian loyalists, or would Tleilaxu invaders imprison them, or worse? Would an Ixian come to notify Rhombur of the death of his parents? Why hadn't the others shown up at the rendezvous point yet? Did they have any idea how much of the capital city of Vernii remained intact? If not, who could find out for them?

The klaxon of an intruder warning interrupted him. Someone was trying to enter the chamber.

Captain Zhaz flipped out a handheld monitor, pressed a button to illuminate the room and activate a videoscreen. Leto saw three familiar faces pressed close to the comeyes in the secondary corridor—Dominic Vernius, and his daughter Kailea, her dress torn and her coppery hair in disarray. Between them they supported the Lady Shando, who seemed barely conscious, her arm and ribs crudely bandaged.

"Permission to enter," Dominic said, his voice tinny and granular across the speakers. "Open up, Rhombur. Zhaz! We need medical attention for Shando." His eyes were shadowed, his teeth very white beneath the bushy mustache.

Rhombur Vernius rushed toward the controls, but the guard captain stopped him with an urgent tug at his arm. "By all the saints and sinners, remember the Face Dancers, young master!" Leto suddenly realized that Tleilaxu shape-shifters could assume familiar guises and walk into the most secure area. Leto held the Ixian Prince's other arm while Zhaz interrogated and received a countersign. Finally, a message appeared from the shielded chamber's biometric identity scanner. *Confirmed: Earl Dominic Vernius.*

"Permission granted," Rhombur said into the voice pickup. "Come in—Mother, what happened?"

Kailea looked stricken, as if the floor had dropped out from beneath her plans for the future and she still couldn't believe she was falling. All of the newcomers smelled of sweat and smoke and fear.

"Your sister was scolding the suboids and telling them to get back to work," Shando said with a bit of mirth shining through her pain. "Very foolish."

"And some of them were about to do it, too—" the young woman said as a flush of anger blossomed beneath the soot smudges on her cheeks.

"Until one pulled a maula pistol and opened fire. Good thing the man couldn't aim." Shando touched her arm and side, wincing at the open wound.

Dominic knocked the guards aside and tore open a medkit to tend his wife's injuries himself. "Not serious, my love. I'll be around to kiss the scars later. But you shouldn't have taken such a risk."

"Not even to save Kailea?" Shando coughed, and her eyes sparkled with tears. "You would have done the same to protect either of our children—or even Leto Atreides. And don't you deny it."

Averting his gaze, Dominic grudgingly nodded. "It still upsets me . . . how close you came to death. Then what would I have left to fight for?" He stroked her hair, and she clasped the palm of his hand against her cheek.

"Plenty, Dominic. You'd still have plenty to fight for."

Watching the exchange, Leto could see what had driven a beautiful young concubine to leave her Emperor, and why a war hero had risked Elrood's wrath to marry her.

Outside in the hidden corridor, half a dozen armed soldiers took up positions again, sealing the access door behind them. On the external-monitor screen, Leto saw the rest of them—shock troops in case of a violent rebel incursion—setting up lascannons, sensors, and sonic defensive equipment in the chamber's access tube.

Relieved to see his family safe at last, Rhombur hugged his parents and sister. "It'll be all right," he said. "You'll see."

Despite her wound, the Lady Shando appeared proud and brave, though salty tracks around her reddened eyes showed evidence of tears. Self-consciously, Kailea glanced over at Leto, then dropped her emerald gaze. She looked defeated now, and fragile, without her usual aloof demeanor. He wanted to comfort her, but hesitated. Everything seemed too unsettled now, too frightening.

"We don't have much time, children," Dominic said, wiping perspiration from his brow, then rubbing his sweaty biceps, "and this time calls for desperate measures." His shaved scalp was smudged with someone else's blood—ally or enemy? Leto wondered. The torn helix insignia dangled from his lapel.

"Then now is not the time to call us *children*," Kailea said with surprising strength. "We're a part of this fight."

Rhombur stood tall, looking unusually regal beside his broad-shouldered father, rather than spoiled and stocky. "And we're ready to help you retake Ix. Vernii is our city, and we have to get it back."

"No, all three of you are going to stay here." Dominic held up a wide, callused hand to silence Rhombur's instant objection. "First order of business is to keep the heirs safe. I'll hear no argument in this. Each moment of arguing takes me away from my people, and they desperately need my leadership right now."

"You boys are too young to fight," Shando said, her delicate face now looking hard and unbreakable. "You're the future of your respective Houses—both of you."

Dominic came forward to stand in front of Leto and looked him directly in the eye for the first time, as if he finally saw the Atreides boy as a man. "Leto, your father would never forgive me if anything happened to his son. We have already sent a message to the Old Duke, notifying him of the situation. In response, your father has promised limited assistance and has dispatched a rescue mission to take you, Rhombur, and Kailea to safety on Caladan." Dominic placed beefy hands on the shoulders of his two children—children who now needed to be much more than that. "Duke Atreides will protect you, give you sanctuary from this. It is all he can do for now."

"That's ridiculous," Leto said, his gray eyes flashing. "You should take refuge with House Atreides as well, m'Lord. My father would never turn you away."

Dominic gave a wan smile. "No doubt Paulus would do exactly as you say—but I *cannot,* because that would doom my children."

Rhombur looked over at his sister in alarm. Lady Shando nodded and continued; she and her husband had already discussed the various possibilities. "Rhombur, if you and Kailea live in exile on Caladan, then you may be safe, not worth anyone's trouble. I suspect that this bloody revolt has been engineered with Imperial influence and support, and all the pieces have fallen into place."

Rhombur and Kailea stared at each other in disbelief, then at Leto. "Imperial support?"

"Why the Emperor wants Ix, I do not know," Dominic said, "but Elrood's grudge is against *me* and your mother. If I go with you to House Atreides, the hunters will come for all of us. They'll find some reason to attack Caladan. No, your mother and I have to find a way to draw this fight away from you."

Rhombur stood indignant. His pale skin flushed. "We can hold out here a while longer, Father. I don't want to leave you behind."

"The deal is done, my son. It's already negotiated. Other than the Atreides rescue operation, there is no help coming—no Imperial Sardaukar to assist us, no Landsraad armies to drive back the Tleilaxu. The suboids are their pawns. We have sent appeals to all the Houses

Major and to the Landsraad, but no one will move fast enough. Someone has outmaneuvered us. . . ."

At her husband's side, Lady Shando held her head high, despite her pain and disheveled appearance. She had been the Lady of a Great House, and an Imperial concubine before that, but first of all she had been lowborn. Shando could be happy even without the riches of an Ixian governorship.

"But what happens to the two of you now?" Leto asked, since Rhombur and Kailea didn't have the courage to inquire.

"House Vernius will go . . . renegade." Shando let the word hang in an astonished silence for a heartbeat.

"Vermilion hells!" Rhombur finally said, and his sister also gasped.

Shando stood and kissed her children.

"We'll take what we can salvage, then Dominic and I will separate and go into hiding. Maybe for years. A few of the most loyal will accompany us, others will flee entirely, still others will stay here, for better or worse. We'll make new lives for ourselves, and eventually our fortunes will turn again."

Dominic gave Leto an awkward handshake, not quite the Imperial clasp of fingers, but more the way Old Terrans used to do it, since the Imperium—from the Emperor to all of the Houses Major—had let House Vernius down. Once they declared themselves renegade, the family Vernius would no longer be part of the Imperium.

Shando and Kailea were crying softly as they hugged one another, while Dominic clasped his son by the shoulders. Moments later, Earl Vernius and his wife hurried out through the chamber's access tube, taking a contingent of guards with them, while Rhombur and his sister held one another and watched them go on the comeye screen.

❦

THE FOLLOWING MORNING, the three refugees sat in uncomfortable but efficient suspensor chairs, eating energy bars and drinking Ixap juice. And waiting.

Kailea said little, as if she had lost her energy for fighting the circumstances. Her older brother tried to cheer her up, but to no avail. Isolated here, walled off, they had heard no word from outside, didn't know if reinforcements had arrived, or if the city continued to burn. . . .

Kailea had cleaned herself up, made a valiant effort to reconstruct her damaged gown and torn lace, and then wore her altered appearance like a badge. "I should have been attending a ball this week," she said, her voice empty as if all the emotion had been scrubbed from it. "The Solstice of Dur, one of the largest social events on Kaitain. My mother said I could attend one when I was old enough." She looked over at Leto and gave a mirthless laugh. "Since I could have gotten betrothed to an appropriate husband this year, I must be old enough to attend a dance. Don't you think?"

She plucked at her torn lace sleeve. Leto didn't know what to say to her. He tried to think of what Helena would have said to the Vernius daughter. "When we get to Caladan, I'll have my mother throw a grand ball to welcome you there. Would you like that, Kailea?" He knew the Lady Helena resented the two Ixian children because of her religious bias, but surely his mother would soften her heart, considering the situation. If nothing else, she would never be seen committing a social faux pas.

Kailea's eyes flared at his suggestion, and Leto shrank back. "What, with fishermen dancing a bawdy jig and rice farmers performing some fertility rite?" Her words cut deep, and Leto felt his world and his heritage to be inadequate for someone like her.

Kailea softened, though, and rested her fingers on Leto's forearm. "I'm sorry, Leto. Very sorry. It's just that I wanted so badly to go to *Kaitain*, to see the Imperial Palace, the wonders of the Court."

Rhombur sat sullen. "Elrood never would have allowed it, if only because he's still angry at Mother."

Kailea got up and paced the small, algae-smelling chamber. "Why did she ever have to leave him? She could have stayed in the Palace, lived her life in luxury—but instead she came here to this . . . *cave*. A cave that's now overrun with vermin. If Father really cared for her, would he have asked her to sacrifice so much? It makes no sense."

Leto tried to console her. "Don't you believe in love, Kailea? I've seen the way your parents look at each other."

"Of course I believe in *love*, Leto. But I also believe in common sense, and you have to weigh one against the other."

Kailea turned her back on them and rummaged in the entertainment files for something to amuse herself. Leto decided not to pursue the matter. Instead, he turned to Rhombur with a suggestion. "We should each take the time to learn how to operate the orship. Just in case."

"No need. I can run it myself," Rhombur said.

After taking a drink of the tart, preserved juice, Leto puckered his lips. "But what if you're injured—or worse? What do we do then?"

"He's right, you know," Kailea said, not even lifting her emerald eyes from the entertainment files. Her voice sounded weary and brittle. "Let's show him, Rhombur."

He stared across the table at Leto. "Well, you know how an ornithopter works? Or a shuttle?"

"I learned to pilot a 'thopter by the time I was ten. But the only shuttles I've seen were robo-controlled."

"Brainless machines, performing set functions the same way every time. I hate those things . . . even though we manufacture them." He took a bite of energy bar. "Well, we *used to*, anyway. Before the Tleilaxu came." He lifted his right hand overhead and rubbed the fire-jewel ring that designated him as heir of the Ixian House.

At his signal, a large square in the ceiling dropped smoothly and came to rest on the floor. Looking up through the aperture, Leto saw a sleek silver shape stored above. "Come with me." Rhombur stepped onto the panel, and Kailea joined him. "We'll do a systems check."

As Leto stepped aboard, he felt an upward thrust. The three of them surged through the ceiling and beyond, up the side of a silver airship to a platform high on the craft's fuselage.

The orship reminded Leto of a space lighter, a small craft with a narrow body and plaz windows. A combination ornithopter-spacecraft, the orship could operate either on-planet or in low orbit. In violation of the Guild's monopoly on space travel, orships were among the most closely held Ixian secrets, to be employed only as a last resort.

A hatch slid open on the side of the craft, and Leto heard the ship's systems surround him with a hum of machinery and electronics. Rhombur led the way into a compact command center with two high-backed chairs and glimmering finger-panel controls in front of each. He slid into one seat, and Leto into the other. The resilient sensiform material conformed to their bodies. Soft green lights glowed on the finger panels. Kailea stood behind her brother, her hands on the back of his chair.

With his fingers dancing over the glowing control panels, Rhombur said, "I'm setting yours on tutorial. The ship will teach you how to pilot it."

Leto's panel changed color to yellow. Wondering again about the machine-mind taboos of the Butlerian Jihad, he scrunched his face in confusion. How much could this craft think for itself? His mother had warned him about accepting too many things, especially Ixian things, at face value. Through the clear plaz windshield he saw only gray rock outside, the rough interior surface of the algae-chamber.

"So it thinks for itself? Like those new training meks you showed me?"

Rhombur paused. "Uh, I know what's on your mind, Leto, but this machine does not emulate human thought processes. The suboids just don't understand. Like our adaptive fighting mek, which scans an adversary to make combat decisions, it doesn't *think*—it only reacts, at lightning speed. It reads your movements, anticipates, and responds."

"That sounds like thinking to me." In the finger-panel zone before Leto, lights danced within lights.

Kailea sighed with frustration. "The Butlerian Jihad has been over for thousands of years, and still humankind acts as if we're terrified rodents hiding from shadows. There is an anti-Ixian prejudice throughout the Imperium because we make complex *machines*. People don't understand what we do, and misunderstanding breeds suspicion."

Leto nodded. "Then help me understand. Let's get started." He looked at the control panel and tried not to be too impatient. After the past few days, they were all feeling the effects of unrelenting stress.

"Place your fingers over the identity plates," Rhombur said. "Don't actually touch the panel. Stay a little above it."

After doing so, Leto's body was surrounded by a pale yellow glow that made his skin tingle.

"It's absorbing the identity components of your body: the shape of your face, tiny scars, fingerprints, hair follicles, retina prints. I've instructed the machine to accept your inputs." When the glow receded, Rhombur said, "You're authorized now. Activate the tutorial by passing your right thumb over the second row of lights."

Leto complied, and a synthetic-reality box appeared in front of his eyes depicting an aerial view that passed over craggy mountains and rocky gorges—the same scenery he had observed months ago, the day he'd been unceremoniously stranded outside by the Guild shuttle.

Suddenly sparks filled the air in the hiding chamber below. Explosions and static bursts inundated his ears. The synthetic landscape image went hazy, came into focus again, and faded. Leto's head rang from the noise.

"Sit down," Rhombur barked. "Uh—this isn't a simulation anymore."

"They've found us already!" Kailea tumbled into a low bulkhead seat behind Leto's and was automatically surrounded by a personal safety field. Leto felt the warmth of another PSF cocooning him as Rhombur tried to lock himself into the piloting seat.

On the orship's surveillance screen, Rhombur saw Tleilaxu soldiers and armed suboids filling the hidden chamber's access tube, firing lasgun bursts to break open the hidden doorways. The attackers were already through the second barrier. Captain Zhaz and a few remaining men lay in smoking mounds on the floor.

"Maybe your parents got away," Leto said. "I hope they're safe."

Rhombur thrust his hands into the finger-control field, removing the orship from tutorial mode and preparing for actual takeoff. Leto sat back, trying to relinquish command. The external simulation still filled his eyes, distracting him with visions of pristine Ixian landscapes.

Blue light flashed from outside the craft. An explosion rocked all of them. Leto heard Rhombur grunt in pain and shook his head to scatter the rest of the tutorial hologram. The Ixian Prince slumped forward in his chair; blood trickled down his face.

"What the hells?" Leto said. "Rhombur?"

"This is real, Leto!" Kailea shouted. "Fly this thing out of here."

Leto jammed his fingers against the panel, struggling to switch from tutorial to active status, but Rhombur hadn't finished prepping the ship. Another explosion blasted through the wall of the chamber, strewing algae-covered shards of rock. Ominous figures surged into the main room below.

Rhombur groaned. From beneath them, suboids shouted and pointed up at the ship that held the three refugees. Lasgun fire scorched the stone walls and the orship's plated hull. Leto activated the auto-launch sequence. Despite his earlier concerns, he now fervently hoped the ship's interactive computer mind would function efficiently.

The orship shot straight up through a channel, then a rock cap, a layer of snow, and finally into an open sky full of dazzling clouds. Steering with his fingers, Leto narrowly avoided a brilliant stream of laser bursts, automated defenses the rebels had commandeered. He squinted against the sudden sunlight.

Looping high in the stratosphere and trying to get a bead on any enemy that might strike them from space, Leto noticed a hulking Heighliner in low-planetary orbit. Two streaks of light shot out of the massive craft in separate V-patterns—a familiar signal to Leto: *Atreides ships*.

From the comboard Leto sent an identifier signal in the special battle language his father and teachers had hammered into him. Rescue craft fell in on each side of the orship, acting as escorts. The pilots signaled him to acknowledge his identity. Bursts of purple from the starboard craft pulverized a cloud below, where enemy ships had been concealed.

"Rhombur, are you all right?" Kailea took a moment to assess her brother's injuries.

The young Vernius heir stirred, put a hand to his head, and groaned. A ceiling-mounted electronics box had struck him on the skull, then shattered on the floor. "Uh, vermilion hells!—didn't get the blasted PSF activated in time." He blinked repeatedly, then swiped dark blood from his eyes.

Using his new skills, Leto followed his escort into the safety of the waiting Heighliner, where he saw two large Atreides battle frigates. As his orship hovered inside the hold, a message came over the comsystem in Galach, but he recognized a familiar Caladanian drawl. "Good thing we got the Heighliner to wait an extra hour. Welcome aboard, Prince Leto. Are you and your companions all right? How many survivors?"

He looked over at Rhombur nursing his battered skull. "Three of us, more or less intact. Just get us away from Ix."

After the orship was parked between Atreides escorts within assigned stalls inside the immense Heighliner hold, Leto looked to each side. Through the portholes of the larger ships he saw uniformed Atreides soldiers in green-and-black livery, familiar hawk crests. He breathed a deep, relieved sigh.

Next he looked with concern at Rhombur, whose sister was wiping blood off his brow with a cloth. Focusing on Leto, the Ixian Prince said, "Well, forget the simulations, friend. It's always best to learn by doing."

Then he passed out and crumpled to one side.

Even the poorest House can be rich in loyalty. Allegiance that must be purchased by bribes or wages is hollow and flawed, and could break at the worst possible moment. Allegiance that comes from the heart, though, is stronger than adamantium and more valuable than purest melange.

— DUKE PAULUS ATREIDES

Far across the galaxy, within the cargo hold of another Heighliner, a single unmarked Ixian space cruiser rested alone and indistinguishable among the crowded ships. The runaway cruiser had hopped from one freight line to another, changing designations each time.

Inside the unmarked ship, Dominic and Shando Vernius sat as passengers amidst the tattered remnants of their armed forces. Many of the family guard had been killed, and many had not made it to the escape ship in time; others had decided to take their chances in the aftermath of the revolution. No one aboard had said anything for a long time.

Lady Shando's personal manservant Omer squirmed, twitching his narrow shoulders; his straight black hair had been cut exactly at the collar line, but now both collar and hair looked a bit ragged. Omer was the only one of her household staff who had chosen to accompany the family into exile. A timid man, he had abhorred the prospect of attempting to make a new life among the Tleilaxu.

Ambassador Pilru's curt reports had made it eminently clear that they could expect no assistance from Landsraad military forces or the Emperor. By declaring themselves renegade they had severed all ties—and all obligations—to Imperial Law.

The seats, storage bins, and lockers aboard the renegade ship were filled with gems and valuable items, anything that could be sold for ready cash. Their flight might last for a long, long time.

Dominic sat next to his wife, holding her small and delicate hand. His hairless brow was creased with concern. "Elrood will send out teams to track us down," he said. "We'll be hunted like animals."

"Oh, why won't he just leave us alone now?" Omer muttered, shaking his straight black hair. "We've already lost everything."

"Not enough for Roody," Shando said, turning to her manservant. She sat straight-backed and regal. "He's never forgiven me for talking him into letting me go. I never lied, but he thinks I tricked him."

She looked out the narrow port edged with gleaming ser-chrome. The Ixian ship was small, with no overt markings of House Vernius: a simple vehicle used for hauling cargo or steerage passengers. Shando squeezed her husband's hand and tried not to think of how far their fortunes had fallen.

She remembered the day of her departure from the Imperial Court, bathed and perfumed and decked with fresh flowers from Elrood's greenhouses. The other concubines had given her gifts of brooches, jewels, radiant scarves that glowed from body heat. She had been young and excited then, her heart swelling with gratitude for the memories and experiences, yet aching to start a new life with a man she desperately loved.

Shando had kept her romance with Dominic secret and left Elrood under what she thought were good terms, terminating her service with his blessing. She and the Emperor had made love one last time, talked fondly of memories they shared. Elrood hadn't understood her desire to leave Kaitain, but he had plenty of other concubines, after all. Her loss had meant little to him . . . until he learned she'd left him out of love for another man.

Now Shando's ragged flight from Ix was far different from her departure from Kaitain. She sighed bitterly. "After a reign of almost a century and a half, Roody has learned how to wait for his revenge."

Long past any shadow of jealousy, Dominic chuckled at the pet name. "Well, now he's gotten even with us. We'll have to be patient ourselves and find some way to restore our House's fortunes. If not for us, then for our children."

"I trust Paulus Atreides to keep them safe," Shando said. "He's a good man."

"We must trust no one else to keep *ourselves* safe, however," Dominic said. "That will be quite enough of a challenge for us."

Dominic and Shando would soon separate, take new identities, and go into hiding on isolated planets, all the while hoping to be reunited one day. They had paid a huge bribe to the Guild, so that no records would be kept of their respective destinations. Husband and wife clung together, knowing that from this point on, nothing in their lives was certain.

Ahead lay uncharted space.

⁕

ALONE WITHIN THE remnants of war-torn Ix, C'tair Pilru buried himself in a tiny transmission-shielded room. He hoped none of the suboids would find him. It seemed to be his only chance to survive the carnage.

His mother had once shown him this place concealed behind a dungeon wall of the Grand Palais, shielded up in the thick crust. As members of the Vernius Court, sons of the Ambassador to Kaitain, C'tair and D'murr had been assigned a place for personal safety should any emergency ever arise. With the same methodical efficiency she employed daily as a Guild banker, S'tina had prepared for every likelihood, and made sure her sons remembered. Sweaty, hungry, and terrified, C'tair had been relieved to find the hiding place intact amidst the chaos, gunfire, and explosions.

Then, safe and numb, the shock of what was happening to his city—his *world*—hit him full force. He couldn't believe everything that had already been lost, how much grandeur had turned to dirt and blood and smoke.

His twin brother was gone, whisked off by the Guild to be trained as a Navigator. At the time he had resented that loss, but at least it meant D'murr was safe from the revolution. C'tair would not wish this ordeal on anyone . . . but he hoped that his brother had somehow received the news by now. Were the Tleilaxu covering it up?

C'tair had tried to contact his father, but the Ambassador had been trapped on Kaitain at the height of the crisis. Amid fires and explosions and murderous suboid gangs, C'tair had found himself with few options other than to hide and survive. The dark-haired young man would be killed if he tried to make it to the Vernius administration chambers.

Their mother was dead already.

C'tair hid in his enclosed room with the glowglobes extinguished, listening to faint tremors of distant fighting and the much louder sounds of his own breathing, his own heartbeat. He was *alive*.

Three days earlier, he had watched the revolutionaries destroy a wing of the Guild facility, the section of the blocky gray building that housed all Ixian banking functions. His mother had been in there. He and D'murr had visited her offices enough times during their childhood.

He knew S'tina had barricaded herself in the records vaults, unable to escape and unwilling to believe the rebellious suboid fighters would dare attack a neutral Guild stronghold. But the suboids did not understand politics or the subtle strands of power. S'tina had sent C'tair a final transmission, telling him to hold out, to stay safe, arranging for where they would meet again once the violence died down. Neither of them had believed the situation could get worse.

But while C'tair had watched, explosions planted by suboid rebels tore part of the building free. The structure broke away from its hold on the cave roof. Burning, groaning, tumbling, the wreckage fell with a monumental crash to the grotto floor, killing hundreds of watching rebels, as well as the Guild bankers and functionaries. Everyone inside.

The air filled with smoke and screams, and the fighting continued. He had known it would be useless to make his way down there to search for his mother. Instead, realizing that his entire world was falling apart, C'tair had run to the only shelter he knew.

Hidden within the transmission-shielded bolt-hole, he slept huddled in a fetal position, then awoke with a vague sense of determination partially dulled by his anger and grief. C'tair found and inventoried provisions laid up in nullentropy storage chambers; he checked outdated weapons in the small armory closet. Unlike some of the larger algae-rooms, this secret place had no orship. He hoped the chamber wasn't on any charts, classified or unclassified. Otherwise, the Tleilaxu and their duped suboid followers would certainly find him.

Stunned and listless, C'tair holed up and passed the time, not certain when he might be able to escape, or even send a message. He didn't think any outside military forces would ever arrive to rescue Ix—it should have happened long before now. His father had departed for good. A few panicked rumors said that House Vernius had fled, gone renegade. The Grand Palais was already abandoned and ransacked, soon to become the headquarters for the new masters of Ix.

Had Kailea Vernius departed with her family, fleeing the destruction? C'tair hoped so, for her sake. Otherwise, she would have been a target for the angry revolutionaries. She was a beautiful young woman bred for Court functions and finery and palace intrigues, never for tooth-and-nail survival.

It made him sick to think of his beloved city, pillaged and trampled. He remembered the crystal walkways, the stalactite buildings, the magnificent achievements of the Heighliner construction, a craft that could be whisked away like magic by the powers of a Guild Navigator. How often had he and D'murr explored long tunnels, looked out at the massive grottoes, watched prosperity spread to all Ix's inhabitants? Now the suboids had ruined everything. And for what? He doubted even they understood.

Possibly C'tair could find a passage to the surface, contact a transport ship, use stolen credits to buy a passage off of Ix and make his way to Kaitain, where he would contact his father. Was Cammar Pilru even still the Ambassador? Of a government in exile? Probably not.

No, C'tair could not leave here and abandon his world to its fate. This was Ix, his home, and he refused to run. He did vow to survive, though . . . somehow. He would do whatever it took. Once the dust settled, he could wear old clothes and meekly pretend to be one of the disaffected Ixians coping with new planetary masters. He doubted he would ever be safe, however.

Not if he intended to continue the fight . . .

In ensuing weeks, C'tair was able to sneak out of his hideout late in the programmed subterranean nights, utilizing an Ixian life-tracer to avoid Tleilaxu guards and other enemy personnel. With disgust he watched magnificent Vernii crumble in front of his eyes.

The Grand Palais was now occupied by the ugly gnome-men, treacherous gray-skinned usurpers who had stolen an entire world under the indifferent eyes of the Imperium. They had flooded the underground city with their furtive, robed representatives. Ferretlike invader teams scoured the stalactite buildings in search of any nobles in hiding. Face Dancer troops proved much more efficient than the reckless lower classes.

Far below, suboids reveled in the streets . . . but they didn't know what else to do. Soon, they grew bored and went sullenly back to their old jobs. Without Face Dancer instigators to tell them what to want or demand, the suboids had no organized meetings, no way to make their own decisions. Their lives became the same again, under different masters, with tighter production quotas. C'tair realized that the new Tleilaxu overseers would have to begin making enormous profits in order to pay the material costs of this takeover.

On the streets of the underground city, C'tair shuffled unnoticed among the defeated populace—shift supervisors and families of mid-ranked workers who had survived the purges and had nowhere to go. Dressed in drab clothes, he crossed damaged walkways into the ruined upper city and took lift tubes down to the rubble of the manufacturing centers. He couldn't hide forever, but he couldn't be seen yet either.

C'tair refused to accept that the battle was already lost. The Bene Tleilax had few friends among the Landsraad, and they certainly couldn't withstand a coordinated resistance. Yet, Ix seemed to offer none.

Standing in a small, cowed group of pedestrians on a sidewalk made of interlocked tiles, he watched blond, chiseled-featured soldiers march by. They wore gray-and-black uniforms—definitely not Ixians or suboids, and certainly not Tleilaxu. Tall and erect, the haughty soldiers carried stunners, wore black riot-control helmets, and enforced order. A new order. With horror, he recognized them.

The Emperor's Sardaukar!

The sight of Imperial troops assisting in the takeover made C'tair furious as he comprehended greater depths to this conspiracy . . . but he masked his emotions in the crowd. He couldn't allow anyone to notice him. Around him, he heard the grumbling of Ixian natives— despite Sardaukar enforcement, even the middle classes were none too content with their changed situation. Earl Vernius had been a good-natured if somewhat preoccupied ruler; the Bene Tleilax, on the other hand, were religious fanatics with brutal rules. Many of the freedoms Ixians took for granted would soon vanish under Tleilaxu government.

C'tair wished he could do something to get even with these treacherous invaders. He vowed to make that his focus for as long as it might take.

As he crept along the gloomy, damaged streets on the grotto floor, it saddened him to see buildings blackened and crumbling from the ceiling. The upper city had been gutted. Two of the diamond pillars supporting the immense rock roof had been blown, and the resulting avalanches had buried entire blocks of suboid dwelling complexes.

With a muffled groan, C'tair realized that virtually all of the grand Ixian public artworks had been destroyed, including the stylized Guild Heighliner model that had graced Plaza Dome. Even the beautiful fiber-optic sky on the rock ceiling was damaged and the projections were splotchy now. The dour and fanatical Tleilaxu had never been known to appreciate art. To them, it simply got in the way.

He remembered that Kailea Vernius had dabbled in painting and motile sculptures. She had talked with C'tair about certain styles that were all the rage on Kaitain and had greedily absorbed any tourist images his father brought back from ambassadorial duties. But now the art was gone, and so was Kailea.

Once again, C'tair felt paralyzed by his aloneness.

Slipping unnoticed into the ruins of a collapsed outbuilding in what had once been a botanical park, C'tair stopped suddenly, transfixed. Something caught his eye, and he squinted to clear his vision.

Out of the smoldering rubble emerged the hazy image of a familiar old man, barely visible. C'tair blinked—could this be his imagination, a stuttering hologram from a diary-disk . . . or something else? He hadn't eaten all day, and he was tense and weary to the point of collapse. But still the image was *there*. Wasn't it?

Through smoke and acrid fumes, he recognized the form of the old inventor Davee Rogo, the crippled genius who had befriended the twins and taught them his innovations. As C'tair gasped, the apparition began to whisper in a frail, creaking voice. Was it a ghost . . . a vision, a mad hallucination? Eccentric Rogo seemed to be telling C'tair what to do, what technological components he needed, and how to put them all together.

"Are you real?" C'tair whispered, stepping closer. "What are you telling me?"

For some reason the blurry image of old Rogo did not respond to questions. C'tair didn't understand, but he listened. Wires and metal parts lay strewn at his feet where a machine had been wrecked by indiscriminate explosives. *These are components I need.*

Bending over and scanning warily for unwanted observers, he gathered the pieces that stood out in his mind, along with other technological remnants: small bits of metal, plaz crystals, and electronic cells. The old man had given him some kind of inspiration.

C'tair stuffed the items into his pockets and beneath his clothing. Ix would change mightily under the new Tleilaxu rule, and any scrap of his civilization's precious past might prove valuable. The Tleilaxu would confiscate everything if they found him. . . .

In the following days of haunted exploration, C'tair never saw the image of the old man again, never truly comprehended what he had encountered, but he worked hard to add to his technological collection, his *resources*. He would continue this battle . . . alone, if necessary.

Each night he passed under the noses of the enemy as they settled in for permanent occupation. He ransacked empty portions of the upper and lower city, before rebuilding teams could clean up and remove unwanted memories.

Remembering what the vision of Rogo had whispered into his imagination, he began to construct . . . *something*.

❦

WHEN THE ATREIDES rescue ships returned to Caladan and approached the spaceport fields of Cala City, the Old Duke made only minimal attempts at a grand welcome. The times and circumstances were too somber for the usual protocol ministers, band, and banner carriers.

Duke Atreides stood in the open air, squinting up into the cloud-dappled sunshine as the ships landed. He wore his favorite cape of spotted whale-fur to block the brisk wind, though it did not match his patterned tunic. All the mustered retainers and household troops waited at attention beside the receiving platform, but he didn't care about his dress, or the impression he might make. Paulus was just glad to have his son home, and safe.

Lady Helena stood beside him, rigid-backed and dressed in a formal gown and cape, her appearance impeccable. As the frigate settled down onto the spaceport landing area, Helena regarded her husband with an "I told you so" expression, then she composed her face into a welcoming smile for all to see. No observer would ever guess at the repeated shouting matches they'd engaged in while the Heighliner was en route, bringing their son home.

"I don't see how you could offer those two sanctuary," she said, her voice quiet but icy. Her lips continued to smile. "The Ixians have gone beyond the strictures of the Jihad, and now they're paying the price for it. It's dangerous to interfere with the punishments of God."

"These two Vernius children are innocents and will stay here as guests of House Atreides for as long as necessary. Why must you keep arguing with me? I have made my decision."

"Your decisions need not be etched in stone. If you listen to me, perhaps this veil will be lifted from your eyes and you can see the peril we all face because of their presence." Helena stood exactly as close to her husband as any observers would expect. "I'm concerned for us, and for our son."

The ship on the landing field extended its struts, and locked down. Exasperated, Paulus turned to her. "Helena, I owe Dominic Vernius more than you can know—and I do not shirk my obligations. Even without the blood-debt we owe each other after Ecaz, I'd still offer to protect his children. I do this as much from my own heart as from a sense of duty. Soften your heart, woman. Think of what those two children have been through."

A gust of wind whipped her auburn hair, but Helena did not flinch. Ironically, she was the first to raise her hand in greeting as the boarding door opened. She spoke out of the side of her mouth. "Paulus, you're baring your throat to the Imperial executioner, and smiling while you're doing it! We'll pay for this folly in ways you can't imagine. I just want the best for everyone."

Around them, the house guards studiously ignored the argument. A green-and-black banner snapped in the breeze. The ship's ramp extended.

"Am I the only one who thinks of our *family honor* instead of politics?" Paulus growled.

"Hush! Keep your voice down."

"If I lived my life only by safe decisions and advantageous alliances, I would be no man at all, and certainly not one worthy of being a Duke."

The soldiers marched out and stood at attention, forming a path for the three who had been rescued from Ix. Leto emerged first, taking a deep breath of the sea-freshened air, blinking in the hazy sunshine of Caladan. He was washed and dressed in clean clothes again, but his manner still conveyed weariness; his skin seemed gray, his dark hair mussed, his brow above the hawklike eyes and nose scarred by memories.

Leto took another huge breath, as if he couldn't get enough of the salt-iodine scents of the nearby sea, the hint of fish and woodsmoke. *Home*. He never wanted to spend time away from Caladan again. He looked beyond the ramp to meet his father's bright gaze—sparkling to see his son again, fiery with indignation and rage at what had happened to House Vernius.

Rhombur and Kailea came out uncertainly to stand beside Leto at the top of the ramp. Kailea's emerald eyes were haunted, and she looked around the new world, as if the sky was far too vast overhead. Leto wanted to comfort her. Again, he held himself back, this time because of his mother's presence.

Rhombur drew himself up and made a visible attempt to square his shoulders and straighten his tousled blond hair. He knew he was now all that remained of House Vernius, the face that all members of the Landsraad would see while his father the renegade Earl went into hiding. He knew the fight was just beginning. Leto put a strong hand on his friend's shoulder and urged him toward the reception platform.

After a moment of stillness, Leto and Paulus moved toward each other at the same time. The Old Duke pressed his salt-and-pepper beard against the side of his son's head; they pounded one another on the back, saying no words. They drew apart, and Paulus placed broad, callused hands on his son's biceps, just looking at him.

Leto looked past his father to see his mother standing behind them, wearing a warm, but forced, smile of greeting. Her glance flicked toward Rhombur and Kailea and then back to him; Leto knew Lady Helena Atreides would receive the two exiles with all the ceremony due important visiting dignitaries. He did note, however, that she had chosen jewelry and colors resplendent with the markings of House Richese, rival to Ix, as if to twist a knife into the Vernius exiles. Duke Paulus didn't seem to notice.

The Old Duke turned to give a vigorous greeting to Rhombur, who still wore a small bandage over his head injury. "Welcome, welcome, lad," he said. "As I promised your father, you and your sister will remain here with us, protected by the might of House Atreides, until all this blows over."

Kailea stared up at the scudding clouds as if she'd never seen open sky before. She shivered, looking lost. "What if it never blows over?"

Following her obligation, Helena came forward to take the Vernius daughter by the arm. "Come, child. We'll help you settle in, just in case this has to be your home for a while."

Rhombur gripped the Old Duke with an Imperial handshake. "Uh, I can't express my appreciation enough, sir. Kailea and I both understand the risk you've taken to shelter us."

Helena glanced over her shoulder at her husband, who ignored her.

Paulus gestured toward the Castle on the cliffs. "House Atreides values loyalty and honor far above politics." He took a hard and insightful look at his exhausted son. Leto drew a deep breath, receiving the lesson like a sword thrust. "Loyalty and honor," Paulus repeated. "That is the way it must always be."

In Birthing Room One of the Wallach IX complex, a screaming newborn girl lay on a med-table. A daughter with the genetic line of Baron Vladimir Harkonnen. The smell of blood and disinfectant hung in the air, wrapped in the rustle of crisp, sterilized clothing. Harsh glowglobes burned down, reflecting from the rough stone walls and polished-metal surfaces. Many daughters had been born here, many new Sisters.

With more excitement than the Bene Gesserit usually exhibited, Reverend Mothers in dark robes poked at the scrawny infant with instruments, talking about her in worried tones. One Sister used a hypo-needle to draw a blood sample, while another took a skin scraping with a shallow curette. No one spoke above a whisper. *Odd skin tone, poor biochemistry, low weight . . .*

Drenched in perspiration, Gaius Helen Mohiam lay nearby in discomfort, attempting to reassert control over the pummeled tissues of her body. Though her preservation hid her actual age, she looked too old to be having babies. This birth had been hard for her, harder than the previous eight children she had borne. By now she felt ancient and used up.

Two acolyte attendants hurried to her bed and wheeled her toward one side of the arched doorway. One laid a cool rag on her forehead, another placed a wet sponge against her lips, squeezing a few drops of moisture into her dry mouth. Mohiam had already done her part in this process; the Sisterhood would do the rest. Though she did not know their plans for this child, she knew the daughter must survive.

On the inspection table, even before the clinging blood and mucus could be wiped from her skin, the baby was turned over and positioned on all sides against a built-in scanner surface. Cold and frightened, the infant wailed, but only intermittently, her voice sounding weaker by the moment.

Electronic signals sent all bioresults into a central-receiving unit, which displayed the data in a column on a large wall monitor for the Bene Gesserit experts to assess. Reverend Mothers studied the results, comparing them with a second column that showed optimal numbers.

"The disparity is quite striking," Anirul said quietly, her eyes wide on her doelike face. The young Kwisatz Mother's disappointment hung like a solid weight on her shoulders.

"And most unexpected," said Mother Superior Harishka. Her birdlike eyes glittered from the wrinkles on her face. In tandem with those taboos that prevented the Bene Gesserit from using artificial means of fertilization in their breeding programs, other taboos kept them from inspecting or manipulating fetuses *in utero*. Sourly, the ancient woman shook her head and flicked a sidelong glance at sweat-soaked Mohiam, still recovering on her table near the door. "The genetics are correct, but this . . . *child* is wrong. We have made an error."

Anirul leaned over the infant girl for a closer look. The child had a sickly pallor and misshapen facial bones, as well as a disjointed or malformed shoulder. Other deficiencies, perhaps chronic, might take longer to assess.

And she's supposed to become the grandmother of the Kwisatz Haderach? Weakness does not breed strength.

Internally, Anirul reeled, trying to determine what could have gone wrong. The other Sisters would call her too young and impetuous again. The projections in the breeding records had been so precise, the information from Other Memory so certain. Though sired by Vladimir Harkonnen, this girl-child wasn't what she was supposed to be. The feeble infant couldn't possibly be the next step in the genetic path that was supposed to culminate—in only two more generations—with the Holy Grail of the Bene Gesserit breeding program, their superbeing.

"Could something be incorrect in the mating index?" Mother Superior said, averting her eyes from the baby. "Or is this an aberration?"

"Genetics is never certain, Mother Superior," Anirul said, taking a step away from the baby. Her confidence was gone, but she tried not to make excuses. She ran a nervous hand over her close-cropped bronze hair. "The projections are correct. I'm afraid the bloodline simply didn't cooperate . . . this time."

Mother Superior looked around the room at the doctors, the other Sisters. Every comment, every move would be recorded and stored in Wallach IX archives—as well as in Other Memory—for perusal by later generations. "Are you suggesting we try again with the Baron himself? He wasn't exactly the most cooperative of subjects."

Anirul smiled faintly. *What an understatement.* "Our projections give us the highest probability. It must be Baron Harkonnen, and it must be Mohiam. Thousands of years of careful selection have led to this point. We have other options, but none as good as this one . . . and so we must try again." She tried to sound philosophical. "Other mistakes have occurred along the way, Mother Superior—we cannot let one failure bring about the end of the entire program."

"Of course not," Harishka snapped. "We must contact the Baron again. Send our best and most persuasive representative while Mohiam recovers."

Anirul stared at the child on the table. Exhausted now, the infant lay silent, tiny hands flexing, legs kicking. The baby couldn't even maintain sustained periods of crying. *Not hardy breeding stock.*

At the doorway arch, Mohiam struggled to sit up on her recovery table, peering with bright eyes at the newborn. Instantly noting the deformity, the weakness, she moaned and fell back on the sheets.

Trying to comfort her, Mother Superior Harishka came over to the table. "We need your strength now, Sister, not your despair. We will make certain you get another chance with the Baron." She folded her arms across her chest, and with a rustling of her robe departed from the birthing room, followed by her aides.

IN HIS BALCONY chambers at Harkonnen Keep, the Baron admired himself naked in the mirror, as he frequently liked to do. There were many mirrors in his extensive apartment wing, and plenty of light, so that he might constantly enjoy the perfection of form that Nature had bestowed upon him. He was lean and muscular, with good skin tone—especially when his male lovers took the time to rub perfumed oils into every pore. He feathered his fingers over the washboard ridges on his abdomen. *Magnificent.*

No wonder the witches had requested that he breed with them a second time. He was, after all, extraordinarily beautiful. With their breeding programs, they would naturally desire the best stock. His first child by that warthog Mohiam must have been so perfect that they wanted another. Though he loathed the prospect, he asked himself if that was truly so horrible.

But he wished he knew how his offspring fit into the long-term plans of those devious, secretive women. They had multiple breeding programs, and no one but a Bene Gesserit seemed to understand any of them. Could this be used to his advantage somehow . . . or did they intend to turn the daughter against him at a later date? They had been careful not to provide any bastard heirs, thus avoiding dynastic squabbles, not that he much cared anyway. But what was in it for him? Even Piter de Vries had been at a loss to offer an explanation.

"You have not given us your response, Baron," Sister Margot Rashino-Zea said from behind him. She seemed not to show any discomfort whatsoever at his nakedness.

In the reflecting glass he saw the beautiful, golden-haired Sister. Did they think her beauty could tempt him, her shapeliness, her fine features? Would he rather mate with her than with the other one? Neither prospect appealed to him at all.

Representing the scheming Sisterhood, Margot had just spoken of the "need" for him to copulate a second time with the witch Mohiam. It hadn't even been a year yet. The gall of these creatures! Margot, at least, used slippery words and a little finesse, rather than the brutish demands Mohiam had made of him that night long ago. At least the witches had sent a better mouthpiece this time.

In front of the beautiful woman, he refused to put on any clothing, especially in the wake of her request. Nude, he flaunted himself for her, but pretended not to notice. *Wouldn't that sleek beauty love to rut with someone like me.*

"Mohiam was rather too plain for my tastes," he said, finally turning to face the Sisterhood's emissary. "Tell me, witch, was my first child a daughter, as I was promised?"

"How could it possibly make any difference to you?" Margot's gray-green eyes remained locked on his, but he could tell she wanted to let her gaze roam over his body, his muscles and his golden skin.

"I didn't say it made any difference, foolish woman—but I am of noble station and I asked you a question. Answer me or die."

"The Bene Gesserit do not fear death, Baron," Margot said, in the calmest of tones. Her serenity both irritated and intrigued him. "Yes, your first child was a girl," she continued. "We Bene Gesserit can influence these things. A son would have been of no use to us."

"I see. So why are you back?"

"I am not authorized to reveal more."

"I find your Sisterhood's second request deeply offensive. I told the Bene Gesserit never to bother me again. I could have you killed for defying me. This is my planet and my Keep."

"Violence would not be wise." Steady tone, with a threatening undercurrent. How could she appear so strong and monstrous in such a deceptively lovely body?

"You threatened to reveal my alleged spice stockpiles last time. Have you come up with anything new, or are you using the same old blackmail?"

"We Bene Gesserit can always provide new threats if you wish, Baron, though evidence of your fraudulent spice-production reports should still be sufficient to bring down the Emperor's wrath."

The Baron raised an eyebrow and finally deigned to snatch a slick black robe from his dressing chair. "I have it on certain authority that several Great Houses have their own stockpiles of melange. Some say even our own Emperor Elrood is not above the practice."

"The Emperor is not in good humor *or* good health these days. He seems to be preoccupied with Ix."

Baron Harkonnen paused to consider this. His own spies at the royal Court on Kaitain reported that old Elrood had been increasingly unstable and short-tempered of late, with signs of paranoia. His mind was going, his health was failing, and this caused him to be more vicious than ever, as evidenced by his blithely allowing the destruction of House Vernius.

"What do you think I am?" the Baron asked. "A prized Salusan bull to be put out to stud?"

He had nothing to fear, because the witches no longer had a scintilla of physical proof against him. He had scattered his stockpile of spice to deep hiding places in the isolation of Lankiveil, and ordered the destruction of every scrap of evidence from Arrakis. It had all been done expertly, by an ex-CHOAM auditor in his employ. The Baron smiled. *Former* employ, actually, since de Vries had already dealt with the man.

These Bene Gesserit could threaten him all they wanted, but had no real hold over him. This knowledge gave him a new power, a new way to resist.

The witch continued staring at him impertinently. He wanted to squeeze Margot's slender throat and shut her up forever. But that wouldn't solve his problem, even if he survived the confrontation. The Bene Gesserit would just send another, and another. He needed to teach the witches a lesson they wouldn't soon forget.

"Send your breeding mother to me, if you insist. I shall prepare for her." He knew exactly what he was going to do. His Mentat Piter de Vries, and probably even his nephew Rabban, would be happy to help.

"Very well. The Reverend Mother Gaius Helen Mohiam will be on her way within a fortnight, Baron." Without another word, Margot left. Her sparkling blonde hair and milky skin seemed too radiant to be contained within the drab robes of the Sisterhood.

The Baron summoned de Vries. They had to get to work.

Without a goal, a life is nothing. Sometimes the goal becomes a man's entire life, an all-consuming passion. But once that goal is achieved, what then? Oh, poor man, what then?

—LADY HELENA ATREIDES,

her personal journals

After his childhood years of repression on Giedi Prime, young Duncan Idaho found the lush world of Caladan a paradise. He'd been landed without a map in a city on the opposite side of the world from Castle Caladan. Janess's friend, the second mate Renno, had discharged his obligations to the boy, then kicked the stowaway out onto the streets of a lowland spaceport.

Paying no further attention to him, the crew off-loaded their cargo of recyclables and industrial scraps and took on a fresh load of pundi rice wrapped in bags made from grain fibers. Without saying goodbye, without offering advice or even wishing Duncan well, the second mate had climbed back aboard his cargo hauler and returned to the Heighliner in orbit.

Duncan couldn't complain: At least he had escaped from the Harkonnens. Now all he had to do was find Duke Atreides.

The boy stood there among strangers, on a strange world, watching the ship ascend into the cloudy sky. Caladan was a planet of rich and compelling smells, the air moist and laden with the salt of the sea, the sourness of fish, and the spice of wildflowers. In all his life on Giedi Prime, he had never encountered anything like it.

On the Southern Continent, the hills were steep and covered with intensely green grasses and terraced gardens hacked into the slopes like drunken stairsteps. Teams of hardworking farmers moved about under the misty yellow sun, not wealthy but still happy. Wearing old clothes, they transported fresh fruits and vegetables on suspensor-borne pallets to the marketplace.

As Duncan stared with hungry eyes at the passing farmers, one kindly old man gave him a small, overripe paradan melon, which the boy ate voraciously. Sweet moisture dripped between his fingers. It was the most delicious meal he'd ever had.

Seeing the boy's energy as well as his desperation, the farmer asked him if he would like to return and work in the rice paddies for a few days. The old fellow offered no pay, only a place to sleep and some food. Duncan readily agreed.

On the long walk back, the boy told him the story of his battles with the Harkonnens, how his parents had been arrested and killed, how he had been chosen for Rabban's hunt, and how he had eventually escaped. "Now I must present myself to Duke Atreides," he said with complete faith. "But I don't know where he is, or how to find him."

The old farmer listened attentively, then gave a grave nod. Caladanians knew the legends of their Duke, had witnessed the greatest of his bullfights at the departure of his son Leto to Ix. The people here honored their leader, and to them it seemed fundamentally reasonable that any citizen could request an audience with the Atreides.

"I can tell you the city where the Duke lives," the old man said. "My sister's husband even has a map of the whole world, and I can show you. But I don't know how you could get there. It's very far away."

"I'm young and strong. I can make it."

The farmer nodded and led his visitor back to the rice paddies.

Duncan stayed four days with the man's family, working up to his waist in flooded fields. He waded through the water, clearing channels, inserting small but hardy seedlings into the loose mud. He learned the songs and chants of the pundi rice planters.

One afternoon spotters in the low-hanging trees banged on pans, sounding an alarm. Moments later, ripples in the peaty water signaled the approach of a school of panther-fish, bog dwellers that swam in packs searching for prey. They could strip the flesh off a farmer's bones in moments.

Duncan scrambled up one of the tangled tree trunks to join the other panicked rice farmers. He hung in the low branches, pushing Spanish moss aside as he looked down and watched the ripples approach. Beneath the water he could see large, many-fanged creatures armored with broad scales. Several of the panther-fish circled around the trunk of the swamp tree in which Duncan had taken refuge.

Some of the creatures rose up on scaled elbows, rudimentary arms with front fins that had developed into clumsy claws. With most of their bodies out of the water, the carnivorous fish stretched upward, large and deadly. They blinked wet, slitted eyes at the young man who hung just out of reach in the branches above. After a long moment of staring them down, Duncan climbed one branch higher. The panther-fish submerged again, swirling away out of sight in the sprawling rice paddies.

The following day Duncan took a spare meal the farmer's family had packed for him and trudged off toward the coast, where he eventually found work as a net-rigger on a fishing boat that plied the waters of the warm southern seas. At least the boat would take him to port on the continent where Castle Caladan lay.

For weeks he worked the nets, gutted the fish, and ate his fill in the galley. The cook used a lot of spices that were unfamiliar to Duncan— hot Caladanian peppers and mustards that made his eyes water and his nose run. The men laughed at his discomfiture, and told him he would never be a man until he could eat food like that. To their surprise young Duncan took this as a challenge, and soon he began asking for extra seasoning. Before long he could endure meals hotter than any other crew member. The fishermen stopped teasing him and began to praise him instead.

Before the end of the voyage, a cabin boy in the next bunk did a calculation for Duncan that showed him that he was nine now, by almost six weeks. "I feel a lot older than that," Duncan responded.

He hadn't expected to take so long to reach his destination, but his life was better now, despite the incredibly hard work he'd taken on. He felt safe, freer in a way than he had ever felt before. The men on the crew were his new family.

Under cloudy skies the fishing boat finally reached port, and Duncan left the sea behind. He didn't ask for pay, didn't take his leave of the captain—he simply departed. The oceangoing sojourn was just a step along the way. Never once during his long journey did he ever deviate from his main goal of reaching the Old Duke. He took advantage of no one and worked hard for the hospitality he received.

In a dockside alley a sailor from another ship once tried to molest him, but Duncan fought back with iron-hard muscles and whip-fast reflexes. The bruised and battered predator retreated, finding this wild boy too much for him.

Duncan began hitching rides on groundtrucks and cars, and sneaked aboard tube trains and short-haul cargo 'thopters. Inexorably, he moved north on the continent, toward Castle Caladan, getting closer and closer as the months passed.

During the frequent rains, he found trees under which he could huddle. But even wet and hungry, he didn't feel so bad, for he recalled the terrible night at Forest Guard Station, how cold he had been, how he had used a knife to cut open his own shoulder. After that, he could certainly handle these brief discomforts.

Sometimes he struck up conversations with other travelers and heard stories of their popular Duke, bits of Atreides history. Back on Giedi Prime, no one had spoken of such matters. People held their opinions to themselves and gave up no information except under duress. Here, however, the locals were happy to talk about their situation. Duncan realized with a shock one afternoon as he traveled with three entertainers that the people on Caladan actually *loved* their leader.

In sharp contrast, Duncan had heard only terrible stories of the Harkonnens. He knew the fear of the populace and the brutal consequences of any real or imagined defiance. On this planet, though, the people respected rather than feared their ruler. The Old Duke, Duncan was told, walked with only a small honor guard through villages and markets, visiting the people without wearing any armor, without shields or fear of attack.

Baron Harkonnen or Glossu Rabban would never dare such a thing.

I may like this Duke, Duncan thought one night, curled up under a blanket one of the entertainers had loaned him. . . .

Finally, after months of travel, he stood in the village at the foot of the promontory that held Castle Caladan. The magnificent structure stood like a sentinel gazing out across the calm seas. Somewhere inside it lived Duke Paulus Atreides, by now a legendary figure to the boy.

Duncan shivered from the chill of morning and took a deep breath. The fog lifted above the seacoast, turning the rising sun into a deep orange ball. He marched away from the village and started up the long, steep road to the Castle. This was where he must go.

As he walked, he did what he could to make himself presentable, brushing the dust from his clothes and tucking his wrinkled pullover shirt into his trousers. But he felt confident about himself, regardless of his appearance, and this Duke would accept him or throw him out. Either way, Duncan Idaho would survive.

When he reached the gates that led into the great courtyard, the Atreides guards tried to bar his way, thinking him a panhandler.

"I'm not a beggar," Duncan announced with his head held high. "I have come across the galaxy to see the Duke, and I must tell him my story."

The guards just laughed. "We can find you some scraps from the kitchen, but no more."

"That would be very kind of you, sirs," Duncan agreed, his stomach grumbling with hunger, "but that isn't why I'm here. Please send a message into the Castle that"—he tried to remember the phrasing one of the traveling singers had taught him—"that Master Duncan Idaho requests an audience with Duke Paulus Atreides."

The guards laughed again, but the boy saw grudging respect seep into their expressions. One went away and came back with some breakfast, tiny roasted eggs for Duncan. After thanking the guard, he wolfed down the eggs, licked his fingers, and sat on the ground to wait. Hours passed.

The guards kept looking at him and shaking their heads. One asked him if he carried any weapons, or any money, both of which Duncan denied. As a steady stream of petitioners came and went, the guards chatted with each other. Duncan heard talk about a revolt that had occurred on Ix, and the Duke's concerns over House Vernius, especially because of the Emperor's acceptance of a bounty on Dominic and Shando Vernius. Apparently, the Duke's son Leto had just returned from war-torn Ix to Caladan with two royal refugees. Everything in the Castle was in quite a turmoil.

Nevertheless, Duncan waited.

The sun passed overhead and slipped below the horizon of the great sea. The young man spent the night curled up in a corner of the courtyard, and with the next morning and a change of guards, he repeated his story and his request for an audience. This time, he mentioned that he had escaped from a Harkonnen world and wished to offer his services to House Atreides. The Harkonnen name seemed to catch their attention. Once again the guards checked him for weapons, but more thoroughly.

By early afternoon, after being frisked and probed—first by an electronic scanner to root out hidden lethal devices, then by a poison-snooper—Duncan was finally ushered inside the Castle. An ancient stone structure whose interior corridors and rooms were draped with rich tapestries, the place bore a patina of history and worn elegance. Wooden floors creaked underfoot.

At a wide stone archway, two Atreides guards passed him through even more elaborate scanning devices, which again found nothing suspicious. He was just a boy, with nothing to hide, but they wore their paranoia as if it were a strange and uncomfortable garment, as if new procedures had just been instituted. Satisfied, they waved Duncan into a large room with vaulted ceilings supported by heavy, dark beams.

At the center of the room the Old Duke sat back and surveyed his visitor. A strong, bearlike man with a full beard and bright green eyes, Paulus relaxed in a comfortable wooden chair, not an ostentatious throne. It was a place where he could be at ease for hours as he conducted the business of state. Atop the chairback, just above the old patriarch's head, a hawk crest had been carved into the dark Elaccan wood.

Beside him sat his olive-skinned son Leto, thin and tired-looking, as if he hadn't fully recovered from his ordeal. Duncan met Leto's gray eyes, and sensed that both of them had much to tell, much to share.

"We have here a very persistent boy, Leto," the Old Duke said, glancing at his son.

"From the looks of him, he wants something different from all the other petitioners we've heard today." Leto raised his eyebrows. He was only five or six years older than Duncan—a large gulf at their ages— but it seemed they had both been thrust headlong into adulthood. "He doesn't look greedy."

Paulus's expression softened as he leaned forward in his great chair. "How long have you been waiting out there, boy?"

"Oh, that doesn't matter, m'Lord Duke," Duncan answered, hoping he used the right words. "I'm here now." Nervously, he scratched a mole on his chin.

The Old Duke flashed a quick scowl at the guard who had escorted him in. "Have you fed this young man?"

"They gave me plenty, sir. Thank you. And I also had a good night's sleep in your comfortable courtyard."

"In the *courtyard*?" Another scowl at the guard. "So why are you here, young man? Did you come from one of the fishing villages?"

"No, m'Lord—I am from Giedi Prime."

The guards tensed hands around their weapons. The Old Duke and his son flashed a glance at each other, disbelief at first. "Then you'd better tell us what's happened to you," Paulus said. Their expressions changed to grim disgust as Duncan told his story, omitting no detail.

The Duke's eyes widened. He saw the guileless expression on this young man's face and looked at his son, thinking that this was no made-up tale. Leto nodded. No boy of nine years could have concocted such a story, however much he might have been coached.

"And so I came here, sir," Duncan said, "to see you."

"You landed in *which* city on Caladan?" the Duke asked again. "Describe it for us."

Duncan couldn't remember its name but recounted what he had seen, and the Old Duke agreed that he must have indeed made his way from across the world.

"I was told to come to you, m'Lord, and ask if you might have something for me to do. I hate the Harkonnens, sir, and I'd willingly pledge my loyalty forever to House Atreides if only I can stay here."

"I think I believe him, Father," Leto said quietly, studying the boy's deep-set blue-green eyes. "Or is this a lesson you're trying to teach me?"

Paulus sat back, hands folded on his lap, and his chest wrenched with spasms. After a moment Duncan realized that the big man was holding in great rumbles of laughter. When the Old Duke could no longer restrain himself, he burst out with a deep chuckle and slapped his knees. "Boy, I admire what you've done. Any young man with balls as big as yours is a man I must have as part of my household!"

"Thank you, sir," Duncan said.

"I'm sure we can find some urgent work for him to do, Father," Leto said with a tired smile. He found this brave and persistent boy to be a hopeful change from everything he had seen recently.

The Old Duke rose from the comfort of his chair and bellowed for retainers, insisting that they supply the boy with clothes and a bath and more food. "On second thought"—he held up a hand—"bring an entire banquet table. My son and I wish to share lunch with young Master Idaho."

They entered an adjacent dining room, where workers scurried and clattered about, setting up everything their Duke had commanded. One servant brushed flat the boy's dark and curly hair, and ran a static cleaner over his dusty clothes. At the head of the table, with Duncan seated on his right and gray-eyed Leto on the left, Paulus Atreides sank his chin into a large fist.

"I've got an idea, boy. Since you proved you could handle those monstrous Harkonnens, do you think a mere Salusan bull is beyond your capabilities?"

"No, sir," Duncan said. He had heard about the Duke's grand spectacles. "If you want me to fight them for you, I'll be happy to do it."

"*Fight* them?" Paulus laughed. "That isn't exactly what I have in mind." The Duke sat back with a huge grin, looking over at Leto.

Leto said, "I think we've discovered a position for you here at Castle Caladan, young man. You can work in the stables, under the guidance of Stablemaster Yresk. You'll help tend my father's bulls: feed them and, if you can get close enough, groom them, too. I've done it myself. I'll introduce you to the stablemaster." He looked over at his father. "Remember, Yresk used to let me pet the bulls when I was Duncan's age?"

"Oh, this boy will do a lot more than pet the beasts," the Old Duke said. Paulus cocked a gray eyebrow as platters and platters of magnificent food were brought to the table. He noted the enchanted look on Duncan's face. "And if you do a good enough job in the stables," he added, "maybe we can find some more glamorous tasks for you."

History has seldom been good to those who must be punished.
Bene Gesserit punishments cannot be forgotten.

—Bene Gesserit Dictum

A new Bene Gesserit delegation bearing Gaius Helen Mohiam arrived on Giedi Prime. Freshly delivered of her sickly Harkonnen daughter, Mohiam found herself in the Baron's Keep for the second time in the space of a year.

She arrived in daylight this time, though the greasy cloud cover and pillars of smoke from unfiltered factories gave the sky a bruised appearance that strangled any hint of sunshine.

The Reverend Mother's shuttle touched down at the same spaceport as before, with the same demand for "special services." But this time Baron Harkonnen had secretly vowed to do things differently.

Stepping in perfect rhythm, a stony-faced regiment of the Baron's household troops marched up to surround the Bene Gesserit shuttle—more than sufficient to intimidate the witches.

The Burseg Kryubi, formerly a pilot on Arrakis and now head of Harkonnen house security, stood in front of the shuttle-debarkation ramp, two steps ahead of his nearest troops. All were dressed in formal blue.

Mohiam appeared at the top of the ramp, engulfed in

her Bene Gesserit robes and flanked by acolyte retainers, personal guards, and other Sisters. She frowned with disdain at the Burseg and his men. "What is the meaning of this reception? Where is the Baron?"

Burseg Kryubi looked up at her. "Do not attempt your manipulative Voice on me or there will be a . . . dangerous . . . reaction from the troops. My orders state that you alone are allowed to see the Baron. No guards, no retainers, no companions. He awaits you in the formal hall of the Keep." He nodded toward the attendants behind her in the shuttle. "None of these others may enter."

"Unthinkable," Mohiam said. "I request formal diplomatic courtesy. All of my party must be received with the respect they are due."

Kryubi did not flinch. "I know what the witch wants," the Baron had said. "And if she thinks she can show up here to rut with me on a regular basis, she's sadly mistaken!"—whatever that meant.

The Burseg stared her down, eye to eye. "Your request is denied." He was far more frightened of the Baron's punishments than of anything this woman could do to him. "You are free to leave if this does not meet with your approval."

With a snort, Mohiam started down the ramp, flashing a glance at those who remained in the ship. "For all his perversions, the Baron Vladimir Harkonnen is somewhat prudish," she said mockingly, more for the benefit of the Harkonnen troops than for her own people. "Especially when it comes to matters of sexuality."

Kryubi, who had not been apprised of the situation, was intrigued by this reference. But he decided that certain things were best left unknown.

"Tell me, Burseg," the witch said to him in an irritating tone, "how would you even know if I was using Voice on you?"

"A soldier never reveals his full arsenal of defenses."

"I see." Her tone was soothing, sensual. Kryubi didn't feel threatened by it, but wondered if his bluff had worked.

Unknown to this foolish soldier, Mohiam was a Truthsayer capable of recognizing nuances of falsehood and deception. She allowed the pompous Burseg to lead her across an overpass on a walkway tunnel. Once inside Harkonnen Keep, the Reverend Mother put on her best air of aloof confidence, gliding along with feigned nonchalance.

But every one of her heightened senses was attuned to the slightest anomaly. The Baron made her extremely suspicious. She knew he was up to something.

PACING RESTLESSLY IN the Great Hall, Baron Harkonnen looked around, his black eyes flashing and intent. The room was large and cold, the harsh light too bright from unfiltered glowglobes clustered in the corners and along the ceiling. As he walked in pointed black boots, his footsteps echoed, making the entire hall sound hollow, empty—a good place for an ambush.

Though the residential portion of the Keep might appear vacant, the Baron had stationed guards and electronic spy-eyes in various alcoves. He knew he couldn't fool the Bene Gesserit whore for long, but it didn't matter. Even if she learned they were being watched, it might give her pause and prevent her from pulling her insidious tricks. The caution might at least gain him a few seconds.

Since he planned to be in control this time, the Baron *wanted* his people to watch. He'd give them a very good show, something they'd talk about in their barracks and troop ships for years to come. Best of all, it would put the witches in their place. *Blackmail me, indeed!*

Piter de Vries came up behind him, moving so swiftly and silently that he startled the Baron, who snapped, "Don't do that, Piter!"

"I've brought what you asked, my Baron." The twisted Mentat extended his hand, offering two small plugs, white-noise transmitters. "Insert these deeply into your ear canals. They're designed to distort any Voice she might try to use. You can still hear normal conversation, but the plugs will scramble the unwanted, preventing it from reaching your ears."

The Baron heaved a deep breath and flexed his muscles. The preparations had to be perfect.

"You just take care of *your* part, Piter. I know what I'm doing." He went to a small alcove, snatched up the decanter of kirana brandy, and took a long deep swig directly from the bottle. Feeling the brandy burn in his chest, he wiped his mouth and the top of the bottle.

The Baron had already imbibed more alcohol than was usual for him, perhaps more than was wise considering the ordeal he was about to face. De Vries, who recognized the Baron's anxiety, looked at his master as if laughing at him. With a scowl, the Baron took another deep swallow, just to spite the Mentat.

De Vries scuttled about, relishing their joint plan, eager to participate. "Perhaps, Baron, the witch is returning here because she enjoyed her first encounter with you so much." He cackled. "Do you think she's been *lusting* after you ever since?"

The Baron scowled at him again—this time sharply enough that the Mentat wondered if he had pushed too far. But de Vries always managed to talk his way out of reprisals.

"Is that the best prime projection my Mentat can offer? Think, damn you! Why would the Bene Gesserit want *another* child from me? Are they just trying to twist the knife deeper, to make me hate them even more than I already do?" He snorted, wondered if that could be possible.

Maybe they needed two daughters for some reason. Or maybe something was wrong with the first one. . . . The Baron's generous lips curved upward in a slight smile. *This child would certainly be the last.*

No evidence remained for the Bene Gesserit to use as blackmail. Lankiveil now hid the largest treasure of Harkonnen melange right under Abulurd's nose. The fool had no inkling of how he was being used to cover the Baron's secret activities. But though softhearted and softheaded, Abulurd was still a Harkonnen. Even if he discovered the deception, he wouldn't dare expose it for fear of destroying his own family holdings. Abulurd revered the memory of their father too much for that.

The Baron walked away from the kirana brandy, and the sweet burning taste turned sour in the back of his mouth. He wore a loose maroon-and-black pajama top tightly sashed across his flat stomach. The pale blue griffin crest of House Harkonnen emblazoned the left breast. He'd left his arms bare to show off his biceps. His reddish hair was cut short, tousled for a rakish look.

He looked hard at de Vries. The Mentat gulped from a small bottle of deep red sapho juice. "Are we ready, my Baron? She's waiting outside."

"Yes, Piter." He lounged back in a chair. His silky pants were loose, and the prying eyes of the Reverend Mother would be able to detect no bulge of a weapon—no *expected* weapon. He smiled. "Go and send her in."

WHEN MOHIAM PASSED into the main hall of the Keep, Burseg Kryubi and his troops closed the doors behind her, remaining outside. The locks sealed with a click. Immediately on her guard, she noted that the Baron had orchestrated every detail of this encounter.

The two of them seemed to be alone in the long room, which was austere and cold, awash in glaring light. The entire Keep conveyed the impression of square corners and unsoftened harshness the Harkonnens loved so well; this place was more an industrial conference room than a sumptuous palace hall.

"Greetings again, Baron Harkonnen," Mohiam said with a smile that overlaid politeness on top of her scorn. "I see you've been anticipating our meeting. Perhaps you're even eager?" She looked away, glancing at her fingertips. "It's possible I shall allow you a bit more pleasure this time."

"Maybe so," the Baron said, affably.

She didn't like the answer. *What is his game?* Mohiam looked around, sensing the air currents, peering into shadows, trying to hear the heartbeat of some other person lying in wait. Someone was there . . . but where? Did they plan to murder her? Would they dare? She monitored her pulse, prevented it from accelerating.

The Baron definitely had more in mind than simple cooperation. She had never expected an easy victory over him, especially not this second time. The heads of some Minor Houses could be crushed or manipulated—the Bene Gesserit certainly knew how to do it—but this wouldn't be the fate of House Harkonnen.

She looked at the Baron's stygian eyes, straining with her Truthsayer abilities, but unable to see what he was thinking, unable to unravel his plans. Mohiam felt a twinge of fear deep inside, barely recognized. Just how much would the Harkonnens dare? This Baron couldn't afford to refuse the Sisterhood's demand, knowing what information the Bene Gesserit held against him. Or would he risk the possibility of heavy Imperial penalties?

Of equal import, would he risk a Bene Gesserit punishment? That, too, was no small matter.

At another time she might have enjoyed playing games with him, mental and physical sparring with a strong opponent. He was slippery and could bend and twist far more easily than he could break. But right now the Baron fell beneath her contempt, serving as a stud whose genes were required by the Sisterhood. She didn't know why, or what importance this daughter might hold, but if Mohiam returned to Wallach IX with her mission unfulfilled, she would receive a severe reprimand from her superiors.

She decided not to waste any additional time. Summoning the full Voice talents the Bene Gesserit had taught her, word and tone manipulations that no untrained human could resist, she said curtly, *"Cooperate with me."* It was a command she expected him to obey.

The Baron just smiled. He didn't move, but his eyes flicked to one side. Mohiam was so startled at the ineffectiveness of Voice that she realized too late the Baron had set a different trap for her.

The Mentat Piter de Vries had already launched himself out of a hidden alcove. She turned, battle-ready, but the Mentat moved as swiftly as any Bene Gesserit could.

The Baron took it all in, and enjoyed what he was seeing.

De Vries held a crude but effective weapon in his hands. The old-fashioned neural scrambler would serve as a brutal high-powered stunning device. He fired a volley before she could move. The crackling waves slammed into her, short-circuiting her mind/muscle control.

Mohiam fell backward, twitching and wrenching with painful spasms, every square centimeter of her skin alive with imaginary biting ants.

Such a delightful effect, the Baron thought as he watched.

She dropped to the polished-stone floor, arms and legs akimbo, as if she had been squashed by a giant foot. Her head struck the hard tiles, and her ears rang from the blow. Unblinking, her eyes stared up at the vaulted ceiling. Even with extreme *prana-bindu* muscular control, she couldn't move.

Finally the mocking face of the Baron loomed over her, pushing itself into her limited field of view. Her arms and legs jittered with random nerve impulses. She felt warm wetness and realized that her bladder had let go. A thin line of spittle trickled from the corner of her lip down her cheek, weaving a path to the base of her ear.

"Now then, *witch*," the Baron said, "that stunner will do no permanent damage. In fact, you'll have bodily control again in about twenty minutes. Time enough for us to get to know one another." He walked around her, smiling, passing in and out of her peripheral vision.

Raising his voice so that electronic pickups would transmit everything to the hidden observers, he continued. "I know what false blackmail material you have fabricated against House Harkonnen, and my lawyers are prepared to deal with it in any court of the Imperium. You have threatened to use it if I don't grant you another child, but that is a toothless threat from toothless witches."

He paused, then smiled as if an idea had just occurred to him. "Still, I don't mind giving you the additional daughter you desire. Really, I don't. But know this, witch, and take my message back to your Sisterhood: You *cannot* twist Baron Vladimir Harkonnen to your purpose without suffering the consequences."

Using all of her training to focus on the output of certain nerves and muscles, Mohiam reconnected her eyes so that she could at least move them to look around. The neural scrambler had been incredibly effective, though, and the rest of her body lay helpless.

Fighting his revulsion, the Baron reached down and tore at her skirts. What a disgusting form she had, without the male muscle patterns he so admired and desired. "My, it looks like you've had a little accident here," he said, frowning at the urine-wet fabric.

Piter de Vries stood over her from behind, looking down at her broad, slack face. She saw the red-stained lips and the half-mad glint in the Mentat's eyes. Below, the Baron knocked her legs apart and then fumbled at his loose-fitting black pants.

She couldn't see what he was doing, didn't want to.

Giddy with the success of his plan, the Baron had no difficulty maintaining an erection this time. Flushed in the afterglow of the brandy he had drunk, he stared down at the unattractive woman, imagined her as a withered old crone that he had just sentenced to the most brutal of the Harkonnen slave pits. This woman, who fancied herself so great and powerful, now lay completely helpless . . . at his mercy!

The Baron took enormous pleasure in raping her—the first time he could ever recall enjoying himself with a woman, though she was just a limp piece of meat.

During the violence of the attack, Mohiam lay supine on the cold floor, furious and impotent. She could feel every movement, every touch, every painful thrust, but she still had no control over her voluntary muscles. Her eyes remained open, although she thought she might have been able to blink if she worked hard enough at it.

Instead of wasting that energy, the Reverend Mother concentrated internally, feeling her biochemistry, changing it. The Mentat's stunner weapon hadn't done a complete job on her. Muscles were one thing, but internal body chemistry was quite another. The Baron Vladimir Harkonnen would regret this.

Previously she had manipulated her ovulation to achieve the peak of fertility in this exact hour. Even raped, she would have no trouble conceiving a new daughter with the Baron's sperm. That was the most important consideration.

Technically, she required nothing more from the vile man. But the Reverend Mother Gaius Helen Mohiam intended to give him something *back*, a slow-acting revenge he would never forget for the rest of his life.

No one was ever allowed to forget a Bene Gesserit punishment.

Though she remained paralyzed, Mohiam was an accomplished Reverend Mother. Her body itself contained unorthodox weapons that remained at her disposal even now, even as helpless as she appeared to be.

With the sensitivities and remarkable functions of their bodies, Bene Gesserit Sisters could create antidotes for poisons introduced into their systems. They were able to neutralize the most hideous strains of diseases to which they had been exposed, and either destroy the virulent pathogens . . . or render them latent in their bodies, keeping the diseases themselves as resources for later use. Mohiam carried several such latencies within her, and she could activate those diseases by controlling her own biochemistry.

Now the Baron lay on top of her, grunting like an animal, his jaw clenched, his lips curled back in a sneer. Beadlets of stinking sweat covered his reddened face. She stared up. Their eyes met, and he thrust harder, grinning.

That was when Mohiam selected the particular disease, an oh-so-gradual vengeance, a neurological disorder that would destroy his beautiful body. The Baron's physique obviously brought him much pleasure, was a source of great pride. She could have infected him with any number of fatal, suppurating plagues—but this affliction would be a deeper blow to him, much slower in its course. She would make the Baron face his own appearance every day as he grew fatter and weaker. His muscles would degenerate, his metabolism would go haywire. In a few years, he wouldn't even be able to walk by himself.

It was such a simple thing for her to do . . . but its effects would last for years. For the rest of his life. Mohiam envisioned the Baron pain-wracked, so obese he couldn't even stand erect unassisted, screaming out in agony.

Finished, smug in the belief that he had shown the witch who was the more powerful, Baron Vladimir Harkonnen withdrew and stood up, frowning at her in disgust now. "Piter, get me a towel, so I can wipe the whore's slime off of me."

The Mentat scuttled out of the room, chuckling. The hall doors were opened again. Uniformed house guards marched in to watch as Mohiam regained the use of her muscles, bit by bit.

Baron Harkonnen admonished the Reverend Mother with a cruel smile. "Tell the Bene Gesserit never to annoy me again with their genetic schemes."

She raised herself to one arm, then gradually gathered her torn clothes and climbed to her feet with nearly full coordination. Mohiam raised her chin proudly, but could not hide her humiliation. And the Baron could not hide his pleasure at watching her.

You think you have won, she thought. *We shall see about that.*

Satisfied with what she had done, and the inevitability of her terrible revenge, the Reverend Mother strode out of Harkonnen Keep. The Baron's Burseg followed her for part of the way, then let her return alone and unescorted to the shuttle like a chastened dog. Other guards remained rigid and at attention, guarding the foot of the ramp.

Mohiam calmed herself as she approached the craft and finally allowed herself a slight smile. No matter what had occurred back there, she now carried another Harkonnen daughter inside her. And that, of course, was what the Bene Gesserit had wanted all along. . . .

How simple things were when our Messiah was only a dream.
—STILGAR, Naib of Sietch Tabr

For Pardot Kynes, life would never be the same now that he had been accepted into the sietch.

His wedding day to Frieth approached, requiring that he spend hours on preparation and meditation, learning Fremen marriage rituals, especially the *ahal*, the ceremony of a woman choosing a mate—and Frieth had certainly been the initiator in this relationship. Many other fascinations distracted him, but he knew he could not make any mistakes in such a delicate matter.

For the sietch leaders, this was a grand occasion, more spectacular than any normal Fremen wedding. Never before had an outsider married one of their women, though Naib Heinar had heard of it happening occasionally in other sietches.

After the would-be assassin Uliet had sacrificed himself, the tale told throughout the sietch (and no doubt spread among other hidden Fremen communities) was that Uliet had received a true vision from God, that he had been directed in his actions. Old one-eyed Heinar, as well as sietch elders Jerath, Aliid, and Garnah, were suitably chagrined for having questioned the impassioned words of the Planetologist in the first place.

Though Heinar gravely offered to step down as Naib, bowing to the man he now believed to be a prophet from beyond the stars, Kynes had no interest in becoming the leader of the sietch. He had too much work to do—challenges on a scale grander than mere local politics. He was perfectly happy to be left alone to concentrate on his terra-forming plan and study the data collected from instruments scattered all around the desert. He needed to understand the great sandy expanse and its subtleties before he could know precisely how to change things for the better.

The Fremen worked hard to comply with anything Kynes suggested, no matter how absurd it might seem. They believed everything he said now. So preoccupied was Kynes, however, that he barely noticed their devotion. If the Planetologist said he needed certain measurements, Fremen scrambled across the desert, setting up collection points in remote regions, reopening the botanical testing stations that had been long abandoned by the Imperium. Some devoted assistants even traveled to the forbidden territories in the south, using a mode of transportation they had kept secret from him.

During those frantic first weeks of information gathering, two Fremen men were lost—though Kynes never learned of it. He reveled in the glorious data flooding to him. This was more than he had ever dreamed of accomplishing in years of working alone as the Imperial Planetologist. He was in a scientific paradise.

The day before his wedding, he wrote up his first carefully edited report since joining the sietch, culminating weeks of work. A Fremen messenger delivered it to Arrakeen, where it was then transmitted to the Emperor. Kynes's work with the Fremen threatened to put him in a conflict of interest as Imperial Planetologist, but he had to keep up appearances. Nowhere in his report did he mention, or even hint at, his newfound relationship with the desert people. Kaitain must never suspect that he had "gone native."

In his mind, *Arrakis* no longer existed. This planet was now, and forever would be, *Dune*; after living in the sietch he could not think of it by anything other than its Fremen name. The more he discovered, the more Pardot Kynes realized that this strangely dry and barren planet held far deeper secrets than even the Emperor realized.

Dune was a treasure box waiting to be opened.

Brash young Stilgar had recovered completely from his Harkonnen sword wound and insisted on helping Kynes with chores and tedious duties. The ambitious Fremen youth claimed it was the only way to decrease a heavy water burden upon his clan. The Planetologist did not feel he was owed such an obligation, but he bent against pressure from the sietch, like a willow before the wind. The Fremen would not overlook or forget a thing like that.

Stilgar's unwed sister Frieth was offered to him as a wife. Almost without the Planetologist noticing, she seemed to have adopted him, mending his clothes, offering him food before he realized he was hungry. Her hands were quick, her blue eyes alive with a lightning intelligence, and she had saved him from many faux pas even before he could react. He had considered her attentions little more than appreciation for saving the life of her brother, and had accepted her without further consideration.

Kynes had never before thought about marriage, for he was too solitary a man, too driven in his work. Yet after being graciously welcomed into the community, he began to understand how quickly the Fremen took offense. Kynes knew he dared not refuse. He also realized that, given the many Harkonnen political restrictions against Fremen on this world, perhaps his marriage to Frieth would smooth the way for future researchers.

And so, with the rising of both full moons, Pardot Kynes joined the other Fremen for the marriage ritual. Before this night was over, he would be a husband. He had a sparse beard now, the first of his life. Frieth, though hesitant to speak her mind about anything, seemed to like it.

Led by pirate-eyed Heinar, as well as the Sayyadina of the sietch—a female religious leader much like a Reverend Mother—the wedding party came down from the mountains after a long and careful journey and out onto the open sands rippled with dunes. The moons shone down, bathing the sandscape with a pearly, glistening luster.

Staring at the sinuous dunes, Kynes thought for the first time that they reminded him of the gentle, sensuous curves of a woman's flesh. *Perhaps I have my mind on the marriage more than I'd thought.*

They walked single file onto the dunes, climbing the packed windward side and then breaking a trail along the soft crest. Alert for wormsign or Harkonnen spycraft, spotters from the sietch had climbed to lookout points. With his fellow tribesmen keeping watch, Kynes felt entirely safe. He was one of them now, and he knew the Fremen would give their lives for him.

He gazed at lovely young Frieth standing in the moonlight, with her long, long hair and her large blue-within-blue eyes focused on him, assessing, perhaps even loving. She wore the black robe that signified she was a woman betrothed.

For hours back in the caves, other Fremen wives had braided Frieth's hair with her metal water rings, together with those belonging to her future husband, to symbolize the commingling of their existence. Many months ago, the sietch had taken all of the supplies from Kynes's groundcar and added his containers of water to the main stores. Once he had been accepted among them, he received payment in water rings for what he had contributed, and Kynes thus entered the community as a relatively wealthy man.

As Frieth looked at her betrothed, Kynes realized for the first time how beautiful and desirable she was—and then chastised himself for not having noticed before. Now the unmarried Fremen women rushed out onto the dunefield, their long, unbound hair flying in the night breeze. Kynes watched as they began the traditional wedding dance and chant.

Rarely did members of the sietch explain their customs to him, where the rituals had come from, or what they signified. To the Fremen, everything simply *was*. Long in the past, ways of life had been developed out of necessity during the Zensunni wanderings from planet to planet, and the ways had remained unchanged ever since. No one here bothered to question them, so why should Kynes? Besides, if he truly was the prophet they considered him to be, then he should understand such things intuitively.

He could easily decipher the custom of binding water rings into the braid of the woman to be married, while the unbetrothed daughters kept their hair loose and free. The troupe of unmarried women flitted across the sands in their bare feet, their footsteps floating. Some were mere girls, while others had ripened to full marriageable age. The dancers whipped and whirled, spinning about so that their hair streamed in all directions like halos around their heads.

Symbolic of a desert sandstorm, he thought. *Coriolis whirlwinds.* From his studies he knew that such winds could exceed eight hundred kilometers per hour, bearing dust and sand particles with enough force to scour the flesh off a man's bones.

With sudden concern Kynes looked up. To his relief, the sky of the desert night was clear and scattered with stars; a precursor fog of dust would be carried up in advance of any storm. The Fremen spotters would see impending weather with sufficient warning to take immediate precautions.

The young girls' dancing and chanting continued. Kynes stood beside his wife-to-be, but he looked up at the twin moons, thinking of their tidal effects, how the gentle flexings of gravity might have affected the geology and climate of this world. Perhaps deep core soundings would tell him more of what he needed to know. . . .

In future months, he wished to take extensive samples from the ice cap at the northern pole. By measuring the strata and analyzing isotopic content, Kynes would be able to draw a precise weather history of Arrakis. He could map the heating and melting cycles, as well as ancient precipitation patterns, using this information to determine where all the water must have gone.

So far this planet's aridity made no sense. Could a world's supply of water somehow be hydrated into rock layers beneath the sands, locking it into the planetary crust itself? An astronomical impact? Volcanic explosions? None of the options seemed viable.

The complex marriage dance finished, and the one-eyed Naib came forward with the old Sayyadina. The holy woman looked at the wedding couple and fixed Kynes with the gaze of her eyes, so dark in the moonlight that they resembled the predatory orbs of a raven: the total blue-within-blue of spice addiction.

After eating Fremen food for months, each taste laced with the richness of melange, Kynes had looked in a reflecting glass one morning and noticed that the whites of his own eyes had begun to take on a sky-blue tinge. The change startled him.

Still, he did feel more alive, his mind sharper and his body suffused with energy. Some of this could be a consequence of the enthusiasm for his research activities, but he knew the spice must also have something to do with it.

Here the spice was everywhere: in the air, food, garments, wall hangings, and rugs. Melange was intertwined with sietch life as much as water.

That day Turok, who still came to take him out on daily explorations, had noticed Kynes's eyes, the new blue tint. "You are becoming one of us, Planetologist. That blue we call the Eyes of Ibad. You are part of Dune now. Our world has changed you forever."

Kynes had offered a smile, but it was only tentative, because he felt some fear. "That it has," he said.

And now he was about to be married—another important change.

Standing before him, the mysterious Sayyadina uttered a series of words in Chakobsa, a language Kynes did not understand, but he gave the appropriate responses he had memorized. The sietch elders had taken extreme care to prepare him. Perhaps one day, with more research, he would understand the rituals surrounding him, the ancient language, the mysterious traditions. But for now he could only make reasoned guesses.

During the ceremony he remained preoccupied, devising various tests he could run in sandy and rocky areas of the planet, dreaming of new experimental stations he would erect, considering which test gardens to plant. He had vast plans to implement and, at last, all the manpower he could possibly desire. It would take an incredible amount of work to reawaken this world—but now that the Fremen shared his dream, Pardot Kynes knew it could be done.

It could be done!

He smiled, and Frieth gazed up at him, smiling in her own right, though almost certainly her thoughts diverged widely from his. Nearly oblivious to the activities around him and paying little mind to their import, Kynes found himself married in the Fremen way, almost before he realized it.

The haughty do but build castle walls behind which they seek to hide their doubts and fears.

—Bene Gesserit Axiom

The dawn mists carried an iodine tang from the sea, rising from the wet black cliffs that supported the spires of Castle Caladan. Normally, Paulus Atreides found it peaceful and refreshing, but today it made him uneasy.

The Old Duke stood out on one of the tower balconies, drawing a deep breath of fresh air. He loved his planet, especially the early mornings; the fresh, pure kind of silence gave him more energy than a good night's sleep ever could.

Even in troubled times such as these.

To ward off the chill he wrapped himself in a thick robe trimmed with green Canidar wool. His wife paused behind him in the bedchamber, hanging on every breath as she always did after they had been fighting. It was a matter of form. When Paulus didn't object, she came closer to stand next to him to gaze out upon their world. Her eyes were tired, and she looked hurt, but unconvinced; he would hold her, and she would warm to him, and then she would try to press the issue again. She still insisted that House Atreides was in grave danger because of what he had done.

From below, shouts and muted laughter and the sounds of exercise drifted upward. The Duke looked down to the

sheltered courtyard, pleased to see his son Leto already out doing his
training routines with the exiled Prince of Ix. Both wore body-shields
that hummed and flickered in the orange early-morning light. The
young men carried blunted stun-daggers in their left hands and training swords in their right.

In the weeks they had lived on Caladan, Rhombur had recovered
quickly and completely from the concussion he'd received during their
escape from Ix. The exercise and fresh air had improved his health, his
muscle tone, his complexion. But the stocky young man's heart and his
mood would take much longer to heal. He seemed all at sea yet from
what had happened to him.

The two circled and parried, slashing down, trying to judge just
how fast they could move their blades without having them deflected
by the protective fields. They challenged and pounced, striking with a
flurry of attacks that had no hope of penetrating the other's defenses.
Blades sang and ricocheted from the shimmering shields.

"The boys have so much energy for such an hour," Helena said,
rubbing her red-rimmed eyes. A safe comment, not likely to raise any
objections. She took half a step closer. "Rhombur's even lost weight."

The Old Duke looked over at her, noting the age-sharpened porcelain of her features, a few strands of gray in her dark hair. "This is the
best time for training. Gets the blood flowing for the entire day. I
taught Leto that when he was just a boy."

From far out at sea he heard the clang of a reef-marking buoy and the
putter of a fishing coracle, one of the local wickerwood boats with water-
proofed hulls. He saw the hazy fog lights of a trawler farther out, cutting
through the low-lying banks of sea mist as it harvested melon-kelp.

"Yes . . . the boys are exercising," Helena said, "but have you noticed Kailea sitting there? Why do you think she's up so early?" The lilt
at the end of her question made him think twice.

The Duke looked down, for the first time marking the lovely daughter of House Vernius. Kailea lounged on a polished-coral bench in the
sunshine, daintily eating from a plate of assorted fruits. She had her
padded copy of the Orange Catholic Bible beside her on the bench—
Helena's gift—but she wasn't reading it.

Puzzled, Paulus scratched his beard. "Does the girl always get up
this early? I suspect she's not adjusted to our Caladan days yet."

Helena watched as Leto pressed with fury against Rhombur's shield and slipped his stun-dagger in, jolting the Ixian Prince with an electric shock. Rhombur howled, then chuckled as he backed off. Leto raised his training sword as if scoring a point. He flashed a gray-eyed glance at Kailea, touching the tip of his sword to his forehead in a salute.

"Have you never seen the way your son looks at her, Paulus?" Helena's voice was stern and disapproving.

"No, I hadn't much noticed." The Old Duke looked from Leto to the young woman again. In his mind Kailea, daughter of Dominic Vernius, was just a child. He had last seen her in infancy. Perhaps his sluggish old mind hadn't seen her adulthood coming so fast. Nor Leto's.

Considering this, he said, "That boy's hormones are reaching their peak. Let me speak to Thufir. We'll find some appropriate wenches for him."

"Mistresses like yours?" Helena turned away from her husband, looking hurt.

"Nothing wrong with it." He prayed with all his heart she wouldn't pursue *that* subject again. "As long as it never becomes anything serious."

Like any Lord in the Imperium, Paulus had his dalliances. His marriage to Helena, one of the daughters of House Richese, had been arranged for strictly political reasons after much consideration and bargaining. He'd done his best, had even loved her for a time—which had come as a genuine surprise to him. But then Helena had drifted away, becoming absorbed in religion and lost dreams instead of current realities.

Discreetly, quietly, Paulus had eventually gone back to his mistresses, treating them well, enjoying himself, and careful not to produce any bastards from them. He never spoke of it, but Helena knew. She always knew.

And she had to live with the fact.

"Never becomes serious?" Helena leaned over the balcony to see Kailea better. "I'm afraid Leto *feels* something for this girl, that he's falling in love with her. I told you not to send him to Ix."

"It isn't love," Paulus said, pretending to pay attention to the movements of the sword-and-shield duel below. The boys had more energy than skill; they needed to work on finesse. The clumsiest of Harkonnen guards would be able to wade in and dispatch both of them in an eyeblink.

"You're sure about that?" Helena asked in a worried tone. "A great deal is at stake here. Leto is the heir to House Atreides, the son of a

Duke. He has to take care and choose his romantic assignations with forethought. Consult with us, negotiate for terms, get the most he can—"

"I know that," Paulus muttered.

"You know it all too well." His wife's voice became cold and brittle. "Maybe one of your wenches isn't such a bad idea after all. At least it'll keep him away from Kailea."

Down below, the young woman nibbled on fruit, eyed Leto with coy admiration, and laughed at a particularly outrageous maneuver he had pulled off. Rhombur countered him, their shields clashing and sparking against each other. When Leto turned to smile back at her, Kailea looked at her breakfast plate with feigned aloofness.

Helena recognized the movements of the courtship dance, as intricate as any swordplay. "See how they look at each other?"

The Old Duke shook his head sadly. "At one time the daughter of House Vernius might have been an excellent match for Leto."

It saddened him to know how his friend Dominic Vernius was being hunted down by Imperial decree. Emperor Elrood, seemingly irrational, had branded Vernius not only a renegade and an exile, but also a traitor. Neither Earl Dominic nor Lady Shando had sent any word to Caladan, but Paulus hoped they remained alive; both were fair game for ambitious fortune seekers.

House Atreides had risked a great deal by accepting the two children into sanctuary on Caladan. Dominic Vernius had called in all his remaining favors among the Houses of the Landsraad, which had confirmed the young exiles in their protected status, so long as they did not aspire to regain the former title of their House.

"I'd never agree to a marriage between our son and . . . *her*," Helena said. "While you've strutted around with bullfights and parades, I've had my ear to the ground. House Vernius has been falling into disfavor for years now. I've told you that, but you never listen."

Paulus said in a mild voice, "Ah, Helena, your Richesian bias keeps you from seeing Ix fairly. Vernius has always been your family's rival, and they roundly defeated you in the trade wars." Despite their disagreements, he tried to accord her the respect due a Lady of a Great House, even when nobody was listening.

"Clearly, the wrath of God has fallen upon Ix," she pointed out. "You can't deny that. You should get rid of Rhombur and Kailea. Send them away, or even kill them—it would be a kindness."

Duke Paulus smoldered. He'd known she'd get back around to the subject before long. "Helena! Watch your words." He looked at her in disbelief. "That's an outrageous suggestion, even from you."

"Why? Their House brought about its own destruction by scorning the strictures of the Great Revolt. House Vernius taunted God with their hubris. Anyone could see it. I warned you myself before Leto went to Ix." She held the edge of his robe, trembling with her passion as she tried to make a reasoned plea. "Hasn't humanity learned its lesson well enough? Think of the horrors we went through, the enslavement, the near extermination. We must never stray from the correct path again. Ix was trying to bring back thinking machines. 'Thou shalt not make a machine in the—' "

"No need to quote verses to me," he said, cutting her off. When Helena dropped into her rigid and zealous mind-set, no rebuttal could penetrate her blinders.

"But if you would just listen and read," Helena pleaded. "I can show you the passages in the Book—"

"Dominic Vernius was my friend, Helena," Paulus said. "And House Atreides stands by its friends. Rhombur and Kailea are *my* guests here at Castle Caladan, and I will hear no more of this talk from you."

Though Helena turned and vanished back into the bedchamber, he knew she would try to convince him again, at some other time. He sighed.

Gripping the balcony railing, Paulus looked back down to where the boys continued their exercises. It was more like a brawl, with Leto and Rhombur battering at each other, laughing and running around and wasting energy.

Despite her self-righteousness, Helena had made some valid points. This was the kind of opening their age-old enemies, the Harkonnens, would use to try and destroy House Atreides. Enemy legal minds were probably already working on it. If House Vernius had in fact violated Butlerian precepts, then House Atreides might be considered guilty by association.

But the die was cast, and Paulus was up to the challenge. Still, he had to make sure nothing terrible happened to his own son.

Below the boys fought on, still playful, though the Old Duke knew Rhombur ached to strike back at the myriad faceless foes who had driven his family from their ancestral home. To do that, however, both young men needed *training*—not only the required brutal instruction in the use of personal weaponry, but in the skills required to lead men, and the abstractions of large-scale government.

Smiling grimly, the Duke knew what he had to do. Rhombur and Kailea had been placed in his care. He had sworn to keep them safe, had given his blood oath to Dominic Vernius. He must give them the best chance they could possibly have.

He would send Rhombur and Leto to his Master of Assassins, Thufir Hawat.

THE WARRIOR MENTAT stood like an iron pillar, glaring at his two new students. They stood atop a barren sea cliff kilometers north of Castle Caladan. The wind smashed against the slick rocks and blasted upward, rustling clumps of pampas grass. Gray gulls wheeled overhead, shrieking to each other, scanning for edible flotsam on the rocky beach. Stunted cypress trees huddled like hunchbacks, bowed against the constant ocean breeze.

Leto had no idea how old Thufir Hawat was. The sinewy Mentat had trained Duke Paulus when he was much younger, and now the Master of Assassins fended off any appearance of age through brute force. His skin was leathery, having been exposed to harsh environments on many worlds during previous Atreides campaigns, from blistering heat to numbing cold, whipping storms and the hard rigors of open space.

Thufir Hawat stared at the young men in silence. He crossed his arms over his scuffed leather chestplate. His eyes were like weapons, his silence a goad. His unsmiling lips were stained the deep cranberry of sapho juice.

Leto stood next to his friend, fidgeting. His fingers were chilled enough that he wished he had brought gloves. *When are we going to begin training?* He and Rhombur glanced at each other, impatient, waiting.

"*Look at me*, I said!" Hawat snapped. "I could have leaped forward and gutted both of you in the instant you exchanged those cute little glances." He took a menacing step toward them.

Leto and Rhombur wore fine clothes, comfortable yet regal-looking. Their capes snapped about in the breeze. Leto's was brilliant emerald merh-silk trimmed in black, while the Prince of Ix proudly sported the purple and copper of House Vernius. But Rhombur looked decidedly uneasy to be out under the towering sky. "It's all so . . . wide-open," he whispered.

After interminable silence, Hawat raised his chin, ready to begin. "First of all, remove those ridiculous capes."

Leto reached up to the clasp at his throat, but Rhombur hesitated just a moment. Within the space of a heartbeat, Hawat had ripped out his short sword and slashed the tiny cord mere millimeters from the Prince's jugular vein. The wind grasped the purple-on-copper cape and carried it like a lost banner over the cliff. The cloth flew like a kite until it drifted to the churning water below.

"Hey!" Rhombur said. "Why did you—"

Hawat sidestepped the indignant outcry. "You came here to learn weapons training. So why did you dress for a Landsraad ball or an Imperial banquet?" The Mentat snorted, then spat with the wind. "Fighting is dirty work, and unless you intend to conceal weapons in those capes, wearing them is foolish. It's like carrying your own burial shroud on your shoulders."

Leto still held his green cape in his hands. Hawat reached forward, grabbed the end of the fabric, snapped it, twirled it around—and in a flash had captured Leto's right hand, his fighting hand. Hawat yanked hard and thrust out with his foot to catch the young man's ankle. Leto sprawled on the rocky ground.

Static spun in front of his eyes, and he gasped to catch his breath. Rhombur laughed at his friend, then managed to restrain himself.

Hawat yanked the cape free and tossed it up in the air, where it blew out on the ocean winds to join Rhombur's. "Anything can be a weapon," he said. "You're carrying your swords, and I see daggers at your sides. You have shields, all of which are obvious weapons.

"However, you should also conceal an assortment of other niceties: needles, stun-fields, poison tips. While your enemy can see the obvious weapons"—Hawat took a long training sword and slashed it in the air—"you can use them as a decoy to attack with something even deadlier."

Leto stood up straight, brushing dirt and debris from himself. "But, sir, it's not sporting to use hidden weapons. Doesn't that go against the strictures of—"

Hawat snapped his fingers like a gunshot in front of Leto's face. "Don't talk to me about pretty points of assassination." The Mentat's rough skin turned more ruddy, as if he barely kept his anger in check. "Is your intention to show off for the ladies, or to eliminate your opponent? This is not a game."

The grizzled man focused on Rhombur, staring so intently that the young man backed up half a step. "Word has it there's an Imperial bounty on your head, Prince, if you ever leave the sanctuary of Caladan. You are the exiled son of House Vernius. Your life is not that of a commoner. You never know when the death blow will fall, so you must be prepared at all times. Court intrigues and politics have their own rules, but oft'times the rules are not known to all players."

Rhombur swallowed hard.

Turning to Leto, Hawat said, "Lad, your life is in danger, too, as heir to House Atreides. All Great Houses must constantly be on the alert against assassination."

Leto straightened, fixing his gaze on the instructor. "I understand, Thufir, and I want to learn." He looked over at Rhombur. "*We* want to learn."

Hawat's red-stained lips smiled. "That's a start," he said. "There may be clumsy clods working for other families in the Landsraad—but you, my boys, must become shining examples. Not only will you learn shield-and-knife fighting and the subtle arts of killing, you must also learn the weaponry of politics and government. You must know how to defend yourselves through culture and rhetoric, as well as with physical blows." The warrior Mentat squared his shoulders and stood firm. "From me you will learn all these things."

He switched on his body-shield. Behind the shimmering field he held a dagger in one hand, a long sword in the other.

Instinctively, Leto switched on his own shield belt, and the flickering Holtzman field glimmered in front of him. Rhombur fumbled to do the same just as the Mentat feigned an attack, pulling back at the last possible second before drawing blood.

Hawat tossed the weapons from hand to hand—left, right, and left again—proving he could use either for a killing strike. "Watch carefully. Your lives may someday depend on it."

Any path that narrows future possibilities may become a lethal trap. Humans do not thread their way through a maze; they scan a vast horizon filled with unique opportunities.

—The Spacing Guild Handbook

J unction was an austere world of limited geographic variations, unadorned scenery, and strict weather control to remove troublesome inconveniences. A serviceable place, it had been chosen as Spacing Guild headquarters because of its strategic location rather than its landscapes.

Here, candidates learned to become Navigators.

Second-growth forests covered millions of hectares, but they were stunted box trees and dwarf oaks. Certain Old Terran vegetables grew in abundance, cultivated by the locals—potatoes, peppers, eggplants, tomatoes, and a variety of herbs—but the produce tended to become alkaloid, edible only after careful processing.

After his mind-opening examination, stunned by the new vistas opened to him through the melange surge, D'murr Pilru had been brought here without a chance to say his goodbyes to his twin brother or his parents. At first he had been upset, but the requirements of Guild training rapidly filled him with so many wonders that he'd disregarded everything else. He found he could now focus his thoughts much better . . . and forget much more easily.

The buildings of Junction—huge bulging shapes with

rounded and angular extrusions—were of standard Guild design, much like the Embassy on Ix: practical in the extreme and awe-inspiring in their immensity. Each structure bore a rounded cartouche containing the mark of infinity. Mechanical infrastructures were both Ixian and Richesian, installed centuries earlier and still functioning.

The Spacing Guild preferred environments that did not interfere with its important work. To a Navigator, any distractions were potentially dangerous. Every Guild student learned this lesson early, as did the young candidate D'murr—far from home and totally engrossed in his studies to the exclusion of any worries about his former planet's troubles.

On a blakgras field he was immersed in his own container of melange gas—half swimming and half crawling as his body continued to change, his physical systems altering to adapt to the bombardment of spice. Membranes had begun to connect his toes and fingers; his body had grown longer than before and more flaccid, taking on a fish shape. No one had explained the extent of the inevitable changes to him, and he neither chose—nor needed—to ask. It made no difference. So much of the universe had been opened to him, he considered it a modest price to pay.

D'murr's eyes had grown smaller, without lashes; they were also developing cataracts. He didn't need them to see anymore, though, since he had other eyes . . . inner vision. The panorama of the universe unfolded for him. In the process, he felt as if he were leaving everything else behind . . . and it didn't bother him.

Through the haze D'murr saw that the blakgras field was covered with neat rows of containerized candidates and their Navigator trainers. One life per container. The tanks vented orange clouds of filtered melange exhaust, swirling around masked humanoid attendants who stood nearby, waiting to move the tanks when told to do so.

The Head Instructor, a Navigator Steersman named Grodin, floated inside a black-framed tank that had been raised high on a platform; the trainees saw him more with their minds than with their eyes. Grodin had just returned from foldspace with a student, whose tank was adjacent to his and connected with flexible tubing, so that their gases merged.

D'murr himself had accomplished short flights on three occasions now. He was considered one of the top trainees. Once he learned to travel through foldspace by himself, he could be licensed as a Pilot, the lowest-ranking Navigator . . . but still vastly higher than he'd once been as a mere human.

Steersman Grodin's foldspace treks were legendary quests of discovery through incomprehensible dimensional knots. The Head Instructor's voice gurgled from a speaker inside D'murr's tank, using higher-order language. He described a time he had transported dinosaur-like creatures in an old-style Heighliner. Unknown to him, the monsters could stretch their necks to incredible lengths. While the Heighliner was in flight, one had chewed its way into a navigation chamber, so that its face appeared outside Grodin's tank, peering in with a curious, wide-eyed expression. . . .

So pleasant in here, D'murr thought without forming words as he absorbed the story. With enlarged nostrils he drew in a deep breath of the sharp, rich melange. Humans with dulled senses compared this pungent scent to strong cinnamon . . . but melange was so much more than that, so infinitely complex.

D'murr no longer needed to concern himself with the mundane affairs of humans, so trivial were they, so limited and shortsighted: political machinations, populations milling about like ants in a disturbed hill, lives flickering bright and dull like sparks from a campfire. His former life was only a vague and fading memory, without specific names or faces. He saw images, but ignored them. He could never go back to what he had been.

Instead of simply finishing his story about the dinosaur creature, Steersman Grodin spoke on a tangent about the technical aspects of what the chosen student had just accomplished on his interstellar journey, how they had employed high-order mathematics and dimensional changes to peer into the future—much the same way the long-necked monster had looked into his tank.

"A Navigator must do more than *observe,*" Grodin's scratchy voice said over the speaker. "A Navigator utilizes what he sees in order to guide spaceships safely through the void. Failure to apply certain basic principles may lead to Heighliner disasters and the loss of all lives and cargo aboard."

Before any of the new adepts like D'murr could become Pilots into foldspace, they must master how to deal with crises such as partially folded space, faulty prescience, the onset of spice intolerance, malfunctioning Holtzman generators, or even deliberate sabotage.

D'murr tried to envision the fates that had befallen some of his unfortunate predecessors. Contrary to popular belief, Navigators did not themselves fold space; the Holtzman engines did that. Navigators used their limited prescience to choose safe paths to travel. A ship could move through the void without their guidance, but that perilous guessing game invariably led to disaster. A Guild Navigator did not guarantee a safe journey—but he vastly improved the odds. Problems still arose when unforeseen events occurred.

D'murr was being trained to the limit of the Guild's knowledge . . . which could not include every eventuality. The universe and its inhabitants were in a state of constant change. All of the old schools understood this, including the Bene Gesserit and the Mentats. Survivors learned how to adjust to change, how to expect the unexpected.

At the edge of his awareness, his melange tank began to move on its suspensor field and fell into line behind the tanks of the other students. He heard an assistant instructor reciting passages from the Spacing Guild Manual; gas circulation mechanisms hummed around him. Every detail seemed so sharp, so clear, so important. He had never felt so alive!

Inhaling deeply of the orange-hued melange, he felt his concerns begin to dissipate. His thoughts drew back into order, sliding smoothly into the neuropathways of his Guild-enhanced brain.

"D'murr . . . D'murr, my brother . . ."

The name swirled with the gas, like a whisper in the universe—a name he no longer used now that he had been assigned a Guild nav-number. Names were associated with individuality. Names imposed limitations and preconceptions, family connections and past histories, they imposed *individuality*—the antithesis of what it meant to be a Navigator. A Guildsman merged with the cosmos and saw safe paths through the wrinkles of fate, prescient visions that enabled him to guide matter from place to place like chesspieces in a cosmic game.

"D'murr, can you hear me? D'murr?" The voice came from the speaker inside his tank, but also from a great distance. He heard something familiar in the timbre, the inflections. Could he have forgotten so much? *D'murr*. He'd almost erased that name from his thoughts.

D'murr's mind made connections that were becoming less and less important, and his slack mouth formed gurgling words. "Yes. I hear you."

Nudged by its attendant, D'murr's tank glided along a paved path, toward an immense, bulbous building where the Navigators lived. No one else seemed to hear the voice.

"This is C'tair," the transmission continued. "Your brother. You can hear me? Finally, this thing worked. How are you?"

"C'tair?" The fledgling Navigator felt his mind fold back into itself, compressing to the remnants of its sluggish, pre-Guild state. Trying to be human again, just for a moment. Was that important?

This was painful and limiting, like a man putting blinders on himself, but the information was there: yes, his twin brother. C'tair Pilru. Human. He got flashes of his father in ambassadorial dress, his mother in Guild Bank uniform, his brother (like himself) with dark hair and dark eyes, playing together, exploring. Those images had been shunted out of his thoughts, like most everything of that realm . . . but not quite gone.

"Yes," D'murr said. "I know you. I remember."

ON IX, IN a shadowed alcove where he used his cobbled-together transmission device, C'tair hunched over, desperate to avoid discovery— but this was worth any risk. Tears streaked down his cheeks, and he swallowed hard. The Tleilaxu and the suboids had continued their rampages and purges, destroying any residue of unfamiliar technology that they found.

"They took you away from me, in the Guild testing chamber," C'tair said, his voice a husky whisper. "They wouldn't let me see you, wouldn't let me say goodbye. Now I realize you were the lucky one, D'murr, considering everything that's happened here on Ix. It would break your heart to see it now." He took a deep, shuddering breath. "Our city was destroyed not long after the Guild took you away from us. Hundreds of thousands are dead. The Bene Tleilax now rule here."

D'murr paused, taking time to slide back into the limited manner of person-to-person communication. "I have guided a Heighliner through foldspace, brother. I hold the galaxy in my mind, I see mathematics." His sluggish words garbled together. "Now I know why . . . I know . . . Uhhh, I feel pain from your connection. C'tair, how?"

"This communication hurts you?" He drew back from the transmitter, concerned, and held his breath, fearful that one of the furtive Tleilaxu spies might hear him. "I'm sorry, D'murr. Maybe I should—"

"Not important. Pain shifts, like a headache . . . but different. Swimming through my mind . . . and beyond it." D'murr sounded distracted, his voice distant and ethereal. "What connection is this? What device?"

"D'murr, didn't you hear me? Ix is destroyed—our world, our city is now a prison camp. Mother was killed in an explosion! I couldn't save her. I've been hiding here, and I'm at great risk while making this communication. Our father is in exile somewhere . . . on Kaitain, I think. House Vernius has gone renegade. I'm trapped here, alone!"

D'murr remained focused on what he considered the primary question. "Communication directly through foldspace? Impossible. Explain it to me."

Taken aback at his twin brother's lack of concern over the horrendous news, C'tair nonetheless chose not to rebuke him. D'murr had, after all, undergone extreme mental changes and couldn't be blamed for the way he was now. C'tair could never understand what his twin had been through. He himself had failed the Guild's tests; he had been too fearful and rigid. Otherwise, he, too, might be a Navigator now.

Holding his breath, he listened to a creaking sound in the passageway overhead, distant footsteps that faded. Whispering voices. Then silence returned, and C'tair was able to continue the conversation.

"Explain," D'murr said again.

Eager for any kind of conversation, C'tair told his brother of the equipment he had salvaged. "Do you remember Davee Rogo? The old inventor who used to take us into his laboratory and show us the things he was working on?"

"Crippled . . . suspensor crutches. Too decrepit to walk."

"Yes, he used to talk about communicating in neutrino energy wavelengths? A network of rods wrapped in silicate crystals?"

"Uhhh . . . pain again."

"You're hurting!" C'tair looked around, fearful of the risk he continued to take himself. "I won't talk much longer."

The tone was impatient. D'murr wanted to hear more. "Continue explanation. Need to know this device."

"One day during the fighting, when I really wanted to talk with you, bits and pieces of his conversation came back to me. In the rubble of a ruined building, I thought I saw a hazy image of him next to me. Like a vision. He was talking in that creaky old voice, telling me what to do, what parts I would require and how to put them together. He gave me the ideas I needed."

"Interesting." The Navigator's voice was flat and bloodless.

His brother's lack of emotion and compassion disturbed him. C'tair tried to ask questions about D'murr's Spacing Guild experiences, but his twin had no patience for the queries and said that he couldn't discuss Guild secrets, not even with his brother. He had traveled through foldspace, and it was incredible. That was all D'murr would say.

"When can we talk again?" C'tair asked. The apparatus felt dangerously warm, ready to break down. He would have to shut it off soon. D'murr groaned with distant pain, but gave no definite response.

Still, even knowing his brother's discomfort, he had a human need to say goodbye, even if D'murr no longer did. "Farewell, for now, then. I miss you." As he spoke the long-overdue words, he sensed an easing of his own pain—odd, in a way, since he could no longer be sure his brother understood him as he once had.

Feeling guilty, C'tair broke the connection. Then he sat in silence, overwhelmed by conflicting emotions: joy at having spoken to his twin again, but sadness at D'murr's ambivalent reactions. How much had his brother changed?

D'murr should have cared about the death of their mother and the tragic events that had befallen Ix. A Guild Navigator's position affected all mankind. Shouldn't a Navigator be *more* caring, *more* protective of humanity?

But instead the young man seemed to have severed all ties, burned all bridges. Was D'murr reflecting Guild philosophy, or had he become so consumed with himself and his new abilities that he'd turned into an egomaniac? Was it necessary for him to behave that way? Had D'murr severed all contact with his humanity? No way to tell yet.

C'tair felt as if he had lost his brother all over again.

He removed the bioneutrino machine contacts that had temporarily expanded his mental powers, amplifying his thoughts and thus enabling him to communicate with distant Junction. Suddenly dizzy, he returned to his shielded bolt-hole and lay down on the narrow cot. Eyes closed, he envisioned the universe behind his lids, wondering what it must be like for his twin. His mind hummed with a strange residue of the contact, a backwash of mental expansion.

D'murr had sounded as if he were speaking underwater, through filters of comprehension. Now, underlying meanings occurred to C'tair—subtleties and refinements. Throughout the evening in the isolation of his hidden room, thoughts percolated through his mind, overwhelming him like a demonic possession. The contact had sparked something unexpected in his own brain, an amazing reaction.

For days he did not leave the enclosure, consumed with his enhanced memories, using the prototype apparatus to focus his thoughts to an obsessive clarity. Hour after hour, the replayed conversation became clearer to him, words and double meanings blossoming like flower petals . . . as if he traversed his own kind of foldspace of mind and memory. Nuances of D'murr's dialogue became increasingly apparent, meanings C'tair hadn't noticed at first. This gave him only an inkling of what his brother had become.

He found it exciting. And terrifying.

Finally, coming back to awareness an unknown number of days later, he noticed that food and beverage packages lay scattered around him. The room stank. He looked in a mirror, shocked to see that he had grown a scratchy dark brown beard. His eyes were bloodshot, his hair wild. C'tair barely recognized himself.

If Kailea Vernius were to set eyes on him now, she would draw back in horror or disdain and send him to work in the dimmest lower levels with the suboids. Somehow, though, after the tragedy of Ix, the rape of his beautiful underground city, his boyish crush on the Earl's daughter seemed irrelevant. Of all the sacrifices C'tair had made, that was among the smallest.

And he was sure there would be harder ones to come.

Before cleaning himself or the hiding place, though, he began preparations for the next call to his brother.

Perceptions rule the universe.
—Bene Gesserit Saying

A robo-controlled shuttle left its orbiting Heighliner in the Laoujin system and streaked toward the surface of Wallach IX, transmitting appropriate security codes to bypass the Sisterhood's primary defenses. The Bene Gesserit homeworld was just another stop on its long circuitous route wandering among the stars in the Imperium.

Her thick hair beginning to turn gray, her body starting to hint at its age, Gaius Helen Mohiam thought it would be good to be home after many months of other duties, each separate assignment a thread in the vast Bene Gesserit tapestry. No Sister understood the entire pattern, the entire weaving of events and people, but Mohiam did her part.

With her advancing pregnancy, the Sisterhood had called her home, to remain at the Mother School until such time as Mohiam delivered the much-anticipated daughter. Only Kwisatz Mother Anirul comprehended her true value to the breeding program, how everything hinged on the child she now carried. Mohiam understood that this baby was important, but even the whispers of her Other Memory, which could always be called upon to offer a cacophony of advice, remained deliberately silent on the subject.

The Guild shuttle carried only her. Working under the spectre of the Jihad, the Richesian manufacturers of the robo-pilot had gone out of their way to make a clunky-looking, rivet-covered device that most vehemently neither emulated the human mind nor looked the least bit human . . . or even sophisticated, for that matter.

The robo-pilot transported passengers and materials from a big ship to the surface of a planet, and back again in a well-rehearsed chain of events. Its functions included barely enough programming flexibility to deal with air-traffic patterns or adverse weather conditions. The robo-pilot took its shuttle in a routine sequence: from Heighliner to planet, from planet to Heighliner . . .

At a window seat in the shuttle, Mohiam reflected on the delicious revenge she had exacted on the Baron. It had been months already, and no doubt he still suspected nothing, but a Bene Gesserit could wait a long time for the appropriate payment. Over the years, as his precious body weakened and bloated from the disease, an utterly defeated Vladimir Harkonnen might even contemplate suicide.

Mohiam's vengeful action might have been impulsive, but it was fitting and appropriate after what the Baron had done. Mother Superior Harishka would not have allowed House Harkonnen to go unpunished, and Mohiam thought her spontaneous idea had been cruelly apt. It would save the Sisterhood time and trouble.

As the ship descended into the cloud layer, Mohiam hoped this new child would be perfect, because the Baron would no longer be of any use to them. But if not, the Sisterhood always had other options and other plans. They had many different breeding schemes.

Mohiam was of a *type* considered optimal for a certain mysterious genetic program. She knew the names of some, but not all, of the other candidates, and knew as well that the Sisterhood didn't want simultaneous pregnancies in the program, fearing this might muddle the mating index. Mohiam did wonder, though, why she had been selected again, after the first failure. Her superiors hadn't explained it to her, and she knew better than to ask. And again, the Voices in Other Memory kept their counsel to themselves.

Do the details matter? she wondered. *I carry the requested daughter in my womb.* A successful birth would elevate Mohiam's stature, might even result in her eventual election as Mother Superior by the proctors, when she got much older . . . depending on how important this daughter really was.

She sensed the girl would be *very* important.

Aboard the robo-piloted shuttle, she felt a sudden change of motion. Looking out the narrow window, she saw the horizon of Wallach IX lurch as the craft flipped over and plunged down, out of control. The safety field around her seat glimmered an unfamiliar, disconcerting yellow. Machine sounds, which had been limited to a smooth whir, now screamed through the cabin, hurting her ears.

Lights blinked wildly on the control module ahead of her. The robo's movements were jerky and uncertain. She had been trained to handle crises, and her mind worked rapidly. Mohiam knew about occasional malfunctions on these shuttles—statistically unlikely—exacerbated by the lack of pilots with the ability to think and react. When a problem did occur—and Mohiam felt herself in the midst of one now—the potential for disaster was high.

The shuttle plummeted, lurching and bucking. Clothlike scraps of cloud slapped the windows. The robo-pilot went through the same circular motions, unable to try anything new. The engine flared out, went silent.

This can't be, Mohiam thought. *Not now, not when I'm carrying this child.* Viscerally, she felt that if she could just survive this, her baby would be healthy and would be the one so badly needed by the Sisterhood.

But dark thoughts assailed her, and she began to tremble. Guild Navigators, such as the one in the Heighliner above her, utilized higher-order dimensional calculations, and they did so in order to see the future, enabling them to maneuver ships safely through the dangerous voids of foldspace. Had the Spacing Guild learned of the secret Bene Gesserit program, and did they fear it?

As the shuttle hurtled toward disaster, an incredible array of possibilities tumbled through Mohiam's mind. The safety field around her stretched and grew more yellow. Her body pressed against it, threatening to break through. Holding her hands protectively over her womb, she felt a frantic desire to live, and for her unborn child to thrive—and her thoughts went beyond the parochial concerns of a mother and child, to a much larger significance.

She wondered if her suspicions might be totally in error. What if some higher force than either she or her Sisters could possibly imagine was behind this? Were the Bene Gesserit, through their breeding program, playing God? Did a real God—regardless of the Sisterhood's cynicism and skepticism toward religion—in fact exist?

What a cruel joke that would be.

The deformities of her first child, and now the impending death of this fetus and Mohiam, too . . . it all seemed to add up to something. But if so, who—or *what*—was behind this emergency?

The Bene Gesserit did not believe in accidents or coincidences.

" 'I must not fear,' " she intoned, her eyes closed. " 'Fear is the mind-killer. Fear is the little-death that brings total obliteration. I will face my fear. I will permit it to pass over me and through me. And when it has gone past I will turn the inner eye to see its path. Where the fear has gone there will be nothing. Only I will remain.' "

It was the Litany Against Fear, conceived in ancient times by a Bene Gesserit Sister and passed on to generation after generation.

Mohiam took a deep breath, and felt her trembling subside.

The shuttle held position momentarily, with her window pointed planetward. The engine sputtered again. She saw the continental mass approaching fast, and made out the sprawling Mother School complex, a labyrinthine white-stuccoed city with sienna roof tiles.

Was the shuttle being sent out of control into the main school, with some terrible explosive force aboard? A single crash could wipe out the heart of the Sisterhood.

Mohiam struggled against the safety field, but could not break free. The shuttle shifted, and the land disappeared from view. The window cocked upward to reveal the blue-white sun on the edge of the atmosphere.

Then her safety field grew clear, and Mohiam realized that the shuttle had righted itself. The engine was on again, a sweet flow of machinery. In the front compartment, the robo-pilot moved with apparent efficiency, as if nothing had happened. One of its programmed emergency routines must have worked.

As the shuttle set down smoothly on the ground in front of the grand plaza, Mohiam breathed a long sigh of relief. She rushed to the doorhatch, meaning to flee into the safety of the nearest building . . . but she paused, took a moment to compose herself, and then strode calmly out. A Reverend Mother had to maintain appearances.

When she glided down the ramp, Sisters and acolytes swarmed

protectively around her. Mother Superior demanded that the shuttle be impounded for a complete overhaul and investigation, seeking evidence of sabotage or confirmation of a simple malfunction. A brusque radio transmission from the Heighliner above, however, prevented this.

Reverend Mother Anirul Sadow Tonkin stood waiting to greet Mohiam, beaming with pride, looking very young with her doelike face and short bronze hair. Mohiam had never understood Anirul's importance, though even the Mother Superior often showed her deference. The two women nodded to each other.

In the midst of her fellow Sisters, Mohiam was escorted to a safe building; a large contingent of armed female guards had been posted to watch her. She would be pampered and observed carefully until the baby was due.

"There will be no more travel for you, Mohiam," Mother Superior Harishka said. "You must remain safely here—until we have your daughter."

In the concubines' wing of the Imperial Palace, throbbing massage machines slapped and kneaded bare skin, using scented oils to caress every glorious contour of the Emperor's women. Sophisticated physical-maintenance devices extracted cellulite, improved muscle tone, tautened abdomens and chins, and made tiny injections to soften the skin. Every detail had to be the way old Elrood preferred, though he didn't seem much interested anymore. Even the eldest of the four women, the septuagenarian Grera Cary, had the figure of a woman half her age, sustained in part through frequent imbibing of spice.

Dawn's light was tinged amber by passing through the bank of thick armor-plaz windows. When Grera's massage was complete, the machine wrapped her in a warm towel of karthan weave and placed a refreshing cloth soaked with eucalyptus and juniper over her face. The concubine's bed changed into a sensiform chair that conformed perfectly to her body.

A mechanized manicure station dropped from the ceiling, and Grera whispered through her daily meditations as her fingernails and toenails were trimmed, polished, and painted a lush green. The machine slid back up into its overhead compartment, and the woman stood and dropped her towel. An electric field passed over her face, arms, and legs, removing barely discernible and unwanted hairs.

Perfect. Perfect enough for the Emperor.

Of the current retinue of concubines, only Grera was old enough to remember Shando, a plaything who had left Imperial service to marry a war hero and settle down into a "normal life." Elrood hadn't paid Shando much attention when she'd been among his numerous women, but once she'd left, he had railed at the others and moaned about his loss. Most of his favorite concubines chosen in succeeding years looked a great deal like Shando.

As she watched the other concubines go through similar body-toning procedures, Grera Cary thought of how things had changed for all the Emperor's harem. Less than a year earlier, these women had congregated only rarely, since Elrood was with one of them so often, performing what he called his "royal duty." One of the concubines, an Elaccan, had secretly given the old goat a nickname that stuck—"Fornicario," a reference from one of the Old Terran languages to his sexual prowess and appetites. The women only used it among themselves, and snickered.

"Has anyone seen Fornicario?" asked the taller of the two youngest concubines at the other end of the room.

Grera exchanged a smile with her, and the women giggled like schoolgirls. "I'm afraid our Imperial oak has turned into a drooping willow."

The old man rarely came to the concubines' wing anymore. Though Elrood spent as much time in bed now as ever, it was for an entirely different reason. His health had declined rapidly, and his libido had already died. His mind was the next thing likely to go.

Suddenly the chattering women grew silent, turning with alarm toward the main entrance of the concubines' wing. Without announcing himself, Crown Prince Shaddam entered with his ever-present companion, Hasimir Fenring, whom they often called "the Ferret" because of his narrow face and pointed chin. The women covered themselves quickly and stood at attention to show their respect.

"What's so funny in here, hm-m-m-m-ah?" Fenring demanded. "I heard giggling."

"The girls were just enjoying a little joke," Grera said, in a cautious tone. Senior among them, she often spoke for the concubines.

It was rumored that this undersized man had stabbed two of his lovers to death, and from his slithery demeanor Grera believed it. Through her years of experience, she had learned how to recognize a man capable of extreme cruelty. Fenring's genitals were supposedly malformed and sterile, though sexually functional. She had never slept with him herself, nor did she wish to.

Fenring studied her with overlarge, soulless eyes, then moved past her to the two new blondes. The Crown Prince remained behind him, near the doorway to the solarium. Slim and red-haired, Shaddam wore a gray Sardaukar uniform with silver-and-gold trim. Grera knew the Imperial heir loved to play military games.

"Please share your little joke with us," Fenring insisted. He addressed the smaller blonde, a petite girl barely beyond her teens who was only slightly shorter than he was. Her eyes resembled Shando's. "Prince Shaddam and I both enjoy humor."

"It was just a private conversation," Grera responded, stepping forward protectively. "Personal things."

"Can't she speak for herself?" Fenring snapped, glaring back at the elder woman. He wore a black tunic trimmed in gold, and many rings on his hands. "If this one's been chosen to entertain the Padishah Emperor, I'm sure she knows how to relay a simple joke, ah-mm-m-m-m?"

"It was as Grera said," the young blonde insisted. "Just a girl thing. Not worth repeating."

Fenring took hold of one of the edges of the towel she had been gripping tightly about her curvaceous body. Surprise and fear covered her face. He jerked at the towel, exposing one of her breasts.

Angrily, Grera said, "Cease this nonsense, Fenring. We are royal concubines. No one but the Emperor may touch us."

"Lucky you." Fenring gazed across the room at Shaddam.

The Crown Prince nodded stiffly. "She's right, Hasimir. I'll share one of my concubines with you, if you like."

"But I didn't touch her, my friend—I was only fixing her towel a little." He let go, and the girl covered herself again. "But has the Emperor been . . . um-m-m-m-ah, utilizing your services much lately? We hear that a certain part of him is already deceased." Fenring looked up at Grera Cary, who towered over the Ferret.

Grera glanced over at the Crown Prince, seeking support and safety, but found none. His cold eyes looked past her. For a moment she wondered what this Imperial heir would be like in bed, if he had the sexual prowess his father had once possessed. She doubted it, though. From the cold-cod look of this one, even the withered man on his deathbed would still be a superior lover.

"Old one, you will come with me, and we will talk more of jokes. Perhaps we can even exchange a few," Fenring commanded. "I can be a funny man."

"Now, sir?" With the fingers of her free hand she indicated her karthan-weave towel.

His gleaming eyes narrowed dangerously. "A person of my station has no time to wait while a woman dresses. Of course I mean *now!*" He grabbed a tuft of her towel and pulled her along. She went with him, struggling to keep the towel wrapped around her. "This way. Come, come." While Shaddam followed passively, amused, Fenring forced her to the door.

"The Emperor will hear of this!" she protested.

"Speak loudly, he has trouble hearing." Fenring gave a maddening smile. "And who will tell him? Some days he doesn't even remember his own name—he certainly won't bother with a crone like you." His tone sent a chill down Grera's spine. The other concubines milled about, confused and helpless as their grande dame was unceremoniously hauled out of their presence and into the corridor.

At this early hour no members of the royal Court were in evidence, only Sardaukar guards standing rigidly at attention. And with Crown Prince Shaddam here, the Sardaukar guards saw nothing at all. Grera looked at them, but they stared right through her.

Since her flustered, stuttering voice seemed to irritate Fenring, Grera decided it would be safest to become silent. The Ferret was behaving strangely, but as an Imperial concubine she had nothing to fear from him. The furtive man wouldn't dare do anything so stupid as to actually hurt her.

Glancing back suddenly, she found that Shaddam had disappeared. He must have scuttled off down another passageway. She was completely alone with this vile man.

Fenring passed through a security barrier and pushed Grera ahead of him into a room. She stumbled onto a black-and-white marbleplaz floor. A large chamber with a stonecrete fireplace dominating one wall, this had once been a visitors' suite but was now devoid of furnishings. It smelled of fresh paint and long abandonment.

Remaining where she was, proud and fearless though wrapped in only a towel, Grera glanced up at him intermittently. She tried not to show defiance or lack of respect. Over her years of service, she had learned to stand on her own.

The door closed behind them. They were alone now, and Shaddam still hadn't appeared. What did this little man want with her?

From his tunic Fenring produced a green-jeweled oval. After he pressed a button on its side, a long green blade emerged, glinting in the light of a glowglobe chandelier.

"I didn't bring you here for questions, crone," he said in a soft tone. He held the weapon up. "Actually, I need to test this on you. It's brand-new, you see, and I've never really liked some of the Emperor's walking meat."

Fenring was no stranger to assassination, and killed with his bare hands at least as often as he engineered accidents or paid for thugs. Sometimes he liked blood work, while on other occasions he preferred subtleties and deceptions. When he was younger, barely nineteen, he had slipped out of the Imperial Palace at night and killed two civil servants at random, just to prove he could do it. He still tried to keep in practice.

Fenring had always known he had the iron will necessary for murder, but he had been surprised at how much he enjoyed it. Killing the previous Crown Prince Fafnir had been his greatest triumph, until now. Once old Elrood finally died, that would be a new feather in his cap. *Can't aim much higher than that.*

But he had to keep himself current with new techniques and new inventions. One never knew when they might come in handy. Besides, this neuroknife was so intriguing. . . .

Grera looked at the shimmering green blade, her eyes wide. "The Emperor loves me! You can't—"

"He *loves* you? A long-in-the-tooth concubine? He spends more time moaning about his long-lost Shando. Elrood's so senile he'll never even know you're missing, and all of the other concubines will be happy to move up a rank."

Before Grera could scramble away, the murderous man was on top of her, showing tremendous speed. "No one will mourn your loss, Grera Cary." He raised the pulsing green blade and, with a dark fire in his flickering eyes, stabbed her repeatedly in the torso. The karthan towel fell away, and the neuroblade struck her freshly creamed and oiled skin.

The concubine screamed in agony, screamed again, then fell into sucking moans and shudders, and finally became silent. . . . No lacerations, no blood, only imagined agony. All of the pain, but no incriminating marks—could murder get better than this?

With pleasure suffusing his brain, Fenring knelt over the senior concubine, studying her shapely body crumpled on top of the disheveled towel. Good skin tone, firm muscles, now slack with death. It was hard to believe this woman was as old as they claimed. It must have required a lot of melange, and quite a bit of body conditioning. He felt Grera's neck for a pulse, then double-checked. None remained. Disappointing . . . in a way.

There was no blood on the body or on the green knife blade, no deep wounds—but he had stabbed her to death. Or so she had *thought*.

An interesting weapon, this neuroblade. It was the first time he had ever used one. Fenring always liked to test the important tools of his trade in noncombat situations, since he didn't want to be surprised in a crisis.

Called a "ponta" by its Richesian inventor, it was one of the few recent innovations Fenring considered worthwhile from that tiresome world. The illusionary green blade slid back into its compartment with a realistic *snick*. The victim had not only thought she was being stabbed to death, but through intense neurostimulation actually *felt* an attack powerful enough to kill. In a sense Grera's own mind had killed her. And now there wasn't a mark on her skin.

Sometimes real blood added an exhilarating cap to an already-thrilling experience, but the cleanup often caused problems.

He recognized familiar noises behind him: an opening door and deactivated security field. Turning, he saw Shaddam staring down at him. "Was that really necessary, Hasimir? What a waste. . . . Still, she had outlived her usefulness."

"Poor old thing had a heart attack, I guess." From a fold of his tunic Fenring brought forth another ponta, this one ruby-jeweled with a long red blade. "I'd better test this one, too," he said. "Your father is hanging on longer than we'd hoped, and this would finish him off neatly. No evidence on the corpse, not a mark. Why wait for the *n'kee* to continue its work?" He grinned.

Shaddam shook his head, as if finally having second thoughts. He looked around, shuddered, and tried to appear stern. "We'll wait as long as we have to. We agreed not to make any sudden moves." Fenring hated it when the Crown Prince tried to think too much.

"Hmmm-mm? I thought you were so anxious! He's been making terrible business decisions, wasting Corrino money every day he stays alive." His large eyes glittered. "The longer he remains in a state like this, the more history will paint him as a pathetic ruler."

"I can't do any more to my father," Shaddam said. "I'm afraid of what might happen."

Hasimir Fenring bowed. "As you wish, my Prince."

They walked away, leaving Grera's body where it lay. Someone would find it, sooner or later. It wasn't the first time Fenring had been so blatant, but the other concubines would know not to challenge him. It would be a warning to them, and they would jockey with each other to become the new favorite of the impotent old man, using the situation to their advantage.

By the time word finally got back to the Emperor, he probably wouldn't even remember Grera Cary's name.

Man is but a pebble dropped in a pool. And if man is but a pebble, then all his works can be no more.

—Zensunni Saying

Leto and Rhombur trained long and hard every day, in the Atreides way. They dived into the exercise routine with all the enthusiasm and determination they could muster. The stocky Ixian Prince regained his vigor, lost some weight, and tightened up his muscles.

The two young men found themselves quite well matched and therefore good sparring partners. Because they trusted one another completely, Leto and Rhombur were able to push their limits, confident that nothing dangerous would happen to them.

Though they trained vigorously, the Old Duke hoped to accomplish more than just turning the exiled Prince into a competent fighter: He also wanted to keep his friend's son happy and make him feel at home. Paulus could only imagine what terrors Rhombur's renegade parents must be enduring out in the wilds of the galaxy.

Thufir Hawat let the two fight with recklessness and abandon, honing their skills. Leto soon noticed remarkable improvement, both in himself and in the heir to what little remained of House Vernius.

Following the Master of Assassins' advice about the

weapons of culture and diplomacy as well as swordplay, Rhombur took an interest in music. He dabbled with several instruments before finally settling on the soothing but complex tones of the nine-string baliset. Leaning against a castle wall, he would strum and play simple songs, fingering melodies by ear that he recalled from childhood or pleasant tunes he made up for himself.

Often, his sister Kailea would listen to him play as she studied her lessons in history and religion that were the traditional fare of young noblewomen. Helena Atreides aided in the teaching, at the insistence of Duke Paulus. Kailea studied with good grace, occupying her mind, resigned to her situation as a political prisoner inside Castle Caladan, but trying to imagine more for herself.

Leto knew that his mother's resentment ran at depths invisible beneath the still waters of her public face. Helena was a hard taskmaster to Kailea, who responded with even greater determination.

Late one evening, Leto went up to the tower room after his parents had retired for the night. He'd intended to ask his father about taking them on one of the Atreides schooners for a day-trip up and down the coast. But as he approached the wooden door to the ducal chambers, he heard Paulus and Helena engaged in deep discussion.

"What have you done to find a new place for those two?" The way his mother said the words, Leto knew exactly whom she meant. "Surely some Minor House on the fringe will take them in if you pay a large enough bribe."

"I don't intend to send those children anywhere, and you know that. They are our guests here, and safe from the loathsome Tleilaxu." His voice dropped to a grumble. "I don't understand why Elrood doesn't just send his Sardaukar in to flush those vermin out of the caves on Ix."

Lady Helena said crisply, "Despite their unpleasant qualities, the Tleilaxu will undoubtedly bring the factories of Ix back to the path of righteousness and obey the strictures established by the Butlerian Jihad."

Paulus gave an exasperated snort, but Leto knew his mother was deadly serious, and that frightened him all the more. Her voice grew more fervent as she tried to convince her husband.

"Can't you see, perhaps all of these events were meant to happen? You never should have sent Leto to Ix—he's already been corrupted by their ways, their prideful thinking, their high-handed ignorance of the laws of God. But the takeover on Ix brought Leto back to us. Don't make the same mistake again."

"Mistake? I'm quite pleased with everything our boy's learned. He's going to be a fine Duke someday." Leto heard the thump of a boot tossed into the corner. "Stop your worrying. Don't you feel at all sorry for poor Rhombur and Kailea?"

Unswayed, she said, "In their pride, the people of Ix have broken the Law, and they have paid for it. Should I feel sorry for them? I think not."

Paulus hit a piece of furniture hard with his hand, and Leto heard wood scraping across stone, a chair shoved aside. "And I'm to believe *you* are familiar enough with the inner workings of Ix to make such a judgment? Or have you already come to a conclusion based on what you want to hear, without being troubled by mere lack of evidence?" He laughed, and his tone turned more gentle. "Besides, you seem to be working well with young Kailea. She enjoys your company. How can you say such things about her to me, and then pretend to be kind to her face?"

Helena sounded eminently reasonable. "The children can't help who they are, Paulus—they didn't ask to be born there, raised there, exposed to anything but proper teachings. Do you think they've ever held the Orange Catholic Bible? It's not their fault. They are what they are, and I can't hate them for it."

"Then what—"

She lashed out at him with such vehemence that Leto took a silent step backward in surprise out in the shadowy hall. "*You're* the one who has made a choice here, Paulus. And you've made the wrong one. That choice will cost you and our House dearly."

He made a rude noise. "There was no choice, Helena. On my honor and my word—there was no *choice*."

"Still it was your own decision, despite my warnings and despite my advice. Your decision alone, Paulus Atreides." Her voice was frighteningly cold. "You must live with the consequences, and be damned by them."

"Oh, calm down and go to sleep, Helena."

Unsettled, Leto crept away, his question forgotten, without waiting to see how soon they extinguished the lights.

THE NEXT DAY, a calm and sunny morning, Leto stood next to Rhombur at an open window, admiring the quays at the base of the promontory. The ocean spread out like a blue-green prairie, curving off to the distant horizon. "A perfect day," Leto said, realizing that his friend was homesick for the lost underground city of Vernii, probably tired of too much weather. "Now it's my turn to show you around Caladan."

The two of them descended the narrow cliffside path and staircase, holding on to rails and vaulting weathered steps, avoiding the slippery moss and the white encrustations of salty spray.

The Duke had several boats tied up at the dock, and Leto chose his favorite coracle, a white motorcraft around fifteen meters in length. With a wide, beamy hull, it featured a spacious cutty cabin in the front and sleeping quarters beneath, reached via a spiral staircase. Aft of the cabin were two decks, at midship and aftship, with cargo holds below: a nice setup for fishing or motor cruising. Additional modules stored on shore could be installed to change the functions of the craft: adding more cabin space or converting one or both cargo holds to additional sleeping or habitation areas.

Servants packed them a lunch while three mariner assistants checked all the onboard systems in preparation for a day-long voyage. Rhombur watched Leto treat these people as friends while they loaded the gear. "Is your wife's leg better, Jerrik? Did you finish the roof on your smoke shed, Dom?"

Finally, as Rhombur looked on with curiosity and trepidation, Leto clapped him on the shoulder. "Remember your rock collection? You and I are going to dive for coral gems."

These precious stones, found in knobby coral reefs, were popular pieces on Caladan, but perilous to handle. Coral gems were said to hold tiny living creatures that caused their inner fires to dance and simmer. Because of the hazards and expense of containment, the gems did not support much of an off-world export market, given the more viable alternative of soostones from Buzzell. But local coral gems were lovely, nonetheless.

Leto thought he wanted to give one to Kailea as a present. With the wealth of House Atreides, he could afford to buy Rhombur's sister many greater treasures if he wished, but the gift might mean more if he procured it himself. She would probably appreciate it either way.

After all preparations were completed, he and Rhombur boarded the wickerwood coracle. An Atreides burgee flew from the stern, snapping in the breeze. As the mariner assistants cast off the lines, one asked, "You can handle this yourself, m'Lord?"

Leto laughed and waved the man away. "Jerrik, you know I've been handling these boats for years now. The seas are calm, and we have a shore-com aboard. But thank you for your concern. Don't worry, we won't go far, just to the reefs."

Rhombur wandered the deck and tried to help, doing whatever Leto told him to do. He'd never been on an open boat before. The engines carried them away from the cliffs, beyond the shielded harbor, and out into open water. Sunlight glittered like sparkflies on the rippled surface of the sea.

The Prince of Ix stood at the bow while Leto worked the controls. Rhombur soaked up the experience of water and wind and sun, smiling. He took a deep breath. "I feel so alone and so free out here."

Looking overboard, Rhombur saw rafts of leathery-leafed seaweed and round gourdlike fruits that held up the plants like air bladders. "Paradan melons," Leto said. "If you want one, just reach over the side and take it. If you've never had paradan fresh from the sea, you're in for a taste treat . . . though the fruit's a bit salty for me."

Far off to starboard a pod of murmons swam like furred logs, large but harmless creatures that drifted with ocean currents, singing to themselves with low, hooting sounds.

Leto sailed the coracle for about an hour, consulting satellite maps and charts, making for a knot of outlying reefs. He handed Rhombur a set of binoculars and indicated a frothy, tumultuous patch on the sea. Isolated black ridges of rock barely poked above the waves like the spine of a sleeping leviathan.

"There's the reef," Leto said. "We'll anchor about half a kilometer away so we don't risk ripping open the hull. Then we can go diving." He opened a compartment and withdrew a sack and a small spatula-knife for each of them. "The coral gems don't grow very deep. We can dive without air tanks." He slapped Rhombur on the back. "It's about time you started to earn your keep around here."

"Just keeping you out of *trouble* is, uh, effort enough," Rhombur countered.

After the coracle was secured on its anchor cord, Leto pointed a scanner overboard to map out the contours of the reefs below. "Look at this," he said, letting his friend view the screen. "See those crannies and tiny caves? That's where you'll find the coral gems."

Rhombur peered at the scanner, nodding.

"Each one is encrusted with a husk, like an organic scab that grows around them. Doesn't look like much until you crack one open and see the most beautiful pearls in all creation, like molten droplets from a star. You have to keep them wet at all times, because the open air oxidizes them instantly and they become extremely pyrophoric."

"Oh," Rhombur said, unsure what the word meant, though he was too proud to ask. Fumbling, he attached his belt, which held the spatula-knife and a small waterlume for probing the darkest caves.

"I'll show you when we get down there," Leto said. "How long can you hold your breath?"

"As long as you," the Prince of Ix said, "naturally."

Leto stripped off his shirt and pants, while Rhombur hurried to do the same. Simultaneously, both young men dived overboard. Leto stroked downward into the warm water, pulling himself deeper until he felt the pressure around his skull.

The large reef was a convoluted, permanently submerged landscape. Tufts of coralweed waved in the gentle currents, the tiny mouths on their leaves snaring bits of plankton. Jewel-toned fish darted in and out of holes in the layered coral.

Rhombur grabbed his arm and pointed at a long purplish eel that drifted by, streaming a rainbow-hued, feathery tail. The Ixian looked comical with his cheeks swollen, trying to hold in his air.

Grasping the rough coral, Leto pulled himself along and peered into cracks and crevices. He shined the beam of his waterlume all around in his search. With his lungs aching, he finally found a discolored knob and signaled for Rhombur, who swam over. But as Leto pulled out his spatula-knife to pry free the coral gem, Rhombur flailed his arms and swam upward as fast as he could, his air exhausted.

Leto remained beneath the water, though his chest pounded. Finally, he pried loose the nodule, which would likely yield a medium-sized coral gem. With it he swam upward, his chest ready to burst, and finally splashed to the surface where Rhombur clung, panting, to the edge of the coracle.

"Found one," Leto said. "Look." Holding the gem underneath the water, he tapped it with the blunt edge of his knife until the outer covering cracked free. Inside, a slightly misshapen ovoid gleamed with self-contained pearly light. Tiny glimmering specks circulated like molten sand trapped within transparent epoxy.

"Exquisite," Rhombur said.

Dripping wet, Leto climbed out of the water and onto the midship deck, by the lifeboat station. He dipped a bucket overboard, filling it with seawater, and dropped the coral gem inside before it could dry out in his hands. "Now you have to find one of your own."

With his blond hair plastered to his head by seawater, the Prince nodded, drew several deep gulps of air, then swam downward again. Leto dived after him.

Within an hour the pair had gathered half a bucket of the beautiful gems. "Nice haul," Leto said, squatting on the deck beside Rhombur, who, fascinated with the treasure, dipped his fingers into the bucket. "You like those?"

Rhombur grunted. His eyes danced with a child's delight.

"I've worked up quite an appetite," Leto said. "I'll go prep the foodpaks."

"I'm starving, too," Rhombur said. "Uh, need any help?"

Leto drew himself up and raised his aquiline nose haughtily in the air. "Sir, I am the resident ducal heir, with a long résumé asserting my competence to prepare a simple foodpak." He strutted to the sheltered galley as Rhombur sorted through the wet coral stones, like a kid playing with marbles.

Some were perfectly spherical, others misshapen and pitted. Rhombur wondered why certain ones had a blazing inner brilliance while others were dull by comparison. He set the three largest stones on the midship deck and watched the sunlight glitter on them, a pale shadow to the brilliance trapped within. He noted their differences, wondered what he and Leto could do with the treasure.

He missed his own collection of gems and crystals, agates and geodes from Ix. He had wandered through caves and tunnels and shafts to find them. He had learned so much of geology that way—and then the Tleilaxu had driven him and his family from their world. He'd been forced to leave everything behind. Although he left it unsaid, Rhombur decided if he ever saw his mother again, he could make a grand gift for her.

Leto leaned out of the galley door. "Lunch is ready. Come and eat before I feed it to the fishes."

Rhombur trotted in to sit at the small table while Leto served up two bowls of steaming Caladanian oyster chowder, seasoned with nouveau wine from House Atreides vineyards. "My grandmother came up with this recipe. It's one of my favorites."

"Well, not bad. Even if *you* made it." Rhombur slurped from his bowl and licked his lips. "It's a, um, good thing my sister didn't come along," he said, trying to hide the joking tone in his voice. "She probably would have tried to wear fancy clothes, and you know she'd never have gone swimming with us."

"Sure," Leto said, unconvinced. "You're right." It was obvious to anyone how he and Kailea flirted with each other, though Rhombur understood—politically speaking—that a romance between them would be unwise at best, and dangerous at worst.

Out on the midship deck just aft of them, the sun beat down, warming the wooden floorboards, drying the splashed water—and exposing the fragile coral gems to the open, oxidizing air. Simultaneously, the three largest gems burst into incandescent flares, merging into a miniature nova of intense heat, hot enough to burn through a metal starship hull.

Leto leaped to his feet, knocking aside his bowl of chowder. Through the broad plaz windowports he could see blue-orange flames shooting up, setting the deck on fire, including the lifeboat. One of the coral gems shattered, spraying hot fragments in all directions, each of which started secondary fires.

Within seconds, two more gems burned completely through the coracle deck and dropped into the cargo hold below, where they ate through crates. One burned open a spare fuel container, igniting it with an explosive burst, while the second gem seared all the way through the bottom hull until it extinguished itself in the refreshing water again. The wickerwood hull, though treated with a fire-retardant chemical, would not hold up against such heat.

Leto and Rhombur rushed out of the galley, shouting at each other but not knowing what to do. "The fire! We've got to get the fire out!"

"They're coral gems!" Leto looked for something with which to extinguish the blaze. "They burn hot, can't be put out easily." Swelling flames licked the deck, and the coracle rocked with an explosion belowdecks. On its davits the lifeboat was a lost cause, completely enveloped in flames.

"We could sink," Leto said, "and we're too far from land." He grabbed a chemical extinguisher, which he sprayed on the flames.

He and his companion took out the hoses and pumps from a front compartment and doused the boat with seawater, but the cargo hold was already engulfed. Greasy black smoke drifted through cracks in the top deck. A warning beep signified that they were taking on large amounts of water.

"We're going to sink!" Rhombur shouted, reading the instrumentation. He coughed from the acrid smoke.

Leto tossed a flotation vest to his friend as he buckled another one around his waist. "Get on the shore-com. Announce our position and send a distress. You know how to operate it?"

Rhombur yelped an affirmative, while Leto used another chemical extinguisher, but soon exhausted its charge without effect. He and Rhombur would be trapped out here, floating with only the debris of the boat around them. He had to reach land and settle where they could wait.

He remembered his father lecturing him: "When you find yourself in the midst of a seemingly impossible crisis, take care of the *solvable* parts first. Then, after you've narrowed the possibilities, work on the most difficult aspects."

He heard Rhombur shouting into the shore-com, repeating the distress call. Leto now ignored the fire. The coracle was sinking, and would soon be underwater, leaving them stranded. He looked toward the port side and saw frothing water around the tangle of the reef. He dashed for the cabin.

Before the fire could reach the aft engines, he started the boat, used the emergency cutoff to sever the anchor, and raced toward the reef. The flaming coracle was like a comet on the water.

"What are you doing?" Rhombur cried. "Where are we going?"

"The reef!" he shouted. "I'll try to run aground there so we don't sink. Then you and I can work to put out the fire."

"You're going to crash us into a reef? That's crazy!"

"You'd rather sink out here? This boat is going down, one way or another." As if to emphasize his point another small container of fuel exploded belowdecks, sending a shudder through the floor.

Rhombur grasped the secured galley table to keep his balance. "Whatever you say."

"Did you get an acknowledgment on the shore-com?"

"No. I, uh, hope they heard us." Leto told him to keep trying, which he did, still without receiving a response.

The waves curled around them, low to the deck rail. Black smoke poured into the sky. Fire licked at the engine compartment. The coracle dipped lower, dragging, taking on water rapidly. Leto pushed the engines, still charging toward the rocks. He didn't know if he would win this race. If he could just run them up on the reef, he and Rhombur could stay safely beside the wreckage. He didn't know how long it would take for rescuers to arrive.

As if driven by a demon, whitecaps rose in front of them, threatening to form a barrier. But Leto held course and did not slacken the acceleration. "Hang on!"

At the last moment, the engines died as fire engulfed them. The coracle cruised forward on sheer momentum and crashed into the jagged reef. The grinding halt threw both Leto and Rhombur to the deck. Rhombur struck his head and stood up, blinking, dazed. Blood trickled down his forehead, very close to the old injury he had received during the orship escape from Ix.

"Let's go! Overboard!" Leto yelled. He grabbed his friend's arm and pushed him out of the cabin. From the forward compartment, Leto tossed hoses and portable pumps into the frothing water. "Dip this end of the hose into the deepest water you can reach! And try not to cut yourself on the reef."

Rhombur scrambled over the rail, while Leto followed, trying to maintain his balance in the churning tide pools and rough surf. The boat was snagged, so for the moment they needn't worry about drowning—just discomfort.

The pumps started, and seawater sprayed out of two hoses, one held by each boy. The water fell in a thick curtain onto the flames. Rhombur swiped blood out of his eyes and kept directing his hose. They doused the coracle with endless torrents until finally, slowly, the flames began to die back.

Rhombur looked bedraggled and miserable, but Leto felt oddly exhilarated. "Perk up, Rhombur. Think about it. On Ix we had to escape from a revolution that nearly destroyed the whole planet. Makes this little mishap seem like child's play, wouldn't you say?"

"Uh, right," the other said, glumly. "Most fun I've had in ages."

The two of them sat waist deep in the surging water, playing their hoses over the fire. Smoke continued to rise into the clear Caladan sky like a distress beacon.

Soon they heard the distant but increasing roar of powerful engines, and moments later a high-speed wingboat came into view, a double-hulled craft capable of reaching tremendous speeds over the water. It drew near and swung clear of the rocks. On the foredeck stood Thufir Hawat, shaking his head at Leto in disapproval.

Among the responsibilities of command is the necessity to punish . . .
but only when the victim demands it.

> —PRINCE RAPHAEL CORRINO, Discourses on
> Leadership in a Galactic Imperium, 12th Edition

Her chocolate hair in disarray, her clothes torn and inappropriate for the desert, the woman ran across the sands, seeking escape.

Janess Milam looked up over her shoulder, blinking sun-scalded tears from her eyes. Seeing the shadow of the suspensor platform that held Baron Harkonnen and his nephew Rabban, she put on a burst of speed. Her feet dug into the powder-sand, making her lose her balance. She staggered toward the open wasteland, where it was hotter, drier, deadlier.

Buried in the lee of a nearby dune, the thumper throbbed, pulsing . . . calling.

She tried to find a refuge of rocks, cool caves, even the shadow of a boulder. At the very least, she wanted to die out of sight so they wouldn't be able to laugh at her. But the Harkonnens had dropped her into a sea of open dunes. Janess slipped and tasted dust.

From their safe vantage on the suspensor platform, the Baron and his nephew watched her struggles, the pitiful flight of a tiny human figure on the sand. The observers wore stillsuits like costumes; their masks hung loose.

They had returned to Arrakis from Giedi Prime only a few weeks before, and Janess had arrived on the previous day's prison ship. At first, the Baron had thought to execute the treacherous woman back at Barony, but Rabban had wanted her to suffer in front of his eyes out on the scorching sands, in punishment for helping Duncan Idaho escape.

"She seems so insignificant down there, doesn't she?" the Baron commented, without interest. Sometimes, his nephew did have unique ideas, though he lacked the focus to carry them through. "This is much more satisfying than a simple beheading, and beneficial to the worms. Food for them."

Rabban made a low sound in his thick throat, remarkably like an animal's growl. "It shouldn't be long now. Those thumpers always call a worm. *Always.*"

The Baron stood tall on the platform, feeling the hot sun, the glistening sweat on his skin. His body ached, a condition he'd been experiencing for several months now. He nudged the suspensor platform forward so they could get a better view of their victim. He mused, "That boy is an Atreides now, from what I hear. Working with the Duke's Salusan bulls."

"He's dead, if I ever see him again." Rabban wiped salty sweat from his sunburned forehead. "Him, and any other Atreides I catch alone."

"You're like an ox, Rabban." The Baron gripped his nephew's strong shoulder. "But don't waste energy on insignificant things. House Atreides is our real enemy—not some insignificant stableboy. *Stableboy . . .* hmmm . . ."

Below, Janess skidded on her face down the slope of a dune and scrambled to her feet again. With a basso laugh the Baron said, "She'll never get far enough away from the thumper in time." The resonant vibrations continued to throb into the ground, like the distant drumbeat of a death song.

"It's too hot out here," Rabban grumbled. "Couldn't you have brought a canopy?" Pulling his stillsuit's water tube to his mouth, he drew in an unsatisfying sip of warm water.

"I like to sweat. It's good for the health, purges poisons from the system."

Rabban fidgeted. When he tired of watching the woman's clumsy run, he looked across the seared landscape, searching for the tracks of an oncoming behemoth. "By the way, whatever happened to that Planetologist the Emperor foisted on us? I took him worm hunting once."

"Kynes? Who knows?" The Baron snorted. "He's always out in the desert, comes in to Carthag to deliver reports whenever he feels like it, then disappears again. Haven't heard from him in a while."

"What happens if he gets hurt? Could we get in trouble for not keeping a better eye on him?"

"I doubt it. Elrood's mind isn't what it used to be." The Baron laughed, a thin, nasal tone of derision. "Not that the Emperor's mind was much even in its prime."

The dark-haired woman, coated now with clinging dust, fought her way across the dunes. She kicked up sand, falling and struggling back onto her feet, refusing to give up.

"This bores me," Rabban said. "No challenge just to stand here and watch."

"Some punishments are easy," the Baron observed, "but *easy* isn't always sufficient. Erasing this woman does nothing to erase the black mark she made on the honor of House Harkonnen . . . with the help of House Atreides."

"Then let's do more," Rabban said with a thick-lipped grin, "to the Atreides."

The Baron felt the heat shimmering on his exposed face, absorbed the thrumming silence of the baked desert. When he smiled, the skin on his cheeks threatened to crack. "Maybe we will."

"What, Uncle?"

"Perhaps it's time to get rid of the Old Duke. No more thorns in our side."

Rabban bubbled with anticipation.

With a calmness designed to agitate his nephew, the Baron focused the oil lenses of his binoculars and scanned the distance at varying magnifications. He hoped to spot the wormsign himself rather than relying on the security ornithopters. Finally he sensed the tremors approaching. He felt his pulse synchronize with the thumper: *Lump . . . lump . . . lump . . .*

Crescent dune tracks spread shadow ripples toward the horizon, an elongated mound-in-motion, a cresting of sand like a big fish swimming just under the surface. In the still, hot air, the Baron heard the rasping, abrasive sound of the slithering beast. Excitedly, he grabbed Rabban's elbow and pointed.

The com-unit at Rabban's ear chirped, and a filtered voice spoke so loudly that the Baron could hear the muffled words. Rabban swatted at the device. "We know! We see it."

The Baron continued his musings as the buried worm approached like a locomotive. "I've kept up my contacts with . . . *individuals* on Caladan, you know. The Old Duke is a creature of habit. And habits can be dangerous." He smiled, his lips hard, his eyes squinting against the glare. "We've already put operatives in place, and I have a plan."

Far out in the dunes ahead of them, Janess spun around and ran in blind panic. She had seen the oncoming worm.

The rippling upheaval of sand reached the thumper in the lee of a whaleback dune. In an explosion like a tidal wave engulfing a dock, the thumper vanished into an immense mouth lined with crystal teeth.

"Move the platform," the Baron urged. "Follow her!" Rabban worked the suspensor controls, floating them up over the desert for a better view of the action.

Following the vibrations of the woman's footsteps, the worm changed course. The sand rippled again as the behemoth dived underground and prowled like a shark searching for new prey.

Janess collapsed on the top of a dune, shuddering, holding her knees up against her chin as she tried not to make any sound that might attract the great worm. Sand skittered around her. She froze, held her breath.

The monster paused. Janess huddled in terror, praying silently.

Rabban brought the suspensor platform above the trapped woman. Janess glared up at the Harkonnens, her jaw clenched, her eyes like daggers, a cornered animal afraid to move.

Baron Harkonnen reached down to grab an empty bottle of spice liquor, drained during their long hot wait for her execution. He raised the brown glass bottle as if in a toast, grinning.

The sandworm waited underground, alert for even a fractional movement.

The Baron tossed the bottle at the dusky-skinned woman. The

glass tumbled in the air, reflecting glints of sunlight, end over end. It struck the sand within meters of Janess's feet with a loud *thunk*.

The worm lunged into motion, toward her.

Screaming curses at the Harkonnens, Janess plunged down the hillside, followed by a small avalanche of sand. But the ground dropped out from underneath her, like a gaping trapdoor.

The mouth of the worm rose up, a cavern of glittering teeth in the sunlight to swallow Janess and everything around her. A puff of dust drifted on the wavering air as the huge worm sank back under the sands, like a whale beneath the sea.

Rabban touched his com-unit, demanding to know whether the spotting craft overhead had taken high-resolution holos. "I didn't even see her blood, didn't hear her scream." He sounded disappointed.

"You may strangle one of my servants," the Baron offered, "if it will make you feel better. But only because I'm in such a good mood."

From the suspensor platform, he gazed down at the placid dunes, knowing the danger and death that lurked beneath them. He wished his old rival Duke Paulus Atreides had been down there instead of the woman. For that, he would have had every Harkonnen holorecorder in operation, so that he could enjoy it from every angle and savor the experience over and over, each time tasting the morsel of human flesh as the worm did.

No matter, the Baron told himself. *I have something just as interesting in mind for the old man.*

Speak the truth. That is always much easier, and is often the most powerful argument.

—Bene Gesserit Axiom

D uncan Idaho stared at the monstrous Salusan bull through the force-field bars of its cage, his child's gaze meeting the multifaceted eyes of the ferocious creature. The bull had a scaly black hide, multiple horns, and two brains that were capable of only one thought: *Destroy anything that moves.*

The boy had worked in the stables for weeks now, doing his best at even the most miserable of jobs, feeding and watering the combat bulls, tending them, cleaning their filthy cages while the beasts were pushed back behind force-barricades to keep them from attacking him.

He enjoyed his job, despite what others considered the degrading meniality of the tasks to be performed. Duncan didn't even think of it as low-level work, though he knew several other stableboys did. These were simply chores to him, and he considered his payment in freedom and happiness more than sufficient. Because of the gracious generosity of his benefactor, Duke Paulus Atreides, he loved the old man dearly.

Duncan ate well now and had a warm place to live and fresh clothes whenever he needed them. Though no one asked him to, he worked hard anyway, driven and dedicated. There was even some time for relaxation, and he and the other workers had their own gymnasium and recreation hall. He could also go splashing in the sea whenever he wished, and a friendly man from the dockside occasionally took him along for a day's fishing.

At present the Old Duke kept five of the mutated bulls for his games. Duncan had sought to befriend the beasts, trying to tame them with bribes of sweet green grass or fresh fruits, but an exasperated Stablemaster Yresk had caught him at it.

"The Old Duke uses them in his bullfights—do you think he prefers them *tame?*" His puffy eyes had widened with anger. The white-haired stablemaster had accepted him on the Duke's orders, but grudgingly, and he gave Duncan no special treatment. "He wants them to attack. He doesn't want the creatures to purr when he's on display in the Plaza de Toros. What would the people think?"

Duncan had lowered his eyes and backed off. Always obedient, he never again tried to make these beasts his pets.

He had seen holorecordings of the Duke's previous spectacles, as well as the performances of other renowned matadors; while he was saddened to witness the slaughter of one of his magnificent charges, he was amazed at the bravery and self-assurance of Duke Atreides.

The last *corrida* on Caladan had been staged to celebrate the departure of Leto Atreides for his off-planet schooling. Now after many months there would be another, as the Old Duke had recently announced a new grand bullfight, this one to entertain his guests from Ix, who had come to stay as exiles on Caladan. *Exiles.* In a sense, Duncan was one, too. . . .

Though he had his own sleeping quarters in a communal outbuilding where many of the Castle workers lived, sometimes Duncan bedded down out in the stables, where he could hear the snorting and simmering beasts. He had put up with far worse conditions in his life. The stables themselves were comfortable, and he enjoyed being alone with the animals.

Whenever he slept out there, he listened to the movements of the bulls in his dreams. He felt himself becoming attuned to their moods and instincts. For days now, though, the creatures had grown increasingly fretful and moody, prone to rampages in their pens . . . as if they knew their nemesis the Old Duke was planning another bullfight.

Standing outside the cages, young Duncan noticed fresh, deep score marks where the Salusan bulls had rammed their enclosures in an attempt to break free, trying to gore imaginary opponents.

This was *not* right. Duncan knew it. He'd spent so much time watching the bulls that he felt he understood their instincts. He knew how they should react, knew how to provoke them and how to calm them—but this behavior was out of the ordinary.

When he mentioned it to Stablemaster Yresk, the gaunt man looked suddenly alarmed. He scratched the shock of thinning white hair on his head, but then his expression changed. He fixed his suspicious, puffy eyes on Duncan. "Say, there's nothing wrong with those bulls. If I didn't know you better, I'd think you were just another Harkonnen, trying to cause trouble. Now run along."

"Harkonnens! I hate them."

"You lived among them, stable-rat. We Atreides are trained to be constantly on the alert." He gave Duncan a nudge. "Don't you have chores to complete? Or do I need to find some more?"

He'd heard that Yresk had actually come from Richese many years before, so he was not truly an Atreides. Still, Duncan didn't contradict the man, though he refused to back down. "I was their slave. They tried to hunt me down like an animal."

Yresk lowered his bushy eyebrows; with his lanky build and wild, pale hair he looked like a scarecrow. "Even among the common people, the old feud between Houses runs deep. How do I know what you might have up your sleeve?"

"That's not why I told you about the bulls, sir," Duncan said. "I'm just worried. I don't know anything about House feuds."

Yresk laughed, not taking him seriously. "The Atreides-Harkonnen breach goes back thousands of years. Don't you know anything about the Battle of Corrin, the great betrayal, the Bridge of Hrethgir? How a cowardly Harkonnen ancestor almost cost the humans our victory against the hated machine-minds? Corrin was our last stand, and we would have fallen to the final onslaught if an Atreides hadn't saved the day."

"I never learned much history," Duncan said. "It was hard enough just finding food to eat."

Behind folds of wrinkled skin, the stablemaster's eyes were large and expressive, as if he was trying to appear to be a kindly old man.

"Well, well, House Atreides and House Harkonnen were allies once, *friends* even, but never again after that treachery. The feud has burned hot ever since—and you, boy, came from Giedi Prime. From the *Harkonnen* homeworld." Yresk shrugged his bony shoulders. "You don't expect us to trust you completely, do you? Be thankful the Old Duke trusts you as much as he does."

"But I had nothing to do with the Battle of Corrin," Duncan said, still not understanding. "What does that have to do with the bulls? That was a long time ago."

"And that's about all the jabber I have time for this afternoon." Yresk removed a long-handled manure scraper from a prong on the wall. "You just keep your suspicions to yourself from now on. Everyone here knows what he's supposed to do."

Though Duncan worked hard and did everything he could to earn his keep, the fact that he had come from the Harkonnens continued to cause him grief. Some of the others working in the stables, not just Yresk, treated him as a barely concealed spy . . . though what Rabban would have wanted with a nine-year-old infiltrator, Duncan couldn't guess.

Not until now, however, had he felt so affronted by the prejudice. "There's something wrong with the bulls, sir," he insisted. "The Duke needs to know about it before his bullfight."

Yresk laughed at him again. "When I need the advice of a child in my business, I'll be sure to ask you, young Idaho." The stablemaster left, and Duncan returned to the stalls to stare at the agitated, ferocious Salusan bulls. They glared back at him with burning, faceted eyes.

Something was terribly wrong. He knew it, but no one would listen to him.

Imperfections, if viewed in the proper light, can be extremely valuable. The Great Schools, with their incessant questing for perfection, often find this postulate difficult to understand, until it is proven to them that nothing in the universe is random.

—From The Philosophies of Old Terra,
one of the recovered manuscripts

I n the darkness of her isolated and protected bedroom in the Mother School complex, Mohiam sat straight up, holding her swollen belly. Her skin felt tight and leathery, without the resilience of youth. Her bedclothes were drenched in perspiration, and the nightmare remained fresh in her mind. The back of her skull pounded with visions of blood, and flames.

It had been an omen, a message . . . a screaming premonition that no Bene Gesserit could ignore.

She wondered how much melange her nurse had given her, and if it might have interacted with some other medication they'd administered. She could still taste the bitter gingery-cinnamon flavor inside her mouth. How much spice was it safe for a pregnant woman to take? Mohiam shuddered. No matter how she tried to rationalize her terror, she could not ignore the power of the sending.

Dreams . . . nightmares . . . prescience—foretelling terrible events that would shake the Imperium for millennia. A future that must never come to pass! She dared not ignore the warning . . . but could she trust herself to interpret it correctly?

Reverend Mother Gaius Helen Mohiam was but a tiny pebble at the beginning of an avalanche.

Did the Sisterhood really know what it was doing? And what about the baby growing inside her, still a month from term? The vision's focus had been centered on her daughter. *Something important, something terrible. . . .* The Reverend Mothers had not told her everything, and now even the Sisters in Other Memory were afraid.

The room smelled damp from the rain outside: The old plaster walls were wet and powdery. Though precise heaters kept her private chamber at a comfortable temperature, the homiest warmth came from the embers in the low fire opposite her bed—an inefficient anachronism, but the aroma of woodsmoke and the yellow-orange glow of coals inspired a sort of primal complacency.

The fires of destruction, the blaze of an inferno sweeping from planet to planet across the galaxy. Jihad! Jihad! That was to be the fate of humanity if something went wrong with the Bene Gesserit plans for her daughter.

Mohiam sat up in her bed, composed herself mentally, and ran a quick check through the systems of her body. No emergencies, everything functioning normally, all biochemistry optimal.

Had it only been a nightmare . . . or something more?

More rationalization. She knew she must not make excuses, but she had to heed what the premonition had shown her. Other Memory knew the truth.

Mohiam remained under close observation by the Sisters—possibly even now. A purple light in the corner of her room was attached to a night-vision comeye, with watchdogs on the other end who reported to Reverend Mother Anirul Sadow Tonkin, the young woman who seemed to carry an importance beyond her years. Finally, though, in Mohiam's dream the secretive Other Memory Voices had hinted at Anirul's place in the project. The nightmare had jarred them loose, shocked the reticent recollections into veiled explanations.

Kwisatz Haderach. The Shortening of the Way. The Bene Gesserit's long-sought-after messiah and superbeing.

The Sisterhood had numerous breeding programs, building upon various characteristics of humanity. Many of them were unimportant, some even served as diversions or shams. None held such prominence as the Kwisatz Haderach program, though.

As an ancient security measure at the beginning of the hundred-generation plan, the Reverend Mothers with knowledge of the scheme had sworn themselves to silence, even in Other Memory, vowing to divulge the full details to none but a rare few each generation.

Anirul was one such, the Kwisatz Mother. She knew everything about the program. *That is why even Mother Superior must listen to her!*

Mohiam herself had been kept in the dark, though the daughter growing in her womb was to be only three steps away from the culmination. By now the real genetic plan had been set in stone, the end of thousands of years of tinkering and planning. The future would ride on this new child. Her first daughter, the flawed one, had been a misstep, a mistake.

And any mistake could bring about the terrible future she had foreseen.

Mohiam's nightmare had shown her what could happen to humanity's destiny if the plan went astray. The premonition had been like a gift, and difficult as the decision was, she could not fail to act on it. She didn't dare.

Does Anirul know my thoughts, too, the terrible act foretold in my dream? A warning, a promise—or a command?

Thoughts . . . Other Memory . . . the multitude of ancient ones within offered their advice, their fears, their warnings. They could no longer keep their knowledge of the Kwisatz Haderach silent, as they had always done before. Mohiam could call to them now, and at their discretion they would come forth, individually or in multitudes. She might ask them for collective guidance, but she didn't want that. They had already revealed enough to awaken her with a scream on her lips.

Mistakes must not be allowed to happen.

Mohiam had to make her own decision, choose her own path into the future and determine how best to prevent the hideous blood-filled fate she had foreseen.

Rising from her bed, straightening her nightclothes, Mohiam moved ponderously through darkness into the next room, the crèche where the babies were kept. Her swollen belly made it more difficult to walk. Mohiam wondered if the Sisterhood's watchdogs would stop her.

Her own churning thoughts made her pause. Inside the dim, warm nursery, she detected the irregular, imperfect breathing of her first Harkonnen daughter, now nine months old. And in her womb the unborn sister kicked and twisted—was this one driving her forward? Had the baby inside triggered the premonition?

The Sisterhood needed a perfect daughter, healthy and strong. Flawed offspring were irrelevant. In any other circumstance, the Bene Gesserit could have found a use even for a sickly and crippled child. But Mohiam had seen her vital place in the Kwisatz Haderach program—and seen what would happen if the program went down the wrong path.

The dream was bright in her mind, like a holo-schematic. She simply had to follow it, without thinking. *Do it.* Heavy consumption of melange often offered prescient visions, and Mohiam had no doubt of what she had seen. The vision was clear as Hagal crystal—billions murdered, the Imperium toppled, the Bene Gesserit nearly destroyed, another jihad raging across the galaxy, sweeping away all in its path.

All of that would happen if the breeding plan went wrong. What did one unwanted life matter in the face of such epochal threats?

Her sickly first daughter by the Baron Harkonnen was in the way, a risk. That girl-child had the potential to ruin the orderly progression along the genetic ladder. Mohiam had to remove any possibility of that mistake, or she could find the blood of billions on her hands.

But my own child?

She reminded herself that this was not really *her child;* it was a product of the Bene Gesserit mating index and the property of every Sister who had committed herself—knowingly or unknowingly—to the overall breeding program. She'd borne other offspring in her service to the Sisterhood, but only two would carry such a dangerous combination of genes.

Two. But there could be only one. Otherwise, the risk was too great.

This weak baby would never suit the master plan. The Sisterhood had already discarded her. Perhaps someday the child could be raised as a servant or cook at the Mother School, but she would never achieve anything of significance. Anirul rarely looked at the disappointing infant anyway, and it received little attention from anyone.

I care about you, Mohiam thought, then chastised herself for the emotion. Difficult decisions had to be made, prices had to be paid. In a cold wave, memories of the nightmare vision washed over her again, strengthening her resolve.

Standing over the child in the nursery, she gently massaged its neck and temple . . . then drew back. A Bene Gesserit did not feel or show *love*—not romantic love, not familial love; emotions were considered dangerous and unseemly.

Once again blaming the chemical changes in her pregnant body, Mohiam tried to make sense of her feelings, to reconcile them with what she had been taught all her life. If she didn't love the child . . . because love was forbidden . . . then why not . . . She swallowed hard, unable to form the horrible thought into words. And if she did love this baby—against all dictates—then that was even more reason to do what she was about to do.

Eliminate the temptation.

Was she feeling love for the child, or just pity? She didn't want to share these thoughts with any of her Sisters. She felt shame for experiencing them, but not for what she was about to do.

Move quickly. Get it over with!

The future demanded that Mohiam do this. If she did not act on the prescient warning, whole planets would die. This new child would be a daughter with an immense destiny, and to ensure that destiny, the other had to be sacrificed.

But still Mohiam hesitated, as if a great maternal weight restrained her, trying to hold back whatever vision had driven her.

She stroked the child's throat. Skin warm . . . breathing slow and regular. In the shadows Mohiam couldn't see the misshapen facial bones and sloping shoulder. The skin was pale . . . the baby seemed so weak. She stirred and whimpered.

Mohiam felt her daughter's breath hot against her hand. Clenching her fist, the Reverend Mother worked hard to control herself and whispered, "I must not fear. Fear is the mind-killer . . ." But she was shaking.

Out of the corner of her eye she saw another comeye, glowing purple to pierce the darkness of the nursery room. She positioned her body between the comeye and the child, with her back to the watchers. She looked into the future, not at what she was doing. Even a Reverend Mother sometimes had a conscience. . . .

Mohiam did what the dream had commanded her to do, holding a small pillow over the child's face until sound and movement stopped.

Finished, still shaking, she arranged the bedding around the little body, then positioned the dead child's head on the pillow and covered her tiny arms and deformed shoulder with a blanket. Suddenly she felt very, very old. Ancient beyond her years.

It is done. Mohiam rested the palm of her right hand on her swollen belly. *Now you must not fail us, daughter.*

In the Plaza de Toros, up in the spectacular box seats reserved for House Atreides, Leto chose a green-cushioned chair beside Rhombur and Kailea. The Lady Helena Atreides, who had no fondness for such public displays, was late arriving. For the occasion Kailea Vernius wore silks and ribbons, colorful veils, and a lush, flowing gown that Atreides seamstresses had made specially for her. Leto thought she was breathtaking.

The gloomy skies did not threaten rain, but the temperature remained cool and the air damp. Even from up here he could smell the dust and old blood in the bullring, the packed bodies of the populace, the stone of the pillars and benches.

In a grand pronouncement carried by the news crier network all over Caladan, Duke Paulus Atreides had dedicated this bullfight to the exiled children of House Vernius. He would fight in their honor, symbolizing their struggle against the illegal takeover of Ix and the blood price that had been placed on their parents, Earl Dominic and Lady Shando.

Beside Leto, Rhombur leaned forward eagerly, his square

chin on his hands as he gazed down at the packed sand of the bullring. His blond hair had been combed and cut, but somehow it still looked mussed. With tremendous anticipation and some concern for the safety of the Old Duke, they waited for the *paseo*, the introductory parade that would precede the fight itself.

Colorful banners hung in the humid air, along with Atreides hawk pennants over the royal box. In this case, however, the leader of House Atreides was not in his prime seat; he was out in the arena, as performer rather than spectator.

All around them, the Plaza de Toros was filled with the humming, chattering sounds of thousands of spectators. People waved and cheered. A local band played balisets, bone flutes, and brassy wind instruments— energetic music that heightened the mood of excitement.

Leto looked around the guarded stands, listening to the music and the happy noises of the crowd. He wondered what could be taking his mother so long. Soon, people would notice her absence.

Finally, with a flurry of female attendants, the Lady Helena arrived, moving through the throng. She walked smoothly, head held high, though her face carried shadows. The ladies-in-waiting left her at the doorway to the ducal box and returned to their assigned seats in the lower level.

Without speaking a word to her son or even looking at his guests, Helena settled herself in the tall carved chair beside the empty post where the Duke sat on those occasions when he watched the matadors. She had gone to the chapel an hour beforehand to commune with her God. Traditionally, the matador was supposed to spend time in religious contemplation before his fight, but Duke Paulus was more concerned with testing his equipment and exercising.

"I had to pray for your father to be saved from his stupidity," she murmured, looking at Leto. "I had to pray for all of us. Someone has to."

Smiling tentatively at his mother, Leto said, "I'm sure he appreciates it."

She shook her head, sighed, and looked down into the arena as a loud fanfare of trumpets played, sounds that blasted and overlapped in resonating echoes from speakers encircling the Plaza de Toros.

Stableboys jogged around the ring in unaccustomed finery, waving bright flags and pennants as they rushed across the packed sand. Moments later, in a grand entrance that he performed so exquisitely, Duke

Paulus Atreides rode out, sitting high on a groomed white stallion. Green plumes rose from the animal's headdress, while ribbons trailed from the horse's mane to flow back around the rider's arms and hands.

Today, the Duke wore a dashing black-and-magenta costume with sequins, a brilliant emerald sash, and a matador's traditional hat, marked with tiny Atreides crests to indicate the number of bulls he had killed. Ballooning sleeves and pantaloons concealed the apparatus of his protective body-shield. A brilliant purple cape draped over his shoulders.

Leto scanned the figures below, trying to pick out the face of the stableboy Duncan Idaho, who had so boldly positioned himself working for the Duke. He should have been part of the *paseo*, but Leto didn't see him.

The white stallion snorted and cantered around in a circle as Paulus raised his gloved hand to greet his subjects. Then he stopped in front of the ducal box and bowed deeply to his wife, who sat rigid in her chair. As expected, she waved a blood-red flower and blew him a kiss. The people shouted and cheered as they imagined fairy tales of romance between their Duke and his Lady.

Rhombur hunched forward on his plush but uncomfortable seat, smiling at Leto. "I've never seen anything like this. I, uh, can't wait."

INSIDE THE STABLES, behind force-field bars, the chosen Salusan bull issued a muffled bellow and charged against the wall. Wood splintered. The reinforced iron supports screeched.

Duncan scrambled backward, terrified. The creature's multifaceted eyes burned a coppery red, as if embers inside the orbs had glowed to life. The bull seemed angry and evil, a child's nightmare come true.

For the *paseo*, the boy wore special white-and-green merh-silks the Duke had given all the stableboys for the day's performance. Duncan had never before worn or even touched such fancy clothes, and it made him uncomfortable to bring them into the dirty stables. But he had a greater sense of uneasiness now.

The fabric felt slick on his clean and lotioned skin. Attendants had scrubbed him, trimmed his hair, cleaned his fingernails. His body felt raw from the cleansing. White lace rode at the wrists above his callused hands. Working in the stables, his pristine condition would not last long.

Safe enough from the bull now, Duncan straightened the cap on his head. He watched the beast as it snorted, pawed the plank floor, and rammed the side of the cage again. Duncan shook his head in dismay and concern.

Turning, he spotted Yresk standing close beside him. The stable-master nodded coolly at the ferocious Salusan bull, his puffy eyes haunted and tired. "Looks like he's eager to fight our Duke."

"Something's still wrong, sir," Duncan insisted. "I've never seen the animal this riled."

Yresk raised his bushy eyebrows and scratched his shock of white hair. "Oh, in all your years of experience? I told you not to trouble yourself."

Duncan bridled at the sarcasm. "Can't you see it yourself, sir?"

"Stable-rat, Salusan bulls are bred to be vicious. The Duke knows what he's doing." Yresk crossed his scarecrow arms over his chest, but he didn't move closer to the cage. "Besides, the more keyed-up this one is, the better he'll fight, and our Duke certainly likes to give a good performance. His people love it."

As if to emphasize Yresk's point, the bull battered itself against the force field, bellowing a deep roar from the vast engine of its chest. Its horned head and leathery hide were gashed in places where it had injured itself trying to trample anything in sight.

"I think we should pick a different bull, Master Yresk."

"Nonsense," the other replied, growing more impatient now. "The Atreides's own stable veterinarian has performed body tissue tests, and everything checked out. You should be ready for the *paseo*, not in here causing trouble. Run along now, before you miss your chance."

"I'm trying to *prevent* trouble, sir," Duncan insisted. He looked defiantly at Yresk. "I'm going to go talk to the Duke myself. Maybe he'll listen."

"You'll do no such thing, stable-rat." Moving like an eel, Yresk grabbed him by the slippery fabric of the costume. "I've been patient enough with you, for the Duke's sake, but I can't let you ruin his bull-fight. Don't you see all the people out there?"

Duncan struggled and cried for help. But the others had already lined up at the gates for the grand parade around the arena. The fanfare sounded a deafening note, and the crowd cheered in anticipation.

Without being unduly rough, Yresk tossed him into one of the empty stalls, turning on the containment field to keep him in it. Duncan stumbled onto piles of trampled feed smeared with green-brown manure.

"You can sit out the event here," Yresk said, looking sad. "I should have known to expect trouble from you, a Harkonnen sympathizer."

"But I hate the Harkonnens!" Duncan stood up, trembling with rage. His silk clothes were ruined. He hurled himself against the bars just as the bull had done, but he had no chance of escaping.

Brushing himself off to look presentable again, Yresk strode toward the arched openings for the *paseo*. The stablemaster flashed a glance over his shoulder. "The only reason you're here, stable-rat, is because the Duke likes you. But I've run his stables for nigh on twenty years, and I know exactly what I'm doing. You just leave it be—I've got work to do."

In the cage beside Duncan, the Salusan bull simmered like a boiler about to explode.

***

DUKE PAULUS ATREIDES stood in the center of the arena. He turned slowly, drawing energy from the enthusiasm of the crowd; residual heat rose from the packed stands. He flashed them all a sparkling, confident grin. They roared with approval. Oh, how his people loved to be entertained!

Paulus switched on his body-shield at partial setting. He would have to maneuver carefully for his protection. The element of danger kept him on his toes, and it made for greater suspense among the spectators. He held the *muleta*, a brightly colored cloth on a pole, which he would use to distract the attacking animal and divert its attention from his body core.

The long barbed staffs, poison-dipped *banderillas*, were wrapped close to the pole for Paulus to use when he needed them. He would get near to the creature and spike them into its neck muscles, injecting a neuropoison that would gradually weaken the Salusan bull so that he could deliver the coup de grâce.

Paulus had been through these performances dozens of times before, often for major Caladan holidays. He was at the top of his form in front of crowds and enjoyed showing off his bravery and skills. It was his way of repaying his subjects for their devotion. Each time, it seemed, his physical abilities rose to their peak as he rode the narrow edge in the contest between living his own life to the hilt and risking it as he fought a raging beast. He hoped Rhombur and Kailea would enjoy the show and feel more at home.

Only once, back when he was younger, had Paulus actually felt threatened: A sluggish, plodding bull had lured him into switching off his shield during a practice session, and then had turned into a whirl-wind of horns and hooves. These mutated creatures were not just vio-lent, but two-brain smart as well, and Paulus had made the mistake of forgetting that—but only once. The bull had slashed him with its horns, laying his side open. Paulus had fallen onto the sand and would have been gored to death had he not been practicing at the same time as a much younger Thufir Hawat.

Seeing the danger, the warrior Mentat had instantly dropped all pretense of protocol in the bullring and leaped forth single-handedly to attack and dispatch the creature. During the ensuing fight, the fero-cious bull had ripped a long wound in Hawat's leg, leaving him with a permanent, curling scar. The scar had become a reminder to all of the Mentat's intense devotion to his Duke.

Now, under the cloudy skies and surrounded by his subjects, Duke Paulus waved and took a long, deep breath. Fanfare signaled that the fight was to begin.

House Atreides was not the most powerful family in the Landsraad, nor the wealthiest. Still, Caladan provided many resources: the pundi rice fields, the bountiful fish in the seas, the kelp harvest, all the fruit and produce from the arable land, and handmade musical instruments and bone carvings done by the aboriginal people in the south. In re-cent years there had been an increased demand for tapestries woven by the Sisters in Isolation, a religious group sequestered in the terraced hills of the eastern continent. In all, Caladan provided everything its people could possibly want, and Duke Paulus knew his family's fortunes were secure. He was immensely pleased that one day he could pass it all on to his son Leto.

The mutated Salusan bull charged.

"Ho, ho!" The Duke laughed and flailed his multihued *muleta*, skit-tering backward as the bull thundered past. Its head tossed from side to side, thrashing with its spiny shovel of a skull. One of the horns moved slowly enough to ripple through the pulsing Holtzman shield, and the Duke slid sideways, just enough so that the bone spike barely scratched his outer armor.

Seeing how close the horn had come to their beloved leader, the audience let out a collective gasp. The Duke sidestepped the bull as it charged past, kicking up powdered sand. The beast skidded to a stop. Paulus held his *muleta* with one hand, jiggling the cloth, and snatched out one of his barbed *banderillas*.

He glanced up at the ducal box, touching the hooked tip of the *banderilla* to his forehead in a salute. Leto and Prince Rhombur had leaped to their feet in excitement, but Helena remained frozen in her chair, her expression clouded, hands clasped in her lap.

The bull wheeled about and reoriented itself. Normally, Salusan bulls became dizzy after missing their target, but this one did not slow a bit. Duke Paulus realized that his monstrous opponent had a greater energy than he had ever seen, keener eyesight, hotter fury. Still, he smiled. Defeating this worthy opponent would be his finest hour, and a fitting tribute to the exiled Ixians in his care.

The Duke played with the bull for a few more passes, dancing beyond the reach of its horns, completing his expected performance for the excited spectators. Around him the partial shield shimmered.

Seeing that the bull did not tire after the better part of an hour, though, and that it remained focused on killing him, Duke Paulus grew concerned enough that he made up his mind to end the contest as swiftly as possible. He would use his shield, a trick he had learned from one of the finest matadors in the Imperium.

The next time the creature shot past, hooves hammering the packed sand, its horns ricocheted off the Duke's personal shield, a collision that finally disoriented the beast.

The Duke grasped the *banderilla* and plunged it into the bull's back like a stake, setting the barbed hook into cable-thick neck muscles. Oily blood spilled out from the slash in its hide. Paulus released the handle of the poisoned spear as he twirled out of the way. The drug on the barbed tip should begin to act immediately, burning out the neurotransmitters in the beast's double brain.

The crowd cheered, and the bull roared with pain. It spun about and stumbled as its legs seemed to give way. The Duke thought this was caused by the poison, but to his surprise the Salusan bull floundered to its feet once more and rocketed toward him. Paulus again side-stepped, but the bull managed to snag the *muleta* on its multiple horns, thrashing its head and tearing the bright ceremonial cloth to shreds.

The Duke narrowed his eyes and released his hold. This was going to be a greater challenge than he had expected. The audience cried out in dismay, and he couldn't stop himself from offering them a brave smile. *Yes, the difficult fights are the best, and the people of Caladan will remember this one for a long, long time.*

Paulus held up his second *banderilla*, slashing it in the air like a thin fencing sword, and turned to face the heavily muscled oncoming bull. He had no cape to distract the animal now, so it would see his body core as its main target. He had only one short, barbed spear as his weapon, and a partial shield for protection.

He saw Atreides guards, even Thufir Hawat, standing at the ring-side, ready to race out and assist him. But the Duke raised his hand, forcing them back. He must do this himself. It simply would not do to have a mob of other fighters rushing to his rescue the moment things got a little sticky.

The Salusan bull pawed the ground, glaring at him with its multi-faceted eyes, and the Duke thought he saw a flash of understanding there. This creature knew exactly who he was—and it intended to kill him. But the Duke had similar thoughts in his own mind.

The bull charged directly toward him and picked up speed. Paulus wondered why the neurotoxin hadn't yet slowed it down. Deadly questions occurred to him: *How can this be? I dipped the* banderillas *in poison myself. But was it really poison?*

Wondering if there had been sabotage, the Duke held out the *banderilla*, its sharp barb glinting in the cloudy sunlight. The bull approached, steaming, frothing. Foam from its nostrils and mouth flew up to fleck its black scaly face.

As they closed to within meters of each other, the bull feinted to the right. Duke Paulus jabbed with his short spear, but the beast instantly swerved and attacked from a different direction. This time the barb caught on a knob of the bull's horny skin, but did not sink in. The small weapon tore out of the Duke's grasp and dropped to the sand as the bull dashed past.

For a moment Paulus was weaponless. He scrambled backward and snatched for the *banderilla* on the ground. Turning his back on the bull, he listened for it to grind to a stop, spin around, and come back—but as he bent over to retrieve his weapon, the huge bull was suddenly there with impossible speed, horns lowered.

The Duke scrambled to one side, trying to get out of the way, but the bull was already within his safety zone, ducking under the partial shield and ramming home. Its long, curved horns gouged deep into the Duke's back, breaking through his ribs and into his lungs and heart.

The bull roared with triumph. To the horror of the crowd, it lifted Paulus up, thrashing him from side to side. Blood sprayed on the sand, red droplets slowed by the concave surface of the small shield. The doomed Duke flailed and twitched, impaled on the forest of horns.

The audience fell deathly silent.

Within seconds, Thufir Hawat and the Atreides guards surged out onto the field, their lasguns cutting the rampaging Salusan bull into piles of smoking meat. The creature's own momentum caused pieces of the carcass to fly apart in different directions. The decapitated but otherwise intact head thumped onto the ground.

The Duke's body pirouetted in the air and landed on its back in the trampled sand.

Up in the ducal box, Rhombur cried out in disbelief. Kailea sobbed. The Lady Helena let her chin sink against her chest and wept.

Leto rose to his feet, all color draining from his skin. His mouth opened and closed, but he could find no words to express his utter shock. He wanted to run down into the arena, but saw from the mangled condition of his father that he would never reach him in time. There would be no gasping and whispering of last words.

Duke Paulus Atreides, this magnificent man of his people, was dead.

Deafening wails erupted from the spectator stands. Leto could feel the vibration rumbling through the ducal box. He couldn't tear his eyes from his father, lying broken and bloodied on the ground, and he knew it was a nightmare vision that would remain with him for the rest of his life.

Thufir Hawat stood next to the fallen Old Duke, but even a warrior Mentat could do nothing for him now.

Oddly, his mother's quiet voice cut through the surrounding din, and Leto heard the words clearly, like ice picks. "Leto, my son," Helena said, "*you* are Duke Atreides now."

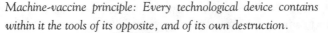

Machine-vaccine principle: Every technological device contains within it the tools of its opposite, and of its own destruction.

—GIAN KANA,
Imperial Patent Czar

It didn't take the invaders long to make permanent changes in the prosperous underground cities. Many innocent Ixians died and many disappeared, while C'tair waited for someone to find and kill him.

During brief sojourns from his shielded hiding room, C'tair learned that Vernii, the former capital city of Ix, had been renamed Hilacia by the Tleilaxu. The fanatical usurpers had even changed Imperial records to refer to the ninth planet in the Alkaurops system as Xuttuh, rather than Ix.

C'tair wanted to strangle any Tleilaxu he found, but instead he developed a subtler plan.

He dressed like a low-level worker and doctored forms to show that he had once been a minor line supervisor, one step above a suboid, who had watched over a labor crew of twelve men. He'd read enough about hull-plate welding and sealing so that he could claim it had been his job. No one would expect much from him.

All around him, the Bene Tleilax were gutting his city and rebuilding it into a dark hell.

He abhorred the changes, loathed the Tleilaxu *gall*. And

from what he could see, Imperial Sardaukar had actually assisted in this abomination.

C'tair could do nothing about it at the moment; he had to bide his time. He was alone here: his father exiled to Kaitain and afraid to return, his mother murdered, his twin brother taken away by the Guild. Only he remained on Ix, like a rat hiding within the walls.

But even rats could cause significant damage.

Over the months, C'tair learned to blend in, to appear to be an insignificant and cowed citizen. He kept his eyes averted, his hands dirty, his clothes and hair unkempt. He could not let it be known that he was the son of the former Ambassador to Kaitain, that he had faithfully served House Vernius—and still would, if he could find a way to do it. He had walked freely through the Grand Palais, had escorted the Earl's own daughter. Acts that, if known, would mean a death sentence for him.

Above all, he could not let the rabid antitechnology invaders discover his shielded hiding place or the devices he had hoarded there. His stockpile might just be the last hope for the future of Ix.

Throughout the grottoes of the city, C'tair watched signs being torn down, streets and districts being renamed, and the little gnomes—all men, no women—occupying huge research facilities for their secret, nefarious operations. The streets, walkways, and facilities were guarded by diligent, thinly disguised Imperial Sardaukar or the invaders' own shape-shifting Face Dancers.

Shortly after their victory was secured, the Tleilaxu Masters had showed themselves and encouraged the suboid rebels to vent their anger on carefully selected and approved targets. Standing back, clothed in a simple workman's jumpsuit, C'tair had watched the smooth-skinned laborers cluster around the facility that had manufactured the new self-learning fighting meks.

"House Vernius has brought this upon themselves!" screamed a charismatic suboid agitator, almost certainly a Face Dancer infiltrator. "They would bring back the thinking machines. Destroy this place!"

While the helpless Ixian survivors had watched in horror, the suboids smashed the plaz windows and used thermal bombs to ignite the small manufactory. Filled with religious fervor, they howled and threw rocks.

A Tleilaxu Master on a hastily erected podium had bellowed into comspeakers and amplifiers. "We are your new masters, and we will make certain the manufacturing abilities of Ix are fully in accord with the strictures of the Great Convention." The flames continued to crackle, and some of the suboids had cheered, but most didn't seem to be listening. "As soon as possible, we must repair this damage and return this world to normal operations—with better conditions for the suboids, of course."

C'tair had looked around, watched the building burn, and felt sick inside.

"All Ixian technology must henceforth be scrutinized by a strict religious review board, to assure its suitability. Any questionable technology will be scrapped. No one will ask you to endanger your souls by working on heretical machines." More cheering, more smashed plaz, a few screams.

C'tair had realized, though, that the cost of this takeover would be enormous for the Tleilaxu, even with Imperial support. Since Ix was one of the major powerhouse economies in the Imperium, the new rulers could not afford to let the production lines remain idle. The Tleilaxu would make a show of destroying some of the questionable products, such as the reactive meks, but he doubted any of the truly profitable Ixian devices would be discontinued.

Despite the promises of the new masters, the suboids had been put back to work—as they were bred to do—but this time they followed only Tleilaxu designs and orders. C'tair realized that, before long, the manufactories would begin pouring out merchandise again; and shiploads of solaris would flow back into the Bene Tleilax coffers to pay them for this costly military adventure.

Now, though, the secrecy and security developed by generations of House Vernius would work against them. Ix had always shrouded itself in mystery, so who would notice the difference? Once the paying customers were satisfied with the exports, no one in the Imperium would much care about internal Ixian politics. Anyone on the outside would forget all that had happened here. It would be cleanly swept under the rug.

That must be what the Tleilaxu were counting on, C'tair thought. The entire world of Ix—he would *never* refer to it, not even in his mind, as Xuttuh—was walled off from the Imperium as an enigma . . . much as the homeworlds of the Bene Tleilax had been for centuries.

The new masters restricted travel off-planet and imposed curfews with deadly force. Face Dancers rooted out "traitors" from hiding rooms similar to C'tair's and executed them without fanfare or ceremony. He saw no end to the repression, but he vowed not to give up. This was his own world, and he would fight for it, in any way he could.

C'tair told no one his name, called little attention to himself—but he listened, absorbed every whispered story or rumor, and he planned. Not knowing whom to trust, he assumed everyone was an informant, either a Face Dancer or simply a turncoat. Sometimes an informant was easily recognizable by the directness of a line of inquiry: *Where do you work? Where do you live? What are you doing on this street?*

But others were not so easy to detect, such as the gnarled old woman with whom *he* had initiated a conversation. He'd only meant to ask directions to a work site where he had been assigned. She hadn't sought him out at all, except to appear harmless . . . somewhat like a child with a grenade in its pocket.

"Such an interesting choice of words," she'd said, and he didn't even remember his own phrasing. "And your inflection . . . you are Ixian nobility, perhaps?" She looked meaningfully at some of the ruined stalactite buildings in the ceiling.

He had stammered an answer. "N-no, although I have been a s-servant all my life, and perhaps I picked up some of their distasteful mannerisms. My apologies." He had bowed and departed quickly, without ever getting directions from her.

His response had been awkward and perhaps incriminating, so he'd thrown away the clothes he'd been wearing and hadn't gone down that narrow street again. Afterward, he had paid more attention than ever before to masking his own vocal identity markers. Whenever possible, he avoided talking to strangers at all. It appalled C'tair that so many opportunistic Ixians had switched allegiance to the new masters, forgetting House Vernius in less than a year.

In the first days of confusion following the takeover, C'tair had hoarded scraps of abandoned technology, from which he had constructed the cross-dimensional "Rogo" transceiver. Soon, though, all but the most primitive technology had been confiscated and made illegal. C'tair still snatched what he could, scavenging anything that might prove valuable. He considered the risk well worth taking.

His fight here might continue for years, if not decades.

He thought back to the childhood he'd shared with D'murr, and the crippled inventor, Davee Rogo, who had befriended the boys. In his private laboratory, secreted inside an ignored coal vein in the upper crust, old Rogo had taught the youths many interesting principles, had shown them some of his failed prototypes. The inventor had chuckled, his bright eyes sparkling as he goaded the boys into disassembling and reassembling some of his complicated inventions. C'tair had learned a great deal under the crippled man's tutelage.

Now C'tair recalled his Navigator brother's lack of interest when he'd told him of the wavy vision he'd seen in the rubble. Perhaps the ghost of Davee Rogo had not come back from the dead to provide instructions. He'd never seen a similar apparition, before or since. But that experience, whether a supernatural message or a hallucination, had permitted C'tair to accomplish a very human purpose: remaining in communication with his twin, maintaining the bond of love as D'murr became lost in the mysteries of the Guild.

Trapped in his various hiding places, C'tair had to live vicariously, soaring across the universe in his brother's mind whenever they made contact via the transceiver. Over the months he learned with excitement and pride of D'murr's first solo flights through foldspace as a trainee Pilot in his own Guild ship. Then, a few days ago, D'murr had been approved for his first commercial assignment, navigating an unmanned colony transport craft that plied the void far beyond the Imperium.

If his outstanding work for the Guild continued, the Navigator trainee who had been D'murr Pilru would be promoted to transporting goods and personnel between the primary worlds of the Houses Major, and perhaps along the coveted Kaitain routes. He would become an actual Navigator, possibly even working his way up to Steersman. . . .

But the communications device exhibited persistent problems. The silicate crystals had to be sliced with a cutteray and connected in a precise manner; then they functioned only briefly before disintegrating from the strain. Hairline cracks rendered them useless. C'tair had used the device on four occasions to reach his brother, and after each time he'd had to painstakingly cut and refit new crystals.

C'tair established careful ties to black market groups that furnished him with what he required. The contraband silicate crystals surreptitiously bore laser-scribed approvals by the Religious Review Board. Ever resourceful, the black marketers had their own means of counterfeiting the approval marks, and had scribed them everywhere, thus frustrating the controlling efforts of the occupation forces.

Still, he dealt with the furtive salesmen as little as possible to reduce his own risk of being caught . . . but that also limited the number of times he could talk with his brother.

C'TAIR STOOD BEHIND a barricade with other restless, sweaty people who studiously refused to recognize each other. He looked out across the sprawling grotto floor to the construction yards where the skeleton of the partially built Heighliner sat. Overhead, portions of the projected sky remained dark and damaged, and the Tleilaxu showed no inclination to repair it.

Suspensor-borne searchlights and speakers hovered over the crowd as the gathered people waited for an announcement and further instructions. No one wanted to ask, and no one wanted to hear.

"This Heighliner is of an unapproved Vernius design," the floating speakers boomed in a sexless voice that resonated against the rock walls, "and does not meet the standards of the Religious Review Board. Your Tleilaxu masters are returning to the previous design, so this craft is to be dismantled immediately."

A soft susurration of dismay crept across the crowd.

"Raw materials are to be salvaged and new work crews established. Construction begins again in five days."

C'tair's mind whirled as maroon-robed organizers marched through the crowds, assigning teams. As the son of an ambassador he'd had access to information that had not been available to others of his age. He knew the old-style Heighliners had a significantly smaller cargo capacity and operated less efficiently. But what possible religious objection could the invaders have to increased profits? What did the Tleilaxu have to gain from less efficient space transport?

Then he remembered a story that his ambassador father had told back in a time of smug assurance, that old Emperor Elrood had been displeased with the innovation, since it curtailed his tariff revenue. Pieces began to fit into place. House Corrino had provided disguised Sardaukar troops to maintain an iron grip on the Ixian population, and C'tair realized that reverting to the old Heighliner design might be how the Tleilaxu intended to repay the Emperor for his military support.

Wheels within wheels within wheels . . .

He felt sick inside. If true, it was such a petty reason for so many lives to have been lost, for the glorious traditions of Ix to have been destroyed, for the overthrow of an entire noble family and a planetary way of life. He was angry with everyone involved—even with Earl Vernius, who should have foreseen this and taken steps not to create such powerful enemies.

The call to work came across the PA system, and C'tair was assigned to join suboid crews as they dismantled the partially finished ship and salvaged its parts in the grotto yard. Struggling to maintain a bland expression on his face as he wielded a construction laser to sever components, he wiped sweat from his dark hair. He wished instead that he could use the laser to attack the Tleilaxu. Other teams hauled the girders and plates away, stacking them for the next assembly project.

With ringing and clanging all around him, C'tair recalled a better, more ordered time, when he'd stood with D'murr and Kailea on the observation deck above. So long ago, it seemed. They had watched a Navigator guide the last new Heighliner out of the grotto. Perhaps it would be the last such ship ever built . . . unless C'tair could help overthrow these destroyers.

The magnificent ship gradually fell to pieces, and the echoing sounds and chemical smells were horrific. Did suboids work this way all the time? If so, he could begin to imagine how they might have been dissatisfied enough to consider a rebellion. But C'tair could not believe the violence had been entirely at the workers' instigation.

Had this all been part of the Emperor's plan? To destroy House Vernius and quash progress? Where and how the Bene Tleilax came into play in the scheme of influences, C'tair wasn't certain. Of all races, these were the most hated people in the known galaxy. Surely, Elrood could have found any number of Great Houses to take over the operations on Ix without disrupting the economics of the Imperium. What else could the Padishah Emperor have in mind for these religious fanatics? Why would he dirty his hands with them?

In disgust, C'tair watched other changes in the grotto, facilities being modified, as he continued the work of dismantling the Heighliner. The new Tleilaxu overlords were busy little creatures, always hurrying about in a mysterious manner, setting up clandestine operations in the largest structures on Ix, locking formerly open facilities, shuttering windows, erecting stun-fences and minefields. *Keeping their filthy little secrets.*

C'tair took it as his mission to learn all those secrets, by whatever means necessary, however long it might take him. The Tleilaxu must fall. . . .

The ultimate question: Why does life exist? The answer: For life's sake.

—ANONYMOUS,

thought to be of Zensunni origin

Two Reverend Mothers stood talking on a treeless knoll: one old, one young. Behind clouds, the waning sun, Laoujin, threw the long shadows of their hooded black robes down the slope. Over the centuries an untold number of other Reverend Mothers had stood on the same spot, under the same sun, discussing grave matters relevant to their times.

If the two women wished, they could revisit those past crises through Other Memory. The Reverend Mother Anirul Sadow Tonkin made such thought-journeys more than most; each circumstance was just another minor step along the long, long road. Over the past year she had let her bronze-brown hair grow long, until its locks hung down to her narrow chin.

At the base of the knoll a whitecrete building was under construction. Like worker bees, female laborers, each one with an entire blueprint in her mind, operated heavy equipment, preparing to lift roof modules into place. To the rare outside observer, Wallach IX with its Bene Gesserit libraries and schools seemed always the same, but the Sisterhood was ever adapting for survival, ever changing, ever growing.

"They're working too slowly. I wanted them finished already," Anirul said, rubbing her forehead; she had been experiencing chronic headaches of late. As Mohiam came closer to term, Anirul's responsibilities as Kwisatz Mother were tremendous. "Do you realize how few days remain until the baby is due?"

"Blame no one but yourself, Anirul. You demanded that this be no ordinary birthing facility," Mother Superior Harishka said sternly. The Kwisatz Mother flushed and looked away. "Every Sister knows how important it is. Many of them suspect this is not just another child to be lost in the web of our breeding programs. A few have even been talking about the Kwisatz Haderach."

Anirul tucked a loose strand of bronze hair behind her ear. "Unavoidable. All the Sisters know of our dream, but few suspect how close it is to reality." She shifted her skirts around her and sat down on the soft grass of the knoll. She gestured toward the construction, where the sounds of carpentry rang clear in the air. "Mohiam is due to deliver in a week, Mother Superior. We don't even have the roof on yet."

"They will finish, Anirul. Calm yourself. Everyone is doing her best to follow your orders."

Anirul reacted as if slapped, then covered her reaction. *Does Reverend Mother see me as an untempered and impetuous girl?* Perhaps she had been too insistent with her instructions for the facility, and sometimes Mother Superior looked at her with a certain amount of resentment. *Is she jealous that Other Memory chose me to lead such an ambitious program? Does she resent my knowledge?*

"I'm not as young as you're treating me," Anirul said, against the better judgment of the voices. Very few of the Bene Gesserit had the weight of history inside them the way she did. Very few knew all of the machinations, every step of the Kwisatz Haderach program, every failure or success over the millennia, every deviation in the plan, for more than ninety generations. "I have the knowledge to succeed."

Mother Superior frowned at her. "Then put more faith in our Mohiam. She's delivered nine daughters for the Sisterhood already. I trust her to control the exact moment at which she chooses to give birth, even to delay her labor if necessary." A scrap of brittle hair blew out of its prim containment and feathered across the old woman's cheek. "Her role in this is more important than any birthing facility."

Anirul challenged the chastising tone. "True. And we must not have another failure, like the last."

Not even a Reverend Mother could master all facets of embryonic development. Through her internal processes she could set her own metabolism, but not the metabolism of the child. Selecting her baby's sex was an adjustment of the *mother's* chemistry, choosing the precise egg and sperm to unite. But once the zygote started growing in the womb, the offspring was effectively on its own, beginning a process of growing *away* from the mother.

Anirul said, "I can feel that this daughter will be vital, a crux point."

A loud thump sounded below, and Anirul grimaced. One of the roof sections had tumbled into the interior of the building, and the Sister workers rushed about to correct the mistake.

Mother Superior uttered a profanity.

THROUGH HERCULEAN EFFORTS the birthing facility was completed, on time, while Kwisatz Mother Anirul marched back and forth. Only hours before the scheduled birth, construction workers and robos put on the finishing touches. Medical equipment was brought in and connected. Glowglobes, beds, blankets . . . even a warm blaze in the archaic wood-burning fireplace Mohiam had requested.

As Anirul and Harishka inspected the job, still smelling of dust and construction materials, they paused to watch the noisy entrance of a motorized gurney bearing an enormously pregnant Gaius Helen Mohiam. She was alert and sitting up, already experiencing increased contractions. Reverend Mothers and white-smocked medical attendants escorted her in, clucking excitedly like hens.

"This was too close, Mother Superior," Anirul said. "I don't appreciate additional stress points in an already-complex task."

"Agreed," said Harishka. "The Sisters will be reprimanded for their lethargy. Though, if your designs had been less ambitious . . ." She let the thought hang in the air.

Ignoring Mother Superior, Anirul noted the trim and decoration of the room, with its intricate ivory and pearl inlays and ornate wood carvings. Perhaps she should have had them concentrate more on functionality than on extravagance. . . .

Harishka crossed her thin arms over her chest. "The design of this new facility is similar to what we had before. Was it really necessary?"

"This is not similar at all," Anirul said. Her face flushed, and she washed the defensive tone out of her words. "The old birthing room simply wasn't functional anymore."

Mother Superior gave a condescending smile; she understood the need for an untainted building, with no old memories, no ghosts. "Anirul, through our Missionaria Protectiva we manipulate the superstitions of backward peoples . . . but we Sisters aren't supposed to be superstitious ourselves."

Anirul took the comment with good humor. "I assure you, Mother Superior, such conjecture is preposterous."

The older woman's almond eyes glittered. "Other Sisters are saying you thought the old birthing room had a curse on it, which caused the first child's deformities . . . and its mysterious death."

Anirul drew herself up straight. "This is hardly the proper time to discuss such a thing, Mother Superior." She scanned the frantic preparations: Mohiam placed on the birthing bed, Sisters gathering warm karthan-weave towels, liquids, pads. An incubator chamber blinked with monitors on the wall. First-ranked midwives bustled around, preparing for unforeseen complications.

On her gurney, Mohiam looked entirely composed now, her thoughts turned inward, meditating. But Anirul noticed how old she appeared, as if the last shreds of youth had been drained from her.

Harishka placed a sinewy hand on Anirul's forearm in a sudden and surprising display of closeness. "We all have our primal superstitions, but we must master them. For now, worry about nothing except this child. The Sisterhood needs a healthy daughter, with a powerful future."

Medical personnel checked equipment and took up their positions around Mohiam, who reclined on a bed, inhaling deeply; her cheeks flushed red with exertion. Two of the midwives propped her up in the ages-old delivery position. The pregnant woman began to hum to herself, allowing only a flicker of discomfort to cross her face as she experienced increasingly severe contractions.

Standing aloof, yet sharply observant, Anirul considered what

Mother Superior had just told her. Secretly, Anirul had consulted a Feng Shui master about the old birthing facility. A withered old man with Terrasian features, he was a practitioner of an ancient Zensunni philosophy which held that architecture, furniture placement, and maximum utilization of color and light all worked to promote the well-being of a facility's inhabitants. With a sage nod, he declared that the old facility had been set up incorrectly, and showed Anirul what needed to be done. They'd had only a month before the expected delivery date, and the Kwisatz Mother had had not a moment to lose.

Now as she observed the abundance of light flowing down upon Mohiam's bed from actual windows and skylights, rather than from clusters of artificial glowglobes, Anirul assured herself she hadn't been "superstitious." Feng Shui was about aligning oneself properly with Nature and being intensely aware of one's surroundings—a philosophy that was, ultimately, very much in the Bene Gesserit way of thinking.

Too much rode on this single birth. If there was a chance, even a small one, Anirul wanted no part in denying it. Using the power of her position, she had demanded a new birthing facility, built according to the Feng Shui master's recommendations. Then she'd sent the old man away, letting the other Sisters believe he had merely been a visiting gardener.

Now she glided closer to Mohiam's bed, looking down at her patient as the time neared. Anirul hoped the old man was right. This daughter was their last, best chance.

IT HAPPENED QUICKLY, the moment Mohiam set her mind to it.

A baby's insistent crying filled the chamber, and Anirul lifted a perfect girl-child in the air for Mother Superior to see. Even the voices in Other Memory cheered at the victory. Everyone beamed triumphantly, delighted with the long-anticipated birth. Agitated, the child kicked and flailed.

Sisters toweled off infant and mother, giving Mohiam a long drink of juice to restore her body fluids. Anirul handed the baby to her. Still breathing hard from the exertion of the delivery, Mohiam took the girl and looked at her, allowing an uncharacteristically proud smile to cross her face.

"This child shall be named *Jessica*, meaning 'wealth,' " Mohiam announced proudly, still panting. When other Sisters moved away, Mohiam stared at Anirul and Harishka, who stood close to her. In a directed whisper that only they could hear, she said, "I know this child is part of the Kwisatz Haderach program. The voices in Other Memory have told me. I have seen a vision, and I know the terrible future if we fail with her."

Anirul and Mother Superior exchanged uneasy glances. In a whisper Harishka responded, looking sidelong as if hoping the spontaneous revelation might weaken the Kwisatz Mother's hold over the program. "You are commanded to secrecy. Your child is to be the grandmother of the Kwisatz Haderach."

"I suspected as much." Mohiam sank back on her pillow to consider the immensity of this revelation. "So soon . . ."

Outside the building, clapping and cheering rang out as news of the birth passed quickly around the training areas. Balconies above the library enclaves and discussion chambers overflowed with acolytes and teachers celebrating the felicitous event, though only a handful knew the full significance of this child in the breeding program.

Gaius Helen Mohiam gave the child to the midwives, refusing to form any sort of parental bond that was forbidden by the Bene Gesserit. Though she maintained her composure, she felt drawn, bone-weary, and *old*. This Jessica was her tenth daughter for the Sisterhood, and she hoped her childbearing duties were now at an end. She looked at young Reverend Mother Anirul Sadow Tonkin. How could she do better than she had already done? Jessica . . . their future.

I am indeed fortunate to participate in this moment, Anirul thought as she looked down at the exhausted new mother. It struck her as odd that of all the Sisters who had worked toward this goal for thousands of years, of all those who now watched eagerly in Other Memory, *she* was the one to supervise the birth of Jessica. Anirul herself would guide this child through years of training toward the critically important sexual union she must have, to carry the breeding program to its penultimate step.

Wrapped in a blanket, the baby girl had finally stopped crying and lay peacefully in the sheltering warmth of its enclosed bed.

Squinting down through the protective plaz, Anirul tried to imagine what this Jessica would look like as a grown woman. She envisioned the baby's face elongating and thinning, and could visualize a tall lady of great beauty, with the regal features of her father Baron Harkonnen, generous lips, and smooth skin. The Baron would never meet his daughter or know her name, for this would be one of the most closely guarded secrets of the Bene Gesserit.

One day, when Jessica was of age, she would be commanded to bear a daughter, and that child must be introduced to the son of Abulurd Harkonnen, the Baron's youngest demibrother. At the moment Abulurd and his wife had only one son, Rabban—but Anirul had set in motion a means of suggesting that they have more. This would improve the odds of one male surviving to maturity; it would also improve the gene selection, and improve the odds of good sexual timing.

A vast jigsaw puzzle remained apparent to Anirul, each of its pieces a separate event in the incredible Bene Gesserit breeding program. Only a few more components needed to slip into place now, and the Kwisatz Haderach would become a reality in flesh and blood—the all-powerful male who could bridge space and time, the ultimate tool to be wielded by the Bene Gesserit.

Anirul wondered now, as she often had without daring to speak of it, if such a man could cause the Bene Gesserit to once again find genuine religious fervor, like the fanaticism of the crusading Butler family. What if he made others revere him as a god?

Imagine that, she thought. The Bene Gesserit—who used religion only to manipulate others—ensnared by their own messianic leader. She doubted that could ever happen.

Reverend Mother Anirul went out to celebrate with her Sisters.

The surest way to keep a secret is to make people believe they already know the answer.

                                —Ancient Fremen Wisdom

U mma Kynes, you have accomplished much," said one-eyed Heinar as the two men sat on a rocky promontory above their sietch. The Naib treated him as an equal now, even with overblown respect. Kynes had stopped bothering to argue with the desert people every time they called him "Umma," their word for "prophet."

He and Heinar watched the coppery sunset spill across the sweeping dunefield of the Great Erg. Far in the distance, a fuzzy haze hung on the horizon, the last remnants of a sandstorm that had passed the previous day.

Powerful winds had washed the dunes clean, scrubbed their surfaces, recontoured the landscape. Kynes relaxed against the rough rock, sipping from a pungent cup of spice coffee.

Seeing her husband about to go above ground, outside the sietch, a pregnant Frieth had hurried after the two men as they waited to bid the sun farewell for another day. An elaborate brass coffee service sat between them on a flat stone. Frieth had brought it, along with a selection of the crunchy sesame cakes Kynes loved so well. By the time he remembered to thank her for her kind attentiveness, Frieth had already vanished like a shadow back into the caves.

After a long moment, Kynes nodded distractedly at the Naib's comment. "Yes, I've accomplished much, but I still have plenty to do." He thought of the remarkably complex plans required to complete his dream of a reborn Dune, a planetary name little known in the Imperium.

Imperium. He rarely thought of the old Emperor now—his own priorities, the emphasis of his life, had changed so greatly. Kynes could never go back to being a mere Imperial Planetologist, not after all he'd been through with these desert people.

Heinar clasped his friend's wrist. "It is said that sunset is a time for reflection and assessment, my friend. Let us look to what we have done, rather than permit the empty gulf of the future to overwhelm us. You have been on this planet for only a little more than a year, yet already you have found a new tribe, a new wife." Heinar smiled. "And soon you will have a new child, a son perhaps."

Kynes returned the smile wistfully. Frieth was nearly through her gestation period. He was somewhat surprised that the pregnancy had happened at all, since he was gone so frequently. He still wasn't certain how to react to his impending role as a first-time father. He had never thought about it before.

However, the birth would fit in neatly with the overall plan he had for this astounding planet. His child, growing up to lead the Fremen long after Kynes himself was gone, could help continue their efforts. The master plan was designed to take centuries.

As a Planetologist, he had to think in the long term, something the Fremen were not in the habit of doing—though, given their long, troubled past, they should have been accustomed to it. The desert people had an oral history going back thousands of years, tales told in the sietch describing their endless wanderings from planet to planet, a people enslaved and persecuted, until finally they had made a home here where no one else could bear to live.

The Fremen way was a conservative one, little changed from generation to generation, and these people were not used to considering the broad scope of progress. Assuming their environment could not be adapted, they remained its prisoners, rather than its masters.

Kynes hoped to change all that. He had mapped out his great plan, including rough timetables for plantings and the accumulation of water, milestones for each successive achievement. Hectare by hectare, Dune would be rescued from the wasteland.

His Fremen teams were scouring the surface, taking core samples from the Great Bled, geological specimens from the Minor Erg and the Funeral Plain—but many terraforming factors still remained unknown variables.

Pieces fell into place daily. When he expressed a desire for better maps of the planet's surface, he was astonished to learn that the Fremen already had detailed topographical charts, even climatic surveys. "Why is it that I couldn't get these before?" Kynes said. "I was the Imperial Planetologist, and the maps I received from satellite cartography were woefully inaccurate."

Old Heinar had smiled at him, squinting his one eye. "We pay a substantial bribe to the Spacing Guild to keep them from watching us too closely. The cost is high, but the Fremen are free—and the Harkonnens remain in the dark, along with the rest of the Imperium."

Kynes was astonished at first, then simply pleased, to have much of the geographical information he needed. Immediately he dispatched traders to deal with smugglers and obtain genetically engineered seeds of vigorous desert plants. He had to design and build an entire ecosystem from scratch.

In large council meetings, the Fremen asked their new "prophet" what the next step might be, how long each process would take, when Dune would become green and lush. Kynes had tallied up his estimates and calmly looked down at the number. In the manner of a teacher answering a child who has asked an absurdly simple question, Kynes shrugged and told them, "It will take anywhere from three hundred to five hundred years. Maybe a little more."

Some of the Fremen bit back groans of despair, while the rest listened stoically to the Umma, and then set about doing what he asked. *Three hundred to five hundred years.* Long-term thinking, beyond their personal lifetimes. The Fremen had to alter their ways.

Seeing a vision from God, the would-be assassin Uliet had sacrificed himself for this man. From that moment on, the Fremen had been fully convinced of Kynes's divine inspiration. He had only to point, and any Fremen in the sietch would do as he bid.

The feeling of power might have been abused by any other person. But Pardot Kynes simply took it in stride and continued his work. He envisioned the future in terms of eons and worlds, not in terms of individuals or small plots of land.

Now, as the sun vanished below the sands in a brassy symphony of color, Kynes drained the last drops of his spice coffee, then wiped a forearm across his sandy beard. Despite what Heinar had said, he found it difficult to reflect patiently on the past year . . . the demands of the labors for centuries to come seemed so much more significant, so much more demanding of his attention.

"Heinar, how many Fremen are there?" he asked, staring across the serene open desert. He'd heard tales of many other sietches, had seen isolated Fremen in the Harkonnen towns and villages . . . but they seemed like the ghosts of an endangered species. "How many in the whole world?"

"Do you wish us to count our numbers, Umma Kynes?" Heinar asked, not in disbelief, simply clarifying an order.

"I need to know your population if I'm to project our terraforming activities. I must understand just how many workers we have available."

Heinar stood up. "It shall be done. We shall number our sietches, and tally the people in them. I will send sandriders and distrans bats to all the communities, and we shall have an accounting for you soon."

"Thank you." Kynes picked up his cup, but before he could gather the dishes himself, Frieth rushed out of the cave shadows—she must have been waiting there for them to finish—and gathered up the pieces of the coffee service. Her pregnancy hadn't slowed her down at all.

The first Fremen census, Kynes thought. *A momentous occasion.*

BRIGHT-EYED AND EAGER, Stilgar came to Kynes's cavern quarters the next morning. "We are packing for your long journey, Umma Kynes. Far to the south. We have important things to show you."

Since his recovery from the Harkonnen knife wound, Stilgar had become one of Kynes's most devoted followers. He seemed to draw status from his relationship with the Planetologist, his brother-in-law. Stilgar served not for himself, though, but for the greater good of the Fremen.

"How long will the journey be?" Kynes inquired. "And where are we going?"

The young man's grin sparkled, a broad display of white. "A surprise! This is something you must see, or you may not believe. Think of it as a gift from us to you."

Curious, Kynes looked over at his work alcove. He would bring along his notes to document this journey. "But how long will it take?"

"Twenty thumpers," Stilgar answered in the terminology of the deep desert, then called over his shoulder as he left, "Far to the south."

Kynes's wife Frieth, now enormously pregnant, nevertheless spent long hours working the looms and the stillsuit-repair benches. This morning Kynes finished his coffee and breakfasted at her side, though they spoke little to each other. Frieth simply watched him, and he felt he didn't understand a thing.

Fremen women seemed to have their own separate world, their own place in the society of these desert dwellers, with no connection to the interaction Kynes had found elsewhere in the Imperium. It was said, though, that Fremen women were among the most vicious of fighters on the battlefield, and that if an enemy were left wounded and at the mercy of these ferocious women, he would be better served to kill himself outright.

Then, too, there was the unanswered mystery of the Sayyadinas, the holy women of the sietch. Thus far Kynes had seen only one of their number, dressed in a long black robe like that of a Bene Gesserit Reverend Mother—and no Fremen seemed willing to tell him much about them. *Different worlds, different mysteries.*

Someday, Kynes thought it might be interesting to compile a sociological study of how different cultures reacted and adapted to extreme environments. He wondered what the harsh realities of a world could do to the natural instincts and traditional roles of the sexes. But he already had too much work to do. Besides, he was a Planetologist, not a sociologist.

Finishing his meal, Kynes leaned forward and kissed his Fremen wife. Smiling, he patted her rounded belly beneath her robes. "Stilgar says I must accompany him on a journey. I'll be back as soon as I can."

"How long?" she inquired, thinking of the baby's impending birth. Apparently Kynes, obsessed with his long view of events on this planet, had not noted his own child's expected due date and had forgotten to allow for it in his plans.

"Twenty thumpers," he said, though he wasn't exactly certain how much distance that meant.

Frieth raised her eyebrows in quiet surprise, then lowered her gaze and began to clean up their breakfast dishes. "Even the longest journey may pass more quickly when the heart is content." Her tone betrayed only the slightest disappointment. "I shall await your return, my husband." She hesitated, then said, "Choose a good worm."

Kynes didn't know what she meant.

Moments later, Stilgar and eighteen other young Fremen decked out in full desert garb led Kynes through the tortuous passages down and out of the barrier mountain and onto the enormous western sea of sands. Kynes felt a pang of worry. The parched expanse seemed too far and too dangerous. Now he was glad he wasn't alone.

"We're going across the equator and below, Umma Kynes, to where we Fremen have other lands, our own secret projects. You shall see."

Kynes's eyes widened; he had heard only grim and terrible stories about the uninhabitable southern regions. He stared into the forbidding distance as Stilgar rapidly checked over the Planetologist's stillsuit, tightening fastenings and adjusting filters to his own satisfaction. "But how will we travel?" He knew the sietch had its own ornithopter, just a skimmer actually, not nearly large enough to carry so many people.

Stilgar looked at him with an expectant expression. "We shall *ride*, Umma Kynes." He nodded toward the youth who had long ago taken a wounded Stilgar back to the sietch in Kynes's groundcar. "Ommun will become a sandrider this day. It is a great event among our people."

"I'm sure it is," Kynes said, his curiosity piqued.

In their desert-stained robes the Fremen marched out across the sand, walking single file. Beneath the robes they wore stillsuits, and on their feet *temag* desert boots. Their indigo-blue eyes gazed out of the far past.

One dark figure raced forward along a dune crest several hundred meters ahead of the rest of his group. There he took a long dark stake and shoved it into the sand, tinkering with controls until finally Kynes could hear the reverberating *thump* of repetitive pounding.

Kynes had already seen such a thing during Glossu Rabban's ultimately frustrating worm hunt. "He's trying to make a worm come?"

Stilgar nodded. "If God wishes."

Kneeling on the sands, Ommun removed a cloth-wrapped bundle of tools. These he sorted and laid out neatly. Long iron hooks, sharp goads, and coils of rope.

"Now what is he doing?" Kynes asked.

The thumper pounded its rhythm into the sand. The Fremen troop waited, carrying packs and supplies.

"Come. We must be ready for the arrival of Shai-Hulud," Stilgar said, nudging the Planetologist to follow as they trudged into position on the sun-drenched dunes. The Fremen whispered among themselves.

Presently Kynes detected what he had experienced only once before, the unforgettable hissing, rushing roar of a sandworm's approach as it was drawn inexorably to the throb of the thumper.

On top of the dune Ommun crouched, grasping his hooks and goads. Long curls of rope hung at his waist. He remained perfectly motionless. His Fremen brethren waited on the crest of a nearby dune.

"There! Do you see it?" Stilgar said, hardly able to suppress his excitement. He pointed off to the south where the sand rippled as if a subterranean warship were heading straight for the thumper.

Kynes didn't know what was going on. Did Ommun intend to battle the great beast? Some sort of a ceremony or sacrifice before their long journey across the desert?

"Be ready," Stilgar said and grasped Kynes's arm. "We will help you in every way we can."

Before the Planetologist could ask another question, a roaring vortex of sand formed around the thumper. Alert and battle-ready, Ommun skittered back, crouching down, ready to spring.

Then the enormous mouth of the sandworm emerged from the depths and engulfed the thumper. The monster's broad-ringed back rose out of the desert.

Ommun sprinted, running with all his might to keep pace with the moving worm, but he wallowed in the loose sand. Then he sprang onto the arched, segmented back using the hooks and claws to haul himself atop one of the worm segments.

Kynes stared in awe, unable to organize his thoughts or comprehend what the daring young man was doing. *This can't be happening,* he thought. *It's not possible.*

Ommun dug one of his scooplike hooks into the crevice between worm segments and then yanked hard, separating the well-protected rings and exposing pinkish flesh underneath.

The worm rolled to keep its sensitive exposed segment away from the abrasive sands. Ommun scrambled up and planted another hook, spreading wide a second segment so that the worm was forced to rise higher out of its secret world beneath the desert. At the highest point on the worm's back, behind its huge head, the young Fremen planted a stake and dropped his long ropes so that they hung from the sides. Now he stood tall and proud on the worm, signaling for the others to come.

Cheering, the Fremen ran forward, bringing Kynes with them. He stumbled to keep up. Three other young men scaled the ropes, adding more of what they called "maker hooks" to keep the worm above the dunes. The big creature began to move forward, but in a confused fashion, as if unable to understand why these bothersome creatures were goading it.

As the Fremen kept pace, they tossed up supplies; packs were lashed to the worm's back with more ropes. The first riders assembled a small structure as fast as they could. Prodded by Stilgar, an astonished Kynes ran up beside the towering worm. The Planetologist could feel friction heat rising from beneath, and he tried to imagine what awesome chemical fires formed a furnace deep within the worm itself.

"Up you go, Umma Kynes!" Stilgar shouted, helping him place his feet into loops in the ropes. Clumsily, Kynes scrambled up, his desert boots finding purchase on the worm's rough hide. He climbed and climbed. The simmering energy of Shai-Hulud caused him to lose his breath, but Stilgar helped him to the top where the other Fremen riders had gathered.

They had assembled a crude platform and seat for him, a palanquin. The other Fremen stood, holding their ropes against the enormous worm as if it were a bucking steed. Gratefully, Kynes took the proffered seat and held on to the arms. He had a disconcerting feeling up here, as if he didn't belong and could easily be toppled off and crushed to death. The rolling movement of the worm made his stomach lurch.

"Normally such seats are reserved for our Sayyadinas," Stilgar said. "But we know you do not have the training to ride Shai-Hulud, and so this shall be a place of honor for our prophet. There is no shame in it."

Kynes nodded distractedly and looked ahead. The other Fremen congratulated Ommun, who had successfully completed this important rite of passage. He was now a respected sandrider, a true man of the sietch.

Ommun pulled on the ropes and hooks, guiding the worm. "Haiiii-

Yoh!" The huge sinuous creature raced across the sands, heading south. . . .

KYNES RODE ALL that day, with the dry, dusty wind blowing in his face and sunlight reflecting off the sands. He had no way of estimating the speed at which the worm cruised, but he knew it must be astonishing.

As the hot breezes whipped around him, he could smell freshets of oxygen and the flinty burned-stone odors of the worm's passage. In the absence of extensive plant cover on Dune, the Planetologist realized the worms themselves must generate much of the atmospheric oxygen.

It was all Kynes could do to hold on to his palanquin. He had no way to access his notes and records in the pack on his back. What a magnificent report this would make—though he knew in his heart he could never give such information to the Emperor. No one but the Fremen knew this secret, and it must remain that way. *We are actually riding a worm!* He had other obligations now, new and far more important allegiances.

Centuries earlier, the Imperium had placed biological testing stations at strategic points on the surface of Dune, but such facilities had fallen into disrepair. In recent months Kynes had been reopening them, using a few Imperial troops assigned to the planet just to maintain appearances; for the most part, though, he staffed them with his own Fremen. He was amazed at the ability of his sietch brothers to infiltrate the system, find things for themselves, and employ technology. They were a marvelously adaptable breed—and adapting was the only way to survive on a place like Dune.

Under Kynes's direction the Fremen workers stripped equipment from the isolated biological stations, took necessary items back to their sietches, and filled out paperwork to report the pieces as lost or damaged; the oblivious Imperium then replaced the losses with new instruments so that the station monitors could continue their work. . . .

After hours of rapid travel across the Great Flat, the enormous worm became sluggish, exhibiting obvious fatigue, and Ommun had difficulty exerting control. The worm showed signs of wanting to bury itself beneath the sand, increasingly willing to risk abrading its sensitive, exposed tissue.

Finally Ommun brought the behemoth around until it ground to a halt, exhausted. The troop of desert men dropped off while Kynes slid down the rough worm segments onto loose sand. Ommun tossed down the remaining packs and dismounted, letting the worm—too utterly tired to turn and attack them—wallow its way into the sands. The Fremen removed the hooks so the worm, their Shai-Hulud, could recover.

The men sprinted to a line of rock, where there would be caves and shelter, and—Kynes was surprised to see—a small sietch that welcomed them for the night with food and conversation. Word of the Planetologist's dream had spread to all the secret places across Dune, and the sietch leader there told them it was his great honor to host Umma Kynes.

The next day the group set off again on another sandworm, and another. Kynes soon gained a more complete understanding of what Stilgar had meant with his assessment of a "twenty-thumper" journey.

The wind was fresh, and the sand was bright, and the Fremen took enormous pleasure in their grand adventure. Kynes sat atop his palanquin like an emperor himself, looking out over the desertscape. For him the dunes were endlessly fascinating, and yet strangely the same at so many latitudes.

Near Heinar's sietch a month earlier, Kynes had flown alone in his small Imperial ornithopter, exploring aimlessly. He had been blown off course by a small storm. He'd held control, even against the gusting winds, but he had been awestruck to look down upon the open sands where the storm had scoured clean a flat white basin—a salt pan.

Kynes had seen such things before, but never here on Dune. The geological formation looked like a white mirrored oval, marking the boundaries of what had once been an open sea thousands of years ago. By his estimate, the pan was three hundred kilometers long. It thrilled him to imagine that in the past, this basin might have been a large inland ocean.

Kynes had landed the 'thopter and stepped out in his stillsuit, ducking low and squinting into the blowing dust. He knelt and dug his fingers into the powdery white surface. He tasted his fingertip to confirm what he'd suspected. *Bitter salt.* Now he could have no doubt that there *had* once been open water on this world. But for some reason it had all disappeared.

As successive sandworms took them below the equator and into the deep southern portion of the wasteland planet, Kynes saw many other such things to remind him of his discovery: glinting depressions that might have been the remnants of ancient lakes, other open water. He mentioned these things to his Fremen guides, but they could explain them only by myths and legends that made no scientific sense. His fellow travelers seemed more intent on their destination.

Finally, after exhausting and long days, they left the last worm behind. The Fremen pushed on into the rocky landscapes of the deep southern regions of Dune, near the antarctic circle where the great Shai-Hulud refused to travel. Though a few water merchants had explored the northern ice caps, the lower latitudes remained primarily uninhabited, avoided, shrouded in mystery. No one came here—except for these Fremen.

Growing more and more excited, the troop walked for a day over gravelly ground, until finally Kynes saw what they had been so eager to show him. Here, the Fremen had created and tended a vast treasure.

Not far from the diminutive polar ice cap in a region where he had been told the weather was too cold and inhospitable for habitation, the Fremen of various sietches had set up a secret camp. Following the length of a wash, they entered a rugged canyon. The floor was composed of stones rounded from long-ago running water. The air was chilly, but warmer than he had ever expected so deep in the antarctic circle.

From a sheer cliff overhead where ice and cold winds at the top gave way to warmer air in the depths, water actually trickled from cracks in the rock—and ran seasonally along the length of the wash they had followed to get there. The Fremen teams had cleverly installed solar mirrors and magnifiers in the cliff walls to warm the air and melt frost from the ground. And there, in the rocky soil, they had nurtured plants.

Kynes was speechless. It was his dream, before his very eyes!

He wondered if the source could be water from hot springs, but upon touching it he found it to be cool. He tasted, and found it not sulfurous but refreshing—easily the best he had drunk since coming to

Dune. Pure water, not recycled a thousand times through filters and stillsuits.

"Behold our secret, Umma Kynes," Stilgar said. "We have done all this in less than a year."

Tufts of hardy grass grew in moist patches on the floor of the arroyo, bright desert sunflowers, even the low, creeping vines of a tough gourd plant. But most amazing of all, Kynes saw rows of stunted young date palms, clinging to life, sucking up the moisture that found its way through cracks in the porous rock and seeped up from a water table beneath the canyon floor.

"Palm trees!" he said. "You've already begun."

"Yes, Umma." Stilgar nodded. "We can see a glimpse of Dune's future here. As you promised us, it *can* be done. Fremen from all across the world have already begun your tasks of scattering grasses on the downwind sides of the dunes to anchor them."

Kynes beamed. So, they had been listening to him after all! Those scattered grasses would spread out their webwork of roots, retaining water, stabilizing the dunes. With equipment stolen from the biological testing stations, the Fremen could continue their work of cutting catchbasins, erecting windstills, and finding other means to grasp every droplet of water borne on the wind. . . .

His group remained in the sheltered canyon for several days, and Kynes felt giddy with what he saw there. As they camped and slept and walked among the palmaries, Fremen from other sietches came at intervals. This place seemed to be a new gathering point for the hidden people. Emissaries arrived to gaze with awe upon the palm trees and plants growing in the open air, upon the faint smear of moisture oozing from the rocks.

One evening a single sandrider came trudging in carrying his gear, looking for Umma Kynes. Breathless, the newly arrived traveler lowered his eyes, as if he didn't want to meet the Planetologist's gaze.

"At your command, our numbering has been completed," he announced. "We have received word from all the sietches, and we now know how many Fremen there are."

"Good," Kynes said, smiling. "I need an approximate number so I can plan for our work." Then he waited expectantly.

The young man looked up and stared at him directly with blue-in-blue eyes. "The sietches are counted in excess of five hundred."

Kynes drew a quick breath. Far more than he had suspected!

"And the number of actual Fremen on Dune is approximately ten million. Would you like me to compile the exact numbers, Umma Kynes?"

Kynes staggered backward with a gasp. Incredible! The Imperial estimates and the Harkonnen reports had implied mere hundreds of thousands, a million at the very most.

"Ten million!" He hugged the astonished young Fremen messenger. So many willing workers. *With such an army of laborers, we can indeed remake an entire planet!*

The messenger beamed and stepped back, bowing at the honor the Planetologist had shown him.

"And there is more news, Umma Kynes," the man said. "I've been instructed to tell you that your wife Frieth has given birth to a strong young son who is sure to be the pride of his sietch one day."

Kynes gasped and didn't know what to say. He was a father! He looked at Ommun and Stilgar and the members of his exploration team. The Fremen raised their hands and shouted congratulations to him. He had not let it penetrate through his consciousness until now, but he felt a flood of pride washing over his surprise.

Considering his personal blessing, Kynes looked at the palm trees, at the growing grasses and flowers, and then up at the narrow slice of blue sky framed by canyon walls. Frieth had given birth to a son!

"And now the Fremen number ten million *and one*," he said.

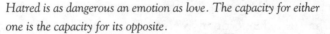

Hatred is as dangerous an emotion as love. The capacity for either one is the capacity for its opposite.

> —Cautionary Instructions for the Sisterhood,
> Bene Gesserit Archives, Wallach IX

The two dim suns of the Kuentsing binary system shone through the murky skies of Bela Tegeuse. The blood-red nearer sun imparted a purplish cast to the afternoon sky, while the icy-white primary—too distant to add much heat or light—hovered like an illuminated hole in the twilit heavens. A scrubby-surfaced and unappealing planet, it was not on any of the main Guild transspace routes, and Heighliners didn't often stop here.

In this dismal place, the Lady supervised her above-ground gardens and tried to remind herself that this was her temporary home. Even after the better part of a year, she felt herself a stranger here.

She stared into the cold gloom and across the agricultural fields at her hired local workers. Under a false name, she had used some of her remaining hoarded assets to buy a small estate, hoping to live here . . . and just survive until she could be reunited with the others. Since her desperate flight, she had not seen or heard from them, nor had she let her guard down for an instant. Elrood still lived, and the hunters were still out there.

Flat glowdisks spread full-spectrum light over the fields,

pampering the rows of exotic vegetables and fruits that would be sold at a premium to wealthy functionaries.

Beyond the edges of the fields, the native vegetation of Bela Tegeuse was bristly and hardy, not welcoming at all. Kuentsing's natural sunlight wasn't bright enough to foster sufficient photosynthesis for the delicate plants in the Lady's crops.

She felt the brisk cold against her face. Her sensitive skin, once caressed by an Emperor, was now chapped and raw from the harsh elements. But she had vowed to be strong, to adapt and endure. And it would have been so much easier to endure if only she could tell the people she cared about that she was alive and safe. She ached to see them, but didn't dare make contact, because of the risk to herself and those who had fled with her.

Harvesting machinery clattered along the neat rows of crops, plucking ripe produce. The brilliant glowdisks cast extended shadows like stealthy creatures that prowled the fields. Some of the shaggy hired workers joined in a singsong chant as they moved about gathering crops too fragile for mechanical picking. Suspensor baskets ready for market waited at the pickup station.

Only a few of her most loyal household retainers had been allowed to accompany her here in this new life. She hadn't wanted any loose ends, no one who could report to Imperial spies—neither had she wanted to put faithful companions in danger.

Only with extreme care did she dare talk with the few familiar people who lived near her on Bela Tegeuse. A handful of furtive conversations, quick glances, and smiles were the most she dared. Comeyes or operatives could be anywhere.

With a carefully laid trail of identity documents, the Lady had become a respectable woman named Lizett, a widow whose fictitious husband—a local merchant and minor official of CHOAM—had left her enough financial resources to run this modest estate.

Her entire existence had altered: no more pampered activities at court, no music, banquets, or receptions, no functions with the Landsraad—not even tedious Council meetings. She simply lived from day to day, remembering old times and longing for them while accepting the reality that this new life might be the best she could ever obtain.

Worst of all, she might never see her loved ones again.

Like an inspector surveying her troops, the Lady walked down the lanes of crops, assessing vermilion spiny fruits that dangled on suspended vines. She had worked hard to memorize the names of the exotic produce she grew. It was important to put up a convincing front, to be able to make idle conversation with anyone and avoid arousing suspicion.

Whenever she appeared outside her manor house, she wore a lovely necklace of Ixian manufacture, a disguised hologenerator. It shrouded her face with a field that distorted her fine features, softened her cheekbones, widened her delicate chin, altered the color of her eyes. She felt safe . . . enough.

Pausing to look up, she saw a glittering rain of shooting stars near the horizon. Across the dim landscape the lights of ranches and a distant village shimmered. But this was something else entirely. Artificial lights—transports or shuttles?

Bela Tegeuse was not a populous planet. Its fortunes and resources were small, its chief claim to history a dark and bloody one: Long ago, it had been the site of slave colonies, hardy but struggling villages from which slaves were harvested and subsequently planted on other worlds. She felt like a prisoner herself . . . but at least she had her life and knew her family was safe.

"No matter what, never let your guard down, my love," her husband had warned as he parted company from her. "Never."

In this constant state of alert, the Lady noticed the spotlights of three ornithopters as they approached from the distant spaceport. The flying craft cruised low across the flat, parched landscape. They had turned on their full nighttime search beacons, though this was the best daylight Bela Tegeuse could manage, at the height of the double afternoon.

She felt cold fingers wrap around her heart, but nonetheless stood tall and drew her dark blue cloak around her. Her House colors would have been preferable, but she no longer dared even keep such items in her wardrobe.

A voice called from the main house. "Madame Lizett! Someone is coming, and they refuse to answer our hails!"

Turning, she saw the narrow-shouldered figure of Omer, one of her primary assistants from the old days, a man who had accompanied her here, not sure what else to do. Certainly nothing else would be as important or fulfilling, Omer had assured her, and she was grateful for his devotion.

The Lady considered fleeing the approaching 'thopters, but dismissed the idea. If these intruders were whom she feared they might be, she had no chance of escape. And if her intuition was wrong, she wouldn't need to run.

The clustered ornithopters arrived overhead, wings fluttering and engines roaring. They set down roughly, indiscriminately, upon her planted fields, knocking her full-spectrum glowdisks out of alignment and crushing crops.

When the doors of the three ships slid open and troops emerged, she knew she was doomed.

In a dreamlike vision, she thought back to a happier time, the arrival of quite different troops. It had been in her younger days at the Imperial Court, when the headiness of being a royal courtesan had begun to fade. The Emperor had spent much time with her for a while, but after his interest waned he had moved on to other concubines. It was to be expected. She hadn't felt snubbed, since Elrood continued to provide for her.

But then one day, after the rebellion on Ecaz had been crushed, she had watched a victory parade of Imperial fighters marching down the streets of Kaitain. The banners were so bright they made her eyes ache, the uniforms perfect and clean, the men so brave. At the head of the column, she had caught her first glimpse of her future husband, a proud warrior with broad shoulders and a broad grin. Even from a distance, his very presence had dazzled her, and she had felt her passions awaken, seeing him as the greatest among all of the returning soldiers. . . .

These soldiers arriving today on Bela Tegeuse were different, though—much more frightening in the dress gray-and-black of Sardaukar uniforms.

A Burseg troop commander stepped forward, flashing his rank insignia. With an upward chop of his hand, he signaled for his men to take up their positions.

Maintaining her pretense with only a shred of hope, the Lady strode forward to meet him, chin high. "I am Madame Lizett, the owner of this estate." Her voice was hard as she scowled over at the destroyed crops. "Do you or your employers intend to make reparations for all the property damage your clumsiness just caused?"

"Shut your mouth!" one of the soldiers snapped, snatching up his lasgun.

Foolish, the Lady thought. *I could have been wearing a shield.* If so, and if he had fired, this section of Bela Tegeuse would have been obliterated in a pseudoatomic explosion.

The Burseg commander held up his hand to silence the soldier, and she recognized the planned gambit: a brash, uncontrolled soldier to intimidate her, a firm military leader showing the face of reason. Good soldier, bad soldier.

"We are here on Imperial orders," said the Burseg. "We're investigating the whereabouts of surviving traitors of a certain renegade House. Through the right of acquisition, we require your cooperation."

"I am unfamiliar with the legalities," the Lady said. "But I know nothing of renegades. I'm just a widow trying to run a modest farm here. Allow my attorneys to consult with you. I'll be happy to cooperate in whatever manner I can, though I'm afraid you'll be disappointed."

"We won't be disappointed," the brash soldier growled.

Around them, her hired workers had ceased their activities, frozen in place. The Burseg stepped forward and stood directly in front of the Lady, who did not flinch. He studied her face, frowning. She knew her holo-masked appearance did not match what the man expected to see. She stared back at him, meeting his flat gaze.

Before she understood his intention, his hand snatched her Ixian necklace and yanked it away. She felt no different, but she knew her disguise had dissolved.

"That's more like it," said the Burseg. "You know nothing of renegades, eh?" He laughed scornfully.

She glared at him. Sardaukar troops continued to file out of the three 'thopters, taking up positions around her. Some of them burst into her manor house, while others searched the barn, sun-silo, and other outbuildings. Did they expect her to be harboring a major military force? Compared to her accustomed lifestyle, it seemed she could barely afford new clothes and hot food.

Another grim-faced Sardaukar grabbed her arm. She tried to pull away, but he pushed up the sleeve of her cloak and, in a flash, scratched her with a small curette. She gasped, thinking the soldier had poisoned her, but the Sardaukar stood back calmly to analyze the blood sample he had stolen.

"Identity confirmed, sir," he said, looking over at his Burseg commander. "Lady Shando Vernius of Ix."

The troops stepped back, but Shando did not move. She knew what was coming.

For over a year, the old Emperor had grown increasingly irrational, his mind failing, his body trembling. Elrood suffered under more delusions than usual, more hatred than one body should have contained. But he remained the Emperor, and his decrees were followed explicitly.

The only question in her mind was whether they would torture her first to acquire information she didn't have about Dominic's whereabouts. Or whether they would just finish the job.

Through a side door of the big house, Omer came running, shouting. His black hair was in disarray. He waved a crude hunting weapon he had found in a storage locker. *Such a fool*, she thought. *Brave, dear, and loyal—but nonetheless a fool.*

"My Lady!" Omer shouted. "Leave her alone!"

A few of the Sardaukar aimed at him and at the shaggy workers in the field, but most kept their weapons trained on her. She looked up to the sky and thought of her loving husband and children and hoped only that they wouldn't meet similar ends. Even at this moment she had to admit that, given the choice, she would do it all again. She did not regret the loss in prestige or riches that leaving the royal Court had cost her. Shando had known a love that few members of the nobility had ever experienced.

Poor Roody, she thought with a flash of pity. *You never understood that kind of love.* As usual, Dominic had been right. In her mind, she saw him again as he was when she had first met the Earl of House Vernius: a handsome young soldier, returned victorious from battle.

Shando raised one hand to touch the vision of Dominic's face one last time . . .

Then all the Sardaukar opened fire.

I must rule with eye and claw—as the hawk among lesser birds.
—DUKE PAULUS ATREIDES,
The Atreides Assertion

Duke Leto Atreides.

Ruler of the planet Caladan, member of the Landsraad, head of a Great House . . . These titles meant nothing to him. His father was dead.

Leto felt small. Defeated and confused, he was not ready for the burdens that had been thrust upon him so cruelly at the age of fifteen. As he sat in the uncomfortable, overlarge chair where the blustery Old Duke had so often held formal and informal court, Leto felt out of place, an imposter.

I am not ready to be Duke!

He had declared seven days of official mourning, during which he'd been able to sidestep most of the difficult business as head of House Atreides. Simply dealing with the condolences from other Great Houses proved almost too much for him . . . especially the formal letter from Emperor Elrood IX, written no doubt by his Chamberlain but signed with the old man's palsied hand. "A great man of the people has fallen," the Emperor's note read. "You have my sincere condolences and prayers for your future."

For some inexplicable reason, this had sounded to Leto like a threat—something sinister in the slant of the signature, perhaps, or in the selection of words. Leto had burned the message in the fireplace of his private quarters.

Most important of all to him, Leto received heartfelt gestures of grief from the people of Caladan: fresh flowers, baskets of fish, embroidered banners, poems and songs written by would-be bards, carvings, even drawings and paintings depicting the Old Duke in his glory, victorious in the bullring.

In private, where no one could see his weakness, Leto cried. He knew how much the people had loved Duke Paulus, and he remembered the feeling of power that had blanketed him the day he and his father had stood holding their bull's-head trophy in the Plaza de Toros. At that time, he had longed to become Duke himself, had felt the love and loyalty wrapped around him. *House Atreides!*

Now he wished for any other fate in the universe.

Lady Helena had locked herself in her chambers and ignored the servants who tried to attend her. Leto had never observed much love or affection between his parents, and right now he couldn't tell if his mother's grief was sincere or merely an act. The only people she agreed to see were her personal priests and spiritual advisors. Helena clung to the subtle meanings she pried loose from verses of the Orange Catholic Bible.

Leto knew he needed to bring himself out of this morass—he had to reach deep for strength and turn to the business of running Caladan. Duke Paulus would have scorned Leto's misery and chastised him for not immediately facing the priorities of his new life. "Grieve during your private time, lad," he would have said, "but never reveal any sign of weakness on the part of House Atreides."

Silently, Leto vowed to do his best. This would be the first of many sacrifices he would no doubt have to make in his new position.

Prince Rhombur came up beside Leto as he sat in the heavy ducal chair in the empty meeting hall. Leto brooded, his eyes fixed on a large portrait on the opposite wall that showed his father in full matador regalia. Rhombur put a hand on his companion's shoulder and squeezed. "Leto, have you eaten? You've got to maintain your strength."

Taking a deep breath, Leto turned to look at his comrade from Ix, whose broad face was filled with concern. "No, I haven't. Would you care to join me for breakfast?" He rose stiffly from the uncomfortable chair. It was time to go about his duties.

Thufir Hawat accompanied them at a morning meal that extended for hours as they laid out plans and strategies for the new regime. During a pause in the discussion, the warrior Mentat bowed his head and met young Leto's gray-eyed gaze. "If I have not yet made it apparent, my Duke, I give you my utmost loyalty and renew my pledge to House Atreides. I will do everything I can to assist and advise you." Then his expression hardened. "But you must understand that all decisions are *yours* and yours alone. My advice may contradict Prince Rhombur's or your mother's, or that of any other advisors you choose. You must decide in each case. *You* are the Duke. You are House Atreides."

Leto trembled, feeling the responsibility hover over him like a Guild Heighliner ready to crash. "I'm aware of that, Thufir, and I'll need all the assistance I can get." He sat up straight and sipped sweet cream from a bowl of warm pundi rice pudding, prepared by one of the chefs who knew it had been his favorite as a boy. Now it didn't taste the same, though; his taste buds seemed dulled.

"How goes the investigation into my father's death? Was it truly an accident, as it appears? Or only made to look that way?"

The Mentat frowned, and a troubled expression clouded his leathery face. "I'm hesitant to say this, my Duke, but I fear it was murder. Evidence is mounting of a devious plan, indeed."

"What?" Rhombur said, pounding his fist on the table. His face flushed. "Who did this to the Duke? How?" He felt affection not only for Leto, but for the Atreides patriarch who had granted sanctuary to him and his sister. A visceral, sinking feeling told Rhombur the motivation might have been to punish Paulus for showing kindness to the Ixian exiles.

"I am the Duke, Rhombur," Leto said, resting a hand on his friend's forearm. "*I* will have to handle this."

Leto could almost hear the wheels humming inside the Mentat's complex mind. Hawat said, "Chemical analysis of muscle tissue in the Salusan bull revealed faint traces of two drugs."

"I thought the beasts were checked before every fight." Leto narrowed his eyes, but for a moment he could not drive away the memory flashes of his younger days, when he had gone to look at the massive bulls in the stables and puffy-eyed Stablemaster Yresk had let him feed the beasts—to the horror of the stableboys. "Was our veterinarian in on a plot?"

"The usual tests were performed as required, before the *paseo*." A frown on his red-stained lips, Thufir tapped his fingers on the table as he marshaled his thoughts and assessed his answer. "Unfortunately, the prescribed analyses tested for the wrong things. The bull had been enraged by a harsh stimulant that gradually built up in its body over days, delivered in time-released amounts."

"That wouldn't have been enough," Leto said, flaring his nostrils. "My father was a good fighter. The *best*."

The Mentat shook his shaggy head. "The bull was also given a neutralizing agent, a chemical that counteracted the neurotoxin in the Duke's *banderillas* and simultaneously triggered a release of the stimulant. When the bull should have been paralyzed, the stimulant was increased instead. The beast became an even more dangerous killing machine, just as the Old Duke was growing tired."

Leto glowered. With an angry lurch he rose from the breakfast table and glanced up at the omnipresent poison-snooper. He paced, letting his rice pudding grow cold. Then he turned and spoke sharply, summoning all the techniques of leadership he had been taught. "Mentat, give me a prime projection. Who would do this?"

Thufir sat motionless as he entered deep Mentat mode. Data streamed through the computer inside his skull, a human brain that simulated the capabilities of the ancient, hated enemies of mankind.

"Most likely possibility: a personal attack from a major political enemy of House Atreides. Because of the timing, I suspect it may be a punishment of the Old Duke for his support of House Vernius."

"My suspicion exactly," Rhombur muttered. The son of Dominic Vernius seemed very much an adult now, hardened and tempered, no longer just a good-natured study companion who had lived a pampered life. Since coming to Caladan he had trimmed down, tightened his muscles. His eyes had taken on a flinty gleam.

"But no House has declared kanly on us," Leto said. "In the ancient rite of vendetta there are requirements, forms to be followed, are there not, Thufir?"

"But we can't trust all of the Old Duke's enemies to adhere to such niceties," Hawat said. "We must be very cautious."

Rhombur reddened, thinking of his own family's ouster from Ix. "And there are those who twist the forms to match their needs."

"Secondary possibility," the Mentat continued. "The target could have been Duke Paulus *himself*, and not House Atreides—the result of a small vendetta or personal grudge. The culprit could perhaps be a local petitioner who didn't like a decision the Duke had made. Though this murder has galactic consequences, its cause could, ironically, be a trivial thing."

Leto shook his head. "I can't believe that. I saw how much the people loved my father. None of his subjects would turn on him, not a single one."

Hawat did not flinch. "My Duke, do not overestimate the strength of love and loyalty, and do not underestimate the power of personal hatred."

"Uh, what's a better possibility?" Rhombur inquired.

Hawat looked his Duke in the eye. "An attack to weaken House Atreides. The death of the patriarch leaves you, m'Lord, in a vulnerable position. You are young and untrained."

Leto drew in a deep breath, but restrained his temper as he listened.

"Your enemies will now see House Atreides as unstable, and could make a move against us. Your allies may also see you as a liability and support you with somewhat . . . limited enthusiasm. This is a very dangerous time for you."

"The Harkonnens?" Leto asked.

Hawat shrugged. "Possibly. Or some ally of theirs."

Leto pressed his hands against his temples and drew another deep breath. He saw Rhombur looking uneasily at him.

"Continue your investigation, Thufir," Leto said. "Since we know that drugs were introduced to the Salusan bull, I suggest you target your interrogations around the stables."

THE STABLEBOY DUNCAN Idaho stood in front of his new Duke, bowing proudly, ready to swear his fealty again. The household staff had cleaned him up, though he still wore stable clothes. The ruined garments he'd been given for the ill-fated final bullfight had been discarded. His curly black hair was disheveled.

A rage burned inside him. He was certain that Duke Paulus's death could have been avoided if someone had only listened to him. The grief struck him sharply, and he agonized over whether he might have done more: Should he have insisted harder or spoken to someone other than Stablemaster Yresk? He wondered if he should reveal what he had tried to do, but for the moment held his tongue.

Looking too small in the ducal chair, Leto Atreides narrowed his gray eyes and skewered Duncan with a gaze. "Boy, I remember when you joined our household." His face looked thinner, and much older than it had been when Duncan had first stood inside the Castle hall. "It was just after I escaped from Ix with Rhombur and Kailea."

Both of the Vernius refugees also sat in the main hall, as did Thufir Hawat and a contingent of guards. Duncan glanced over at them, then returned his attention to the young Duke.

"I heard stories of your escape from the Harkonnens, Duncan Idaho," Leto continued, "of how you were tortured and imprisoned. My father trusted you when he gave you a position here at Castle Caladan. You know how unusual it was for him to do that?" He leaned forward on the dark, wooden chair.

Duncan nodded. "Yes, m'Lord." He felt a hot flush of guilt on his face at having failed the benefactor who had been so kind to him. "Yes, I know."

"But someone drugged the Salusan bulls before my father's last fight—and you were one of those tending the beasts. You had ample opportunity. Why didn't I see you at the *paseo* when all the others marched around the arena? I remember looking for you." His voice became much sharper. "Duncan Idaho, were you sent here, all innocent-looking and indignant, as a secret assassin in the employ of the Harkonnens?"

Duncan stepped back, appalled. "Indeed not, m'Lord Duke!" he cried. "I tried to warn everyone. For days I knew something was wrong with the bulls. I told Stablemaster Yresk again and again, but he wouldn't do anything. He just laughed at me. I even argued with him. That's why I wasn't at the *paseo*. I was going to go warn the Old Duke myself, but instead the stablemaster locked me in one of the dirty stalls during the fight." Tears welled up in his eyes. "All the fine clothes your father gave me were ruined. I didn't even see him fall in the arena."

Surprised at this, Leto sat up in his father's large chair. He looked over at Hawat.

"I will find out, m'Lord," the Mentat said.

Leto scrutinized the boy. Duncan Idaho stood before him showing no fear, only deep sadness. As he studied him, Leto thought he recognized an openness and a heartfelt devotion on the young face. By appearances, this nine-year-old refugee seemed truly glad to be part of Castle Caladan, despite his demeaning, thankless chores as a stableboy.

Leto Atreides did not have many years of experience in judging devious people and weighing the hearts of men, but he had an intuition that he could trust this earnest boy. Duncan was tough and intelligent and fierce—but not treacherous.

Be cautious, Duke Leto, he told himself. *There are many tricks in the Imperium, and this could be one of them.* Then he thought of the old stablemaster; Yresk had been with Castle Caladan ever since the arranged marriage of Leto's parents. . . . *Could such a plan have been so many years in germination?* Yes, he supposed it could. Though he trembled at the implications.

Unaccompanied, the Lady Helena glided into the reception hall, taking furtive steps. Deep shadows hovered around her eyes. Leto watched his mother slip into the empty chair beside his, the one reserved for times when she had sat beside her husband. Straight-backed and without words, she examined the young boy before them.

Moments later, Stablemaster Yresk was unceremoniously brought into the hall by Atreides guards. His shock of white hair was mussed, and his baggy eyes seemed wide and uncertain. When Thufir Hawat finished summarizing the story Duncan had told, the stablemaster laughed and his bony shoulders sagged with exaggerated relief. "After all the years I served you, would you believe this stable-rat, this *Harkonnen?*" He rolled his puffy eyes in indignation. "Please, m'Lord!"

Overly dramatic, Leto thought; Hawat saw it, too.

Yresk placed a finger to his lips, as if considering a possibility. "Now that you mention it, m'Lord, it could well be that the boy himself was poisoning the bull. I couldn't watch him every moment."

"That's a lie!" Duncan shouted. "I wanted to tell the Duke, but you locked me in a stall. Why didn't you try to stop the bullfight? I warned you and warned you—and now the Duke is dead."

Hawat listened, his eyes distant, his lips moist and cranberry-stained from a fresh swallow of sapho juice. Leto saw he had entered Mentat mode again, racing through all the data he recalled of the events involving young Duncan and Yresk as well.

"Well?" Leto asked the stablemaster. He forced himself not to think of old times with the lanky man who had always smelled of sweat and manure.

"The stable-rat may have prattled some at me, m'Lord, but he was afraid of the bulls. I can't simply cancel a bullfight because a child thinks the beasts are terrifying." He snorted. "I took care of this pup, gave him every chance—"

"Yet you didn't listen to him when he warned you about the bulls, and now my father is dead," Leto said, noting that Yresk suddenly seemed afraid. "Why would you do that?"

"Possible projection," Hawat said. "Through the Lady Helena, Yresk has worked for House Richese all his life. Richese has had ties to the Harkonnens in the past, as well as an adversarial relationship with Ix. He may not even be aware of his part in the overall scheme or—"

"What? This is absurd!" Yresk insisted. He scratched his white hair. "I have nothing to do with the Harkonnens." He flashed a glance at the Lady Helena, but she refused to meet his gaze.

"Don't interrupt my Mentat," Leto warned.

Thufir Hawat studied Lady Helena, whose icy stare was leveled at him. Then his gaze slid to her son, where it remained as he continued to lay out his projection: "Summary: The marriage of Paulus Atreides to Helena of House Richese was dangerous, even at the time. The Landsraad saw it as a way to weaken Richese/Harkonnen ties, while Count Ilban Richese accepted the marriage as a last-ditch effort to salvage some of his family fortune at the time they were losing Arrakis. As for House Atreides, Duke Paulus received a formal CHOAM directorship and became a voting member of the Council—something this family might never otherwise have achieved.

"When the wedding party came here with Lady Helena, however, perhaps not all of her retainers granted their full loyalty to Atreides. Contact could have been made between Harkonnen agents and Stablemaster Yresk . . . without Lady Helena's knowledge, of course."

"That's wild conjecture, especially for a Mentat," Yresk said. He looked for support from anyone in the room, Leto noticed—with the exception of Helena, whose eyes he now seemed to avoid. On his thin throat, his Adam's apple bobbed up and down.

Leto stared at his mother sitting in silence beside him, at the set of her jaw. A sharp cold sliced unbidden down his spine. Through the carved wood of their closed bedroom door, Leto had heard her words concerning his father's Vernius policy. *You're the one who's made a choice here, Paulus. And you've made the wrong one.* Now the words echoed in Leto's head. *That choice will cost you and our House dearly.*

"Uh, nobody really watches a stablemaster, Leto," Rhombur pointed out in a low voice.

But Leto continued to observe his mother. Stablemaster Yresk had come to Caladan as part of Helena's wedding entourage from Richese. Could she have turned to him? What sort of hold did she have on the man?

His throat went dry as all the pieces interlocked in his mind with a sudden realization that must have been similar to what a Mentat experienced. *She* had done it! Lady Helena Atreides herself had set the wheels in motion. Oh, perhaps she'd had some outside assistance, possibly even from Harkonnens . . . and most certainly Yresk had been the one to carry out the actual details.

But she herself had made the decision to punish Paulus. He knew it in the core of his soul. With her fifteen-year-old son, she would now control Caladan and make the decisions *she* believed best.

Leto, my son, you *are Duke Atreides now.* Those had been his mother's words only moments after her husband's death. An odd reaction for a shocked and grief-stricken woman.

"Please stop this," Yresk said, wringing his hands. "M'Lord, I would never betray the House I serve." He pointed at Duncan. "But you *know* this stable-rat must be a Harkonnen. He came from Giedi Prime not that long ago."

Lady Helena sat rigidly, and when she finally spoke, her voice cracked, as if she hadn't used it much in recent days. She leveled a challenging look at her son. "You've known Yresk since you were a child, Leto. Would you accuse a member of my entourage? Don't be ridiculous."

"No accusations yet, Mother," Leto said very carefully. "It's just discussion at this point." As leader of House Atreides, he had to work hard to distance himself from his childhood, from when he had been an eager boy asking the white-haired stablemaster if he could see the bulls. Yresk had taught him how to pet various animals, ride some of the older mounts, tie knots, and fix harnesses.

But the wide-eyed child Leto was the new Duke of House Atreides.

"We must study the evidence before we draw any conclusions."

Emotions roiled across Yresk's face, and suddenly Leto was afraid of what the stablemaster might say. Pressed into a corner and afraid for his life, would he implicate Helena? The guards in the hall listened attentively. Kailea watched, drinking in every detail. Others would no doubt hear and repeat everything that was spoken here. The scandal would rock Caladan, perhaps the Landsraad itself.

Even if his mother had arranged for the accident at the bullfight, even if Yresk had done it under orders—or because he had been bribed or blackmailed somehow—Leto did not dare let the man confess it here. He required the truth, but in private. If word got out that Lady Helena had been behind the Old Duke's death, it would tear House Atreides apart. His own rule could be damaged beyond repair . . . and he would have no choice but to deal out the harshest possible justice to his own mother.

He shuddered as he thought of the play *Agamemnon*, and the curse of Atreus that had dogged his family since the dawn of history. He drew a deep breath, knowing he must be strong.

"Do what you must, lad," his father had said. "No one can blame you for that, as long as you make the right decisions."

But what was the right decision now?

Helena stood up from her chair and spoke to Leto in a cool maternal tone. "The death of my husband was no treachery—it was a punishment from God." She gestured toward Rhombur and Kailea, who seemed stunned by the proceedings. "My beloved Duke was punished for his friendship with House Vernius, for allowing these children to live in our Castle. Their family has broken the commandments, and Paulus still embraced them. My husband's pride killed him—not a lowly stablemaster. It's as simple as that."

"I've heard enough, Mother," Leto said.

Helena gave him an indignant, withering glare, as if he were a child. "I am not finished speaking. There is much to being a Duke that you couldn't possibly understand yet—"

Leto remained seated, putting all the power he could muster into his voice and composure. "I *am* the Duke, Mother, and you *will* be silent, or I shall have the guards forcibly evict you from the hall and lock you in one of the towers."

Helena's skin paled, and her eyes went wild as she fought to contain her shock. She couldn't believe her own son had spoken to her in this manner, but thought better of pressing him. As usual, she struggled to maintain appearances. She had seen similar expressions on the Old Duke's face and didn't dare bring the storm closer.

Though it would have been better for him to remain silent, Yresk shouted, "Leto, boy, you can't believe this fatherless stable-rat over me—"

Leto looked at the frantic, scarecrowish man and compared his demeanor with the proud young Duncan's. Yresk's puffy-eyed face sparkled with perspiration. "I do find him more credible, Yresk," Leto said slowly. "And never call me 'boy' again."

Hawat stepped forward. "We might retrieve further information through deep interrogation. I shall personally question this stablemaster."

Leto's gaze fell on his Mentat. "In private would be best, Thufir. No one but you." He closed his eyes for the briefest moment and swallowed hard. Later, he knew, he would have to send a message to Hawat that the stablemaster must not be allowed to survive the interrogation . . . for fear of what else he might reveal. The Mentat's fractional nod told Leto that he understood much that had been left unsaid. All information Hawat extracted would remain a secret between himself and his Duke.

Yresk howled as the guards grasped his thin arms. Before the stablemaster could shout anything, Hawat clapped a hand over his mouth.

Then, as if it had been timed to occur during the moment of greatest confusion, the guards opened the main hall doors to allow the entry of a uniformed man. He strode in, eyes fixed on Leto and Leto alone, who sat on the chair at the end of the hall. His electronic identity badge marked him as an official Courier, newly disembarked from a lighter at Cala City Spaceport. Leto stiffened, knowing this man could not possibly bear good tidings.

"M'Lord Duke, I bring terrible news." The Courier's words sent an electric shock through everyone in the Court. The hall guards holding Yresk captive stood still, and Hawat gestured for them to leave before the announcement.

The messenger marched up to the chair and stood straight, then drew deep breaths to prepare himself. Knowing the situation here on Caladan with the new Duke and the exiled Ixians, he chose his words carefully.

"It is my sad duty to inform you that the Lady Shando—branded as a renegade and traitor by Emperor Elrood IX—has been tracked down and, in accordance with Imperial decree, executed by Sardaukar on Bela Tegeuse. All members of her entourage have also been killed."

Rhombur, looking as if the wind had been knocked from him, slumped in shock onto the polished marble step beside the ducal chair. Kailea, who had watched the entire proceedings in silence, now sobbed. Tears spilled unchecked from her emerald eyes. She leaned against a wall, pounding a stone pillar with a fragile fist until blood blossomed from her hand.

Helena looked at her son with sadness and nodded. "You see, Leto? Another punishment. I was right. The Ixians and all those who assist them are cursed."

Giving his mother a look of hatred, Leto snapped to the guards, "Please take my mother to her chambers and instruct her servants to pack for a long journey." He fought to keep his voice from trembling. "I believe the stress of recent days requires that she take a quiet rest, someplace far, far from here."

In adverse circumstances, every creature becomes something else, evolving or devolving. What makes us human is that we know what we once were, and—let us hope—we remember how to change back.

—AMBASSADOR CAMMAR PILRU,
Dispatches in Defense of Ix

The hiding chamber's silent alarm system woke him again. Damp with sweat from recurring nightmares, C'tair sat bolt upright, ready to fight and fend off the invaders hunting for him.

But the Bene Tleilax hadn't found this place yet, though they had come close, using their damnable scanners. His transmission-shielded bolt-hole was equipped with an automatic internal monitor that should have operated for centuries without trouble, but the fanatical investigators used technology-scanning devices to detect the operation of unapproved machines. Sooner or later they would catch him.

Working with quiet efficiency, he scrambled to shut everything down: all the lights, ventilation, heating elements. Then he sat in the stifling utter darkness, sweating, waiting. He heard nothing except his own breathing. No one pried at the concealed door. Nothing.

After a long time, he allowed himself to move.

The random scanners would cause serious harm to his shield's ability to continue hiding him and his stockpile. C'tair knew he had to steal one of the devices. If he could analyze how the Tleilaxu technology worked, he might set up a system to counter its effects.

Most mornings, the halls and public rooms of the former Grand Palais (now a Tleilaxu government office building) were empty. C'tair slipped out of a concealed access shaft and into a storage room near the main corridor. From there, it was only a short distance to a lift tube that led straight out of the building, across to other stalactite structures, and even down to the lower levels. He could keep moving, keep up appearances—and keep himself alive. But his chances would be better if he could foil the technology scanners.

The routine investigator might still be in this facility, or the man might have already moved to a different level. C'tair sprinted out on the hunt, listening, watching corridor lights, creeping along. He had already learned all the secrets of this part of the building.

Although C'tair carried a stun-pistol and a lasgun at his side, he feared that Tleilaxu sensor nets would detect their use. Then dedicated teams would be sent out specifically to find him. That was why he held a long, sharp blade in one hand. It would be efficient and silent. The best choice.

Setting up his trap, he finally spotted a balding, pinch-faced Tleilaxu man who approached down the hallway. With two hands he held a little screen that spewed the hues and patterns of fireworks. The investigator was so intent on the readings he did not at first notice C'tair—until the dark-haired man raced forward with the knife blade extended.

C'tair wanted to shout his hatred, scream out a challenge, but he only hissed instead. The Tleilaxu man's mouth dropped open in an O to reveal little white teeth like pearls. Before the investigator could cry out, C'tair had slashed his throat.

The man tumbled to the floor in a spray of blood, but C'tair caught the scanning device before it could strike the hard surface. He stared hungrily at the scanner, barely noticing his dying enemy's convulsions as a slowing lake of blood spread across the ornate, polished tiles of what formerly had been the Grand Palais of House Vernius.

C'tair felt no remorse whatsoever. He had already committed plenty of crimes for which he would be executed if the fanatics ever got hold of him. What did one more matter, so long as his conscience was clear? How many people had the Tleilaxu annihilated? How much

Ixian history and culture had their takeover destroyed? How much blood did *they* already owe?

Moving quickly, C'tair dragged the body into the access shaft that led up to his secret quarters inside the solid rock, then cleaned up the leftover blood. Exhausted, sticky with crusting red liquid, C'tair froze for a moment as a flash of his former life pierced his hardened conscience. Looking down at his bloody hands, he wondered what the delicate and lovely Kailea Vernius would think if she saw him now. Every time they had known they would see her, C'tair and his brother had taken extraordinary care to groom themselves properly, wear dashing clothes, add a dab of cologne.

He spared just an instant to mourn what the Tleilaxu had forced him to become . . . and then wondered if Kailea had been changed as well, by whatever ordeals she had endured. He realized he didn't even know if she was still alive. C'tair swallowed hard.

But he wouldn't survive long, either, if he didn't erase the evidence of his crime and disappear back into his hiding chamber.

The Tleilaxu investigator was surprisingly heavy for his size, suggesting a dense bone structure. He dumped the gray-skinned body into a nullentropy bin; the sun would burn out in the Ixian sky before the corpse began to rot.

After wiping himself clean and changing his clothes, C'tair set to work on the primary task at hand. He eagerly took the stolen scanner back to his workbench.

It was fairly easy to figure out how to operate the unit. Its controls were rudimentary: a black touch pad and an amber screen that identified machines and technological traces. Markings were in a Tleilaxu code language, which he deciphered easily by speaking the words into a decrypter he had smuggled into the shielded room during the first frantic days after the takeover.

Understanding the innards of the Tleilaxu scanner posed a far more difficult problem. C'tair had to work with extreme caution because of the probable existence of a proprietary antitampering system that could melt down interior parts. He didn't dare take a tool to the scanner and attempt to pry it open. He would have to use passive methods.

Again he wished the spirit of old Rogo might reappear to provide valuable advice. C'tair felt very much alone in this all-but-forgotten room, and at times had to fight off the temptation to feel sorry for himself. He found strength in the realization that he was doing something extremely important. The future of Ix might rest on what covert battles he managed to win.

He had to survive and keep his hiding place intact, since his protective cocoon housed the important transspace communicator. Before long, he might also find a way of locating the survivors of House Vernius and render valuable assistance to them. Perhaps he was the only survivor who could liberate his beloved world.

And to protect the shielded room, C'tair needed to figure out the damnable Tleilaxu scanner. . . .

Finally, after days of frustration, he used a sounding device in the hope of creating a reflected schematic of the scanner's interior. To his surprise something clicked. He set the scanner down on the workbench and backed away. Then, approaching again to examine the device closely, C'tair found that a seam had opened on one side. He applied pressure on each side of the split and pulled.

The scanner opened without exploding or melting down. Before his delighted eyes he discovered not only the guts of the unit, but also a pin-activated holoprojector that caused a User Guide image to appear in the air—a dapper holo-man happy to explain everything about the scanner.

Helpful and cheery, the User Guide had no concerns about a competitor stealing the technology of the unit, since it depended upon the rare and precious "Richesian mirror," which no outsider had been able to duplicate. Constructed of unknown minerals and polymers, such mirrors were thought to contain geodome prisms within prisms.

As C'tair studied the scanner, he grudgingly admired its construction, and for the first time suspected Richesian involvement in the plot against Ix. The hatreds were long-standing, and Richesians would have gladly assisted in the destruction of their chief rivals. . . .

Now C'tair had to use his own intuitive knowledge, the scraps of components, and this Richesian mirror to create a disabling device to block the scanner. After repeated queries to the annoyingly solicitous Guide, he began to unravel a solution. . . .

THE EVENING MEETING with the black marketers had been nerve-wracking again, with many frightened glances over his shoulder, but what choice did C'tair have? Only these illicit traders had been able to procure the few components he needed for his scan-blocker.

Finally, after making his purchases, he returned to the quiet building overhead, using a biometric ID scrambler card to trick the entrance station into thinking he was a Tleilaxu technician. As he rode the lift tube up through the former Grand Palais toward his hiding room, C'tair thought of the numerous drawings he had left scattered across his workbench. He was eager to return to work.

When he stepped out into the corridor, though, C'tair realized he had arrived on the wrong floor. Instead of windowless doors and storage rooms, this level held a number of offices separated by clear plaz. Dull orange night-lights burned in the offices; bold, ominous signs on the doors and windows were written in an unknown Tleilaxu language.

He paused, recognizing the place. He hadn't gone far enough up into the solid rock layers. Once, he thought angrily, these rooms had been conference chambers, ambassadorial offices, meeting rooms for members of the Court of Earl Vernius. Now they looked so . . . so functional.

Before he could retreat, C'tair heard something on his left—a clank of metal and a scuffing noise—and ducked back toward the lift tube to return to his own floor. Too late. He'd been seen.

"You there, stranger!" a shadowy man called out in Ixian-accented Galach. "Come out where we can see you." Probably one of the collaborators—an Ixian turncoat who had sold his soul to the enemy at the expense of his own people.

Fumbling with his bioscram card, C'tair trembled at hearing the heavy sounds of approaching boots. He swiped the card through the lift-control reader. More voices called out. He expected weapons fire at any moment.

After an interminable instant, the lift tube opened—but as he dashed through the doorway, C'tair accidentally dropped the bag containing the parts he had just purchased. No time to retrieve it.

With a muttered curse he dived into the lift and ordered the correct floor in a harsh, commanding whisper. Just in time, the door clicked shut, and the sound of voices faded. He worried that the guards might disable the lift or call in Sardaukar—so he needed to exit quickly. It seemed to take forever to reach his floor.

The door opened, and C'tair peered out carefully, looking right and left. No signs of anyone here. Reaching back into the lift tube, he programmed it to stop at four other floors, then sent it off empty to soar even higher into the crustal passages.

Seconds later, C'tair stood sweating in the sanctuary of his shielded chamber, thankful to have escaped with his life, but angry at himself for his carelessness. He had lost the precious components, and also given the Tleilaxu a clue as to what he had been up to.

Now they would be looking for him specifically.

We all live in the shadows of our predecessors for a time. But we who determine the fate of planets eventually reach the point at which we become not the shadows, but the light itself.

—PRINCE RAPHAEL CORRINO,
Discourses on Leadership

As an official member of the Federated Council of Great and Minor Houses, Duke Leto Atreides embarked on a Heighliner and traveled to Kaitain for the next Landsraad meeting. Wearing his formal mantle off-planet for the first time, he thought he had recovered enough from the loss of his father to make a major public appearance.

After Leto had made his decision to attend, Thufir Hawat and several other Atreides protocol advisors had locked themselves with him in Castle meeting rooms to give him crash courses in diplomacy. The advisors hovered around him like stern teachers, insisting that he be brought up to speed on all the social, economic, and political factors a Duke must take into account. Harsh glowglobes lit the stone-walled room, while a sea breeze drifted in through the open window, bringing with it the sound of crashing waves and screaming gulls. Despite the distractions, Leto attended to the lectures.

For his turn, the new Duke had insisted that Rhombur sit beside him during the training sessions. "One day he will need to know all these things, when his House is restored,"

Leto had said. Some advisors had looked skeptical, but they did not argue.

As he departed from Cala City Spaceport, accompanied only by Thufir Hawat as his escort and confidant, Leto's counselors had warned him against rash behavior. Leto had pulled his cloak tighter around his shoulders. "I understand," he said, "but my sense of honor drives me to do what I must do."

By ancient tradition it was Leto's right to appear in the Landsraad forum and put forth his demand. A demand for justice. As the new Duke, he had an agenda, and enough anger and youthful naïveté to believe he just might succeed, no matter what his advisors might tell him. Sadly, though, he remembered the few times when his father had petitioned the Landsraad; Paulus had always returned home red-faced, expressing scorn and impatience at the bumbling bureaucracy.

But Leto would start fresh, with high hopes.

Under the eternally sunny skies of Kaitain, the massive Landsraad Hall of Oratory stood high and imposing, the tallest peak in a mountain range of legislative edifices and government offices surrounding an ellipsoidal commons. The Hall had been erected by contributions from all the Houses, each noble family trying to outdo the others in grandeur. Representatives from CHOAM had helped to procure resources from across the Imperium, and only by special order of a former Emperor—Hassik Corrino III—had the exorbitant Landsraad construction plans been curtailed, so as not to overshadow the Imperial Palace itself.

Following the nuclear holocaust on Salusa Secundus and the relocation of the Imperium's seat of government, everyone had been anxious to establish an optimistic new order. Hassik III had wanted to show that even after the near obliteration of House Corrino, the Imperium and its business would continue at a more exalted level than ever before.

Banners of the Great Houses rippled like a rainbow of dragon scales along the outer walls of the Landsraad Hall. Standing there in the glittering commons surrounded by towering metal-and-plaz buildings, Leto was hard-pressed to locate the green-and-black flag of House Atreides, but finally found it. The purple-and-copper colors of House Vernius had been taken down and publicly burned.

Thufir Hawat stood beside the young Duke. Leto longed for the presence of his friend Rhombur, but it was not yet safe for the exiled Ixian Prince to leave the sanctuary of Caladan. Dominic Vernius still had not emerged from hiding, even following reports of Shando's death; Leto knew the sharp-eyed man would be mourning in his own way. And plotting revenge. . . .

In any case, Leto would have to do this himself. His father would have expected no less of him. So, under the bright Kaitain sunshine, he squared his shoulders, thought of his family history and all that had occurred since the dark days of Atreus, and fixed his gaze forward. He marched ahead along the flagstoned streets, not allowing himself to feel small in the face of the Landsraad's grandeur.

As they entered the Hall of Oratory in the company of other family representatives, Leto spotted the colors of House Harkonnen, with its pale blue griffin symbol. Just looking at the banners, he could name a few other families: Houses Richese, Teranos, Mutelli, Ecaz, Dyvetz, and Canidar. In the center of all the flags hung the much larger Imperial banner of House Corrino, in striking scarlet and gold with its central lion symbol.

The fanfare surrounding his entrance, and that of the other arriving representatives, was deafening and constant. As the men and a few women entered, a crier announced each person's name and position. Leto saw only a few true nobles; most arrivals were Ambassadors, political leaders, or paid sycophants.

Even though he himself carried a royal title, Leto did not feel powerful or important. After all, what was the Duke of a mid-level House compared with even the prime minister of one of the wealthy families? Though he controlled the economy and population of Caladan and the other holdings of Atreides, many Great Houses held dominion over far more wealth and worlds. He envisioned himself for a moment as a small fish among sharks, then quashed such thoughts before they could diminish his confidence. The Old Duke had never allowed him the luxury of feeling small.

In the enormous Hall he wondered where he might find the empty seats formerly occupied by House Vernius; he took only small satisfaction in knowing that, though they now held Ix, the Bene Tleilax would never receive any such honors. The Landsraad would not allow despised Tleilaxu representatives into this exclusive club. Normally

Leto would have had no patience for such wholesale prejudice, but in this case he made an exception.

As the Council meeting commenced with interminable formalities, Leto took his seat in a plush black-and-maroon booth along one side, similar to those provided for the dignitaries of other Houses. Hawat joined him, and Leto watched the business unfold, eager to learn, ready to do his part. But he had to wait until his name was called.

The real family heads could not be bothered to attend every such meeting, and as a number of trivial matters were heard—items that dragged on for far longer than was necessary—Leto soon understood why. Little business was accomplished despite all the talking and arguing and niggling over fine points of protocol or Imperial law.

Newly installed in his title, though, Leto would make this his formal reception. When the scrolling agenda signaled his turn to speak at long last, the young man crossed the dizzying expanse of polished floor in the cavernous chamber, unaccompanied by the warrior Mentat or any other assistant, and climbed to a central lectern. Trying not to look like a mere teenager, he remembered his father's powerful presence and recalled the cheers as they stood in the arena, holding a bull's-head high.

Gazing across the sea of bored, dignified representatives, Leto took a deep breath. Amplifiers would snatch his words and transmit them so that all listeners could hear; shigawire recordings were made for documentation purposes. This would be a vital speech for him—most of these people had no inkling of his personality, and few even knew his name. Realizing that they would form their impression of him from the words he said that day, Leto felt the weight on his shoulders grow even heavier.

He waited to be certain he had everyone's attention, though so late in the Council meeting he doubted anyone had the mental energy required to concentrate on anything new.

"Many of you were friends and allies of my father, Paulus Atreides," he began, then dropped his bombshell, "who was recently murdered through a heinous and cowardly act of assassination." He glanced pointedly over at the seats held by representatives of House Harkonnen. He didn't know the names or titles of the two men there representing the enemy household.

His implication was clear enough, though he made no specific ac-cusation, nor did he have any specific proof. Stablemaster Yresk, who had not survived his interrogation as Leto had requested, had con-firmed Helena's complicity, but could give no further details about co-conspirators. So the new Duke Atreides simply used his statement to gain the attention of the bored people in the chamber—and now he certainly had it.

The Harkonnens whispered among themselves, casting nervous and angry looks at the podium. Leto ignored them and turned back to the central cluster of representatives.

Directly in front of him in the seat of House Mutelli he recognized old Count Flambert, an utterly ancient gentleman whose memory was said to have failed him many years before. With his long-term recol-lection gone, he kept at his side a squat former Mentat candidate with blond hair, who served as a portable memory for the Count. The failed Mentat's sole duty was to remind the ancient Flambert of things, pro-viding every bit of data the nobleman might require. Though he had never completed his training as a human computer, the failed Mentat served the senile Count's needs well enough.

Leto's voice carried across the assemblage, as clear and concise as the pealing of buoy bells on a cool Caladan morning: "A sign over the Emperor's own door declares that 'Law is the ultimate science.' Thus, I stand here not on my own behalf, but on behalf of a former Great House, one that can no longer come here to speak. House Vernius was a close ally of my family."

Several people on nearby benches groaned. A few others fidgeted impatiently. They had already heard too much about Vernius.

Boldly, the young Atreides continued: "Earl Dominic Vernius and his family were forced to declare themselves renegade after the illegal takeover of Ix by the Bene Tleilax—whom all here know to be a de-praved and disgusting breed, and unworthy of representation before this august body. While House Vernius cried out for help and support against this outrageous invasion, all of *you* hid in the shadows and dal-lied until such assistance became irrelevant." Leto was careful not to point the finger at Elrood himself, though it was clear in his mind that the Emperor had encouraged the stalling.

A great murmur arose in the Landsraad Hall, accompanied by expressions of confusion and outrage. Leto could see that they now viewed him as a young upstart, a brash and ill-mannered rebel who didn't know the true order of things in the Imperium. He'd had the bad form to bring such unpleasant matters out into the open.

Leto was unswayed, though. "You all knew Dominic Vernius as an honorable, trustworthy man. You all traded with Ix. How many of you did not call Dominic your friend?" He looked around quickly, but spoke again before anyone could get up the nerve to raise a hand in public.

"Though I am not a member of the Vernius family, the Tleilaxu invaders threatened my own life, and I barely escaped through my father's assistance. Earl Vernius and his wife also fled, forsaking all their possessions—and recently the Lady Shando Vernius was murdered, hunted down like an animal!" His vision spun with anger and grief, but he took a deep breath and continued.

"Know, all who can hear me, that I express grave reservations about the Bene Tleilax and their recent outrageous actions. By any means, kanly or otherwise, they must be brought to justice. House Atreides is no ally of the illegal government of Ix—how dare they rename the planet Xuttuh? Is the Imperium civilized, or do we drown in a sea of barbarians?" He waited. His pulse pounded loudly in his head. "If the Landsraad ignores this incredible tragedy, can you not see that this could happen to any one of *you?*"

A representative of House Harkonnen spoke without even the courtesy of standing to announce his intention. "House Vernius declared itself renegade. By ancient law, the Emperor's Sardaukar and any other bounty hunters had a perfect right to hunt down and eliminate the renegade's wife. Have a care, young pup of a Duke. We're only granting you the right to give her children asylum out of the goodness of our hearts. There is no requirement that we do so."

Leto believed the Harkonnen was wrong, but did not wish to argue a point of law, especially without Thufir's guidance. "So any House can be persecuted, their members assassinated by Sardaukar on a whim, and no one here believes it is *wrong?* Any power can crush a Great House of the Landsraad, and the rest of you will simply cover your eyes and hope it doesn't happen to you next?"

"The Emperor does not act on a whim!" someone shouted. A number of voices of assent called out . . . but not many. Leto realized this bit of patriotism and loyalty was probably a consequence of Elrood's severely failing health. The ancient man had not been seen at functions for months, was supposedly bedridden and near death.

Leto put his hands on his hips. "I may be young, but I'm not blind. Consider this, members of the Landsraad, with your shifting alliances and false loyalties—what pledge can you offer one another if your promises blow away like dust?" He then repeated the words his father had greeted him with when he'd stepped off the rescue ship from Ix. "House Atreides values loyalty and honor far above politics."

He raised a hand, and his voice took on a sweeping, commanding resonance. "I admonish each of you to remember House Vernius. It *can* happen to you, and it will if you are not careful. Where can you place your trust if each House turns upon the other at the slightest opportunity?" He saw his words strike home to some of the representatives, but he knew in his heart that when he called for a vote to advocate removal of the blood price on House Vernius, few would stand in his support.

Leto took a long breath. He turned, pretending to be finished, but called back over his shoulder. "Perhaps you would all be better advised to think about your own situations. Ask yourselves this: *Whom can you really trust?*"

He stalked toward the arched doorway of the Landsraad Council chamber. There was no applause . . . no laughter either. Only shocked silence, and he suspected he had gotten through to some of them. Or perhaps he was just being optimistic. Duke Leto Atreides had much to learn about statecraft—as no doubt Hawat would tell him on the trip home—but he vowed not to become like the lip-service imposters in that chamber. For all of his days, for as long as he could draw breath, Leto would remain reliable and faithful and true. Eventually the others would see that in him . . . perhaps even his enemies would.

Thufir Hawat joined him at the colonnaded portals, and they both passed out of the enormous Hall of Oratory as the Landsraad continued its business without them.

History demonstrates that the advancement of technology is not a steady upward curve. There are flat periods, upward spurts, and even reversals.

—Technology of the Imperium, 532nd Edition

While two shadowy figures watched, a bland-faced Dr. Yungar passed a Suk scanner over the old man, who lay ashen-faced on the bed as if drowning in voluminous coverings, embroidered sheets, and diaphanous netting. The diagnostic instrument hummed.

He won't be needing his concubines ever again, Shaddam thought.

"The Emperor is dead," Yungar announced, tossing his long iron-gray ponytail over his shoulder.

"Ah, yes. At least now he's at peace," Shaddam said in a low, husky voice, though a superstitious chill ran down his spine. Had Elrood known, at the very end, who had been responsible for his demise? Just before death, the ancient man's reptilian eyes had focused on his son. With a twisting in his gut, the Crown Prince remembered the terrible day when the Emperor had discovered Shaddam's complicity in the murder of his elder son Fafnir . . . and how the old man had chortled upon discovering that his younger child had been slipping contraceptives into the food of his own mother, Habla, so she couldn't conceive another son and rival to him.

Had Elrood suspected this? Had he cursed his own son and heir with his dying thoughts?

Well, it was certainly too late to change his mind now. The ancient ruler was dead, at last, and Shaddam had been the cause of it. No, not him. *Fenring.* Let him be the scapegoat, if necessary. A Crown Prince could never admit such guilt.

Soon he would no longer be Crown Prince—he would be Emperor, at last. Padishah Emperor of the Known Universe. It was imperative, though, that he not show his excitement or triumph. He would wait until after the formal coronation.

"Not that this is unexpected," Hasimir Fenring said at his side, his large head bowed low, weak chin tucked against his throat. "The poor man has been degenerating for some time, ah-mm-m-m-m."

The Suk doctor folded his scanning instrument shut and slipped it into the pocket of his tunic. Everyone else had been ordered out of the room: the concubines, the guards, even Chamberlain Hesban.

"Something odd about this case, though," Yungar said. "For days now I've had a feeling of unease . . . something more here than an old man dying of natural causes. We must be exceedingly cautious with our analysis, since it is the Emperor—"

"*Was* the Emperor," Shaddam said, too quickly. Fenring made a subtle warning gesture to get his attention.

"My point exactly." The Suk doctor brushed a hand across the black-diamond tattoo on his forehead. Shaddam wondered if he was just distressed that he would no longer receive extravagant fees for continuing treatment.

"My good Doctor, Emperor Elrood was ancient and under a great deal of stress." In an odd benediction, Fenring bent down and placed his fingertips on the old man's cold brow, which reminded Shaddam of a parchment-covered rock. "We who were closest to him saw visible changes in his health and mental capacity in, say, the past two years. It would be best if you do not voice innuendos and unfounded suspicions that could only damage the stability of the Imperium, especially in this difficult time, hm-m-m-m? Padishah Emperor Elrood IX was more than a hundred and fifty years old, with one of the longest reigns in the history of the Corrinos. Let us leave it at that."

Shaddam cleared his throat. "What else could it be, Doctor? The security around my father is impenetrable, guards and poison-snoopers everywhere. No one could possibly have harmed him."

Yungar looked uneasily past the Crown Prince to the ferretlike man behind him. "Identity, motive, and opportunity. Those are the questions, and though I'm not a police investigator, I'm certain a Mentat could provide answers to all three. I will compile my data and provide it to a review board. It is strictly a formality, but it must be done."

"Who would do such a thing to my father?" Shaddam demanded, stepping closer. The doctor's abruptness made him stiffen, but this Suk had already demonstrated his pompous nature. The dead man on the bed seemed to be watching them, his clawed fingers pointing in accusation.

"More evidence needs to be gathered first, Sire."

"*Evidence?* Of what sort?" He calmed himself. Sweat broke out on his brow, and he ran a hand across his carefully styled reddish hair. Perhaps he was carrying the act too far.

Fenring seemed entirely calm and moved to the other side of the bed, near where the remains of the Emperor's last glass of spice beer sat.

In a whisper that only Shaddam could hear, the doctor said, "It is my duty as a loyal Suk to warn you, Prince Shaddam, that you, too, may be in extreme danger. Certain forces . . . according to reports I've seen . . . do not want House Corrino to remain in power."

"Since when does the Suk School obtain reports about Imperial alliances and intrigues?" Fenring asked, slithering closer. He had not heard the specific words, but years ago he had taught himself the valuable skill of reading lips. It helped greatly with his spying activities. He had tried to teach Shaddam the trick, but the Crown Prince had not caught the knack of it yet.

"We have our sources," the Suk doctor said. "Regrettably, such connections are necessary even for a school such as ours dedicated to healing." Recalling the doctor's insistence on full payment before even looking at a patient, Shaddam frowned at this irony. "We live in perilous times."

"Do you suspect anyone in particular?" Shaddam husked, following the direction of the doctor's gaze. Perhaps they could set up Chamberlain Hesban to take the fall—plant evidence, start rumors.

"In your position it would be safest to suspect everyone, Sire. I would like to conduct an autopsy on Emperor Elrood. Working with a partner from the Inner School, we can scanalyze every organ, every tissue, every cell . . . just to be safe."

Shaddam frowned. "It seems a terrible disrespect to my father, slicing him up into little pieces. He had quite a . . . a horror of surgery. Ah, yes. Better to let him lie in peace. We must prepare immediately for the funeral of state. And my coronation ceremony."

"On the contrary," Yungar persisted, "we show respect for Elrood's memory by trying to determine what happened to him. Perhaps something was implanted in his body some time ago, when his behavior began to change—something that caused his slow death. A Suk doctor could find the subtlest traces, even after two years."

"The very thought of an autopsy sickens me," Shaddam said. "I am the heir to the Imperium, and I forbid it." He looked down at the dead old man, and his arms broke out in gooseflesh, as if the ancient creature's ghost hovered over his head. He glanced warily at shadows in the corners and in the cold fireplace.

He had expected to experience elation when his father finally passed the Golden Lion Throne to him—but now, knowing that his own chaumurky had been the cause of the Emperor's death, Shaddam's skin crawled.

"According to Imperial Law, I could formally insist upon it, Sire," the Suk doctor explained, his voice still low and calm. "And for your own good I must do exactly that. I see that you are inexperienced in the ways of intrigue, since you have grown up protected in the Court. You undoubtedly think I'm being foolish, but I assure you I am not wrong about this. I feel it in the pit of my stomach."

"Perhaps the good doctor is right," Fenring said.

"How can you . . ." Seeing a peculiar gleam in Fenring's eyes, Shaddam cut himself short, then glanced at the doctor and said to him, "I must confer with my advisor."

"Of course." Yungar watched them move off to one side, by the door.

"Are you mad?" Shaddam whispered, when he and Fenring were a distance away.

"Go along with him for the moment. Then through a . . ." Fenring smiled, selected just the right word. " . . . misunderstanding . . . old Elrood will be cremated before they can cut him open."

"I see," Shaddam said, with sudden understanding. Then, to Yungar, he said, "Send for your associate and complete your autopsy. My father will be moved to the infirmary, where you may complete the procedure."

"A day will be needed to bring in the other doctor," the Suk said. "You can arrange to keep the body chilled?"

Shaddam smiled politely. "It shall be done."

"By your leave then, Sire," the Suk said, bowing and retreating hastily. The doctor hurried away with a rustling of medical robes. His long steel-gray hair dangled in its ponytail, clasped by a silver ring.

When they were alone, Fenring said with a crafty smile, "It was either that or kill the bastard, and we didn't dare risk that."

An hour later, through an unfortunate series of events, Emperor Elrood IX was reduced to ashes in the Imperial crematorium, and his remains were misplaced. A Court orderly and two medical attendants paid for the mistake with their lives.

Memory and History are two sides of the same coin. In time, however, History tends to slant itself toward a favorable impression of events, while Memory is doomed to preserve the worst aspects.

—LADY HELENA ATREIDES,
her personal journals

Father, I was not ready.

The nighttime seas on Caladan were rough, and wind-driven rain pelted the windows of the Castle's east tower. Another sort of storm raged within Duke Leto, though: concern for the future of his troubled House.

He had avoided this duty for too long . . . for months, in fact. On this isolated evening, he wanted nothing more than to sit in a fire-warmed room in the company of Rhombur and Kailea. Instead, he had decided at last to go through some of the Old Duke's personal items.

Storage chests containing his father's things were brought in and lined up along one wall. Servants had stoked up the flaming logs in the fireplace to a fine blaze, and a crock of mulled wine filled the room with the spicy scents of terrameg and a bit of expensive melange. Four small glowglobes provided enough light to see by.

Kailea had found a fur cloak in storage, taken it as her own, and wrapped herself just to keep warm—but it also made her look stunning. Despite the radical changes in her life, how far she had fallen from her dreams of sparkling at the Imperial Court, the Vernius daughter was a survivor.

Through sheer force of will Kailea seemed to bend the environment around herself, making the best of things.

Despite the political drawbacks of any romance with the renegade family, Duke Leto—now ruler of his Great House—found himself even more attracted to her. But he remembered his father's primary admonition: *Never marry for love, or it will bring our House down.* Paulus Atreides had hammered that into his son as much as any other leadership training. Leto knew he could never shrug off the Old Duke's command; it was too much a part of him.

Still, he was drawn to Kailea, though thus far he hadn't found the courage to express his feelings to her. He thought she knew, even so; Kailea had a strong, logical mind. He saw it in her emerald eyes, in the curve of her catlike mouth, in the contemplative looks she gave him when she thought he wouldn't notice.

With Leto's permission, Rhombur searched curiously through some of the massive storage chests, looking for old wartime mementos of the friendship between Duke Paulus and Dominic Vernius. Reaching deep into one chest, he brought out an embroidered cape and unfolded it. "What's this? I never saw your father wear it."

Leto studied the design and knew instantly what it was—the hawk of House Atreides embracing the Richesian lamp of knowledge. "I believe that's his wedding cloak, from when he and my mother were married."

"Oh," Rhombur said, his voice trailing off in embarrassment. "Sorry." He folded the cape and stuffed it back into the box.

Shaking his head, Leto took a deep breath. He'd known they would encounter many such memory land mines, and he would just have to endure them. "My father didn't choose to die and leave me in this position, Rhombur. My mother made her own choices. She could have been a valued advisor to me. Under other circumstances I would have welcomed her assistance and wise counsel. But instead . . ." He sighed and looked bitterly over at Kailea. "As I said, she made her own choices."

Only Leto and the warrior Mentat knew the truth about Helena's complicity in the murder, and it was a secret Leto vowed to carry with him to his grave. With the death of the stablemaster during interrogation, Duke Leto Atreides had fresh, bright blood on his hands—his first, but certainly not his last. Not even Rhombur or Kailea suspected the truth.

He had sent his mother out of Castle Caladan with two of her servants, chosen by him. For her "rest and well-being," Lady Helena had been taken to the Eastern Continent where she would live under primitive conditions with the Sisters in Isolation, a retrogressive religious commune. Haughtily, but without bothering to demand explanations for her son's behavior, Helena had accepted her banishment.

Though he put up a strong front, Leto privately mourned the loss of his mother, and was astounded to find himself without both parents in the space of a few months. But Helena had committed the most abhorrent act of betrayal against her own family, her own House, and he knew he could never forgive her, could never see her again. Killing her was out of the question; the thought had barely crossed his mind. She was, after all, his mother, and he was not like her. Besides, getting her out of his sight was a practical matter, for he'd been left with vast holdings to manage, and the welfare of the citizens of Caladan had priority. He needed to get down to the business of running House Atreides.

From a chest of items, Rhombur brought out a set of old-fashioned handmade playing cards and some of the Old Duke's awards, including military badges of honor, a chipped knife, and a small bloodstained banner. Leto discovered seashells, a colored scarf, an unsigned love poem, a lock of auburn hair (not Helena's color), then a lock of blonde hair, and enameled brass armbands designed for a woman, but he had no idea how to explain the items.

He knew his father had taken mistresses, though Paulus had brought none of them into the Castle as bound concubines. He'd merely enjoyed himself, and had no doubt showered the women with trinkets or fabrics or sweetmeats.

Leto ignored those items and closed the heavy lid of the box. Duke Paulus was entitled to his own memories, his past, and his secrets. None of these mementos had any bearing on the fortunes of House Atreides. He needed to concern himself with politics and business. Thufir Hawat, other Court advisors, and even Prince Rhombur were doing their best to guide him, but Leto felt like a newborn, having to learn everything from scratch.

As the rain continued outside, Kailea poured a mug of the mulled wine and handed it to Leto, then drew two more for herself and her brother. Thoughtfully the Duke sipped it, savoring the spicy flavor. Warmth seeped into his bones, and he smiled when he thanked her.

She looked down at the odd paraphernalia and adjusted one of the gold combs in her deep copper hair. Leto noticed that her lower lip was trembling. "What is it, Kailea?"

She took a deep breath and looked at her brother, then at Leto. "I'll never have a chance to go through my mother's things like this. Not from the Grand Palais, not even the few precious items she took with her when we fled."

Rhombur came forward and held his sister, but she continued to look at Leto. "My mother had keepsakes from the Emperor himself, treasures he gave her when she left his service. She had so many memories, so many stories left to tell me. I didn't spend enough time listening to her when she was alive."

"It'll be all right," Rhombur said, trying to console her. "We'll make our own memories."

"And we'll make them remember *us*," Kailea said, her voice suddenly brittle.

Feeling sick inside, and deeply weary, Leto rubbed the ducal signet ring on his finger. It still felt strange and heavy there, but he knew he would never remove it until someday far in the future, when he would pass it to his own son to continue the traditions of House Atreides.

Outside, the storm flung more rain at the walls and windows of the ancient stone Castle, while the sea shushed a foamy lullaby against the cliffs far below. Caladan felt very large and overwhelming around him, and Leto seemed incredibly small. Though it was still an inhospitable night, when the young Duke exchanged smiles with Kailea and Rhombur, he felt warm and comfortable in his home.

LETO LEARNED OF the Emperor's death as he and three attendants were struggling to hang the mounted Salusan bull's-head in the dining hall. Workers used ropes and pulleys to haul the monstrous trophy onto a spot on the previously unadorned, highly polished walls.

A grim Thufir Hawat stood by, watching with hands clasped behind his back. Absently, the Mentat touched the long scar on his leg, a souvenir of the time when he had rescued a much younger Paulus from another rampaging bull. This time, however, he had not acted swiftly enough. . . .

Kailea shuddered as she looked up at the ugly creature. "It's going to be hard to eat in this hall, with that thing staring down at us. I can still see the blood on its horns."

Leto regarded the bull's-head with an appraising eye. "I see it as a reminder that I must never let my guard down. Even a dumb animal—albeit with the interference of human conspirators—can conquer the leader of a Great House of the Landsraad." He felt a shiver. "Think of that lesson, Kailea."

"I'm afraid that's not a very comforting thought," she murmured, her green eyes bright with unshed tears. Blinking to clear her vision, she turned back to her own activities.

With a ridulian crystal report folder open before her on the table, she devoted her energies to studying the household accounts. Using what she had learned in the Orb Office on Ix, Kailea analyzed the income streams for Atreides holdings in order to determine how work and productivity were distributed on Caladan's continents and seas. She and Leto had been discussing the matter in depth, despite their youth. The exiled Kailea Vernius had an excellent head for business, Leto was delighted to discover.

"Being a good Duke is not all swordplay and bullfighting," Thufir Hawat had told him once, long before all the latest troubles and challenges. "Management of little things is often a more difficult battle." For some reason the statement had stuck in Leto's mind, and now he was discovering the wisdom of the words. . . .

When the Imperial messenger marched into the dining hall, fresh off a Guild Heighliner, he stood tall, formally dressed in scarlet-and-gold Imperial colors. "I request an audience with Duke Leto Atreides."

Leto, Rhombur, and Kailea all froze, remembering the horrible news they'd received the last time a crier had entered the great receiving room. Leto prayed that nothing had happened to the fugitive Dominic Vernius in his continued flight. But this official messenger wore House Corrino colors, and looked as if he had delivered his announcement a dozen times already.

"It is my duty to announce to all members of the Great and Minor Houses of the Landsraad that the Padishah Emperor Elrood Corrino IX has died, struck down by an extended illness in the one hundred thirty-eighth year of his reign. May history fondly remember his long rule, and may his soul find eternal peace."

Leto stepped back, astounded. One of the workers almost let the mounted bull's-head slip from its position on the wall, but Hawat shouted for the man to attend to his tasks.

The Emperor had been a fixture in the galaxy for two normal life-times. Elrood lived on Kaitain, surrounded by guards, protected from all threats, and heavily addicted to the geriatric spice. Leto had never considered that the old man might die someday, though in the past year or two he'd heard that Elrood had been growing increasingly frail.

Leto turned to the messenger, nodded formally. "Please give Crown Prince Shaddam my condolences. When is the funeral of state to be held? House Atreides will attend, of course."

"Not necessary," the Courier replied in a crisp voice. "At the request of the throne, there will only be a small private ceremony for the immediate family."

"I see."

"However, Shaddam Corrino, soon to be crowned Padishah Emperor of the Known Universe, Shaddam IV, graciously requests your appearance, and your oath of fealty, when he formally ascends to the Golden Lion Throne. Details of the coronation ceremony are being arranged."

Leto glanced briefly at Thufir Hawat and replied, "It shall be done."

With a curt nod, the messenger said, "When the protocol has been set and all schedules are made, proper word will be brought to Caladan." He bowed, sweeping his scarlet-and-gold cape around his arms, and spun about with a neat click of his shoes. He marched back out of the hall, bound for a flitter that would take him back to the spaceport for his trip to the next Imperial planet, where he would deliver his report again.

"Well, uh . . . that was good news," Rhombur said sourly. His face was pale but hard. He stood quietly in the doorway, absorbing the information. "If it hadn't been for the Emperor's petty jealousy and intervention, my family could have recovered from the crisis on Ix. The Landsraad would have sent help."

"Elrood didn't want us to recover," Kailea said, glancing up from her accounting records. "I'm just sorry my mother couldn't have lived to hear those tidings."

Leto's lips turned upward in a smile of guarded optimism. "Wait, this gives us an unexpected opportunity. Think about it. Elrood alone bore personal animosity against House Vernius. He and your mother had their painful past, which we know to be the true reason behind his refusal to erase the blood price on your family. It was *personal*."

Standing under the bull's-head, Hawat looked closely at Leto. He listened in silence, waiting to see what his new Duke would suggest.

"I've tried speaking to the Landsraad Council," Leto said, "but they're useless, noncommittal. They won't do anything to help us. But my distaff cousin Shaddam . . ." He passed his tongue over the inside of his lower lip. "I've only met him three times, but my maternal grandmother was also a child of Elrood's. I can claim blood ties. When Shaddam becomes the new Emperor, I will petition him to offer you amnesty as a gesture of forgiveness. When I swear the eternal loyalty of House Atreides, I will ask him to remember the great history of House Vernius."

"Why would he assent to that?" Kailea wanted to know. "What's the advantage for him?"

"It would be the right thing to do," Rhombur said. "The fair thing." His sister looked at him as if he had lost his mind.

"He'll do it to establish the tenor of his reign," Leto said. "Any new Emperor wants to create an identity, show how he's different from his predecessor, not locked into old ways and old decisions. Shaddam just might be in a forgiving mood. Word has it that he was not on the best of terms with his father anyway, and he'll certainly want to show his own colors after more than a century under Elrood."

Kailea threw herself into Leto's arms, and he hugged her awkwardly. "It would be so wonderful to have our freedom back, Leto— and our family holdings! Maybe there's something we can salvage from Ix after all."

"Let's all keep our hopes up, Kailea," Rhombur said with cautious optimism. "Try to envision it, and it just might happen."

"We must not be afraid to ask," Leto said.

"All right," Rhombur said. "If anyone can accomplish this, it's you, my friend."

Fiery with determination and optimism, Leto began to develop plans for his formal procession to Kaitain. "We'll do something they won't expect," he said. "Rhombur and I will show up for the coronation, together."

He met the Mentat advisor's alarmed gaze. "It is dangerous to bring the son of Vernius, m'Lord."

"And precisely what they will not expect."

What senses do we lack that we cannot see or hear another world all around us?

—The Orange Catholic Bible

S ome considered the rocky wilderness of Forest Guard Station to be beautiful, a pristine and natural wonderland. But Baron Vladimir Harkonnen disliked being so far from enclosed buildings, sharp angles, metal, and plaz. The cold air smelled harsh and unpleasant without the familiar fumes of industry, lubricants, and machinery. Too raw, too hostile.

The Baron knew the importance of their destination, though, and entertained himself by watching the even greater discomfort exhibited by his twisted Mentat. With a dirty robe and mussed hair, Piter de Vries struggled to keep up. Though his mind operated like a powerful machine, his body was pampered, scrawny, and weak.

"Everything is so *primitive* out here, my Baron, so filthy and cold," de Vries said, his eyes feral. "Are you certain we have to go this far? Have we no alternative, other than jaunting out into the forest?"

"Some people pay dearly to visit places like this," the Baron said. "They call them *resorts*."

"Piter, shut your mouth and keep up with us," Rabban

said. They trudged up a steep hillside toward an ice-glazed and cave-pocked wall of sandstone.

Scowling, the Mentat returned the jab with his own barbed words. "Isn't this the place where that little boy bested you and all your hunting team, Rabban?"

The Baron's nephew turned back, his thick-lidded eyes staring at de Vries, and growled, "I'll hunt *you* next time if you don't watch your tongue."

"Your uncle's priceless Mentat?" de Vries said in a carefree tone. "But how would he possibly replace me?"

"He has a point," the Baron agreed, with a chuckle.

Rabban muttered something to himself.

Earlier, the Baron's guards and hunting experts had combed the isolated hunting preserve, a security check so that the three men could walk alone, without their usual entourage. Carrying a maula pistol on his hip and a heat-scattering rifle slung over his shoulder, Rabban insisted that he could take care of any gaze hounds or other predators that might attack. The Baron didn't share such complete confidence in his nephew, considering the fact that a small boy had indeed outwitted him—but at least out here they could stay away from prying eyes.

At the top of a bluff the three of them rested on a ledge, then ascended another slope. Rabban led the way, clawing aside thick scrub brush until they reached more exposed sandstone. There, a low crack yielded a black space between crumbling stone and the ground.

"It's down here," Rabban said. "Come on."

The Baron knelt and shined a ring-light into the opening of a cave. "Follow me, Piter."

"I'm not a spelunker," the Mentat replied. "Besides, I'm tired."

"You're just not physically fit enough," the Baron countered as he took a deep breath to feel his own muscles. "You need more exercise. Keep yourself in shape."

"But this isn't what you purchased me for, my Baron."

"I purchased you to do anything I *tell* you to do." He bent and crawled through the opening; the tiny but powerful beam of light on his finger probed the darkness ahead.

Though the Baron tried to maintain his physique in a perfect condition, he had been plagued with body aches and unexpected weakness over the past year. No one had noticed—or perhaps no one had dared mention—the fact that he'd also begun to gain weight, through no change in his diet. His skin had a thicker, pastier appearance. He had considered discussing his problem with medical experts, maybe even a Suk doctor, no matter the incredible expense of consulting one. Life, it seemed, was an endless string of problems.

"It smells like bear piss in here," de Vries complained as he squirmed through the hole.

"How would you know what bear piss smells like?" Rabban said, pushing the Mentat deeper inside to make room for himself.

"I've smelled *you*. A wild animal can't be any more rank than that."

The three men stood up inside, and the Baron illuminated a small glowglobe, which floated up to shine against the near wall in the back of the low cave. The place was rough and moss-covered, smudged with dust, showing no sign of human habitation.

"Quite a good mimetic projection, isn't it?" the Baron said. "The best work our people have done." He reached forward with a ring-studded hand, and the image of the wall blurred, became indistinct.

Rabban located a slight protrusion of rock and pushed; the entire rear wall rumbled back and fell away to reveal an access tube.

"A very special hiding place," the Baron said.

Lights flared on, illuminating a passage that led into the heart of the bluff. After they stepped inside and sealed the false-wall projection behind them, de Vries looked around in amazement. "You kept this a secret even from me, my Baron?"

"Rabban found this cave on one of his hunts. We've . . . made some modifications using a new technology, an exciting technique. I think you'll see the possibilities, once I explain it all to you."

"Quite an elaborate hiding place," the Mentat agreed. "One can't be too careful about spies."

The Baron raised his hands toward the ceiling and shouted at the top of his lungs, "Damn Crown Prince Shaddam to the cesspits! No—make that to the lowest depths of a filth-encrusted, lava-blasted hell-grotto!"

The treasonous outburst shocked even de Vries, and the Baron chuckled. "Here, Piter—and nowhere else on Giedi Prime—I'm not in the least worried about eavesdroppers."

He led them into a main chamber. "We three could hide here and resist an attack even from contraband atomics. No one would find us. Nullentropy bins hold supplies and weapons to last forever. I have placed everything vital to House Harkonnen in here, from genealogical records to financial documents, to our blackmail material—all the nasty, fascinating details we have on the other Houses."

Rabban took a seat at a highly polished table and punched a button on a panel. Suddenly the walls became transparent, glowing yellow to spotlight distorted corpses, twenty-one in all, hanging suspended in the gaps between plaz sheets, on display.

"Here's the construction team," Rabban said. "It's our special . . . memorial to them."

"Rather pharaonic," the Baron said, in a lighthearted tone.

The flesh of the corpses was discolored and bloated, the faces contorted in macabre death grimaces. The victims' expressions contained a larger measure of sad resignation than terror of impending death. Anyone building such a secret chamber for the Harkonnens must have realized they'd be doomed from the start.

"They'll be unpleasant enough to look at while they rot," the Baron said, "but we'll eventually have nice clean skeletons to admire."

The remaining walls were layered with intricate scrollwork showing blue Harkonnen griffins as well as gross and pornographic images of human and human-animal copulation, suggestive designs, and a mechanical clock that would have offended most observers. Rabban looked at it and chuckled as the male and female parts interacted in a steady, eternal rhythm.

De Vries turned around, analyzing the details and applying them to his own Mentat projection.

The Baron smiled. "The room is surrounded by a shielding projection that renders an object invisible in all wavelengths. No scanner can detect this enclosure by sight, sound, heat, or even touch. We call it a *no-field*. Think of it. We're standing in a place that doesn't *exist* as far as the rest of the universe is concerned. It's the perfect spot for us to discuss our . . . delicious plans."

"I've never heard of such a field—not from the Guild, not from Ix," de Vries said. "Who invented it?"

"You may remember our . . . visiting researcher from Richese."

"Chobyn?" the Mentat asked, then answered his own question. "Yes, that was his name."

"He came to us in secret with a cutting-edge technique the Richesians had developed. It's a new and risky technology, but our friend Chobyn saw its possibilities. He wisely brought it to House Harkonnen for our private exploitation, provided we give him sufficient remuneration."

"And we've certainly paid him enough," Rabban added.

"Worth every solari," the Baron continued. He drummed his fingers in a habitual rhythm on the tabletop. "Inside this no-globe, not a soul can overhear us, not even a Guild Navigator and his damnable prescience. We've now got Chobyn working on . . . something even better for us."

Rabban impatiently slumped back in one of the seats. "Let's get on with what we need to talk about."

De Vries sat down at the self-scrubbing table, eyes bright, Mentat capabilities already whirling and grasping the implications of an invisibility technology. How it could be used . . .

The Baron shifted his gaze from his blunt-featured nephew to his twisted Mentat. *What an utter contrast these two are, representing the extremes of the intellectual spectrum.* Rabban and de Vries both needed constant supervision, the former because of his thick skull and short fuse, and the latter because his brilliance could be equally dangerous.

Despite his obvious deficiencies, Rabban was the only Harkonnen who could possibly succeed the Baron. Certainly Abulurd wasn't qualified. Other than those two bastard daughters the Bene Gesserit had forced from him, the Baron had no children of his own. He therefore had to train his nephew in the proper uses and abuses of power, so he could eventually die content with the knowledge that House Harkonnen would continue as it always had.

It would be even better, though, if the Atreides were destroyed. . . .

Perhaps Rabban should have two Mentats to guide him, instead of the customary one. Because of his bullish nature, Rabban's rule would be especially brutal, perhaps on a scale never before seen on Giedi Prime, despite the Harkonnens' long history of torture and harsh treatment of slaves.

The Baron's expression became grim. "Down to business. Now listen, both of you. Piter, I want you to use your full Mentat abilities."

De Vries removed his small bottle of sapho juice from a pocket inside his robe. He gulped, and smacked his lips in a manner that the Baron found repulsive.

"My spies have reported very distressing information," the Baron said. "It involves Ix and some plans that the Emperor seems to have made before he died." He drummed his fingers in time to the little ditty that always ran through his head. "This plot has serious implications for our family's fortunes. CHOAM and the Guild don't even know about it."

Rabban grunted. De Vries sat up straight, awaiting more data.

"It seems that the Emperor and the Tleilaxu have made some kind of an alliance to do unorthodox and highly illegal work."

"Sligs and shit go together," Rabban said.

The Baron chuckled at the analogy. "I've learned that our dearly departed Emperor was personally behind the takeover on Ix. He forced House Vernius to go renegade and set the Tleilaxu up so they could begin research, adapting their methods to sophisticated Ixian facilities."

"And what research is that, my Baron?" de Vries asked.

The Baron dropped his bomb. "They seek a biological method to synthesize melange. They think they can produce their own spice artificially and cheaply, thereby cutting Arrakis—us—out of the distribution channels."

Rabban snorted. "Impossible. Nobody can do that."

But de Vries's mind spun as related information clicked into place. "I would not underestimate the Tleilaxu—especially when combined with the facilities and technology on Ix. They'll have everything they need."

Rabban drew himself up. "But if the Emperor can make synthetic spice, what happens to our holdings? What happens to all the spice stockpiles we've spent years building up?"

"Provided the new synthetic is cheap and effective, Harkonnen spice-based fortunes would evaporate," de Vries said stonily. "Practically overnight."

"That's right, Piter!" The Baron slammed a ringed fist on the table. "Harvesting spice from Arrakis is incredibly expensive. If the Emperor has his own source of cheap melange, the market will collapse and House Corrino will control the rest—a new monopoly held entirely in the hands of the Emperor."

"CHOAM won't like that," Rabban said with surprising insight.

De Vries suggested, "Then we will have to get this information to the Spacing Guild. We must reveal to them what the Emperor was doing, and see to it that Shaddam ceases all such investigations. CHOAM and the Guild won't want to lose their investment in spice production either."

"But what if the new Emperor makes a treaty with them first, Piter?" the Baron asked. "CHOAM is partially owned by House Corrino. Shaddam will be out to make his mark as he begins his reign. What if CHOAM presses him into giving *them* access to the synthetic spice at an extraordinary discount, as the price of their cooperation? The Guild would love to have a cheaper, reliable supply. They might abandon Arrakis altogether if it's too difficult."

"Then we'll be the only ones left out in the cold," Rabban growled. "House Harkonnen gets stepped on by everybody."

The Mentat's eyes fell half-closed as he droned on. "We can't even file a formal complaint with the Houses of the Landsraad. Knowledge of a spice substitute would create a feeding frenzy among the Federated families. Political alliances have shifted recently, and a number of Houses wouldn't mind if our monopoly were broken. They couldn't care less if the price of melange plummets. The only ones to lose would be those who had invested heavily in secret and illegal spice stockpiles, or those who invested heavily in the expensive spice-harvesting operations on Arrakis."

"In other words, *us* again—and a few of our closest allies," the Baron said.

"The Bene Gesserit, and your little sweetheart among the witches, would probably like an inexpensive supply, too."

The Baron glowered at his nephew. Rabban merely chuckled. "So what can we do about it?"

De Vries answered without consulting the Baron. "House Harkonnen will have to take care of this by itself. We can expect no outside assistance."

"Remember that we're only a quasi-fief on Arrakis," the Baron said. "It was given to us on sufferance from CHOAM and the Emperor. And now it's like a hook on which they've hung us out to dry. We must be extremely careful."

"We don't have enough military strength to fight all those enemies," Rabban said.

"We'll have to be subtle," de Vries said.

"Subtlety?" The Baron raised his eyebrows. "All right, I'm willing to try new things."

"We must disrupt this Tleilaxu research on Ix," de Vries said, "preferably destroy it. I suggest that House Harkonnen also liquidate various assets, build up a reserve of cash, and milk our current spice production for as much hard profit as possible, because it may disappear at any moment."

The Baron looked over at Rabban. "We need to squeeze. Oh, and I'll have your idiot father step up whale-fur harvesting on Lankiveil. We need to stuff our coffers. The upcoming battles may be quite taxing to our resources."

The Mentat wiped a red drop from his lips. "We must do this in utmost secrecy. CHOAM watches our financial activity carefully and would detect if we suddenly started doing something unusual. For now it's best we don't tip our hand about the Tleilaxu research. We don't want CHOAM or the Guild joining forces with our new Emperor against House Harkonnen."

"We've got to keep the Imperium properly dependent upon us," the Baron said.

Rabban scowled, trying to wrestle his way through the implications by brute force. "But if the Tleilaxu are entrenched on Ix, how do we destroy this research without exposing it for what it is? Without giving away our own involvement and bringing all of our enemies against us?"

De Vries sat back to stare at the sexual designs on the walls. The rotting corpses hung in their display cases like hideous eavesdroppers. His mind churned through Mentat calculations until finally he said, "We must have someone else fight for us. Preferably without their knowledge."

"Who?" Rabban asked.

"That's why we brought Piter here," the Baron said. "We need suggestions."

"Prime projection," de Vries said. "House Atreides."

Rabban's mouth dropped open. "The Atreides would never fight for us!"

De Vries shot back a response. "The Old Duke is dead, and House Atreides is currently unstable. Paulus's successor Leto is an impetuous young pup. He has no friends in the Landsraad and recently gave a rather embarrassing speech at the Council. He went home humiliated."

The Baron waited, trying to see where his Mentat was going with this.

"Second data point: House Vernius, staunch ally to Atreides, has been ousted from Ix by the Tleilaxu. Dominic Vernius remains at large with a price on his head, while Shando Vernius has just been killed, based on her renegade status. House Atreides has offered sanctuary to the two children of Vernius. They're in thick with the victims of the Tleilaxu."

De Vries raised a finger to assemble the points. "Now, brash young Leto is a close friend of the exiled Prince of Ix. Duke Leto blames the Tleilaxu for the takeover of Ix, for the bounty on the mother, and for the ruined situation of their family. 'House Atreides values loyalty and honor far above politics,' Leto said to the Landsraad. He may see it as his duty to help Rhombur Vernius regain his position on Ix. Who better to strike a blow for us?"

The Baron now smiled as he followed the implications. "So . . . start a war between House Atreides and the Tleilaxu! Let them tear each other apart. That way House Atreides *and* the synthetic-spice research will both be destroyed."

Rabban was clearly having trouble envisioning this. From the intense look on his face, the Baron could see that his nephew was thinking as hard as he could, just trying to keep up.

The Mentat nodded. "If played properly, we could accomplish this in such a manner that House Harkonnen remains completely apart from the hostilities. We get what we want, and our hands stay entirely clean."

"Brilliant, Piter! I'm glad I didn't execute you all those times when you were so annoying."

"So am I," de Vries said.

The Baron opened one of the nullentropy chambers to remove a flagon of expensive kirana brandy. "We must have a toast." Then he smiled slyly. "Because I've just realized when and how we can make all this happen." His two listeners couldn't have been more attentive.

"The new Duke is overwhelmed with the complexities of running his holdings. Naturally, he will attend the coronation of Shaddam IV.

No Great House could risk offending the new Padishah Emperor by scorning him on his greatest day."

De Vries caught on immediately. "When Duke Leto travels to the coronation . . . that will be our chance to strike."

"On Kaitain?" Rabban said.

"Something more interesting than that, I suspect," de Vries said.

The Baron sipped the warm sweetness of the aged brandy. "Ahhh, it will be delicious revenge. And Leto won't even see it coming, won't know which direction it came from."

Rabban's eyes lit up. "We'll make him squirm, Uncle?"

The Baron handed crystal snifters to his nephew and his Mentat. Rabban drained his brandy in a single gulp, while de Vries simply stared at it as if performing a chemical analysis with his eyes.

"Yes, Rabban, he'll squirm and squirm until a big Imperial boot steps on him."

No one but a Tleilaxu may set foot in Bandalong, holiest city of the Bene Tleilax, for it is fanatically guarded hallowed ground, purified by their God.

—Diplomacy in the Imperium,
a Landsraad publication

The burn-scarred building had once been an Ixian fighting-mek factory . . . one of the sacrilegious industries that defied the holy commandments of the Butlerian Jihad. *But not anymore.* Hidar Fen Ajidica gazed at the rows of tanks and attendants, satisfied now to see that the place had been fully cleansed and put to good use. *God will approve.*

Following the Tleilaxu victory, the facility had been emptied of its poisonous machinery and blessed by fully robed Masters, so that it could be used for the exalted purposes of the Bene Tleilax. Despite the commandment and support from old Emperor Elrood, now dead, Ajidica had never considered this an Imperial project. The Tleilaxu did not act for the benefit of anyone but themselves and their God. They had their own purposes, which would never be understood by the unclean outsiders.

"Tleilaxu strategy is always woven within a web of strategies, any one of which may be the real strategy," he intoned the axiom of his people. "The magic of our God is our salvation."

Every axlotl tank contained the ingredients of a different experiment, each representing an alternate avenue for solving the artificial melange problem. No outsider had ever seen a Tleilaxu axlotl tank, and none understood their true function. To produce the precious spice, Ajidica knew he would have to use unsettling means. *Others would be horrified, but God will approve*, he repeated in his secret soul. Eventually, they would mass-produce the spice.

Realizing the complexity of his challenge, the Master Researcher had brought in technological adepts from Tleilax One—learned men who had widely divergent views on how that goal might be attained. At this early point in the process, all options must be considered, all evidence studied for clues to be inserted directly into the DNA code of organic molecules, which the Tleilaxu called the Language of God.

All of the technological adepts agreed that artificial spice must be grown as an organic substance in an axlotl tank, because the tanks were holy sources of life and energy. Master Researchers had nurtured countless previous programs with astonishing results, from sligs to clones and gholas . . . though there had been many unfortunate failures, as well.

These exotic vessels were the most sacred of Tleilaxu discoveries, with their workings shielded even from Crown Prince Shaddam, his aides, and his Sardaukar. Such secrecy and security here on Ix—now Xuttah—had been a requirement of the original bargain with Emperor Elrood. The old man had agreed with deprecating amusement, must have assumed he could take those secrets whenever he wished.

Many people made such ridiculous assumptions about the Tleilaxu. Ajidica was accustomed to being dismissed by fools.

No one other than a Tleilaxu Master or a full-blooded Tleilaxu Researcher would ever have access to this knowledge. Ajidica drew a deep breath of the rank chemicals, the unpleasant humid stink that was an inevitable consequence of the functioning tanks. Natural odors. *I feel the presence of my God*, he thought, forming the words in Islamiyat—the arcane language that was never spoken aloud outside of *kehls*, the secret councils of his race. *God is merciful. He alone can guide me.*

A glowglobe floated in front of his eyes, blinking red . . . long, long, short, pause . . . long, short, color change to blue . . . five rapid blinks and back to red. The Crown Prince's emissary was anxious to see him. Hidar Fen Ajidica knew not to keep Hasimir Fenring waiting. Though he had no noble title of his own, the impatient Fenring was the Imperial heir's closest friend, and Fenring understood the manipulations of personal power better than most great leaders in the Landsraad. Ajidica even bore a certain amount of respect for the man.

With resignation Ajidica turned and passed easily through an identity zone that would have been deadly to anyone not properly sanctioned. Even the Crown Prince himself would be unable to pass through safely. Ajidica smiled at the superiority of his people's ways. Ixians had used machinery and force fields for security, as the ruthless and clumsy suboid rebels had discovered . . . causing messy detonations and collateral damage. Tleilaxu, on the other hand, used biological agents, unleashed through ingenious interactions—toxins and nerve mists that rendered *powindah* infidels lifeless the moment they set foot where they didn't belong.

Outside in the secure waiting area, a smiling Hasimir Fenring greeted Ajidica as the researcher exited the identity zone. From some angles the weak-chinned man looked like a weasel and from others a rabbit, innocuous in appearance, but oh so dangerous. The two faced each other in what had once been an Ixian lobby connected through an intricate network of clear-plaz lift tubes. This deadly Imperial killer stood more than a head taller than the Master Researcher.

"Ah, my dear Fen Ajidica," Fenring purred, "your experiments go well, hm-m-m-m-ah? Crown Prince Shaddam is eager to receive an update as he begins the work of his Imperium."

"We make good progress, sir. Our uncrowned Emperor has received my gift, I presume?"

"Yes, very nice, and he sends his appreciation." He smiled tightly as he thought of it: a silver-furred hermafox, capable of self-replication, an unusual living bauble that served no useful purpose whatsoever. "Wherever did you come up with such an interesting creature?"

"We are adepts with the forces of life, sir." *The eyes,* Ajidica thought. *Watch his eyes. They reveal dangerous emotions. Vicious now.*

"So you enjoy playing God?" Fenring said.

With controlled indignation, Ajidica retorted, "There is but one God All High. I would not presume to take His place."

"Of course not." Fenring's eyes narrowed. "Our new Emperor sends his gratitude, but points out one gift he would have greatly preferred— a sample of artificial spice."

"We are working hard on the problem, sir, but we told Emperor El-rood from the outset that it would take many years, possibly even de-cades, to develop a completed product. Much of our labor heretofore has simply been consolidating our control on Xuttah and adapting the existing facilities."

"You've made no tangible progress, then?" Fenring's scorn was so extreme that he couldn't conceal it.

"There are many promising signs."

"Good, then may I tell Shaddam when he should expect his gift? He would like to receive it prior to his coronation, in six weeks' time."

"I don't think that is possible, sir. You brought us a supply of melange as a catalyst less than a Standard Month ago."

"I gave you enough of the stuff to buy several planets."

"Of course, of course, and we *are* moving as quickly as possible. But the axlotl tanks must be grown and modified, probably through several generations. Shaddam must be patient."

Fenring studied the little Tleilaxu, looking for signs of deception. "Patient? Remember, Ajidica, an Emperor does not have unlimited patience."

The dwarf-sized man did not like this Imperial predator. Something in Fenring's overlarge dark eyes and his speech carried a threatening undertone, even when discussing mundane subjects. *Make no mistake. This man will be our new Emperor's enforcer—the one who will murder me if I fail.*

Ajidica took a deep breath, but concealed it in a yawn to avoid showing fear. When he spoke, it was in the calmest of tones. "When God wills our success, it will happen. We move according to His schedule, not our own, and not Prince Shaddam's. That is the way of the universe."

Fenring's huge eyes flashed dangerously. "You realize how impor-tant this is? Not only to the future of House Corrino and the economy of the Imperium . . . but to your personal survival, as well?"

"Most certainly." Ajidica did not react to the threat. "My people have learned the value of waiting. An apple plucked too soon may be green and sour, but if one merely waits until it is ripe, then the fruit is sweet and delicious. When perfected, the artificial spice will alter the entire power structure of the Imperium. It is not possible to engineer such a substance overnight."

Fenring glowered. "We have been patient, but that cannot continue."

With a generous smile, Ajidica said, "If you wish, we can convene regular meetings to display our work and progress. Such distractions, however, would only slow our experiments, our substance analyses, our settings."

"No, keep on," Fenring growled.

I've got the bastard where I want him, Ajidica thought, *and he doesn't like it one bit.* Still, he had the distinct impression that this assassin would do away with him without a second thought. Even now, despite the tightest security scans, Fenring no doubt carried a number of weapons concealed within his clothing, skin, and hair.

He will make the attempt as soon as I'm not needed, when Shaddam thinks he has everything he wants.

Hidar Fen Ajidica had his own concealed weapons, though. He had set up contingency plans to deal with the most dangerous of outsiders . . . to ensure that the Tleilaxu remained in control at all times.

Our laboratories may indeed come up with a substitute for the spice, he thought. *But no* powindah *will ever learn how it is made.*

Our timetable will achieve the stature of a natural phenomenon.
A planet's life is a vast, tightly interwoven fabric. Vegetation and
animal changes will be determined at first by the raw physical
forces we manipulate. As they establish themselves, though, our
changes will become controlling influences in their own right—and
we will have to deal with them, too. Keep in mind, though, that
we need control only three percent of the energy surface—only
three percent—to tip the entire structure over into our self-sustaining
system.

— PARDOT KYNES, Arrakis Dreams

When his son Liet was a year and a half old, Pardot
Kynes and his wife embarked on a journey into the
desert. They dressed their silent child in a custom-fitted
stillsuit and robes to shield his skin against the sun and
the heat.

Kynes was delighted to spend time with his family,
to show them what he had accomplished in the transformation of Dune. His entire life rested on sharing his
dreams.

His three apprentices, Stilgar, Turok, and Ommun, had
tried to insist on going along to protect and guide him, but
Kynes would hear none of it. "I've spent more years alone
in the wilderness than any of you have been alive. I can
handle a few days' sojourn with my family." He made a
shooing gesture with his hands. "Besides, haven't I given
you enough work to do—or shall I find additional tasks?"

"If you have more for us to do," Stilgar said, "we will
gladly do it for you."

"Just . . . just keep yourselves busy," Kynes said,
nonplussed, then set off on foot with Frieth and young
Liet. The baby rode one of the sietch's three kulons, a

domesticated desert ass that had been brought to Dune by smugglers and prospectors.

The animal's water price was high, despite its inbred adaptation to a harsh, arid environment. The Fremen had even developed a modified four-legged stillsuit for the beast, which saved some of the moisture the animal exuded. But in such a contraption the kulon had difficulty moving—in addition to the fact that it looked ridiculous— and Kynes decided not to bother with such extreme measures. This required taking extra water on the journey, which the animal carried in literjons attached to its back.

In the shadow of morning, the tall, bearded Kynes led his small party up a winding thread that only a Fremen would have called a path. His eyes, like Frieth's, were the blue of the Ibad. The desert ass picked its way up the precipitous slope, but made no sound of complaint. Kynes didn't mind walking; he had done so for much of his life, during his years of ecological study on Salusa Secundus and Bela Tegeuse. His muscles rippled, whipcord-tough. Besides, when he went on foot he could keep his eyes focused more on the pebbles and varying grains of sand beneath his boots than on the distant mountains or the sweltering sun.

Eager to please her husband, Frieth turned her attention every time Kynes pointed out a rock formation, studied a spot of ground for its composition, or assessed sheltered crannies as possible sites for planting future vegetation. After a time of uncertainty, she also pointed things out to him. "A Fremen's greatest strength is in observation," Frieth said, as if quoting an old proverb for him. "The more we observe, the more we know. Such knowledge gives us power, especially when others fail to see."

"Interesting." Kynes knew little about his Fremen wife's background. He'd been too busy to ask her for many details about her childhood and her own passions, but she didn't seem in the least offended by his preoccupation with the terraforming work. In Fremen culture, husbands and wives lived in different worlds connected by only a few narrow and fragile bridges.

Kynes knew, however, that Fremen women had a reputation as ferocious fighters—deadly on the battlefield and feared above even Imperial soldiers in one-on-one combat. So far, he had managed to avoid uncovering Frieth's vicious streak, and he hoped never to see it for himself. Fiercely loyal, she would make as formidable a foe as she did a friend.

As he trudged along, a small piece of vegetation caught his eye. Halting the kulon behind him, he knelt to inspect the small, pale green plant that grew in a shaded niche where dust and sand had collected. He recognized the specimen as a rare root plant and brushed the dust from its tiny waxy leaves.

"Look here, Frieth," he said, like a teacher, his eyes shining. "Marvelously tenacious."

Frieth nodded. "We have dug those roots in times of need. It is said a single tuber can yield half a liter of water, enough for a person to survive for several days."

Kynes wondered how much desert knowledge Stilgar's sister held within her Fremen mind; until now she had shared virtually none of it with him. It was his own fault, he told himself, for not paying enough attention to her.

Eager to eat the fresh leaves of the struggling plant, the kulon lowered its muzzle to the ground, nostrils flaring as it sniffed. But Kynes nudged it away. "That plant is too important to be a snack for you."

He scanned the ground, intent on finding other tubers, but noticed none in the immediate vicinity. From what he had learned, these plants were native to Dune, survivors of whatever cataclysm had drained or diverted the moisture from this world.

The travelers took a short break to feed their child. As Frieth set up a shade-floater on a ledge, Kynes recalled the work of recent months and the tremendous progress he and his people had already made as they began their centuries-long project.

Dune had once been a botanical testing station, an isolated outpost with a few sample plantings placed centuries ago in the days of Imperial expansion. This had been done even before the prescient and geriatric properties of melange were discovered . . . back when this world had been a desert hellhole with no discernible use. But the botanical stations had been abandoned; the sparse plantings as well as animal and insect life-forms were left to fare as best they could in the rough environment.

Many species had survived and diversified, demonstrating remarkable durability and adaptability . . . mutated sword grasses, cacti, and other arid-country vegetation. Kynes had already arranged with smugglers to bring in cargoes of the most promising seeds and embryos. Fremen workers then set about sowing the sands and spreading the precious seeds, each one a vital kernel of life, a grain of Dune's future.

From a water merchant, Kynes had learned of the death of Emperor Elrood IX. That had brought back vivid memories of his audience on Kaitain, when the ancient ruler had given him his assignment to come here and research the ecology of Arrakis. The Planetologist owed his entire future to that one meeting. He owed Elrood a great debt of gratitude, but he doubted the ancient Emperor had even remembered him in the last year or so.

Upon hearing the startling news, Kynes had considered trudging back to Arrakeen, booking passage on a Heighliner, and attending the state funeral—but decided he would have felt entirely out of place. He was a desert dweller now, rugged, hardened, and far from the niceties of Imperial politics. Besides, Pardot Kynes had much more important work to complete here.

In the deep south, far from Harkonnen watchers, the Fremen had planted adaptive poverty grasses along the downwind sides of chosen dunes, anchoring them across the prevailing westerly winds. Once the slipfaces were held stable, the windward faces of the dunes grew higher and higher, trying to overcome the plantings, but the Fremen moved their grasses to keep pace, eventually building gigantic sifs that rose as a sinuous soft barrier for many kilometers, some of them more than fifteen hundred meters high. . . .

As he contemplated, Kynes heard his wife stirring under the shadefloater. She talked gently to the child as young Liet suckled her breast through a stillsuit flap.

Next, Kynes pondered the second phase of the ecological transformation process, in which he and his team would plant tougher sword grasses, add processed chemical fertilizers, build windtraps and dewprecipitators. Later, careful not to pressure the fragile new ecology, they would add deeper plantings, including amaranth, pigweed, scotch broom, and dwarf tamarisk, followed by familiar desert icons such as saguaro and barrel cactus. The timetable scrolled out toward the horizon, decades and centuries hence.

In Dune's northern inhabited areas, the Fremen had to content themselves with small plantings and hidden growths. The vast population of Fremen knew the terraforming secret and labored with their

collective sweat and lifeblood . . . and managed to keep the monumental task and its accompanying dream hidden from prying eyes.

Kynes had the patience to see the metamorphosis take place little
by little. The Fremen had intense faith in their "Umma." Their un-
questioning belief in one man's dreams and cooperation with his difficult demands warmed his heart, but Kynes was determined to give
them more than just grand lectures and empty promises. The Fremen
deserved to *see* a brilliant glimmer of hope—and he had accomplished
just that.

Others knew about his place in Plaster Basin, of course, but he
wanted to be the first to show it to Frieth and their baby son Liet. "I'm
taking you to see something incredible," Kynes said as his wife dismantled the minicamp. "I want to show you exactly what Dune can be.
Then you'll understand why I work at it so hard."

"I already understand, husband." Frieth smiled knowingly, then
zip-sealed her pack. "You cannot keep secrets from me." She looked at
him with a strange confidence, and Kynes realized that he did not
need to rationalize his dreams to the Fremen. Any Fremen.

Surveying the increasing steepness and hazards of the trail, Frieth
didn't place the child back on the kulon, but chose to carry him in her
arms instead.

Caught up in his thoughts again, Kynes began speaking aloud to
Frieth as if she were one of his most dedicated students. "The thing
the ecologically illiterate don't realize about an ecosystem is that it's a
system." He grabbed on to a rock on the rough mountain wall and
hauled himself forward. He didn't look back to observe the kulon's difficulties in negotiating the tight turn. Its hooves stumbled on loose
rock, but it followed.

In his mother's arms, the baby Liet whimpered, then silenced himself. Frieth continued to listen to her husband.

"A system maintains a certain fluid stability that can be destroyed
by a single misstep in only one niche. Everything comes crashing
down with the slightest of mistakes. An ecological system flows from
point to point . . . but if something dams that flow, then the order col-
lapses. An untrained person might miss the impending collapse until it
is too late."

Already the Fremen had introduced insect forms, populations of tunneling creatures to aerate the soil. Kit fox, kangaroo mouse, and larger animals such as desert hares and sand terrapin, along with their appropriate predators, desert hawk and dwarf owl, scorpions, centipedes, and trapdoor spiders . . . even the desert bat and biting wasps—every small point interconnected on the web of life.

He couldn't tell if Frieth understood what he was saying or if she was interested. In her silence, she agreed with him wholeheartedly. Just once, though, he wished his wife would debate with him. But Pardot Kynes was her husband and considered a prophet among the Fremen. Her own ingrained beliefs were too strong for her to question anything he said.

Kynes drew a deep breath through his nose filters and continued up the side of the mountain. If they didn't reach the cave opening before afternoon, the sun would pass overhead and bake them. They'd have to find shelter and wouldn't get to Plaster Basin until the following day. Anxious to show them his ecological treasure vault, Kynes picked up the pace.

The rocks stood above them and to their right like the knobbed spine of a starving lizard, casting shadows, muffling sounds. The kulon plodded along, sniffing the ground for something to eat. Frieth, who carried the baby boy without complaint, suddenly froze. Her blue eyes grew wide, flashing from side to side. She cocked her head to listen.

Kynes, weary and hot, but with a spring of eager anticipation in his step, went for five meters before he noticed that his wife had paused. "Husband!" she said in a quick, harsh whisper. Frieth looked up into the blue-white sky, as if trying to see through the mountainous barricade.

"What?" he asked, blinking.

An armored scout 'thopter thrummed over the ridge and rose high from the other side of the mountain wall. Kynes stared up at it, standing out in the sunlit open path. He noted the sandstorm-scarred Harkonnen markings, the scratched paint of the blue-griffin symbol.

Frieth clutched the baby close and scrambled for cover. "Husband! This way!" She tucked their baby into a sheltered cranny of rock far too small for either of the adults, then ran back to get Kynes before he'd managed to react. "Harkonnens—we must hide!" She grabbed his stillsuit sleeve.

The two-man 'thopter circled around close to the cliffside. Kynes realized they had been seen; he and his family made obvious targets on the exposed ridge. Harkonnen troops often made sport of attacking lone Fremen, hunting them down with impunity.

Weapons emerged from the snub nose of the craft. The plaz side window slid open so that one grinning soldier in Harkonnen uniform could extend his lasgun rifle. He had room to swing the stock and take aim.

As his wife passed the desert ass, she gave a bloodcurdling shriek and slapped the kulon hard on its hindquarters. The startled animal brayed and bucked before galloping off up the winding path, spraying loose rocks with its hooves.

Frieth turned the other way and ran downhill, her face hard and intent. Kynes did his best to follow. They stumbled back down the slope, dodging boulders, seeking shadows. Kynes couldn't believe she had left Liet alone, until he realized that his young son was far more protected than either of them was. The baby folded into the shadows, instinctively falling silent and remaining still.

He felt clumsy and exposed, but Frieth seemed to know what to do. She had been raised as a Fremen and understood how to melt into the desert.

The 'thopter roared past them and targeted on the panicked kulon. Frieth must have known the Harkonnens would pick off the animal first. The side gunner leaned out of his open window, his sunburned face smiling. He fired a near-invisible bolt of white-orange fire from the lasgun, which sliced the desert ass into slumping hunks of meat, several of which tumbled down the steep cliffside, while the head and forelegs lay steaming on the path.

Then lasgun explosions began to track down the rock wall, sparking chips of stone that flew off. Barely able to keep their footing, Kynes and Frieth ran pell-mell. She threw him against the wall behind the barest protrusion of lava rock, and the lasgun bolts ricocheted off, missing them by centimeters. Kynes could smell the fresh ozone and stone smoke in the air.

The 'thopter came closer. The side gunner leaned out, aiming his weapon, choosing this kind of sport rather than letting the pilot target them with the heavier weaponry built into the craft itself.

At that moment Kynes's guardian troops opened fire.

From hidden battlements in the camouflaged cliff wall near the cave, Fremen gunners shot the armored hull of the 'thopter. Brilliant lasers dazzled the cockpit viewport. One unseen defender used an old-fashioned artillery launcher, shoulder-mounted, to fire small explosives obtained from smugglers. The artillery shell struck the underbelly of the scout craft, making it lurch and rock in the air.

The sudden jolt knocked the precariously balanced side gunner from his seat. He tumbled out of the craft, screaming, and fell through the air to shatter in an explosive spray of red flesh against the rocks far below; his abandoned lasgun rifle clattered after him.

Frieth huddled against the cliff wall, holding Kynes close, astonished at the unexpected Fremen defense. He could tell she had expected to fight the attackers single-handedly—but he had other protectors as well.

As the Harkonnen 'thopter reeled in the sky, Fremen defenders opened fire on its vulnerable engine components. The air smelled of fire and burned metal. The pilot desperately attempted to stabilize, while black smoke spewed from exhaust ports and lifeblood lubricants sizzled out of severed transport lines. The craft spun, whined, and lumbered toward the ground.

The 'thopter struck the side of the cliff, split open, and continued to scrape down the rock wall. In vain, the articulated wings kept beating, twitching like involuntary muscles, until the craft smashed into the base of the ridge.

"I know of no sietch up here," Frieth said, breathless and confused. "Who are these people? What tribe claims them?"

"Troops of mine, defending the project."

Below, he noticed that the Harkonnen pilot had survived the crash. Part of the canopy popped open, and the wounded man began to crawl out, holding one dangling arm. Within moments camouflaged Fremen troops boiled out of the rocks and swarmed over the wreckage.

The pilot tried to duck back into the dubious safety of his craft, but two Fremen pulled him out. A flash of blue-white crysknife, then a splatter of crimson, and the pilot was dead. Watermen—consecrated body handlers—whisked away the corpse to where its water could be recovered. Kynes knew any moisture or fertilizer chemicals derived from this victim would be devoted to the Plaster Basin project, rather than to enriching any particular family unit.

"But what could be so important up here?" Frieth asked. "What is it you are doing, husband?"

He rewarded her with a sparkling smile. "You will see. I wanted you to be our first visitor."

Frieth hurried back to retrieve their child from his sheltered hiding place. She picked up the baby, checked him for injuries. Young Liet had not even begun to cry. "He's a true Fremen," she said proudly, holding him up for Kynes to see.

Below, organized teams began dismantling the ruined 'thopter, stripping away the metal, the engines, the stash of supplies. Younger Fremen crawled up the dangerous cliff face to retrieve the fallen lasgun rifle.

Kynes led his wife past the remains of the butchered kulon. He gave a sad sigh. "We'll have meat at least—that's a rarity. And I think there's good cause for celebration, once we get to the cave."

The Fremen worked furiously to scour away all traces of the crash, dragging the heavy components into hidden tunnels, repairing scars in the rock, even combing the sand on the desert floor. Though Kynes had been with these people for some time, their hardened efficiency still astonished him.

Striding in the lead now, he led Frieth to the low, shielded opening shortly past noon. The sun burned down, its line of yellow fire sharpening the jagged crest of the mountains. Drifting out of the cave, the smell of cool, rock-moist air was like a refreshing breath.

Kynes plucked out his nose plugs and inhaled deeply, gesturing for his wife to do the same, though she seemed reluctant to shuck her desert survival instincts. Then she grinned in amazement as she looked deep into the shadows. "I smell water, my husband."

He took her arm. "Come with me. This is something I want you to see."

As they rounded a sharp corner whose purpose was to block light and evaporation from the grotto, Kynes gestured magnanimously to indicate the Eden he had made in Plaster Basin.

Yellow glowglobes hovered at the ceiling. The air was rich with humidity, redolent with the scents of flowers, shrubs, trees. The sweet sound of running water chuckled from narrow grooved troughs. In a carefully arranged appearance of randomness, flower beds burst with magenta and orange blossoms.

Irrigation systems trickled droplets into algae-packed tanks, while fans stirred the air to keep the moisture level constant. The grotto was alive with flittering patches of color, butterflies, moths, and bees, heady with the treasure of pollen and nectar around them.

Frieth gasped, and for a moment Kynes saw through the porcelain mask of her face, saw much more than he had ever noticed before. "This is paradise, my love!"

A hummingbird hovered in front of her with a tiny blur of wings, then darted off again. In their own euphoria Fremen gardeners moved about, tending the plants.

"One day gardens like this will grow all across Dune, out in the open air. This is a showcase with growing crops and plants and open water, fruit trees, decorative flowers, green grasses. We have here a symbol for all Fremen, to show them my vision. Seeing this, they'll understand what they can accomplish."

Moisture ran down the walls of the cavern, touching parched rock that had known nothing but thirst for uncounted eons. "Even I did not truly comprehend," Frieth said, ". . . until now."

"Do you see why all this is worth fighting for? And dying for?"

Kynes walked around, inhaling the scents of the leaves, sniffing the perfume of the flowers. He found a tree from which dangled orange globes of ripening fruit. He plucked one, large and golden. None of the workers would question his right to the fresh produce.

"A portygul," he said, "one of the fruits I was talking about back at Red Wall Sietch." He gave it to Frieth as a gift, and she held it reverently in her tanned hands as the greatest treasure she had ever been offered.

Kynes waved expansively at the enclosed grotto. "Remember this well, my wife. All the Fremen must see this. Dune, *our* Dune, can be like this in only a few centuries."

Even innocents carry within them their own guilt in their own way. No one makes it through life without paying, in one fashion or another.

—LADY HELENA ATREIDES,
her personal journals

Immediately after hearing the announcement of the first Imperial coronation ceremony in almost a century and a half, House Atreides began work on their family preparations. From dawn until the fall of darkness, the servants in Castle Caladan went from wardrobe to storeroom, gathering the clothing, trinkets, and gifts necessary for the formal journey to the Imperial Court.

Meanwhile, Leto wandered through his rooms, trying to refine his plan and decide the best way to obtain a dispensation for Rhombur and Kailea. *The new Emperor Shaddam must hear my plea.*

His protocol advisors had bickered for hours over the proper colors of capes, armbands, and merh-silk tunics . . . whether the jewelry should be gaudy or understated, expensive imported Ecazi stones or something simpler. Finally, because of his memorable times with Rhombur, Leto insisted on wearing a small coral gem suspended in a transparent sphere filled with water.

Kailea desperately wanted to go. Visiting the Palace on Kaitain, where her mother had once served the Emperor, had been a lifelong dream of hers. Leto could see the longing in her green eyes, the hope on her face, but still he had no choice but to forbid it. Rhombur had to accompany the entourage, to make his family's case, but if they failed, the Vernius heir could be executed for having left his sanctuary. Kailea's life would be forfeit as well.

If their mission succeeded, though, Leto vowed to take Kailea to the capital world himself, a glamorous vacation that would be all she imagined it to be.

Now, in the quiet hour before dawn, he paced back and forth on the wooden floors of his upper room, listening to the old beams creak. It was the comforting sound of home. How many times had other Dukes paced the same floor pondering decisions of state? Duke Paulus had undoubtedly done so time and again, troubled as he was by uprisings of the primitives in the southern continent or by requests from the Emperor to put out brushfire rebellions on outer worlds. In those times, Paulus Atreides had first blooded his sword, and had become a comrade-in-arms with Dominic Vernius.

Throughout his years the Old Duke had served with talent and finesse, knowing when to be hard and when to be lenient. He had employed the ingredients of dedication, ethics, and economic stability to create a population devoutly loyal to and proud of House Atreides.

How could Leto ever hope to do the same?

His voice filled the room. "Father, you left large shoes for me to fill." He drew a deep breath, angrily forcing away his self-pity. He could do no less than his very best, for Caladan and for the memory of the Old Duke.

On calmer dawns, he and Rhombur might have gone down to the practice courtyard to train with knives and shields under the watchful eye of Thufir Hawat. Today, though, Leto had hoped to get more rest, a hope that hadn't materialized. He'd slept badly, haunted by the weight of decisions that seemed to make the stones of the tall Castle grind together under the burden. Far below, the sea crashed like gnashing teeth—uneasy water that reflected Leto's churning thoughts.

Wrapping himself in a robe lined with expensive imported whale-fur, he cinched the sash at his waist and padded barefoot down the curving steps toward the main hall. He smelled bitter coffee brewing and the faint hint of melange that would be added to his cup. Leto smiled, knowing the cook would insist on the young Duke receiving an extra boost of energy.

He could hear noises from the distant kitchen, food-prep units being primed, breakfast being prepared, old-fashioned fires being stoked. The Old Duke had always preferred real crackling fires in some of the rooms, and Leto had continued the tradition.

When he passed on bare feet through the Hall of Swords on the way to the banquet hall, he stopped upon encountering an unexpected person.

The young stableboy, Duncan Idaho, had removed one of Paulus's tall and ornately carved ceremonial swords from the rack. He held it, point downward, resting against the flagstoned floor. Though the long weapon was nearly as tall as the ten-year-old, Duncan gripped its pommel with determination. The inlaid rope pattern on the hilt gave him all the leverage he needed.

Duncan spun around, startled at being discovered here. Leto's voice caught in his throat in time to squelch a chiding speech. He meant to demand what the boy was doing here, unsupervised and without permission. Then Leto saw Duncan's wide eyes with the tracks of tears running like salty tributaries down his face.

Embarrassed but filled with pride, the young man stood up straighter. "I am sorry, m'Lord Duke." His voice was full of sorrow and much deeper than any child's had a right to be. He looked down at the sword and then through the arched columns into the dining hall, where the portrait of dashing Paulus Atreides hung on the far wall. The hawkish patriarch stared from the painting with burning green eyes; he wore his gaudy matador clothes as if nothing in the universe could knock him from his intended course.

"I miss him very much," Duncan said.

Feeling a lump in his throat that gradually expanded to become a leaden weight in his chest, Leto approached the boy.

Paulus had left his mark upon many lives. Even this youth who worked with the bulls, a mere boy who had somehow managed to outwit Harkonnen hunters and escape from Giedi Prime, felt the loss like a mortal wound.

I am not the only one who still feels the pain of my father's death, Leto realized. He clasped Duncan's shoulder, and in silence they spoke more than hours of conversation could have communicated.

Duncan finally pulled away and leaned on the tall sword as if it were a crutch. His flushed skin returned to its normal tone, and he drew a deep breath. "I came . . . I came to ask you a question, m'Lord, before you go to Kaitain."

Pots clanged in the distance, and servants moved about. Before long, someone would come up to Leto's room bearing a breakfast tray. They would find his room empty. "Ask," he said.

"It's about the bulls, sir. With Yresk gone now, I've been tending them every day, me and some of the other stableboys—but what do you mean to do with them? Will you fight the bulls just like your father?"

"No!" Leto said quickly, as a bolt of fear shot through him. He pushed the reflex away. "No," he repeated more calmly. "I think not. The days of bullfighting on Caladan are over."

"Then what shall I do, m'Lord?" Duncan said. "Do I still need to tend the animals?"

Leto tried not to laugh. At his age the boy should be playing, doing a few chores, and filling his head with imaginings of the grand adventures that awaited him in life.

But when Leto looked into Duncan's eyes, he saw that the person before him was far more than just a boy. He was much older inside. "You've eluded Harkonnens in their prison city, correct?"

Duncan nodded, biting his lower lip.

"You fought them in a forest preserve when you were only eight years of age. You killed several, and if I remember your story right, you cut a tracking device out of your own shoulder and laid a trap for Harkonnen hunters. You humiliated Glossu Rabban himself."

Again Duncan nodded, not with pride, but simply confirming the summary of events.

"And you found your way across the Imperium, coming here to Caladan because this is where you wanted to be. Even the distance of several continents didn't divert you from our doorstep."

"All that is true, m'Lord Duke."

Leto indicated the large ceremonial sword. "My father used that blade for training. It's overlarge for you—at least for now, Duncan—but perhaps with some instruction, you could become a formidable fighter. A Duke is always in need of trustworthy guards and protectors." He pursed his lips, considering. "Do you think you're fit to be one of mine?"

The boy's blue-green eyes shone and he grinned, crinkling his skin around the drying tracks of tears. "Will you send me to the weapon schools of Ginaz so I can become a swordmaster?"

"Ho, ho!" Leto gave a booming laugh that startled his own ears, because it sounded so much like his father's. "Let's not get ahead of ourselves, Duncan Idaho. We'll train you here to the limit of your abilities—then we'll see if you're good enough for such a reward."

Duncan nodded solemnly. "I *will* be good enough."

As Leto heard servants bustling by in the dining room, he raised a hand to signal them over. He would breakfast with this boy and chat some more.

"You can count on me, my Duke."

Leto drew a long, deep breath. He wished he could share the unshakable confidence of this young man. "Yes, Duncan, I believe you."

Innovations seem to have a life and a sentience of their own. When conditions are right, a radical new idea—a paradigm shift—may appear simultaneously from many minds at once. Or it may remain secret in the thoughts of one man for years, decades, centuries . . . until someone else thinks of the same thing. How many brilliant discoveries die stillborn, or lie dormant, never to be embraced by the Imperium as a whole?

—OMBUDSMEN OF RICHESE, Rebuttal to the Landsraad,
The True Domain of the Intellect—
Private Property, or Resources for the Galaxy?

The tube transport dropped its two passengers into the depths of Harkonnen Keep and then, with programmed precision, shot them across an access rail.

The capsule, with the Baron and Glossu Rabban inside, raced toward the swarming morass of Harko City, a smoky blot on the landscape where buildings crowded together. To the Baron's knowledge, there was no detailed map of the city's underworld, since it continued to grow like a fungus. He wasn't sure exactly where they were going.

While scheming against the Atreides, he had insisted that Piter de Vries find extensive yet confidential laboratory space and fabrication facilities in the armpit of Harkonnen influence. The Mentat said he'd done so, and the Baron didn't ask further questions. This tube transport, dispatched by de Vries, was taking them there.

"I want to know the whole plan, Uncle," Rabban said, fidgeting next to him in the compartment. "Tell me what we're going to do."

Up front in the piloting cubicle, a deaf-mute vehicle specialist hurried them along. The Baron paid no attention to the dark and blocky buildings flashing by, the clouds of exhaust and residue spilling from the factories. Giedi Prime produced sufficient goods to pay for itself, and tidy sums came in from the whale-fur trade on Lankiveil and mineral excavation on various asteroids. The really big profits for House Harkonnen, however—dwarfing all the others combined—were from spice exploitation on Arrakis.

"The plan, Rabban, is simple," he answered finally, "and I intend to offer you a key part in it. If you can handle it."

His nephew's heavy-lidded eyes lit up, and his thick lips twisted his generous mouth into a grin. Surprisingly, he knew enough to re-main quiet and wait for the Baron to continue. *Maybe, eventually, he'll learn. . . .*

"If we succeed in this, Rabban, our fortunes will increase dramati-cally. Better still, we can take personal satisfaction in knowing that we have at last ruined House Atreides, after all these centuries of feuding."

Rabban rubbed his hands in delight, but the Baron's black stare be-came harder as he continued. "If you fail, however, I'll see to it that you're transferred back to Lankiveil, where you'll be trained any way your father wishes—complete with singalongs and the recitation of poems about brotherly love."

Rabban glowered. "I won't fail, Uncle."

The tube car arrived at an armored high-security laboratory, and the deaf-mute motioned for them to exit the vehicle. The Baron couldn't have found his way back to Harkonnen Keep if his life had depended upon it.

"What is this place?" Rabban asked.

"A research establishment," the Baron said, waving him forward. "One where we are preparing a nasty surprise."

Rabban marched ahead, eager to see the facility. The place smelled of solder and waste oils, blown fuses, and sweat. From the cluttered, open floor, Piter de Vries came up to greet them, stained lips smiling. His mincing footsteps and slithery, jerky movements gave him the de-meanor of a lizard.

"You've had weeks here already, Piter. This had better be good. I told you not to waste my time."

"Not to worry, my Baron," the Mentat answered, gesturing for them to come deeper into the building's high bay. "Our pet researcher Chobyn has outdone himself."

"And I always thought Richesians were better at cheap imitations than actual innovations," Rabban said.

"There are exceptions everywhere," the Baron said. "Let's see what Piter has to show us."

Filling most of the chamber was what de Vries had secretly promised the Baron: a modified Harkonnen warship, 140 meters in diameter. Sleek and highly polished, this craft had been used to good effect in conventional battles to strike hard and escape quickly. Now it had been converted according to Chobyn's exacting specifications, with the tail fins trimmed, the engine replaced, and a section of the troop cabin cut away to make room for the required technology. All records of the craft's existence had been expunged from Harkonnen ledgers. Piter de Vries was good at manipulations like that.

A rotund man with a bald pate and steel-gray goatee emerged from the engine compartment of the attack ship, stained with grease and other lubricants.

"My Baron, sir, I'm pleased you have come to see what I've accomplished for you." Chobyn tucked a tool into the pocket of his overalls. "Installation is complete. My no-field will operate perfectly. I've synchronized it with the machinery of this ship."

Rabban rapped his knuckles on the hull near the cockpit. "Why is it so big? This hulk is large enough to carry an armored groundcar unit. How are we going to do any secret work with this?"

Chobyn raised his eyebrows, not recognizing the burly young man. "And you are . . . ?"

"This is Rabban, my nephew," the Baron said. "He raises a valid question. I asked for a small stealth ship."

"This is the tiniest I could make it," Chobyn answered with a huff. "A hundred and forty meters is the smallest cloak of invisibility the no-field generator can project. The constraints are . . . incredible. I—"

The inventor cleared his throat, suddenly impatient. "You must learn to think beyond your preconceptions, sir. Realize what we have here. Naturally, the invisibility more than makes up for any diminished maneuvering capability." He wrinkled his brow again. "What difference does the size make, if no one can see it anyway? This attack craft will still fit easily inside the hold of a frigate."

"It will do, Chobyn," the Baron said. "If it works."

De Vries scuttled back and forth along the length of the ship. "If no one knows to *look* for the ship, Rabban, you won't be in any danger. Imagine the chaos you can create! You'll be like a killer ghost."

"Oh, yes!" Rabban paused as realization flooded across his face. *"Me?"*

Chobyn closed an access hatch behind the engines. "Everything is simple and functional. The ship will be ready by tomorrow when you depart for the Padishah Emperor's coronation."

"I have verified it, my Baron," de Vries said.

"Excellent," the Baron said. "You have proven yourself most valuable, Chobyn."

"I'm going to pilot it?" Rabban said again, as if he still couldn't believe the idea. His voice cracked with excitement. Baron Harkonnen nodded. His nephew, despite his shortcomings, was at least an excellent pilot and an excellent shot, along with being the Baron's heir apparent.

The inventor smiled. "I believe I made the correct choice in coming to you directly, Baron. House Harkonnen has immediately seen the possibilities of my discovery."

"When the new Emperor learns of this, he'll demand a no-ship for himself," Rabban pointed out. "He might even send the Sardaukar in to take it away from us."

"Then we must make sure Shaddam doesn't find out. At least not yet," Piter de Vries replied, rubbing his hands together.

"You must be a brilliant man, Chobyn," the Baron said. "Coming up with all this."

"Actually, I just adapted a Holtzman field to our uses. Centuries ago Tio Holtzman's mathematics were developed for shields and foldspace engines. I simply carried the principles several steps further."

"And now you expect to become wealthy beyond your wildest dreams?" the Baron mused.

"Deservedly so, would you not agree, Baron?" Chobyn said. "Look what I've done for you. If I'd stayed on Richese and gone through channels, I would have had to endure years of legalities, title searches, and patent investigations, after which my government would have taken the lion's share of profit derived from my own invention—not to speak of the imitators who would set to work once they got wind of what I was doing. A minor adjustment here, another there, and then someone else has a different patent, one that accomplishes essentially the same thing."

"So you kept it a secret until you came to us?" Rabban said. "No one else knows of the technology?"

"I'd have been foolish to tell anyone else. You have the only no-field generators in the universe." Chobyn crossed his arms over his stained jumpsuit.

"Perhaps for the time being," the Baron said, "but the Ixians were a clever lot, and so are the Tleilaxu. Sooner or later someone else will have something like this, if they don't already."

Rabban maneuvered himself closer to the unwary Richesian.

"I see your point, Baron," Chobyn said, with a shrug. "I am not a greedy man, but I would like to profit from my own invention."

"You are a wise man," the Baron said, flashing a meaningful glance at his burly nephew. "And deserve to be paid in full."

"It's good to keep secrets about important things," Rabban chimed in.

He stood directly behind the rotund inventor, who beamed at the praise and wiped his hands on his pant legs.

Rabban moved swiftly, like a whiplash, wrapping his muscular fore-arm around Chobyn's neck, then squeezed tightly like a vise. The inventor gasped but could make no other sound. Rabban's face reddened with the strain as he pulled back with his arm until he was rewarded with the loud *crack* of a crushed spine.

"We must all be more careful with our secrets, Chobyn," the Baron muttered, smiling. "You haven't been careful enough."

Like a broken doll, Chobyn collapsed with only a rustle of his clothes to the oil-stained floor. Rabban had been so forceful that Chobyn gurgled no death rattle, gasped out no final curses.

"Was that wise, my Baron?" de Vries asked. "Shouldn't we have tested the ship first, to make sure we can reproduce the technology?"

"Why? Don't you trust our inventor . . . the *late* Chobyn?"

"It works," Rabban said. "Besides, you've had him under comeye surveillance, and we have the detailed plans and holorecordings he made during the construction process."

"I've already taken care of the workers," the Mentat said, nodding in agreement. "No chance for leaks there."

Rabban smiled greedily. "Did you save me any of them?"

De Vries gave a jittering shrug. "Well, I've had my fun, but I'm not a pig. I did leave a few for you." He nodded toward a bank of solid doors. "Second room on the right. Five of them are in there on gurneys, drugged. Enjoy yourself." The Mentat patted the beefy Harkonnen on the shoulder.

Rabban took a couple of steps toward the door, then hesitated and looked back at his uncle, who had not yet given permission for him to leave. The Baron was studying de Vries.

The twisted Mentat furrowed his brow. "We are the first with a no-ship, my Baron. With the advantage of surprise, no one will ever suspect what it is we intend to do."

"What *I'm* going to do," Rabban said gruffly.

De Vries used a handheld com-unit to speak to several sluggish workers in the lab. "Clean up this mess and get the attack ship moved to the family frigate before departure time tomorrow."

"I want all technical notes and records confiscated and sealed," the Baron ordered as the Mentat switched off the communicator.

"Yes, my Baron," de Vries said. "I'll see to it personally."

"You may go now," the Baron said to his anxious nephew. "An hour or two of relaxation will do you good . . . it'll get your mind in order for the important work ahead."

They demonstrate subtle, highly effective skills in the aligned arts
of observation and data collection. Information is their stock-in-
trade.

—Imperial Report on the Bene Gesserit,

used for tutoring purposes

This is most impressive," Sister Margot Rashino-Zea
said, as she gazed at the imposing buildings on each
side of the enormous oval of the Imperial-Landsraad Commons. "A spectacle for all the senses." After long years on
the cloudy, bucolic world of Wallach IX, her eyes now
ached from so many sights.

A refreshing, fine mist rose from the fountain at the
center of the Commons, an extraordinary artistic composition that towered a hundred meters overhead. In the design
of a glittering nebula swirl, the fountain was replete with
oversize planets and other celestial bodies that spurted perfumed streams in myriad colors. Tightbeam spotlights refracted from the water, creating loops of rainbows that
danced silently in the air.

"Ah, yes, you have never been to Kaitain, I see," Crown
Prince Shaddam said, strolling casually beside the lovely
blonde Bene Gesserit. Sardaukar guards hovered in the
background, assuming they were near enough to prevent
any harm from coming to the Imperial heir. Margot suppressed a smile, always pleased to see how much other people underestimated the Sisterhood.

"Oh, I've seen it before, Sire. But familiarity does not lessen my admiration for the magnificent capital of the Imperium."

Dressed in a new black robe that rustled stiffly as she moved, Margot was flanked by Shaddam on one side and Hasimir Fenring on the other. She did not hide her long golden hair, her fresh face, or her pristine beauty. Most of the time, people expected the Bene Gesserit to be old hags shrouded in layers of dark garments. But many, like Margot Rashino-Zea, could be stunningly attractive. With a precise release of her body's pheromones and carefully selected flirtations, she could use her sexuality as a weapon.

But not here, not yet. The Sisterhood had other plans for the Emperor-to-be.

Margot was nearly Shaddam's height, and much taller than Fenring. Behind them, out of hearing range, an entourage of three Reverend Mothers followed, women who had been investigated and cleared by Fenring himself. The Crown Prince did not know what these others had to do with this meeting, but Margot would convey the reason presently.

"You should see these gardens at night," Shaddam said. "The water looks like a meteor shower."

"Oh, yes," Margot said with a faint smile. Her gray-green eyes glittered. "This is my favorite place to be in the evenings. I have come twice since my arrival here . . . in anticipation of this private meeting with you, Sire."

Though he tried to make casual conversation with this representative of the powerful Bene Gesserit, Shaddam felt ill at ease. Everyone wanted something, everyone had a private agenda—and every group thought it was owed favors or held sufficient blackmail material to sway his opinion. Fenring had already taken care of several of those parasites, but more would come.

His current uneasiness had less to do with Sister Margot than with his concerns over mounting mistrust and turmoil among the Great Houses. Even without an autopsy by the Suks, several important members of the Landsraad had raised uncomfortable questions over the Emperor's mysterious, lingering death. Alliances were shifting and re-forming; important taxes and tithes from several wealthy worlds had been delayed, without adequate explanation.

And the Tleilaxu claimed to be years away from producing their promised synthetic spice.

Shaddam and his inner council would discuss the brewing crisis again this morning, a continuation of meetings that had gone on for a week. The length of Elrood's reign had forced a stability (if not stagnation) across the Imperium. No one remembered *how* to implement an orderly transition of power.

All across the worlds, military forces were being increased in strength and placed on alert. Shaddam's Sardaukar were no exception. Spies were busier than ever, in all quarters. At times he wondered if his reassignment of Elrood's trusted Chamberlain Aken Hesban might have been a mistake. Hesban now sat in a tiny, rock-walled office deep in the gullet of an asteroid mine, ready to be recalled if things ever got too bad.

But it'll be a cold day on Arrakis before that happens.

Shaddam's unease made him jumpy, perhaps a little superstitious. His old vulture of a father was dead—sent to the deepest hell described in the Orange Catholic Bible—yet still he felt the invisible blood on his hands.

Before departing the Palace to meet with Sister Margot, Shaddam had, without much thought, grabbed a cloak to warm his shoulders against an imagined chill in the morning air. The gold mantle had hung in the wardrobe with many other garments he had never worn. Only now did he remember that this particular article had been a favorite of his father's.

Realizing this, Shaddam's skin crawled. He felt the fine material prickle him suddenly, making him shiver. The fine gold chain seemed to tighten at his throat like a noose.

Ridiculous, he told himself. Inanimate objects did not carry spirits of the dead, couldn't possibly harm him. He tried to put such concerns out of his mind. A Bene Gesserit would certainly be able to read his discomfort, and he couldn't allow this woman so much power over him.

"I love the artwork here," Margot said. She pointed toward a scaffold fixed to the face of the Landsraad Hall of Oratory, where fresco painters worked on a mural depicting scenes of natural beauty and technological achievement from around the Imperium. "I believe your great-grandfather Vutier Corrino II was responsible for much of this?"

"Ah, yes—Vutier was a great patron of the arts," Shaddam said with some difficulty. Resisting an urge to remove the haunted cloak and throw it to the ground, he vowed to wear only his own clothes henceforth. "He said that spectacle without warmth or creativity meant nothing."

"I think you should make your point, please, Sister," Fenring suggested, noting his friend's discomfort, but guessing incorrectly as to its cause. "The Crown Prince's time is valuable. There is much turmoil after the Emperor's death."

Shaddam and Fenring had murdered Elrood IX. That fact could never be erased, and they hadn't escaped suspicion entirely, not according to rumors. War between the Landsraad and House Corrino might result unless the Crown Prince consolidated his position, and soon.

Margot had been so persistent about the importance of a certain matter, using all the quiet clout of the Bene Gesserit, that an audience had been granted to her on short notice. The only time open was during one of Shaddam's morning walks, an hour he normally reserved for quiet personal reflection ("grief for his dead father," according to the Court gossip Fenring had fostered).

Margot favored the weasel-faced man beside her with a pretty smile and a casual toss of her honey-blonde hair. Her gray-green eyes studied him. "You know very well what I wish to discuss with your friend, Hasimir," she said, employing a familiar tone that astonished the Imperial heir. "Didn't you prepare him?"

Fenring shook his head jerkily, and Shaddam saw him weaken in her presence. The deadly man wasn't his usual forceful self. The Bene Gesserit delegation had been here for some days, waiting, and Margot Rashino-Zea had spent a great deal of time with Fenring in close discussions. Shaddam cocked his head, sensing some affection—or at least mutual respect—between the two. Impossible!

"Hmm-m-m-ah, I thought you might phrase it better than I could, Sister," Fenring said. "Sire, the lovely Margot has an interesting proposal for you. I think you should listen to her."

The Bene Gesserit looked at Shaddam strangely. *Has she noticed my distress?* he wondered, suddenly panicked. *Does she know the reason for my feelings?*

The sigh of the fountain drowned out their words. Margot took Shaddam's hands in hers, and they were pleasingly soft and warm to him. Gazing into her sensual eyes, he felt her strength flow back into him, a comfort. "You must have a wife, Sire," she said. "And the Bene Gesserit can provide the best match for you and House Corrino."

Startled, Shaddam glanced over at his friend and snatched his hands back. Fenring smiled, uneasily.

"Soon you will be crowned Emperor," Margot continued. "The Sisterhood can help you secure your power base—more than an alliance with any single Great House of the Landsraad. During his life, your father married into the Mutelli, Hagal, and Ecaz families, as well as your own mother from Hassika V. However, in these difficult times, we believe you would gain the greatest advantage by allying your throne with the power and resources of the Bene Gesserit Sisterhood." She spoke firmly, convincingly.

He noticed that the entourage of Sisters had stopped a distance away and stood watching them. Out of earshot, the Sardaukar remained watchful but motionless, like statues. He looked at Margot's perfectly formed face, her golden hair, her hypnotic presence.

She surprised him by turning back to the entourage and pointing. "Do you see the woman in the center over there? The one with bronze hair?"

Noting the gesture, a robed Reverend Mother stepped forward. Shaddam squinted, assessing her features, her doelike face. Even from a distance, he found her rather attractive, though she was not a classic beauty. Not as lovely as Margot, unfortunately, but she did seem young and fresh.

"Her name is Anirul, a Bene Gesserit of Hidden Rank."

"What does that mean?"

"It's just one of our titles, Sire, quite common in the Sisterhood. It means nothing outside the order and is irrelevant to your work as Emperor." Margot paused a beat. "You need only know that Anirul is one of our best. We are offering her to you in marriage."

Shaddam felt a jolt of surprise. "What?"

"The Bene Gesserit are quite influential, you know. We can work behind the scenes to smooth over any difficulties you currently have with the Landsraad. This would free you to perform the work of being Emperor and secure your place in history. A number of your grandfathers have done this, to good effect." She narrowed her gray-green eyes. "We are aware of the troubles you currently face, Sire."

"Yes, yes, I know all that." He looked over at Fenring, as if the weasel-faced man could explain himself. Then Shaddam beckoned for

Anirul herself to come forward. The guards looked at one another un-easily, not knowing whether they should accompany her.

In front of him, Margot's gaze intensified. "You are now the most powerful man in the universe, Sire, but your political rule is balanced between yourself, the Landsraad Council, and the powerful forces of the Spacing Guild and the Bene Gesserit. Your marriage to one of my Sisters would be . . . mutually beneficial."

"Besides, Sire," Fenring added, his eyes even larger than usual, "an alliance with any other Great House would bring with it certain . . . baggage. You would join with one family at the risk of spurning an-other. We don't want to trigger another rebellion."

Though surprised by the suggestion, Shaddam rather liked the sound of it. One of his father's adages about leadership indicated that a ruler needed to pay attention to his instincts. The haunted cloak hung heavy on his shoulders like a crushing weight. Maybe the witching powers of the Sisterhood could ward off whatever malevolent force in-habited the garment and the Palace.

"This Anirul of yours does have an appealing look to her." Shad-dam watched as the proffered woman stepped forward and stood at silent attention, eyes averted, five paces from his royal person.

"Then will you consider our proposal, Sire?" Margot asked and took a respectful step back, awaiting his decision.

"Consider it?" Shaddam smiled. "I already have. In my position, decisions must be made quickly and decisively." He looked at Fenring, narrowing his eyes. "Wouldn't you agree, Hasimir?"

"Ah-hm-m-m, that depends upon whether you're choosing a new garment or a wife."

"Wise counsel on the surface," Shaddam said to Fenring. "But disingenuous, I think. You are obviously Sister Margot's friend, and *you* arranged this meeting, knowing full well the request she would make. I must, therefore, presume you concur with the Bene Gesserit position."

Fenring bowed. "The decision is yours, Sire, no matter my personal opinion or feelings toward this beautiful woman beside me."

"Very well, my answer is . . . yes." Hearing this from where she stood, Reverend Mother Anirul did not even smile. "Do you believe I have made the right choice, Hasimir?"

Unaccustomed to being caught off-balance, Fenring cleared his throat several times. "She is a fine lady, Sire, and will no doubt make a superb wife. And the Bene Gesserit should make excellent allies, especially in these difficult transition times."

The Crown Prince laughed. "You sound like one of our diplomats. Give me a yes or a no, without equivocation."

"Yes, Majesty. That is, I give you a yes, without hesitation. Anirul is a woman of fine breeding and disposition . . . a bit young, but she has a great wisdom about her." With a glance at Margot beside him, Fenring said, "You assured me that she can indeed bear children?"

"Royal heirs will flow from her loins," Margot quipped.

"What an image!" Shaddam exclaimed, with another hearty laugh. "Bring her to me so I can meet her myself."

Margot raised her hand, and Anirul hurried to the Crown Prince's side. The rest of the Bene Gesserit entourage buzzed with conversation.

Shaddam looked at the woman closely, noted that Anirul—his wife-to-be—had delicate features. He noted tiny lines around the doe eyes, though her gaze was youthful and her movements lithe. At the moment she continued to lower her head with its ruffled bronze hair. As if being coy, she looked at the Crown Prince and then away again.

"You have just made one of the best decisions of your life, Sire," Margot said. "Your reign will have a strong foundation."

"This is cause for celebration, with all the pomp and splendor the Imperium can muster," Shaddam said. "In fact, I plan to announce that the marriage will take place on the same day as my coronation."

Fenring beamed. "It will be the grandest spectacle in Imperial history, my friend."

Shaddam and Anirul exchanged smiles, and touched hands for the first time as he reached out to her.

When the center of the storm does not move, you are in its path.
—Ancient Fremen Wisdom

The Atreides frigate departed from Cala City Spaceport for the Padishah Emperor's coronation, loaded with an abundance of banners, exquisite clothes, jewels, and gifts. Duke Leto wanted to make sure he contributed visibly to the magnificence of the Imperial ceremony.

"It is a good tactic," Thufir Hawat agreed with a grim nod. "Shaddam has always reveled in the trappings of his position. The more finery you wear and the more gifts you present him, the more impressed he'll be . . . and therefore the more inclined to grant your request."

"He appears to value form over substance," Leto mused. "But appearances can be deceiving, and I dare not underestimate him."

Kailea had worn her own gorgeous sky-blue-and-lilac dress to see them off, but she would remain at the Castle, with no one to see her finery. Leto could see how much she longed to go to the Imperial Court, but he refused to bend in his decision. Old Paulus had taught him stubbornness as well.

Rhombur emerged into the staging area wearing pantaloons, a synthetic merh-silk shirt, and a billowing cape of purple and copper, colors of the lost House Vernius. He stood proudly, while Kailea gasped at her brother's bravery for flaunting his family heritage. He seemed much more a man now, muscular and tanned, without the gentle roundings of baby fat.

"Some might see that as arrogance, my Duke," Hawat said, nodding toward Rhombur's clothes.

"This is all a gamble, Thufir," Leto said. "We need to hark back to the grandeur that was lost when Tleilaxu treachery forced this noble family to go renegade. We must show the shortsightedness of Emperor Elrood's malicious decision. We must help Shaddam see what a great ally House Vernius could be to the Imperial throne. After all"—he gestured to the proud Rhombur—"would you rather have *this man* as your ally, or the filthy Tleilaxu?"

The Master of Assassins favored him with a small, contained smile. "I wouldn't come out and say that directly to Shaddam."

"We'll say it without words," Leto replied.

"You are going to make a formidable Duke, m'Lord," Hawat said.

They walked together from the staging area to the landing field, where twice the usual complement of Atreides troops had just finished boarding the frigate that would take them up to the waiting Heighliner.

Kailea came forward and gave Leto a brief, formal hug. Her pastel dress rustled with her movements, and he pressed his cheek against one of the gold combs in her copper-dark hair. He could feel the tension in her arms, and sensed that they both wanted to share a much more passionate embrace.

Then, with tears in her eyes, the daughter of Dominic and Shando Vernius clutched her brother even more desperately. "Be careful, Rhombur. This is so dangerous."

"This may be the only way we can restore our family name," Rhombur answered. "We must throw ourselves upon the mercy of Shaddam. Perhaps he'll be different from his father. He has nothing to gain by maintaining the sentence against us, and much to lose—especially with the restlessness in the Imperium. He needs all the friends and strength he can get." He smiled and swirled the purple-and-copper cape.

"Ix is wasted on the Bene Tleilax," Kailea noted. "They don't have an inkling about how to run a galactic business."

Leto, Rhombur, and Hawat would be representatives from Caladan. Brash perhaps, and showy in their impertinence—or would it be seen as calm confidence? Leto hoped for the latter.

As Duke, he knew that flying in the face of Court politics was unwise. But his heart told him to gamble when the stakes were important enough, when he was on the side of righteousness—where he always intended to be. The Old Duke had taught him no less.

His father had shown him that a gambit filled with bravado often paid off far more substantially than a conservative and unimaginative plan . . . so why not this? Would the Old Duke have done something similar, or would he, guided by his wife, have taken a safer course? Leto had no answer for that, but was thankful that he didn't have anyone like the stern and inflexible Lady Helena getting in his way now. When he decided to marry, it would never be to anyone like her.

He had sent a formal Courier to the Sisters in Isolation compound on the Eastern Continent, notifying his mother that he and Rhombur would journey to Kaitain. He didn't delineate their plan or comment on the obvious risk involved, but he wanted her to be prepared for the worst. With no other heirs, Lady Helena would become the ruler of House Atreides should things go wrong, should Leto find himself executed or "accidentally" killed. Though he knew she had instigated the murder of his father, he had no choice in this circumstance. It was a matter of form.

The final pieces of Atreides luggage and trunks were loaded aboard, and within seconds the big frigate leaped into the gray-locked skies of Caladan. This would be different from his previous trips—the future of Rhombur's bloodline hung in the balance . . . and perhaps his own as well.

With all the ceremonial fanfare, Leto was fortunate to have been granted an Imperial audience four days after the coronation. At that time he and Rhombur would make a formal petition to Shaddam, stating their case and throwing themselves on his mercy.

In the glorious first days of his regime, would the new Padishah Emperor risk casting a dark pall upon the festivities by renewing a sentence of death? Many Houses still saw omens in every action, and Shaddam was rumored to be as superstitious as any of them. This omen would be clear enough. By his own decision, Shaddam would establish the tenor of his reign. Would the Emperor want to begin by denying justice? Leto hoped not.

The ducal frigate took its assigned position inside the Heighliner's cavernous but crowded cargo bay. Nearby, shuttles full of passengers moved delicately into position, along with transports and cargo ships filled with the trading goods of Caladan: pundi rice, medicinals from processed kelp, handmade tapestries, and preserved fish products. Privately owned lighters were still loading merchandise into the hold, ferrying up from the surface to the Heighliner. This huge Guild ship had gone from world to world on its roundabout route to Kaitain, and the province-sized cargo bay was dotted with ships from other worlds in the Imperium, all on their way to the coronation.

While they waited, Thufir Hawat looked at the chronometer mounted on a bulkhead of the frigate. "We still have three hours before the Heighliner completes loading and unloading and is ready to depart. I suggest we use this time for training, m'Lord."

"You always suggest that, Thufir," Rhombur said.

"Because you are young and require considerable instruction," the Mentat countered.

Leto's plush frigate was so full of amenities that he and his entourage could forget they were even off-planet. But he'd had enough of relaxing, and the anxiety of impending events filled him with a nervous energy that he wanted to discharge. "You have a suggestion, Thufir? What can we do out here?"

The Master of Assassins' eyes lit up. "In space, there are many things a Duke—and a Prince—" he said with a nod to Rhombur, "can learn."

⁕

A WINGLESS COMBAT pod the size of an ornithopter dropped out of the hold of the Atreides frigate and descended away from the Heighliner, into space. Leto worked the controls with Rhombur sitting in the copilot's seat to his right. It reminded Leto for a moment of their brief training attempt in the Ixian orship, a near disaster.

Hawat stood behind them wearing a mobile crash restraint. In his harness he looked like a pillar of wisdom, frowning down at the two young men as they felt their way through the combat pod's controls for the first time. An emergency override panel floated in front of Hawat.

"This craft is different from a coracle at sea, young sirs," Hawat said.

"Unlike the larger ships, we're in zero gravity here, with all the flexibility and constraints that implies. You have both done the simulations, but now you are about to discover what real space combat is all about."

"I get to fire the weapons first," Rhombur said, repeating their prior arrangement.

"And I'm piloting," Leto added, "but we switch in half an hour."

Behind him, Hawat spoke in a monotone: "It's not likely, m'Lord Duke, that you will find yourself in a situation that requires space combat, but—"

"Yes, yes, I should always be prepared," Leto said. "If I've learned anything from you, Thufir, it's that."

"First you must learn maneuvering." Hawat guided Leto through a series of cruising curves and sharp arcs. He stayed sufficiently far from the enormous Heighliner, but close enough that he felt it constituted a genuine obstacle at this speed. Once, Leto reacted too quickly and plunged the combat pod into an uncontrolled spin, which he pulled out of by firing reaction jets to stop them without sending the craft spiraling in the opposite direction.

"Reaction and counter-reaction," Hawat said, with approval. His now-tilted mobile crash restraint righted itself. "When you and Rhombur had your boating accident on Caladan, you were able to run aground on a reef to stop things from getting worse. Here, though, there is no safety net to catch you. If you spin out of control, you will continue to do so until the proper countermeasures are taken. You could fall and burn up in the atmosphere, or in deeper space you might hurtle into the void."

"Uh, let's not do any of that today," Rhombur said. He looked over at his friend. "I'd like to try some practice shots now, Leto, if you can keep this thing flying straight for a few minutes."

"No problem," Leto said.

Bending to the weaponeer station between the boys, Hawat said, "I loaded skeet-drones into the hold. Rhombur, try to fire and nullify as many of them as you can. You have free range to use whatever weaponry you wish. Lasbeams, conventional explosives, or multiphase projectiles. But first, m'Lord"—Hawat squeezed Leto's shoulder— "please take us around to the other side of the planet where we won't have to worry about hitting the Heighliner when Rhombur's shots go wild."

With a chuckle, Leto did as he was instructed, cruising high above the clouds of Caladan to the nightside, where the planet lay black below them except for necklaces of city lights strung along the distant coasts. Behind them, the glare of Caladan's sun formed a halo against the dark eclipse of the planet.

Hawat launched a dozen spinning, glittering globes that flew off on random paths. Rhombur grabbed the weapons control—a stilo bar with multicolored panels—and blasted shots in all directions, most of which missed entirely, although he did remove one drone with a spray of multiphase projectiles. They all knew the bull's-eye was a mere accident, and Rhombur took no pride in it.

"Patience and control, Prince," Hawat said. "You must use each shot as if it were your last. Make it count. Once you've learned to hit things, then you can be more liberal with your expenditures."

Leto chased after the drones as Rhombur fired with the full array of weapons available to him. When Rhombur had finally succeeded in eliminating all the targets, he and Leto switched positions and went through more practice maneuvers.

Two hours passed swiftly, and finally the Mentat instructed them to return to the Guild Heighliner so they could make themselves comfortable before the Navigator folded space and guided the ship to Kaitain.

SETTLED IN, LOUNGING on his plush hawk-crested chair, Leto stared out the window into the crowded cluster of ships inside the Heighliner bay. He sipped a mug of mulled wine that reminded him of Kailea and the stormy night when they had rummaged through the Old Duke's possessions. He longed for peaceful interludes and warm companionship, though he knew it would be a long time before his life became settled again.

"The ships are so close together in here," he said. "It makes me uneasy." He watched two Tleilaxu transports take positions near the Atreides frigate. Beyond the transports a Harkonnen frigate hung in its Guild-assigned place.

"Nothing to worry about, my Duke," Hawat said. "By the rules of warfare dictated by the Great Convention, no one can fire a weapon inside a Heighliner. Any House breaking that rule faces permanent forfeiture of its access to Guild ships. No one would risk that."

"Are our shields up anyway?" Leto asked.

"Vermilion hells, no shields, Leto!" Rhombur said, with alarm in his voice. He laughed. "You should have learned more about Heighliners on Ix—or were you looking at my sister the whole time?"

Leto flushed crimson, but Rhombur explained quickly. "Aboard a Heighliner, shields interfere with the ship's Holtzman propulsion system, preventing it from folding space. An active shield disrupts a Navigator's ability to hold his navigation trance. We'd be dead in space."

"It is also forbidden under our Guild transport contract," Hawat said, as if the legal reason might somehow carry more weight.

"So we're all here unprotected, naked, and trusting," Leto grumbled, still seeing the Harkonnen ship through the plaz ports.

Rhombur said with a defeated smile, "You're making me remember how many people wish me dead."

"All ships inside this Heighliner are equally vulnerable, Prince," Hawat said. "But you should not concern yourself just yet. Your greatest peril lies ahead, on Kaitain. For now, even I intend to rest a bit. Here on board our frigate, we are as safe as we can be."

Leto looked out and up at the distant roof of the Heighliner hold. High above in a minuscule navigation chamber, a single Navigator in a tank of orange spice gas controlled the enormous bulk of the ship.

Despite Hawat's assurances, he remained uneasy. Beside him, Rhombur fidgeted as well, but struggled to cover his anxiety. With an agitated breath the young Duke sat back, trying to let his tension drain away and prepare for the political crisis he was about to initiate on Kaitain.

Storms beget storms. Rage begets rage. Revenge begets revenge. Wars beget wars.

—Bene Gesserit Conundrum

The Guild Heighliner's external hull hatches were sealed, the cavernous openings closed, and the vessel made ready to depart. Soon the Navigator would go into his trance, and the ship would be under way. The next and final destination on this route would be Kaitain, where representatives of the Great and Minor Houses of the Landsraad had begun arriving for the coronation of Padishah Emperor Shaddam IV.

The Navigator maneuvered the enormous vessel away from the gravity well of Caladan and out into open space, preparing to engage the huge Holtzman engines that would carry it in wild leaps across foldspace.

The passengers aboard family frigates within the liner's holding bay discerned no movement whatsoever, no motion from the engines, no change in position, no sound. The packed ships hung in their isolated spaces like data bricks in a secure library complex. All Houses followed the same rules, putting their faith in the ability of a single mutated creature to find a safe course.

Like giedi-cattle in a slaughter pen, thought Rabban as he climbed into his invisible attack ship.

He could have wiped out a dozen frigates before anyone figured out what was going on. Given free rein, Rabban would have enjoyed causing such mayhem, the exhilarating sensation of extravagant violence. . . .

But that was not in the plan, at least not for now.

His uncle had developed a scheme of beautiful finesse. "Pay attention and learn from this," he'd said. *Good advice*, Rabban admitted to himself. He had been discovering the benefits of subtlety and the enjoyment of a revenge long savored.

This didn't mean Rabban would forsake the more blunt forms of violence at which he excelled; on the contrary, he would simply add the Baron's methods to his homicidal repertoire. He'd be a well-rounded person by the time he took over the leadership of House Harkonnen.

In an unobtrusive movement, the hatches of the Harkonnen family frigate slid open, and the containment field faded just long enough to let Rabban's sleek warship descend into the sealed vacuum within the Heighliner hold.

Slowly, quietly, patiently.

Before anyone could see his fighter craft, he engaged the no-field, working the controls the way Piter de Vries had shown him. He felt no different, saw no change in the view transmitted from his monitors. But now he was a killer ghost: invisible, *invincible*.

From anyone else's viewpoint, and from external sensors, all electromagnetic signals impinging on the no-field would reflect off and bend around, transforming his ship into an empty spot. The attack craft's engines, more silent than the softest whisper, made no detectable sound or vibration.

No one would suspect a thing. No one could even imagine an invisible ship.

Rabban activated the no-ship's attitude jets, silently coaxing the deadly craft away from the innocent-looking Harkonnen frigate, toward the Atreides vessel. This attack ship was too big for his liking, not very maneuverable and rather bulky for a quick fighter, but its invisibility and stone-silence made all the difference.

His thick fingers danced over the control panels, and he felt a measure of glee, of power, glory, and satisfaction yet to come. Soon a ship full of nasty, brutish Tleilaxu would be destroyed. Hundreds of them would die.

Always before, Rabban had used his position in House Harkonnen to get what he wanted without question, to manipulate other people and kill those few who were unfortunate enough to stand in his way. But that had been mere play for his personal amusement. Now he was performing a vital function, an act upon which the future of House Harkonnen depended. The Baron had picked him for this mission, and he vowed to do it well. He certainly didn't want to be sent back home to his father.

Rabban maneuvered the ship into place slowly, gently—no hurry, now. He had the entire transspace voyage in which to start a war.

With the no-field around his attack craft, he felt like a hunter concealed in a blind. This was a different kind of hunting, though, requiring more sophistication than blowing up sandworms on Arrakis, more finesse than chasing children in the Harkonnen forest preserve. Here, his trophy would be a change in Imperial politics. In the end he would hang the trophies of greater power and fortunes for House Harkonnen on his wall, stuffed and mounted.

The invisible attack craft approached the Atreides frigate, almost close enough to touch.

Noiselessly, Rabban powered up his weapons systems, making sure his full array of multiphase projectiles was ready to launch. He would rely on manual targeting in a case like this.

At point-blank range, he couldn't possibly miss.

Rabban turned his no-ship, pointing the gunports toward two nearby vessels, Tleilaxu transports that had, through a substantial Harkonnen bribe paid to the Guild, been ordered to park adjacent to the Atreides frigate.

Bound from Tleilax Seven, the ships undoubtedly carried genetic products, the specialty of the Bene Tleilax. Each ship would be commanded by Tleilaxu Masters, with a crew of Face Dancers, their shape-shifting servants. The cargo might be slig meat, animal grafts, or a few of those abominable gholas—clones grown from the flesh of dead humans, copies nurtured in axlotl tanks so that bereaved families could once again see fallen loved ones. Such products carried high price tags and made the gnomelike Tleilaxu extremely wealthy, despite the fact that they undoubtedly would never be granted Great House status.

This was perfect! With all the Landsraad listening, young Duke Leto Atreides had declared his vendetta against the Tleilaxu, swearing vengeance for what they had done to House Vernius. Leto had not been circumspect with regard to the statements he'd made on the record. Everyone knew how much he must hate the occupants of these Tleilaxu ships.

As a bonus, the renegade Rhombur Vernius was at this very moment aboard the Atreides frigate, yet another person to be caught in the Harkonnen web, yet another victim in what would soon be a bloody Atreides-Tleilaxu war.

The Landsraad would accuse Duke Leto of being a hothead—brash, impetuous, and violent, pushed to ill-advised acts by his misplaced Ixian friendships and his inconsolable grief over the death of his father. Poor, poor Leto, so inadequately trained to cope with the pressures bearing down on him.

Rabban knew full well what conclusions the Landsraad and the Imperium would draw, because his uncle and the twisted Mentat had explained it to him in detail.

Hovering immediately in front of the Atreides frigate, invisible and cloaked in anonymity, Rabban targeted the nearby Tleilaxu ships. With a smile on his generous lips, he reached for the controls.

And opened fire.

Tio Holtzman was one of the most productive Ixian inventors on record. He often went on creative binges, locking himself up for months on end so that he could work without interruption. Sometimes upon emerging he required hospitalization, and there were constant concerns over his sanity and well-being. Holtzman died young—barely past thirty Standard Years—but the results of his efforts changed the galaxy forever.

—Biographical Capsules, an Imperial filmbook

W hen Rabban departed from the Harkonnen frigate, full of his important duty, the Baron sat in a high observation chair, looking out into the enormous Heighliner hold. The Navigator had already initiated the engines, sent the gigantic craft through foldspace. The smaller ships sat arrayed like so much cordwood, unaware of the fire that was rushing toward them. . . .

Even knowing where to look, he couldn't see the invisible ship, of course. But the Baron glanced at his chronometer, knew the time was approaching. He stared out at the unsuspecting Atreides frigate, silent and arrogant in its assigned berth, and kept his eyes on the nearby Tleilaxu craft. Tapping his fingertips on the arm of the chair, he watched and waited.

Long minutes passed.

Planning the attack, Baron Harkonnen had wanted Rabban to use a lasgun on the doomed Tleilaxu ships—but Chobyn, the Richesian designer of the experimental craft, had left a murky warning scrawled in his notes. The new no-field had some relationship with the original Holtzman Effect that formed the foundation for shields. Every child knew that when a lasgun beam struck a shield, the resulting explosion resembled an atomic detonation.

The Baron didn't dare take that risk, and since the Richesian inventor had already been disposed of, they couldn't ask further questions. Perhaps he should have thought of that ahead of time.

No matter. Lasguns weren't needed to damage the Tleilaxu vessels anyway, since ships transported in a Heighliner hold were prohibited from activating their shields. Instead, multiphase projectiles—the high-powered artillery shells recommended by the Great Convention to restrict collateral damage—would do the job. Such shells penetrated the fuselage of a target craft and destroyed the interior of the vessel in a controlled detonation, after which the phased secondary and tertiary explosions snuffed onboard fires and saved the remains of the fuselage. His nephew hadn't understood the technical details of the attack; Rabban only knew how to aim and fire the weapons. That was all he needed to know.

Finally the Baron saw a tiny burst of yellow-and-white fire, and two deadly multiphase projectiles streaked out, as if fired from the front of the Atreides frigate. The projectiles shot like gobbets of viscous flame, then impacted. The doomed Tleilaxu transport vessels shuddered and glowed bright red inside.

Oh, how the Baron hoped other ships had been watching this!

A direct hit on one ship left it a hollow, incinerated hull in only a few seconds. By design, the other projectile hit the tail section of the second Tleilaxu ship, disabling it without killing everyone aboard. This would give the victims an excellent opportunity to fire back at the Atreides aggressors. Then things would escalate nicely.

"Good." The Baron smiled, as if he could speak directly to the frantic Tleilaxu crew. "Now you know what to do. Follow your instincts."

AFTER LAUNCHING THE projectiles, Rabban's no-ship darted away, passing between parked frigates that loomed high overhead.

On an emergency frequency, he heard the damaged Tleilaxu ship transmit urgent distress messages: "Peaceful Bene Tleilax transports attacked by Atreides frigate! Violation of Guild law. Assistance urgently requested!"

At that moment, the Guild Heighliner was *nowhere*—in transit between dimensions. They could expect neither retaliation nor enforcement until they emerged from foldspace and arrived at Kaitain. By then, it would be far too late.

Rabban hoped this would be more like a tavern brawl; he and his friends often marched into drinking establishments in outlying Giedi Prime villages and stirred up trouble, cracked open a few heads, and had a fine old time.

A control-panel screen in the no-ship showed him a graphic of the immense cargo hold, with a gray dot representing each ship. The dots changed to orange as the ships of various Houses Major powered up their weapons, prepared to defend themselves in what would become an all-out brush war.

Feeling like an unseen mouse on the floor of a crowded dance hall, Rabban piloted the no-ship behind a Harkonnen freighter, around to where no one in any other craft could see the Harkonnen ship open a hatch and allow the guerrilla craft inside.

Within the safety of the mother ship, Rabban switched off the no-field, making the attack craft visible to the Harkonnen crew. His hatch opened, and he stepped forth onto the platform, wiping sweat from his forehead. His eyes sparkled with excitement. "Have the other ships started shooting yet?"

Klaxons sounded. Panicky conversation spat out of the comsystem like shrapnel from a maula pistol. Frantic voices in Imperial Galach and battle code sounds spilled over from the crowded comlinks inside the Heighliner: "The Atreides have declared war on the Tleilaxu! Weapons fired!"

Smug about his successful attack, Rabban shouted to the crew, "Activate our frigate's weapons array. Make sure no one fires on us—those Atreides are ruthless, you know." He chuckled.

Cargo-handling equipment gripped the small craft, then lowered it into a space between false bulkheads. Panels snicked shut over the opening, which even Guild scanners could not detect. Of course no one would search for the craft anyway, since there was no such thing as an invisible ship.

"Defend yourselves!" another pilot shouted over the comsystem.

A Tleilaxu whine ensued. "We give notice that we intend to fire back. We are well within our rights. No provocation . . . blatant disregard for Guild rules."

Another voice, coarse and deep: "But the Atreides frigate shows no weapons. Maybe they were not the aggressors."

"A trick!" the Tleilaxu screeched. "One of our ships is destroyed, another severely damaged. Can you not see with your own eyes? House Atreides must pay."

Perfect, Rabban thought, admiring his uncle's plan. From this crux point, several events could occur, and the plan would still work. Duke Leto was known to be impetuous, and everyone now believed he had committed a heinous and cowardly act. With any luck, his ship would be destroyed in a retaliatory attack, and the Atreides name would go down in infamy for Leto's treacherous deed.

Or this could just be the beginning of a long and bloody feud between House Atreides and the Tleilaxu.

In either case, Leto would never be able to untangle himself.

ON THE COMMAND bridge of the Atreides frigate, Duke Leto struggled to calm himself. Because he knew his ship had not fired, it took him some seconds even to understand the accusations being shouted at him.

"The shots came from very nearby, my Duke," Hawat said, "from right under our bow."

"So that was no accident?" Leto said, as a dismal feeling came over him. The destroyed Tleilaxu ship still glowed orange, while the pilot of the other vessel continued to scream at him.

"Vermilion hells! Somebody actually fired on the Bene Tleilax," Rhombur said, peering out the armor-plaz porthole. "And it's about time, if you ask me."

Leto heard the cacophony of radio traffic, including the outraged Tleilaxu distress calls. At first he wondered if he should offer assistance to the damaged ships. Then the Tleilaxu pilot started howling the *Atreides* name and demanding *his* blood.

He noted the burned-out hull of the destroyed Tleilaxu craft—and saw the guns on its wounded companion swiveling *toward him*. "Thufir! What's he doing?"

The open comlink blared a furious debate between the Tleilaxu and those who refused to believe in Atreides culpability. Increasingly, voices supported the Tleilaxu position. Some claimed to have seen what happened, claimed to have witnessed the Atreides ship firing upon the Tleilaxu. A dangerous momentum was building.

"Vermilion hells, they think *you* did it, Leto!" Rhombur said.

Hawat had already dashed to the defensive panel. "The Tleilaxu have powered up weapons for a counterstrike against you, my Duke."

Leto ran for the comsystem and threw open a channel. In only a few seconds his thoughts accelerated and compressed in a manner that astonished him, for he was not a Mentat capable of advanced reasoning powers. It was like dream-compression, he realized . . . or the incredible array of visions that reportedly flashed across a person's mind when faced with imminent death. *That's a grim thought.* He had to see a way out of this.

"Attention!" he shouted into the voice pickup. "This is Duke Leto Atreides. We did not fire upon the Tleilaxu ships. I deny all accusations."

He knew they would not believe him, would not cool down soon enough to avoid an eruption of open hostilities that could result in a full-scale war. And in a flash he knew what else he had to do.

Faces from his past scrolled across his mind, and he locked on to a memory of his paternal grandfather Kean Atreides gazing at him with expectation, his face a crease-map of his life experiences. Gentle gray eyes like his own held a disarming strength that his enemies often overlooked, to their great peril.

If only I can be as strong as my ancestors. . . .

"Do not fire," he said, addressing the Tleilaxu pilot and hoping all the other captains would listen.

Another image took shape in his mind: his father, the Old Duke, with green eyes and the same expression, but on a face that was Leto's age now, in his teens. In a microflash, more images appeared: his Richesian uncles, aunts, and cousins, the loyal servants, domestic, governmental, and military. All of them carried the same blank expression, as if they were one multiplexed organism, studying him from different perspectives, waiting to make a judgment about him. He saw no love, approval, or disrespect in their faces—just a nothingness, as if he had truly committed a heinous act and no longer existed.

The sneering face of his mother appeared, faded.

Don't trust anyone, he thought.

A feeling of despondency settled over Leto, followed by extreme, bitter loneliness. Deep inside himself, in a lifeless and bleak place, Leto saw his own emotionless gray eyes, staring back at himself. It was cold here, and he shivered.

"Leadership is a lonely task."

Would the Atreides lineage stop here with him at this nexus-moment, or would he father children whose voices would be added to those of all the Atreides since the days of the ancient Greeks? He listened for his children in the cacophony, but did not sense their presence.

The accusing eyes did not waver.

Leto spoke the words to himself. *Government is a protective partnership; the people are in your care, to thrive or die based upon your decisions.*

The images and sounds faded, and his mind became a quiet, dark place.

Barely a second had passed in his tension-spawned mental journey, and Leto knew exactly what he had to do, regardless of the consequences.

"Activate shields!" he shouted.

☙

PEERING AT AN observation screen in the belly of the seemingly innocent Harkonnen frigate, Rabban was surprised by what he saw. He raced up from one deck to the next, until finally he stood red-faced and puffing in front of his uncle. Before the indignant but timid Tleilaxu pilot could open fire, a shield began to shimmer around the Atreides ship!

But shields were forbidden by Guild transport contract, because they shattered a Navigator's trance and disrupted the foldspace field. The Heighliner's enormous Holtzman generators would not function properly with the interference. Rabban and the Baron both cursed.

The Heighliner shuddered around them as it plunged out of foldspace.

☙

IN THE NAVIGATION chamber high atop the cargo enclosure, the veteran Navigator felt his trance crumble. His brain waves diverged and circled back into themselves, spinning and twisting out of control.

The Holtzman engines groaned, and foldspace rippled around

them, losing stability. Something was wrong with the ship. The Navigator spun in his tank of melange. His webbed feet and hands flailed, and he sensed darkness ahead.

The massive ship veered off course, hurled back into the real universe.

❧

WHILE RHOMBUR WAS thrown to the carpeted deck of the frigate in a tumble of purple-and-copper cloth, Leto grabbed a bulkhead rail to keep his balance. He uttered a silent prayer. He and his valiant crew could only ride this out and hope the Heighliner didn't emerge inside a sun.

Like a tree beside Leto, Thufir Hawat somehow maintained his balance by sheer force of will. The Mentat teacher stood in a trance sorting through veiled regions of logic and analysis. Leto wasn't certain how such projections could benefit them now. Perhaps the question— the odds of disaster following shield activation inside a Heighliner— was so complex that it required layers and layers of mentation.

"Prime projection," Hawat announced, at long last. He licked his cranberry-colored lips with a tongue of matching hue. "Thrown out of foldspace at random, odds of encountering a celestial body are calculated at one in . . ."

The frigate jerked, and something thudded belowdecks. Hawat's words were drowned out in the commotion, and he slipped back into the secret realm of his Mentat trance.

Rhombur stumbled to his feet, tugging an earclamp headset in place over his tousled blond hair. "Activate shields on a moving Heighliner? That's as crazy as, uh, someone firing on the Tleilaxu in the first place." With wide eyes he looked at his friend. "This must be a day for crazy events."

Leto leaned over a bank of instruments, made a number of adjustments. "I had no choice," he said. "I see it now. Someone is trying to make it look like *we* attacked the Tleilaxu—an incident that could spark a major war among the factions of the Landsraad. I can envision all the old feuds coming into play, and battle lines being drawn here on the Heighliner." He wiped his brow, smearing sweat away. The intuition had come from his gut level, like something a Mentat might have realized. "I had to stop everything *now*, Rhombur, before it escalated."

The Heighliner's erratic motion finally ceased. The background noise quieted.

Hawat finally snapped out of his trance. "You are right, my Duke. Almost every House has a representative ship aboard this Heighliner, en route to the Emperor's coronation and wedding. The battle lines drawn here would extend out into the Imperium, with war councils called and planets and armies aligning themselves on one side or another. Inevitably more factions would arise, too, like the branches of a jacaranda tree. Since the death of Elrood, alliances are already shifting as Houses look for new opportunities."

Leto's face flushed hot; his heart jackhammered. "There are powder kegs all over the Imperium, and one of them is right here within this cargo hold. I'd rather see everyone on this Heighliner die—because it would be nothing compared to the alternative. Conflagrations in every corner of the universe. Billions of deaths."

"We've been set up?" Rhombur asked.

"If war breaks out here, no one will care whether or not I really fired. We've got to stop this cold, and then take the time to sort out the real answers." Leto opened a comlink and spoke into it, his voice brisk and commanding. "This is Duke Leto Atreides calling Guild Navigator. Respond, please."

The line crackled, and an undulating voice came back, ponderous and distorted, as if the Navigator could not recall how to converse with mere humans. "All of us could have been killed, *Atreides*." The way he pronounced the House name—A-*tray*-a-dees—brought to Leto's mind the word "traitor." "We are in unknown sector. Foldspace gone. Shields negate navigation trance. Shut down Atreides shields immediately."

"Respectfully, I must refuse," Leto said.

Across the comsystem he could hear other messages being shouted to the navigation chamber—accusations and demands from the ships aboard. Muffled, angry tones.

The Navigator spoke again. "Atreides must shut off shields. Obey Guild laws and regulations."

"Refused." Leto stood firm, but his skin had gone pale and cold, and he knew his expression just barely concealed his terror. "I don't think you can get us out of here as long as my shields are on, so we stay here, wherever we are, until you accede to my . . . request."

"After destroying a Bene Tleilax ship and activating your shields, you are in no position to make any *requests!*" cried an accented voice, a Tleilaxu.

"Impertinent, Atreides." It was the mutated Navigator's rumbling, underwater-sounding voice.

More muffled communications ensued, which the Navigator abruptly silenced. "State . . . request . . . Atreides."

Pausing, Leto met the inquiring but respectful gazes of his friends, then spoke into the comsystem. "First, we assure you we did *not* fire upon the Tleilaxu, and we intend to prove it. If we lower our shields, the Guild must guarantee the safety of my ship and crew, and transfer jurisdiction of this matter to the Landsraad."

"The Landsraad? This ship is under Spacing Guild jurisdiction."

"You are bound by honor," Leto said, "as are the members of the Landsraad, as am I. There is in the Landsraad a legal procedure known as Trial by Forfeiture."

"My Lord!" Hawat protested. "You can't mean to sacrifice House Atreides, all the centuries of noble tradition—"

Leto shut off the voice pickup. Placing a hand on the warrior Mentat's shoulder, he said, "If billions have to die for us to keep our fief, then Caladan isn't worth the price." Thufir lowered his gaze in acquiescence. "Besides, we know we did *not* do this—a Mentat of your stature shouldn't have much difficulty proving that."

Reactivating the comlink, Leto said, "I will submit myself to Trial by Forfeiture, but all hostilities must cease immediately. There must be no retaliation, or I will refuse to deactivate my shields, and this Heighliner will remain here, nowhere."

Leto thought of bluffing, threatening to fire lasguns at his own shields to cause the dreadful atomic interaction that would leave the gigantic Heighliner nothing but bits of molten flotsam. Instead, he tried to be reasonable. "What is the point in further argument? I have surrendered, and will submit myself to the Landsraad on Kaitain for a Trial by Forfeiture. I am merely trying to prevent a full-scale war over a mistaken assumption. We did not commit this crime. We are prepared to face the accusations *and* the consequences if we are found guilty."

The line went dead, then crackled back on. "Spacing Guild agrees to conditions. I guarantee safety of ship and crew."

"Know this, then," Leto said. "Under the rules of Trial by Forfeiture, I, Duke Leto Atreides, intend to give up all legal rights to my fief and will place myself at the mercy of the tribunal. No other member of my House may be subjected to arrest or to any legal proceeding. Do you acknowledge the jurisdiction of the Landsraad in this matter?"

"I do," the Navigator assured him, in a firmer tone, more accustomed to speaking now.

Finally, still nervous, Leto switched off the frigate's shields and sagged into his chair, trembling. The other ships in the immense hold powered down their weapons, though the tempers of their crews continued to flare.

Now the real battle would begin.

In the long history of our House, we have been constantly shad-
owed by Misfortune, as if we were its prey. One might almost be-
lieve the curse of Atreus from ancient Greek times on Old Terra.

—DUKE PAULUS ATREIDES,
from a speech to his generals

On the prism-lined promenade of the Imperial Palace, the Crown Prince's new fiancée Anirul and her companion Margot Rashino-Zea strode past three young women, members of the Imperial Court. The showpiece city extended all the way to the horizon, and massive works filled the streets and buildings, colorful preparations for the upcoming spectacular coronation ceremony and the Emperor's wedding.

The trio of young Court women chattered excitedly, barely able to move in their stuffed gowns, sparkling orna-mental feathers, and kilograms of gaudy jewelry. But now they fell silent as the black-robed Bene Gesserit drew near.

"Just a moment, Margot." Pausing in front of the elabo-rately coiffed women, Anirul snapped with the barest hint of Voice, "Don't waste your time gossiping. Do something productive for a change. We have much to prepare before all the representatives arrive."

One of the young women, a dark-haired beauty, glared for a moment with large brown eyes, but then had second thoughts. Her manner took on a conciliatory expression and tone. "You are right, Lady," she said, and abruptly led her companions down the promenade toward a wide, arched doorway of pitted Salusan lava rock that led to the Ambassadors' apartments.

Exchanging smiles with the secret Kwisatz Mother, Margot quipped, "But aren't Imperial Courts about gossiping, Anirul? Isn't that their primary business? The ladies were performing their duties admirably, I'd say."

Anirul glowered, looking much older than her young features. "I should have given them explicit instructions. Those women are merely decorations, like the jeweled fountains. They don't have the slightest idea *how* to be productive."

After her years on Wallach IX, knowing through her Other Memory just how much the Bene Gesserit had accomplished over the landscape of Imperial history, she considered human lives precious, each one a tiny spark in the bonfire of eternity. But such courtesans aspired to be no more than . . . than morsels for the appetites of powerful men.

In reality, Anirul had no jurisdiction over such women, not even as the Crown Prince's future wife. Margot placed a soft hand on her forearm. "Anirul, you must be less impulsive. Mother Superior recognizes your talent and skill, but says you must be tempered. All successful life-forms adapt to their surroundings. You are now at the Imperial Court, so adapt to your new environment. We Bene Gesserit must work *invisibly*."

Anirul gave her a wry smile. "I always considered my outspokenness to be one of my primary strengths. Mother Superior Harishka knows that. It enables me to discuss matters of interest and to learn things I might not have learned otherwise."

"*If* others are capable of listening." Margot raised her pale eyebrows on her flawless forehead.

Anirul continued down the promenade, head held high, like an Empress. Precious gems glittered in a headpiece that covered her bronze hair like a spiderweb. She knew the courtesans gossiped about her, wondering what secret tasks the Bene Gesserit witches were performing at Court, what spells they had woven to lure Shaddam. *Ah, if they only knew.* Their gossip and speculations would only serve to enhance Anirul's mystique.

"It seems that we have things to whisper about, ourselves," she said.

Margot brushed a lock of honey-blonde hair out of her eyes. "Of course. Mohiam's child?"

"And the Atreides matter as well."

Anirul drew a deep breath from a hedge of sapphire roses as they reached a patio garden. The sweet perfume awakened her senses. She and Margot sat together on a bench, where they could observe anyone approaching, though they spoke in directed whispers, secure from any spies.

"What can the Atreides have to do with Mohiam's daughter?" As one of the Bene Gesserit's most accomplished operatives, Sister Margot possessed inner-circle details on the next stage of the Kwisatz Haderach program, and now Mohiam herself had been briefed as well.

"Think in the long term, Margot, think of genetic patterns, of the ladder of generations we have plotted. Duke Leto Atreides lies imprisoned, in peril of his life and title. He may *seem* to be an insignificant noble of an unimpressive Great House. But have you considered what a disaster this situation could be for us?"

Margot took a deep breath as pieces fell into place for her. "Duke Leto? You don't mean he is needed for . . ." She couldn't utter the most secret of names, *Kwisatz Haderach.*

"We must have Atreides genes in the next generation!" Anirul said, echoing the agitated voices in her head. "People are afraid to support Leto in this matter, and we all know why. Some of the key magistrates can be made sympathetic to his cause for political reasons, but no one truly believes in Leto's innocence. Why would the young fool do such an unwise thing? It goes beyond comprehension."

Margot shook her head sadly.

"Although Shaddam has publicly expressed his neutrality, he speaks against House Atreides in private. He certainly doesn't believe in Leto's innocence," Anirul said. "Yet there could be more to it. The Crown Prince may have some relationship with the Tleilaxu, something he isn't revealing to anyone. Do you think it possible?"

"Hasimir has said nothing to me of it." Margot realized she had used the familiar name, and smiled back at her companion. "And he *does* share some secrets with me. In time, your man will share them with you as well."

Anirul frowned, thinking of Shaddam and Fenring with their never-ending schemes, like games of politics. "So, they're up to something. Together. Maybe Leto's fate is part of their plan?"

"Perhaps."

Anirul leaned forward on the stone bench to be more sheltered by the rose hedge. "Margot, our men want House Atreides to fall, for some reason . . . but the Sisterhood must have Leto's bloodline for the culmination of our program. It is our best hope, and the work of centuries hangs on this."

Not entirely understanding, Margot Rashino-Zea gazed at Anirul with her gray-green eyes. "Our need for Atreides offspring is not dependent on their status as a House Major."

"Isn't it?" Anirul patiently explained her greatest fears. "Duke Leto has no brothers or sisters. If he fails in his gambit—the Trial by Forfeiture—he could very well commit suicide. He's a young man of tremendous pride, and it would be a terrible blow to him so soon after the loss of his father."

Margot narrowed her eyes skeptically. "This Leto is exceptionally strong. With his character, he'll fight on, no matter what."

Kitebirds flew overhead, their songs like broken crystal. Anirul looked up into the cloudless sky and watched them. "And what if a vengeful Tleilaxu assassinates him, even if the Emperor pardons him? What if a Harkonnen sees an opportunity to create an 'accident'? Leto Atreides can ill afford to lose the protection of his noble status. We need to keep him alive, and preferably in his position of power."

"I see your point, Anirul."

"This young Duke must be protected at all costs—and to begin, we must protect the status of his Great House. He cannot lose this trial."

"Hm-m-m, there may be a way," Margot said with a tight-lipped smile. She spoke in a low, musing tone. "Hasimir might even admire my idea, if he learns of it, despite his instinctive opposition. Of course we don't dare breathe a word of it to him, or to Shaddam. But it will throw all the players into complete confusion."

Anirul waited in silence, but her eyes burned with bright curiosity. Margot moved closer to her Bene Gesserit companion. "Our suspicion of . . . the Tleilaxu connection. We can use that for a convoluted bluff within a bluff. But can we do it without harming Shaddam or House Corrino?"

Anirul stiffened. "My future husband—and even the Golden Lion Throne itself—are secondary to our breeding program."

"Of course you're right." Margot nodded in resignation, as if shocked at her own gaffe. "But how should we proceed?"

"We begin with a message to Leto."

Truth is a chameleon.
—Zensunni Aphorism

On the second morning of Leto's confinement in Landsraad Prison on Kaitain, an official arrived with important documents for him to sign—the official demand for a Trial by Forfeiture, and Leto's formal surrender of all property held by House Atreides. It was the moment of truth for him, the point at which he had to certify the dangerous course of action he had demanded.

Though undeniably a prison, the cell had two rooms, a comfortable sling couch, a desk made of polished Ecaz jacaranda, a filmbook reader, and other fine appointments. These so-called courtesies had been granted to him because of his status in the Landsraad. No leader of a Great House would ever be treated as a common criminal—at least, not until he either lost everything through due process, or went renegade like House Vernius. Leto knew he might never again be surrounded by such elegant trappings, unless he could prove his innocence.

His cell was warm, the food sufficient and palatable, the bed comfortable—though he had hardly slept at all while preparing for his ordeal. He had little hope of a swift and simple resolution to this matter. The Courier could only be bringing more problems.

The official, a Landsraad courtech with security clearance, wore a brown-and-teal Landsraad uniform with silver epaulets. He referred to Leto as "Monsieur Atreides," without the customary ducal title, as if the forfeiture documents had already been processed.

Leto chose not to make a point of this faux pas, though officially he remained a Duke until the papers were signed and the sentence thumbprint-sealed by the magistrates of the court. In all the centuries of the Imperium, Trial by Forfeiture had been invoked previously only three times; in two of those cases, the defendant had lost, and the accused Houses were ruined.

Leto hoped to beat those odds. He could not allow House Atreides to crumble to dust less than a year after his father's death. That would earn him a permanent place in the Landsraad annals as the most incompetent House leader in recorded history.

Wearing his black-and-red Atreides uniform, Leto took a seat at a blueplaz table. Thufir Hawat, acting as Mentat-advisor, lowered himself ponderously into a chair beside his Duke. Together, they examined the sheaf of legal documents. Like most formal matters of the Imperium, the evidence forms and trial documents were inscribed on microthin sheets of ridulian-crystal paper, permanent records that could last for thousands of years.

At their touch, each sheet illuminated so that Leto and Hawat could study the fine text. The old Mentat used his skills to imprint each page onto his memory; he would absorb and comprehend it all in greater detail later. The documents spelled out precisely what was to occur during the preparations and the actual trial. Each page bore the identification marks of various officers of the court, including Leto's own attorneys.

As part of the unorthodox procedure, the crew of the Atreides frigate had been released and permitted to return to Caladan, though many loyal followers remained on Kaitain to offer their silent support. Any individual or collective culpability had been shouldered entirely by the commander, Duke Atreides. In addition, the guaranteed sanctuary of the Vernius children would continue, regardless of the status of the House. Even with the worst possible outcome of the trial, Leto could take comfort in that small victory. His friends would remain safe.

Under the forfeiture provision—which even his estranged mother could not countermand from her retreat with the Sisters in Isolation—Duke Leto surrendered all of his family assets (including the House atomics and stewardship of the planet Caladan itself) to the general supervision of the Landsraad Council, while he prepared for a trial before his peers.

A trial that might be rigged against him.

Win or lose, though, Leto knew he had averted a major war and saved billions of lives. His action had been the right one, regardless of the consequences to himself. Old Duke Paulus himself would have made no other choice, given the alternatives.

"Yes, Thufir, this is all correct," Leto said, turning the last page of shimmering ridulian crystal. He removed his ducal signet ring, snipped the red armorial hawk from his uniform, and handed the items over to the courtech. He felt as if he had just cut away pieces of himself.

If he lost this desperate gambit, the holdings on Caladan would become the prize in a Landsraad free-for-all, the citizens on the watery world no more than helpless bystanders. He had been stripped, his future and fortune placed in limbo. *Perhaps they'll give Caladan to the Harkonnens,* Leto thought in despair, *just to spite us.*

The courtech handed him a magnapen. Leto pressed his forefinger against the soft side of the tiny inking device and signed the crystal documents in a wide, flowing script. He felt a faint crackle of static electricity on the top sheet, or perhaps that was just his own anxiety. The courtech added his own ID print to witness the papers. With obvious reluctance, Hawat did the same.

As the courtech departed in a swirl of brown-and-teal livery, Leto announced across the table, "I am a commoner now, without title or fief."

"Only until our victory," Hawat said. With the faintest tremor in his voice, he added, "Regardless of the outcome, you will always be my Honored Duke."

The Mentat paced the length of the cell like a captive marsh panther. He paused with his back to a tiny window that looked out on the immense flat black plain of an outbuilding to the Imperial Palace. The morning sun flowing from behind him cast Hawat's face in shadow.

"I have studied the official evidence, the data taken by scanners in the Heighliner hold, and eyewitness accounts. I agree with your attorneys that it looks very bad for you, m'Lord. We must begin with the assumption that you did not instigate this act in any way and extrapolate from there."

Leto sighed. "Thufir, if *you* don't believe me, we have no chance whatsoever in the Landsraad court."

"I take your innocence as fact. Now, there are several possibilities, which I will list in the order of least likelihood. First, though it is a remote possibility, the destruction of the Tleilaxu ship *may have been* an accident."

"We need something better than that, Thufir. No one will believe it."

"More likely, the Tleilaxu blew up their own ship simply to incriminate you. We know the small value they place on life. The passengers and crew on the destroyed craft may have only been gholas, and thus expendable. They can always grow more duplicates in their axlotl tanks."

Hawat tapped his fingers together. "Unfortunately, the problem is lack of motive. Would the Tleilaxu concoct such a complex and outrageous scheme merely to get petty revenge against you for harboring the children of House Vernius? What would they gain by this?"

"Remember, Thufir, I did declare my clear enmity against them in the Landsraad Hall. They see me as an enemy as well."

"I still don't think that is sufficient provocation, my Duke. No, this is something bigger, something for which the perpetrator was willing to risk all-out war." He paused, then added, "I am unable to determine what the Bene Tleilax could possibly gain by the embarrassment or destruction of House Atreides. You are a peripheral enemy to them, at best."

Leto wrestled with the conundrum himself, but if even the Mentat could not find a chain of associations, then a mere Duke wouldn't be able to follow such subtle threads. "All right, what's another possibility?"

"Perhaps . . . Ixian sabotage. The result of an Ixian renegade who sought to strike back against the Tleilaxu. A misguided attempt to assist the exiled Dominic Vernius. It's also possible that Dominic himself was involved, though there have been no sightings of him since he went renegade."

Leto digested this information, but the practical question nagged him. "Sabotage? By what means?"

"Difficult to say. The gutting of the Tleilaxu ship's interior suggests a multiphase projectile. Chemical residue analysis also confirms this."

Leto leaned back in the uncomfortable chair. "But how? Who could have fired such a projectile? Let's not forget that witnesses claim to have seen shots launched from the direction of *our* frigate. The Heighliner hold was empty in the vicinity. You and I were both watching. Ours was the only ship close enough."

"The few answers I can suggest are extremely unlikely, my Duke. A small attack craft could have fired such a projectile, but it is not possible to hide such a vessel. We saw nothing. Even an individual suited up with breathing apparatus would have been noticed in the cargo hold, so that rules out shoulder-launched missiles. Besides which, no one is allowed outside the ships during foldspace transit."

"I'm no Mentat, Thufir . . . but I smell Harkonnens in this," Leto mused as he ran his finger in circles on the slick, cold surface of the blueplaz table. He had to think, had to be strong.

Hawat gave him a concise analysis. "When a foul deed occurs, three principal trails invariably lead to the responsible party: money, power, or revenge. This incident was a setup, designed to destroy House Atreides—possibly linked to the scheme that killed your father."

Leto heaved an enormous sigh. "Our family had a few quiet years under Dmitri Harkonnen and his son Abulurd, when the Harkonnens seemed to let us live in peace. Now I'm afraid the old feud has resurfaced. From what I hear, the Baron revels in it."

The Mentat smiled grimly. "Exactly what I was considering, m'Lord. I am absolutely baffled as to *how* they might have accomplished such an ambush with so many other ships watching. Proving such a conjecture in Landsraad court will be even more difficult."

A guard appeared at the force-barred cell and entered, carrying a small parcel. Without uttering a word or even looking Leto in the eyes, he placed the package on the slick table and departed.

Hawat ran a scanner over the suspicious parcel. "Message cube," he said. Gesturing for Leto to stand back, the Mentat removed the wrapping to reveal a dark object. He found no markings, no indication of the sender, yet it seemed to be important.

Leto held up the cube, and it glowed after recognizing his thumbprint. Words flowed across its face in synchronization with his eye movements, two sentences that spoke volumes of provocative information.

"Crown Prince Shaddam, like his father before him, maintains a secret and illegal alliance with the Bene Tleilax. This information may prove valuable to your defense—if you dare use it."

"Thufir! Look at this." But the words dissolved before he could shift the face of the cube toward the Mentat. Then the message cube itself crumbled to brittle debris in his palm. He had no idea who could have sent such a bombshell to him. *Is it possible that I have secret allies on Kaitain?*

Suddenly uneasy, even paranoid, Leto switched to Atreides hand signals, the secret language Duke Paulus had taught close members of his household. The young man's hawklike face darkened as he recounted what he had read and asked who could have sent it.

The Mentat considered for just a moment, then answered with his own flickering hand gestures: "The Tleilaxu are not known for their military prowess, but this connection might explain how they could so easily crush the Ixians and their defensive technology. Sardaukar might secretly maintain control over the downtrodden populace underground." Thufir finished: "Shaddam is mixed up in this somehow, and doesn't want that fact revealed."

Leto's fingers flashed in inquiry: "But what does that have to do with the attack inside the Heighliner? I don't see a connection."

Hawat pursed his stained lips and spoke aloud in a husky whisper. "Maybe there isn't one. But it might not matter, so long as we can use the information in our darkest hour. I propose a bluff, my Duke. A spectacular, desperate bluff."

In a Trial by Forfeiture, the normal rules of evidence do not apply.
There are no disclosure requirements that evidence be revealed to
the opposition or to the magistrates prior to the court proceedings.
This places the person with secret knowledge in a uniquely power-
ful position—commensurate with the extreme risk he takes.

      —Rogan's Rules of Evidence, 3rd Edition

A s Crown Prince Shaddam read the unexpected message cube from Leto Atreides, a wave of crimson rage
tinted his face.

"Sire, my defense documentation includes a full disclosure of
your relationship with the Tleilaxu."

"Impossible! How could he know?" Shouting an ob-
scenity, Shaddam smashed the cube against the wall, chipping the indigo-veined marble. Fenring scuttled forward to
pick up the pieces, anxious to preserve the evidence and
read the message for himself. Shaddam glared at his advisor,
as if this were somehow Fenring's fault.

It was early evening, and the two of them had left the
Palace to go to Fenring's private penthouse for a few moments of peace. Now Shaddam paced the perimeter of the
spacious room, with furtive Fenring following the other like
a shadow. Shaddam, though not yet formally crowned, settled onto a massive balcony chair as if it were a throne.
With royal reserve, the Crown Prince eyed his friend. "So,
Hasimir, how do you suppose my cousin learned about the
Tleilaxu? What evidence does he have?"

"Hm-m-m-m, he may simply be bluffing. . . ."

"Such a guess can't be pure coincidence. We don't dare call his bluff—if it is one. We can't risk letting the truth come out in Landsraad court." Shaddam groaned. "I don't approve of this Trial by Forfeiture business at all. Never did. It shifts responsibility for the allocation of a Great House's assets away from the Imperial throne, away from *me*. I think it's very bad form."

"But there's nothing you can do about it, Sire. It's an established law, dating back to Butlerian times when House Corrino was appointed to rule the civilizations of mankind. Take heart that in the thousands of years since, this is only the fourth time forfeiture has ever been invoked, mm-m-m-m? It seems the all-or-nothing gambit is not very popular."

Shaddam continued to scowl, looking across the evening skies at the prismatic domes of the faraway Palace, his gaze distant. "But how could he possibly know? Who talked? What did we miss? This is a disaster!"

Fenring stopped at the edge of the balcony, looking out at the stars with his close-set, glittering eyes. He dropped his voice to an ominous whisper. "Maybe I should pay Leto Atreides a little visit in his cell, hm-m-m-m-ah? To find out exactly what he knows and how he learned of it. It's the most obvious solution to our little dilemma."

Shaddam slouched low in the balcony chair, but it felt too hard against his back. "The Duke won't tell you anything. He's got too much to lose. He may be grasping at straws, but I've no doubt he'll carry out his threat."

The huge eyes darkened. "When I ask questions, Shaddam, I get answers." Fenring clenched his fists. "You should know that by now, after all I've done for you."

"That Mentat Thufir Hawat won't leave Leto's side, and he is a formidable adversary. He's called the Master of Assassins."

"My talent, too, Shaddam. We can find a way to separate them. You command it, and I shall see that it is done." He revealed eagerness at the prospect of killing, with his pleasure heightened by the challenge at hand. Fenring's eyes shone, but Shaddam cut him off.

"If he's as smart as he seems, Hasimir, he'll have established many guarantees for himself. Ah, yes. The moment Leto suspects a threat, he could announce whatever he knows—and there's no telling what sort of insurance he's set up for himself, especially if this has been his plan all along."

. . . full disclosure of your relationship with the Tleilaxu . . .

A cool breeze drifted across the balcony, but he did not go back inside. "If word of our . . . project . . . comes out, the Great Houses could block me from the throne and a Landsraad attack force would be dispatched against Ix."

"They've named it Xuttah now, Sire," Fenring muttered.

"Whatever they call it."

The Crown Prince ran a hand through his pomaded reddish hair. The Atreides prisoner's single line of text had shaken him more than the overthrow of a hundred worlds. He wondered how much this would have disturbed old Elrood. More than the huge revolt in the Ecaz sector early in his reign?

Watch, and learn.

Oh, shut up, you old vulture!

Shaddam's brow furrowed. "Think on it, Hasimir—it seems almost too obvious. Is there any chance at all that Duke Leto *didn't* destroy the Tleilaxu ships?"

Fenring ran a finger along his pointed chin. "I doubt that very much, Sire. The Atreides ship was there, as confirmed by witnesses. The weapons had been fired, and Leto has made no secret of his anger toward the Bene Tleilax. Remember his speech at the Landsraad? *He is guilty.* No one could believe otherwise."

"I'd think even a sixteen-year-old could be more subtle than that. Why would he demand a Trial by Forfeiture, then?" Shaddam hated it when he couldn't understand people and their actions. "A ridiculous risk."

Fenring let a long pause hang in the air before he dropped his idea like a bombshell. "Because Leto knew all along he would send you *that message?*" He gestured toward the shrapnel of the message cube. He had to point out the obvious, since Shaddam often let his rage get the best of his reasoning faculties. He continued quickly.

"Perhaps you are thinking backward, Sire. It may be that Leto purposely struck out at the Tleilaxu, knowing he could use the incident as a pretext to demand a Trial by Forfeiture—a public forum in the Landsraad court during which he could expose what he knew about us? All the Imperium will be listening."

"But why, *why?*" Shaddam studied the well-manicured nails on his fingers, flushed with confusion. "What does he have against me? I am his cousin!"

Fenring sighed. "Leto Atreides is in thick with the ousted Prince of Ix. If he learned about our hand in the overthrow there and the Tleilaxu synthetic-spice work, wouldn't that be motive enough? He inherited a deep, misplaced sense of honor from his father. Consider this, then: Leto took it upon himself to punish the Bene Tleilax. But if we let him stand trial now before the Landsraad, he plans to tell of our involvement and take us down with him. It's as simple as that, hm-m-m-m? He committed the crime, all the while knowing we would have to protect him . . . to protect *ourselves*. Either way, he'll have punished us. At least he left a way out."

"Ah, yes. But that's—"

"Blackmail, Sire?"

Shaddam drew an icy breath. "Damn him!" Now he stood up, looking Imperial at last. "Damn him! If you're right, Hasimir, we have no choice but to help him."

The written Law of the Imperium cannot be changed, no matter which Great House holds dominion or which Emperor sits on the Golden Lion Throne. The documents of the Imperial Constitution have been established for thousands of years. This is not to say that each regime is legally identical; the variations stem from subtleties of interpretation and from microscopic loopholes that become large enough to drive a Heighliner through.

—Law of the Imperium: Commentaries and Rebuttals

Leto lay supine on the sling bed in his cell, feeling the warm throb of a massage mechanism beneath him as it worked the stress-tightened muscles of his neck and back. He still didn't know what he was going to do.

So far he had received no response from the Crown Prince, and Leto was now convinced that his wild bluff would not work. Relying on the secret message had been a long shot anyway, and Leto himself had no idea what it meant. Instead, for hour after hour, he and the Mentat had continued to discuss the merits of their case and the necessity of relying on their own skills.

Personal articles and comforts surrounded him for his use during the long hours of anticipation, contemplation, and boredom: filmbooks, fine clothing, writing instruments, even Couriers waiting outside his cell to carry personal message cubes to any recipients he chose. Everyone knew how much was at stake in this trial, and not everyone on Kaitain wanted Leto to win.

Technically, because of the legal procedures in which he was embroiled, he no longer owned any personal items; still, he appreciated the use of them. The filmbooks and clothing provided a sense of stability, a link with what he thought of as his "former life." Since the mysterious attack inside the Heighliner, he had been thrown into a state of chaos.

Leto's whole future, the fate of his House, and his holdings on Caladan hung precariously on the Trial by Forfeiture, all or nothing. If he failed here, his Great House would be even worse off than the renegade family Vernius. House Atreides would no longer exist—at all.

At least then, he thought with forced wryness, *I won't have to worry about negotiating an appropriate marriage to make the best Landsraad connections.* He released a deep sigh, thinking of copper-haired Kailea and her dreams for a future that would never come to pass. If he was stripped of his titles and possessions, Leto Atreides could choose to marry her without considering dynasties and politics . . . but would she, with her dreams of Kaitain and the Imperial Court, want him if he wasn't a Duke?

Somehow, I always manage to find advantages, Rhombur had said. He could use a little more of his friend's optimism now.

At the crowded blueplaz desk, deep in silent concentration, Thufir Hawat flipped through holo-pages projected in front of his eyes—a compilation of the probable evidence that would be used against Leto, as well as analyses of Landsraad law. This information included the input of Atreides attorneys and the Mentat projections Hawat himself had made.

The case rested entirely on circumstantial evidence, but it was highly compelling, beginning with Leto's own angry statement in front of the Landsraad Council. He had an obvious motive, having already declared a verbal war on the Tleilaxu.

"It all points to my guilt, doesn't it?" Leto said. He sat up in the swaying bed, and the massage unit automatically paused.

Hawat nodded. "Too perfectly, my Lord. And the evidence continues to grow worse. The multiphase projectile launchers on our combat pods were checked during the investigation, and found to have been fired. Quite a damning result, and it adds to the body of evidence."

"Thufir, we *know* the projectiles were fired. We've reported that from the beginning. Rhombur and I went out on skeet-drone practice before the Heighliner folded space. Every member of our crew can testify to that."

"The magistrates may not believe us. The explanation sounds too convenient, as if it were a concocted alibi. They'll think we practiced in order to establish a reason for the weapons results, because we *knew* we would fire upon the Tleilaxu. A simple enough trick."

"You were always good at the intricate details," Leto said with a gentle smile. "It's your security-corps training. You pore over everything repeatedly, searching each layer, making calculations and projections."

"That is exactly what we need right now, my Duke."

"Don't forget that we have *truth* on our side, Thufir, and that's a powerful ally. Holding our heads high, we will stand before the tribunal of our peers and tell them everything that happened, and most of all what *didn't* happen. They must believe us, or else centuries of Atreides honor and honesty will mean nothing."

"I wish I had your strength . . . your optimism," Hawat responded. "You show remarkable steadiness and composure." A bittersweet expression crossed his weathered face. "Your father taught you well. He would be proud of you." He flicked off the holoprojector, and the dancing pages of evidence disappeared in the heavy prison air. "So far, among the magistrates and voting members of the Landsraad jury, we do have a few who are likely to find you innocent, thanks to past allegiances."

Leto smiled, but noted how uneasy his Mentat was. He swung out of bed onto the floor. Wearing a blue robe, Leto left his feet bare as he paced. A chill ran up his arms, and he adjusted the temperature in the cell. "There'll be more believers after they listen to my statement and see the evidence."

Hawat looked at Leto as if he were a mere child again. "One advantage we have is that most of your allies will vote to acquit you solely because they despise the Tleilaxu. Regardless of what they think you may have done, you are of noble blood from a respected Landsraad family. You are one of *them*, and they would not destroy you to reward the Bene Tleilax. Several Houses have given us their support because of prior respect for your father. At least one magistrate was impressed by the boldness of your initial presentation at the Landsraad Council months ago."

"But everybody still believes I did such a terrible thing?" He frowned dejectedly. "Those other reasons are incidental."

"You are unknown to them, little more than a boy, reputed to be brash and impulsive. For now, my Duke, we must be more concerned with the verdict itself, and less with the reasons. If you succeed, you will have many years to rebuild your reputation."

"And if I lose, it won't matter a bit."

Nodding solemnly, Hawat stood like a monolith. "There are no set rules for conducting a Trial by Forfeiture. It is a freestyle forum without rules of evidence or procedures, a container without contents. Without a disclosure process, we don't have to reveal to the court what evidence we'll present—but neither does anyone else. We can't know the lies our enemies may tell, or what exhibits they may have doctored. We won't see ahead of time what alleged proof the Tleilaxu possess, how their main witnesses will testify. Many ugly things will be said about House Atreides. Prepare yourself for it."

Looking up at a noise, Leto saw a guard shut down the humming confinement field to let Rhombur enter. The Ixian Prince wore a white shirt with a Vernius helix on the collar. His face was flushed from a session in the gym, his hair wet from a shower. On his right hand, the fire-jewel ring glinted.

Leto thought of the similarities between his situation and his friend's, with their Houses in disarray and near annihilation. Rhombur, who had received the temporary protection of the court, came at the same time each day.

"Finish your exercises?" Leto inquired, forcing a hearty tone despite Hawat's grim pessimism.

"Today I broke the physical-training machine," Rhombur responded with an impish smile. "The device must have been built by one of those disreputable Houses Minor. No quality control. Certainly not good Ixian stuff." Leto laughed as he and Rhombur interlocked fingertips in the half handshake of the Imperium.

Rhombur scratched his damp, tousled blond hair. "The hard exercise helps me to think. These days it's difficult enough to concentrate on anything. Uh, my sister sends her support, by the way, via a fresh Courier from Caladan. I thought you'd like to know. It might cheer you up."

His expression grew serious, and revealed the layered strain of his long ordeal, the subtle signs of stress and instant maturity that a boy of sixteen shouldn't have had to endure. Leto knew his friend was concerned about where he and Kailea would end up if House Atreides lost this trial . . . two great noble families destroyed in a frighteningly short time. Perhaps Rhombur and Kailea would go in search of their renegade father. . . .

"Thufir and I were just discussing the merits of our case," Leto said. "Or as he might put it, the *lack* of merits."

"I wouldn't say that, my Duke," Hawat protested.

"Well, then, I bring good news," Rhombur announced. "The Bene Gesserit wish to provide Truthsayers at the trial. Those Reverend Mothers can draw falsehoods out of anyone."

"Excellent," Leto said. "They'll end this whole problem in a moment. Once I speak, they can verify I'm telling the truth. Can it be that simple?"

"Normally a Truthsayer's testimony would be inadmissible," Hawat cautioned. "An exception may be granted here, but it's doubtful. Witches have their own agendas, and legal analysts posit that they can therefore be bribed."

Leto blinked in surprise. "Bribed? Then they don't know very many Reverend Mothers." He began to think more about this, though, considering various possibilities. "But secret agendas? Why *would* the Bene Gesserit make such an offer? What do they have to gain by my innocence—or my guilt, for that matter?"

"Be cautious, my Duke," Hawat said.

"It's worth a try," Rhombur said. "Even if it isn't binding, a Truthsayer's testimony would lend weight to Leto's version of events. You and all the people around you—including Thufir, me, the frigate crew, and even your servants from Caladan—can all be scrutinized by Truthsayers. And we know the stories will be consistent. They'll prove your innocence beyond a shadow of a doubt." He grinned. "We'll be back on Caladan before you know it."

Hawat, though, remained unconvinced. "Exactly who contacted you, young Prince? Who among the Bene Gesserit made this *generous* offer? And what did she ask in payment?"

"She, uh, didn't ask for anything," Rhombur said, surprised.

"Not *yet*, maybe," Hawat said, "but those witches think in the long term."

The Ixian Prince scratched his temple. "Her name is Margot. She's in Lady Anirul's entourage, here for the Imperial wedding, I suppose."

Leto drew a quick breath as an idea occurred to him. "A Bene Gesserit is to be married to the Emperor. Is this Shaddam's doing, then? In response to our message?"

"The Bene Gesserit aren't errand girls for anyone," Hawat said. "They're notoriously independent. They made this offer because they wanted to, because it benefits them somehow."

"I didn't stop to wonder why she would come to me, of all people," Rhombur said. "But think about it: Her offer could be of no advantage to us, unless Leto is indeed innocent."

"I am!"

Hawat smiled at Rhombur in admiration. "Of course. But now we have proof that the Bene Gesserit know Leto's telling the truth, too, else they would never have made such a suggestion." He wondered what the Sisters knew, and what they hoped to gain.

"Unless they were testing me," Leto suggested. "Just by accepting their Truthsayer, they'd know I wasn't lying. If I turned them down, they'd be convinced I have something to hide."

Standing by the cell wall, Hawat gazed through an armor-plaz window. "Be mindful that we're in a trial that is a shell only. Prejudices exist against the Bene Gesserit as well and their arcane weirding ways. Truthsayers might betray their oath and lie for a greater purpose. Witchcraft, sorcery . . . Perhaps we should not be so quick to accept their help."

"You think it's a trick?" Leto asked.

"I always suspect deception," the Mentat said. His eyes flashed. "It's in my nature to do so." He switched to Atreides hand signals and signed to Leto, "These witches may be on an Imperial errand after all. What alliances are hidden from us?"

The worst sort of alliances are those which weaken us. Worse still is when an Emperor fails to recognize such an alliance for what it is.

—PRINCE RAPHAEL CORRINO,
Discourses on Leadership

Crown Prince Shaddam did as little as possible to make the Tleilaxu representative feel comfortable or welcome in the Palace. Shaddam hated even being in the same room with him, but this meeting could not be helped. Heavily armed Sardaukar escorted Hidar Fen Ajidica through a back passageway, through maintenance corridors, down unmarked stairways, and finally behind a succession of barred doors.

Shaddam chose the most private room, a chamber so discreet it appeared on no printed floor plans. Long ago, a few years after the death of Crown Prince Fafnir, Hasimir Fenring had uncovered this place during his usual skulking around. Apparently, the hidden room had been used by El-rood in the early days of his interminable reign, when he had taken numerous unofficial concubines as well as those he formally adopted into his household.

A single table remained in the chill room, illuminated by new glowglobes dragged in for the occasion. The walls and floor smelled of dust. The sheets and blankets on the narrow bed against the wall were now little more than frayed fibers and lint. An ancient bouquet, now petrified into a clump of blackened leaves and stems, lay in a corner where it had been tossed decades ago. The place conveyed the desired impression, though Shaddam knew the Bene Tleilax were not known for their attention to subtleties.

Across the plain table, Hidar Fen Ajidica, swathed in his maroon robes, folded his grayish hands on the wooden surface. He blinked his close-set eyes and looked across at Shaddam. "You summoned me, Sire? I came from my researches at your command."

Shaddam picked at a plate of glazed slig meat one of the guards had brought him, since he'd had no time today for a formal dinner. He savored the buttery mushroom sauce, then grudgingly nudged the platter toward Ajidica to offer his guest a morsel.

The diminutive man drew back and refused to touch the food. Shaddam frowned. "Slig meat is of your own manufacture. Don't you Tleilaxu eat your own delicacies?"

Ajidica shook his head. "Though we breed those creatures, we do not consume them ourselves. Please forgive me, Sire. You need offer me no amenities. Let us discuss what we must. I am anxious to return to Xuttah and my laboratories."

Shaddam sniffed, relieved that he didn't have to make any further attempts to be polite. He had no interest in displaying proper etiquette to this man. Instead, he rubbed his temples, where his long-standing headache threatened to grow even worse within the hour. "I must make a request—no, a demand as your Emperor."

"Forgive me, my Lord Prince," Ajidica interrupted, "but you have not yet been crowned."

The guards at the door stiffened. Shaddam's eyes flew open wide in astonishment. "Does any man's command bear more weight than mine? In all the Imperium?"

"No, m'Lord. I was merely correcting a matter of semantics."

Shaddam pushed the food platter to one side and leaned over the table like a predator, so close that he could smell the man's unpleasant odors. "Listen to me, Hidar Fen Ajidica. Your people must withdraw your charges in the trial of Leto Atreides. I don't want this matter to come to open court." He sat back again, took another bite of slig meat, and continued with his mouth full. "So, just drop your accusations, I'll send some treasure your way, and everything will settle down."

He made the solution sound so simple. When the Tleilaxu man did not respond immediately, Shaddam rambled on, trying to be gracious. "After discussing this with my advisors, I have decided that the Tleilaxu can be compensated, paid blood money for their losses." Shaddam brought his reddish eyebrows together in a stern expression. "*Real* losses only, though. Gholas don't count."

"I understand, Sire, but I am sorry to say that what you ask is impossible." Ajidica's voice remained low and smooth. "We cannot ignore such a crime committed against the Tleilaxu people. It strikes to the heart of our honor."

Shaddam nearly choked on another bite of his food. " 'Tleilaxu' and 'honor' aren't words usually used in the same conversation."

Ajidica brushed the insult aside. "Nevertheless, all of the Landsraad is aware of this horrible event. If we withdraw our objections, then House Atreides will have attacked us openly—destroyed our ships and people—with impunity." The pointed tip of his nose twitched. "Surely you have enough statecraft, Sire, to know that we cannot back down on this matter."

Shaddam fumed. His headache was getting worse. "I'm not asking you. I'm *telling* you."

The little man considered this for some time, his dark eyes glittering. "Might I inquire as to why the fate of Leto Atreides is so important to you, Sire? The Duke represents a relatively unimportant House. Why not throw him to the wolves and give us our satisfaction?"

Shaddam growled deep in his throat. "Because somehow Leto knows about your artificial-spice activities on Ix."

Alarm finally registered on Ajidica's masked features. "Impossible! We have maintained the utmost security."

"Then why did he send me a message?" Shaddam demanded as he half stood from his seat. "Leto is using this knowledge as a bargaining chip, to blackmail me. If he is found guilty at trial, he will expose all of your work, and our collusion in it. I'll be faced with a rebellion in the Landsraad. Think of it—my father, with my help, allowed a Great House of the Landsraad *to be overthrown*. Unprecedented! And not just by any rival House, but by you . . . the Tleilaxu."

Now the researcher seemed to take offense, but still did not respond.

Shaddam groaned, then remembered appearances and glowered instead. "If it becomes known that I did all this in order to have access to a private source of artificial spice, thereby cutting the Landsraad and the Bene Gesserit and the Guild out of their profits, my reign won't last a week."

"Then we are at an impasse, m'Lord."

"No, we are not!" Shaddam roared. "The pilot of the surviving Tleilaxu ship is your key witness. Get him to change his story. Perhaps he didn't see everything as clearly as he thought at first. You will be well rewarded, both from my coffers and from those of House Atreides."

"Not sufficient, Sire," Ajidica said with a maddeningly impassive expression. "The Atreides must be humiliated for what they have done. They must be embarrassed. Leto must pay."

The Emperor looked down his nose in disdain at the Tleilaxu researcher. His voice was cold and controlled. "Would you like me to send more Sardaukar to Ix? I'm sure another few legions walking the streets would keep a very close eye on your activities there."

Ajidica still revealed no emotion.

Shaddam's gaze turned stony. "For month after month I've waited, and still you haven't produced what I needed. Now you say it could take decades more. Neither of us will last that long if Leto exposes us."

The Crown Prince finished eating the slig morsels and pushed the plate away. Though the dish had been prepared perfectly, he had barely tasted it because his mind was elsewhere, distracted by the throbbing within his skull. Why did being Emperor have to be so difficult?

"Do what you will, Sire," Ajidica said, his voice more strident than Shaddam had ever heard it. "Leto Atreides is not forgiven and must be punished."

Wrinkling his nose, Shaddam dismissed the little man, gesturing for the Sardaukar to haul him away. Since he would soon be the Emperor of the Known Universe, he had many other things to do, important things.

If only he could get rid of this damned headache.

The worst sort of protection is confidence. The best defense is suspicion.

                                          —HASIMIR FENRING

Thufir Hawat and Rhombur Vernius could leave the cell at their leisure, while Leto was honor-bound to remain, in part for his own safety. The Mentat and the Ixian Prince often went out to discuss testimony with various crew members from the Atreides frigate and anyone else who might help their cause in any way.

Leto, meanwhile, sat at the desk alone in his cell. Although the old Mentat had always trained him never to sit with his back to a door, Leto felt that he should be safe enough inside a maximum-security cell.

For the moment he reveled in a few moments of silence and concentration as he pored over the copious evidence projections that had been prepared for him. Even with Sardaukar guards as escorts, he would have been reluctant to walk through the Imperial Palace knowing that the shadow of accusation still hung over him. He would face his peers soon enough and proclaim his innocence.

He heard a noise at the cell confinement field behind him, but delayed looking back. With a humming scriber in his hand, he finished a paragraph about the complete destruction of the first Tleilaxu ship, noting a technical detail he hadn't considered before.

"Thufir?" Leto asked. "Have you forgotten something?" Casually, he glanced over his shoulder.

A tall Landsraad guard stood there in a colorful, billowing uniform. The man wore a strange expression on his broad face, especially in the dark eyes. His skin looked pasty, as if painted on. And Leto spotted something different about the body, an odd lumpiness in the man's peculiar, jerky movements. A disturbing, grayish tone to the skin on the hands, but not the face . . .

Reaching under his desk, Leto slid his fingers over the handle of a knife that Hawat had sneaked into the cell for him. It hadn't been difficult for the warrior Mentat. Leto felt the hilt, gripped it without shifting his position or changing the placid and expectant expression on his face.

Every lesson the weapons master had ever taught him simmered in his muscles, alert and ready. Spring-coiled, Leto didn't speak, didn't challenge the intruder. But he knew something was wrong, and his life was on the line.

In a heartbeat the tall man slipped out of the voluminous uniform, maneuvering the static-seals that held the cloth together—and when the fabric slid away, so did the dull, expressionless face. *A mask!* The hands and lower arms went, too, dropping in a pile on the floor of the cell.

Dizzy with confusion, Leto threw himself to one side, tumbled off the chair onto the floor, and crouched beside the slim shelter of the desk. He held the knife ready, still out of the intruder's view, and considered his options.

The tall guard's body split at the waist, as if breaking in half—and a pair of Tleilaxu men spun around to face him, each a leathery-faced dwarf. One leaped down from the shoulders of the other and tumbled to the floor. They were both dressed in tight black outfits that showed every rippling, thick muscle.

The Tleilaxu assassins moved away from one another, circling him. Their tiny eyes glittered like buckshot. Something gleamed in each of their hands—four weapons, indistinct but assuredly deadly. Leaping wildly at Leto, one of the Tleilaxu screeched, "Die, *powindah* devil!"

In a flash, Leto considered crawling under the desk or the cart, but first he decided to even the odds by killing one of the attackers . . . to keep them from acting in a coordinated plan. With well-practiced aim, he hurled Hawat's knife. It found its mark, pierced the dwarf's jugular and knocked him backward.

A silvery dart whizzed by Leto's ear, and now he rolled behind the holo-cart, which continued to project images above the desk. A second dart struck the wall beside his head, chipping the stone.

Then he heard the hum of a lasgun. An arc of purple light filled the room.

The second Tleilaxu's body slammed into the holo-cart, knocking it over. His face oozed onto the floor, liquefied by the hot beam of light. His body collapsed near Leto's hiding place.

Thufir Hawat and a Landsraad guard captain strode into the cell and looked down at Leto. Behind them, guards inspected the two black-clad bodies. A burned-meat odor hung in the air.

"Somehow they got past our security," the captain said.

"I wouldn't call that *security*," Hawat snapped at him.

One of the guards said, "This one's got a knife in his throat."

"Where'd the knife come from?" The captain helped Leto to his feet. "Did you throw it, sir?"

Leto glanced at his Mentat, but left it for Hawat to answer. "With all your *security*, Captain," Hawat said with a withering sneer, "how could anyone possibly smuggle a weapon in here?"

"I wrested it from one of the attackers," Leto said, his expression confident. "Then I killed him with it." He blinked his gray eyes. His body trembled with the after-rush of adrenaline. "I guess the Bene Tleilax couldn't wait for the trial to be over."

"Vermilion hells!" Rhombur said, stepping in and looking around at the mess. "On the, uh, bright side, this won't look good for the Tleilaxu in the trial. If they were so sure of winning, why should they try to take justice into their own hands?"

Flushing in embarrassment, the guard captain turned to his men and directed them in the removal of the bodies and in the cleanup.

"The assassins fired two darts," Leto said, pointing to where the needles had stuck.

"Be careful handling them," Hawat said. "They're probably poisoned."

When Leto, Rhombur, and Hawat were alone again, the Mentat slipped a smuggled maula pistol into a bottom drawer of the desk.

"Just in case," he said. "Next time a dagger might not be sufficient."

As seen from orbit, the world of Ix is pristine and placid. But beneath its surface, immense projects are undertaken and great works are achieved. In this way, our planet is a metaphor for the Imperium itself.

—DOMINIC VERNIUS,
The Secret Workings of Ix

Smug and very satisfied, Hasimir Fenring extended to Shaddam a sheaf of covert documents written in the private language he and the Crown Prince had developed during their childhood. The grand audience hall echoed with every whisper and sound, but they could be confident in their own secrets. Shaddam sat wearily on the heavy throne, and the Hagal-crystal dais shone with inner illumination like a firelit aquamarine.

Fenring twitched with enough nervous energy for both of them. "These are files for the Major Houses of the Landsraad who will be sitting at the Atreides Trial by Forfeiture." His large eyes were like black holes into the labyrinth of his mind. "I believe I've found something either embarrassing or illegal about each one of concern. All told, I believe we have the means of persuasion we need."

Lurching forward on the throne, Shaddam looked as if he'd been taken completely by surprise. His eyes became wild and concerned, red from lack of sleep and flashing with anger.

Fenring had seen him on the verge of panic before, just as when they had arranged for the death of his older brother

Fafnir. "Calm yourself, Shaddam, hm-m-m-m-m?" he said quietly. "I've taken care of everything."

"Damn you, Hasimir! If word ever gets out about any bribery attempts, it would ruin House Corrino. We can't allow anyone to see our connection to this!" Shaddam shook his head as if the Imperium was already crumbling around him, and he hadn't even been crowned yet. "They'll wonder why we would go to such lengths to save an insignificant Duke."

Fenring smiled, trying to steady Shaddam with his own confidence. "The Landsraad is composed of Great Houses, many of which are already your allies, Sire. A few carefully phrased suggestions among the nobles, a bit of melange exchanged, some well-placed bribes and threats . . ."

"Ah, yes. I've always gone along with you—perhaps too often, as if I had no brain of my own. Soon I will be Emperor of a Million Worlds, and I'll have to think for myself. I'm doing that now."

"Emperors have advisors, Shaddam. *Always.*" Fenring suddenly realized he had to be more cautious. Something had unsettled Shaddam, something recent. *What does he know that I don't?*

"For once we won't use your methods, Hasimir." He was firm, insistent. "I forbid it. We will find some other way."

Intense now, Fenring climbed the steps to stand beside the Crown Prince, like an equal. For some reason, though, the atmosphere was uncomfortably changed. What had gone wrong? As babies had they not both sucked on the same breast when Fenring's mother had been Shaddam's wet nurse? As boys, hadn't they been tutored side by side? Had they not concocted plots and schemes together as they grew older? Why was Shaddam suddenly refusing to listen to his advice?

Fenring leaned close to the Crown Prince's ear. He sounded as contrite as he could be. "My apologies, Sire, but, hm-m-m-ah, it has . . . already been done. I was certain of your approval, and so the notes were cleverly delivered to the appropriate representatives, asking for them to support their Emperor when it comes time to call for a vote in the trial."

"You dared that? Without consulting me first?" Shaddam purpled with outrage and could not find his voice for some moments. "You just thought I'd follow your lead? In whatever schemes you might contrive?"

Shaddam had grown incensed, *too* incensed. What else was bothering him? Fenring backed one step away from the throne. "Please, Sire. You're overreacting, losing perspective."

"On the contrary, I believe I'm *gaining* perspective." His nostrils flared. "You don't think I'm terribly bright, do you, Hasimir? Since we were children you've had a snide way of explaining things to me in training class, of helping me on examinations. And you were always the faster thinker, more intelligent, more ruthless—or so you made it appear. But, believe it or not, I *can* handle situations by myself."

"I've never doubted your intelligence, my friend." Fenring's overlarge head bobbed on his thin neck. "With your standing in House Corrino, your future has always been guaranteed, but I've had to fight for my position every step of the way. I want to be your sounding board and confidant."

Shaddam sat forward on the massive crystal throne that threw sparkle-fire from the glowglobes around the chamber. "Ah, yes. You thought you'd be the power behind the throne, with me as your puppet?"

"Puppet? Certainly not." Fenring backed another step away now. Shaddam was terrifyingly unstable, and Fenring didn't know how he had strayed onto such uncertain ground. *He knows something I don't.* Shaddam had never questioned his friend's actions before, had never wanted to know the details of bribery and violence. "Hm-m-m-m . . . I have always considered how best I might help you to become a great ruler."

Shaddam rose to his feet, slow and regal, looking down his nose at the weasel-faced man who stood at the foot of the dais. Fenring decided not to back farther away. *What does he know? What news?*

"But, I'd never do anything at your expense, old friend. We've, ahhhh, known each other too long. Indeed, we share too much blood on our hands." He held his hand over his heart, in the way of the Imperium. "I am aware of how you think, and of your . . . limitations, hm-m-m-m-ah? In fact, you're exceptionally bright. The problem is, you often find it hard to make the difficult but necessary decisions."

Shaddam climbed down from the Golden Lion Throne and stalked across the floor of polished stones from a million Imperial worlds. "A hard decision is needed right now, Hasimir, and it regards your service to me in the immediate future."

Fenring waited, afraid of what ill-advised ideas the Crown Prince might have gotten into his head. But he dared not argue.

"Know this—I won't forget the grievous breach of conduct you have committed. If this bribery scheme comes back to bite us, your head will roll. I would have no qualms about signing an execution order for treason."

Fenring paled, and the startled look on his narrow face sent a wave of pleasure through the Crown Prince. In Shaddam's present mood, Fenring realized that his friend just might be capable of issuing such an order.

The fidgety man's jaw clenched, and he decided to put an end to this foolishness immediately. "What I've said to you about friendship is the truth, Shaddam." He measured his words carefully. "But I'd be a fool if I hadn't taken certain precautions that could expose your involvement in certain . . . mm-m-m-m . . . shall we call them, ah . . . adventures? If anything happens to me, all will be revealed: how your father really died, the artificial-spice activities on Ix, even the assassination of Fafnir when you were a teenager. If I hadn't poisoned your brother, *he* would be sitting on the throne right now, not you. We're in lockstep, you and I. Up or down . . . together."

Shaddam looked as if he had expected to hear nothing else. "Ah, yes. Very predictable, Hasimir. You always warned me not to be predictable."

Fenring had the good grace to look embarrassed. He held his silence.

"You're the one who got me into this risky scheme in the first place, and who knows when we'll see any payback from our dangerous investment on Ix." Shaddam's eyes flashed fire. "Synthetic spice, indeed! I wish we'd never allied with the Tleilaxu. And now I'm stuck with the unpleasant aftermath. See where your scheming has gotten us?"

"Hm-m-m-m-ah, I won't be drawn into an argument with you, Shaddam. It wouldn't be productive. But you knew the risks from the outset, and the enormous possible gains. Please be patient."

"Patient? At the moment we're faced with two distinct possibilities." Shaddam sat back down and hunched forward on the throne, hawklike. "As you said, either I will be crowned, and you and I can rise to the top together—or we go down together . . . into exile or death." He let his breath out in a slow whistle. "At the moment we're both in mortal danger, all because of your infernal spice scheme."

Fenring pressed his last desperate idea, large eyes flicking from side to side in search of some escape. "You have had some disturbing news, Sire. I can sense it. Tell me what has happened." Few things in the Imperial Palace or the capital city occurred without Fenring knowing about them immediately.

Shaddam clasped his long-fingered hands together. Fenring flushed and leaned forward, his dark eyes widening with interest. The Crown Prince sighed in resignation. "The Tleilaxu sent two assassins to kill Leto Atreides in his protected cell."

Fenring's heart leaped, wondering if this was good news or bad. "And did they succeed?"

"No, no. Our young Duke somehow managed to smuggle a weapon in and protected himself. But this causes me great concern."

Fenring hunkered down, astonished at the news. "That's impossible. I thought you'd already spoken to our Tleilaxu contact and told him in no uncertain terms—"

"I did," Shaddam snapped. "But apparently you aren't the only one who no longer listens to my commands. Either Ajidica ignored my instructions, or he has no power to control his own people."

Fenring growled, happy to divert the Crown Prince's anger. "We need to strike back in a similar manner: Let Hidar Fen Ajidica know that he must heed all orders from his Emperor, or the price will grow much higher."

Shaddam looked at him, but his eyes were weary now and no longer as warm or open as they had once been. "You know exactly what to do, Hasimir."

Fenring seized the chance to restore himself to the Crown Prince's good graces. "I always do, Sire." He scuttled away across the long reception hall.

Shaddam paced the polished floor in front of the crystalline throne, trying to calm himself and put his thoughts in order. Just as Fenring reached the archway, he called out, "This isn't over between us, Hasimir. Things must change once I am crowned."

"Yes, Sire. You must . . . hm-m-m-m, do as you see fit." Bowing deeply, Fenring backed out of the audience chamber, relieved to depart with his life.

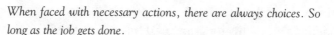

*When faced with necessary actions, there are always choices. So
long as the job gets done.*

—COUNT HASIMIR FENRING,
Dispatches from Arrakis

The Tleilaxu pilot who had survived the Atreides attack inside the Heighliner was a material witness at
the trial, and thus had been forced to remain on Kaitain.
He wasn't a prisoner, and his needs were taken care of,
though no one sought out his company. The Bene Tleilax
hadn't even made his name commonly known. He wanted
to be back on his ship, back at work.

However, because of the huge influx of guests arriving
for Shaddam's upcoming coronation ceremony and the Imperial wedding, accommodations were difficult to find.
Shaddam's protocol ministers had taken great pleasure in
finding only an austere and unpleasant room for the man.

Much to the protocol ministers' annoyance, the Tleilaxu
pilot didn't seem to mind. He said nothing in complaint
while he waited, and sulked and stewed until he could bring
the foul criminal Leto Atreides to justice. . . .

Kaitain nights were perfect, clear and full of stars and
moons. Through shimmering curtains of auroras, complete
darkness never fell. Even so, most of the capital city slept
during certain hours.

Hasimir Fenring easily crept into the sealed room that

held the Tleilaxu man. He moved stealthily, like a shadow on a sus-
pensorlift, and made no sound, used no illumination. He was accustomed to the night; it was his friend.

Fenring had never seen a Tleilaxu asleep before—but as he stepped
closer to the bed, he found the pilot already sitting up, totally awake.
The gray-skinned man stared at him through the darkness as if he
could see better even than Shaddam's henchman.

"I have a fléchette pistol trained directly at your body core," the
Tleilaxu said. "Who are you? Have you come to kill me?"

"Hm-m-m-m-ah, no." Fenring recovered quickly and used his sweetest, silkiest voice to introduce himself. "I am Hasimir Fenring, boon
companion to Crown Prince Shaddam, bearing a message and a request."

"What is it?" the pilot said.

"Crown Prince Shaddam beseeches you to reconsider the details of
your testimony, hm-m-m-m? He desires peace among the Houses of
the Landsraad, and does not wish for such a shadow to fall upon House
Atreides, whose members have served the Padishah Emperors since
the time of the Great Revolt."

"Nonsense," the Tleilaxu snapped. "Leto Atreides fired upon our
sovereign ships, destroying one, damaging mine. Hundreds are dead.
He has created the largest political firestorm in recent decades."

"Yes, yes!" Fenring said. "And you can prevent it from escalating
further, hmmm? Shaddam wishes to begin his reign with quiet and
prosperity. Can you not consider the larger picture?"

"I think only of my people," the pilot said, "and how we have been
wronged by one man. Everyone knows the Atreides is guilty, and he must
pay the price. Only then will we be satisfied." He smiled with thin lips.
The fléchette pistol in his hand did not move a millimeter. Fenring
could see how this man could have risen to the rank of pilot; he clearly
had the stomach to command ships. "After that happens, Shaddam may
have as quiet a reign as he chooses."

"You make me sad," Fenring said, sounding disappointed. "I will
take your answer back to the Crown Prince." He crossed his arms over
his chest and bowed in farewell, extending his palms forward. The motion triggered two needle guns mounted to his wrists. In silence, they
fired deadly paralytic darts into the pilot's throat.

The Tleilaxu clenched in a spasm, reflexively firing the fléchette
pistol. Fenring easily ducked out of the way. The long spikes hammered

into the wall and hung there quivering. A second later, an occupant in the adjacent room pounded on the wall for quiet.

Still in darkness, Fenring studied his work. The evidence was all here, and the Bene Tleilax would understand what had happened. After the outrageous assassination attempt on Leto Atreides—despite Shaddam's specific orders for them to drop the matter—Hidar Fen Ajidica had much to atone for.

The Tleilaxu prided themselves on their ability to keep secrets. No doubt they would discreetly remove the pilot's name from the witness list and not mention him again. Without his testimony, their case would be weaker.

Fenring hoped, though, that this murder wouldn't make the little men even more vengeful. How would Hidar Fen Ajidica respond?

Departing from the locked room, Fenring slid through the shadows. He left the body, just in case the Bene Tleilax wanted to resurrect him as a ghola. After all, despite the little man's failings, he might have been a good pilot.

.

In plotting any course of revenge, one must savor the anticipation phase and all its moments, for the actual execution often differs widely from the original plan.

Dispatches from Arrakis

The Baron Vladimir Harkonnen couldn't have been more delighted at the way events were turning out. He might have taken deeper pleasure if the rest of the Imperium could *appreciate* the delicious complexities of what he had done—but of course he could never reveal those.

As an important House, as well as the current stewards of spice production on Arrakis, the Harkonnens received fine accommodations in a distant wing of the Imperial Palace. Tickets for reserved seats at the coronation and the wedding had already been delivered to their quarters.

And, of course, before all the pomp and ceremony, it would be the Baron's sad duty to watch the terrible trial of Leto Atreides. He tapped his fingers against his leg and pursed his generous lips. Ah, the burdens of nobility.

He lounged in a plush indigo chair, cradling a crystal sphere in his lap. From the depths of the transparent ball shone holo-images of fireworks displays and light shows, previews for the spectacle that would shower Kaitain in a few days' time. In a corner of the room a musical fireplace whispered quiet notes, making him yawn. Lately, he felt tired so often, his body weak and shaky.

"I want you to leave the planet," the Baron told Glossu Rabban without looking up from the crystal sphere. "I don't want you here during the trial or the coronation."

The broad-shouldered, thick-lipped man bristled. His brown hair had been hacked short, without finesse, for the public appearance, and he wore a padded dra-leather vest that made him look even more like a barrel than usual. "Why? I did everything you asked, and our plans turned out beautifully. Why send me away now?"

"Because I don't *want* you here," the Baron said, running a hand along his widow's peak to smooth down his thick hair. "I can't have anyone taking a look at you and thinking you might have had something to do with poor, dear Leto's plight. You have that . . . gloating manner about you."

The Baron's nephew frowned and drew a deep breath, still defiant. "But I want to be there so I can look in his eyes when he receives his sentence."

"That is exactly why you must be gone. Can't you understand? You'll give something away."

With a deep breath and a grunt, Rabban finally backed down. "May I come to the execution at least?" He sounded dangerously close to pouting.

"It depends on the timing." The Baron stared at his ring-studded fingers and tinkled their metal against the smooth surface of the sphere in his lap in his habitual rhythm. "At the very least I'll make sure the event is recorded for your enjoyment."

The Baron got out of his chair with an effort and cinched the sash around his tighter-than-usual lounge robe. With a sigh he circled the elaborate room on bare feet, saw the ornate bathtub with its complicated temperature and massage controls. Since his body continued to be plagued by mysterious pains, he decided to take a long and luxurious bath—if he could find someone to serve him properly here on Kaitain.

Rabban, still displeased, stood on the threshold of the Baron's opulent guest quarters. "What shall I do, then, Uncle?"

"Take a lighter and board the first available Heighliner. I want you to go to Arrakis and watch over the spice production there. Keep adding to our profits." The Baron smiled at him, then waggled his fingers to shoo the nephew away. "Oh, don't look so gloomy. Go hunt a few more Fremen if you like, just to amuse yourself. You've already done your part in this plot, and done it well." He made his voice sound soothing. "But we have to be very careful. Especially now. Just pay attention to what I do and try to learn from it."

Grabbing something to eat from a sampling tray that hovered by the archway, Rabban departed. Alone at last, the Baron began to contemplate how best to find a young, soft-skinned boy to tend him in his bath. He wanted to be completely relaxed and prepared for the following day.

Tomorrow, he would have nothing to do but observe and enjoy the event as young Leto Atreides found himself caught in more traps than he could begin to understand.

Soon there would be no more House Atreides at all.

What matters more, the form of justice or the actual outcome? No matter how a court may dissect the evidence, the foundation of genuine truth remains unblemished. Unfortunately for many of the accused, such genuine truth is often known only to the victim and the perpetrator. All others must make up their own minds.

—Landsraad Law, codicils and analyses

On the morning of the trial in Landsraad court, Leto Atreides chose his wardrobe carefully. Others in the same situation might have worn their most expensive finery, the grandeur of merh-silk shirts, pendants and earrings, along with whale-fur-lined capes, and stylish caps adorned with feathers and baubles.

Instead, Leto dressed in plain dungarees and a blue-and-white-striped shirt with a navy blue fisherman's cap—the simple garb he would have to wear if he could no longer be a Duke. In a sash at his waist he carried a pouch of fishing lures and an empty sheath for a knife. He wore no Atreides insignia and no ducal signet ring. An ordinary commoner—which was all he would be if found guilty—Leto showed the Landsraad by his humble demeanor that he would survive, somehow. Even simple things would be enough for him.

Following his father's example, he had always tried to treat his loyal men well, to such an extreme that many of the servants and soldiers considered Leto one of their number, a comrade-in-arms. Now, as he groomed himself for trial, he began to think of himself as a plain man . . . and discovered that the feeling wasn't so bad. It made him realize the tremendous burden of responsibility he had shouldered since the death of the Old Duke.

Being a poor fisherman might actually be a relief, in certain ways. He wouldn't have to worry about plots, shifting alliances, and betrayals in the Imperium. Unfortunately, though, Kailea would never want to be a fisherman's wife.

And I cannot let my people down.

In a curt letter from Caladan, his mother had expressed her complete disagreement with his demand for a Trial by Forfeiture. To her, the loss of stature associated with the destruction of House Atreides would be a huge blow, even though she now (temporarily, in her mind) lived an austere life among the Sisters in Isolation.

With the decline of House Richese, Helena had married into House Atreides as a way to stabilize her family's waning fortunes, after Emperor Elrood had withdrawn their quasi-fief of Arrakis and turned it over to the Harkonnens.

As for Helena's dowry, House Atreides had received political power, a CHOAM directorship, Landsraad voting privileges. But Duke Paulus had never brought his wife the fabulous riches she had wanted, and Leto knew she must harbor hopes of returning to the former glories of her family. All of that would be forever impossible if he lost this gambit.

After receiving the early-morning summons, Leto met his legal team in the corridor outside his cell: two brilliant Elaccan lawyers, Clere Ruitt and Bruda Viol—women renowned for their criminal-defense work. They had been offered by the Ixian Ambassador-in-exile, Cammar Pilru, and thoroughly interviewed by Thufir Hawat.

The attorneys wore dark business suits and would follow the legal forms, though in this unusual trial Leto knew it would be primarily up to him and his own personality. He certainly had no hard evidence in his favor.

Clere Ruitt handed him a thin sheet of ridulian crystal that contained a brief legal pronouncement. "I am sorry, Lord Leto. This came to us only moments ago."

Already feeling dread, Leto scanned the words. Beside him, Hawat's shoulders sagged, as if he had guessed the document's contents. Rhombur pressed close, trying to read the etchings on the crystal. "What is it, Leto? Let me see."

"The tribunal of magistrates has ruled that no Bene Gesserit Truthsayers may speak on my behalf. Such testimony will not even be introduced."

Rhombur sputtered in indignation. "Vermilion hells! But everything is admissible in a Trial by Forfeiture! They can't make such a ruling."

The other Elaccan attorney shook her head, and her expression remained bland. "They have taken the position that the weight of all other Imperial Law argues against it. Numerous rules and statutes explicitly forbid Truthsayer testimony. The requirements of evidence may be loosened in a forfeiture proceeding such as this, but the magistrates have determined that even loose rules must not go too far."

"So . . . no Truthsayers." Rhombur scowled, fully sullen now. "That was the best thing we had going for us."

Leto held his head high. "Then we'll just have to do this on our own." He looked at his friend. "Come now, I'm not usually the one to shore up *your* optimism."

"On a brighter note," Bruda Viol said, "the Tleilaxu have removed the pilot of their attacked frigate from the witness list. They provided no explanation."

Leto heaved a long sigh of relief, but Hawat cautioned him, "We will still hear plenty of damning testimony, my Duke."

Silently, he accompanied his advisors into the crowded Landsraad courtroom. At the head of a long aisle he took a seat between them at the defense table below a towering bench for the magistrates who would hear the case. Ruitt whispered in his ear, but he didn't focus on her words. Instead he closely studied the names of the assigned magistrates: seven Dukes, Barons, Earls, Counts, and Lords randomly chosen from among the Great and Minor Houses of the Landsraad.

These men would decide his fate.

Since the Tleilaxu belonged to no royal House and had been spurned for membership even after their takeover of Ix, they were not represented in the Landsraad. In the days preceding the trial, outraged Bene Tleilax dignitaries had shouted in the Palace courtyards, demanding justice—but after the Tleilaxu attempt on Leto's life, Sardaukar guards had kept them silent.

Now, with a rustle of robes and formal uniforms, the chosen magistrates filed solemnly into the courtroom. They took seats at the curved stonewood bench that loomed over the defense table. The colorful banners and crests of their Houses hung behind each chair.

Having been coached by his attorneys and Thufir Hawat, Leto recognized all of them. Two of the magistrates, Baron Terkillian Sor of IV Anbus and Lord Bain O'Garee of Hagal, had been strong economic trading partners with House Atreides. One, the black-haired Duke Prad Vidal of Ecaz, was an avowed enemy of the Old Duke, an ally of the Harkonnens. Another, Count Anton Miche, was reputed to be susceptible to bribery, making him easily adaptable to the needs of the Harkonnens, since neither Rhombur nor the loyal Mentat had gotten to him first.

Two to two, he thought. The other three magistrates could go either way. But he detected the rank odor of betrayal in the air; he saw it in the cold expressions of the judging panel, the way they avoided making eye contact with him. *Have they already decided my guilt?*

"We have more bad news . . . Duke Leto." Bruda Viol hesitated before using his former title. Her face was squarish and stern, but oddly passionless, as if she'd seen so much injustice and manipulation that nothing bothered her anymore. "We've only just discovered that one of the three undecided magistrates, Rincon of House Fazeel, lost an immense fortune to Ix in a secret trade war. It had to do with ring-asteroid mining in the Klytemn system. Five years ago, Rincon's advisors barely kept him from declaring a blood feud against Dominic Vernius."

The other attorney nodded and lowered her voice. "We have heard a rumor, Monsieur Atreides, that Rincon sees your personal downfall as his only chance to get even with Ix, now that House Vernius has gone renegade."

Leto broke out in a cold sweat and made a disgusted sound. "Does any part of this trial concern what actually happened in the Heighliner?"

Both Bruda Viol and Clere Ruitt looked at him as if he had uttered the most ridiculous comment imaginable.

"Three to two, my Duke," Hawat said. "We must therefore win over both of the undecided judges and lose none of the tentative support we've counted on."

"It'll turn out all right," Rhombur said.

The windowless, armored courtroom had once been a ducal chancery during the construction work on Kaitain. Its vaulted Gothic ceiling was inset with military paintings and the designs and shields of the Great Houses. Leto focused on the red hawk crest of the Atreides among the other shields and coats of arms. Though he tried to remain stoic, a terrible feeling of loss swept over him, a longing for what might never be again. In a short time he had brought down everything his father had left him, and House Atreides was crashing toward ruin.

When he felt tears welling in his eyes, he cursed himself for the momentary weakness. All was not lost. He could still win. He *would* win! Iciness infused him, and he stemmed the threatening flow of despair. The Landsraad was watching, and he had to be strong enough to face whatever needed to be done here. He could ill afford despair, or any other emotion.

Behind him, observers filed into the courtroom, speaking in low, excited tones. Two larger tables flanked the defense table at which he sat. His enemies took seats at the table on the left—designated representatives of the Tleilaxu, probably sponsored by the Harkonnens and other Atreides foes. But the hated Baron and his entourage sat far back in the simple spectator seats, as if to keep their hands completely clean of the matter. At the other table sat allies and friends of the Atreides. Leto nodded to each of them with a confident smile.

But his thoughts were far from brave, and he had to admit he didn't have much of a case, even now. The prosecutors would present the evidence of weapons fired from the Atreides combat pod, firsthand accounts of dozens of neutral parties who claimed the shots couldn't have come from anywhere but the tiny craft berthed in Leto's ship. Even without the Tleilaxu pilot as a witness, the other observers would be sufficient. The offsetting testimony of his companions and crew wouldn't be enough, nor would the numerous family friends who would act as character witnesses.

"Perhaps the denial of Truthsayers will give us sufficient grounds for an appeal," Clere Ruitt suggested, but Leto took no comfort from this.

Then, through a side passage, the somber Tleilaxu prosecution team entered with their own attorneys and twisted Mentat scholars. They came with minimal fanfare, but much clanking and commotion as they brought with them a diabolical-looking machine. It rolled in on creaking wheels with a clatter of hinges and bars. A hush fell over the room as the spectators craned forward to get a better look at the most frightening contraption any of them had ever seen.

This has to be intentional, Leto thought, *to make me more uneasy.*

The Tleilaxu ponderously hauled the ominous machine past Leto's defense table; the gray-skinned men glared at him with fiery, dark eyes. The audience began to buzz and whisper. Presently the Tleilaxu team stopped, leaving their device in the center of the main speaking floor, below the curved stonewood bench of the chosen judges.

"What is this?" One of the central magistrates, Baron Terkillian Sor, leaned forward, scowling.

The leader of the Tleilaxu team, a wiry man who had not been introduced by name, looked hatefully at Leto, then gazed up at the questioner. "My Lords, in all the recorded annals of Imperial Law, the specific subsections pertaining to Trial by Forfeiture are few, but clear. 'Should the accused not succeed in his legal bid, he shall lose everything he possesses, without exception.' *Everything.*"

"I can read." Terkillian Sor continued to scowl. "And what does this have to do with your contraption here?"

The Tleilaxu spokesman drew a deep breath. "We intend to claim not only the holdings of House Atreides, but also the actual person of the heinous criminal Duke Leto Atreides himself, down to his cells and genetic material."

While the audience muttered in shock, the Tleilaxu attendees worked controls on the machine, causing hidden saw blades to whir, and electrical arcs to crackle from one long needle to another. The ominous machine was outrageous and exaggerated—obviously by design.

"With this device, we will exsanguinate Duke Leto Atreides in this very courtroom, draining him of every drop of his blood. We will flay the skin from his body, and remove his eyes for our testing and experimentation. Every cell will be ours, for whatever purposes the Tleilaxu determine to use them." He sniffed. "It is our right!"

Then the grayish little man smiled at Leto.

Leto held steady and tried desperately not to show the discomfort raging inside. A trickle of cold sweat ran down his back. He wanted his lawyers to say something, but they held their damnable silence.

"Perhaps the accused can even see an advantage to this fate," the Tleilaxu spokesman suggested with a wicked grin, "since he has no heirs. If he loses, there will be no more House Atreides. With his cells, however, we have the option of resurrecting him as a ghola."

To do their bidding, Leto thought, with horror.

At the defense table, Rhombur glared defiantly at the Tleilaxu, while Thufir Hawat sat beside him like a statue. Flanking Leto on either side, the two Elaccan attorneys scribbled notes.

"Enough of this showmanship," boomed Lord Bain O'Garee. "We can decide this matter later. Let us get on with the trial. I want to hear what the Atreides has to say for himself."

Though he fought not to show it, Leto suddenly knew he was lost. Every person present in the hall knew his professed hatred for the Tleilaxu, his clear support of the ousted Ixian family. He could summon character witnesses, but no one here really *knew* him. He was young and untried, thrust by tragedy into his role as Duke. The only time these members of the Landsraad had seen Leto Atreides was when he'd spoken before the Council, revealing a glimpse of his hot temper.

Sparks crackled from the Tleilaxu vivisection and execution device, like a hungry, waiting beast. Leto knew there would be no appeal.

Before the first witness could be called, though, the immense brass-inlaid doors at the rear of the hall slammed open against the stone walls. A hush fell over the courtroom, and Leto heard the crisp cadence of metal-heeled boots on the marbleite floor.

Looking back to the grand entrance doors, he saw Crown Prince Shaddam, dressed in scarlet-and-gold Imperial fur-satins instead of his customary Sardaukar uniform. Followed by an escort of his elite force, the soon-to-be-crowned Emperor strode forward, commanding the full attention of those in the hall. Four heavily armed men scanned the crowd in all directions, every muscle poised for violence.

The Trial by Forfeiture was already highly unusual for the Landsraad court—but the appearance of the future Padishah Emperor himself was unprecedented.

Shaddam made his way up the long aisle and passed Leto with hardly a glance. The Sardaukar took positions behind the defense table, increasing Leto's feeling of uneasiness.

Shaddam's face was stony, his upper lip slightly twisted. He gave no sign of his intentions. *Did my message offend him?* Leto wondered. *Does he mean to call my bluff? Will he crush me here in the hall before all the Landsraad? Who could oppose him if he did?*

Reaching the towering bench, Shaddam looked up and announced,

"Before this trial actually begins, I have a statement to make. Will the court recognize me at this time?"

Though Leto didn't trust his distaff cousin, he had to admit that Shaddam looked especially regal and elegant. For the first time, he saw this man as a genuine presence in his own right, not just the shadow of his ancient father Elrood. Shaddam's coronation was set for two days hence, to be followed immediately by his magnificent wedding to Anirul—events that Leto might never live to see. The powerful Bene Gesserit faction had thrown its support to Shaddam's upcoming reign, and all of the Great and Minor Houses of the Landsraad wanted to stay on his good side.

Does he feel threatened by me?

The head magistrate bowed deeply and made an expansive gesture. "Sire, we are honored by your presence and your interest in this case. Of course the Landsraad tribunal will hear you." Leto knew only the most basic facts about this magistrate, the Baron Lar Olin from the titanium-rich planet of Risp VII. "Please speak."

Shaddam pointed over his shoulder, in Leto's direction. "With the permission of the court, I'd like my cousin Leto Atreides to stand with me. I wish to address the matter of these malicious accusations and, I hope, prevent the court from wasting the valuable time of all its members."

Leto's mind raced, and he looked over at Hawat. *What is he doing? "Cousin"? The way he says it, the word sounds like a term of endearment . . . but he and I have never been close.* Leto was merely the grandson of one of Elrood's daughters, by the ancient Emperor's second wife, not even Shaddam's mother. The Corrino family tree sprawled among the Houses of the Landsraad; any blood connection should have meant little to Shaddam.

The head magistrate nodded. At the table beside Leto, his lawyers sat in astonishment, not knowing how to respond. Warily, Leto levered himself to his feet. With shaking knees, he marched forward to join the Crown Prince, standing a pace away from his side, on his left. While of similar height and facial appearance, the men were dressed in radically different fashion, representing two social extremes. Leto stood in his rough fisherman clothes, feeling like a dust mote in the middle of a whirlwind.

He made a formal bow before Shaddam closed the gap between them, placing a hand on Leto's shoulder. The fine, loosely fitted satin of the Crown Prince's tunic cascaded over the arm of the young Atreides.

"I speak from the heart of House Corrino, the blood of the Padishah Emperors," Shaddam began, "with the supportive voices of all my ancestors who have ever associated with House Atreides. This man's father, Duke Paulus Atreides, fought bravely for the Imperial cause against the rebels on Ecaz. Through battle and high peril, the Atreides family has never to my knowledge committed any treasonous or dishonorable act—all the way back to their heroism and sacrifice at the Bridge of Hrethgir during the Butlerian Jihad. Never! Never have they been cowardly murderers. I challenge any of you to disprove this." He narrowed his eyes, and the magistrates looked away uncomfortably.

Shaddam stared from magistrate to magistrate. "Who among you, knowing the histories of your Houses, can make the same claim? Who has displayed the same loyalty, the same unblemished honor? Few of us, if the truth be told, can compare with noble House Atreides." He let the silence hang, disturbed only by a sharp static discharge from the ominous Tleilaxu vivisection machine. "Ah, yes. And that is why we are here today, is it not, gentlemen? Truth and honor."

Leto saw some of the magistrates nod in agreement, because they were expected to. But they looked perplexed. Imperial leaders never voluntarily addressed Landsraad courts. Why was Shaddam involving himself in such a relatively minor matter?

He read my message! Leto thought. *And this is his response.*

Still, he waited for the trap to appear. He didn't understand what he had gotten himself into, but Shaddam couldn't intend just to march in and rescue him. Of all the Great Houses in the Landsraad, the Corrinos were among the most devious.

"House Atreides has always taken the high road," Shaddam continued, his regal voice growing more powerful. "Always! And young Leto here has been indoctrinated into this family code of ethics, forced into his royal station early because of the senseless death of his great father."

Shaddam removed his arm from Leto's shoulder and took a step forward, closer to the magistrates. "In my opinion, it would be impossible for this man, from this House, to intentionally fire upon Tleilaxu ships, as he has been accused of doing. Such an act would be abhorrent to everything House Atreides believes. Any evidence to the contrary must be false. My Truthsayers have confirmed this after speaking to Leto and his fellow witnesses."

A lie, Leto thought. *I spoke to no Truthsayers!*

"But Royal Highness," Magistrate Prad Vidal said, with a dark scowl that lowered his black eyebrows, "the guns on his frigate showed evidence of having been fired. Are you suggesting the Tleilaxu ships were damaged by a convenient accident? A mad coincidence?"

Shaddam shrugged. "As far as I am concerned, Duke Leto has explained this satisfactorily. I, myself, have taken a combat pod into orbit for skeet-drone practice. The remainder of the investigation is inconclusive. Perhaps an accident, yes, but not caused by the Atreides. It must have been a mechanical malfunction."

"But on *two* Tleilaxu ships?" Vidal said, in an incredulous tone.

Leto looked around, speechless, watching the events play themselves out. Shaddam was about to begin his reign. If the Emperor himself threw his weight indisputably in support of Leto, would any of the representatives declare themselves enemies of the crown? The repercussions could be severe and long-lasting.

This is all politics, Landsraad power plays, favors exchanged, Leto thought, struggling to keep his expression calm. *None of this has anything to do with the truth.* Now that the Crown Prince had made his stance clear, any magistrate who voted to convict Leto would be openly defying the next Emperor. Even the enemies of House Atreides would be loath to risk that.

"Who can say?" Shaddam responded, with a toss of his head that labeled the question irrelevant. "Perhaps debris from the first accidental explosion hit the companion craft, damaging it less severely." No one believed the explanation for a moment, but the Crown Prince had given them a way out, a paper platform on which to stand.

In low tones the magistrates conferred among themselves. Some of them agreed that Shaddam's line of reasoning was plausible—they *wanted* to find some way to agree with the new Emperor—but Vidal was not one of them. Sweat ran down his brow.

Looking over his shoulder, Leto saw the Tleilaxu spokesman shaking his head in silent disapproval. In the tall chair that had been rigged for him at the prosecution table, he looked like a displeased child.

The Crown Prince continued. "I am here, as is my right and duty as your Supreme Commander, to personally vouch for my eminent cousin, Duke Leto Atreides. I urgently request an end to this trial and the restoration of his title and properties. If you grant this . . . request, I promise to send a contingent of Imperial diplomats to the Tleilaxu to convince them to drop the matter and not to retaliate against the Atreides in any way."

Shaddam fixed a long glance at the Tleilaxu, and Leto had the distinct impression that the Emperor also had the gnomish men over a barrel. Somehow. Seeing that Shaddam stood by House Atreides, their hauteur crumbled.

"And if the complainants won't agree?" Vidal inquired.

Shaddam smiled. "Oh, they'll agree. I am even willing to open the Imperial coffers to pay generous, ah, disaster relief for what was, undoubtedly, an unfortunate accident. It is my duty as your new ruler to maintain peace and stability throughout the Imperium. I cannot allow such a feud to destroy what my dear father built during his long reign."

Leto caught Shaddam's gaze, and detected a glimmer of fear beneath the statesmanship and bravado. Without words Shaddam told Leto to keep his mouth shut, making Leto even more curious about what alarms his mysterious bluff had triggered.

So he held his tongue. But could Shaddam afford to let him live afterward, not knowing what proof Leto might have against him?

Following a short conference among themselves, Baron Lar Olin cleared his throat and announced, "It is the finding of this duly sworn Landsraad Council that all evidence against Leto Atreides is circumstantial and unprovable. Given such extreme doubts, there are insufficient grounds to proceed with a trial of such devastating consequences, especially in light of the extraordinary testimony of Crown Prince Shaddam Corrino. We therefore declare Leto Atreides fully exonerated and restore to him his title and property."

Stunned at his sudden good fortune, Leto found himself congratulated by the Emperor-to-be and then mobbed by his friends and supporters. Many of them were delighted to see him win, but despite his youth Leto was not naive; he knew just as many of them were happy simply to see the Tleilaxu *lose*.

All around him the courtroom erupted in cheers and thunderous ovations, with the exception of a few in attendance who remained conspicuously silent. Leto marked them for further consideration, and knew Thufir Hawat would be doing the same.

"Leto, there is one more thing I must do," Shaddam said, his voice cutting through the din.

Out of the corner of his eye, Leto saw something glint in the light. Shaddam's hand moved, snatching a jewel-handled knife from his sleeve—translucent blue-green like the Hagal quartz of the Imperial throne. He raised it, moving quickly.

Back at the bench, Thufir Hawat leaped to his feet, but too late. The crowd fell into an instant hush.

Then, with a smile, Shaddam slipped the knife into the empty sheath at Leto's waist. "My congratulatory gift to you, Cousin," he said in the most pleasant of tones. "Carry this blade as a reminder of your service to me."

We do what we must. Friendship and loyalty be damned. We do what we must!

—LADY HELENA ATREIDES,
her personal journals

Hasimir Fenring brooded in his private apartments, in shock. *How can Shaddam do this to me?*

The message capsule with the formal Imperial seal—the wax lion of House Corrino—lay discarded on his bed. He had torn Shaddam's formal decree to shreds, but not before memorizing every word.

A new assignment—a banishment!—a promotion?

"Hasimir Fenring, in acknowledgment of your unfailing service to the Imperium and the throne of the Padishah Emperors, you are hereby appointed to a newly created post as official Imperial Observer on Arrakis.

"Because of this planet's vital importance to the Imperial economy, you shall have all necessary resources made available to your station."

Blah, blah, blah.

How could he dare do this? What a useless waste of his talent. What petty revenge to send Fenring off to a sand-hole festering with worms and unwashed people. He fumed, wishing he could discuss the matter with the fascinating Margot Rashino-Zea, whom he trusted more than he should. She was, after all, a Bene Gesserit witch. . . .

Because of the planet's vital importance! He snorted in disgust, then set about smashing everything breakable he could get his hands on. He knew Shaddam had banished him in a fit of pique. For a man with Fenring's capabilities, the new job was an insult, and it removed him from the center of Imperial power. He needed to be *here*, on Kaitain, at the hurricane's eye of politics, not lost out in some forgotten corner of space.

But Shaddam's decree could not be questioned or denied. Fenring had thirty days to report to the notorious arid planet. He wondered if he would ever return.

*All persons are contained within a single individual, just as all time
is in a moment, and the entire universe is in a grain of sand.*

—Fremen Saying

On the day of Shaddam IV's coronation and wedding,
a carnival air prevailed on all the worlds of the Imperium. Jubilant crowds immersed themselves in drinking,
dancing, sporting events, and fireworks exhibitions. Old
Emperor Elrood had held his throne for so long that few
people could remember the last time a new ruler had been
crowned.

In Kaitain's capital city, throngs gathered along the
magnificent boulevards, lining up beside the route the royal
procession would take. It was a sunny day—as usual—and
vendors did a brisk business hawking souvenirs, commemo-
rative items, and refreshments.

Royal Corrino flags fluttered in the breeze; everyone
wore their scarlet and gold to mark the occasion. Sardaukar
soldiers guarded the convoluted route, wearing ceremonial gold brocade over their dress gray-and-black uniforms.
Standing like stone guardians, they held their lasrifles in
the present-arms position, unmoved by the blaring fanfare
or the roar of the crowd. But they remained ready to react
with deadly force at the slightest hint of threat to the Imperial presence.

Boisterous cheers rose from thousands of throats as Crown Prince Shaddam and his betrothed Lady Anirul rolled by in a velvet-cushioned coach pulled by six golden lions from Harmonthep; braided with jewels, the animals' magnificent manes ruffled in the gentle breeze. Royal footmen and pikemen jogged alongside the carriage, which was barely obscured by the gossamer shimmer of a protective shield.

Looking intensely regal, Anirul waved and smiled; she had shed her black Bene Gesserit robes and wore a waterfall of laces, ruffles, and pearl drops. Her tiara dazzled with prisms and jewels, catching the sunlight from the ever-cloudless sky. Beside her, Shaddam looked magnificent with his reddish hair perfectly pomaded, his military-style uniform decked with braids and shoulder boards and clanking medals.

Since the Crown Prince's marriage displayed no favoritism to any Great or Minor House, the Landsraad had accepted Anirul as the Imperial consort, though many questioned her mysterious background and "hidden rank" in the Bene Gesserit. After the death of Elrood, though, followed by this grandiose coronation and wedding, the Imperium was awash in a sea of changes. Shaddam hoped to use that to his advantage.

With a paternal smile fixed on his face, he scattered solari coins and packets of gemdust to the crowd, following a tradition of Imperial largesse that was believed to bring blessings upon a new reign. The people loved him; he was surrounded by wealth; with the snap of his fingers he could obliterate entire worlds. This was exactly how he had imagined the role of Emperor would be.

A flourish of trumpets made joyful clarion sounds.

***

"WON'T YOU SIT with me, Hasimir?" the willowy blonde asked, giving him a coquettish smile during the pre-coronation reception. Fenring couldn't tell if Margot Rashino-Zea had purposely made her voice sultry, or if it just came naturally to her. He held a plate of food containing exotic hors d'oeuvres. Poison-snoopers fluttered like hummingbirds over the crowded guests. The day's ceremonies would last for hours upon hours, and the guests could relax and partake of refreshments at their leisure.

Sister Margot Rashino-Zea stood taller than Fenring, and leaned

Brian Herbert and Kevin J. Anderson

intimately close to him when she spoke. Her coral-and-jet dress shimmered around the exquisite perfection of her form and features. She wore a Caladanian pearl necklace and a brooch encrusted with gold and precious stones. Her skin looked like rich, honeyed milk.

Around them in the balcony lobby of the Grand Theatre, elegantly dressed noblemen and ladies chatted and drank *grand cru* wines from tall-stemmed glasses. The octave-crystal hummed as glasses were touched together in repeated toasts. Within the hour, the assemblage would witness the climactic double event that would be held on center stage: the coronation of Padishah Emperor Shaddam Corrino IV and his wedding to the Lady Anirul Sadow Tonkin of the Bene Gesserit.

Fenring nodded his large head and executed a brief bow to her. "I would be honored to sit next to you, lovely Margot." Balancing his plate, Fenring lowered himself onto the bench beside her. She inspected the hors d'oeuvres he had chosen and, without asking, reached over to pluck one of them for herself.

It was a cheerful gathering, Fenring thought, without the whisperings of discontent that had so poisoned the Palace in recent months. He was satisfied with his own efforts in this regard. Key alliances had been solidified, and the Federated Houses no longer made any serious talk of revolt against Shaddam. The Bene Gesserit had thrown their public support behind the Corrino reign, and no doubt the witches had continued their machinations behind the scenes at other Great Houses. Fenring found it curious that many of those who'd been the most suspicious and outspoken nobles were no longer counted among the living—and even more curious that he'd had nothing to do with it.

The trial of Leto Atreides had ended by fiat, and the only ones openly dissatisfied with the verdict were the Bene Tleilax. He and Shaddam would work to quiet them quickly, though. The greatest mystery in Fenring's mind was that no one seemed to know exactly what *had* happened inside the Guild Heighliner.

The more he observed and the more he considered the strange sequence of events, the more he began to believe the possibility that young Leto Atreides had been framed after all—*but how and by whom?* No other House had come forward to gloat, and since virtually everyone had believed in Atreides culpability, even the most imaginative and loose tongues had not bothered to spread additional rumors.

564

Fenring would dearly love to know what had happened, if only to add the technique to his own repertoire. But, once he went off to his new assignment on Arrakis, he doubted he would have any opportunity to unravel the secret.

Before he could advance his pleasant conversation with Margot, though, he heard thunderous crowds outside and resonating trumpets. "Shaddam and the royal entourage are coming," Margot said with a toss of her honey-blonde hair. "We'd best go find our seats."

Fenring knew the Crown Prince's carriage would now be entering the quadrangle containing the theatre and Imperial government buildings. He tried to cover his disappointment. "But you'll be in the Bene Gesserit section, my dear." He stared at her with glittering dark eyes as he dipped a piece of pheasant Kaitain into a bowl of plum sauce. "Would you like me to dress in one of those costumes and pretend to be in the Sisterhood?" He swallowed the morsel, savored its sweetness. "I'd do it, to be next to you, hm-m-m-m?"

She tapped him on the chest playfully. "You aren't what you appear to be, that's for certain, Hasimir Fenring."

His overlarge eyes narrowed. "Meaning?"

"Meaning . . . we have much in common, you and I." She pressed one of her soft breasts against his arm. "Perhaps it would be wise for the two of us to continue—and formalize—this alliance we seem to be forming."

Fenring glanced around to see if anyone was eavesdropping. He didn't like snoopers. Leaning close to her, he spoke in a passionless voice. "I never intended to take a wife. I am a genetic-eunuch and cannot father children."

"Then we may be required to make certain sacrifices, each in our own ways. That need be nothing personal." She arched her golden eyebrows. "Besides, I imagine you have your ways of pleasing a woman? I, too, have had extensive . . . training."

A cruel smile slashed his face. "Ah-um-m-m-m. Is that so? My dear Margot, it sounds as if you're presenting me with a business plan."

"And you, Hasimir, seem to be a man who prefers practicality over romanticism. I think we're well matched," she said. "Both of us are skilled at recognizing layered plans, the labyrinthine ways in which seemingly unrelated actions are actually connected."

"The results are often quite deadly, aren't they?"

She reached over with her napkin to wipe plum sauce from the side of his mouth. "Mmm, you need someone to take care of you."

He studied her, the finishing-school way she held her chin high, the perfection and steady tempo of her speech—such a contrast to his occasional slurs and verbal hesitations. Her gray-green eyes gazed at him without apparent concealment. But he could see the sparkle of secrets held behind those lovely pupils . . . so many secrets.

And he could spend years and years reveling in the challenge of uncovering them.

Fenring reminded himself how clever these witches were; they did not take individual action. Nothing was as it seemed. "You and your Sisterhood have a larger purpose in mind, Margot, my dear. I know something of the ways of the Bene Gesserit. You are a group organism."

"Well, I've informed the organism of what I wish to do."

"Informed them, or asked them? Or did they send you after me in the first place?"

The Dame of House Venette strolled by, leading a brace of small, coiffed dogs. Her gilded dress was so voluminous that other guests had to back out of her way. With each step, the noblewoman fixed her blank gaze forward, as if just concentrating on keeping her balance.

Margot watched the spectacle, then turned back to Fenring. "There are obvious advantages to all of us, and Mother Superior Harishka has already given me her blessing. You would gain a valuable connection with the Sisterhood, though I wouldn't necessarily tell you *all* of our secrets." She nudged him playfully, nearly causing him to spill his plate of food.

"Mm-m-m-m," he said, looking over the perfection of her figure, "and I am a key to the power of Shaddam. He trusts no one more than me."

Bemused, Margot raised her eyebrows. "Oh? Is that why he sent you away to Arrakis? Because you're so close to him? I'm told that you aren't happy with the new duty."

"How did you find out about that?" Fenring scowled, felt the uncomfortable sensation of losing his balance. "I just learned of the assignment myself two days ago." This clever witch had more to say, and he waited for her.

"Hasimir Fenring, you must learn to use every circumstance to your advantage. Arrakis is the key to melange, and the spice opens the universe. Our new Emperor may think he has merely reassigned you, but in reality he has entrusted you with something vitally important. Think of it—Imperial Observer on Arrakis."

"Yes, and the Baron Harkonnen won't like it one bit. I suspect he's been hiding many small details all along."

She graced him with a lush, full smile. "No one can hide such things from you, my dear. Or me."

He smiled back at her. "Then we can while away the miserable days ferreting out his secrets."

She ran her long, thin fingers along his sleeve. "Arrakis is a most difficult place in which to live, but . . . perhaps you would enjoy it more in my company?"

He grew wary, as was his nature. Though the crowd was filled with extravagant costumes and exotic plumage, Margot was the most beautiful woman in the entire hall. "I might. But why would you want to go there? A horrible place, by all accounts."

"My Sisters describe it as a planet of ancient mysteries, and my spending time there would greatly increase my standing among the Bene Gesserit. It could be an important step in my training to become a Reverend Mother. Use your imagination: sandworms, Fremen, spice. It could be most interesting if you and I were to solve those mysteries together. I'm stimulated by your companionship, Hasimir."

"I'll give your . . . proposal some thought."

He was drawn to this woman physically and emotionally . . . bothersome feelings. When he had experienced such strong emotions in the past, he had felt compelled to dismiss the attraction, get rid of it in any manner necessary. This Sister Margot Rashino-Zea was different, though—or seemed to be. Only time would tell.

He'd heard stories of Bene Gesserit breeding programs, but because of his congenital deformity, the Sisterhood would not be after his genetic line; there had to be something else to it. Obviously Margot's motives went beyond her personal feelings—if she truly had any feelings for him. This woman had to see the *opportunities* in him, both for herself and for her order of Sisters.

And Margot offered him something as well—a new avenue to power he'd never dreamed existed. Until now, his only advantage had rested with Shaddam, his fortuitous childhood companion. But that status had been recently damaged when the Crown Prince began behaving strangely. Shaddam had stepped beyond his abilities, attempting to make his own decisions and think for himself. A dangerous, foolhardy course of action, and he didn't even seem to know it yet.

Given the circumstances, Fenring needed new contacts in powerful places. Such as the Bene Gesserit.

With the arrival of the Imperial carriage outside, guests began streaming into the Grand Theatre. Fenring discarded his plate on a side table, and Margot slipped her arm through his, saying, "You'll sit with me, then?"

"Yes," he said with a wink, "and maybe a little more than that."

She smiled prettily, and he thought of how difficult it would be to kill this woman. If it ever came to that.

❦

EACH HOUSE MAJOR had received a dozen tickets to the double event in the Grand Theatre, while the rest of the population in the Imperium watched over planetary relays. Everyone would talk about the details of the magnificent ceremony for at least the next decade— exactly as Shaddam intended.

As the representative of his restored House, Duke Leto Atreides sat with his entourage in blackplaz seats in the second row, main level. The Emperor's "beloved cousin" had maintained pretenses since the ending of the Landsraad trial, but Leto did not believe the feigned friendship would last beyond his return to Caladan—unless, of course, Shaddam intended to collect on the favor. *Beware of what you buy,* the Old Duke had said, *for there may be hidden costs.*

Thufir Hawat sat on Leto's right and a proud and effusive Rhombur Vernius on his left. On the other side of Rhombur sat his sister Kailea, who had joined the delegation after Leto was freed. She had rushed to Kaitain to see the coronation and to stand beside her brother—her emerald eyes dazzled with every fresh sight. Not a moment went by without Kailea gasping or exclaiming in delight at some new marvel. Leto's heart warmed to see such utter joy in her, the first he'd noticed since their flight from Ix.

While Rhombur wore Vernius purple and copper, Kailea chose to drape her creamy shoulders with an Atreides cloak sporting red hawk armorial crests, like Leto's. Clutching his forearm and letting him escort her to their seats, Kailea told him with a soft smile, "I chose these colors out of respect for the host who granted us sanctuary, and to commemorate the restored fortunes of House Atreides." She kissed him on the cheek.

Since the matter of the death sentence on House Vernius still hung like a thick cloud on the horizon, the siblings attended the festivities at considerable personal risk. In the present atmosphere of celebration, however, Thufir Hawat surmised that they were probably safe, provided they didn't overstay their welcome. When Leto first heard this, he laughed. "Thufir, do Mentats ever provide guarantees?" Hawat did not find this amusing.

Though the coronation and Imperial wedding were among the safest places in the universe because of the intense public attention, Leto doubted that Dominic Vernius would show his face. Even now, after vindictive Elrood's death, Rhombur's father had not ventured out of hiding, had not sent them any sort of message whatsoever.

Across the rear of the cavernous theatre, on both the main and upper levels, sat representatives of Houses Minor and various factions among CHOAM, the Spacing Guild, the Mentats, the Suk doctors, and other power bases scattered across the million worlds. House Harkonnen had their own segregated section in an upper balcony; the Baron, attending without his nephew Rabban, refused even to glance in the direction of the Atreides seats.

"The colors, the sounds, the perfumes—it's making me dizzy," Kailea said, drawing a deep breath and leaning closer to Leto. "I've never seen anything like this—on Ix, or on Caladan."

Leto said, "No one in the Imperium has seen anything like this in almost a hundred and forty years."

In the first row, directly in front of the Atreides, sat a contingent of Bene Gesserit women in identical black robes, including withered Mother Superior Harishka. On the other side of the aisle from the quiet and manipulative women stood fully armed Sardaukar in ceremonial uniforms.

The Bene Gesserit delegation greeted fresh-faced Reverend Mother Anirul, the Empress-to-be, as she passed the group, accompanied by a large honor guard and garishly dressed ladies-in-waiting. Rhombur searched for the stunning blonde woman who'd given him the mysterious message cube, and found her sitting with Hasimir Fenring instead of with the other Sisters.

An air of expectation filled the high-ceilinged, tiered facility. Finally, a hush fell over the Grand Theatre, and everyone stood respectfully, holding their hats and caps.

Crown Prince Shaddam, attired in a formal Sardaukar commander's uniform with silver epaulets and the Golden Lion crest of House Corrino, marched down the aisle on a carpet of velvet and damask. His red hair was pomaded with glitter. Members of his royal Court followed him, all of them wearing scarlet and gold.

Bringing up the rear was the green-robed High Priest of Dur, who had by tradition crowned every Emperor since the fall of the thinking machines. Despite the varying fortunes of his ancient religion, the High Priest proudly sprinkled the iron-red holy dust of Dur right and left onto the audience.

Seeing Shaddam's stately pace and how smartly uniformed he was, Leto recalled when the Crown Prince had marched up another aisle only days earlier to testify on his behalf. In a way, it seemed to him that his royal cousin had looked even more regal then, swathed in the fine silks and jewels of an Emperor. Now he looked more like a soldier—the commander in chief of all Imperial forces.

"An obvious political move," Hawat said, leaning over to mutter in his ear. "Do you notice? Shaddam is letting the Sardaukar know that their new Emperor considers himself a member of their organization, that they are important to his reign."

Leto nodded, understanding this practice well. Like his father before him, the young Duke fraternized with his men, dining with them and joining them in everyday functions to show that he would never ask his troops to do what he wouldn't do himself.

"Looks to me like more show than substance," Rhombur said.

"In ruling a vast empire, there's a place for show," Kailea said. With a pang, Leto recalled the Old Duke's penchant for bullfights and other spectacles.

Shaddam reveled in the grandeur, bathed himself in glory. He bowed as he strutted past his future wife and the Bene Gesserit contingent. His coronation would come first. At the designated place, Shaddam came to a stop and turned to face the High Priest of Dur, who now held the glittering Imperial crown on a gilded pillow.

Behind the Crown Prince, a wide curtain opened to reveal the royal dais, which had been moved here. The massive Imperial throne, empty now, had been carved from a single piece of blue-green quartz— the largest such gem ever found, dating back to the days of Emperor Hassik III. Hidden projectors shot fine-tuned lasers into the depths of the block of crystal, refracting a nova of rainbows. The audience gasped at the translucent beauty of the throne.

Indeed, there is a place for ceremony in the daily workings of the Imperium, Leto thought. *It has a unifying influence, making people feel they belong to something significant.*

Such ceremonies cemented the impression that Humanity, not Chaos, reigned over the universe. Even a self-serving Emperor like Shaddam could do some good, Leto felt . . . and fervently hoped.

Solemnly, the Crown Prince climbed the steps of the royal dais and seated himself on the throne, staring fixedly ahead. Following time-honored procedure, the High Priest moved behind him and raised the jeweled crown high in the air.

"Do you, Crown Prince Shaddam Raphael Corrino IV, swear fidelity to the Holy Empire?"

The priest's voice carried throughout the theatre, over speakers of such high quality that everyone in the audience heard completely natural, undistorted sounds. The same words were transmitted around the planet of Kaitain, and would be spread throughout the Imperium.

"I do," Shaddam said, his voice booming.

The High Priest lowered the symbol of office onto the seated man's brow, and to the gathered dignitaries he said, "I give you the new Padishah Emperor Shaddam IV, may his reign shine as long as the stars!"

"May his reign shine as long as the stars!" the audience intoned in a thunderous response.

When Shaddam rose from the throne with the glittering crown on his head, he did so as Emperor of the Known Universe. Thousands inside the chamber applauded and cheered him. He looked across the audience that was a microcosm of everything he ruled, and his gaze came to rest on doe-eyed Anirul, who had moved to stand just below the dais with her honor guard and ladies-in-waiting. The Emperor extended a hand, beckoning her.

Harishka, Mother Superior of the Bene Gesserit, guided Anirul to

Shaddam's side. The magnificent women moved with the faultless glide-walk of the Sisterhood, as if Shaddam were a magnet drawing them into his presence. Then ancient Harishka returned to her seat with the other Bene Gesserit.

The priest said words over the couple, while the new Emperor slipped two diamond rings onto the marriage finger of Anirul's hand, followed by a breathtaking red soostone band that had belonged to his paternal grandmother.

When they were pronounced Emperor and Lady, the High Priest of Dur presented them to the assemblage. In the audience, Hasimir Fenring leaned over and whispered to Margot, "Shall we step forward and see if the High Priest can squeeze in another quick ceremony?"

She giggled, nudged him playfully.

THAT EVENING, HEDONISM in the capital city reached a fever pitch of adrenaline, pheromones, and music. The royal couple attended a sumptuous dinner banquet followed by a grand ball and then by a magnificent culinary orgy that made the earlier meal appear to have been no more than an appetizer. As the newlyweds departed for the Imperial Palace, they were showered with merh-silk roses and chased by the nobles.

Finally Emperor Shaddam IV and Lady Anirul retired to their marriage bed. Outside their room drunken noblemen and ladies rang crystal bells and floated bright glowglobes at the windows—the traditional shivaree that would bring blessings of fertility upon the union.

These festivities continued much as they had for millennia, going back to pre-Butlerian days, to the very roots of the Imperium. More than a thousand expensive gifts were arrayed on the lawn of the Palace. These offerings would be gathered by Imperial servants and distributed later to the populace, in conjunction with an additional week of festivities on Kaitain.

After all the celebrations were complete, Shaddam would finally be able to get down to the business of ruling his Empire of a Million Worlds.

In the final analysis, the legendary event called Leto's Gambit became the basis of the young Duke Atreides's immense popularity. He successfully projected himself as a shining beacon of honor in a galactic sea of darkness. To many members of the Landsraad, Leto's honesty and naïveté became a symbol of honor that shamed many of the Great and Minor Houses to alter their behavior toward each other . . . for a short time, at least, until familiar old patterns reemerged.

—Origins of House Atreides: Seeds of the Future
in the Galactic Imperium, by Bronso of Ix

Furious that his plot had failed, Baron Harkonnen raged up and down the halls of his family Keep on Giedi Prime. He screamed demands that his personal staff find a dwarf for him to torture; he needed a creature to dominate, something he could crush entirely.

When Yh'imm, one of the Baron's entertainment monitors, complained that it wasn't exactly sporting for him to persecute a man solely on the basis of his physical size, the Baron ordered Yh'imm's legs amputated at the knees. In that way, the soon-to-be-shortened entertainment monitor would fit the Procrustean bill nicely.

As the howling, pleading man was hauled away to the Harkonnen surgeons, the Baron summoned his nephew Glossu Rabban and the Mentat Piter de Vries to attend him for a vital discussion, to be held in the Baron's workroom.

Waiting for them at a worktable spread with papers and ridulian crystal reports, the Baron boomed in his basso voice, "Damn the Atreides, from the boy-Duke to his bastard ancestors! I wish they'd all died in the Battle of Corrin."

He whirled when de Vries entered the workroom doorway, and the Baron nearly lost his balance with suddenly clumsy muscle control. He grasped the edge of the table to steady himself. "How could Leto survive that trial? He had no proof, no defense." Muted glowglobes floated overhead in the room. "He still doesn't have a clue what really happened."

The Baron's bellow echoed through the enclosure and out an open door into the halls, which were lined with polished stone and brasswork. Rabban hurried down the corridor. "And damn Shaddam for his meddling! Just because he's Emperor, what gives him the right to take sides? What's in it for him?"

Both Rabban and de Vries hesitated at the iron-arched entrance to the workroom, not anxious to step into the maelstrom of the Baron's wrath. The Mentat closed his eyes and rubbed his thick eyebrows, trying to think of what to say or do. Rabban went to an alcove and poured himself a strong glass of kirana brandy. He made slurping animal noises as he drank.

The Baron stepped away from the table and paced the floor, his movements oddly jerky, as if he were having difficulty controlling his equilibrium. His clothes seemed tight on him from his recent weight gains.

"It was supposed to start a sudden war, and after the carnage who could pick up the pieces? But somehow the damned Atreides kept everyone from killing each other. By insisting on a risky Trial by Forfeiture—ancient rites be damned!—and his willingness to sacrifice himself just to protect his precious friends and crew, Leto Atreides has gained favorable attention in the Landsraad. His popularity is soaring."

Piter de Vries cleared his throat. "Perhaps, my Baron, it was a mistake to pit them against the Tleilaxu. Nobody cares about the Tleilaxu. It was difficult to foster a general sense of outrage among the Houses. We never planned for this matter to come to trial."

"We made no mistakes!" Rabban grunted, immediately defending his uncle. "Do you value your life, Piter?"

De Vries didn't respond, nor did he show any fear. He was a formidable fighter in his own right, with tricks and experience that could undoubtedly defeat Rabban's brawn, should it come to physical combat.

The Baron looked at his nephew, disappointed. *You never seem to grasp anything buried beneath even a single layer of subtlety.*

Rabban glared at the Mentat. "Duke Leto is just an impetuous young ruler from an unremarkable family. House Atreides makes its income through selling . . . pundi rice!" He spat the words.

"The fact is, Rabban," the twisted Mentat said smoothly, with the voice of a snake, "that the other members of the Landsraad Council actually seem to *like him*. They admire what this boy-Duke has accomplished. We've made him a hero."

Rabban finished his drink, poured another, slurped it.

"The Landsraad Council becoming *altruistic?*" The Baron snorted. "That's even more unbelievable than Leto winning his case."

From the surgery rooms down the long, dim halls, grisly noises could be heard, screams of agony that echoed along the corridors all the way to the Baron's workroom. The muted glowglobes flickered, but maintained their low level of illumination.

The Baron looked piercingly at de Vries, then gestured toward the operating rooms. "Perhaps you'd better attend to this yourself, Piter. I want to make certain that idiot entertainment monitor survives his surgery . . . at least until I've made sufficient use of him."

"Yes, my Baron," the Mentat said and scuttled down the halls to the medical chambers. The screams grew higher-pitched and womanish. The Baron heard the sounds of sizzling cutterays and a grinding saw.

The Baron thought of his newly shortened plaything and what he would do to Yh'imm as soon as the painkillers began to wear off. Or could it be possible the doctors had managed their task without using any painkillers? Perhaps.

Rabban let his thick-lidded eyes fall closed in supreme pleasure, just listening and enjoying. Given the choice, he would rather have hunted the man down in Giedi Prime's wilderness preserve. But the Baron thought that sounded like too much trouble—all that running and chasing and climbing snow-covered rocks. He could come up with far better ways of spending his time. Besides, the Baron's limbs and joints had been growing increasingly sore of late, his muscles were weakened and trembled, his body was losing its edge. . . .

For now the Baron would simply make up his own sport. Once Yh'imm's stumps were cauterized and sealed, he would pretend the hapless monitor was Duke Atreides himself. That would be fun.

The Baron paused and realized how foolish it was for him to be so upset over the failure of a single plan. For uncounted generations the

Harkonnens had spun subtle traps for their hated mortal enemies. But the Atreides were difficult to kill, especially when their backs were to the wall. The feud extended all the way back to the Great Revolt, the betrayal, the accusations of cowardice. Since that time, Harkonnen had always hated Atreides, and vice versa.

And so it would always be.

"We still have Arrakis," the Baron said. "We still control melange production, even though we're under CHOAM's thumb and the watchful eye of the Padishah Emperor." He grinned at Rabban, who grinned back at him, strictly out of habit.

Deep in the heart of the dirty and dark grandeur of Harkonnen Keep, the Baron clenched his fist and raised it high in the air. "As long as we control Arrakis, we control our own fortunes." He clapped a hand on his nephew's padded shoulder. "We will wring spice from the sands until Arrakis is nothing more than an empty husk!"

On the Spacing Guild world of Junction, the one who had been D'murr Pilru was brought before a tribunal of Navigators. They didn't tell him the reason, and even with all his intuition and conceptual understanding of the universe, he could not fathom what they wanted from him.

No other trainees joined D'murr, none of the new Pilots who had learned the ways of foldspace with him. On a huge open parade ground of stunted blakgras, the sealed spice-filled tanks of the high-level tribunal were arrayed in a semicircle on grooved flagstones, where tracks from thousands of previous convocations could still be seen.

D'murr's smaller tank sat in front of them all, solitary at the center of the semicircle. Relatively new to his life as a Navigator, still a low-ranking Pilot, he retained much of his human shape inside the enclosed tank. The members of the tribunal—Steersmen all, each inside his own tank—showed only bloated heads and monstrously altered eyes peering out through the murk of cinnamon-orange.

I will be like them someday, D'murr thought. At one time he would have recoiled in horror; now he accepted it as inevitable. He thought of all the new revelations he would have along the way.

The Guild tribunal spoke to him in their shorthand, higher-order mathematical language, thoughts and words communicated through the fabric of space itself—vastly more efficient than any human conversation. Grodin, the Head Instructor, acted as their mouthpiece.

"You have been monitored," said Grodin. By long-standing procedure, Guild Instructors set up holorecording devices in every Heighliner navigation chamber and every training tank of the new and unproven Pilots. Periodically in the ships' circuitous routes between the stars, these recordings were removed from the transports and cargo ships and delivered to Junction.

"All evidence is studied in detail as a routine matter." D'murr knew that Guild Bank officials and their economic partners in CHOAM had to make certain that important navigation rules and safeguards were being followed. He questioned none of it.

"The Guild is perplexed by targeted and unauthorized transmissions being directed to your navigation chamber."

His brother's communication device! D'murr reeled inside his tank, floating free, seeing all the dizzy possibilities, the punishments and retributions he might face. He could become one of those pathetic failed Navigators, stunted and inhuman—the physical price paid, but the benefits not reaped. But D'murr knew his ability was strong! Perhaps the Steersmen would forgive. . . .

"We are curious," Grodin said.

D'murr told them everything, explained everything he knew, gave them every detail. Trying to remember what C'tair had told him, he reported on the conditions inside sealed Ix, the Tleilaxu decision to return to more primitive Heighliner designs. The Heighliner decision disturbed them, but the tribunal was more interested in the functioning of the "Rogo transceiver" itself.

"Never have we had instantaneous foldspace transmission," Grodin said. For centuries all messages had been carried by Couriers, in physical form, on a physical ship that traveled through foldspace much faster than any known method of transmission could skim across space. "Can we exploit this innovation?"

D'murr realized the military and economic potential of such a device, if it could ever prove feasible. Though he didn't know all the technical details, his brother had created an unprecedented system, and one most intriguing to the Spacing Guild. They wanted it for themselves.

A senior tribunal member suggested the possibility of using a mentally enhanced Navigator on both ends, rather than a mere human, like C'tair Pilru. Another questioned whether the link was more mental than technological, an enhanced connection because of the former closeness of the twins, the similarity of their brain patterns.

Perhaps, among the vast pool of Pilots, Navigators, and Steersmen, the Guild could find others with similar mental connections . . . though it would likely be rare. Nevertheless, despite the cost and difficulty, this method of communication was perhaps a service that could be tested, and then offered at great expense to the Emperor.

"You may retain your status as Pilot," Grodin said, releasing him from the inquiry.

FOR SEVERAL WEEKS after returning in triumph from Kaitain, Duke Leto Atreides and Rhombur Vernius had awaited a response from the new Emperor to their request for an Imperial audience. Leto was prepared to board a shuttle and travel to the Imperial Palace the moment a Courier arrived with a confirmed slot in the Emperor's calendar. He had vowed to make no mention of his bluff message, decided not to pursue the matter of a Corrino-Tleilaxu connection . . . but Shaddam IV had to be curious.

If another week passed without a response, however, Leto would go there even without an appointment.

Attempting to ride the momentum of his increasing stature and popularity, Leto wished to discuss amnesty and reparations for House Vernius. He believed this would be the best chance to bring the situation to a fortuitous conclusion, but as the days passed in Imperial silence, he saw the opportunity slipping like silt through his fingertips. Even optimistic Rhombur became agitated and frustrated, while Kailea grew more and more resigned to their limited options in life.

Finally, in a standard communiqué via human Courier bearing a message cylinder, the Emperor suggested—since he had very little free time for conversation with his cousin—that they make use of a new and untried method being offered by the Spacing Guild, an instantaneous process called Guildlink. It involved the mental connection of two Guild Navigators positioned in separate star systems; a Heighliner in orbit around Caladan and another over Kaitain could theoretically arrange a conversation involving Duke Leto Atreides and Emperor Shaddam IV.

"At last I'll be able to speak my piece," Leto said, though he had never before heard of this communication method. Shaddam seemed anxious to try it for his own purposes, and this way no one would see him actually meeting with Duke Leto Atreides.

Kailea's emerald eyes lit up, and she even ignored the distasteful bull's-head that hung in the dining hall. She went to change her dress into proud Vernius colors, though it wasn't likely she would be seen in the transmission at all. Rhombur came at the appointed hour, accompanied by Thufir Hawat. Leto sent all the other retainers, guards, and household staff out of the room.

The Heighliner that had brought the original Courier remained in geostationary orbit over Caladan; another already waited over Kaitain. The sophisticated Guild Steersmen aboard each ship—separated from one another by vast distances—would use an unfathomable procedure that allowed them to stretch their minds across the void, joining thoughts to form a connection. The Guild had tested hundreds of their Navigators before finding two that could establish a tentative direct link—through telepathy, melange-fostered prescience, or some other method, to be determined.

Leto took a deep breath, wishing he had more time to practice his words, though he had already waited far too long. He dared not request another delay. . . .

From a magnificent hedge-lined arboretum at the Imperial Palace, Shaddam spoke into a tiny microphone on his chin, which transmitted to speakers in the navigation chamber of the Heighliner over his planet. "Can you hear me, Leto Atreides? It's a sunny morning here, and I've just returned from my morning walk." He took a sip from a goblet of syrupy juice.

As the Emperor's words reached the navigation chamber of the ship orbiting Kaitain, the Steersman in the other Heighliner over Caladan experienced them in his mind, in an echo of what his compatriot had heard. Breaking the link temporarily, the Steersman over Caladan repeated the Emperor's words into the glittering speaker globe that floated within his spice-filled chamber. In turn, standing in the echoing dining hall of Castle Caladan, Leto heard the words over his own speaker system, distorted and slow, without the nuances of emotion. But still, they were the Emperor's own words.

"I've always preferred the morning sun of Caladan, Cousin," Leto responded, using the familiar form of address, trying to begin on friendly terms. "You should visit our humble world someday."

By the time Leto said this, the Navigator above Caladan was again in Guildlink with his associate, and Leto's words were heard in the other ship, then transmitted down to Kaitain.

"This new communication is marvelous," Shaddam said, avoiding the meat of Leto's request. He did, however, seem to be enjoying the possibilities of Guildlink, as if it were a new toy for him. "Much faster than human messengers, though it'll likely be prohibitively expensive. Ah yes, we have here the makings of another monopoly for the Guild. Hopefully they won't charge too much for urgent messages."

Receiving the words in his dining hall, Leto wondered if that message was for his benefit, or the Guild eavesdroppers.

Shaddam coughed uneasily, sounds that were not repeated in the translation process. "There are so many important issues on Imperial planets, and such a shortage of time in which to address them. I have too little time for friendships I'd like to nurture, such as yours, Cousin. What is it you wish to talk with me about?"

Leto drew a sharp breath, and the hawklike features on his narrow face darkened. "Exalted Emperor Shaddam, we beseech you to grant amnesty to House Vernius and restore them to their rightful place in the Landsraad. The world of Ix is economically vital and must not remain in the hands of the Tleilaxu. They have already destroyed important manufacturing facilities and have curtailed products vital to the security of the Imperium." Then he added, with just another hint of his bluff, "We both know what is really going on there, even now."

The Tleilaxu connection again, Leto thought. *Let's see if I can make him believe I know more than I really do.* Standing beside him in the room, Prince Rhombur fixed him with a wary gaze.

"I cannot discuss such matters through intermediaries," Shaddam said quickly.

Leto's eyes widened at the possible mistake Shaddam had just made. "Are you suggesting that the Guild can't be trusted, Sire? They haul armies for the Imperium and the Great Houses; they know or suspect battle plans before they are implemented. This Guildlink is even more secure than a face-to-face discussion in the Imperial audience chamber."

"But we haven't studied the merits of the matter," Shaddam protested, clearly stalling. He had been watching the rising popularity and influence of Duke Leto Atreides. Did this upstart have connections that extended even to the Spacing Guild? He looked around his empty gardens, wishing Fenring were with him after all, but the ferret-like man was preparing for his journey to Arrakis. *Perhaps it was a mistake to save Leto after all.*

Keeping his phraseology lean and to the point, Leto presented the noble case of the Ixians, asserting that House Vernius had never manufactured forbidden technology. Despite their promises, the Tleilaxu had brought no case and no evidence to the governing body of the Landsraad, and had instead taken matters into their own hands in their greed to acquire the riches of Ix. Based upon conversations he'd had with Rhombur, Leto provided a value for the fief and how much damage the Tleilaxu had caused.

"That sounds excessive," Shaddam said, too quickly. "Reports from the Bene Tleilax indicate a much lower figure."

He's been there himself, Leto thought, *and is concealing it.* "Of course the Tleilaxu would try to establish a low number, Sire, in order to reduce reparations, if they are ever forced to pay them."

Leto went on to estimate the loss of Ixian life, and even commented on Elrood's unwarranted blood price for the death of the Lady Shando. Then, in an emotion-filled voice, he conjectured about the desperate plight of Earl Vernius, who remained in hiding on some unknown, distant world.

During an extended pause on his end of the conversation, Shaddam seethed. He desperately wondered how much this brash Duke truly knew about the Tleilaxu matter. There had been hints, nuances . . . but was he bluffing? As new Emperor, Shaddam needed to do something quickly, to keep the situation under control—but he could never afford to allow House Vernius to return to its ancestral home. The Tleilaxu synthetic-spice research was vital and not easily moved. The

Vernius family was an unfortunate casualty—Shaddam didn't care about his father's stung pride or petty revenge—but those people could not be rescued now, as if nothing had happened.

Finally the Emperor cleared his throat and said, "The best we can offer is limited amnesty. Since Rhombur and Kailea Vernius are in your personal care, Duke Leto, we grant them our full protection and pardon. From this day forth there shall be no price on their heads. They are absolved of any wrongdoing. You have my guarantee on this."

Seeing a look of disbelieving exultation on the faces of the two ex-iled Ixians, Leto said, "Thank you, Sire, but what about reparations to the family fortunes?"

"No reparations!" Shaddam said in a much sterner tone than the Guildsman managed to duplicate. "And no restoration of House Vernius to its position on Xuttah, formerly Ix. Ah, yes. The Bene Tleilax have in fact presented extensive, conclusive documentation *to me*, and I am satisfied as to its veracity. For reasons of Imperial security I cannot divulge details. You have taxed my patience enough."

Irritated, Leto growled, "Any evidence that is denied scrutiny is no evidence at all, Sire. It should be presented before a court."

"What about my father and other surviving members of House Vernius?" Rhombur said into the microphone Leto had been using. "Can he have your amnesty as well, wherever he is? He's not hurting anybody."

Shaddam's response, directed at Leto, was swift and stinging, like the bite of a venomous serpent. "I've been lenient with you, Cousin— but I caution you not to press your luck. If I weren't so favorably in-clined toward you, personally, I would never have committed myself by testifying on your behalf, nor would I have granted this impromptu audience today—or the concessions for your friends. Amnesty for the two children, and that is all."

Hearing the harsh relayed words, Leto reeled, but maintained his composure. It was clear he could not push Shaddam further.

"We suggest you accept these terms while we remain in a mood to grant them," Shaddam said. "At any moment additional evidence could be presented to me against House Vernius, causing me to judge them less kindly."

Away from the voice pickup, Leto conferred with Rhombur and Kailea. Reluctantly, the siblings leaned toward acceptance. "At least we've won a small victory, Leto," Kailea said in her soft voice. "We'll have our lives, and our personal freedom—if not our heritage. Besides, living here with you is not so terrible. Like Rhombur always says, we can make the best of things."

Rhombur put a hand on his sister's shoulder. "If that's good enough for Kailea, it'll be good enough for me."

"The bargain is sealed then," Shaddam said; their acceptance had been sent through the Guildlink intermediaries. "The official papers will be prepared." Then his words became like razors. "And I expect never to hear of this matter again."

Abruptly, the Emperor ended the Guildlink, and the two separated Navigators broke their mental contact. Leto drew both Rhombur and Kailea into a hug, knowing that at last they both were safe.

Only fools leave witnesses.

—HASIMIR FENRING

I am going to miss Kaitain," Fenring said in an odd, somber tone. Within the day, he was scheduled to report to Arrakis as Shaddam's Imperial Observer. *Exiled into the desert!* But Margot had told him to see the opportunities . . . Fenring was good at that. Could the Emperor have more in mind than simple punishment? Could this be turned into a powerful position after all?

Fenring had grown up at the side of Shaddam, both of them more than two decades younger than Fafnir, the former heir apparent to the Golden Lion Throne. With an elder Crown Prince in place and a brood of daughters by his various wives, Elrood had not expected much from the junior Prince, and on the quiet suggestion of his Bene Gesserit mother, Fenring had been allowed to attend classes with him.

Over the years Fenring had made himself into an "expediter," a person willing to complete necessary tasks for his friend Shaddam, no matter how unpleasant they might be—including the murder of Fafnir. The companions shared many dark secrets, too many for them to split up now without serious repercussions . . . and both men knew it.

Shaddam owes me, dammit!

Given time to reconsider, the new Emperor would understand that he couldn't afford to have Fenring as an enemy, or even as a disgruntled Imperial servant. Before long, Shaddam would summon him back from Arrakis. It was only a matter of time.

Somehow he would find a way to turn every circumstance to his advantage.

Lady Margot, whom he had married in a simple ceremony three days earlier, took command of the subchamberlains and unattached servants. Issuing orders with every breath, she created a whirlwind of packing and shipping. As a Bene Gesserit Sister, she had few needs and no extravagant tastes. But understanding the importance of trappings and public appearances, she arranged to send a cargo ship full of amenities, including House Corrino clothing and furniture, Imperial tableware, fine tapestries, and linens. Such possessions would increase her husband's standing in Arrakeen, where they would set up a private residence, many kilometers from the Harkonnen seat of power in Carthag. This show of independence and luxury would emphasize to the Harkonnen governors and their functionaries the power of Shaddam and his omnipresent watchful eyes.

Smiling, Fenring watched Margot go about her finishing tasks. She was a flow of bright colors and lovely honey-blonde hair, encouraging smiles, and sharp words for anyone who moved too slowly. *What a magnificent woman!* He and his new bride kept such fascinating secrets from each other, and the process of mutual discovery was proving most enjoyable.

By nightfall they would be dispatched to the desert planet, which the natives called Dune.

LATER IN THE day, during a relaxed hour in which neither the Emperor nor his lifelong friend would utter the apologies that needed to be said, Fenring sat at the shield-ball console, waiting for Padishah Emperor Shaddam IV to make the next move. They sat alone in a plaz-walled retiring room at the top of one of the Palace pinnacles. Flitter-thopters buzzed by in the distance, higher than ribbon-festooned kites and gleam-bubbles.

Fenring hummed to himself, though he knew Shaddam hated the mannerism. Finally, the new Emperor slid a rod through the shimmering shield at precisely the correct speed—not too fast and not too slow. The aimed rod engaged a spinning interior disk, causing the black ball in the center of the globe to float into the air. Focusing hard, Shaddam yanked the rod free, and the ball plunked into the number "9" receptacle.

"You've been practicing, Sire, hm-m-m-m?" Fenring said. "Doesn't an Emperor have more pressing duties? But you'll need to do better than that to beat me."

The Emperor stared at the rod he had just used, as if it had failed him.

"You want to change sticks, Sire?" Fenring offered, in a taunting tone. "Something wrong with that one?"

Shaddam shook his head stubbornly. "I'll stay with this one, Hasimir—this will be our last game for some time." He drew a deep breath, flaring his nostrils. "I told you I could handle things on my own." He fumbled a bit. "But that doesn't mean I no longer value your advice."

"Naturally, Sire. That's why you sent me to a dust pit populated by sandworms and unwashed barbarians." Dispassionately, he stared past the shield-ball at Shaddam. "I think it's a grave mistake, Highness. In these first days of your rule, you will require good, objective counsel more than ever before. You can't handle it alone, and whom can you trust more than me?"

"Well, I handled the Leto Atreides crisis rather well. I alone avoided disaster."

Delaying his turn at the shield-ball station, Fenring said, "I agree the result was favorable—but we still haven't learned what he knows about us and the Tleilaxu."

"I didn't want to appear overly worried."

"Um-m-ah-m-m. Maybe you're right, but if you solved the problem, then tell me this: If not Leto, who really *did* fire on the Tleilaxu ships? And how?"

"I'm considering alternatives."

Fenring's overlarge eyes flashed. "Leto is incredibly popular now, perhaps even a threat to your throne one day. Whether he engineered the crisis or not, Duke Atreides has turned it into an undeniable victory for himself and the honor of his House. He overcame an insurmountable obstacle and behaved with marvelous grace. The members of the Landsraad notice things like that."

"Ah yes, true, true . . . but nothing to worry about."

"I'm not so certain, Sire. The discontent among the Houses might not have dissipated entirely, as we were led to believe."

"We do have the Bene Gesserit on our side, thanks to my wife."

Fenring sniffed. "Whom you married at *my* suggestion, Sire—but just because the witches say a thing, does not make it true. And what if the alliance isn't sufficient?"

"What do you mean?" Shaddam slid back from the game station and impatiently motioned for Fenring to take his turn.

"Think about Duke Leto, how unpredictable he is. Maybe he's setting up secret military alliances for an assault on Kaitain. His tremendous acclaim translates into bargaining power for him, and he's obviously ambitious. Leaders of Great Houses are eager to talk with him now. You, on the other hand, have no such popular basis of support."

"I have my Sardaukar." But creases of doubt crept into the Emperor's face.

"Watch your legions to make certain they aren't infiltrated. I'm going to be away on Arrakis, and I worry about such things. I know you said you could handle it all yourself, and I believe you. I'm just giving you my best advice—as I always have, Sire."

"I appreciate that, Hasimir. But I cannot believe my cousin Leto created the Heighliner crisis in order to achieve this particular end. It was too clumsy, too risky. He couldn't have known I'd testify for him."

"He knew you'd do something, once you learned he had secret information."

Shaddam shook his head. "No. The potential for failure was enormous. He nearly lost his family's entire holdings."

Fenring held out a long finger. "But consider the potential glory he reaped, hm-m-m-m? For proof, just look at what has happened to him in the meantime. I doubt he could have planned it this way, but Leto's a hero now. His people love him, all the nobles admire him—and the Tleilaxu have been made to look like whining fools. I'd suggest, Sire—since you insist on doing this alone—that you keep a careful eye on the ambitions of House Atreides."

"Thank you for your advice, Hasimir," Shaddam said, turning back to study the game console. "Oh, by the way, did I mention that I'm . . . promoting you?"

Fenring gave a quiet snort. "I wouldn't exactly call the Arrakis assignment a promotion. 'Imperial Observer' doesn't sound terribly exalted, does it?"

Shaddam smiled and raised his chin in a very Imperial gesture. He had intended to do this all along. "Ah, yes . . . but how does *Count Fenring* sound?"

Fenring was taken aback. "You're . . . making me a *Count?*"

Shaddam nodded. "Count Hasimir Fenring, Imperial Observer assigned to Arrakis. Your family fortunes are improving, my friend. Eventually, we'll see about establishing you in the Landsraad."

"With a CHOAM directorship, as well?"

Shaddam laughed. "All in good time, Hasimir."

"That makes Margot a Countess, I presume?" His large eyes glittered as Shaddam nodded to him. He tried to hold his pleasure inside, but the Emperor could see it clearly on his face.

"And now I'll tell you why this is such a critically important assignment, for you and for the Imperium. Do you remember a man named Pardot Kynes—the Planetologist my father stationed there several years ago?"

"Of course."

"Well, he hasn't been much help lately. A few erratic reports, incomplete and seemingly censored. One of my spies even sent word that Kynes has grown too close to the Fremen, that he may have crossed the line and become one of them. Gone native."

Fenring's eyebrows arched. "An Imperial servant mixing with that nasty, primitive brood?"

"I hope not, but I'd like you to uncover the truth. In essence, I'm making you my Imperial Spice Czar, secretly overseeing the melange operations on Arrakis as well as the progress of our synthetic-spice experiments on Xuttah. You'll shuttle back and forth between those planets and the Imperial Palace. You will transmit only coded messages, and only to me."

As the magnitude of the task and its repercussions sank in, Fenring felt a renewed fervor that burned away his discontent. Yes, he did see the possibilities now. He couldn't wait to tell Margot—with her Bene Gesserit mind, she would no doubt see additional advantages.

"That sounds provocative, Sire. A challenge worthy of my particular talents. Um-m-m-m, I might actually enjoy it."

Turning back to the game, Fenring engaged the spinning interior disk and guided the floating shield-ball. It dropped into the number "8" receptacle. Dissatisfied, he shook his head.

"Too bad," Shaddam said. With a deft movement he dropped his final ball into number "10," winning the game.

*Progress and profit require a substantial investment in personnel,
equipment, and capital funding. However, the resource most often
overlooked, yet which can often provide the greatest payoff, is an
investment in* time.

—DOMINIC VERNIUS,
The Secret Workings of Ix

Nothing left to lose.
Nothing left at all.

The renegade Earl and war hero once known as Dominic Vernius was dead, erased from records and removed from the bosom of the Imperium. But the man himself lived on in different guises. He was a person who would never give up.

Dominic had once fought for the glory of his Emperor. In war, he had killed thousands of enemies with fighter craft and handheld lasguns; he had also felt the blood of his victims up close when he used bladed weapons, or even his bare hands. He fought hard, worked hard, and loved hard.

And the payment for his lifetime's investment was dishonor, banishment, the death of his wife, the disgrace of his children.

Despite all that, Dominic was a survivor, a man with a purpose. He knew how to bide his time.

Though the bitter vulture Elrood was already dead, Dominic felt no glimmer of forgiveness within him. The power of the Imperial throne itself had brought about such abuses and such pain. Even the new ruler Shaddam would turn out no better. . . .

He had watched Caladan from a distance. Rhombur and Kailea seemed safe enough; their sanctuary was holding, even without the charismatic presence of the Old Duke. He had mourned the death of his friend Paulus Atreides, but he dared not attend the funeral or even send coded messages to the young heir Leto.

He had, though, been sorely tempted to arrive on Kaitain during the Trial by Forfeiture. Rhombur had foolishly left Caladan and come to the Imperial Court to lend support to his companion, though in doing so he had risked capture and summary execution. If things had gone wrong, Dominic would have gone there and sacrificed himself to buy the life of his son.

But that had been unnecessary. Leto had been freed, given amnesty, impossibly forgiven—and so, too, Rhombur and Kailea. How had it all come about? Dominic's mind was in a turmoil and his brow furrowed on his shaved-smooth head. Shaddam himself had saved young Leto. Shaddam Corrino IV, son of the despicable Emperor Elrood who had destroyed House Vernius, had—seemingly on a whim—dismissed the case. Dominic suspected enormous bribes and coercion had gone into that resolution, but he couldn't imagine what a sixteen-year-old untried Duke could possibly use to blackmail the Emperor of the Known Universe.

One risk, though, Dominic decided he had to take. Against good judgment but blinded by grief, he had dressed in shabby clothes, tinted his skin a ruddy copper, and traveled alone to Bela Tegeuse. Before he could go anywhere else, he felt compelled to see where his wife had been slaughtered by Elrood's Sardaukar.

Using air and ground vehicles he searched the planet in silence, not daring to ask questions, though many reports hinted at where the massacre had taken place. Finally he found an unmarked spot where the crops had been leveled, plowed under, and then salted so that nothing would ever grow there again. A manor house had been burned to the ground and then covered with syncrete. Of Shando's grave there was nothing, but he felt her presence.

My love has been here.

Under the dim double suns, Dominic knelt on the ruined land and wept until he lost all track of time. And when the tears had run out of him, his heart was filled with a great, hard emptiness.

Now he was at last ready for the next step.

And so Dominic Vernius traveled the backwater worlds of the Imperium, gathering loyal men who had escaped from Ix—men who would prefer to work with him, no matter his goals, than drowse through quiet lives on agricultural planets, eking out mundane livings.

He rounded up fellow officers who had fought with him during the Rebellion on Ecaz, people to whom he owed his life a dozen times over. In searching out these men, he knew he put himself at great peril, but Dominic trusted his former comrades. Despite the large bounty that remained on his head, he knew none of them would be willing to pay the price in conscience of betraying their former commander.

Dominic hoped that the overwhelmed new Padishah Emperor Shaddam IV would not think to track down the subtle movements and disappearances of men who had fought under Vernius back when Shaddam had barely been in his teens and not even the heir apparent to the throne . . . back in the days when Crown Prince Fafnir had been first in the line of succession.

Many years had passed now, long enough that most of those veterans sat around talking about the glory days, convincing themselves the war and the bloodshed had been more exciting and more glorious than it really was. About a third of them chose not to join him, but the others quietly signed on and awaited further orders. . . .

When Shando had gone into hiding, she'd erased all records, changed her name, used unmarked credits to buy a small estate on the gloomy world of Bela Tegeuse. Her one mistake had been in underestimating the persistence of the Emperor's Sardaukar.

Dominic would not make his wife's mistake. For what he had in mind, he would go where no one could see him . . . a place where he could prey upon the Landsraad and be a thorn in the Emperor's side.

That was about the only weapon he had left.

Ready to begin his real work, Dominic Vernius took the pilot controls of an unregistered smuggler's craft loaded with a dozen loyal men. These comrades had gathered up hoarded cash and equipment in order to join him in striking a blow for glory and honor—and perhaps vengeance along the way.

Then he went to the Vernius family's stockpile of atomics—forbidden weapons, nevertheless held in reserve by every Great House of the Landsraad. Absolutely restricted by the articles of the Great Convention, the Ixian atomics had been secreted away for generations, sealed on the dark side of a moonlet orbiting the fifth planet in the Alkaurops system. The Tleilaxu vermin on Ix knew nothing of this.

Now Dominic's smuggler ship carried enough doomsday firepower to annihilate a world.

"Vengeance is in the hands of the Lord," stated the Orange Catholic Bible. But after what he had gone through, Dominic did not feel terribly religious, nor did he care to be bound by the niceties of law. He was a renegade now, and beyond the touch—or protection—of the legal system.

He envisioned himself as the greatest of all smugglers, hiding where no one would find him, yet where he could inflict great economic damage on all the powerhouses that had betrayed him and refused to offer help.

With these atomics, he could make his mark on history.

Shielded from the outdated weather-satellite network maintained by the Guild, Dominic brought his ship and his atomic stockpile down in an uninhabited polar region of the desert planet Arrakis. A brisk, cool wind whipped the ragged uniforms of his men as they stepped onto desolate land. *Arrakis.* Their new base of operations.

It would be a long time before anyone heard of Dominic Vernius again. But when he was ready . . . the entire Imperium would remember.

A world is supported by four things: the learning of the wise, the justice of the great, the prayers of the righteous, and the valor of the brave. But all of these are as nothing without a ruler who knows the art of ruling.

—PRINCE RAPHAEL CORRINO,
Discourses on Galactic Leadership

eto worked his way down to the shore alone, zigzagging along the steep cliffside path and staircase to reach the old quays below the edifice of Castle Caladan.

Through cloud patches, midday sunlight glimmered off the placid water that stretched to the horizon. Leto paused on the sheer, black-rock cliff, shading his eyes to look beyond the aqueous kelp forests, the fishing fleets with their chanting crews, and the line of reefs that sketched a hard topography onto the sprawling sea.

Caladan—his world, rich in seas and jungles, arable land and natural resources. It had belonged to House Atreides for twenty-six generations. Now it belonged to him, uncontested.

He loved this place, the smell of the air, the salt of the ocean, the tang of kelp and fish. The people here had always worked hard for their Duke, and Leto tried to do his best for them as well. If he had lost his Trial by Forfeiture, what would have happened to the good citizens of Caladan? Would they even have noticed if these holdings had been given over to the surrogate governorship of, say, House Teranos, House Mutelli, or any other reputable member of the Landsraad? Perhaps. . . . Perhaps not.

Leto, though, could not imagine being anyplace else. This was where the Atreides belonged. Even if he'd been stripped of everything, he would have returned to Caladan to live out his life near the sea.

Though Leto knew he was innocent, he still did not understand what had happened to the Tleilaxu ships inside the Heighliner. He had no evidence to prove to anyone else that he *hadn't* fired the blasts that nearly triggered a major war. On the contrary, he'd certainly had sufficient motive, and because of this, the other Houses had been reluctant to speak strongly in his defense, allies or not. Had they done so, they would have risked their share of the spoils if the Atreides holdings were forfeited and divided. Yet even during that time, many Houses had sent silent expressions of approval for the way Leto had protected his crew members and friends.

And then, by some miracle, Emperor Shaddam had saved him.

On the flight home from Kaitain, Leto had spoken at length with Thufir Hawat, but neither the young Duke nor the warrior Mentat could fathom Emperor Shaddam's reason for coming to the aid of the Atreides, or why he had so feared Leto's desperate bluff. Even as a boy, Leto had known never to trust an explanation of pure altruism, no matter what Shaddam said in his moving statement before the court. This much was certain: The new Emperor had something to hide. Something involving the Tleilaxu.

Under Leto's guidance, Hawat had dispatched Atreides spies to many worlds, hoping to uncover further information. But the Emperor, forewarned by Leto's mysterious, provocative message, would no doubt be more careful than ever.

In the vast spectrum of the Imperium, House Atreides was still not particularly powerful and had no hold on the Corrino family, no apparent reason to be protected. The blood ties were not in themselves enough. Though Leto himself was a cousin to Shaddam, many in the Landsraad could trace their bloodlines at least peripherally back to the Corrinos, especially if one went all the way back to the days of the Great Revolt.

And where did the Bene Gesserit fit in? Were they Leto's allies, or his enemies? Why had they offered to help him? Who had sent the information about Shaddam's involvement in the first place? The coded message cube had disintegrated. Leto had come to expect hidden enemies—but not *allies* who remained so secretive.

And, most enigmatic of all, who really *had* destroyed the Tleilaxu ships?

Alone for the moment, but still troubled, Leto stepped away from the cliffs and crossed a gentle downslope along the gray-black shingle at the water's edge, until he reached the quiet docks. All the boats had been taken out for the day, save for one small beached coracle and a yacht at anchor, flying a faded pennant with the hawk crest of the Atreides.

That hawk had come perilously close to extinction.

In bright sunlight, Leto sat at the end of the main dock, listening to the lapping waves and the songs of gray gulls. He smelled salt and fish and the sweet, fresh air. He remembered when he and Rhombur had gone out together to dive for coral gems . . . the accidental fire and the near disaster they had suffered out on the distant reefs. A small matter in comparison with what had occurred later.

Peering into the water below him, he watched a rock crab as it clung to the dock piling, then disappeared into the blue-green depths.

"So, are you satisfied to be a Duke, or would you rather be a simple fisherman, after all?" Prince Rhombur's loud voice sounded bright, blustering with good cheer.

Leto turned, feeling the sun-warmed dock boards beneath the seat of his trousers. Rhombur and Thufir Hawat trudged across the crunching shingle toward him. Leto knew the Master of Assassins would chide him for sitting with his back vulnerable to the open beach, where the white noise from the ocean might mask any stealthy approach.

"Perhaps I can be both," Leto said, standing and brushing himself off. "The better to understand my people."

" 'Understanding your people paves the road to understanding leadership,' " Hawat intoned—an old Atreides maxim. "I hope you were meditating upon statecraft, as we have much work to do, now that all is returning to normal."

Leto sighed. "Normal? I think not. Someone tried to start a war with the Tleilaxu and blame my family in the process. The Emperor fears what he *thinks* I know. House Vernius is still renegade, and Rhombur and Kailea remain exiled here, though at least they were pardoned and the blood price on their heads has been lifted. Moreover, my name was never actually cleared—a lot of people still think I attacked those ships."

He scooped up a beach pebble that lay on the dock and tossed it far out on the water where he couldn't discern the splash it made. "If this is a victory for House Atreides, Thufir, it's bittersweet, at best."

"Perhaps," Rhombur said, standing next to the beached coracle. "But better than a defeat."

The old Mentat nodded, his leathery skin reflecting the harsh sun. "You handled yourself with an air of true honor and nobility, my Duke, and House Atreides has gained widespread respect. That is a victory you must never discount."

Leto looked up at the tall towers of Castle Caladan looming high on the cliff. *His* Castle, his home.

He thought of the ancient traditions of his Great House, and how he would build on them. In his royal station he was an axis upon which millions of lives revolved. The life of a simple fisherman might have been easier, after all, and more peaceful—but not for him. He would always be Duke Leto Atreides. He had his name, his title, his friends. And life was good.

"Come, young masters," Thufir Hawat said. "It's time for another lesson."

In high spirits, Leto and Rhombur followed the Master of Assassins back up to the Castle.

AFTERWORD

For more than a decade there had been rumors that I would write another novel set in my father's Dune universe, a sequel to the sixth book in the series, CHAPTERHOUSE: DUNE. I had published a number of acclaimed science fiction novels, but wasn't sure I wanted to tackle something so immense, so daunting. After all, DUNE is a magnum opus that stands as one of the most complex, multilayered novels ever written. A modern-day version of the myth of the dragon's treasure, DUNE is a tale of great sandworms guarding a precious treasure of melange, the geriatric spice. The story is a magnificent pearl with layers of luster running deep beneath its surface, all the way to its core.

At the time of my father's untimely death in 1986, he was beginning to think about a novel that carried the working title DUNE 7, a project he had sold to Berkley Books, but on which there were no known notes or outlines. Dad and I had spoken in general terms about collaborating on a Dune novel one day in the future, but we'd set no date, had established no specific details or direction. It would be sometime after he completed DUNE 7 and other projects.

In ensuing years I thought about my late father's uncompleted series, especially after I concluded a five-year project writing DREAMER OF DUNE, a biography of this complex, enigmatic man—a biography which required that I analyze the origins and themes of the Dune series. After long consideration it seemed to me that it would be fascinating to write a book based upon the events he had described so tantalizingly in the Appendix to DUNE, a new novel in which I would go back ten thousand years to the time of the Butlerian Jihad, the legendary Great Revolt against thinking machines. That had been a mythical time in a mythical universe, a time when most of the Great Schools had been formed, including the Bene Gesserit, the Mentats, and the Swordmasters.

Upon learning of my interest, prominent writers approached me with offers of collaboration. But in tossing ideas around with them I couldn't visualize the project coming to fruition. They were excellent writers, but in combination with them I didn't feel the necessary synergy for such a monumental task. So I kept turning to other projects, avoiding the big one. Besides, while Dad had sprinkled many provocative loose ends in the fifth and sixth books of the series, he had written an afterword for CHAPTERHOUSE: DUNE that was a marvelous dedication to my late mother, Beverly Herbert—his wife of nearly four decades. They had been a writing team in which she edited his work and acted as a sounding board for his overflow of ideas . . . so with both of them gone it seemed a fitting conclusion to leave the project untouched.

The trouble was, a fellow named Ed Kramer kept after me. An accomplished editor and sponsor of science fiction/fantasy conventions, he wanted to put together an anthology of short stories set in the Dune universe—stories by different, well-known authors. He convinced me that it would be an interesting, significant project, and we talked about coediting it. All the details weren't finalized, since the project had a number of complexities, both legal and artistic. In the midst of this, Ed told me he had received a letter from best-selling author Kevin J. Anderson, who had been invited to contribute to the proposed anthology. He suggested what he called a "shot in the dark," asking about the possibility of working at novel length, preferably on a sequel to CHAPTERHOUSE: DUNE.

Kevin's enthusiasm for the Dune universe fairly jumped off the pages of his letter. Still, I delayed answering him for around a month, not certain how to respond. Despite his proven skills, I was hesitant. This was a big decision. By now I knew I wanted to be involved closely in the project, and that I needed to participate to such a degree in order to ensure the production of a novel of integrity, one that would be faithful to the original series. Along with J.R.R. Tolkien's LORD OF THE RINGS and a handful of other works, DUNE stood as one of the greatest creative achievements of all time, and arguably the greatest example of science fiction world-building in the history of literature. For the sake of my father's legacy, I couldn't select the wrong person. I read everything I could get my hands on that Kevin had written, and did more checking on him. It soon became clear to me that he was a brilliant writer, and that his reputation was sterling. I decided to give him a telephone call.

We hit it off immediately, both on a personal and professional level. Aside from the fact that I genuinely liked him, I felt an energy between us, a remarkable flow of ideas that would benefit the series. After obtaining the concurrence of my family, Kevin and I decided to write a prequel—but not one set in the ancient times, long before *DUNE*. Instead we would go to events only thirty or forty years before the beginning of *DUNE*, to the love story of Paul's parents, to the Planetologist Pardot Kynes being dispatched to Arrakis, to the reasons for the terrible, destructive enmity between House Atreides and House Harkonnen, and much more.

Before writing a detailed outline, we set to work rereading all six Dune books my father had written, and I took it upon myself to begin assembling a massive DUNE CONCORDANCE—an encyclopedia of all the characters, places, and wonders of the Dune universe. Of primary concern to us, we needed to determine where Dad had been heading with the conclusion of the series. It was clear that he was building up to something momentous in *DUNE 7*, and without intending to do so he had left us with a mystery. There were no known notes or other clues, only my memory that Dad had been using a yellow highlighter on paperback copies of *HERETICS OF DUNE* and *CHAPTERHOUSE: DUNE* shortly before his death—books that no one could locate after he was gone.

In early May 1997, when I finally met Kevin J. Anderson and his wife, the author Rebecca Moesta, new story ideas fairly exploded from our minds. In a frenzy the three of us either scribbled them down or recorded them on tape. From these notes, scenes began to unfold, but still we wondered and debated where Dad had been going with the series.

In the last two books, *HERETICS OF DUNE* and *CHAPTER-HOUSE: DUNE*, he had introduced a new threat—the reviled Honored Matres—who proceeded to lay waste to much of the galaxy. By the end of *CHAPTERHOUSE*, the characters had been driven into a corner, utterly beaten . . . and then the reader learned that the Honored Matres themselves were running from an even greater mysterious threat . . . a peril that was drawing close to the protagonists of the story, most of whom were Bene Gesserit Reverend Mothers.

A scant two weeks after our meeting, I received a telephone call from an estate lawyer who had handled matters involving my mother and father. He informed me that two safety-deposit boxes belonging to Frank Herbert had turned up in a suburb of Seattle, boxes that none of us knew existed. I made an appointment to meet with the bank authorities, and in an increasing air of excitement the safety-deposit boxes were opened. Inside were papers and old-style floppy computer disks that included comprehensive notes from an unpublished DUNE 7—the long-awaited sequel to CHAPTERHOUSE: DUNE! Now Kevin and I knew for certain where Frank Herbert had been headed, and we could weave the events of our prequel into a future grand finale for the series.

We turned with new enthusiasm to the task of putting together a book proposal that could be shown to publishers. That summer I had a trip to Europe scheduled, an anniversary celebration that my wife Jan and I had been planning for a long time. I took along a new laptop computer and a featherweight printer, and Kevin and I exchanged FedEx packages all summer long. By the time I returned at the end of the summer, we had a massive 141-page trilogy proposal—the largest that either of us had ever seen. My allied DUNE CONCORDANCE project, the encyclopedia of all the marvelous treasures of the Dune universe, was a little over half-completed, with months of intensive work remaining before it would be finished.

As we waited to see if a publisher would be interested, I remembered the many writing sessions I had enjoyed with my father, and my early novels in the 1980s that had received his loving, attentive suggestions for improvement. Everything I had learned from him—and more—would be needed for this huge prequel project.

—*Brian Herbert*

I never met Frank Herbert, but I knew him well through the words he wrote. I read *DUNE* when I was ten years old, and reread it several times over the years; then I read and enjoyed all of the sequels. *GOD-*

EMPEROR OF DUNE, hot off the presses, was the very first hard-
cover novel I ever purchased (I was a freshman in college). Then I
worked my way through every single one of his other novels, diligently
checking off the titles on the "Other Books By" page in each new
novel. THE GREEN BRAIN, HELLSTROM'S HIVE, THE SANTA-
ROGA BARRIER, THE EYES OF HEISENBERG, DESTINATION:
VOID, THE JESUS INCIDENT, and more and more and more.

To me, Frank Herbert was the pinnacle of what science fiction
could be—thought-provoking, ambitious, epic in scope, well-researched,
and entertaining—all in the same book. Other science fiction novels
succeed in one or more of these areas, but DUNE did it all. By the
time I was five years old, I had decided I wanted to be a writer. By
the time I was twelve, I knew I wanted to write books like the ones
Frank Herbert wrote.

Throughout college, I published a handful of short stories, then began to write my first novel, RESURRECTION, INC., a complex tale
set in a future world where the dead are reanimated to serve the living.
The novel was full of social commentary, religious threads, a large cast
of characters, and (yes) a wheels-within-wheels plot. By this time, I
had enough writing credits to join the Science Fiction Writers of
America . . . and one of the main benefits was the Membership Direc-
tory. There, before my eyes, was the home address of Frank Herbert. I
promised myself that I would send him the very first signed copy. The
novel sold almost immediately to Signet Books . . . but before its publication date, Frank Herbert died.

I had avidly read the last two Dune books, HERETICS and
CHAPTERHOUSE, in which Herbert had launched a vast new saga
that built to a fever pitch, literally destroyed all life on the planet Arrakis, and left the human race on the brink of extinction—that's
where Frank Herbert left the story upon his death. I knew that his son
Brian was also a professional writer with several science fiction novels
under his belt. I waited, and hoped, that Brian would complete a draft
manuscript, or at least flesh out an outline his father had left behind.
Someday soon, I hoped, faithful DUNE readers would have a resolution to this cliffhanger.

Meanwhile, my own writing career flourished. I was nominated for
the Bram Stoker Award and the Nebula Award; two of my thrill-
ers were bought or optioned by major studios in Hollywood. While I

continued to write original novels, I also found a great deal of success in dipping my toes into established universes, such as *Star Wars* and *X-Files* (both of which I love). I learned how to study the rules and the characters, wrap my imagination around them, and tell my own stories within the boundaries and expectations of the readers.

Then in the spring of 1996 I spent a week in Death Valley, California, which has always been one of my favorite places to write. I went hiking for an afternoon in an isolated and distant canyon, wrapped up in my plotting and dictating. After an hour or so I discovered that I had wandered off on the wrong trail and had several extra miles to hike back to my car. During that unexpectedly long walk, out in the stark and beautiful desert scenery, my thoughts rambled over to *DUNE*.

It had been ten years since Frank Herbert's death, and by now I had pretty much decided that *DUNE* was always going to end on a cliffhanger. I still very much wanted to know how the story wrapped up . . . even if I had to make it up myself.

I had never met Brian Herbert before, had no reason to expect he would even consider my suggestion. But *DUNE* was my favorite science fiction novel of all time, and I could think of nothing I would rather work on. I decided it would do no harm to *ask.* . . .

We hope you have enjoyed revisiting the Dune universe through our eyes. It has been an immense honor to sift through thousands of pages of Frank Herbert's original notes, so that we might re-create some of the vivid realms that sprang from his research, his imagination, and his life. I still find *DUNE* as exciting and thought-provoking as I did when I first encountered it many years ago.

—*Kevin J. Anderson*

A requirement of creativity is that it contributes to change. Creativity keeps the creator alive.

— FRANK HERBERT, unpublished notes